"... A FIRST RATE NOVEL: TOUGH, FASTMOVING ... DON'T MISS IT." —NEWSDAY

This extraordinary novel is a trip into the world of prison, where men live together in fear and violence and unnatural passion, and convicts and guards share a mutual corruption . . . into the world of the urban jungle outside, where vicious criminals and political idealogues mingle, and women give their bodies for kicks or for a cause . . . into the simmering underground world just below the surface of America today—a world like a human volcano about to explode.

HERE IS THE MOST POWERFUL WRITING TALENT SINCE JAMES JONES, DESCRIBING A WORLD HE INTIMATELY KNOWS. IT IS A TOTALLY GRIPPING, SHOCKING, COMPULSIVELY READABLE EXPERIENCE —THE YEAR'S MOST POWERFUL TRIUMPH.

THE RAP

Ernest Brawley

A Dell Book

To my mother and father

Published by
DELL PUBLISHING CO., INC.
1 Dag Hammarskjold Plaza
New York, New York 10017

Moke, small, comely and brown, came out only at dark, like a nocturnal fish. She loved night and black water and U.S. dollars. They were her lovers, and her prey. She was their queen. Her eyes shone like diamonds. Alone among her race she defied the sun, which held sway over all the wide Pacific, alone to her came sleek ambition and a supreme distaste for napping under coconut palms at midday.

Alone among all the moneylovers and junkies of the world she knelt too at the throne of the deep, sought gold at its source in watery darkness, undeceived by sunny appearance.

At home on Oahu, after her 8 P.M.—3 A.M. job at the Prince Kuhio Grill, she had nightly swum the Makapuu Straits, naked through the shoals of her gray brothers, moon-basking sharks, naked through the inky waters, octopus waters, sparks of phosphorescence shooting out from her green-painted toenails. Far out to Manana she had swum, to Rabbit Island and beyond, into the swift swirling Kaiwi Channel, the Molokai Current, fearless, caressed, aroused, on and on into the throat of the blackness till she felt it consume her, till she could hear the seaweed speak, the rumble of the submerged volcano, the killer whales sounding, the music of a million pounds of pressure, the call of the oceanic canyon without end, the thirty-eight-thousand footer: "Eh, Moke! Weah you go, eh?"

Swimming back into shore, past the Coast Guard station and the Makapuu Lighthouse with its petty-strong beam of white that lost itself so quick, so pathetic in the curve of the immense sea, she had known in every golden pore of her body, her sane body, that the light would never have its way.

Not till she gave the word.

"Never, never, never!"

Daytime was for sleeping, for sleep without dreams and for digesting huge predawn breakfasts of rice and poi and passion fruit and wheat bread toast. Here on the West Coast it was the same. Only thing she had to give up was the poi. Here it was fried rice and eggs and expensive canned pineapple juice and imported guavas at five o'clock in the morning, sitting alone on her tatami floor, feet tucked up under her low cable spool table. Silence, and listening to the work-bound traffic pick up on the freeway bridge that ran right over her roof. Resting up after work at the restaurant and a long night's run on her Honda 250 to the first clean water within her range, China Cove (opaque, mud-ridden, but free till now of floating garbage and oil gunk). Relaxing after her night-time's new regimen: the marathon swim to Iguana Rock and back, her black rubber dry-suit carrying her high in the icy flow, her long hair heating up in the tight rubber hood, eyes sealed and green behind hermetic goggles, blackfins kicking hard out behind, knees locked, legs rigid, slow-popping bubbles boiling up behind. No sparks, no fire in the night, no fish, no depth-diving whales, but still she was queen of the deep!

And if by chance she ever had to live through a light-time day, she would drag the night along with her. Last P.M.'s eyeballs, pinned, beaned, amphetamined, round and pitiless and wide, cached in very dark glasses. She would regard the waking workaday world through the perspective of time gone, a black hole in the day. And do it all through the next night until the yellow-jacket sun-up tomorrow.

Moke ate slow, munching careful on her breakfast toast with bad teeth, teeth that were white and bright as a toothpaste ad but rotten at the core, the result, she was convinced, of an almost proteinless childhood in a tropical rain forest above Honolulu, but probably had more to do with the heroin, the smack she carefully put into her fit, her outfit, her works, her cooker and eyedropper and point, and skin-popped four times daily into the muscle tissue of her pretty brown buttocks.

Eating her toast, mixing her rice and soya with her fingers, she often thought of that valley without protein.

Manoa, it was called, a valley surrounded on three sides by towering volcanic cliffs covered with lush vegetation. Miles past the city, past the University of Hawaii campus, past the middle-class housing developments, at the very top of the valley, there was a heavy rain forest, a Chinese graveyard, and three waterfalls that plunged from the top of the northwestern cliffs, from the green blackrock spine of the Koolau Range, the backbone of the island. In this rain forest, a place where the sun never shone and the rain came three times daily with gale force winds that whirled down from the peaks, bending even the banyan trees, rattling the bamboo, there lived a few poor families, *da kine*, as they called themselves in Pidgin—"The Kind"—a mixed Chinese-Hawaiian, Filipino-Portuguese potpourri mostly. They scraped a living growing and selling taro root, passion fruit, mangos, guavas, bananas, bamboo shoots, papayas, and Manoa lettuce, a particularly succulent variety, to the wholesalers on River Street in Honolulu. Others lived on welfare checks, or worked as houseboys, waitresses, maids or musicians in the city. Most of them refused to work, however, and managed a meager living off the land. Moke grew up with her Tutu (Auntie) Cereza, a barefoot, obese, happy-go-lucky, Primo-drinking lady renowned over the island of Oahu as one of the last great Hawaiian slack-key guitarists and singers of the old school. Moke's beloved quarter-breed father had died of overeating at a Sunday pig fest when Moke was just a little girl. And her mother, less loved, less white, almost Kanaka black, in fact, had followed him two years later of love and overdrink.

Tutu loved her little Moke more than anything, and would have died for her without a moment's thought. Moke hated Tutu. She was so tacky black and fat and lazy. Moke hated the Islands and her race, and loved them at the same time. And loved her Tutu too, hating her, resenting her, and the lax Hawaiian way of taking all possessions for granted, sharing everything. Moke was jealous, jealous of her own time, her own money, her own place, her room, her things, her possessions. She held them dear. And this was just the commodity which in Hawaii was cheapest, cheap as air and wind and sunlight and salt sea. Moke felt like nothing belonged to her alone. Even the fruits on the trees belonged to everyone in common. This she detested. This she resented and grudged and ridiculed about Island living. Nothing was *hers,* and, by extension, Moke felt almost as if nothing was *her,* either. Tutu would come and take anything of hers without apologies. In an effort to create something of her own, that would belong only to her, Moke once cultivated a little garden out in back, in an open space she cleared between the flame trees. Just a little thing of ten or twelve, she spent a whole year getting it in shape. She carefully plowed up the black volcanic earth, dug her furrows to drain the excess rain water, brought in the best fertilizers she could find, patiently watched her plants grow and bloom and flourish, picking the bugs off the leaves one by one. And when she had her garden growing high, ready for eating, or sale, or whatever she chose to do with it, her Tutu dug it up, sold the taro and Manoa lettuce Moke had cared for day and night for weeks, sold it down on River Street, took the money and went on a drunken rampage on the Windward Side, out at Waimanalo with her relatives the Puhanuis, singing and playing her guitar at a Sunday pig party in the Hawaiian Homelands tract.

Moke had her own little corner of the shack where she secreted her sewing box with her treasures. She hid money there, pennies she saved from baby-sitting and peddling the *Sunday Advertiser.* Tutu, whenever she wanted to get a six-pack of Primo, would take it, every time, Moke's precious things, her money and possessions. One day Moke took her treasures out and hid them in the far back yard, under the monkeypod tree. She dug a hole and put the box deep in the black earth. There she hid all the buttons, tacks, nails, thread, glass jewelry, cheap Montgomery Ward necklaces, earrings, brooches, and pins that she stole whenever she got the chance. She was an utterly fearless thief, a kleptomaniac almost, and only rarely got caught. One day she dug up her box and all her treasures were gone. Tutu swore she hadn't taken them. Moke never found out who did. "Maybe eet da deevil take eet," Tutu said. Maybe she was right. For from that moment on, Moke was out for herself alone and nobody else. The rest of the world became fair game, the enemy, prey. She coldly exploited even her Tutu, and cheerfully defrauded friends, relatives, and classmates, hiding her booty away, counting it by flashlight in the middle of the night, fingering it, holding it to her small shapely breasts, trembling with desire. Her body, she knew from the first, was her dearest and most precious and valuable commodity. No man touched her. No man even got near. It was her treasure too, hidden from all eyes, cached in ankle-length muumuus, stashed, waiting while its value rose, waiting.

When Moke graduated from the Kamehameha School, a private institution for "children of native blood," she was offered a scholarship at the University of Hawaii (she'd won the state high school forensics championship for "The Black Dove," a brilliant, original, ironic, and highly comic mock defense of the Vietnam peace movement). She declined the offer, however. She had no interest in higher education, certain as she was that she could educate herself a hell of a lot faster than the University of Hawaii, and make a hell of a lot of money by the time she would have been graduating.

She lied about her age and got a job as a waitress at the Prince Kuhio Grill on Beretania Street, selling Primo and Asahi and Kirin beer, deep-fried shrimp, and spicy half-cooked vegetables with rice and sweet mahi mahi, making good tips, cultivating steady customers, teasing and flirting, but holding herself aloof, playing hard to get, sucking them in deeper and deeper, hauling in *da 'Merican dollah*. She worked nights, stepping unconcernedly over the giant rats that resided in the restaurant kitchen, hurrying to sweep up her tips, hurrying to provide the smilingest, fastest, best service in the place. She was always the last to leave, the ideal employee, riding the last city bus home, walking the last mile through the rain forest and the Chinese graveyard (a graveyard of many-colored stones, red and blue and yellow, each one with a picture of the deceased forever imprinted above the name), in the warm rain, in the darkness and the wind. all the way home to her Tutu's tin-roofed shack among the weather-bent Norfolk pine and monkeypod and banvan trees, listening for the sound of Cereza's loved and hated golden-throated slack-key guitar:

Oh she da wahini
Wi da hula hula heah
An da hula hula deah
An a hot of gold
Oh she da kine
All a time
Make da local boy bold . . .

Moke saved her money diligently through her teens, husbanding it secretly at the Central Pacific Bank in the Moiliili Shopping Center. When she had enough she bought a car, a classic, a good investment, an ancient Model A touring car in perfect condition, and drove it with great pleasure, secret pleasure, every night around the narrow southwest end of the island past Diamond Head, along Maunalua Bay, the Hawaii Kai housing tract, the yacht basin, Koko Head, the National Guard Firing Range, Sandy Beach, and Makapuu Point. All the way to the Windward Side, under the mountains of Koolaupoko. All the way to her nighttime cove. The desert island, Rabbit Island, just a gray smudge in the heart of the blackness.

At times during the summer, when the waves came up to twenty feet riding the south swell, and swimming or even wading became impossible, she lit cigarettes and watched and listened till dawn, soaking through her muumuu, watching the mist rise, the spray coming off the gigantic surf, breakers that rolled thundering in waves one after the other all the way from Tahiti and the Marquesas Islands, like her ancestors, only to break up on the rocks of the fiftieth state.

In all the time in Hawaii she never had a man. Her lover was sublime, and found only at late hours.

One day she stopped at the Central Pacific Bank, took a change of clothes and a suitcase to work, asked the Japanese bossman for her pay, rode a taxi out the Moana Loa Highway to the Honolulu International Airport, and by the time she would have been getting off work, she was sitting in the garish fluorescent light of the Los Angeles Air Terminal, feeling not at all unhappy or lost or foreign in her bright flower-patterned muumuu, waiting for opportunity to come knocking. She had patience, enormous unending patience, the patience of a woman convinced she'll never die. She believed in her star, her destiny, her considerable talent for money. But mostly she believed in that star, her dark dwarf star that did not shine.

A young GI she'd met on the plane, a boy just back from the Vietnam War, asked her if she wouldn't like to come out to Corona with him and stay with his family. She accepted this turn of fate with great alacrity. And he was very sweet, and his family liked her in spite of the fact that they'd never met "no Haywayans before," and within a fortnight they'd gotten her a job with a relative who ran a small roadside bar and grill at Elsinore Lake. She phoned her Tutu and said she had a job and was doing fine and not to worry. Tutu said:

"Eh! I geev you one yeah, Meez Prosperitee, den I come look. An you watch out da *Haole* boys, eh?"

"Right, Tutu!" she said.

Mr. Holloway, the bar owner, an earnest Iowan, gave her a clean room upstairs. She worked nights by choice.

Elsinore had once been a clear and beautiful lake but was lately drying up. All the streams that once fed it had been dammed up to irrigate the nearby truck gardens. Elsinore was usually, nowadays, just an enormous flat mud basin five miles long and two miles wide. But the year Moke happened to work there was one of those extremely wet seasons that hits southern California every decade or so.

It rained buckets every day all winter long. Moke was delighted. She never saw the sun. She worked and saved her money, waiting for her star. And by February the lake was brimming over with fresh muddy water from the mountains in the Cleveland National Forest. She bought a rubber wet suit down in Riverside and nightly slithered like a salamander down the bank. The incline was treacherous. The mud was deep and sucked like quicksand. She crawled on her belly, froggy, through the rain and slush and water, kicking her feet, treading lightly with her hands, dog-paddling it, the headlights of cars on the highway shining out over the lake when they turned the curve, driving her farther into the darkness and damp. Down and down she went, out to the deep water, the chop, the waves, the stinging spray, the wind-driven rain. Kicking with her blackfins. Nothing ahead. Seeing nothing. Striking out for the deep middle and then, after the long exhausting swim, being alone in the brown black water of mid-lake, mid-valley, with the clouds backed up and dropping torrents on the Santa Ana Range all around her. And then riding the wind back, riding the little breaking lake waves, over the mud, the quicksand, dogging it up the bank, stripping her fins, walking barefoot up the highway. Sometimes a car would catch her in its beams for an instant, and she would see the driver's eyes go blank with fear, behind his seal beams, and he would rocket away into the night, disbelieving.

Up in her room she'd slap her whole body down and take a nice long hot shower and then she'd cook up some rice and vegetables for her dawntime breakfast.

What did she do with her time? She never knew. Apart from cleaning her room and reading paperback art books and random novels and air-mailed editions of the *Honolulu Advertiser*, and going down to the Bank of America in Arlington every week to salt away her check, all she did was work, eat, sleep, and swim. . . . And yet, she could go days without doing any of those things, if she chose to . . . days that were lost and unremembered. . . . Time, Moke always knew, was on her side. . . .

In May she gave notice to Mr. Holloway and wrote her Tutu she was coming home for a visit on a June 2nd flight. She missed the valley, she said, and the climate, and the sea. But the truth was that Tutu had confessed she was very ill, and Moke wanted to make sure that she inherited (to the exclusion of hordes of other relatives) the family house if Tutu passed away.

On the 1st of June Moke's fellow waitresses talked her into the bright spring sunlight and gave her a going-away party out of doors. They drove to an abandoned farm on the other side of the lake. It was a lovely ruin of a place, situated at the mouth of a wide, deep canyon. The abode walls of the house were covered with huckleberry and gooseberry vines. The fallow fields had run to manzanita, horse chestnut, blue sage, and chaparral. A big old canyon maple grew in the yard. After the picnic they went picking the dead farmer's household flowers that had gone wild in the yellow grass and scrub oak: white jonquils, violets, pale yellow daffodils, wild red lilies, golden California poppies. They found a stand of half-dead pomegranate trees and filled a plastic picnic basket with their surprisingly sweet fruit. They had just sat down again, biting into the pomegranates, fingering for the tasty seeds, when all the dogs at the beekeeper's place down the highway began to howl. They looked up and listened, and from way around the other end of the lake they heard the mufferless roar of a gigantic Harley-Davidson 74 resounding off the pale placid waters of the lake. . . .

Wasco!

He thundered up in a melodramatic cloud of dust, on

his way north from a dope run over the Mexican border, spitting fire and smoke and exhaust fumes from the twin pipes of his lacquered black and gold three-wheeled chopper, his giant chopped Hog with the fat chrome rear wheels and the tiny bicycle front wheel leading far out ahead on a fifty-inch fork. A small metallic plaque hanging from the wide stainless steel back axle proclaimed the beast's name: CHERRYETTE.

Wasco hoisted a thick leg over the tiny egg-shaped gasoline tank and grinned at them where they lay on the hill, in the yellow hay, and his leering broken-toothed smile sent the fear of Beelzebub into their quaking women's hearts. Their mouths hung open. Only their eyes moved, up and down his squat ugly body, his panting rumbling beast.

What did he wear? Moke remembered but she wasn't sure whether the memory held from that first moment. He never changed his clothes. Surely he was wearing what he always wore: black engineer's boots with sharp metal studs, a beer can opener hanging from the strap. Greasy, piss-stained, come-stained Levis with a red lightning rod sewed down the seam from waist to ankle. A polished motorcycle drive chain for a belt. A filthy sleeveless Levi jacket open at the front, showing the rank red hair on his massive dust-encrusted chest.

Four pseudo-military patches decorated the jacket: the three smaller ones read 69, 1%er, and 13, and a big one that ran from shoulder to shoulder, a considerable distance, in the shape of a death's head, proclaimed his membership in the:

MOTOPSYCHO
M.C.
NEW SONORA

. . . And Mercurochromed red hair, shoulder length, lank and dirty. A black leather headband with silver diamond-shaped studs. A long forked beard dyed indigo blue. A single earring in his pierced left ear. A clip-on nose ring that hid his cruel moustache.

Their lipsticked barmaids' mouths hung open long after the dust cleared and the huge throbbing motor died, stayed awake and wide. until he dropped to the ground, startlingly light on his feet, and said with a vague and almost languorous wave of his heavily muscled arm:

"Hey, babies! Which way to the Santa Ana Freeway?"

And Moke knew in her Hawaiian heart, her self-serving money-loving mystic's soul, in that single instant, that she'd finally met her master, her prince, her bad-ass dad, whom she would always know in her belly by his secret Kanaka name, a name never to be divulged to nobody, not even him, not at least until several days later when, working over his fiery red pubic hair, she catapulted off him ass-backwards to the ceiling and screamed it till the rafters rung and shuddered and shattered the roof, impelling it outward to the great night sky: HALEAKALA! . . . Snorting blowing metal-melting volcano born at the bottom of the sea . . .

And within an hour she was on her way north with him to New Sonora.

And never again did she have to swim. Not at least until Wasco was locked up in state prison.

And that very afternoon, cruising at an unstoppable sixty-five miles an hour out of L.A. on the speed-cop-infested Ventura Freeway, she had dared ask him his secret:

"Eh, *Haole,* wha da numbah means, eh?" she shouted into the wind.

"Never ask a Motopsycho his number, woman," he growled back at her through his flying blue beard, "else he'll get yours . . ."

And it was only much later, after she knew him better, and his sinister friends, that she broke his cipher. It was obvious when you got to know him:

69   is sixty-nine
1%   is the one per cent of the baddest
13   is the thirteenth letter of the alphabet, "M,"
        signifying:
      Murder
      Money
      Mayhem

. . . to which later, in a sentimental moment, she appended:

      Moke

. . . and even later, in a more reflective mood, after reading the Bible Interpretation section of the magazine *Awake,* reduced in its entirety to:

Moloch

And on June the 2nd Tutu Cereza sat out on the modernistic open terrace of the Honolulu International Airport for nine hours and nine minutes (magical time limit set by her primitive faith in certain local Kanaka lore), in wind and hot Kona rain, awaiting the known and preordained nonarrival of her lost Moke.

Within a month a series of want ads began appearing in the personal sections of the *Berkeley Barb,* the L. A. *Free Press,* the *New Sonora Oracle,* and other West Coast underground newspapers: SOMEBODY KNOW WHEREABOUTS MISS PROSPERITY PUHANUI TODD MIXED HAWAIIAN 20 YEAR PHONE CEREZA PUHANUI COLLECT HONOLULU 988-7286.

Tutu finally got wind of Moke through a two-faced friend who ran into her in the street and went back to the Islands and told. Tutu wrote a letter begging her to come back. But by then Moke had herself a smack cutting-room operation and a fifteen-dollar-a-day habit at wholesale prices and was salting away $1,000 a week and she had her daddy-man and he was the only dude with a ready supply of everything her heart desired. She wasn't going to answer Tutu, but Wasco insisted on writing her himself: "Dear Tutu I am Wasco G. Weed Mokes new friend now you dont mess with us auntie I will send her home to you a couple a times a year."

Tutu wrote back thanking him "for to consider bereave of old wahini."

A year later when Moke was eight months along with Flo, Wasco's greatest error (conceived by rectal fluke . . . but that's another story), Wasco sent Moke to Hawaii on a Continental Airlines 747 with a full piece of smack, an ounce of five-cut heroin, packed into a Sheik prophylactic and stuffed to the cervix up her vagina.

. . . *an all away cross da watah I wonner tru high if da kine rubbah bust if it go like da supposiitree an how long it take an what it feel like to die fuck to death wi da kine smack up da cunt.* . . .

Part I

One

Wasco dug his baldy. They gave it to him the first day. He remembered it, old Wasco did, riding chained to another scalped convict in a Commission of Corrections bus. They lined them up on the asphalt outside the institution barber shop and two mainline Chicanos with gorgeous pompadours sheared it off, thirty seconds to a man. His beautiful long outrageous red mercurochromed hair oh it fell! It fell free and hit the black linoleum like a picture, the Mexican standing in it while he worked on him, shuffling around on it, mixing it up with the hundred other varieties of hair lying there in deep ratty piles on the floor: black, blond, gray, red, brown, strawberry, curly, kinky, wavy, nappy, straight, thin, thick, coarse, fine, long, short, normal, Afro, dry, greasy, hennaed, peroxided, iodined, processed, conked, and dixie-peached.

He would remember it always and always, Wasco would: his electric hair falling . . . falling and falling . . .

Now he dug feeling the little bristle. He dug lathering it up in the shower. Oh the showers at the State Joint! Wasco lined up first at shower time and he was the very last to leave. He loved to get clean. Outside of the Joint he never washed. Never. Went months without changing his filthy Levi's. Here he washed himself four times over. And he wasn't the only one who changed his habits in the Slam. He watched the others. They held the hard-scraping institution soap bars tightly, rubbing them like whetstones against their soft flesh, against their bare skulls, into the secrets under and around their members and holes. Oh the loving care they took of the cracks of their asses. The ten-minute lather in the pubic hair, the hair of their chest, their legs, their armpits. The friction with the wirelike wash rags. Many of them, many times, Wasco seen them goosing themselves with a soapy thumb, a long clean index finger with short clean nails; he too experimented.

The Haley Reception Center, where prisoners from all over the state were processed upon coming into the custody of the Commission of Corrections, smelled of disinfectant and pine oil and urine and stale sweat and bad breath and farts. Brand new, modernistic, with long swept, mopped, waxed corridors, and miles and miles of spotless green and eggshell tiled shower baths, it smelled like the New Sonora County Hospital in Mission Santa Bonita where his Mexican grandpa died. Wasco always felt a shiver of delight when he was locked up again, locked out of those dirty streets outside.

His twice a week shower time Wasco had made into a science. Everything he truly dug was a "science," or a "philosophy." He dug definitions too, "fine distinctions." He thought up a new pearl of wisdom now, looking out the window of the prison bus: *Science is nothing but business. Philosophy is pleasure. A real scientific philosophy is nothing but just mixing business with pleasure.* He'd have to remember that one. He'd know the right moment to spring it on someone. That day, in the shower, standing there soaping and wetting, drying and patting, rubbing, rubbing away for three delicious hours while seven hundred milling sweating convicts came and went, he'd had a lot of time to conduct his first scientific experiment of this his latest state penitentiary sentence. He had the whole thing down now: *Seven hundred men. Seven hundred swinging pricks. Fourteen hundred hanging perspiring balls. Seven hundred indigo-veined ballbags. On the thesis of this afternoon's observation, conducted absolutely impartial, this conclusion been figured out by Professor Wasco G. Weed, Behavior Scientist: the human race is hung in sizes that get littler and littler progressive in the following order: black, white, brown, yellow. Thereby: a shrimpy little Spick is bigger than the grandest Gook. A pee-wee Whitie is larger than the spiffiest Spic. And the itty-bittiest nigger is hung, man, hung a whole peck heavier than the wildest Whitie in the block. Other observations noted: the cock area of all races, creeds, and colors is darker than the remainder of the body. Therefore, by way of example, Chinks and Japs pack sacks the color of Monterey Jack. Greasers got gunmetal grays. Hon-*

*keys're hung the hue of honey. Mojo motate with mid-
night monsters. Filipinos I even seen in aquamarine . . .*

Yeah, old Wasco, he loved the Reception Center. One
day it was a physical: Wasserman, X-rays, tetanus shot,
analysis of caca/peepee, counting of scars; then the next
day it was the IQ tests, education tests, vocation tests, interest tests, tests to figure out what you wanted to do, why
you wanted to do it, whether you could do it if you
wanted, and whether it was against the law of man or
state if someday you actually did go ahead and do what
you was willing and able to do. All very scientific. Everything was taken care of in the Jam. That's what Wasco
dug.

If you mind your own business and tend to your own
affairs the Joint ain't so bad at all. After the last nightmare month on the street, with the dope war and all, the
old Motopsycho M.C. pitted against the combined forces
of the law, the Mafia, the Spic and spade smack dealers,
and what with, moreover, the crime rate going up every
day, with muggings, rapes, murders, even your best
friends . . . And what with the Russians and the Chinese
and the Cubans and the Vietnam War. And the A-rabs
and the Yids, and the H-bombs, A-bombs, chemical warfare, bacteriologic warfare, weather warfare, and the
demonstrations, airplane hijacks, the radicals, liberals,
fairies, and the welfare con-men and women and the
unemployed and the spades and the Chicanos and the students and all that . . . and threatened all around, from
everywhere, not paranoid, man . . . true, true, true, that
you was aimed at from all angles. . . . After all that, after them danger-filled streets in the Freeworld, the Joint
looked like home sweet home to Wasco. Oh that was a
horrific fucking last month on the street when you was
both scared shitless and happy at the same time that you
knew you was going to do time again. The net closing in.
The world about to shut down again. Narcs, Wops and
niggers and Spics after you. All of them wanting you
snuffed, blown off, zapped, greased, burnt, dusted, dead.
Asking questions all around. Looking for you even at
sweet Moke's place. Threatening your baby's ass. Threatening the life of your sweet child Flo so much that you
was happy you'd had the foresight the year before to ship
that kid of yours, only three and a half years old, off to

her Great-aunt Tutu in the Hawaiian Islands where she'd
be safe from the harm that was coming down all around.
. . . Oh yeah, and the fear! Oh, the shaking and shivering
and the nervous giggles that you had to admit to, even
now! The waiting, waiting to get taken off, waiting to beat
or be beat, the heart just a-palpitating . . . one potater
. . . two potater . . . palp pitater! Running high and running low with no chance to get a breath. Heavy fucking
dudes after you, Uncle Ben Black, and others, big Wops,
blaming an unsolved murder on you. A dealer's band,
rubber, always around your wrist; running light, a .38
caliber special at fingertip, and six big-ass Motopsychos
around you at all times. And then high speed chases, dope
battles, gang battles, police battles, shootouts, and getting
separated, Willy and Peaches getting iced, all alone suddenly, with your sure-fire death a matter of minutes away,
and then the bullets, the tracers, rocketing into your
chopped Hog, the long-forked chopper, splitting the gold-
painted gas tank, splitting your head like a pomegranate
*everything closed down and shut up and went sticky and
green and I couldn't see nothing but chlorophyll like
chewing gum stuck to my lids.* And then the capture,
which you knew was coming, which is always a drag,
even though you're feeling lucky, in a way, that it was
the Man that got you. And then the in-between place
what I call the Purge that you got to go through, that
you know got to be rough, but worth it: the shakedown
leaning out against the heavy chromed three-wheeled machine, the little punk rookie hitting you in the balls, toe-
ing it at your heel tendons. And then the real shit kicking,
the stomping in the prowl car on the way in . . . "So you
fucking animals think you're tough, huh? You motorcycle
motherfuckers. Well let's find out!" Wham! Blam! Slam!
And then the tank, the hole, the hours of questioning,
more stompings, the packed county jail *in there with all
kinds of criminals . . . petty thieves, cheap crooks, two-bit
hustlers, crazies, hippies. . . .*Trying to cop a plea, write a
cheap beef, anything but do time behind a life tops, with
a heavy silent beef in your jacket for the parole board to
read. Finking, lying, snitching on your best buddies, in-
forming on everyone but Moke, who you'd never fink on,
no matter what, dealing for an easy trey with a dime tops,
turning your best coke connection at his stash pad for the

narcs just to beat the heavy bit. Abandon ship, motherfucker, every man for himself when the shit comes down!
And then the dirty punk young Assistant D.A., the liar,
the Ivy League weenie, pricklicking cheating dog, double-
crossing swine, laughing at you while he wrote the indictment, the indictment that Wasco's frankly admittedly
criminal heart, his vengeance-ridden soul remembered verbatim, would remember till his violent dying day word for
word, sentence for sentence, paragraph by paragraph, with
murder in mind, and no remorse *I would blow him off
without blinking or flinching or thinking twice, would
crack up with giggles while the dude's blood splattered the
marble of City Hall:*

P. Jasper Brown
Asst. District Attorney
County of New Sonora
500 Courthouse   (ENDORSED)
1223 Fuller Street   FILED
New Sonora, N.S.   March 21, 1972
Phone: 6540986   Billy J. McNeer
                                  County Clerk

IN THE SUPERIOR COURT OF THE STATE OF NEW
SONORA IN AND FOR THE COUNTY OF NEW SONORA

THE PEOPLE OF THE STATE
OF NEW SONORA,
                Plaintiff,   56487
          v.   No————————
WASCO GARLAND WEED   INDICTMENT
          Defendant.

The Grand Jury of the County of New Sonora
hereby accuses WASCO GARLAND WEED of a
felony, to wit: Murder, a violation of Section 187 of
the Penal Code of New Sonora, in that on or about
the 21st day of February, 1972, in the County of
New Sonora, State of New Sonora, said defendant
did then and there murder PROVERB JEFFERSON
DUPREE, a human being.

SECOND COUNT

The Grand Jury of the County of New Sonora by this second count of this Indictment further accuses WASCO GARLAND WEED of a felony, to wit: a violation of Section 11500.5 of the Health and Safety Code of New Sonora. in that on or about the 26th day of February, 1972, in the County of New Sonora, State of New Sonora, said defendant did then and there possess for sale a narcotic, to wit: Heroin.

The Grand Jury of the County of New Senora further charges that at the time of the commission of the offense charged in Count No. One of this Information, the defendant was armed with a deadly weapon, to wit: a handgun.

Prior Conviction Against Wasco Garland Weed

The Grand Jury of the County of New Sonora further charges that before the commission of the offenses charged in this Indictment, and on or about the 20th day of May, 1966, the said WASCO GARLAND WEED was convicted in the Superior Court of the State of New Sonora in and for the County of New Sonora, of a felony, to wit: FORCIBLE RAPE, and that in pursuance of said conviction the said defendant served a term in the New Sonora State Prison, a penal institution.

Prior Conviction Against Wasco Garland Weed

The Grand Jury of the County of New Sonora further charges that before the commission of the offenses charged in this Indictment, and on or about the 12th day of October, 1962, the said WASCO GARLAND WEED was convicted in the Superior Court of the State of New Sonora, in and for the County of New Sonora, of a felony, to wit: ATTEMPTED MURDER. and that in pursuance of said conviction the said defendant served a term in the Youth Authority facility at Prill, a penal institution.

Prior Conviction Against Wasco Garland Weed

The Grand Jury of the County of New Sonora fur-
ther charges that before the commission of the of-
fenses charged in this Indictment, and on or about
the 6th day of January, 1964, the said WASCO
GARLAND WEED was convicted in the Superior
Court of the State of California, in and for the
County of San Francisco, of a felony, to wit:
GRAND THEFT, and that in pursuance of said con-
viction, the said defendant served a term in Dewayne
Vocational Institution, a penal institution.

> **A TRUE BILL**
> /s/   William McDermott
> Foreman of the Grand Jury
> of the County of New Sonora,
> State of New Sonora.

> *P. Jasper Brown, ASST. D.A.*
> County of New Sonora

. . . And then the first trial, a killer . . . *guilty on all
counts* . . . and then the waiting, the appeals, sitting up in
the county jail with no possibility of bail . . . and then finally talking with a fine and decent and sensitive gentleman of the old school, an upstanding man in all that
scum, the grandfatherly silver-haired D.A. himself, who
made an interesting and lucrative offer. . . . "Let me appeal to your better instincts, Wasco," he said, sitting there
behind that big impressive mahogany desk in the County
Courthouse building trying to impress Wasco with all that
majesty of state behind him *but drumming his manicured
fingernails nervous and sweaty on the clean green blotter
on his desk* . . . while Wasco, choosing humility for the
moment, stood there cap in hand before him on the dark
blue rug, thinking *you ain't as confident as you put out,
Jack!* . . . "Let me appeal to your belief in a better
America and racial harmony within this state," he said,
stroking his dignified Anglo-Saxon ski-nose . . . *real
nice-looking older fellah, looked like Bob Hope a little bit*
. . . And the more the old cat laid down his patter, the
more and more nervous and spit-lipped he got . . . till
Wasco, sheeeeit, his confidence, feeding like a bloodsucker

bird off the D.A.'s loss, soared up and took control of the field, like a real marauder, a fighter plane, a bat above the sparrow tree . . . "Now, I'm going to be real frank with you, Wasco. You're facing some very serious charges here, I believe, charges so serious, as a matter of fact, that you could well spend the rest of your natural life behind bars," he said, "however, since your particular case has come to my attention, I have studied your record with great thoroughness, and I firmly believe that with the proper guidance you are capable of true rehabilitation as a productive member of society. Now . . . this is only between you and me, Wasco . . . a group of . . . er . . . prominent and patriotic citizens of this state . . . men whose identity will necessarily remain secret . . . wishes to offer you every assistance, including legal and financial aid, in return for your wholehearted cooperation in . . ." and then the elegant but high-strung old aristocrat lowered his voice to the merest quailing whisper *chickenshit little anxious and birdy whisper and trying not to show how scared he was of his own dangerous words* . . . "er . . . every assistance . . . in . . . er . . . in *neutralizing*," he said, choosing his words real careful, starting over again, "what this group of citizens wants, speaking very candidly, Wasco, is, put in simple terms, for you to use all your re . . . your *resourcefulness* . . . to . . . to . . . *counteract* the influence of an extremely dangerous enemy of the state, a man who has frankly confessed his desire to bring about the downfall of this nation through force and violence, a man who has been, until now, beyond the reach of lawful punishment, a man who has, with the collusion of certain liberal-radical lawyers, judges, and politicians, consistently been permitted to carry out his treasonous agitation and conspiracy with impunity . . . making a mockery of American justice," he said, but his quivery old man's voice, it kind of lessened the impact, in a way, the impact of the *evil* in his words, showed that he was just another fucking lackey, when you got down to it, a slave to someone even higher up, someone faceless and nameless somewhere up at the state capital or somewhere even higher in political circles . . . *he didn't scare me a fucking bit . . . I knew I had the mother from the first . . . he needed me!* . . . "Now," the old man said, "anything

you may need to accomplish your mission within the
prison will be placed at your disposal . . . There is only
one minor obstacle in your path. The Honorable Warden
Miniver. But after a close scrutiny of your records,
Wasco, I can think of no better man . . . in view of your
courage and ingenuity, your ability to keep a secret, and,
most important, your youth spent on the prison grounds,
your numerous contacts and relations among the correctional officers, and your long personal acquaintanceship
with Warden Miniver . . . I can think of no better man,
Wasco, than yourself," the well-groomed old D.A. finished up, adjusting his round wire-rimmed dark glasses
which he wore day and night, carefully patting back a
stray lock of his longish white hair, a bit less sweaty-
handed and blinky now, like he was kind of happy to be
over this dangerous and ticklish business, ". . . no better
man to rapidly overcome this one minor obstacle . . ."

And then the sweet old D.A., taking heart from
Wasco's eager smile, honorably converted his generous offer into a firm oral promise of executive clemency (in the
remote event of trouble), a promise of $25,000 "upon
completion of assignment," and cold cash, $25,000, de-
posited as a down payment in the name of Prosperity
Weed in the Bank of New Sonora.

Well, sheeeeit, old Wasco, he didn't have to think twice
about that offer: "Oh you bet, sir! I'm your man, alright!"
he said, thinking: *Neutralize? Neuuuuutraliiiiize? Sheeeeit,
that "neutralize," I know what that is, that's just a fucking
made-up word for the old bastard's guilt complex, so
when the shit comes down he can tell the world and himself that he never knew a damn thing about it . . . tell his
wife and kids with a lily-white conscience that his hands
are clean . . .* "Yes *sir*," Wasco said, "why, hell, I'll have
the whole damn thing over and done with in ten days, sir,
I promise! I been real well acquainted with everyone in
that Joint all my life, sir, just like you say . . . and old
Lobo Miniver, sheeeeit, if I don't have that wishy-washy
old reformer eating out of my hand inside of a week, my
name ain't Wasco G. Weed! Take it from me, sir. I know
just how to handle him . . . *a thing of value* . . . that's
how we'll get him, sir. You can count on me . . . as long
as I can . . . a . . . as long as I can be sure you'll . . .
behind the scenes, of course . . . back me up to the hilt

. . . a . . . no matter what . . . no matter what it might
become necessary for me to . . . to . . . oh, you know
what I mean, sir!"

"By all means, Wasco," the kindly D.A. said, crinkling
up the tanned corners of his eyes behind the dark glasses,
much more relaxed now, now that he thought Wasco was
his man, smiling at Wasco just as nice as you please,
showing his even rows of bright false teeth. . . .

And then after that there wasn't no sweat at all with the
law. Wasco beat the one eighty-seven, the murder beef
. . . "Insufficient evidence." He was pronounced guilty
(as prefigured and planned) on the other counts. And
then they shipped him out to the Haley Reception
Center. . . .

Well, after that whole long process, that Purge, whew!
Yes sir! You goddamn Fucking A John! It sure was a real
pleasure to get locked up again in a smooth-running institution where you could walk around a little, bullshit with
the boys, cruise the Yard (Ooh but there was some
fine ass in that yard!), get the latest off the vine with no
danger in it for yourself . . . "Hey, man! Telegraph say
Miller been burnt at Viaduct and Ortega; he was holding
and a little fifteen-year-old hippy kid come along and run
off with the whole piece!"

. . . Sure! And you could read the paper, catch up on
the news, receive private visits from your cute little wife
with no guards listening in (the D.A.'s grease was already
working!) . . . "Hey Moke! Your man's gone and done it
again! Turned adversity into fortune, like always! Now
dig this, I already got it worked out, my Grand Design.
And you're in it! Here's what you're gonna do, you're
gonna get real friendly with a certain young guard at the
Joint. We'll run the Slow Shuck on him. I got him all
picked out for you. A real cutie. Meanwhile you're gonna
be running our old dope scam across the border to Evie's.
Yeah! We're gonna make our fucking fortune this time,
baby! If you don't believe me take a peek in your old
bank account some time, over at the Bank of New Sonora!"

. . . And you could watch a little tube, listen to the radio, and even, if you wanted, from time to time, for a certain price, get a good piece of ass off a pretty Flip kid
with a prick the size of a clit who did it open-legged and

frontways and kissed as sweet as any fox on the Street.

. . . And you could receive lawful visits from your next-nearest of kin too, your apple-cheeked old mama . . . long cozy mother and son tête-à-têtes just like back at her home in Mexican Town, and rough and tumble give-and-take sessions too, cussing and fighting with each other like cats and dogs, just like you always done . . .

"Evie, Mama dear, this time I'm gonna retire you for the rest of your natural life in queenlike splendor!"

"Sheeeeit, boy! I'll believe *that* when I see it! You always did talk a good game. . . . But . . . well, god-damnit, you *do* say the sweetest things, kid. And I like a man with a little confidence in hisself . . ."

"Yeah," Wasco said, the last time she talked to him in the Haley Visiting Room, "now listen, honey, I'm gonna need your help on this one . . ."

"Sure!" she said, playing like she was real skeptical, just like she always did, "as if I hadn't already guessed as much . . ."

"Har har! Yeah!" Wasco said, laughing deliberately. "Well, just this one last time, darlin'. But you ain't gonna mind. I'll tell you that for sure!"

"How do you know?"

"It ain't any rougher than the dope thing we been working right along, Mom."

"Who says that ain't rough? You ain't the one holding the shit in your own home."

"The profits are gonna be ten times higher, dig?"

"Who says so?"

"I say so, damnit!" Wasco said, getting real angry, "and the D.A. of New Sonora says so, and that $25,000 in Moke's bank account says so, just for openers!" And then, playing her game, the game she'd taught him as a kid, Wasco stoked his anger higher, letting her believe she'd been successful in provoking it. He ran the whole story about the D.A. and the dope scam down for her, letting her believe that it was her cunning and not his that had got him to reveal the secret . . . playing her game.

"Sonofagun!" Evie exclaimed when he was finished. "Now you're talking turkey, boy!"

"I knew I'd get you to see reason, Mom. Now, lookie here, you're gonna have to organize a little help for us out your way."

"Always *my* place, for Christ's sake! How come?"

"Now wait a minute, Evie. You got two guys out there working for you that we're gonna need."

"Who's that?"

"Come on! You only got two guys working for you! We're gonna need Uncle Big Arv in on the scam with us. And you're the only one who can get to the sonofabitch. Shit, Mama, he's been hung up on you for thirty years! Should be easy as Christmas pie. And we need Fast-Walking in on this too, the Warden's kid. So it's just gotta be! Now, I got other plans for old Fast-Walking eventually," Wasco said, continuing rapidly once he saw that Evie wasn't going to put up much more major resistance, "but we might as well make use of him while we can. He shouldn't be too hard to win over either, since, like you told me last visit, the poor slob is having money troubles as usual."

"Alright, alright!" Evie said cantankerously, but you could tell she'd go for it. The twenty-five down and twenty-five on delivery was what sold her. And all this defensive crap that she was laying down, all this objection and feistiness, that was just old Evie being Evie, as far as Wasco could tell.

"Good!" Wasco said, smiling warm as toast at his old redheaded mom, "now, dear, you handle them guys any way you want . . . use your own imagination in recruiting their services. Knowing you, honey, and your power, I figure they oughta be in the palm of your hand within a week. Remember, the key with them is this: they're both born gamblers, Mom, and a *born gambler is a born loser,* a walking mark, just looking to get took off . . ."

"Shitfire, kid!" Evie fumed, "don't you go giving old Evie advice about *people!* I'm the one that taught you the truth of them very words when you was just half past a duck's ass!"

But Wasco, he just laughed. Cause he knew he had her. "Well, damn if you ain't right, now that I think of it!" he said, but he knew that there wasn't going to be no problems with his mom. Her powerful greed would see to that. "So, anyway," he went on quickly, "after we don't have any more need of Fast-Walking's services, Mom, I want you to engage Uncle Sanger too, on this deal. You won't have no trouble with him either. You couldn't meet a nicer fellah, but, I mean, you and me know that he's so fucking punch-drunk he'd do anything anybody told him. Okay?"

"Why sure, son," Evie said, smiling her crocodile smile for him, the one he loved, "you know, dear, that I'd do anything for my baby!"

. . . So, anyway, after Wasco's relaxing month at the Country Club, which is what he called the Haley Reception Center, and with that happy knowledge always with him—the solid state contract and the twenty-five thou down and twenty-five on delivery—Wasco felt kind of fat, a little sassy, and ready to do business when the bulls slipped the leg irons, the handcuffs and chains and shackles on him and led him and fifty-five other fish, fifty-five other clean bald new convicts, out of the Main Gate and into the hot Center Valley sunlight, into the old Greyhound-type streamliner with the twin vents at the rear. And when they locked him in his wire-mesh cubicle, chained up to another white dude, a crazy little jive-talking junkie of nineteen, Wasco figured he was going home, heading on home to his pad to settle in and do business for the next three to ten . . .

Aside from carrying out the operation for which he'd been contracted by legal state authority, Wasco fully intended to get into the same business he always entered when he was behind bars: the contraband business. He figured it this way: *Twenty-five down and twenty-five on delivery . . . plus parole at my discretion, ain't nothing to sniff at. But who said I wanted out? Last time me and Moke was making so much Inside I thought we'd be able to buy the place* out! *Parole Board come by asking if I want to go home.* "Sheeeit, I said, "can't afford it, man!" Nope, fifty thou ain't hay, but it ain't what Wasco called a lifetime stash either.

Wasco had big plans for his stay in the Slam. He always had big plans. He was gonna retire himself and his entire family as wealthy and landed gentry by the time he was thirty years old. He loved his wife Moke and their little dark-haired daughter Flo and his poor family of prison guards and fruit tramps. They were what he called the "down-trodden masses," they were the victims of the World Jew, the World Nigger and the World Communistic conspiracy. He figured all his family needed was a few breaks, a push in the right direction, leadership, to bring them glory, power, money, cars, beautiful people around them, servants, houses, European travel. . . . Now, he was going to have to use them, use his family's help, a certain way, maybe without them knowing it, except for Evie, this one last time, for their own good, to further his grand design. But the way it'd end up they'd see it was all worth it. Why shit! It'd be worth it to them even while they worked the scam from him. *I'll offer each man what he's got to have:* one wants love, one wants money, one wants to get away, and one *(me)* wants positive action in defense of racial harmony and a better America. Aside from that, like Evie was saying just last visit, all they wanted was "some damn woman or other." Well, old Wasco, he'd see that they got it, everything they wanted.

Wasco always liked to accentuate the positive, eliminate the negative, just like in the song. He figured the world was rough, but it didn't have no grudge against him personally. There was no sense getting all paranoid about everything and everyone being against you, like dudes in the Jam was always doing. "Shit, man, I just ain't never had no breaks," they were always moaning. But Wasco figured you made your own breaks. Luck could be manufactured. There wasn't anything you couldn't do with a little self-confidence, a little faith in your star. Wasco's mom taught him that when he was still in the crib, and he still believed it. If he took it into his head he felt perfectly capable of cracking rocks with his bare hands, splitting the atom with his skull, healing the sick with his middle finger, hypnotizing people with his eyes. Wasco loved his own eyes. They were the most remarkable blue anyone'd ever seen. They were so fucking blue they were almost purple, so purple sometimes they were bald-ass red. He sometimes felt he could drill holes through solid tempered steel with them fucking orbs of his. Nobody he'd ever met had as much confidence in himself as Wasco. Nobody. He was unbeatable. The world was his for the taking. This way of thinking was at once the secret of his considerable success, and the reason he was always ending up in the Jam. But that didn't matter. What mattered was guts, and calculated risks, and not getting into a rut, and going way the fuck out beyond the ordinary limitations of ordinary chickenshit human beings. "Just look at me," he always said to them punks in the Joint, pointing at his brawny body bursting with vibrant good health, "I'm in perfect shape cause I believe in myself, and my body shows it. You take a weak-kneed, lily-livered, pale-ass skinny little weakling and ask him 'do you believe in yourself?' He'll always say 'no.' You know why? Cause he don't follow in his star!"

Now, you take the old Motopsycho M.C. When Wasco met up with them they was mean-ass motherfuckers. But they didn't have no class. No style. "The Whisky Go-Go's," they called themselves. But they weren't going nowheres. Wasco cased out several top clubs for a few months before he settled on the Go-Go's as his own. Walked into the Dipsy-Doodle Bar one night, their hangout, and made the acquaintance of the chief, a great big strong and dumb type, a Lithuanian cat from Pittsburgh, Pa. Struck up a friendship over beer and Polack jokes and pretzels. Within a week of hanging out at the Dipsy-Doodle they all dug Wasco's act so much, and his bad-ass three-wheeled chrome machine, and his dynamite plans for making a million in the dope trade, that they asked him if he wanted to join up. He said, "Sure, man," knowing that only a member could challenge the leader for chiefdom of the club. Anybody else got ganged and offed right on the spot. Wound up in the West Hazelton Hills with a motorcycle drive chain wrapped around his neck. Well, like, another week went by and Wasco turned the whole club on to his fine Ecuadorian cocaine and a sure-fire scheme for making their fortune on the Mexican run. After he had everyone wowed with his rap and his good coke he said to the prez, "Hey Andy, I heard you give the best head in town. A faggot told me. How about . . ." Wham! Crash! Blam! Pow! It wasn't even a contest. Wasco'd been ready for him with brass knucks. He'd kept his hand in his pocket the whole time he was talking. And anyway, that fucking Lithuanian, he had eyes, after all. He could see who the club was rooting for. The winner. He could see that they all knew where their damn bread was buttered, and wouldn't be too broke up if Andy had a little . . . bad luck. So, old Andy, the poor sonofabitch, he came flailing across the bar real stupidlike, swinging wild haymakers. Wasco just laughed, ducked, and broke his kneecap with his steel-toed stomper boots. After that it

was easy. Andy was real nervous and scared-looking,
seeing that he was abandoned by his only friends, and all.
. . . And he couldn't stand up right, with his knee problem, so Wasco could take him at his leisure. He did.
Them fucking Whisky Go-Go's never seen anything like
it. Wasco took him slow, took him easy and bad, made it
last, extended it for the pleasure of his audience. Broke
his other fucking knee. Got his nose. His front teeth. Got
him crying like a baby, begging for mercy. "Should I give
it to him?" Wasco asked the Whisky Go-Go's. "Fuck no!"
they all yelled. "Never give mercy to a faggot!" The cli-
max of the show was when Wasco made him crawl out
onto Fifth Street on his belly over a thirty-foot bed of
broken beer bottles. . . . Later on, a month or so afterwards, Andy made some incautious threats from his hospital bed. So it was Wasco's unpleasant duty as prez of
the newly rechartered Motopsycho M.C. to send a man
over to put the poor Lithuanian slob out of his misery.
. . . And within a year after that Wasco had delivered to
the boys of the club just what he'd promised he would,
just what they wanted: a new name, a new image, a new
style, heavy new financial resources, talk-show spots on
national TV . . . press conferences . . . the works!
    . . . The driver wheeled the big old prison bus out the
sally port and along the bumpy blacktop road that was
shimmering in the sun. Wasco watched the almond
orchards and walnut groves and alfalfa fields going by with
interest but no desire. He didn't at all want to be out
there, free and chainless. Even out in the bucolic Center
Valley, with all those trees and open fields and irrigation
canals, danger was sure to be waiting. Even Middle River,
lazy and brown, looked like danger water to Wasco.
    Riding out in the Center Valley reminded him of old
Evie again, his light-foot, fruit tramp mama, who left him
and his old man in their little wood cottage on the prison
grounds when Wasco was just a little guy and never came
back. She soon became the richest tramp on the circuit.
The fastest tomato packer in the history of the West: her
record she made one day on the winter crop down in the
Coachella Valley, California: 1,088 double boxes of
Medium Green Rounds in ten hours and thirteen minutes.
The record still held to this day. And she still kept the
plaque commemorating the event. It was sitting on top of

her portable TV in her house trailer, a fancy aluminum streamliner job that she pulled with a big pink and black Cadillac Coupe de Ville. She doubled as a revivalist whenever she could find a tent meeting. That's where she made all her extra. Every once in a while she'd flash into town for a day or two, bringing everybody, including the old man, a whole shitload of presents, plus cake and candy and ice cream. If she didn't have a man with her at the time, she'd sleep with old Dad for the night, and then be on her way early the next morning, heading out to the tomato circuit in the Center Valley, and then down to California, to the Sacramento, San Joaquin, and Imperial valleys, following the later and later crops till finally, at the Mexican border, she'd hit the winter crop and January the year out. Then she'd head slowly back up north, following the season, following her fortune. Wasco always dug her more than the old man because she wasn't so steady. When she wanted to do something, why, she just went out and did it! And that was that. The old man, he was quiet and slow and cautious. A secret drunk who always threw stones at Mom cause she would tipple a bit in the barrooms. He was a hypocrite, as far as Wasco was concerned. And that's one thing that old Evie never was. If a spade was a spade, why, she'd call the motherfucker right there. He'd heard her do it once in a trailer court when he was spending the summer with her down in Turlock . . . "Get outa here, you dirty nigger!" she yelled, and the cat, real dark complected, he did it. He split posthaste.

Oh, but she was good people, old Evie, Wasco was thinking. Even though he knew in his heart he couldn't trust her as far as he could throw her. She was out for old Numero Uno. Wasco figured he could never trust her like he trusted Moke. Even though he knew this about old Evie, knew that the bitch would help him out only so far as she could help herself, would fink on him, cop a plea at his expense without batting an eye if she ever got caught, even so, despite her cold-bloodedness and her treachery, there was something about her that Wasco loved above all else. Even though Evie'd screwed him up a hundred times, turned him into the police more than once, turned him out of her trailer too more than once, refused him money when he was broke, beat the shit out of him with a razor strap when he was still just a baby. . . . Maybe the main reason he loved her so much was that you always love the one most who will stab you in the back. Makes it more kinky that way, Wasco thought.

One time Wasco went out with her on the road for a whole summer. Down in Porterville she picked up this cat at an Okie bar and took him home for a one nighter and got what she wanted out of the sonofabitch and then kicked him out the next morning. Wasco listened to the whole thing from the trailer's front-room couch. Next night he came by wanting some more nookie. But she was tired of his stuff, she said. And it was too late to be coming around pounding at her door. Her and Wasco, a great big kid of fifteen, was laying up in her big double trailer bed together, tireder than shit, after a day's packing at the Hayman-Culver shed. So she said, "Hey, son, make your voice real deep, pretend like you're a mean-ass Texan stud and tell that cocksucker to vamoose!" So Wasco, he did it, he yelled out in a deep Texas voice that would've struck fear into the heart of Jesus, he yells out, "Hey, Okie! Get the fuck outa here before I come out with my thirty ought six!" And the dude. he split faster than a nigger boy splits watermelon with a Monkey-Ward ax. And Wasco and his old mom, old Evie, they laughed all night long.

She was like that. Different from the old man. She was always full of life. Now she was richer than shit. Fixed up fine with her own store and whorehouse in Nueva Ronda. She wrote him once in a while, and came to visit him from time to time when he was in the Joint. This time he'd already received several visits from her, but you couldn't count that cause they had business to talk about now. Wasco admired his mama, especially for the way she got her new whorehouse and general store. Evie was always fixed up nice with a man. She made damn sure. Been through at least six husbands, as far as Wasco could figure. She used to read the obituary column every day in the newspaper. When she read about the death of a lady of, say forty to fifty-five years old, she used to go down and attend the funeral, looking the husband over real careful. If he looked like money, she'd fall by his house a week or so later, selling permanent plastic flowers for the grave. She'd knock, and Wasco's mama, she was real sexy and big-hipped and buxom, with red hair and kewpie-doll blue eyes, and an ass on her that'd drive a gelded mule to distraction. So, nine times out of ten she'd have the dude bedded down that very night. And if it looked like real money (she could tell by their bellies, she always said), and they were good in bed (she insisted on a good fuck all her life, regardless of the financial end of matters), she'd be married again within a month. When she felt like leaving she'd never bother with a divorce. She'd just wait till she had enough of his bread in her name and swoop out. "The law don't bother with women or niggers," she always said, and Wasco figured she was right. Cause neither his mama nor any nigger he knew had ever been prosecuted for bigamy. So, anyway, the last dude in her lineup was a Spic with a little store and wetback camp in Nueva Ronda. It wasn't much, just a little brokendown wooden place in Chile-Town, but she had plans for it, and she'd found out he had cancer just like his wife had. Sure enough, he passed on within six months. And she was even sad to see him go, she said. He was a fine upstanding man who always treated her right, even if he was Mexican. Now she had settled in there, with her own business at last. Just the thing she'd always dreamed of. And she'd fixed the place up, and brought in some girls for the wetbacks, and hired Uncle Big Arv and Fast-Walking to drive a VW minibus around to all the labor camps in the neighborhood and bring in the braceros, and, well, the way Wasco saw it, she was pretty well set up. Although, he'd never dream of asking her for anything out of her little nest egg, even for bail money. He knew, if he did, all her respect would be lost. She always told him, "You know, kid, I never did respect a man who couldn't stand up on his own two feet." And Wasco, by God, had always done just that, ever since he was ten years old. He'd never asked or given quarter to anyone, not to save his fucking soul, not unless it was a matter of life and death. Then he'd ask for quarter, beg for it on his knees, and when it was given, give none in return. "It's a dog eat dog world," Evie always said. And Wasco listened.

The big old Commission of Corrections bus speeded up and swung up the on-ramp of the freeway and started climbing the hills of the Coast Range. Wasco became aware that the little punk junkie next to him was itching to break in upon his delicious daydream. It seemed like he

wanted to talk. But Wasco, with a lifetime's experience
with punks, knew how to handle that right quick.

"Hey, Jim!" the junkie said, "what's shaking in the
Joint? You done time over there? Hey, man, you heard?
There's a big nigger on this here short!"

Wasco leaned down as far as he could and raised his
hand as high as the chains permitted and got out with
great difficulty a pack of cigarillos from his denim shirt
pocket and offered the punk one, the squeeze. That's what
he was, if Wasco ever seen one. The kid was a born
squeeze, servant class, spouse class, a born cellmate.

"You like these, sweetheart?"

"Yeah."

"You sure they ain't too strong for your constitution,
Squeezy?"

"Sure."

"Here then, take two of them . . . go on!"

"Thanks."

"Now light them up."

"What?"

"Light them up."

"Both of them?"

"Do it!"

The squeeze lit them both and tried to smile and smoke
them but he got red in the face and sick and looked like
he wanted to put them out. Wasco wouldn't let him. He
made the skinny little junkie smoke them down to little
butts and then he said, "I feel like giving you another couple of smokes, or something else, just as a kind of gift.
Anything else you want, sugar?"

"Uh . . . no . . . I just . . ."

And Wasco cracked his best meat-eating grin and sent
the fear of Jesus into the squeeze's quivering thin addict
skin, and his weak Irish nose started running from withdrawal sickness or too much cigar and he couldn't wipe
it and it ran down onto his blue little lips and he left Wasco
alone all the rest of the way through the valley and west
through the green rainy-season hills and oak groves and
mesquite and cattle ranch country. Wasco watched the
cows grazing and an occasional horse or two, and a few
sheep, and ranch houses, Okie settlements with wrecked
cars in the front yards and rabbit hutches in back, and
roadside stands, billboards, wine-tasting rooms, Frosty

Freezes, fruit stands, waiting for the bus to cross over the Coast Range.

At Ajo there was a big airfield. Burney Air Force Base. It was huge, built for the heavy stuff, big MATS freighters and tankers and SAC stuff, four, six and eight and ten engine babies. You could see them stacked up in layers in the sky, shining like glass in the sun, running in from Hawaii, from Okinawa, from Thailand and Japan and Vietnam. They glided in for miles, one on top of the other, coming in low over the parking lots and hangars and barracks and dependents' housing areas and PX's, quiet, hitting the blacktop without a sound, in slow motion. It was beautiful. All silver and all black. Silver planes and buildings, reflecting the sun. Black roads and runways and parking lots, absorbing it. *Little Arv rode in from Vietnam here. Mom closed the store for the occasion. Aunt May took the day off from her waitressing job at Bert's Beanery. They were waiting for him when the plane landed. Looked good, Aunt May said. Had a nice tan, Mom said. Put on weight. They made a real man out of my boy, Aunt May said . . . Sheeeit! Take more than just that to make him a man!* Wasco sometimes truly regretted the fact that he never graduated from high school or went to college, cause something he'd always wanted to do was fly one of them big-ass silver babies, them birds. But one thing, he didn't have to worry about no competition from Little Arv, his little cousin. Arv used to just hang around on his coattails all the time, tagging along, trying to figure out what Wasco had that he was missing. Always flirting around with the cool world, the world of motorcycles and rock music and fistfights and beer drinking, but never really letting go, never would you see the little shrimp with greasy dirty hands. He was like a lot of book readers and fairies who want to sniff around the real world, the street world. But then, when it came right down to it, he always chickened out. He liked to smoke a little grass, maybe, on Saturday night, but he'd never blow his mind. He liked to break a law once in a while, exceeding the speed limit or throwing a rock at a cop in a big crowd of longhairs. But you talk to him about blowing off a narc with a .45 and he shut up fast . . . even though, you had to say, the little turd was a real good marksman, if you came right down to it, an expert with

sidearm or rifle. Not that he'd ever dreamed of using one
on anything but targets and bottles and tin cans. Even
over in Vietnam . . . Aunt May said, "Well sir, I'm
proud to say that my boy never had to fire a shot in anger
. . ." Anyway, that old Little Arvie . . . Marvie-Arvie,
all the kids used to call him, he liked to maybe ride
around on a little stroked Triumph T-Bird in tennis shoes,
laughing and giggling. But it you showed him a pack of
filthy Hog riders tooling down the freeway stinking up the
world, chug-a-lugging beer cans and throwing them at
pedestrians, he lost interest fast. All he wanted to do was
bop around real innocent, and then check out, hoping he
wouldn't get burnt. Yeah, that old Arv. Wasco felt a real
fondness for the little squirt. Like to see him get on in the
world. Was figuring on helping him along as much as he
could. Loved the kid like a brother. Grew up together.
Wasco wanted to liberate his cousin. Arv thought he was
going to get free through going to college, hanging out
with them mod kids and hippies. That was just more middle-class shit! That was just conforming! Wasco would
show him freedom. Wasco would show him what real rebellion was! Funnily enough, Arv had never dug Wasco
too much. And now, riding along in the prison bus, crossing the Coast Range, Wasco couldn't really figure out
why. Except for a little hazing now and again as a kid,
just pantsing him and giving him Indian burns and shit
like that, he hadn't done much at all to Arv, that he could
remember. But, years ago, Arv had had the nerve to
throw out a challenge on the football field . . . "You just
wait, Wasco! One of these days I'll get you back, you
bastard!" he'd cried through his tears, "one of these days
I'll be the boss and you'll be the lackey!" Wasco thought
of that old challenge now. He intended to hold Arv to it.
He truly loved his little cuz, but the kid had to grow up
sometime, had to find out what the real world was like
. . . and it ain't no picnic! Wasco had determined to initiate him this time, bring him out in a big way . . . the biggest of all . . . Wasco had even set the plan in motion,
had even, with sweet Moke's zealous aid, set into motion
the forces that would irresistibly sweep him into direct
participation in that initiation . . . self-initiation. It was
all part of Wasco's grand design, a design inspired by the
kind old D.A.'s generosity and foresight, perhaps, but

turned into a thing of perfection, a work of the finest art, by the genius of Mr. Wasco Fucking G. Weed! Yeah!

That old Arv. He always used to say, "Come on! Let me go with you, you guys," when Wasco and Wesley wanted to go out to the levee and drink beer and jack off. And then, when they'd get out there, and try to get him to blow them, he wouldn't, even though he was drunk. So Wasco, this one time, he says, "Okay, then beat me off."

"No!" Arv said, real shocked, like nobody ever did that kind of nasty thing.

"Alright, I'll beat you if you beat meeeee off," Wasco said, real kewpie-doll, blinking his red eyelashes at him, rolling his eyes, laughing, winking at Wesley.

"Okay," the little shrimp said, and tried to get his hand around the gigantic loaf that Wasco had by that time. Wasco went for Arv's little peepee, but couldn't find it. "Where do you keep that little weenie?" he roared. Wesley like to split his beer belly. Finally Wasco found the little thing where it was hiding in the zipper fold of his Levis and shook it at Wesley between his thumb and forefinger, laughing to beat all git out. "Hey Wesley," he yelled, "ever seen meat like that?"

"Why sure," Wesley said, doubling over with the giggles, "I got a banty rooster out at the dairy looks maybe only a half inch longer!"

"Shut up, Wesley," Wasco hollered, "or you'll make him disappear it!"

The bus veered off the freeway now and followed along the northern edge of Refugio Bay going along the salt flats and dirty sloughs and swampy tule land and bird refuges to Colina Linda, where it turned and went down Highway 61 going south through more and more little towns and modern housing tracts that nestled back into the green and yellow hills and then past Montclair Field where Phantom fighter planes squatted white and shiny and long and low as basking sharks in rows. Wasco couldn't see a one of them in the air yet.

The squeeze finally got up enough of his mealymouthed cowardly nerve to lean over in Wasco's direction again.

"You seen him yet?"

"Seen who?"

"I told you, that bad-ass spade cat. That's him up there."

"You like to chat, don't you?" Wasco said, narrowing his eyes.

"Listen . . ."

"Sure! You got some more info for me, honeylamb?"

"I was . . ." he started, but gave up when he saw that Wasco was ignoring him on purpose, looking forward to where he'd been pointing, staring at that mild-looking little brown black man of early middle age, sitting alone in one of the wire cages smoking a cigarette. He seemed to be, like Wasco, just watching the landscape, not interested in the other convicts on the bus. Wasco caught him in profile when he turned to look at one of them sharks, them pretty Phantoms, taking off. Then he bent over and started writing something. It looked like he was writing a letter. Funny, a guy writing a letter on the bus, like that. After a while a guard came back and took something away from him. It was a book. Wasco couldn't see the title. He didn't look mean at the guard at all. Didn't look bad-ass, not what Wasco'd expected. He had this real mild expression on his face. That meant it didn't say nothing. He had a mouth that could tremble. That was all. He could shiver and shake with fear, just like anybody. His eyes could cry. Once maybe he was happy. Or once he used to laugh a lot, you could see it in his wrinkles around the eyes. He had damp brown eyes. That kind of person is never dumb. They might or might not be weak. But they're never dumb. Don't think for a minute that they got to be weak-livered if they got them wet brown cow eyes. Wasco seen that type kill, real chilly. And dry-eyed ones peeing into their socks. No sir! Wet eyes got to do with smarts. You got to watch out with a dude like that. Cause you never know. *I'm going to watch that nigger real close, cause he's my man. . . .*

Wasco, in secret, had nothing against niggers. Nothing at all. Like everything else in life, he merely used racism as a tool and weapon for self-improvement and advancement.

Wasco was just sitting there quiet thinking like that but the little junkie just couldn't contain himself. All in a breathless panting teenage flush, or a smack withdrawal flush, he rushed out with it: "That's Galliot! They're transferring him up to the Main Joint. They set up them militants down at Brown Max. He's the only one left alive. They figure he wants to pick off another Pig to get even. He already got one, but they can't prove it. There's rumors out that the suedes are going to riot when he gets in, take hostages, and get him released to fly to Cuba . . ."

"Say," Wasco said, real icy, "I don't want you to ever call an officer of the law a 'Pig' around me again. You dig? Never. I don't want to ever hear that kind of nigger talk around me either. Remember your race, man. You ain't one of them jungle bunnies."

But the squeeze went on, not listening, "Look, I heard that in the Joint the Man almost got the militants contained, see? He's the last one . . ."

"Say man," Wasco said, "I want to thank you, sweet-meat, for running it down for me . . ."

"Sure! And you know what? They say that pretty soon, old Galliot, he's gonna be on ice, man, ice!"

"I'll tell you what," Wasco said, "I'm going to remember your nice young face. Inside I'm going to make it a point to get to know you better. You can fill me in on the latest off the vine. And I'll pay you back, some time, in the shower room, with a few friends . . ."

And after that the little punk shut his pinched mackerel-snapping face. His junkie-yellow simpering little girl's jaw clamped down tight, and he never said another word all the way to Quintana Sound, all the way to the front gate of the Joint. Wasco watched him close to make sure. He almost shut his eyes, Wasco did, he narrowed them down to heredity, Cherokee slits, Indian Territory, two mean bright-hot little redskin jewels, burning twin cigarette holes into the junkie's pale-haired temples, thinking *the punk's got the skinny. Never let a squeeze know when he's right. You do, and he uses it. Never let a punk know he can use it. Keep those snake eyes on him, the Okie-Mexican orbs, them fiery Indian beans; keep him quiet and still. Put the fear of Jesus into him, the fear of the burning Weed. Hold him still and tense at the top of his toes. Then lead him where you want by his chin . . .*

Crossing the last range of hills before the Joint, above the salt flats, after passing the town of Mission Santa Bonita on the freeway, Wasco remembered Little Arv's donkey. Canary, they used to call it, Rocky Mountain Canary. But just Canary for short. Wasco used to creep around in back of Arv's place and untie it and haul ass for the hills above the salt flats and the Joint. These same familiar low green sound-side hills before him now, these good windy coastal hills with sparse stands of pine trees and hidden groves of stunted oak trees. Used to ride it for hours in the moonlight, telling it his troubles, riding slow, bareback, through the wild oats, through the grass and fern, the pine and oak, to a secret place he knew, singing to the donkey to pass the time. It was just a little old yellow donkey, but Wasco did truly dig and admire that smelly beast, more than anything or anybody he could remember, till Moke came along. . . . Wasco used to sing it, he would sing:

> You keep me waiting till it's getting aggravating
> You're a slow poke
> I wait and worry but you never seem to hurry
> You're a slow poke, dear.
>
> Why should I keep trying to change you
> It's not the thing to do
> I guess I'll have to learn to be a slow poke too!

Two

After driving home from City College, Little Arvin Weed, part-time student, full-time prison guard, always liked to take a good long shit while he read the *New Sonora Times* from cover to cover. It was the only time he could really relax. Every other minute of the day was covered, booked solid, overbooked. Up in semidarkness for his eight o'clock class, Humanities 167. Then a pat required course, Speech II, so he could get his B.A. degree in June. Then his favorite course, Creative Writing I, with Elaine, his friend, or his almost friend, his teacher, a stutterer, a thick-haired freak, a mad persecuted young survivor of the New Left of the mid-'60's, scarred untiring radical of the '70's, national coordinator of the Free Galliot Committee (and rumored ex-lover of the great black radical himself), the Fair Shake for Black Fence Committee, and member in good standing of dozens of other far-out organizations. And then a quick burger and a shake in the Dining Commons with Moke, his classmate in Creative Writing, his newfound friend, adversary, seductress, lover, envying her and all the other long-haired free people hanging out in there with nothing but time on their hands. Then bye bye, baby! See you after work. And out to the parking lot and his Merc. Down 18th Avenue with its row upon row of double-decker white and pink stucco modern houses with carefully tended twenty-foot-square lawns and neat clean thin palm trees that leaned uniformly backward, away from the wide bright Pacific. Then over the Scully Peak Road with its perfect view of Quintana Sound and the Alvarez Straits and the small hillside cities on the other side of the Estuary. And then he drove into the broken-down Victorian neighborhoods to Orchard Street, Blueville, the Black Belt, niggertown, to his low-rent two-room apartment in the ghetto and a long anticipated shit, and a leisurely read-through of the *New Sonora Times* before he went to work at the Joint:

PEACE TALKS BREAK DOWN
KISSINGER RETURNS TO US

One o'clock. Two hours to do a number. Little Arv lay back on his bed on his war surplus army blanket looking up at the stained curleycues on the ornate Victorian ceiling. He lay there perhaps fifteen minutes contemplating and smoking a joint, making lists in his head. Arvin was a lister. He made lists of *things to do, things I want, things I don't want, things to read, to think about, to write about, to investigate, to experience, to avoid.* He wrote them down on scraps of paper which he saved for months and then finally lost or threw away, he made them in his head and then promptly forgot them.

Arv had just recently, through a stroke of fortune, found a way to begin clearing himself of all the debts he'd incurred since his unfortunate shotgun marriage. He'd done it by accepting a commission, an *illegal* commission, and taking a great risk, a risk so serious, so dangerous, that he preferred not to think of it, preferred to think of his other alternatives, which seemed to him even worse: working two jobs while attending college full time, as he'd done until very recently, working his ass to the bone, sleeping only four or five hours a night in order to meet his obligations of child support. . . . Yes, old Arv, he preferred to make lists in his head, looking forward to a future in his life that until just a week or so before he'd believed to be beyond hope:

MONEY TO BE SAVED	
Jan.	$200
Feb.	200
Mar.	200
Apr.	200
May	200
June	200
July	200
Aug.	200
Sept.	200
Oct.	200

Nov.	200
Dec.	200
Jan.	200
Total:	$2,600

Arv counted it up again, listing each month in his head
. . . it seemed such a pathetic sum of money when he
thought about the enormity of his risk: *the law prescribes
a sentence of five years minimum for the correctional
officer convicted of carrying uncensored mail to or from
an inmate in state custody.* Considering the notoriety of
the black militant Galliot, the intended recipient of the
letter Arv would smuggle into the Joint for the first time
today, and considering also the recent ascendancy of an
archconservative wing of the Republican Party on the political scene in New Sonora, Arv knew that if he were
caught he would get no mercy, no suspended sentence, no
copping a plea as a first offender, none of that at all. Yet,
somehow, the very severity of the possible consequences of
his actions gave Arv some comfort: the great risk was a
measure of his desperate resolve, his lifetime desire to escape from New Sonora, the Joint, his family and friends,
and all that they represented to him—unhappiness, repres-
sion, decay—to leave them all behind forever. . . .

All the time that Arv was thinking like this, he continued making lists in his head. One of the great things about
his lists, he felt, was the fact that they were a form of
recreation. They relaxed you. Got the little things in life
into some kind of order, afforded you a modicum of perspective, objectivity, in regard to your own life, made it
"official," as it were. And there is nothing more objective
than a list. So, meanwhile, Arv was able to catalogue the
things in his rather barren room. The room was almost
empty. There was only:

1. a map of the globe
2. a map of Paris streets
3. a typewriter
4. a table
5. a mattress
6. sheets and blankets
7. a bedspread
8. two tatami mats

9. two windows
10. a light bulb
11. a reading lamp

It wasn't that Arv didn't like nice things. When he was married he used to take a lot of trouble fixing up his little home on the prison grounds, decorating it and redecorating it with his young wife, Deanna. And even in the army, inside his locker he'd made a private miniature world all his own, with a tiny vase, and fresh flowers, and small framed pictures and maps. And he'd kept it there inviolate, hidden from the eyes of everyone in the platoon, until he was caught, and the sergeant made him throw it all out. But anyway, it hadn't been for show; he wasn't a man for that kind of display. It had been for himself alone, his own inner gratification in things of beauty. But now, of course, he was keeping himself light, minimizing possessions, camping out, in a way, to remind himself on purpose at every moment of the day that he was leaving soon, that he was going away, to Europe, or Africa, or Asia, or Australia, it didn't even matter where, that he was splitting, swooping, fading out, as soon as humanly possible, as soon as he had the funds, the bread, the ill-gotten gains, the moo to do it! Because he was sick to death of the horrible, dreary, jive-ass life he'd been leading since he was born . . . Deanna, the bitch, would oppose him, naturally. The law would oppose him, as a matter of course: *Child Abandonment, Willful Withdrawal of Child Support, New Sonora Health and Safety Code #654-K and #655-B.* And Deanna's parents would oppose him, and his parents, the world, society, even his little daughter Wendy would oppose him and end up hating him when she grew up. But . . . to hell with them all! For them it would be perhaps a slight inconvenience. Deanna would have to accept money from her well-set dad, Lobo Miniver, Warden of the Slam. Big fucking deal! Everyone would get all hot and bothered. So what? To Arv it would be salvation, literally. If he stayed on they'd all be a bit happier, but Arv would die, truly die. It would be the end of him, to stay on at the Joint, and no bullshit about it. . . .

Blam! The downstairs door slammed, rattling the windows. It was Arv's unwelcome house guest coming in, his ex-brother-in-law Fast-Walking Miniver, whose hardnosed

French wife had just kicked him out of the house. Found out his salary'd been attached for secret gambling debts, and he'd lost his stripes again.

Now Fast-Walking, dishonored prison guard, son of a penitentiary warden, junior college grad, who'd once had a brilliant career ahead of him in the state penal service, worked an extra job over across the estuary for Arv's Aunt Evie, trying to pay off his debts so his old lady'd let him back in the house.

Though happy to offer his hospitality on a temporary basis, Arv found the whole thing depressing, and would be delighted when Fast-Walking's wife relented. The truth was that Arv feared the spendthrift sonofabitch would get wind of his brand new savings account at the Bank of New Sonora.

Arv glanced at his watch. He began looking over at his second-hand uncovered Smith-Corona typewriter nervously. Then he got up and stalked it. It was time. He circled it, feinted, jabbed at it, getting a kick out of his own act, the rather belabored drama of this daily game. And then quick he stepped back, shadowed it, boxed it, twirled away, the old footwork, the fast-walk, like Fast-Walking was always doing, going slow but looking like fast. Finally he attacked it frontally, overcame it by force, sat at it and madly pounded it for the allotted one hour and forty-five minutes without another thought in the world, not even caring what hit the flying pages. He did this every day, including days off and holidays, never looking at the finished product until later, as if a stranger wrote it. He could achieve greater objectivity that way. "Objectivity" was one of the most important and frequently employed words in Little Arv's vocabulary. A working-class kid, prison guard's son, up from the bottom, he'd only recently learned what it meant. He'd looked it up a hundred times in the dictionary before it finally sank in. He had a difficult time with learning. It came hard. But once he had it, well, goddamn! It was learnt, Jack, for good! Old Elaine liked Arv's stuff. Said so all the time. But Elaine was prodding at him all the time, trying to make him "think seriously" about things. She was always talking politics, trying to get Arv to think about his job in the Joint, and what it meant. "Why don't you bring your personal experience into your writing?" she was always asking. But he hadn't been able to write about the Joint until very re-

cently. He hated it too much. He hated it with all his
heart and all his soul because it was boring and depressing. Elaine said, "Why do you work there, anyway?" Arv
couldn't imagine why not. He needed the money. And
even Albert Camus once said: *Part of becoming a man is
spending time in prison.*

"First of all," Elaine said in reply, "that reactionary
colonialist Camus didn't have the foggiest notion what
real 'manhood' was . . . and second . . . you're not *in*
prison."

"Oh, but I am!" he insisted, "and I've been there all my
life!"

Anyway, somebody had to work there. Besides, everyone he knew, everyone he'd grown up with, and even
most of his family worked there. As far as Arv could see,
no matter where or when, under no matter what kind of
political system, capitalism or socialism or Communism,
there would always be a need for prisons. There would always be cons, always be guards. Of that he was sure. But
old Arv himself, by God, he had no intention of being either one ever again. Because the Joint was a disgusting
horrible place. Not so much because of the guards, or the
administration, or the inmates (who all seemed, on a general moral comparison, more or less alike, as far as Arv
could tell: uniformly, unthinkingly, mundanely evil). The
problem was, and always would be, the human condition
itself, the problem of evil, the fact that there would always be a society, of one kind or another, and there
would always be the dude who would transgress the arbi-
trary rules of that society. So, the way Arv saw it, given
this flaw in the scheme of things, the human scheme,
you'd just have to always accept the necessity of prisons, a
permanent but necessary evil.

Arv was just getting warmed up, getting this all down
on an essay for his Humanities course, getting excited
about himself, and the sweet pattern of his mind's work,
work that was new and fresh and wonderful to him, when
at exactly three o'clock the alarm went off, catching him
in mid-sentence. He stopped there, however, right in the
middle of the sentence, took off his civilian shirt, and
went across the hall to the bathroom where he stood on
tiptoe regarding himself in the mirror for a moment.
What does a fucking prison guard look like? Short, squat,
and irredeemably ugly was this state employee, or at least

that's what his mirror said: squinting little slitlike slant
eyes, Weed eyes, the heritage of his half-breed family. An
off-kilter bashed-in flat boneless nose with skin stretched
taut to display to horrible advantage its black and bristly
moist innards. A low simian forehead upon which fell in
hysterical and unattractive confusion his coarse curly dull
black hair. A pink premature bald spot in the center of
his crown. Thick bettle-ridged eyebrows: the eyebrows of
an Australoid. A fat insipid mouth. Quivering chicken-
sensitive Mexican lips that collected spittle habitually in
their corners. A tiny pink pointed tongue, the tongue of a
rat, a furtive darting drippy tongue that flicked outside his
mouth constantly, nervously, uncontrollably. The scars of
teenage acne. And, covering it all, all this ghastly face, in
redneck Okie profusion, were scattered millions of obscene and assinine little brown splotchy freckles, from
forehead to chin, and then from neck to asshole, from
toes to fingertip. . . .

That's how Arv's mirror saw him as he busily brushed
his teeth *ugly crooked wide-gapped teeth*, shaved quickly
and carefully, trimming his dark modified Pancho Villa
moustache (severely modified moustache: the only kind
the prison authorities permitted), combed his fringe of
black hair artfully sideways to camouflage the trauma of
his young life, and got into his prison guard's uniform
Come on, man! You ain't that bad looking, are you?

At this time Arv decided to have a look out the window
at the Alatri Art School across the street. Class was just
letting out, and whole flocks and coveys of beautiful black
and white birds came flooding out onto the sunny pavement, holding their sketch pads and books against their
high young breasts, chirping excitedly to each other about
the day's lessons. Arv could see Fast-Walking too, the
lecherous bastard, peeking out of the window of the other
room, digging it too, supremely! They waved at each
other and Fast-Walking's loose lascivious gesture with his
short skinny arms made Arv snigger. And then they snig-
gered together . . . SNUCKSNUCK! . . . and this gift of
Fast-Walking's that made Arv laugh, this sweet wanton
moment they shared that proved Fast-Walking was no
better than Arv, just as nasty, just as ugly-minded and
piggy, immediately reconfirmed Arv in his basic affection
for his ex-brother-in-law.

Little Arv got his uniform on. It wasn't the real

McCoy, actually. It wasn't the official Commission of Corrections uniform that Fast-Walking wore. Arv wore his ex-army garb: forest green dress pants, black shoes, brass clasp belt, black tie, tan shirt. The prison uniform was similar, but a little lighter green in color. And the official prison belt was much wider, and brown instead of black, and the buckle was iron, heavy iron, with double tongues. This, of course, was an insignificant detail to Arv, but it caused him no end of difficulty in the Joint. Fast-Walking, and Arv's father, and his Uncle Sanger, and every other half-assed official he came up against were always saying, "Say there, when ya gonna get yourself a uneeform, buddy?" Even the inmates bugged him about it, as if he were masquerading under false colors, or something. "That ain't no Joint uneeform, Officer!" they'd yell from the safety of a crowd of prisoners, as if that were somehow immoral or unsavory. But a real uniform cost a hundred and twenty dollars. And, since Arv had no intention of making the C of C a career, there wasn't anyone who could shame him into buying one.

It caused Arv some embarrassment though, in spite of himself. He liked to blend in. Don't make waves. That way you got away with more. If you seemed to fit in, well, then it left you more room to be a true individual. What counts is what's inside. And what you do. Having recently been assigned Aristotle's *Poetics* in his Humanities course, Arv bent the teacher's lesson somewhat, as he often did, and thought: *your actions, goddamnit, that's what you're finally judged by!* And Arv's actions, within the next few months, would prove his mettle, his real worth, his difference from the herd. Because, by God, he was committed, he would risk all for freedom. He would escape his hated environment or die trying. He'd once been trapped. Lucky it hadn't been for life. But now he'd get free! He'd wail away, split, cut out, out of the country, off the whole fucking continent! And it didn't even matter where. Tokyo, Capetown, Bombay, Paris! "Yow!" he shouted into the mirror, straightening his U.S. Army tie, "it don't even matter where! Yow!"

Arv put on his Commission of Corrections cop-style billed cap. It was the sole article of his attire that conformed to official specifications. And that's only because they gave it to him free. Then he picked up the risky illegal letter on his table, a letter written on Free Galliot

Committee stationery, folded it double, put it in his pants pocket, went down the hall and knocked on the living-room door. Fast-Walking was lying stoned and silent on the tattered green and red davenport, cutting out articles from the *New Sonora Times:*

N.Y. STOCKS FALL
IN REACTION TO BREAKDOWN
IN PARIS PEACE TALKS

Fast-Walking loved to read the newspaper too. He was an obsessive cutter. He never read the *New Sonora Times* without a pair of scissors in his hand. He'd been that way as a kid, too, when they were growing up together on the grounds of the Joint. Just like Arv had always been a lister. Every time Fast-Walking found an interesting arti-cle, something he wanted to save, something, as he said, "that you'd want to remember and would forget if you didn't cut it out," old Fast-Walking, he'd just cut it out and paste it in the one permanent possession he could call his own: a huge old leather-bound picture album that his father the Warden had given him as a child.

Fast-Walking was all dressed up in his uneeform, and ready to go. When he spotted Arv in the doorway, after his light knock, he rose up like a tall stork from the couch, seemingly without effort, to his full spindly-legged six foot two inches. Fast-Walking moved like no other earthly creature. As he started across the room Arv watched with wonder while Fast-Walking did his stork-walk; it was something incredible to behold. He had these stiltlike legs and largish hips and then he had these narrow little shoulders and these short little skinny arms. Arv watched while he went down the stairs, his knees knock-ing, unsteady, jerky, pigeon-toed, but surprisingly fast, surprisingly smooth, like he was riding on stagecoach springs, with his little blond head rocking back and forth, perched up there on top of that impossibly long neck.

Fast-Walking paused on the front steps and Arv caught up. "Should we do it, man?"

"Sho nuff, Jim! let's do it!" Fast-Walking said, dipping low when he talked, as if he were swooping down on a basketball. "Oohie! Let's do it, Sylvester!" he said, like he'd learned it at the Joint, like he imagined Wilt the Stilt did it, like a lot of guards did, trying hard to get the black prison jargon down right, and almost succeeding, but not quite. And all the time keeping it just a tiny bit ironic, so you could never call him on it. Like maybe he was shucking, but underneath it all, under the jive, he was serious, deadly daddy-ass dead fucking sincerely serious Jim about being as cool as he had long ago understood *they* were, *dey*, the black cons, the setters of prison trends. There were essentially only two kinds in the Joint, among both guards and cons, there were the niggerlovers, and the niggerhaters. Fast-Walking was the only man in the Joint who fell in between somewhere. It annoyed Arv to see niggerhating and niggerbaiting in his father, and other guards. But Fast-Walking he had to tolerate, even sometimes had to join in with him. Because he was somewhere out of the ordinary, in his attitudes toward the black men. With the other guards it was mockery they were after, however unachieved. But with Fast-Walking, even though the mockery was there, you could tell he was going for something else too. He went for soul. And he didn't quite make it. But you did have to tip your hat to a cat who appreciated real style when he saw it.

So Arv and Fast-Walking went out onto Orchard Street and into the dazzling winter sunlight. It reflected brightly on the asphalt and broken bottles and candy wrappers and dully on the banged-up second-hand cars parked up on the curb. The day was chiaroscuro, with deep shadows and green greens in the small grass yards. A dog barked in someone's apartment in the white wooden building next door. Music drifted from an open window across the street: James Brown. A nippy little breeze blew in east off the Pacific, mitigating somewhat the car sounds from Chase Boulevard down the hill. There were other sounds too: the sound of a skyful of airplanes, jets and propeller-driven, even a little pusher-type turboprop high up in the blue. A flock of pigeons rose fluttering wildly off the street as four little black girls with cotton-rolled hair and skinned knees rode screaming down the steep blacktop hill on homemade ball-bearing scooters. darting in and out of traffic, making elderly Negro pedestrians jump for cover.

Fast-Walking glided ahead of Arv, crossing Orchard Street, going up the hill. There was no way you could keep up with old Fast-Walking. He was the fastest man in the entire State Slam. Clocked by Arv at true time doing sixteen seconds crossing the Big Yard—a hundred yards—his limber wobbling legs seeming to float in space. Still a young man, only seven or eight years older than Arv, with a handsome face and bright blue eyes and a hawklike curved nose and a high pale brow and straight pretty teeth and a strong forthright jaw like his father's and a thin dry mouth, the mouth of an aristocrat of the Joint, and all of that laid over that tiny head atop that impossible body, Fast-Walking seemed at once as young and old as creation. Women found his atavistic freshness irresistible.

Arv and Fast-Walking got into Arv's gray 1958 Mercury Hardtop that ran like a charm, cranked it over, and headed out Bird Street past the park to 18th Avenue and over the fog-bound hills and back out into the sun and through the tall elegant wind-shaped cypress trees of Fort Riley and over the Alvarez Straits Toll Bridge, leaving the city far behind.

Nobody said anything for a while and then Fast-Walking lit up another joint on the car cigarette lighter, puffing away at it furiously while it was still stuck to the hot electric coils, rapping to Arv at the same time. He had a deep low voice, but clear and even and soft-edged, the voice of a reasonable man. You expected that sure, logical-sounding voice to speak in measured cadences, giving the speaker time to puff at a pipe and rationally consider his next sensible phrase. But that isn't the way Fast-Walking did it at all. Fast-Walking's words came out jumbled and crazy and amazingly fast. Almost no visible effort did he expend. Inert-eyed, phlegmatic, he laid down a mad smokescreen of words that soon diverted your attention from their meaning to their sound and flow. But somehow, in the end, that voice gave you quickly the essence of Fast-Walking, made sense of him: he was water and clouds and dreaming and there was no fire or soil in him at all. His senseless words told you also that none of his dreams would ever be achieved, and that in spite of this fact he would always go on talking, old Fast-walking. . . . In this way his rap was surprisingly accurate.

"Well this is how I figure it Arv baby we're gonna get ourselves out of this here fucking Joint as soon as I get it together again get myself out of debt get Marie-Claude back on the track and get the kids in shape a little bread in the bank I've been thinking I think we oughta go in together on a ranch up in Oregon I been looking at these

brochures of the eastern desert corner down in the far
southeast of the state . . ." Fast-Walking said. Arv, realizing it wouldn't do any good, raised his hand.

"Hold it, man. We already been through that five times
in the last two days!" But Fast-Walking didn't hear.
Wouldn't. He was a man who never ever listened to other
people. If you started talking he'd interrupt you in the
middle of your phrase, inadvertently, without animosity,
completely unaware of what you were saying, and start off
on one of his monologues. But he had such a smile, such
a shiny all-American set of white teeth, and such
wholesome western blond good looks, that you let him get
away with it.

"Listen, man, down in that there corner of Oregon they
only get about ten inches of rain a year it comes in the
form of snow in the winter with all that aridity nobody
wants the land now here's what I figure, I figure to take
its drawbacks and make virtues out of them my plan
is . . ."

Arv hated Fast-Walking's plans, all of them, and especially this current one about Oregon. But they'd long ago
established a tacit understanding between themselves that
Fast-Walking could talk all he wanted, or at least to the
limits of auditory endurance, and Arv would be permitted
to only pretend he was listening.

"Listen to me, goddamnit man, listen to this fucking
plan cause it's the hottest thing you ever hear of it'll make
our fortunes for us I guarantee it solid gold guarantee
baby here's how we're gonna do it . . ." Fast-Walking
continued as on and on they drove in the Merc past little
suburban communities with Spanish names. Past eucalyptus groves, stands of pine and oak and poplar trees, past a
million flowerbeds and tiny plots of lawn. And past hundreds and hundreds of cars riding low in back with trunks
packed with garden implements and winter vacation gear
and supermarket groceries and dead human bodies. Cars
and cars and cars riding stuffed and weighty and low, but
fast, like fat mama woodticks cigarette-hot off a dog,
trailing gore and bloody Indian guts going both ways in
heavy rapid traffic on the freeway, eating up the miles of
country with their skidding burning nylon tires, slicing
through the mountains with their chromed cut-out pipes,
dual carbs, wild raked front ends, magnesium hubs, super-
charger airvents. Flattening out the miles, heating it all

up. Arv purled that hot old fast-riding Merc in overdrive down along the Sound. Radio turned up high to the Top Ten. Wheels just sizzling on the blacktop. Through the long cuts and tunnels and the superb reaches of wide-ass Highway 61 at top speed, laying down a smokescreen of fumes with their oil-burning engine, laying down a smokescreen of words out of Fast-Walking's mind-burning mouth . . .

"Goddamnit man when we get up in there with all the kids . . . and you get yourself another old lady, the hell with Deanna, even if she is my own sister, baby we'll have us some fun we'll run it communal, dig? We'll put everything in common split up all the work and money and shit why not even the fucking wives!"

. . . All the way down to Point Paradise and the Joint they rapped, rapping their pipes, rapping their mouths. Loving it, hating it: the speed, the cars sweeping alongside, the stretch of big roadway, the magnificence of the American vistas, the ponderous rag-tag fart of a landscape, and the banked high-speed turns, the grades, the embankments, interchanges, on-ramps, off-ramps, the cloverleafs, the wire mesh fences that always ran alongside, and the signs:

WATERSIDE PRISON
Point Paradise, ½ mile
Commission of Corrections
MAXIMUM SECURITY FACILITY
*No Alcoholic Beverages or
Dangerous Drugs Allowed*

You could see the gray and bile-yellow walls of the Joint long before you got there. You could see it six miles away from the top of the second range of hills coming from the city. Peninsular, bent and long, it thrust out into the vaporous mudwaters of the Sound like an old bald-headed dork, diseased and dangling, the genital end of the Pacific Ocean. Massive, lonely, squalid it was, with bilious umber-colored smoke rising in slow spirals from it like a swarm of flies off a putrid corpse. The peninsula had once been the abode of miserable and degenerate West Coast Indians, the Mud-Hen Indians, who had lived naked, scabrous, wind-lashed, and utterly without hope on the clams and worms they dug from the fetid mud flats. Later the peninsula had been used by the Mexican governor as a mooring place for his prison ship, where he kept and tortured the most vile and unrepentant convicts of the early nineteenth century. When the gringos arrived they had converted it into a permanent walled and moated fortress that dominated the outer reaches of the Sound. With the coming of statehood it had been refortified and expanded and strengthened to the point that now you knew for sure that it, or its memory, would always be there, always! The Joint, Arv was thinking, the Joint is the livest place in the world, in spite of its smell, its deathly clean smell.

It is where I came into the world. It is where I live.

And Arv, knowing a scream would do it, a shout, knowing only a cry from the depths would break through Fast-Walking's rapidly accelerating monologue, a monologue that paralleled exactly the momentum of the automobile, Arv yelled out at the top of his lungs, "HEEEEEEY MAN! What you want, man? What you want?" in the mocking voice of a black prisoner, a voice that mocked and was in turn mocked itself, an authentic prison guard's affectation that his father had taught him while he was just a little boy. And Fast-Walking blinked, his eyes opened to the outside, he turned, and . . . and . . . responded!

"What I want?" he asked, in the same black man's tones.

"Yeah! What you need, brother? Whatever it is, the Joint got it, right?"

"Oohie! You right on there, motherfucker!" said Fast-Walking, "you name it, man, the Joint got it, sho nuff!" and, just before they pulled up at the Front Gate, Fast-Walking quick pulled his khaki sleeve back, turned his pale white hand over, and reached for air, reached for skin, and repeated it, just as Little Arv remembered it from his prison childhood, he said . . . "Oohie, Jim! Soul on!" And Little Arv took his right hand fast off the steering wheel and hit Fast-Walking with what he wanted, hit him with five, gave him loud-ass skin . . . WHAM! . . . and Fast-Walking . . . ZAP! . . . gave him rebound skin that resounded throughout the tattered inside of the old Merc . . .

"Oohie! Sock it *to* me, baby! That what I call *sin*-skin!"

Three

On the bus, the rickety creaking old streamliner from Haley Reception Center, riding chained to another black man in a wire-mesh cubicle, riding along the salt flats outside the Joint, Galliot finished up his letter and signed it carefully, slowly, letting his pen ride up high on the curve of the capital G in his name, letting it soar six full lines up into the body of the letter and then descend gracefully to the little *a* and the *lliot*.

NSCC-125 (34256)	Name	William S. Galliot
	Number	240976
	New Sonora Maximum Security Facility	
	Mission Santa Bonita, N.S. 86611	
	Date	18 December 1972

Ms. Harriet Hayes
West Hazelton Sun-Times
3321 March Blvd.
West Hazelton, N.S. 86645

Dearest Harriet:

In response to your query as to why I have begun writing on a professional basis, I can only rejoin, "Why not?" It is a self-evident verity that if you will only mute yourself, remain anon., "do your time," as they say, they will not discommode you in any manner. It is equally veritable that the moment you manifest your law-given rights they will severely chastise you, reminding you in the process of another immemorial truth: might makes right, i.e., the goon squad invades your cell at all irreverent hours, compels you to stand in the buff on the cold metal tier while they rifle your private belongings, mangling them intentionally. And dead flies, cockroaches, microscopic flecks of sharp glass, and eventually urine, feces, and lye will appear "accidentally" in your slop-tray, your already foul-smelling provender. But there is a catch, Catch 69, as we call it (if they don't transfix you one way they'll turn you around and do it ass-backwards). The catch is this: if you endure in silence (I am speaking of political cases) they will forget about you; they will obliterate your very memory; they will never let you out; you will abide till doomsday in the bowels of Isolation. On the other hand, if you complain, if you lament, mutter, grumble, write your congressman, or yell, they will become enraged at your ungratefulness and the result will be the same: they will never allow you your freedom. And they are perfectly within their rights, legally speaking. As you know, most sentences in this state are "open-ended." That is to say, you are sentenced to a period in prison of six months to life, or one year to life. In prison jargon it is known as a "Life Tops," and cons will do anything to avoid doing time behind it. If the governor's appointed Parole Board doesn't like your political beliefs, then it is a simple administrative decision to keep you behind bars until you die of old age. Therefore, I make the existentialist choice: in spite of all appearance I refuse to give up hope, I strongly and steadfastly endeavor to make my voice heard, to curse the Pig, the Main Cop, the Man, to make active plans for his rapid dispatch, his demise, to extract some kind of meaning from my incarceration, and my inevitable violent end at the hands of the oppressor behind these walls.

Several events of the past week I find extremely sinister: first of all, the Pigs surrounded my prison psychiatrist inside Haley Reception Center. He was just returning from a session with me. They pinned him up against a wall with five large heavily armed guards and seized his confidential records of the discussion and therapy sessions we have been conducting. They presented a search warrant from the D.A., apparently laboring under the rather ludicrous misapprehension that they would find secret admissions of guilt on my part, for the alleged murder of that guard at Brown Max. If that is what they were aiming for, they were sadly mistaken. However, it shows the illegal and unconstitutional lengths the Pig will go to, to get me iced. Nixon's recent tergiversation at the Paris Peace Talks, and his subsequent blackmail and threats to bomb Hanoi and mine Haiphong Harbor again, against all reason and all international law, is not irrelevant in this connection. Nor is last month's state referendum vote to reinstate the death penalty, since you and I know whom it will be used against: the poor, the black, and the revolutionary. What all this proves is something I've known all along, and always taught my cadres: it is not the Amerikan government that has imposed its evil will upon the subjugated people. It is the Amerikan people themselves who are inherently evil. Witness their espousal of Nixon's murderous policy in Vietnam, their self-satisfied silence at the time of My Lai, and now during this infamous Watergate scandal. People tend to maintain the government they deserve. If the majority of the people do not quickly rise up and destroy an evil government, then they must share in the responsibility for its actions. Therefore the white man as a single citizen, and as a group, I find culpable of genocide and slave mongery, and punishable, one and all. The black man, of course, is not Amerikan at all, having never truly participated in Amerika's governing, having never received its benefice, having never been granted its vaunted advantages and riches. This goes also for the other nonwhite minorities, our yellow and brown brothers who will, when the day of revolutionary judgment comes, alongside the black man, be judged by their fellow world citizens exactly as German citizens of Jewish ancestry were after World War II: they were not guilty as Germans because not only did they not participate in or gain advantage from that government, but they were actually exploited and murdered and oppressed as if they were the wartime enemies of the state. That is our situation today, here in prison, and on the Outside too.

Numerous hip and political white inmates here, and guys on the Outside too, have asked me how come they share the blame with the oppressor. But what they don't realize is that there is a fundamental difference between them and us. You know, I recently saw the great white rock star George Harrison, of the Beatles, on TV. One of the sharpies from NBC was interviewing him. George came across as a very groovy, hip, relaxed cat. And I can relate to his music, on a nonvisceral level—it is sweet and gentle and harmless—but anyway, the TV guy asked him, "Say George, what do you think about the world situation," or something to that effect, "what's with the Vietnam War, Arabs/Jews, Black Liberation," etc. And do you know what hip groovy old George said? He said, quoting the words of his hit song, you see?, being smart-ass, you see, thinking he was being funny, but under it very sincere, you could tell, he said to the cat, and you had to laugh, he said: "I must admit its getting bettah, a little bettah all the time . . ." And there, in a nutshell, is the rub, for us, the crux of the matter, the evidence that establishes the guilt of all white men. Because, you know, Baby, it sure as shit ain't getting any "bettah" for the black man, no sir!

Another sinister thing happening lately is this, Harriet: I have found irrefutable proof that the rumored (see the *New Sonora Times, San Francisco Chronicle,* and *Village Voice*) new "Maximum Psychiatric Unit" on the premises of Brown Max is an actual fact. It has been set there, on one floor of the West Block which connects with the Hospital Wing, for the "study and implementation" of what is euphemistically termed "behavior modification." The means for this projected modification of the mind are: psycho-surgical alteration, electrocauterization brain surgery, electroshock, soundwave control, sex hormone injections, and aversion therapy with powerful drugs such as lithium carbonate. These methods of character modification are to be employed upon "hyperaggressive, destructive inmates," and those who are "serious management problems." You can readily imagine who they mean by that. I know this must all sound like some kind of fantasy, or science fiction, but I assure you it is true, and that they are deadly serious about it. If you find it difficult to believe me, please have a look at Bernard Weiner's beautiful investigative reporting of a similar program down in California in the *Village Voice*, "Prison & Psychosurgery—'The New Biology' of Brain Corrections" (I don't remember the exact date on that, you'll have to look it up). Of course, what all the State's euphemistic hocus-pocus means is that (believe me!) they fully intend to lobotomize, in one way or another, all militant or activist inmates.

The third sinister thing is the fact that they have suddenly and inexplicably released me from my closely supervised isolation at Haley, and are now transferring me (I'm writing you from on board a prison bus in transit) into the general population of the New Sonora Maximum Security Facility at Mission Santa Bonita. This of course would be welcome under any other circumstances, since I can keep a typewriter there, and can have access to the library, and talk to comrades and friends, etc. But in view of the authorities' well-known wish for my immediate liquidation as a "dangerous and treasonous subversive," I can only look upon this recent benediction as a direct threat to my life. It is much, much easier for an "accident" to befall me out there in the teeming Big Yard, or during TV time in the crowded East Block.

Doubly sinister, I find the fact that all my requests for a cellmate at New Sonora have been refused. A cellmate, of course, is a necessity for me because he would act as a witness in case of any funny business. I've asked the brothers at New Sonora, through the interprison grapevine, to contact the men who will be on either side of me to keep a sharp lookout, and they, Black Fence members all, have agreed with alacrity.

Again, I do not find it irrelevant that this escalation in the authorities' war against our Black Fence organization takes place at a time when, in a larger

context, they are threatening to escalate the war in
Indochina. It's all part and parcel of the same global
ripoff. The prison scene is merely a microcosm of the
world outside. Now that Nixon's reached an "understanding" with the Russians and the Chinese, he feels
even more confident to crack down on liberation
forces all over the world.

I anticipated this reaction, against our group in
particular, as soon as I made my recent well-publicized renunciation of nonviolence. I knew this would
be the result when the black man, driven to the wall
(all his leaders but Galliot dead or dying or bought
out), cold and deadly in his ultimate desperation,
turned around and faced his murderous assailant with
force of arms. So I am not surprised, nor am I even
particularly sorry, that Nixon has drawn the lines of
battle. Everything is out and in the open now—except our future policy in the Black Fence movement.
What's our next move? Where will we strike? What
kind of weapons will we use, now that we have finally endorsed armed conflict as the only remaining
means to resist our oppressor? The Man doesn't
know that, and that's where we've got it all over him.
The initiative is still in our hands! How will we
strike? With plastic bombs like the IRA? Or kidnap-
ping, like the Tupumaros or the Black September?
No one knows but me!

Which doesn't mean, dearest Harriet, that I do not
harbor grave doubts as to the success of our endeavors. As a matter of fact, between you and me, I'm incapable of continuing this letter, sweet woman, because I'm sick at heart thinking of the overwhelming
odds against our survival, and my own chances of
living, of even lasting out the few remaining days of
this year . . . and because I'm ninety-nine per cent
certain that they will not send this letter, or it will be
censored beyond recognition. It will be a miracle if it
somehow slips through the bureaucracy. But I'll try
anyway since I've got no other hope and, as you
know, we've not been without good fortune in this
respect in the past.

Since we're driving by a gigantic U.S. Air Force
Base right now, and the power of the Pig's machines

almost has reduced me to tears, tears of hatred while I watch those shark-nosed evil birds take off, with sleek murderous missiles slug under their razor-sharp wings, and since I'm just about scared to death, and don't want to die at only forty-three because I feel as if I've only just begun to live, and since I'm terribly perilously alone right now, and since I'm probably not even going to get through to you, I have the guts (or I'm desperate enough) to confess my true love for you, and my mind-bending almost insufferable loneliness, and my desire for your beautiful black body, to make love with you, over and over again, to make you pregnant with my child. Magnificent black woman! More than I fear my death, which I feel rapidly approaching, I fear that I will never see you again, never touch your hand, never awaken with you on a bright morning after a night of black magic, of love and carnal passion. I love you, warrior woman, and if I ever get out of here, out of this vile filthy evil stinking hole, I promise you, our black sons will conquer the earth and the stars! All Power to the People!

Yours in revolution,
Galliot

Four

Arv whipped the Merc into the employees' parking lot down by the Sound and they locked up, grabbed their lunch pails, and shagged up toward the barber shop for their required daily shoeshine.

A convict who was on his knees clipping the grass looked up at their approach and asked Arv for a cigarette.

"Sorry, you know it's against the rules."

"Don't you remember me, sir?" the convict asked, looking at Arv with pale gray Scandinavian-American eyes from where he knelt on the trimmed edge of the lawn, "I used to be tier man in your section in the South Block."

"Oh, yeah!" Arv exclaimed, "but wait a minute! Didn't I just run into you out on the Street in the city the other day, man? It seems just like yesterday."

"That's right, sir. Fast, huh? Parole officer violated me. I freaked out on meth crystals up on the roof of a whore-house and woke up in the Joint!"

"Here," Arv said consolingly, "take a couple of cigarettes. But don't ask again. Alright?"

Inside the barber shop Sergeant Big Arvin Weed, Arv's old man, a short, fat, low-browed and slack jawed dude who was one of the rare guards who conformed to the liberal-minded public's notion of what a guard should look like, was lying up on a barber chair getting a beautiful shave from a little old wizened black inmate named Yuba. Yuba was the most renowned barber in the Joint. It was said that over the years he'd gotten rich from his business Inside, and had a huge bank account in the city. He passed the money to his beautiful young wife when she came to see him in the Trusties' Visiting Room. He'd hold a tight-rolled wad of tens in his mouth all through the visit, talking like a man at the dentist's office with cotton stuffed between his gum and cheek, and then when he kissed her good-bye he'd pass it over into her mouth in a fast illegal French kiss which the "tipped" Visiting Room officer overlooked. In the Joint they even had a name for the technique. It was called the Yuba Pass. Some said they passed smack that way too.

Yuba was working away on Big Arv's throat with the straight razor and all the time Big Arv was putting him on, expounding his "theories" on the great political-social issue of the day, racial busing. Big Arv went on and on about "them weak sisters, them fucking pinkos, them radicals, old Galliot we got coming in from Haley today, this Black Fence thing, and the goddamn Jews that's to blame for it all," to the assembled members of the swing shift as they sat around on benches, the barbers' chairs, and the shoeshine stand, jawboning, squinting out the bay window across Quintana Sound at the city all pretty in the sunlight, white as anybody's Tunis.

It was all supposed to be tongue in cheek, but it fooled no one.

Yuba just laughed, diplomatically, wiping the shiny stainless steel blade on his starched white towel.

"That's right, laugh, you black-ass sonofabitch! With your money I'd be laughing too! But you better look out for Brother Galliot, your buddyboy, cause, I tell you, if you don't he's gonna be on ice, boy, fast as you say Martin Luther King!" Big Arv shouted it, rapping, enjoying himself, the charade, the familiarity of it all, knowing his rep as a jailhouse humorist permitted it.

"Easy now, settle down, Sarge," Yuba said, mock serious now, "we don't want this here shank to slip and get you red neck, do we now?" and the entire swing shift including sleepy-eyed old Fast-Walking laughed to beat the devil.

Little Arv sat on the shoeshine stand and big Roundo did up his U.S. Army shoes to a lustrous black. He'd been doing Arv's shoes since Arv was a very little boy, when his old man used to bring him in. Roundo was a permanent fixture in the Joint's barber shop, more or less. He sometimes got out, hit the Street for a while, but it was never more than six months at a time. As a kid Arv would miss him, and ask about him when he got paroled, from time to time, as if the fragile stability of his childish world were threatened by his absence. "When's Roundo coming back, Daddy?" he'd ask. "Aw, don't worry," Big Arv would say, "he'll be back soon, the poor old bastard."

And it was true. He always came back, a great big shit-eating grin on his leather brown face.

"I shot-time now, sonny boy," he used to say every few years, when he was about to go out onto the streets again, "but I be back directly. Y'all can count on that." And Arvin did, and Roundo never failed him.

"So, what is it, Roundo?"

"Hey! Outside of the big news, old Galliot coming in, nothing to it. Same ole same ole. Dig it? Parole Board pass me one more time. Look like I be pulling the whole dime."

"You mind?"

"Naw. It that old blindfolded lady with the scales. Anyway, that only two more years. And it ain't like something new. I been beat for the yolk all my life-long days, scoffing fishheads and scrambling for the gills. Nothing but slops and slugs and trickeration all the way. Anyway . . . Say! You know what? I hear your cousin coming back in, old Wasco!"

"Oh yeah? Which one is it this time?"

"They say he graduating."

"How high up?"

"Right on up to the top, and a heavy slat to boot. Trey bottom, dime tops."

"Hey!"

"Sho. He be showing up today, they say. With Galliot, with that Haley shipment. Shit! And I use to do up them little brown high-tops of his, right along with yours, them Buster Browns, 'member?"

"Wow! You hear that, Fast-Walking?" Arv yelled. "Old Wasco's showing up! What'd they get him on this time, Roundo?"

"Eleven five hundred," Big Arv cut in, shouting it from where he lay with his feet in the air on the barber's chair, "and an eleven five o one. He beat the one eighty-seven cause nobody would testify against him on a heavy number like that, murder beef. You mean you ain't heard about all that, kid? Well, you know, I didn't find out myself till just the other day. Seems like family is the last to know. Just like when you get married. Ain't that right, Yuba? . . . By the way, how's that good-looking young wife of yours doing over in the city with all that bread of yours?"

"Say there, Sarge," Yuba said, "you better hush you mouth or I tell some stories I know about you old Sister Evie!"

But Big Arv wasn't listening. Talking fast, rubbing his fat belly that hung over his thick belt, showing off his "inside" information, his command of the prison vine, he went on: "Picked him up with that motorcycle gang of his. Holding a fortune of someone else's junk, a dead man's junk. Lucky the Man got him first. Ain't that right, Roundo?"

"That still ain't sho," Roundo said, "lot of ole dope hands in this here Jam."

"Yeah," Big Arv said, laughing, while Yuba gingerly shaved the back of his thick neck, "well, I tell you what. If I know that old Wasco, and I known him all his goddamn criminoid life, he'll be on top of that in no time!"

"Right on!" Yuba said, putting him on, working the razor around the back of his bluish earlobe, "that right, Sarge! If I know that oiler, he handle that right fast! They didn't tag his play with the slammer issue for nothing! And it seem jus' like only a deuce of dims and darks on the cutback what that colt was sitting right here in this chair," he pursued, acting up, having Big Arv on some more, laying down the '40's hipster talk that him and Roundo always employed to confound the popeyed sergeant, "yes sir! That kack, ole Wasco, he a regular if I ever seen one!"

"You ain't just a woofing there, boy, oh yeah!" Fast-Walking seconded, waked suddenly from his drowse, oblivious as the Sarge to Yuba's heavy irony. "How about that time over at Dewayne Vocational? They say he had the biggest contraband operation in history. Came out with a fortune. Didn't even want to come out, they say. Couldn't afford it, he told the Parole Board. They had to let him out cause they couldn't afford him!" he said. And, with immense respect for Wasco, with the kind of understanding the two guards imagined exists between first-class law officers and first-class lawbreakers, the kind of *esprit de corps*, they preferred to believe, that exists between white enemies on the field of honor, Big Arv loudly reaffirmed it, "Oh yeah! Neutralize that old opposition, Fast-Walking, right?"

"Oohie! That right, sir!" Yuba cut in, "you a solid

sender! You tell 'em Sarge, and you too, Mr. Miniver,
cause you know!" he continued, with a flourish of the razor stroking downward from Big Arv's beefy moled nose,
sweeping out over his plump red lip. "Yes sir! Jus' like I
always saying, ain't nobody in this here Slam know the
criminal mind like Big Arvin Weed and old ex-Sergeant
Fast-Walking Miniver!" he shouted, gleeful, going too far,
and exulting because it looked like he might get away with
it. . . .

"Yeah," said Little Arv, laughing, joining in on purpose
so they'd get by with it, aiding, condescending on purpose
so Big Arv'd think it was just nigger jive, and nothing
more.

"Right on!" Roundo said wisely, lending his support too.
"They real solid senders!"
"Jus' like the song!"
"Oohie!"
"Sing it!"
"Yeah!"
Roundo sang it:

> Oh my Linda
> You a solid sender
> You know I never surrender
>
> Oh my Linda
> You a solid sender
> You know I never surrender
>
> Oh baby I been told
> That you been bold
> Ain't gonna be yo fool no mo'

He sang it good.
"Yeah!" Yuba and Little Arv kept yelling, getting it on,
so Roundo wouldn't bring the Man down on hisself.

All the other guards just a-laughing and clapping their
hands . . . "Yippee!" stomping their cowboy boots and
their jodhpur boots on the hairy asphalt tile.

Roundo ragging it as he sang and did up Little Arv's
army issue shoes.

"Yeah!" they all hollered. "Wow!"
"Shabadoobee-bop-bop,   shabadoobee-bop-bop,"   went

Roundo's shoeshine rag, his ragmop, and everyone but Fast-Walking and Big Arv laughed fit to kill.

In the dining room Little Arv and Fast-Walking were fortunate enough to get a table by themselves. But Fast-Walking started up on his fucking obsession again.

"Now the way I see it, the water table in southern Oregon is going through a rapid change now . . ."

Arv turned off his ears, within the terms of the unspoken agreement, let Fast-Walking spout out his drivel to his heart's content, and amused himself by scanning the menu and listing his selection in his head:

1. Oyster Soup
2. Crackers
3. Salad
4. Chicken à la King
5. Angel Food Cake
6. Coffee

Conklin, the inmate maître d', came over, took their order, and relayed it to the waiters (all of them, despite the variety of their races, carbon copies of Irish Conklin: short, fast, slick-haired ex-pimps, quick on their toes, homosexuals to a man). Conklin was terribly brusque with his help, terribly efficient, quite conscious of the great distance between maître and mere garçon.

"I hope you left that shit in the car," Arvin said as soon as Conklin had bustled away to the kitchen.

"Don't worry about it," Fast-Walking said, cutting his monologue for a second, just long enough to respond, and then plunging back into the wilds of the arid southeastern corner of Oregon where something that Arv could never figure out, quite, was going to take place someday in the far remote future, long after both he and Fast-Walking were dead and buried.

Arv was seriously concerned that the crazy bastard was going to forget someday and inadvertently bring a joint into the Joint, and get caught, with disastrous consequences. Arv felt he bore some of the responsibility. He was the one who'd introduced Fast-Walking to grass, just after he came back from Vietnam. Arv had become a weekend smoker over there, inhaling the weed simply for relaxation and pleasure. But Fast-Walking had soon developed a psychological dependence on the stuff, reaching for a roach as soon as he woke up in the morning, unable to sleep without a joint before bedtime. Arv worried about him. Especially since his wife and kids had kicked him out. Arv had a soft place in his heart for the bastard, even if sometimes it was hard to figure out why. They had almost nothing in common anymore, apart from smoking an occasional joint together. Sometimes Arv felt they were almost from different generations. Fast-Walking and all those assholes from the '50's often times acted as bad as the real antiques, the old World War II farts, like Big Arv. But in the old days, growing up, Fast-Walking had often helped Arv out, protecting him, kicking the shit out of schoolyard bullies like Wasco who picked on Arv because he was little. Just as Arv began to reflect upon his bitter anguished childhood, a sentimental habit of his, Big Arv came in and called them into the Briefing Room where he gave his usual pep talk dealing with current events in the Joint. Today it was Galliot's arrival:

"Now, boys, we got a real toughie coming in today. And there's a lot of talk about the colored in here planning to raise some kind of racial ruckus or riot or something, maybe take a few hostages and bargain to get Galliot outside free and on a plane for Cuba, something like that. Now, we all know they're always planning one thing or another in here, and if all their plans had been carried out I for one wouldn't be standing up here today. So we can take it all with a grain of salt as usual, but at the same time we can tighten up our ship and maintain proper surveillance of all areas within our responsibility with double alertness. Now, the grapevine says that the militant colored within these here walls have heard some ridiculous silly rumor about someone putting a contract out on their hero, and that's what's stirred them all up. So, no matter how foolish them colored might be, thinking anyone in here would want to harm even a hair on his nappy head, we got to be on our guard. Don't matter what we believe. *They* believe somebody's gunning for him. Well, I don't believe in any rumors, but I want you on your toes all the same. Got it? I want all access doors and sally ports double checked and double locked. I want everyone and I mean everyone including tier men, water boys, kitchen and laundry help, locked up at ten P.M. on the dot. I want any and all infractions or rebellious actions or backtalking no matter how trivial sounding or unimportant reported to me on the double. Alright? Okay!"

Big Arv then read out their assignments for the evening:

"Miniver, Frank R.: Wall Post #8 . . . Weed, Arvin Jr.: Main Gate."

And little Arv cursed his old man under his breath, figuring exactly why he put him at the Main Gate. With Wasco coming in, and all. Intimately acquainted with the prick's sense of sport, his idea of a good time. Remembering the line drives, the blistering power hits coming at him at short stop on a Little League size field. Big Arv, the oaf, his muscles bulging out of his sweat shirt, coach of the institution resident dependents' team. And Arv only twelve years old. All the kids laughing. Little Arv with the split skin, the bloody palm, the broken hand, trying not to be a cry baby, not succeeding *there's something wrong with his prick we seen it in the shower room the knife slipped Grandma Dora Lee says when they were circumcising him as a baby . . . they sewed it up wrong now it looks half-circumcised with a little skin flap hanging down on the end like a goat's beard. Mom complained to Betty one time said she didn't like it cause . . . I forget . . . why didn't she like it? Did it tickle too much?* Remembering the boxing ring he set up in the back yard where he used to make Arv train every day telling all the kids that Arv was the champ, would take on all comers and when Arv balked at huge Wasco's challenge he took the strap to Arv and made him fight with a sinking heart, knowing how stupid and pointless it was, knowing he was not only going to get his ass kicked, but would have to endure worse, the ridicule of his peers *the old man's shorts always smelled of come Mom used to hound him to the shower once a month but he hated it like poison why did he always have those come stains and smells in his shorts I don't leak now that I'm grown up why did he?*

Big Arv finished up with the assignments and then asked, "Any questions?"

When there were none he yelled out, "Remember Attica!" as he always did when he drew the swing-shift sergeant slot. And all the boys hollered it back at him, their

voices carrying out even into the Yard, where they were
wanted to carry, where it was meant they would sound,
and carry, and warn . . . "REMEMBER ATTICA!" the New
Sonora State Maximum Security Facility swing shift
screamed in unison, their mouths, all their mouths save
Arv's, Little Arv's, hanging open for what seemed like
minutes as they thundered those death-defying six sylla-
bles . . . "REMEMBER ATTICA!"

On the way over to his post at the Main Gate, a post
set between two gigantic reinforced steel doors, a kind of
"lock" set between the outer and inner edges of the thick
prison wall, Arv began to list carefully in his head the
names of the towns that Galliot and old Wasco would be
passing through on their way into the Joint:

1. Center Valley
2. Mesa Verde
3. Mendoza River
4. Farmingdale
5. Palm Hill
6. Ajo
7. Colina Linda
8. Mission Santa Bonita

Five

Fast-Walking sat up in Wall Post #8 listening, against prison regulations, to Merle Haggard on a transistor radio and smoking a joint. No one but the seagulls remained on the Big Yard. Even the pigeons had gone home. All the convicts had been herded in an hour before for the first count. A winter storm had sprung up suddenly and come flying in off the Pacific Ocean. Rain now streaked the bird shit on the gunwalk, making it dangerous to negotiate, streaked also the black macadam in the Big Yard, lonely, slicking it down in long waves and quick showering sprays from west to east.

Out over Paradise Cove, and coming in from Miguel Island and beyond, from the Alvarez Straits and the open North Pacific, line upon line of rain clouds came marching, with this afternoon's bright sunlight shining through in long fingers pointing at Sheepshead Island, at the Santa Caterina Peninsula, at Funland Amusement Park across the Sound in the city, at Holly Island and Malayerba.

Fast-Walking, relieved of his task of scanning the Yard, moved his binoculars from due west in a circle around the Sound going south and around to due east, letting his tightly rolled joint hang at the corner of his mouth: patches of sun too on the hills of West Hazelton, another at Point Edmonds on the huge metal oil storage tanks, and the last one he saw struck the purple-black roof of a Commission of Corrections bus, an ancient reconverted streamliner, swept-back airvents at the rear, as it rode in slow motion across the empty salt flats from Mission Santa Bonita. He beat time to the country boogie sound of the music with the barrel of his Winchester Rim-Fire on the metal windowsill as he followed that old bus in through the Front Gate and down Front Street past the pump station and the Warden's Mansion and the Employees' Service Station and the In-Service-Training Center and up in front of the yellow stucco Administration Building where it stopped with a lurch. The Reception Center boys right away opened up the exit door and the prisoners began climbing awkwardly out onto the wet pavement, chained together two by two. Quickly they were herded inside the third fence, their leg irons and handcuffs and chains and shackles clanging. They went up past the Employees' Association Building and the malt shop and the barber shop and across the lawn to the Main Gate where Little Arv was waiting to bring them into custody. Then they disappeared from view.

After that bit of excitement, or what passed for excitement in Wall Post #8, Fast-Walking was left with a whole hour on his hands, an hour the thought of which drove him nearly to despair. Fast-Walking, after growing up on the grounds of the Joint, after having worked there for almost thirteen years, still hadn't gotten used to it. He hated it. He hated to be alone, hated to be cooped up, hated this wall post and gunwalk duty worse than all the hated jobs in the prison. The idea, the very notion that he still had six hours and forty-seven minutes to go on this shift drove him nearly insane. He began pacing up and down, three steps up, three steps back, swinging the Winchester, slapping his holstered .38 Police Special in time to old Merle Haggard. He felt constricted. He *was* constricted. The weapons were fastened to his long-legged body in an elaborate and uncomfortable set of straps and belts and metal buckles, to prevent them from falling into the "wrong hands." It was difficult to sit with all that gear on. It put your limbs to sleep, cut into your groin and your shoulder muscles. In the tiny wall post, set alone on the stone wall between the Big Yard and the Isolation Yard, the effect was claustrophobic. The place was cluttered with all kinds of things: a commode, a heater, the transistor, a Mickey Spillane he'd brought along (which he read by flashlight in his lap with his coat covering it so the Sarge wouldn't catch him), a long rope with a key on the end, a large bucket with a rope on it too. And all this stuff got in his way, bothered him terribly. It was like there was no place for his legs. And the chair was too low for him. His knees buckled. Even when he sat down in the corner on the toilet he had to be on his guard, looking out the windows, with his rifle propped up on his naked knees. Fast-Walking's only comfort was the grass he brought along at great personal risk. He never carried in really good stuff, Gold, or hash, for work. He couldn't function straight with that stuff. The sober and straight world eluded him. Somehow all this workaday shit seemed so stupid and pointless. *What the fuck am I doing up here on this wall all alone in the middle of the night? And what are all those dudes below doing locked up behind walls and wire and iron bars?* It all seemed so silly, when you were really stoned. So Fast-Walking, he brought in only the very smooth light stuff, native stuff, that Evie's Mexican whore grew in her back yard in Nueva Ronda. Happy Grass, that's what she called it. It gave you a lift without zonking you out of your gourd. But the truth was, up in Wall Post #8, even Happy Grass didn't work.

Fast-Walking looked at the little traveler's alarm clock he'd set up on the heater. Only three minutes had passed. He always brought that little clock along so that when it got bad, unendurable, he could get a little sleep. It was against the rules too, of course, and very dangerous. That's how Fast-Walking had lost his stripes the first time. He'd been up all night the night before and all day too gallivanting with an Armenian woman named Tandy over in the city, and got tired, and Lieutenant Willis had caught him sleeping in the guard's shanty in the South Block. Big Arv too, he loved to sneak up on you, catch you napping, or reading, or listening to an illegal radio, and fire you on the spot. Fast-Walking had seen him do it three times. He was ingenious. He'd crawl up on his belly along the wall, even, dragging his slack fat on the cement. It's a wonder the motherfucker hadn't been shot as an escapee. . . .

Big Arv and Fast-Walking had always been archrivals at the Joint. It was taken for granted, therefore, that Big Arv would have no mercy on Fast-Walking when he lost his stripes, that Big Arv would consistently place him in the worst jobs, like the wall posts, jobs he knew from years of experience that Fast-Walking couldn't endure. And it was taken quite as a matter of course too that when Fast-Walking's salary was attached for debts and it was essential that he take a second job immediately or lose everything, Big Arv would come to him with a malicious grin and ask him if he needed a job at "his" store in Nueva Ronda. No matter that the store belonged in reality to his sister-in-law Evie, Big Arv's victory was confirmed in this round of their ongoing battle when Fast-Walking, at the end of his tether, unable to get back into his own home, bowed his head in the Briefing Room and unconditionally surrendered before the eyes of the entire swing shift: "Hey, Big Arv, did you say you needed an extra man out at *your* place?"

"Say now, you're in luck, Honcho, I was just going to fill it with a nigger kid . . . should be right up your alley . . ."

At the same time, the two prison guards profoundly respected each other. They were two remaining men in the world who would give no quarter, two mavericks, *machos*, men of the old school. Each of them had started out with grand illusions, dreams of great success. Big Arv had come home from both World War II and Korea as a highly decorated war hero, a combat-promoted top sergeant. Fast-Walking was the junior-college-educated son of a high state official, a company sergeant in the New Sonora National Guard. Neither had gone anywhere. The years had slipped by, faster for Big Arv because he was older, but they had slipped by for both of them nonetheless. Both had surrendered most of their illusions of success within the state penal system years before, blaming all the trouble on exterior causes having nothing to do with themselves personally. Each of them knew in his heart that he was merely making excuses. Both were perfectly aware that in their own terms they were failures at life.

One of the very few things in their world that gave their lives meaning, that gave their lives a certain shape, a kind of "dignity" of purpose, was this cut-throat business of trying to exterminate each other. Of the two of them, only Fast-Walking was perceptive enough to see this, and only admitted it to himself when he was up in that fucking Wall Post #8 and had nothing else he could do with his time but think, goddamn think, think, think!

Fast-Walking sat cooped up in his tiny wall post wondering why life had dealt him such a difficult hand. There he was, ex-sergeant, stripped of his prison honor, salary attached for debts, kicked out of his own house by an un-grateful foreign bride who threatened divorce. . . . Did he really deserve it? He just couldn't see how. As he did every night on this wall post, Fast-Walking began to take stock of himself. He was forced to. He didn't really want to. But there was really and truly nothing else in the world to do with his time. Nothing! How had he gone wrong? At seventeen, going off to J.C. to study law en-forcement and criminology, the world had been his oyster. His family and friends had every expectation that he would follow in his father's illustrious footsteps, would one day too become Warden of the Joint. What had he done to deserve his sad fate, his low estate? He'd always done right by his wife, despite their differences in tem-perament. He'd given her four kids, provided her with a low-rent state home near his work and near a school, and they'd never gone hungry, though at times it had been touch and go. He'd done alright by the old U.S. too, god-damnit. He'd served ten years in the National Guard, ris-ing all the way to E2. No matter that he'd done it to get away from the old lady on weekends, it was still service, as he saw it. And he'd done alright by the state too, by God. He'd slaved his butt off working in a boring, de-pressing, dangerous prison filled with bloodthirsty criminals for thirteen years at starvation wages.

Fast-Walking wasn't suited to the Joint. He was a dreamer. And the only other dreamers in the Joint were on the opposite side of the law. His mind wandered. He couldn't keep his attention fixed on his job. Because of this he got into trouble with his superiors who reported him to his dad who accused him of being a failure, a bum. Because he believed his father, believed he had failed at the Joint, he developed a hatred for it, which paralleled exactly his hatred of his father. And year by year his hatred and bitterness grew. Trying to forget his hated job, he began to ramble, to gamble and stay out late at night. That got him into trouble with his wife, and got him into heavy financial debt. Because he lived on the grounds of the Joint, and there was no privacy there, no secrecy, all of Fast-Walking's problems and failures both on and off the job eventually found their way into his Job Efficiency Reports which, getting worse and worse every year, snowballing with his increasing frustration, going round in a full circle, contributed again to his endless failing, failing, failing.

Fast-Walking, gazing out at the flat, gray, empty Big Yard, thought again of success, a natural success, Lobo, his old man, Warden of the Joint . . .

Lobo, despite his wolfish nickname (bestowed upon him by an errant eloquent Chicano inmate gardener in the '50's), was known as a well-read, highly cultured gentleman, in spite of his lack of formal education. This false rumor had taken root one time when a magazine reporter who was interviewing him left a copy of his *Sewanee Review* lying on his desk. Later in the day a TV crew, filming his response to recent allegations of "corruption in the prison system," panned in on the literary review and asked if he'd read it. "Of course!" Lobo replied without batting an eye, "what do you think? That prison officials are all sadistic brutes? Why, I take great pleasure in reading contemporary poetry magazines, literary reviews and journals of intelligent opinion every night!" After that Lobo always made sure his office and waiting rooms were furnished with a wide variety of highbrow magazines, and the library behind his desk stuffed with classical lit and avant-garde psych and philosophy.

And Lobo's appearance did not belie the impression his library conveyed. Tall and rather natty and British looking, sixtyish, with light brown hair graying slightly at the temples, he had a naturally elegant demeanor, a grave and truly commanding presence, and a keen quick wit (an assumption Fast-Walking made not with any hard evidence but through the process of deduction; against all odds his dad had managed to survive and prosper for thirty years in the complex and dangerous arena of the Joint and big-time state politics).

Lobo's stare was perhaps the most remarkable thing about him. He'd perfected it with years of training, and it was highly effective. Fast-Walking was convinced that it could wilt flowers, curdle milk, melt women, burn through iron bars, persuade black men they were white, and white men they were wrong, that it could immediately dispossess a man of his will and the contents of his bowels. But Fast-Walking was just projecting, trying to figure out something he couldn't explain: why his father still had such a profound influence upon him, why Fast-Walking was still stuck in the Joint against his own will. . . .

Anyway, Lobo was a man with a tremendous capacity to survive. That you had to admit, whether you liked him or not. He was a man who knew exactly what he wanted, how to obtain it, and he almost always got it. Fast-Walking was his only failure in a long career (and he let Fast-Walking know it every chance he got). Lobo had achieved his high position in the Commission of Corrections through a canny, almost nautical ability to ride the winds of political change. At the present juncture of political affairs in New Sonora, Lobo found himself in the slightly awkward but unalarming position he found himself in after every election: his sails furled, he was coasting along for the moment, awaiting the most opportune hour to change direction . . . to run up his spinnaker and go hell for leather before the wind exactly the way it was blowing: Right. At present he was still handicapped with his holdover rep from former days, his embarrassing image as a prison reformer, liberal humanist, an "antipunitive Care and Treatment man," as some of his Rightist enemies had characterized him before the inauguration of the present governor.

Fast-Walking knew that at this particular moment in New Sonora penal history, with a brand new archconservative Republican administration in the state house, and a tremendous upsurge of highly combustible political consciousness among the black and Chicano prison population, it would be only a short time before Warden Lobo Miniver got rid of all those highbrow liberal magazines in his rack and replaced them with more suitable material. Not that this would bother Fast-Walking at all. He'd never been a liberal on penal reform (as his father had pretended to be when he was under moderate and liberal Democratic governors). Fast-Walking believed like Big Arv and most of the other guards. He believed that prisons were built for detention and punishment, pure and simple. He firmly believed in separating criminals from the general population, and in the notion of prison as a deterrent: if you made prisons bad enough, criminals, fearing severe conditions and corporal punishment, would think twice before they committed any more crimes.

To poke fun at liberal schemes for prison reform and the "rehabilitation" of inmates and, at the same time, to

ridicule his father, Fast-Walking often told a story about
Lobo when he'd been known (ironically by convicts, seriously by liberals he was trying to impress on the Outside)
as "Warden Miniver, the Inmates' Friend." The story had
to do with the manner in which, ten years before, Lobo
had finally succeeded in obtaining his long-desired post as
Warden of the Joint. Lobo became Warden because in
1962 he won the coveted New Sonora State Peace Officers' Association Award, the most prestigious award in
state law enforcement. He got this prize, outpolling all
other nominees by an enormous margin, for his original
idea "Project Relevance." He'd conceived of it one late
night of fitful sleeplessness, lying next to Mom, who, as
usual, at two o'clock in the morning, was still watching
her bedside TV set. First thing in the morning Lobo went
into his Associate Warden's office and had the inmate
secretary type it up and put it into the prison suggestion
box in front of Warden Finnegan's office.

Project Relevance was suggested to Lobo because at
that particular time, the year 1962, with a liberal New
Frontier-oriented administration in the state capital, the
terms "relevance" and "relate" and "dialogue" were enjoying a great vogue in the Joint, with both cons and cops. In
addition, these words were in great favor with the all-pow-
erful Adult Authority and the Parole Board, for whom everyone in the Joint had enormous respect. "I just can't
relate to that dude," a guard would say about a man he'd
just beaten with a rubber truncheon. "That ain't relevant
to my needs at the moment," a con would say when he really meant, "You gotta up the ante, man, if you want me
to snitch on my friend." Or, "Let's have a little constructive dialogue in relation to that matter," a guard would
say instead of, "Listen, buddy, if you give me any more lip
I'm gonna kick the living shit outa you!" That's what suggested Project Relevance to Lobo, that kind of thing. It
was a great idea, and it got Warden Finnegan all excited.
He promptly instituted Project Relevance into the normal
prison routine, praising Lobo to the sky, and eventually
nominating him for the award. But this was the kicker
. . . a few years later Fast-Walking asked his old man,
"Say Dad, that Project Relevance thing, what exactly was
it?"

"Well, son, Project Relevance, for which, as you'll

remember, I won the New Sonora State Peace Officers' Association Award, was . . . was . . . er . . . I like that title, don't you? Has a great little ring to it! 'Project Relevance!' Yes, it was . . . er . . . what was it? I got it right on the tip of my tongue . . ." But Lobo couldn't remember to what exactly "Project Relevance" was relevant to save his damned soul. . . .

Looking out over the stone walls of the prison, with his high-powered binoculars, over the water tower, over the industrial area with its black smokestacks and tangles of wire and machinery, over the prison dairy, past the second wire fence, Fast-Walking spied his honey-haired wife Marie-Claude coming in the Back Gate heading home from work, his frail French wife, walking quick-step, small fast steps, down the sidewalk past the schoolhouse and the tennis courts and the football field and ball diamond of the dependents' housing area.

Through the juniper trees and eucalyptus he could see her moving, this tall thin frail woman, his wife from another nation, who now, after he'd not spoken with her in a month, seemed almost exotic to him. Her long light-boned olive-skinned legs switched fast and nervous, slithering almost audibly on her nylon stockings under the skirts of her yellow airline ticket agent's uniform. The bus had just let her off, a suburban Greyhound. He narrowed in on it with his binoculars and watched it climbing over the low pine- and oak-clad hills to Mission Santa Bonita, spewing clouds of diesel smoke. Back again in the housing area he brought Marie-Claude right up close, twisting the lens knob tight as it would go, saw those flashing white feet he knew so well. She always wore those white wedgies, old Marie-Claude, claimed they eased her feet on the job. She cleaned them every night with horrible chalk-colored polish the consistency of semen. She cleaned her shoes and she washed her yellow drip-dry uniform dress and she washed her nylon stockings and hung them all up to dry over the gas heater when it was foggy and hung them outside in the wind when the sun came out.

Marie-Claude had begun her career at the city airline office a couple of years after their marriage, a few months after Ralph, unwanted, had popped in upon them, destroying their youth, their rapture, their pleasure in each other, destroying even Marie-Claude's delightful foreign qualities, her Frenchness which had charmed Fast-Walking's soul, stirred his pride. After the twins were conceived she had become just cow-eyed and knocked-up and ugly and stupid looking, like all women.

When they met in France, during his active duty military service, they had fallen in love at first sight. The future had lain before them like a great unmapped country, rich, virgin, and free for the taking. It was in Poitiers, a medieval university town with large spiring churches, tall graystone houses, a lazy shallow river so green with water lilies it hid the spare tires and tin cans on the bottom, that they had met. He was stationed at the local U.S. Army Quartermaster Depot. They met on the principal square, the Place de Notre Dame la Grande, on a warm August evening after a chilly day of wind and rain. The tall Gothic cathedral gleamed almost silver in the floodlights at its base. She came walking long-legged in a hooped skirt with many petticoats across the slick black cobblestones with her ponytail blowing and her lips pursed and she was very tall for a French girl, tall enough even for Fast-Walking, and he loved her suddenly and madly with no hope. He didn't know how to tell her. Was afraid she wouldn't like it if he did tell her. French girls of good family were not seen with GI's. Fortunately, however, she had been struck with the same clap of lightning, the same *coup de foudre* and, what's more, had picked up enough English in school and working at her aunt's *brasserie* to understand quite well enough what he was conveying when he finally got up the nerve to open his trembling mouth:

"I don't know how to say this . . ." he began, as she dallied in front of him on the cobbles, pretending to adjust her sandal.

"Say it!" she said suddenly, rising up before him, tall and lithe and lovely, and all pretenses gone.

"I'm afraid I . . ." he said, looking looking looking hard, trying to say with his eyes and expression what his voice would not.

"I know," she said, laughing, aiding him, taking pity on him, in his terrible lovestruck fix, swinging her white leather handbag delightedly.

"I think I . . ." he said.

"I know," she repeated in her accent, an accent that

rang in his head like a small poison arrow smacking a
small bell, charming him fatally.

Sitting in the Café de la Libération on the Grande Rue,
sitting outside beneath a chestnut tree so venerable that its
limbs sagged to head level with the weight of its fragrant
heavy leaves, they spoke all in a rush, frankly, crazily,
cutting directly through all the bullshit, all the niceties.
They confessed their crazy love, and their immense physical attraction, and the fact that they had seen each other
often before, and yearned insanely for each other from a
distance, across the slate-colored square, the courtyard of
the old university, across the river. And they got rid of
the past in a few brief words, as if to rid themselves of its
hold.

"On va débarrasser tout ça," she said, "I am an *orphe-
line,* from Oradour sur Glane, my mozer and my fazer
was *fusilés* by zee Zhermans in my town. I work in zee
brasserie of my haunt Denise."

They rode on her motor-driven Velo bicycle to a little
Basque restaurant and had, with careless thoughtless un-
originality, *poulet Basquaise* on a terrace overlooking the
green choked river. A happy band of wandering singers,
young men from St. Jean de Luz, arrived in an ancient
black Citroën and sat at the bar singing Basque folk songs
good-naturedly. The bartender wouldn't let them stop.
They heated even the terrace with their hearty good will,
the terrace that had become chilled by a brisk night wind.
The lovers sat and watched those good red sweating round
faces and laughed, and crept into each other's arms over
the table with their elbows heedless of the gravy bowl,
kissing, kissing, kissing shamelessly while the songs went
up around them under the red and yellow lanterns, kissing
till he was drunk with it, and the white Bordeaux, and her
honey hair, lilac-scented, and her small precious breasts
pounding against his pounding chest, and her rich olive-
colored skin, her curved Roman nose, her elegant pursed
French mouth, her soft brown earlobes, the lobes of a
child . . . It seemed a billion years ago to Fast-Walking
now as he sat in the guard post, dreaming the remainder
of his life away. He watched her still going. . . .

Now Marie-Claude was going home, she was almost
home, old Marie-Claude was, with this large brown paper
bag full of supermarket groceries, stuff she bought special

on her lunch hour at a high-class gourmet supermarket in the city, setting their budget back almost past redemption. Fast-Walking knew, as he spied her with his binoculars, the contents of that brown bag like he knew the back of his own hand: inside there were fresh artichokes or brussels sprouts or endives or fennel or *pisenlit*, a head of lettuce, a pound of narrow-necked Italian *pomodoro* tomatoes, a cucumber, a green pepper, two or three different kinds of cheese, but for sure a Brie or a Camembert and a Boursault, a pound and a half of some lean red meat, two quarts of unpasteurized milk, and a small bottle of a good red wine. Fast-Walking spied on Marie-Claude this way, his wife, now that he was no longer living with her, and loved her again as they had loved for three or four or maybe five bright hours in the enchanted French countryside of 1958. He laughed to himself, and his laugh held no rancor, as she crossed the sparse yellow lawn of the family home, Prison Residence #71, stepping over the careful inmate-trimmed little hedge along the walk, as she climbed the wooden stairs of the old prison-gray row house and fumbled for the key balancing her package on her knee, her worried but still pretty and pursed small mouth contorted with the effort. Finally she got in. Fast-Walking laughed to watch her and he couldn't say why. It was like the way you laugh watching a little dog locked out in the rain trying to get in. He didn't know, really. He couldn't explain it. But the laughter was sweet to him and brought bitter-sweet tears to his eyes, fogging the binoculars. He put them down on the heater in front of him and wiped his eyes with the tan blond-haired back of his hand, wondering: *Is it just because I want home again? Naw. It's funny cause she couldn't wait to get in there and cook up some of her good chow even for just her and the kids . . .* but he realized that that didn't quite explain his tears either, and left it for the time being, left it to unzip his uniform pants and sit down on the commode with the Winchester propped across his naked knees and dream of that seventeen-year-old French country maiden, and him only nineteen himself (while his eyes, still alert. still scanned the Yard in carrying out his officially constituted duties), and how they drove to the country for the first time in a borrowed American car, drove to her native village destroyed by Nazi fire and bullets where her mom

and dad were interred, drove there and walked around the
gray and black burnt-out streets, along the deserted
streetcar track, with the wind blowing her hair, and towering French thunderheads skidding high above them, and
the green of the grass between cracks in the blown-up
pavement, the knocked-over stone houses, and then he
said "Jesus! That's enough!" and she cried and he knew
she was his and they left the horrid little atrocious dead
town and drove up the flashing afternoon by the summer
River Vienne past Confolens and L'Isle Jourdain. Found a
forest full of straight-rowed cultivated poplar trees. And
later in the night full of thunderstorms and lightning
flashes he had to motate the supply sergeant's Edsel
bouncing through the wide-spaced trees of the poplar forest. Bouncing Marie-Claude naked in the back seat. When
the night-irrigating farmer-forester caught them in his bicycle beams. Trespassing. And Fast-Walking hauling ass
across the still-dry furrows spinning rubber, stripped nekkid behind the brody-knobbed and throbbing wheel of the
Edsel, laughing his young eyes out. Marie-Claude laughing too, always a good sport that way: European. And the
Forester with his cigarette and his shotgun strung over his
back. Pounding his bicycle pedals frantically, shouting,
"Arrête! Arrête!" And then they hit the highway doing
sixty, with the forester's pathetic little bicycle light still
flickering on the trunk of that big-ass Edsel. Headed up
the river, hightailing it, to another place, a dark purple
field of *cassis* berries when the moon came out. And Fast-
Walking spread her long white moonlit legs with firm decision, legs with no hair, not even peach fuzz. And he ate
her perfect black-haired Gallic untouched-by-human-hand
pussy and it tasted like the berries they later sampled in the
night: bitter-sweetly delicious . . . and she lay back on the
back seat with her head crinked up against the arm rest
and she moaned then, and writhed, and pumped, called
his name in her adorable Froggie accent, and then he . . .
and then . . . he . . .

And then Fast-Walking had to quick put away his loaf
and button up his fly and get up off the toilet and pretend
to pace the wall post alertly because his privacy was being
invaded. . . .

Six

Officer Little Arvin Weed, traitorous, nervous, fast on his feet, was already shaking down the fifteenth prisoner before he realized it was his cousin Wasco.

"Jesus H. Fucking Christ!"

"Sheeeeit! Relax, baby, ain't nobody gonna harm you."

The Lock, a high echoing vaultlike chamber between the walls, was filled with cigarette smoke, milling convicts, and the shouts of guards.

"Come on, line up, goddamnit! Line up!"

Two gigantic steel doors led out; one went inside the walls, the other went outside. Sparrows twittered in the rafters and flew in and out every time one door opened. The mechanism was fixed in such a way that only one could be opened at a time.

Arv was working in there with heavy heart, feeling guilty, working fast, scared and worried: he had contraband on him, damnit, after all! That highly suspect and illegal letter he carried in his back pocket felt very heavy to him now, weighed like five years. . . . He'd worked up quick from Wasco's shackles to his huge thighs to his hips, waist, his muscled underarms. his heavy shoulders, and his big bull neck. He'd worked all the way up that tough hard bod. Then he found himself looking him right in his mean little eyes. And they struck him dumb, struck him stupid and open-mouthed incompetent for five full seconds, just like they did when they were kids and Wasco was the schoolyard bully. Just like they did when Arv was in high school and Wasco reduced him to slavery, abject lackeydom that was only mitigated on the rare times when Fast-Walking, Arv's old protector, happened to be hanging around. And Arv, finally, driven to despair after Fast-Walking's departure for the army, had said those fateful words which hung now between them like a storm cloud, time cloud, spanning space and experience:

"You just wait, Wasco! Someday when I'm big . . ."

"Sheeeeeit! You're never gonna be big enough, you fucking little fairy!"

"Tsk, tsk, it's only me, you old cuz, relax, man, relax!" Wasco said, in present time, snapping Arv back, while all the cons in the lineup snickered at the officer's shrinking, his instinctive cowardice in the face of the enormous barrel-chested inmate. Leaning back, arching, grinning like a big bald-headed cat, like a caged and dangerous feline, Wasco mocked his little cousin, just like he'd always done, right there in the Lock, right there before the facetious eyes of the black convicts, the ironic eyes and elbows of the whites and Spics. Today, Arv thought, Wasco's got the face of the devil. . . .

"Don't know why I'm so surprised," Little Arv managed, after those agonizing seconds.

"Thought you might say something stupid like that," Wasco said, guffawing again, displaying his broken-toothed smile like the head of a chopper, bouncing on the balls of his big feet, playing to his locked-in audience. "You about finished?"

And Little Arv let him get away with it.

Or did he? *Who the hell is boss here now?*

Arv pointed Wasco through the metal door to the lineup in front of the Sign-in Desk, gave him a little shove (important shove, this first one of their lives, perfectly gauged shove, figured out in advance and made not too strong and not too gentle either), and said, "In there, on the double!"

Wasco turned around and evil-eyed him.

But who had the power now?

It was Wasco who had to go in and take off his clothes and stand naked while prison guards rifled his belongings. It was Wasco who had to wait in a smelly musty line of multiracial convicts while two beefy gunmen armed with nasty-looking sawed-off shotguns paced the gunwalk inches above his scalped head. It was Wasco, the dumb shit, the stupid asshole, the criminoid motherfucker, who was going to get sprayed like an animal with antilouse disinfectant, who had to stand there, humiliated in front of his own relatives, first on one foot and then on the other while his Uncle Big Arv, his own uncle, delivered in a bored and monotonous voice a lecture he'd memorized by rote twenty years before: "Swearing, cursing, fighting, disrespect to officers, loud arguments, sodomy, masturbation, homosexuality, drugs, unnatural acts and political agitation will not be tolerated. . . ." It was his flunk-out cousin Wasco G. Weed himself, and not Little Arv, who had to stand there sick with depression and boredom with those stale-smelling cons for one hour waiting for the clothes he would wear his whole three to ten years in the Joint, worn used ugly denims, clothes with a number stenciled on them, a number once used by another prisoner now discharged or deceased.

Yeah! Who's lower on the pecking order now? Arv exulted to himself when Wasco was safely out of the vault.

Then Arv, he started working on the rest of the inmates. He finished with the whites, got through the Spics, and started working on the stiff surly black men, shaking down twenty-seven of them real careful, methodical, thoroughly official, taking his time, making sure not to create a bottleneck at the desk or in the hallway, keeping the lineup real straight and tight, keeping them moving slow and easy and very even, doing a good job. In this way he was able to contain his agony.

He went over each black man with grave attention, real close, minutely, from head to foot. They resented it. It was probably their third or fourth shakedown of the day. But none of them said a word. Stiff, stubborn, they submitted to his probing fingers, his rough handling with insubordination only in their eyes, nigger eyes that narrowed down to the size of a welding-torch flame, and burnt right into you.

He was afraid of them, though he was on their side.

They knew he was afraid, but not that he was on their side. His fear did not tempt them.

Had they seen his fear?

Dark eyes, African eyes, know who's master. They saw.

In his deepest heart Arv hated the bastards, though he loved them *I'm on your side and you will know it even though you don't know it yet.*

Arv's attention fastened on the name Galliot, which he'd read in the *New Sonora Times,* fastened on a face, milk chocolate brown, under which he'd read:

WILLIAM GALLIOT, MILITANT LEADER OF BLACK FENCE
MOVEMENT, INDICTED FOR MURDER OF PRISON GUARD.

Shaking his black men down, spooky eyes, spooky
scowls, reaching into their shoes and socks, sticking his
fingers up their pant legs, running his hands up their slim
negroid hips and into their heavy-weight nigger crotches,
going up along the skinny ribs, under the sinewy arms, the
defined pectoral muscles, smelling them, sniffing their difference, smelling their musky African smell, feeling them,
their texture, their composition and disposition, in a way
he had felt only a very few women in his young life, Little
Arv searched for Galliot the militant, the last one, the
leader of his people.

Like with Wasco, he discovered him only when he was
looking at him eyeball to eyeball. He looked down into his
deep-set brown eyes and wondered, and wondered, and
didn't see anything special. Galliot was just a little colored
dude, high brown, wearing thick glasses, square light-
weight gold frames. He looked like a railway clerk or a
telegraph operator. Compared to some of the giant hulking Negroes that surrounded Arv in the Lock, this one
looked like he couldn't harm a flea. He submitted to Arv's
search quite docilely, letting Arv go over him much more
thoroughly than usual, permitting him even to run his
hands up his sleeves and down his shirt front through his
short wiry chest hair.

"Now unloosen your belt," Arv commanded, thrilled
with his role. Arv was putting on a show. He had to, in
order to deflect suspicion from Galliot and himself. The
ambiguity of Arv's feelings toward Galliot, however, and
his race (love, hate, well-wishing, death-wishing) made
the show real. And Arv realized that he was becoming too
well what he played: the Pig.

"How come?" the black man asked, not belligerent, not
knowing who Arv was, or what his commission was, not
suspecting that Arv might be his man.

"Never mind, just do like I say," Arv said, determined
to create a disturbance.

"Look, man," Galliot said, opening his brown hands,
turning them upwards in their handcuffs, "they're gonna
strip search us in the next room, what's the sense?"

"You heard me, goddamnit!" Arv yelled, a little fright-

ened by his own playacting, but fixed on earning a reputation as a nigger-hating, hard-nosed, Galliot-hating prison
ruffian, for the good of the cause he espoused, and . . .
because . . . somewhere, deep within himself, there dwelt
an evil murderous whiteman, seriously enjoying this act,
this game the other (which other?) was playing.

"Aw, for Christ's sake, kid, you guys going to already
start giving me shit?" Galliot asked, moving backward,
rebelling, a couple of steps, upsetting the lineup, moving
them all back a few paces, upsetting Arv . . . *Oh Jesus!
Wait a minute, man! It's all an act!* The last man in the
line clanged up against the iron gate with his chains.
Wham!

"Hey, what the fuck's going on?" they all yelled, rattling their chains and shackles, scuffling on purpose, upsetting the other inmates, the whites and Spics, creating dis-
sension, discord, setting the sparrows to skitting nervously
in the rafters.

"Come over here and take off that belt!" Arv shouted,
not sure now where he was, Pig or Pigeon, not sure who
was actor and what was acted upon and who was acted
for and what against . . .

Arv was scared shitless.

His real fear was instantaneously communicated to every black man in the vault. They broke ranks, lawlessly,
began milling around in the narrow passageway, cursing
and knocking their chains up against the stone wall, perfectly ready for rebellion, though it was a bit premature.
. . . The noise echoed in the closed Lock so much that it
was like the echo inside your skull when you've been hit
over the head with a metal object. Arv was living a prison
guard's nightmare: he'd lost control of those in his charge.
It was the one unforgivable sin in the Joint, the one thing
that provoked instant ridicule: "Shit, that little dude can't
even control inmates!"

Arv had failed as a traitor, and failed as the Man. And
was lost somewhere in between. And needed one or the
other.

"Fuck you!" the black men raged, delighted to find an
outlet for their hungry outrage, their highly combustible
hatred, their righteous anger.

"Chuck sucks!" they screamed.

"Ice Whitey!"

Galliot jerked his chain partner forward out of the crowd again, trying to reach Arv again *did he want to talk or what?* but Arv jumped back fast, afraid. All the blacks wailed and yodeled with ridicule: "Oohie! You got him going! Turn that cat out! Yeah!"

"What the fuck is going on up there?" the gate officer yelled.

Arv, pressed into a corner, up against the wall, cowering, tears welling up in his eyes, summoned his deepest voice, from the bottom of his little heaving lungs, reached deep deep for it, to make it manlike, not afraid, not scared of the dark or the dark men's violence, their unknowable nigger hate, reached far into himself for a grownup's authority and came out with a squawking chicken croak, a loud humiliating shriek that set them laughing at him all the more, "I . . . uh . . . I got a man here . . . uh . . . he won't submit to a . . . search!"

"Well call the Sergeant, goddamnit!"

Arvin, pinned against the stone wall, surrounded by twenty-seven big pissed-off niggers, yelled in desperation, "Sergeaaaaaaaaaaant!" It was a miracle he hadn't called out what he'd almost started to: *Daaaaaad!* A fucking miracle.

Inside the reception office he could see the heads turn. Wasco turned too, triumphant, smirking at the scared-ass tone in Arv's voice.

Big Arv, stout and middle-aged and graying and coplike, came out and coolly, professionally, realizing that Arv had lost control of the situation, asked, "What seems to be the trouble here?" to the room at large.

Before Arv could say anything Galliot spoke up.

"Sergeant," he said politely, "this young officer here wants me to take my pants off even though there's going to be a strip search in the next room. Now, though I realize that might be fun . . . I've just reminded him that it's just going to make the whole process here longer and a hell of a lot more difficult for us all."

"Difficult, shit!" Arv yelled from where he was pinned up against the wall on the other side of the room, forgetting himself, his face going red, "he wouldn't . . ."

"Alright," Big Arv cut in, "move ahead to the Sign-in Desk, move ahead! And that'll be enough of this racket out here!" Big Arv was old enough, and he said it politely, fatherly, almost, and all the black men moved fast into the reception room, leaving Arv limp against the cold gray stone of the vault.

"Dad, I . . ." Arv began, following his squat uniformed shadow after the inmates, but his father continued into the other room without turning, ignoring him, and his degradation was complete. Standing guard over the slow-moving line of convicts he tried to shrink into his uniform, tried to fold himself inside out and hide, would have if he could. Everybody but Big Arv and Wasco stared at him, whispered about him, laughed. He resented those fucking niggers. How he resented them! While they stood there naked in the lineup they had more dignity than he, Arv, who was fully dressed, and in a military getup as well! How'd they do it? *Why don't people respect me more?* he wondered, and wondering, he watched Big Arv and his favorite nephew Wasco shucking and jiving and fooling around, making jokes without a thought in the world: "Hey Unckus, how you doing?"

"Shit, couldn't be better kid. Looks like you had a spell of downs."

"What makes you think so, Unck? I'm here on business! Gonna make my fortune in the Joint, you watch! It's the world's greatest market area! Captive consumers. All you got to do is figure out the right product . . ."

The inmates started laughing at their rap. It was just the right thing to break the tension. And perfect for their audience. They realized it and continued their chatter. "Well," Big Arv said, beaming, red-faced, squinting his eyes up like Wasco's, leaning casually on the stacked denims, "the way I figure it, you're right. But you got to remember one thing. I tell you, in here you got to make sure your merchandise is properly oiled or your profit margins are just gonna dry right up in your fingers . . ."

"Don't worry, Unck, I just acquired myself a fine well-greased piece of machinery on the way over from Haley," Wasco said, jubilant, crowing, pointing to the skinny little junkie punk standing next to him, setting the room to rocking and rolling with good laughter, blowing off steam with his antics, conspiring without words with his uncle, diminishing the tension neatly. Big Arv appreciated it, you could see, just like he'd always appreciated Wasco, even when he was a kid. Wasco did have one thing, and Big

Arv loved him for it, Wasco had no fear, and a sense of timing. And in the Joint there's nothing more important. Both Big Arv and Wasco, as far as Arv could tell, were real success stories within their own lower echelon prison milieu. Each of them was completely relaxed and totally in command of his own seamy environment. Never had Arv been in command of his. And he admired with his whole heart Big Arv and Wasco and Galliot, and all men of strong wills. Arv himself, he just didn't have the balls. That's the truth, he thought bitterly. Just no balls, crying in his chest, trying not to show it, Arv thought with bitter self-hatred of when they were kids, and the two of them, Big Arv and Wasco, father and spiritual son, had laughed together often over secrets, secrets that the younger frailer more innocent boy was never let in on. And secrets, Little Arv was early convinced, and reconvinced himself now, were all of life that really counted. Blood, sex, hate, love, money, all were secret . . . *Big Arv, he brought a broken-winged woodpecker home one day and with great care and endless patience he nursed it back to health. Then Wasco drowned it in a milk bottle one day. Stuck its head in the cream at the top, holding on to its wings and legs while it twitched and jumped and blew frantic white bubbles of froth. All the kids thought Dad would come home and beat Wasco to a pulp. We all waited, happily anticipating Wasco's comeuppance. But Big Arv listened impassively to Wasco's phony story about the danger of "bringing a sick bird into the house . . . might have rabies or something," and said he was probably right. Big Arv will go to his grave believing Wasco, a four-time loser, murderer, heroin dealer, motorcycle gang prez, sodomist, is just a good boy gone wrong. They are brothers under the skin.* And Arv loved them. He loved them both and they rejected him. All his life. From tiniest childhood. It was simple. And the more they rejected him, the more he loved them. The more he loved them, the more they rejected him, hated and ridiculed and even tortured him. He got so desperate for their warmth as a kid that sometimes he'd creep up into his dad's warm spot in bed just after he got up. "What to hell you doing?" his old man would demand angrily. What could he say in response? *That I have learned from you that women are worthless creatures. By your example I've learned who the*

*gods of creation are. Men. And you and Wasco are the
only men, by your definition of men, which is mine. That
I want to be one, a man, and if I sniff and sniff and smell
enough of men maybe I will become one too?* What could
he say? He could never say that. Any time Wasco took a
shit at their place, Little Arv would run into the bathroom
to sniff his powerful shit, powerful stink . . . and to sit
content on his still man-warm toilet seat. . . . Wasco
called him a "fairy," but that wasn't it. He liked girls well
enough. But he had eyes. He saw that men judged each
other not by the way women looked at them, but by the
way men looked at them. Men were the valued ones. And
Arv was never allowed into that secret and exclusive club.
The more he awkwardly tried to get in, the harder they
held the door against him. It was still that way. . . .

Fast-Walking, a loser too, had been Little Arv's only
friend as a kid. Together they had made a pact: if the
people at the Joint didn't dig them, they would rise above
them. They would succeed on their own terms. Arv especially felt this. He was younger than Fast-Walking, stood
more of a chance. He dreamed every night, every day,
from the time he first understood that he was smarter
than most kids, from the time in the fourth grade the
teacher said, "You know what? Next to Deanna you got
the highest IQ in the whole school!" Arv dreamed. He
would rise up out of the morass, rise above his class, his
past, his family. He would be the first Weed in all of history to get away, to finish high school, go on to college,
graduate school, get a Ph.D., travel in Europe, learn languages, foreign ways. He would marry a beautiful woman.
He would make money on his own terms. He'd be a
writer or an artist or an architect or a professor. He'd buy
a fine big home, go to the opera, the symphony, the ballet,
the theater. He'd go on and on and on till his despicable
weedy origins, his prison-bred childhood, his degenerate
low-class middle-American family life were only a remote
memory, like man's memory of when he crawled out of
the primeval funk. Little Arv would be somebody! He
would!

But what had happened? Fast-Walking had gotten married, had kids too soon, ended up stuck in the Joint, getting deeper and deeper into debt every year, with no hope
of ever getting out. Arv had knocked up Fast-Walking's
sister and ended up the same way.

But, Arv was thinking, watching Wasco and Big Arv cutting up in the lineup, making everyone, even the niggers, laugh, *it still ain't too late, is it?*

When Big Arv finished handing out clothes and stuff, he led the troops out the Lock door and out onto the Isolation Yard. Little Arv slammed and locked the vault door behind them with an audible sigh. Wheeeew!

Arv's only cheer came now when he remembered that he was the traitor. But it was the smallest cheer, and gave him no pleasure at all.

"Weren't nothing to it," said Barney, the other officer, when he heard Arv's sigh. Barney was a young junior-college student who was still full of enthusiasm, whose clear young twenty-one-year-old eyes watched Arv with honest recognition of his inferior qualities, and felt sorry for him.

"Hey man, don't worry about this here little ruckus in the Lock," he said, "could've happened to the best of us!"

"Worry about what?" Arv asked, twisting the double lock on the huge reinforced steel door, sealing them into the vault.

Seven

Fast-Walking, squatting up in the wall post, had to put his cock away because his privacy was being invaded. He wiped his hand with his blue cowboy handkerchief and stood and zipped up and straightened his belt. Sergeant Weed had let the new prisoners into the Isolation Yard and duty called. His duty, according to Wall Post #8 rules and regulations, was to stand out on the gunwalk with Winchester in hand and oversee all movement in the Isolation Yard. This he promptly did, watching Barry Hutchins, the gaunt hollow-chested young swing shift runner, lope up to Big Arv to help escort the new convicts down along the asphalt walkway across the carefully manicured lawn in front of the Isolation building. All the cons looked the same to Fast-Walking, with their baldy haircuts and their dark blue C of C jeans and their light loose-fitting open-collared blue denim shirts, and the pack of cigarettes each of them carried in the upper righthand pocket of his shirt. With all that uniformity you couldn't tell one from the other, Wasco from Galliot, or black from brown from white from yellow.

Fast-Walking watched them turn left around the modernistic yellow Isolation building and go by the institution library, a dilapidated old green two-story building donated by some do-gooder in the '40's. Down the flower-lined walk to the "Pig Pen," the Yard Control Center, as it was officially known. There the Sergeant pulled them up short.

They were much closer now, and Fast-Walking finally recognized Wasco. Maybe he'd recognized him even before, coming down the walk, a great big muscle-bound dude, doing a crazy little bop step instead of a march, acting smart as usual, smoking a cigar in a long black holder, holding it at a jaunty up-turned angle, a smirky smart-ass smile on his red squinty Okie face. Everybody but this one dude was wearing prison issue high-top black work shoes. But this cat, who had to be Wasco, was sporting ten-inch black motorcycle boots with spiked toes and high-style stomper heels. And up close you could see that under his baldy his hair was red, and receding already, even though he was still young, more than six years younger than Fast-Walking himself, who'd watched the motherfucker grow up, watched him terrorize the neighborhood of the employees' housing area for years.

Though Fast-Walking had shared Arv's hatred and jealousy of Wasco when they were all kids together, for years now Fast-Walking had felt almost a kind of pride *well goddamn here comes a cat with some spirit by God some fucking balls!,* a pride in Wasco's style, his daring, his nonconformity, his well-publicized exploits in banditry and gangland warfare, a pride that almost everyone in the housing area felt *local boy makes good makes a name for himself like Jesse James, Billy the Kid, Baby Face Nelson, Bonnie and Clyde, Free-Wheeling Frank, Hell's Angels.* There was something in Fast-Walking and indeed the entire population of the prison housing area that saw Wasco's activities as merely the shenanigans of a lusty brawling boy *after all, why, shit, he's a* white *kid!*

Half the men were blacks. They all looked exactly alike. Any one of the twenty-five or so tall and short and fat and skinny suede dudes could have been Galliot. Even though Fast-Walking had seen his picture in the paper a hundred times, even cut it out and pasted it in his scrapbook, there was no telling. Galliot had a kind of strong face; whether you agreed with his politics or not, you had to hand it to him. You had to admit to yourself that there *was* something that the spooks saw in the stud, whether white men did or not. Denying it, like Big Arv did, was just crazy. And short-sighted too. There was something in his eyes, and his brow. He had the face of a black prophet, or an old-time nigger camp healer, Fast-Walking figured. You could see that he really did have a kind of power, that the coons latched on to real solid.

But anyway, right now Fast-Walking couldn't see any face like that in the lineup down in the Isolation Yard. Not a prophet or a poet there. They looked just like ordinary Clinks to him, plain old shuffle-footed brothers, standing out in the cold rain, smacking their black fists

into their pink palms and blowing on their hands to keep
warm.

Sergeant Weed climbed up on the front steps of the Pig
Pen shanty, puffing and blowing steam into the rainy air,
his big soft belly heaving, and yelled out, "Alright! Quit
your jiving!" because some of the blacks had begun to
murmur among themselves. They all fell silent. Big Arv lit
up a cigarette. Everyone, cons and bulls, is always smoking in the Joint. There ain't much else to do, except jack
off. Fast-Walking himself, in fact, up on the gunwalk, lit
up a joint. Nobody could smell it, he knew, the wind and
rain would carry it right away over their heads.

The inmates seemed displeased. Especially the black
ones. They didn't go for the tough talk, Big Arv's usual
stupid troublemaking number. They didn't seem to dig it
at all. They leaned over and started muttering among
themselves. Fast-Walking even imagined he heard the
whispered epithet "Pig" waft up with a sudden lull in the
squall. But finally they calmed down a bit and just stood
there shivering in the rain, freezing in their light denim
clothing, for quite a long time, while Big Arv walked
down the line, looking them over one by one. Many of
them knew him from before. Some of the white inmates
even greeted him.

"Hiya, Sarge! How's it going?"

"Fine, Carl, what you doing back in here?"

"Aw, you know the Freeworld nowadays."

"Oh yeah, do I ever! Ain't much better than Inside, is
it?"

Some poor black devil up in a strip cell in Isolation
could see them down there too, apparently, and he yelled
out at the top of his lungs:

"WHERE'S GALLIOOOOOOOOOOT!"

and it was like a death rattle that went all the way around
the yard, bouncing off the stone walls, shaking everyone,
even the convicts, even the black ones, and they all looked
around trying to figure out who did it.

Fast-Walking knew who did it.

He did it again.

"WHERE'S GALLIOOOOOOOOT!" he shrieked at the
top of his lungs, lungs that seemed riddled with hatred

and fear, afflicted with some kind of horrible pulmonary ailment. Somebody in the closely packed group of black men yelled back in a strong loud voice, an extraordinary voice with deep, resonant, almost messianic power:

"I'M WITH YOU, BROTHER!"

And they all cheered wildly.

"Right on!"

"That yo bad self!"

"Blow Black Fence!"

Bald black domes turned down backwards, howling at the sky, faces to the rain, teeth grinding, lips jutted out, threatening, aggressive, taking no shit, the black men continued to shout . . .

"I'm gon' fall out!"

"Soul on, brother!"

"Alright, goddamnit, that'll be enough of that!" Big Arv hollered, and turning up toward Fast-Walking, "Hey! Fast-Walking! You see who done that?"

Fast-Walking cupped his hands and yelled, "Strip cell number three. Isolation!"

Big Arv sent Barry hustling over to Isolation with instructions to "Cool that gunsel, and fast!"

The niggers huddled together and spoke excitedly among themselves. The whites and Chicanos started sidling to the background.

"Shut up!" Big Arv shouted.

Fast-Walking, up in the wall post, couldn't even figure out why he told, why he copped to the bastard. He didn't owe Big Arv any favors. He could've just as easily said he didn't know. But it came so sudden it just kind of popped out. Now Big Arv, always jealous of his authority, was just gonna get everybody into a whole shitload of trouble with that temper of his.

Fast-Walking flicked off the safety on his Winchester.

Barry came back from Isolation real nervous-looking, hearing the yard buzzing and whistling with potential violence. Big Arv said, "Okay, Barry, take these here gentlemen inside and skin search them again. Lock 'em up and wait around for chow. Then escort them all the way through the line. See to it that they get fed and don't give anybody any shit. Tuck 'em in good for the night. Then report to the Pig Pen sergeant. Alright?"

Barry looked scared and uncertain, as if he was thinking, *What the fuck am I gonna do all alone with twenty-
seven wild niggers?* but he nodded anyway, and said,
"Right, Sarge!"

"But leave *Mister* Galliot with me," Big Arv said, like
an idiot. Like a stupid fucking idiot he slurred the "Mister," leading up to the end of the word slow and then,
making fun of nigger talk, leaving the "r" off on the end.
"Yeah, leave old Mistah Galliot here with me," he repeated insultingly, "we got different plans for him."

"Okay, Sarge!" Barry yelled again, scared to death, and
started moving off as fast as he could.

Fast-Walking had tensed up when Big Arv started teasing. He figured that Big Arv, goddamn his soul to hell,
was going too far. Them blacks were in an ugly mood. *But
that's the thing,* Fast-Walking was thinking, *a lot of these
here old-time guards don't understand the new nigger. The
new nigger ain't like the old one. He don't care if he dies.
And nothing's more dangerous.*

But when Big Arv pointed over at a very ordinary looking little slump-shouldered studious-looking spade cat who
looked like he wouldn't or couldn't harm a flea, Fast-
Walking relaxed.

"Sheeeit!" he said out loud, puffing on his stubby roach,
diphthonging the expletive to entertain himself and contain his nervousness. "Well, appearances, they sure are de-
ceptive!"

Shepherded by Barry, the whites and Chicanos started
off toward the Big Yard. But the black men, with the will
of one person, without a word spoken, remained standing
in the center of the yard in a tight angry circle, the circle
of hobbled but pissed-off musk oxen, grouped around Galliot.

"Oh fuck!" Fast-Walking shouted out loud, stumbling
over his own feet.

Big Arv's jaw dropped. Fear-struck, his brown full eyes
went goggle-round.

"Now you got us into it, you stupid fucking Spic!"
Fast-Walking moaned, regaining his balance, watching the
Tower #3 man and the Wall Post #7 man running out on
their gunwalks across the yard, rifles at the ready.

Fast-Walking just stood there where he was for several

seconds trying to comprehend what Big Arv had gotten them all into.

Big Arv himself, comprehending too well, stood speechless in front of the rebellious mob of black men, trembling for his life.

Fast-Walking moved, finally, with a fast-walking effortless lurch; moving without seeming to move, he clanged over the metal walkway in his flying jodhpur boots. Stood outside on the gunwalk at the point closest to the action, leaning on the iron railing with the Rim-Fire propped up in front of him, deadly gunmetal gray, safety securely off. He pointed its mean snout right into the angry black flower in the yard, right into the glowering crowd of restive niggers, right dead center into the heart of the circle, the honeybee heart of the flower, right into the black nectareous heart of Galliot, knowing in his rifleman's soul that Miley and Peters at #3 and #7 were aiming for the same place, and only waiting for a word from the proper authority to liven up their cheerless lives, brighten up their boring hours, their lonely unloved existences on the wall. Fast-Walking's hands sweated, his eyes popped bulbous out of his head, perspiration dripped too between his long skinny legs, tickling his excited scrotum. His pulse beat madly. His spirits leapt!

ACTION! *Goddamn sonofabitching cocksucking motherfucking* ACTION! ACTION!

Big Arv, feeling murder crawling out of the very air around him, blood and gore seeping up from the asphalt beneath his quivering toes, raised his hands, turning around in a circle toward all three gunmen, squinting up his little Mexican-Indian eyes to avoid the big raindrops that began coming down harder now, pounding on the grass on the Isolation lawn like dum-dums, gathering suddenly in puddles on the blacktop, soaking everyone.

"Hold it boys!" he yelled, to whom, no one ever knew, to both gunmen and blacks, perhaps . . . "Holdit Holdit Holdit Holdit HOLDIT!"

Then he turned to the black men confronting him and tried to placate them, knowing he'd gotten himself into something he wouldn't be able to handle. Or rather, Fast-Walking figured, assessing what would happen if the shit did hit the fan: Galliot would go down deader than a doornail within two seconds and before we could squeeze

off three more shots (three more niggers) they'd be on
Big Arv and they wouldn't give him any mercy, he could
count on that. They'd eat him right up.

"Hey! Whoa down now!" Big Arv yelled, "listen fellahs, we don't want no trouble. Listen, maybe I was
wrong but I was just kidding, see? Look, just head on into
your cells and we'll forget the whole thing . . ."

But they just stood there, them bushboogies. Nobody
said a word. The rain came down harder and harder,
blowing up against the windows of the Pig Pen below.
The silence got Fast-Walking jittery up on the wall. His
leather strap kept getting caught in the trigger guard of
his rifle. He had to take his eyes off the Yard each time
for precious seconds to remove it. Across the Yard, above
on the other side, he could see Miley sweating it too, on
the wall, his face drained an icy white you could see a
half a hundred yards away. *Like lions that get used to the
trainer's whip, the new nigger is deadly.*

"Okay?" Big Arv went on nervously, shifting his big
feet. "Here! Wait a minute! Barry, you take them other
boys over to the gate, okay?" he said, politer than usual,
motioning to the gawking white and Chicano convicts.
"Now look," he said, swinging around again in the direction of the scowling black men, "we got no intention
whatsoever of harming or bothering Mr. Galliot here in
no manner whatsoever . . ."

"How we know that?" Galliot asked, cutting in, very
calm and easy, his arms chained up to the next nigger, a
little cocky now, superspady, sure that he'd outbluffed the
swart gray-haired sergeant. The other blacks clustered
tighter around him, linking arms, linking chains and handcuffs, clanging metal, beating their heavy black feet, rumbling deep, rumbling bad, bad-ass, groaning, moaning
their jungle-nigger beat, "Oh Lord," and "Yea!" "Oohie!"
slave talk, field calls, field nigger talk, shuffling and clink-
ing in the Yard, rubbing musk, rubbing black musky bods
up close, hearing those chains, listening, digging it, prideful now, the black-ass motherfuckers, dangerous proud of
those ringing banging sounds of bondage, ancestry,
slaveships, blackblood, blackmud, beating their feet,
beating time to the rhythm, "Blow it Black!"

"Soul on!"

"Blow it Black Fence!"

They called, they sang, getting into it, ignoring the Sergeant, ignoring the bloodlusting white-ass gunners on the wall, ignoring old Fast-Walking himself, negating his pounding bloodhungering honkey fucking heart, negating the whole goddamn Joint and the walls around them, negating the entire white world, negating it all in affirmation and prideful nigger-love of their painful piss-poor peola-pussy peanut-picking past! Socking it to the old Sarge, socking it to the gunners, swaying now, wigging it, jiving, swaying together, shucking it, but serious too, deadly dead-ass dirty down and determined, them black mother-fuckers, doing the Black Fence, the famous dance, that had started the movement. "Black Fence!" they shouted, dancing it, doing it, "Do it! Do it! Do it!" doing that mad contagious dance that had swept America before Galliot went to prison the first time, that still swept from coast to coast, echoed from one fucking end of the country to the other, raged through the squalid needle-infested, crime-prone, high-murder-rate ghettos from Bedford-Stuyvesant to Harlem to Mo-Town to South Side Chi-Town to Watts, Hough, Hunter's Point, West Oakland to Fillmore like wildfire, ideological conflagration. The Black Fence, Black-ass Fence, a song, a lilting springy West Indian kind of bopping song that came into being spontaneously one day right in the leader's wiggy black brain, the papers said. Big Black Fence, Numbah One, a song that just popped into his natural nappy head by chance, mystically, a song out of the past somewhere, out of Trinidad or Jamaica or Louisiana or Brazil, or a combination of all. Maybe he'd heard it as a kid, the magazines speculated, maybe he made it up. It was an impossible song, impossibly perfectly sweepingly rhythmic. Jamaican perhaps. Reggae-like. Voodoo, Ras Tafarian, Black Camp, religious, mystic, violent. It was like a Ghost Dance. "The New Ghost Dance," the papers called it, provoking hysteria in the boarded-up watch-doggied, locked-in white-butt population of the land. Like the Ghost Dance of the American Indians in the 1890's, like those same wild Wovoka dances, those magic, mysto, epic dances that stormed across the country from Paiute to Sioux and brought broken-down reservation Indians out on a great warpath that set Washington and the entire white race trembling with mortal trepidation. That's what old Galliot did, he scared

the White Man shitless. . . . His was a wild wonderful
song, a blues song, a chant, a field cry, a call to arms. The
melody was magically catchy. Once you'd heard it you
never forgot it. Fast-Walking would never forget it, never!
The beat too, it was infectious, startlingly so. It was a
dance too, with intricate but spontaneous shouting and
stamping in a flowerlike exploding pattern which, viewed
from an apartment window, looked like ritual warfare,
looked like danger, looked like them black bastards were
gearing up for the showdown, Armageddon, the Day of
Last-ass Judgment. Black Fence! They were doing it now.
Fast-Walking watched them with Winchester at hand, .38
caliber Police Special at fingertip. They were doing it now,
flowering it out, the Black Fence, setting up their funny
weirdo nigger flower that was a fence, that said, "Don't
come in, whitey!" Flowering, the fence grew around Sergeant Arvin Weed. "Wham-chooga-chooga, Wham-chooga-chooga, Wham-chooga-chooga. Wham!" they started,
turning Big Arv's shit to melted dripping Shinola. They
were doing it now, them black-bottomed slave-boys,
them fucking cons, convicts, prisoners, inmates, incarcerated within the State Joint, them fucking big-footed nigger
slaves. Fast-Walking watching. They all watched, them
Sylvesters, them Chucks, them scared white-balled cocksuckers, scared pee-peeless, chills running up and down
their chicken-pale spines, round and round their hairy
white bellies. Cause them dudes out there in the Yard,
flowering it, Fencing it, flower-power, black lilies, smelling, perfuming up the Isolation Yard with their musk-cat
reek, musk-rat smell, musky nigger boy scent, they was
some angry fucking niggers, scary ones, who didn't care
nothing about dying, jungle bunnies, lost in their chant,
hypnotized by their mysto leader, Galliot, doing the Black
Fence. "Do the Black Fence!" someone yelled. And they
did it.

"Do it! Do it! Do it!"

Did they really do it? You bet your sweet white ass
they did.

> Black Fence
> Black Feeence
> Blaaaack Feeeeence
> Blaaaaaaaaaaaaaaaack!

While Big Arv, transfixed, mentally crucified, pissed slow and sour down his uniform pantleg, dribbling it, spotting his pig-khaki crotch. . . . *The new nigger got nothing to lose, he figures.*

"Do it! Do it! Do the Black Fence!"

They did it. Them fucking negro niggers. They did the Black Fence, a scam, a slam, a shuffle-shuffle-shuffle-boom! Shuffle-shuffle-shuffle-boom! Soft-shoe, voodoo, jungle magic, shashashasha, sha ba da, shabada shaba da, a samba-like slow-walking bop that had sent them black-boys out into the streets all over this American land, a carnival dance that you could step out to, get lost in, get hung up on, revolt to, rape and murder and pillage to, a killer's song, a sexual black negroid lover's song. Fast-Walking thought about it now. A Mau Mau song, Jomo's dance, Black Terror, Black September, Black Peril, Black Plague, Black Black Black Black Black Black . . . Black Fence! Sha sha sha sha sha . . . extending it out, they went, down in the Isolation Yard, going beyond endur-ance, beyond whiteman's hearing, beyond white experi-ence, higher than his ear could follow, them fucking ani-moids, criminoids, negroids, them fucking Afro-apes, Ivory Coasters, Cameroon Cowboys, Angola Army Ants, Liberian Lightfoots, far off and away out beyond Fast-Walking and the other Joint guards, taking them out to the farthest hairy edge of the universe, out past reality, out to where man began, out to the tent poles and the midnight gardens, out to the piss hole of caca, out to the dinosaur shit whence sprang the humanoid kind, the fat black turd that nurtured the Homo sapiens race. They went *too far*. Just like they did on the outside. The whiteman felt like *he* was up against the wall. And that wouldn't do at all. His age-old nigger fears came out to the fore: the menace, the other, the unknown, alien, out-sider. Up in the towers, up in the wall posts and gunwalks all over America, and right here in the Joint, the Man, Chuck, Charley, the Kack, the Hack, the Main Cop, Fast-Walking Miniver, prison aristo, son of the great Warden, snapped his sphincter FLOMP! in fear, and nar-rowed his fucking rifle sight down to a one-inch square in the middle of Galliot's Black Fencing heart.

Nobody said a word against them.

"Blow Black Fence!"

"Tell it!"

Then there was silence and blowing rain and shiny wet black faces for five full minutes while the light got dimmer and dimmer.

Finally Big Arv summoned the courage to speak.

"Well . . ." he began.

"Well, nothing!" the little black man said, his small frame growing in stature with every word, magicianlike, possessor of the black magic, "here's what we're going to ask for." Galliot paused and looked around slowly at the gunmen in the towers, on the walls, confronting each and every one, eye to fucking eye, so there'd be no shunting or shifting the guilt . . . confronting even the Warden's only begotten son.

"We're going to ask only what it is in your power to grant, Sergeant. No impossible demands. We're going to ask that I be allowed to continue right along with the Brothers, unbothered, un-roughed-up, un-tortured or intimidated or bullied as you had planned, and no questions asked . . . on either side."

Old Galliot, he had a real voice, a powerful preacher-like voice that you had to stand up and listen to.

Big Arv raised his hands in the air, palms up, and shrugged his shoulders in an authentic Latin gesture indicating honest inability to perform what's asked for. The Mexican prisoners picked up on it and laughed together. The tension in the air had diminished considerably.

"Look fellahs, I can't do that," Big Arv said, pleading, "it's against the rules. I got to put you in a holding cell, Mr. Galliot, in Isolation, and ask you a few questions. Then you can proceed over to your cell in the East Block."

"Well, I think it might behoove you to make an exception this time," Galliot said, through his clenched yellow teeth, taking a step forward, a step that Big Arv awkwardly shrank from, almost tripping over his large fat feet, a step followed without discussion by every black in the group. They seemed to obey Galliot's silent commands almost like limbs of his own body. Their prison-made shoes splashed water, stomping in the puddles of rainwater on the asphalt. Their breath rose up steamy in the humid air. Big Arv comically shrunk away, cringing.

"I'll lose my job!" he wailed, almost believable, his

hands turned up to the sky. He was eloquent, in his fear, in his infinite cunning. And Fast-Walking had his bead now down to a half-inch square area in the center of Galliot's heaving chest, just above his third shirt button.

"Call and ask."

"Whoooo?" Big Arv groaned.

"Call the Warden. Isn't that the Warden's kid up there?" he asked, pointing up to where Fast-Walking stood, knees a-knocking, on the gunwalk *how the fuck'd he know?* "Get him to call up his old man!"

"Hold it! Hold it! I'll tell you what," Big Arv said, speaking rapidly, as if he'd suddenly come upon a solution to their quandary, their standoff in the yard, their highly uncertain truce. "We don't want no trouble, man. I'll send you up with my runner. When you get up there you just stick your hand out the bars and wave. They'll see it and head on into the Big Yard cause they'll know you're okay. How's about that?"

"I'm sorry, but the Brothers just wouldn't have it," Galliot said, "they'd be afraid of what might happen to me later. I'm sure you understand, Sergeant?"

Fast-Walking, looking down the long rifle barrel at Galliot's pounding nigger ventricle, laughed to himself. Galliot's way of speaking seemed to him impossibly quaint, comic . . . "just wouldn't have it," indeed!

"Okay. Let's go," Big Arv said, the wheels almost visibly turning in his fat-necked head.

"Go where?"

"You got it," Big Arv said, all business now, motioning Barry over. "Okay Barry, run them over to the East Block. Galliot too. And don't harm a hair on his head!"

"Oohie!"

"Got this round, motherfuckers!"

"Blow Black Fence!"

"Yeah!"

"Sing it!"

"Do it! Wham-chooga-chooga! Wham-chooga-chooga! Wham-chooga-chooga! Wham!" And those black sons-ofbitches did the Black Fence all the way out of the Isolation Yard.

Fast-Walking let down the key on the rope and Barry opened the gate to the Big Yard and let the convicts all in, whites, blacks, and Chicanos, relocked it, and Fast-

Walking wound the key back up, sighing loudly, letting
his heart wind down finally . . . "Wheeeeew! Goddamn!"

Barry escorted the excited inmates across the Big Yard,
under the high tin roof of the rain shed that ran down the
middle of the yard. Fast-Walking, according to regulations, followed them above on the gunwalk. The rain
came down on the tin roof like ten thousand skeletons
fucking. The inmates, quieter now, suffering the perils of
anticlimax (after all, the motherfuckers were still in
prison!), hurried toward the enormous steel gate of the
East Block. Even the blacks' enthusiasm seemed damp-
ened by the cold wet wind off the Sound. Very shortly
they disappeared.

That was the end of that. "Wheeeew!"

Later, much later, Fast-Walking stood up above the
Yard alone, the wind whipping at his war surplus overcoat, ruffling his fine longish blond hair under his uniform
cap. Nothing moved within the walls. Even the sea gulls
had gone home to roost on the sea, or wherever it was
they slept. The Yard stood as long and empty as his own
death before him. An approaching sure death that he
hated, hated without knowing it, without being acquainted
with it (death being one of the few things in the world
that even the fairest-minded individual detests without
even giving it a decent chance). Suddenly he was miserable, as he always was after a big to-do in the Joint, after
big prison excitement. Because "excitement" in the Joint
usually meant some kind of eventual misery for someone
else. There was, therefore, a certain measure of guilt in
Fast-Walking's present response. Galliot's inevitable misery and early death now sorrowed Fast-Walking, who had
just been looking down at his heart through a rifle sight,
who had just been ready, willing and able to pull that
hair-pin trigger and kill him deader than a fucking doornail. It got to him, though, all of a sudden. Fast-Walking
was not a man without sentiment. It worked at him. Got
into his backbone, bent it, slumped him down, curled his
posture on the gunwalk *shit what did they get the poor asshole for anyway the first time? Nothing but smoking a
joint!* And the tears of pity came into his clear still-young
eyes, blue eyes, eyes that could suffer too, just like them
black eyes, *the blue-eyed daddy of four kids,* eyes that

could get wet too, with tears, like Galliot's damp brown high-yellow eyes that he'd seen in a picture once, a colored picture in a magazine, a picture he had cut out and pasted somewhere, and still possessed somewhere, in one drawer or another in his prison residence.

Often after violence, or its threat, in the Joint, Fast-Walking, and other guards too, when they were alone, got maudlin, sentimental, felt sorry for what they'd done, or might have done, or wanted to do, usually after it was too late. Felt sorry for the poor criminals locked up in the Joint, cons and bulls alike. For they were all criminals, all of them, each in his own way, greater or smaller. Fast-Walking pitied Galliot, and himself, and everybody, everybody everywhere, but most of all he pitied himself and Little Arv and all the guards and all the prisoners stuck in that terrible horrible Joint, that filthy dripping diseased old Joint sticking out into the shitwater Sound, the mud-smell, the oily cove.

And all the long way up along the metal gunwalk, the corrugated iron walkway above the empty wet yard, he cried for himself and his poor immigrant wife and his poor kids, cried for the entire human race, for his brothers and sisters of all kinds and colors: the white ones, the brown and yellow ones, and the loved and hated, despised and envied nigger-black ones too. And he couldn't imagine how he could endure another minute on his wall post, another hour, and the five hours and thirty-eight minutes remaining on his shift stretched on in front of him like the end of space, like a gap in time and the stars, and he was sure, dead sure, that he could never summon the courage to come to work again tomorrow. Because he knew one thing. He knew Galliot's life wasn't worth a plug Confederate nickel. Hadn't been since the day he left Brown Max. And he knew Galliot knew it. Knew Galliot knew that the only reason he was breathing right now this minute was because Big Arv had been his hostage in the Yard, and because Galliot would of course have insisted on taking Big Arv with him on his journey to infinity *not that that would bother me at all.* And he knew Big Arv knew all that too, and wouldn't hesitate two seconds letting Galliot know what he knew, once he got him in his cell helpless in the East Block . . . not only was it that Big Arv *knew,* but he'd do everything in his power to help

it along, activate it, what he knew. And now, after Big
Arv's abject humiliation in the Yard, in front of all those
people, it was sure. Cause, what you know, well, that can
be reckoned and worked out. Knowing is possibility. And
possibility, well, that only remains to be attained!

Galliot was no pushover. And he had an almost hypnotic power over his brothers. But Fast-Walking knew that
no matter what the black man worked up in defense, no
matter what his frantic attempts to survive turned out to
be, even those attempts themselves, riot, escape, or whatever, they'd just play right into the Man's hands. Cause
the Man was out to get him. And nobody beats the Man!
Nobody! Let's say he was even successful as them black
dudes at Attica. They'd get him in the end, with English!
Just like the Man did over in New York State. The Man
would not only ice that motherfucker, they'd dry-ice him,
force freeze him, instant zero him! No question about
that. He never had a chance.

Poor old Galliot. Captive slave. Resident nigger. One of
our own. What you going to do now?

And the dark and irreconcilable ambiguity of Fast-
Walking's quavering white-skinned Americano response to
that question, and his attitude (tragic: equivocal too)
toward that proud and brave and crazy black man Galliot,
overwhelmed the prison guard with terror, the terror of
possibility: the possibility of chaos, the possiblity of unre-
ality, the possibility of his residence in an empty and
meaningless yet permanently walled universe. . . .

Eight

Sergeant Weed banged on the steel vault door with his big porcine fist, a fist so stuffed and red and meaty, with unhealthy tautly stretched skin cushioning its knuckles, its joints and nails and palm, that you'd think it feeble. But it was hard and powerful as tempered steel. WANG! WANG! WANG! Arv snapped to. He spun the lockwheel and turned the giant bronze key. The massive gate swung open, screeching a horrendous metallic SCREEEEEECH and Big Arv stepped over the low iron bar and walked straight by and into the Lock without taking the least notice of his open-mouthed son. Oh-oh! Look out! Big Arv's large red lips were clamped down tight, his jowly pink face twitching, his right eye, the greener one, flickering involuntarily the way it always did when the pressure came down. Arv didn't know what'd happened outside with Galliot and them but he did know that it'd been heavy and not at all pleasant in the Yard and that made his heart skitter with happy vindication *let* him *find out what it feels like for a change!* And, thinking of Big Arv's certain humiliation out in the Isolation Yard, Little Arv's previous failure in the lineup was somehow canceled out. It made him feel great all of a sudden.

Big Arv walked straight through the Lock to the outside gate and banged on it. When no one came immediately he walked back toward Arv, still not looking at him, not aware of him, distracted, pacing the stone floor with his jaw set, mouth twitching.

Then, apparently to no one in particular, he said, "Got to go over and see Lobo."

Barney, the outside gate man, came in from the Sign-in Room and, clanging his keys around, opened up. Big Arv, still distracted, unconscious, walked through without a word, and Barney, a tough little Irishman from the Mis-

sion District, San Francisco, slammed the gate and locked
up. CLANG!

WHAM! WHAM! WHAM! There went Big Arv again,
pounding on the gate from the outside.

"Jesus Christ! Make up your fucking mind!" Barney
yelled when the Sergeant was still out of earshot.

Arv couldn't figure out what had got his old man shook
up. But he knew this mood, and it made him glow with
malicious pleasure and, simultaneously, with affection and
concern for his father. Arv knew, as Barney spun the
lockwheel, as he fumbled for his big key among the many
at his belt, that Big Arv in this mood was as useless and
ineffective as a child, lost to reason . . . all he could do in
this mood was sputter and rage and run around in circles.

"Goddamnit, come on!" he shouted in Little Arv's direction as soon as he stepped in the door. Barney winced
and shook his head at the Sarge's volume.

"What?"

"You heard me, goddamnit! Give Barney your keys and
come with me. Barney, you phone the reserve man and
get him over here to take over Little Arv's job while he's
gone. We got to go over and see Lobo. Then we're going
over to the East Block and give Mistah Galliot," he said
venomously, "a little help moving into his new cell . . ."

"Right, Sarge!" Barney said. "Oh boy! Look out nigger
here come de Man!"

Arv didn't say a word. Just did like he was told.

Barney let them out and they marched across the
squishy lawn in the rain to the Third Fence Gate. Big Arv
led the way. His enormous buttocks went FLONK FLONK
FLONK up and down hard and crooked like two pig-iron
pistons on a broken barnyard drive wheel.

Arv, malicious-minded now, felt it necessary to break
the silence.

"Say, Dad!" he said spitefully, vindictively, reaching his
fleeing beefy old man, "what do you think about this Galliot thing?"

"Whaddaya mean?"

"I mean, like, do you think he dusted that guard down
at Brown Max?"

"Shit, he done it, he done it, alright."

"How do you know for sure?"

"You think they'd go to all that trouble with the black
sonofabitch if they didn't have him down cold?"

"Lot of people say they just wanted to get rid of the last militant, put a stop to that Black Fence stuff," Arv said.

"Good idea," Big Arv said irrelevantly, "good iiiiiiidea!"

Arv laughed, just to be polite, just to play it close to the table. Anyway, after that statement, reaffirmed twice, there was nothing more to say. This kind of logical short circuit in Big Arv's reasoning was one of the things that always put even topical conversation between them to flight. What could you say to an assertion like that? Arv, who knew he had almost no influence on his father, less influence than almost anyone, less even than his brow-beaten mother, thought that nevertheless, in the interests of conscience, perhaps he ought to try and point out the error in Big Arv's pattern of reasoning. But he just couldn't. First of all, he wouldn't listen. Second, he was too prejudiced to change even if he did hear. Third, the solace and safety implicit in Arv's "understanding" with his father was too precious to jeopardize. Arv and his old man had a tacit understanding between themselves that they'd ignore each other's real existence as much as pos-sible when they were forced to be alone together. When they were together in a crowd Big Arv could bluster about and be free of his son, even make wisecracks about him, ridicule his "weakness" and "cowardice." Arv could snicker callowly behind his father's back. But alone to-gether they were always sheepish, unable to talk about anything that really counted, required by the terms of their unspoken accord to remain forever offhand with one another. It was a most uncomfortable situation, and one of the reasons Arv hated to spend one minute alone with his dad. But it was a necessity if they were to avoid outright warfare with each other. This uncomfortable state of affairs had come about when Arv returned from his army service at Air Cav Headquarters in Vietnam. Big Arv had been for once in his life proud of his kid (though, if the truth be known, all he'd been was a clerk/typist at G-2) and had taken it for granted that he couldn't treat him like a little boy anymore, since he was now a decorated veteran (phony Purple Heart for flaming incendiary gonorrhea acquired during the Tet offensive of '68 when the entire staff was trapped for three days inside G-2 with fourteen Nammie hooch maids and canteen

girls), since he was now a married man, father, son-in-law
to Warden Miniver . . . couldn't scold or strap him anymore with his thick leather double-tongued uniform belt,
so now he'd have to treat him like a grownup. But Big
Arv hadn't been able to make the change. Didn't seem to
know what to do with Arv, how to treat him, now that he
was a man. When Arv was a kid his old man had ignored
him completely, had never recognized his individual humanity, like any other father in the Joint. Now that Arv
was big he still ignored his separate identity, but was a little bit embarrassed by the whole thing. That was the difference.

So now, crossing the moat bridge, Arv said nothing
more, afraid that if he abrogated this understanding of
theirs his old man would reclaim his "right" to give out
free "advice" to Arv all the time. And then they'd be back
on the same old whirlwind again, arguing all the time,
making life miserable for everyone. Though Big Arv almost never remarked his son's physical presence, for some
reason the official and written and statistical details of the
boy's life—bills, draft cards, driver's licenses, report cards,
work reports, college transcripts, money, marriage papers,
divorce papers, bank statements, etc.—had always fas-
cinated him. *I wonder what he'd say to the letter in my
pocket right now?* No, Arv didn't want to get back into all
that again, all that verbal fencing *my rapier, his bludgeon*
they used to get into on the rare times they spoke, nor did
Little Arv desire to say those unretractable words again,
those words that had been forced from his lips by his father's barrage of nagging advice on the occasion of Arv's
quicky Mexican divorce: "Now, kid, you oughta try to
make it up, oughta go over and talk to her dad the
Warden, oughta talk to her again, oughta try and patch
things up, oughta talk to her brother, he's one of your
best friends" . . . oughta do this, oughta do that . . .
And Arv'd had to say those sad unforgivable, unforgiving
words, words that begged for concrete active response,
now that Arv carried that highly irregular letter in his
right shirt pocket, buttoned securely, words that rang now
in both their ears like their heavy-booted, metal-toed footsteps as they rang rapidly over the antique bronze drawbridge, as they went across the slick rainy blacktop road
and through the neat inmate-tended rose garden to the Ad
Building one after the other . . . "Who are you, a fat

slob, a failure, to give me advice?" *And then* PLOW! *he hit me and had another heart attack . . . and they rushed him to the County Hospital where he nearly died like his old dad in an institution bed. . . .*

In the foyer outside the Warden's office Big Arv asked the secretary, a slick wavy-haired white inmate by the name of Barnes ("Ma" Barnes, as he was known in prison homosexual circles) for Official Form 3342, which was Arv quickly learned, entitled:

(NSCC-3342) 660

FRIEND OR RELATIVE IN STATE CUSTODY

1. Name of Officer _____
2. Rank _____
3. Years of Service _____
4. Relation to Inmate _____
5. Name of Inmate _____
6. Sentence _____
7. Crime _____
8. Your confidential assessment of character and re-habilitative prospects of inmate (use separate sheet if necessary). _____

Sergeant Weed filled out the first five lines and then said, "Pull his jacket, will you, Barnes?"

Barnes went to the huge metal filing cabinet and pulled the drawer marked "W." He read off the information to the Sergeant in a crisp clear voice:

"Weed, Wasco Garland, Number 876543. Three to ten years. Convictions on an eleven five one, an eleven five hundred and a three forty-two, plus Parole Violation. There's a silent beef here too: charged but not convicted of a one eighty-seven, first degree. Priors: a three forty-five and a four eighty-four A six down in California as an Adult Offender, and a silent one eighty-six, reduced to Aggravated Assault, with the New Sonora Youth Authority."

Little Arv looked over his old man's heavy bisonlike shoulder, the shoulder of an animal force-fed for meat, as he digested Barnes's cryptic information, information rendered in the code that only lawyers and judges, cons and bulls, in the whole world could understand, information that Little Arv had barely understood himself . . . except perhaps the salient facts: Wasco'd been tried for murder and selling heroin. He'd beat the murder beef, and was convicted on the other, and would now do three to ten years in the Slam.

Little Arv watched his old man as he wrote:

> Being the prisoner's uncle I seen him over the years he is not to my way of thinking a born criminal as some in here I believe if he learns a good trade and a little control with the right kind of supervision and discipline he can be a useful member of the community . . .

As he stood hovering over Big Arv's familiar and almost edible shoulder in that high-ceilinged room, Arv's mind wandered from the stolid remote figure below him to a far more real father figure. It wandered to the figure imprinted in Arv's startlingly unique imagination, an imagination originating, as far as he could see, from no discernible source in the regressive, degenerate heredity of his family.

My father, who is he?

Your father? Arv thought, thought it out, rapped it to himself as he could later rap it, winding it out, telling it, locked in a Hawaiian woman's embrace in a broken-down fleabag motel in San Felipe, Baja California:

Sergeant Weed is a dishonest cop, a Democrat for Nixon, and a World War II and Korean War infantry veteran. He's got a bad heart . . .

Big Arv's present voice, his unreal voice, his exterior voice broke through Little Arv's reverie for a moment as he whisperingly repeated one of the lines he'd just written in his report:

> I will explain here that his first offense as a Youth Offender is as far as this officer can see more like a 185, Self Defense, than a 186 Murder the prejudice in this case happened because the victim was the prioner's father well known in Custody as a hard drinking man since deseaced . . .

Little Arv did not deign to correct his father's spelling of that word meaning "dead" because it somehow ex-

pressed the bent weird place where the "deseaced," Arv's
ignorant, reclusive, soulless Uncle Big Wasco, now most
probably dwelt. The Sergeant's squat, bull-like, Weed-like
brother was a man of few words. Worse! He was a man
of almost *no* words! He never had an opinion about anything. He never chatted, gossiped, laughed, cried, or even
farted so far as anyone in the Joint knew. Even when
Wasco stabbed him that time when he was a kid, more
out of surprise than deviltry, he hadn't let out a peep, not
a cry, not a tear, even as they hauled him off to the
Joint's Emergency Operating Room! Arv had watched, behind the low hedge, lying flat against the inmate-trimmed
grass. He'd seen: Big Wasco never said a fucking thing.
And Wasco, the tough little sonofabitch, he hadn't either.
Not a word did he say, as they clapped the handcuffs on
him and led him away, the county sheriffs, led him away
to another Joint for kids where he stayed for three years,
growing into adulthood there, a stunted state-trained,
criminoid adulthood, for sure, but adulthood, full and sexual, nonetheless. . . . But old Big Wasco, the old man,
he'd remained a total nonentity all his life, even when
they stitched up his gut and let him out of the hospital.
Even Big Arv admitted he never knew him, from the time
they were kids together. "He was a real secret, that guy,"
Big Arv said of his brother. Which was the understate-
ment of his life. Although Big Wasco worked twenty-five
years in the Joint, until the day of his death on the job by
arteriosclerosis, a hereditary danger with the Weeds, nobody ever knew what his exact job was, or what he did after hours, or anything about his private life. Very few
people in the Joint even knew his name, or that he even
existed. The kids used to talk about it amongst themselves,
and ask Wasco about it, whether Big Wasco was the same
at home, whether he was a lush like everyone said.

"Hey Wasco!" they'd ask, "what's your old man like at
home?"

"What old man?" Wasco would reply.

There was only one thing in the world that could bring
Big Wasco out of his lifelong seclusion, and that was a
hot bowl of Big Arv's fabled genuine Mexican
chilibeans. . . .

Little Arv watched his father now, his father who, pencil in his mouth, was trying to figure out what to write
down on the official form to make life easier for Wasco in

the Joint. Latin in his sense of loyalty to his criminoid nephew, WASP in his loyalty to the printer of that official form, Big Arv personified to his son the terrible ambiguous fix that America was in, the terrible fix of his old man's generation.

And Little Arv's heart opened up to the old fart *what would you have done? would you have done any better?*, this aging betrayer of trusts, violator of his own ethics, this heart-attack-prone survivor of cultural shocks, this devout believer, unquestioning acceptant of The Great American Lie, this survivor of holocausts: the Great Depression, World War II, the Korean War, the Vietnam War, the Great Death Row Riot of '62, all through which he had stolidly persevered, carried onward and onward, never upward, never succeeding, even on his own terms, but ever onward forward into progress with his great American ship of State—and Arv's great love for his father and his father's land, this land through which the very North American Indian marrow of his and Big Arv's bones had been sifted, and his resolution to leave that father, that land, and never ever come back, were reconfirmed for Arv now, as he watched with tears in his eyes his poor old prison guard dad painfully spell out words relating to blood and bondage on a printed and stamped piece of paper in the State Prison Warden's outer office:

And this here individual come home under the influence of alcoholics and he and his dependent was having a lot of trouble at this time and the dependent retained a sharp pointed instrument of hunting knife size near his bed in case of prowlers he said. The inebriated individual he commences to striking the youth offender in a slapping motion for no reason while asleep the dependent jumps up half groggy stabs the drunk father in the abdomen and groin but when the dependent seen it was his provider and father he kind of lost sanity temporary and left weapon protruding and retired outside where officers later found him hiding in area of Refuse Dump #6. To my professional mind when the youth offender was remanded to Prill Vocational Institution custody this is what started him on the road to crime before that it was minor . . .

Big Arv kept writing but Little Arv quickly lost interest. He started leafing through the old *New Yorkers, Harper's, Atlantics, Saturday Reviews* and *Poetry* magazines that Lobo Miniver, Warden of the Joint, Arv's ex-father-in-law, had laid out on the magazine rack for visitors to browse through. . . .

Little Arv had known Lobo all his life, from the time when Lobo was still a mere captain in the Custody Department. Arv had always liked him, even when they became related through marriage, and Lobo had seemed to reciprocate that affection. He had never failed to pick Arv, among all the other kids at the prison housing area, to be his caddy when he went out to the Mission Santa Bonita Country Club. He played golf like he did everything else. Excellently. A four handicapper at the age of fifty-three. Driving three hundred yards against a strong wind off the Alvarez Straits. Dropping sixty-five-yard nine-iron birdies right into the pin. Plowing out of deep and sand hazards like a volcanic eruption. Yet, all the time, a "good guy," as Arv used to think of him. Always asking Arv's advice as a caddy, whether he really needed it or not . . . "Say! What should I use here, Little Arv? The six iron, or the five?" Smiling at him when his choice was correct, saying nothing when it wasn't, teaching him a lot . . . "Now, on this shot, Little Arv, I'm going to use the two iron and I'll tell you why. I know we've got that little hill in front of us. But that wind is blowing to beat all get out. So we'll go in soft and low over the crest and let the incline on the other side roll it right up to the pin. You see what I mean?" . . . Lobo had impressed Arv like no other adult in his childhood and teens. He had all the qualities that Arv admired. By the time Arv was a junior in high school he had persuaded himself that Lobo liked him because they had a lot in common: both of them came from the lowest rung of the working class, but both were basically enlightened humanists, intelligent and imaginative, and both would go far in life. And Arv was never disappointed in this judgment. Lobo had always been extremely civil to Arv. Even after Arv went into the Army, and he and Deanna had to get married, and then had their trouble when Arv came back from Nam, Lobo'd always been real philosophical about it, and always treated Arv nice. He'd even taken Deanna and the kid back into

the Warden's Mansion when the divorce was filed, and
now he positively doted on his little granddaughter, calling
her "the light of my declining years," and spent hours
with her playing childish games before the fireplace.

Arv had grown up with Deanna, had, as a matter of
fact, often chased her retreating blond and nubile form
out across the employees' parking lot down by the Sound,
playing tag and "hide and go seek," and "ditch 'em." Oh
but she was fast! He never caught up with her. Still hadn't
really. She was on her own trip to this very day. Arv
remembered one time when they were about thirteen and
twelve. Big Arv caught a wild burro in the New Sonora
Alps on a deer hunting trip (it still lived, detested by Arv,
that smelly little donkey, unridden, unchanged, happily
aging, ageless perhaps, tied up in retirement out in back
of Aunt Evie's place in Nueva Ronda), and brought it
home to him and his sisters. Even then, just when Arv
was the eyepiece of the entire neighborhood, the butt of
all conversation, with Wasco and all the other kids green
with envy, and he was sure he could get that fast-running
Deanna now, with her long legs . . . even then old Lobo
had bought her a saucy pretty white mare, and she'd run
her all over the country, far out in front of Arv, far more
elegant, from the Sound to Paradise Slough to Red Hill to
the Soundside Hills to Mission Santa Bonita and back. She
even rode her mare to school, the little local prison grade
school, tying it up to the acacia tree in back, when they
wouldn't allow Arv to ride his burro because it would
hee-haw when it was rutting and its shit smelled so bad
that the odor would come in through the windows and
distract the pupils from their lessons.

But she once gave him a ride. Unforgettable ride! She'd
developed into a stately blonde and fully-bloomed four-
teen-year-old beauty by then, with elegant smooth eyelids
that never drooped or sagged, the typical Miniver nose,
high-bridged and classic, and long tapered aristocratic fingernails like talons. That same eagle-footed Deanna he'd
known as a child, busting out of her zipper-bottomed
playsuits, early-budded, ripening at eleven and twelve. At
fourteen she was built like a warrior woman, with tits like
Amazonian breastplates, engines of war. She put him up
behind her on the Western saddle and galloped off across
the salt flats on Paradise Cove, kicking up salty dust all
white behind them. Titi-rump, titi-rump, titi-rump they

had rattled, her boyish teenage buttocks coming down with every titi-rump on Arv's hard apparatus. She wouldn't consent to get down, to lie in the yellow grass on the other side, or in the sage, or the salt lick, no matter how he begged.

"Aw, come on, Deanna, just once! It means so little to you and so much to me!" he wailed, like he'd read somewhere in a forbidden adult novel. But never would she give in.

Wasco got to know her much better a year or so later. Took her out one day for a ride to the Giant Oak Tree four miles down the China Bank Road and didn't come home till after dark. She arrived back at the Joint stained from head to butt to toes in pure white alkali. Old Lobo found out all about it within minutes. His convict houseboy, a tiny big-toothed Filipino by the name of Ignazio, phoned him. He came out of the Ad Building uncharacteristically flustered and vermilion-faced (this is one of the very few times anybody ever saw Lobo lose his head, usually even a national disaster couldn't break his calm) and chased Wasco clean around the prison, all the way around Point Paradise. Wasco on the purloined mare. Lobo motating his big old black Buick Roadmaster in low drive all the way out to the abandoned World War II airstrip on Paradise Cove. Finally he treed Wasco on the sagging wing of the war surplus C-46 that some anonymous donor, misconstruing the then current euphemism for the Joint (State Vocational Training Institute), had long ago bequeathed for "aeronautical training for the young gentlemen." Then he gave Wasco ten to get down. Then when he wouldn't come down he called Gun Towers #3, #4, #5, #6, and #7 and commanded them loud on his radio to open fire if Wasco didn't come down in ten seconds. One . . . two . . . three . . . four . . . and Wasco came down, his head hanging and his hands in the air, repeating, "I'm sorry, Mr. Miniver, we didn't do nothing; we just went for a . . . really, only for a . . ." and then he started getting the giggles (Wasco was never really afraid of anything), and he couldn't stop and he knew his only alternative was to make a run for it so he broke and ran for the institution refuse dump which he knew like the back of his hand (him and Arv and Fast-Walking and others, Wesley, and others, used to go out there and shoot rats when they were little guys, shoot rats and sea gulls

with their BB guns: Arv always bagged the most . . .
never missed once he had one in his sights . . . once he
even got a swan, and it fell spiraling in slow motion like a
bomber, like one of those B-52's over Hanoi), and hid
there overnight till things cooled down, till Deanna, with
many tears, finally convinced Lobo (without even having
to undergo the physical exam he threatened) that nothing
happened, nothing really did happen.

So that's why both Big Arv and Little Arv faced this
coming audience with more than a little trepidation.

Yet, funnily enough, when Lobo walked in and Big Arv
laid it on the line for him and handed over Official Form
#3342, duly signed and stamped, Lobo merely confirmed
his faith in the two of them, "on the basis of a lifetime's
experience and twenty-five years of friendship and personal observation . . . first-rate officers, both father and
son."

"And . . . Wasco?" Big Arv timidly began.

"Wasco? Oh yes! Well, of course, we all saw this coming years ago, starting with that time when he knifed his
own father. The only reason it took this long is the len-
ience of these new young D.A.'s, the permissiveness of
contemporary judges, and the hamstringing rulings of
Warren's Supreme Court," the Warden said, and Little
Arv realized suddenly that what Fast-Walking had recently intimated, that Lobo was undergoing a political
"conversion of expedience" to please the new conservative
powers in the state capital, was true. But, in a way, this
realization didn't bother Little Arv as much as it might
have. It seemed to him that Lobo's heart wasn't in it. It
sounded to Arv like Lobo was merely voicing that
Birchite line without any real conviction. He was doing it
just to survive, Arv was sure, to keep his job, support his
family, and pay his bills for the three years left before his
mandatory retirement date. At least this is what Arv chose
to believe about Lobo . . . *Sometimes,* he thought, *damn
it, you really just have to "suspend disbelief" about certain
childhood myths and heroes. Otherwise, your whole world
will come tumbling down at once. And no one can support that . . .*

" . . . Too bad," Lobo continued, "that Wasco's a
'member of the family,' as it were. But such is life. It was
just a matter of time . . . just a matter of time. Now, as I
see it, our duty is to try our utmost to rehabilitate the lad,

right? Spend a little extra time with him, give him a break or two, and see if he shapes up. If so, well and good. If not, then we'll just have to wash our hands of him. What do you think, Big Arv? Is that a fair enough shake?"

"You bet, sir!"

"Great," Lobo said, starting for the door, "was that everything, Sarge?"

"Well," said Big Arv, rather shyly, looking down at his huge wide feet, "we had a minor little problem out in the Isolation Yard this afternoon I thought I'd better tell you about, sir."

"Yes? Nothing serious, I hope."

"Well, we had some trouble with that . . . that new . . . *Mister* Galliot. Didn't want to go to his cell," Big Arv said, and Little Arv could tell he was feeling Lobo out. He'd heard those local rumors too, about Lobo's sudden political switch, and wanted to find out how far he'd be allowed to go in his cruelty . . . in seeking his revenge for whatever slight Galliot had given him this afternoon in the yard.

"I see," Lobo said, but you could tell right away that he would be playing it very close to the table, would reveal nothing, condone nothing . . . at least, nothing he could ever be pinned down on. "But—knowing you, Big Arv— the problem was resolved successfully, was it not?"

"Oh yeah, Warden," Big Arv affirmed, glaring, theatrically fierce, still testing, cunningly, still trying to get some kind of hint out of Lobo, some kind of silent "Okay" for his intended violence, "sure we did! With a little help from our friends on the gunwalk!"

"I'm happy to hear the situation is under control," Lobo said, choosing his words carefully, still noncommittal.

The disappointment showed plainly now on Big Arv's face.

"Anyway," Lobo went on, changing the subject deftly, smiling his good-looking British smile, cracking his thin dry lips widely across his long narrow face, "about this Wasco thing, I want you to carry on with your duties as usual, fellows . . . no reflection upon either of you, nothing on your records. In fact, Big Arv," Lobo said, and from the sudden chill in his voice Arv knew he would finally give Big Arv the clue, the hint he wanted, "in fact, as a sign of my approval of you and your work here at the prison, and in light of the extraordinary nature of this Galliot case, I'm placing you as East Block sergeant on the swing shift tomorrow. I'll need my very best men there now with this . . . er . . . agitator . . . this . . . uh . . . proven troublemaker, Galliot . . . because I most definitely would not want anything *serious* to befall him. . . ."

Lobo pronounced every word of the last sentence precisely, so there would be no mistaking his exact meaning, no mistaking the apparent truth of the rumor Fast-Walking'd confided. . . . And Arv, who'd followed the old Warden a long way, all the way from earliest childhood, just couldn't keep up with him anymore, just couldn't. And his heart fell behind Lobo, lagged, bitterly disappointed in the man, though he understood *them poor old fuckers, it was rougher for them . . . I never had it as bad, never had to go through the changes they did. . . .*

Shit! Arv thought, *there goes another idol!*

Would his generation be granted not even one?

"I'd be real glad to accept, sir!" Big Arv exclaimed.

"Fine," the Warden said, conducting them to the door, "and remember, don't worry about Wasco being locked up here with you. It's really nothing. Why, hell!" he said heartily, shaking their hands, "I got a no-good brother-in-law myself down on some county road camp in California! You know what? Very few people in this country don't have some kind of closet-case hidden away somewhere. You'd be surprised at the number of employees who come in here notifying me about friends, relatives, and even spouses who are being incarcerated within the walls of penal institutions."

Outside on the sidewalk Big Arv took off for the Main Gate like a bat out of hell, fired up with what he had in mind for Galliot, double-fired with the Warden's surprising endorsement of whatever it turned out to be . . . short of murder.

Arv, thinking again suddenly of the letter he carried in his pocket, a letter that would send him into this prison with his cousin, if he got caught, started worrying, wondering how he, with the dangerous liability of the letter, could prevent that thing his old man had in mind . . . to prevent it . . . with his small resources . . . and the extreme danger . . . how the fuck was he supposed to stop Big Arv now that he even had the backing of that chickenshit, hypocritical, turncoat Warden Miniver?

Arv watched his old man going, watched him going way out ahead, not waiting, watched him turn the corner of the fence sharply, springy for his weight and age and cardiac problems, quick on his toes, even if they were fat toes. It occurred to Little Arv now that, strangely enough, given the proper upbringing, the right kind of direction in youth, and culture, and money, and all the things that come with it, things might have been different with the Weed family! Things might have been different with his father. He might have been, of all things . . . a dancer!

Arv followed his father across the moat bridge and the grass in the rain that now fell harder and harder. Arv had a heavy heart, thinking about his old man as he might have been, if he hadn't been a prison guard, thinking, with tears in his young eyes, traitorous eyes *what can I do to stop the fucking Pig?* Oh yes, how different it all might have been, with Big Arv as a dancer, slim and powerful. Renowned dance master. Ballet virtuoso. Choreographer extraordinaire! They were all natural dancers in the family. Champions at everything from the Varsity Drag to the Jitterbug to the Bop to the Frug, depending on their ages. Wasco, Mom and Dad, Arv himself, and Judy and Carol, his married sisters, and Libby, and Aunt Evie, and Uncle Sanger, even old Grandma Dora Lee! All of them! What if Dora Lee'd had the imagination of an Isadora Duncan, back in the old days? What if, instead of coming out to the West Coast, she had dragged her dancing ass out of the West and all the way back east to New York, London, Paris, Rome! What might they all have been? With the proper breaks, forty or fifty years ago. Oh, what those Weeds couldn't have done!

But all Arv could see now, hastening after his rapid-moving homicide-minded old man, of the past or future, looking out across the gray cloud-socked Sound, was just rain coming in, maudlin, more and more rain, Weed-gray, driving the spots of sun away, at Holly Island and the Santa Caterina Peninsula, at Funland in the city, rain, rain, rain, all the way across the Alvarez Straits, all the way from the open North Pacific Ocean.

Nine

After he let Big Arv and Little Arv into the Yard, after
he'd watched them go across the whole long wet expanse
of blacktop in the rain, watched them disappear into the
East Block steel gate in the far southwest corner, Fast-
Walking sat up in the shanty, his place of exile and disgrace, listening to the radio and smoking joints until the
First Count was over. Watching his sister Deanna heading
up toward the schoolhouse for her nightly trampoline
practice, dragging her three-year-old blond daughter
Wendy along by the hand, Fast-Walking listened to a
song he hadn't heard since shortly after his sister was
born. Hank Snow sang it. Or was it Hank Williams or
Lefty Frizell? He could never remember which was which.
He sang:

> Poor old Kalaija
> He had a wooden head . . .

Fast-Walking followed her progress along the macadam
road from the Warden's Mansion with vague brotherly
distaste, his attention still captured . . . Kalaija was an
Indian, he remembered . . . he had a wooden head . . .
is it any wonder that his face was red? Isolated as he was,
with nothing to do, perched high in his tiny room above
the prison world, Fast-Walking narrowed in on her. . . .

Because Deanna was handsome and self-confident, reso-
lute, independent, and had enormous ambitions, and because she would most certainly achieve those ambitions,
become a lawyer, practice criminal law, go into politics,
through her great strength of will, despite her handicaps
as a woman, a mother, a divorcee . . . because Deanna
was serious-minded and cautious, because she was the
most accomplished and intelligent of the Miniver children,

star of her high school and junior college gym teams,
Honor Society, sports editor of her J.C. newspaper, because of all that, and because she much more nearly conformed to Lobo's notion of what a child of his should be
like, Fast-Walking liked his sister least of all the people he
knew. Less even than Big Arv, less than his old man.

There was something in Fast-Walking, something not as
simple as mere jealousy or envy, that hated well-earned
success in all its forms. He'd even advised Deanna once
when she was growing up, as respected older brother, that
it'd be a waste of time for her, a girl, to go to college and
law school. He did it in complete confidence that it would
make her feel very bad. And it did. Hurt her terrible. He
could see it . . . and secretly rejoiced . . . and hated himself.

Because Deanna more than any other in Fast-Walking's
circle of friends and family in the Joint truly loved him
and admired him (his wife merely loved him . . . sometimes; Lobo merely sought in him the fulfillment of his
dreams, a kind of immortality) for the small kernel of reality deep within him, almost lost to sight, almost covered
over with floods of words, layers of phony plans and
dreams, loved him for that tiny aching germ of
unachieved, unachievable but great potential within him.

Oh but it was a burden to him, that Deanna'd always
understood him, looked up to him, listened to his words
of counsel, respected him. Such a burden! No one else in
the world burdened him with respect. Fast-Walking found
her love of him, and her qualities of honesty, integrity, industry and perseverance, so unendurable that it was difficult not to show it. He'd talked this over frankly with
Arv, many times, even while they were still married, and
Arv'd admitted that she made him feel the same way . . .
"She's so fucking uptight all the time!" Arv'd hollered out
one time over a mug of beer at Bert's Beanery. *And it's
true, goddamnit!*

Both men felt guilty about their feelings toward poor
Deanna. Yet both confessed there was nothing they could
do about it.

In the final analysis, what they both appreciated and admired most in a person was the totally fortuitous: luck
and style. And Deanna was unfortunate enough to be too
busy at the moment to cultivate either.

There was something in them both; Fast-Walking and Little Arv, something wild and dark and anarchic, something quintessentially plebeian and western American that hated itself.

Fast-Walking liked to pretend that his distaste for his sister was a secret. But everyone knew. His father never forgave him for it. Deanna herself knew, and had long ago forgiven him for it, had long ago seemed to conclude that his antipathy was right and just, and berated herself and reviled herself. *Hateful fat and ugly despicable, despicable, despicable!* she used to repeat over and over in front of her mirror. And then went out to work harder than anyone to succeed at life. She would succeed. If it killed her. And the more she achieved in life, the harder she'd find it getting into that hard heart of Fast-Walking Miniver.

Not that Fast-Walking did not suffer pangs of conscience, even now: *you just get her off her high-horse some, knocked up again, barefoot and eight months gone to belly, standing in a torn flower-print dress on the brokedown stoop of an unpainted wood shack in Okieville, and I would give all my natural brotherly condolence and affection . . .*

On alongside the football field she walked, her head full of thoughts, plans, dreams for her and her kid. On she walked, still loving her old bud, her brother, who hated her *hated himself hated her exactly as he hated himself,* still loving her brother Fast-Walking and his buddy Little Arv her ex-hubby, she walked, like a bitch dog, loving the hands that beat it, her sorrel-colored coarse hair, wire hair, dog's hair, wound up in a bandanna.

Tall and blond and powerful as a strong young man, she moved without effort down the road by Mrs. Gibb's chrysanthemums, not swaying her hips, not wiggling her strong young man's buttocks, handsome rather than pretty, masculine as she guessed she was. *And yet which one of us don't secretly in his heart believe that what he guesses about himself can't possibly be true, that some dreamy older brother or lover will come along and tell us that we're wrong about ourselves. "Why, no! You ain't at all that way, honey! You're real pretty and feminine,"* Mama used to say, trying to make everything okay. Poor thing! In a land that loves its soft curves, its moist large

lips, turned-up noses—there Deanna was with her thin dry
lips, freckles and high masculine brow and Miniver's eagle
beak and washed-blue eyes, colorless hair. Poor thing!
Fast-Walking could see her with his powerful glasses; she
walked with grave purpose, easily, but thinking all the
time, trying to keep her feet from touching the lines in the
cement, dragging little blond Wendy behind, and doing it!
Never letting the kid trip her up, never having to skip a
step or jump a square, judging the terrain from afar, and
pacing herself just right, like the true athlete she was.
Never slipping up, never looking backward, never awkward. Never! How Fast-Walking hated that girl! How he
hated her!

The only person in the immediate family who did not
fall under Fast-Walking's decidedly unpowerful malig-
nance was his mom, Patsy. Dad and Deanna he actively
disliked. His mother Fast-Walking rarely even thought of
. . . *except up here in this goddamned wall post where
there ain't nothing else to do!*

Nobody, not even Lobo or Deanna, thought much
about Mom anymore. Even friends avoided discussing her
situation. Lobo never invited people over anymore. He'd
made Deanna his official hostess and held state functions
in the In-Service-Training building or Rec Hall. The truth
of the matter was that Fast-Walking's old lady had sat in
front of the TV in a virtual state of hypnosis or catatonia
for the last fifteen years. Day and night. Week in and
week out. Snatching catnaps between her favorite programs. Yelling at Ignazio to empty her bed pan twice a
day: once in the morning between the Eight O'Clock
News and the first soap opera, and once in the evening
between the Six O'Clock News and the Beverly Hillbillies.

Patsy's severe mental problems had begun shortly after
Deanna was born. Rumor had it that she had become barren after Deanna's birth, had taken thalidomide, and had
given birth to a monstrous freak that had to be immediately placed in an institution. It was born without arms or
legs, purportedly. Inmate wags had it as being born with
the horns and head of a bull. But people only laughed at
that story. Fast-Walking never knew the truth of the matter because his father refused to discuss it, as if it were
some kind of shameful secret. At any rate, after the
"freak" came into the world Patsy was never the same.

She believed that the reason for the ghastly birth was that Lobo had been unfaithful to her in China during the war, and had come home with a terrible Asiatic disease: every time he ejaculated into her, instead of shooting sperm, he released a swarm of noxious insects in her womb. It was only Lobo's tremendous desire to avoid even the breath of another scandal, especially in these extremely ticklish times of political changeover, that kept the unfortunate lady out of a mental home. Fast-Walking could therefore look at his lifetime of scandalous behavior—epic drunks, wanton women, statutory rape charges, illegitimate children, salary attachments, losing his stripes, getting caught sleeping on the job—in an ironic light: he was his mom's savior, in a way. If it hadn't been for Fast-Walking causing all that trouble for the old man, he could've afforded a little scandal, and he'd have had Patsy locked up in the bughouse five years ago.

Fast-Walking was thinking like that, just to pass the time away, when Betty Weed came walking down from her place, Prison Residence #35, past the long gray lines of prison homes each with its little patch of lawn and its straight concrete sidewalk and its low hedge (private fences weren't allowed). Fast-Walking never spoke much to Arv's Aunt Betty, punch-drunk old Uncle Sanger's wife. Never had much call to. She was Marie-Claude's friend. That's where she was headed now, fast, now that her hubby was fed and taking his after-dinner nap in front of the TV, she was going up there to Fast-Walking's place to sit up with Marie-Claude watching the news in the living room and sipping coffee having a gay old time with no men around.

When Fast-Walking was working as Control Tower sergeant, a couple of years ago, he used to see her come walking down at this same time, old Betty. She used to take care of the twins while Marie-Claude was working and then she'd bring them home about this time of evening.

The twins were afterthoughts, born six years after Ralph, the next kid up the ladder. "The accident twins," they used to call them in the family, for a flaw in Fast-Walking's prophylactic in the rainy winter of 1967 had caused them to take hold in Marie-Claude's unwilling, unready and unforgiving Gallic womb.

Their sad eyes knew it. Dully, question marks written
there always, under perpetually incredulous horned simian
eyebrows, they regarded the world with the unblinking
stares of the retarded. . . . By the time they were four
years old they seemed to understand intuitively the struggle going on in Marie-Claude's mind: whether to give
them up to the State Home or not. And, just as intuitively, they seemed to know what she did not. Seemed to
dig what Fast-Walking had never himself faced up to:
that they were already dead, as far as the rest of the
family was concerned, especially the other kids. Never to
be seen again, after a year or so of rare visits. After that
they would abide together forever, alone in the Home
above the Pacific, in the redwood groves, unvisited and
happy together, playing their crazy twins games, games
that nobody in the family ever figured out, or wanted to.
Silent, bug-eyed, they would yank each other's middle fingers for hours at a certain gait, a certain rhythm, a certain
number of times, waiting for the other to respond. A ritual of which no one ever ascertained the significance.

They had already taken their leave.

They'd never been at home. Would never care that no
one cared. They were born as strangers. Went out that
way too.

Fast-Walking figured they were lucky in a lot of ways.

Slowly they used to walk along, Fast-Walking would
watch them, Betty Weed holding the little motherfuckers
by their misshapen little hands: six fingers on one twin,
four fingers on the other. Fast-Walking never determined
which twin was which, Henry or Harry. Never even
sorted out which one had six fingers and which one had
four.

Betty Weed used to walk them awkward up the road
and Fast-Walking used to sit up there in the Control
Tower dry-eyed thinking just like he was thinking now:
*I'll never know them . . . never know my own flesh and
blood.*

Bored, bored, bored, Fast-Walking tried to concentrate
on his latest plan, the one about that wild and wonderful
southeastern corner of Oregon. But he couldn't. None of
the pieces fell into place, now that he was alone. With
other people Fast-Walking always had a plan, some fantastic plan that took up all his conversation. But alone he

could rarely think of these plans. Other things, mostly his troubles, and his more concrete hopes for their eventual dissolution, took up his thoughts. Fast-Walking's celebrated "plans" were in reality just for listeners, for friends and coworkers, his captive audience.

Fast-Walking was intensely shy. Actually. In a desperate effort to "relate" to people, he concocted these plans of his, and spouted them out as mere entertainments. Most of the time he had no intention of carrying them out. They were the show he put on for life.

Fast-Walking alone was a very different dude from Fast-Walking in public.

In this way he figured he was like most everyone else.

Soon he went over to where his overcoat was hanging, pulled out the scissors and the afternoon newspaper he always kept in his inside pocket, and sat down again, clipping the latest news stories to pass the time:

COMEDIAN BOB HOPE GETS WARM WELCOME IN TOKYO
        He and his troupe arrive for annual
        Christmas tour of U.S. military bases

When he cut them out he folded them neatly and put them in his wallet alongside the dollar bills, preserving them that way for the day he'd have time to paste them in at the very end of his 1972 notebook.

It occurred to him, as he carefully worked the small sharp scissors up the margin of the Bob Hope story, that within a fortnight it would be next year. And, without some outrageous stroke of good fortune, he wouldn't have the bread to get 1973's news notebook.

That thought drove him deeper into his despair than anything in days. . . .

RIIIIIING! The dinner bell rang and then, one cell block at a time, the inmates were released to go to the Dining Hall, and Fast-Walking had to go out under the rain shed and pace the gunwalk again, supervising all movement. Several of the cons going by yelled up a greeting.

"Hey, Fast-Walking," the white dudes would say, "how you doing, man?" And Fast-Walking would respond, "Shitty, Phil, this here is the worst fucking job in the Slam. But how about yourself?"

"Outa sight! Got my date yesterday!"

"Oh yeah? When's that?"

"First of June!"

"Say, man, wisht I could get outa here that fast!"

Fast-Walking himself would initiate the exchange with the black cats:

"Hey man, what is it?" he would say, changing his dialect to suit the occasion. And they would reply:

"Same ole same ole . . ."

"It gonna get better."

"Sho."

"Jus' keep on keepin' on."

"Right on, man!"

Other convicts, hidden in the long chow lines, yelled up threats and curses at him, in black and white English, and in Spanish, knowing he couldn't place them.

"Ese! Chingado! Me cago en el coño de tu madre!"

"Eat shit, Pig!"

"Fuck you, Hack!"

"Ice Chuck!"

"Muerte al jabalí!"

"Off Sylvester!"

He could never be sure who did it. There were too many cons in the yard. It might just as well be the same dude who, moments before, yelled up a cheerful greeting to him. You can never trust a con. You can never trust a screw either; and if you can never trust a screw-ass guard, well, then you can be bull's-eye sure you can never trust a con. Their infinite capacity for duplicity always amazed him. If they lied to and betrayed the confidence of the guards, they did it even more to their own *compadres*. They ratted on each other, gossiped, socked and finked. They knifed each other, gunned each other down with zipguns, gave one another hotshots of heroin, lye in their homebrew, glass in their chow, pissed and shit under each other's pillows, and spit in each other's coffee. They blew each other off to the staggering average tune of fourteen murders a year in this one Joint. They raped and buggered each other with astounding frequency. They had race wars, religious wars, dope wars, sex wars, ideological wars and even laundry wars.

Laundry is very important in the Joint. Theoretically everyone wears the same threads in the Jam. That's the

law. And your number is stenciled on everything you own
from shoes to shorts to caps. But in practice it's just like
on the Street. There are certain distinctions, certain subtle
variations unnoticed by the outsider, that make all the difference. And there are many men who will pay for these
distinctions, will pay highly to separate themselves from
the *hoi polloi*. You see a dude with razor sharp creases in
his denim pants, impeccably starched and pressed shirts
made of the finest denim that money can buy, with Eck-
stein collars and French cuffs with diamond links, a cat
with patent-leather loafer shoes, or black Chelsea boots,
or flying jodhpurs, a stud with gold-rimmed sunglasses, or
bee-bop shades, well then you know for sure that mother's
on the game, got something going for himself, working
some scam. He's a pimp, a dealer, a bag man, numbers
man, a connection, second-story man, porno dealer, porno
artist, gunsmith, goldsmith, locksmith, jeweler, expert
forger, marijuana farmer, chemist, pill man, tailor, queen,
punk, whore, fairy, informer, laundry man, plant, snitch,
agent provocateur, hit man, counterfeiter, or any one of a
million other possible lucrative vocational specialists. He's
upper class. And he lets you know it. Just like on the
Street. All the rest is just beggars and winos, baggy pants,
smelly underwear, unstarched and torn pants and shirts,
raggedy socks, cast-off high-top prison work shoes. They
just shuffle along, the prison poor, the working people and
the unemployed, just like on the Street, their hands in
their pockets, heads hanging down. You can spot the
scruffy bastards a mile away.

After dinnertime and the movie, and night school, there
was no movement on the Yard until the Last Count.
Fast-Walking went back into the wall hut. He was all
alone. He couldn't see another human being. He might as
well have been guarding a ruin, a forgotten city, a
wrecked ship. The rain quit. The hours went by slow and
sickly, like waves of nausea, dragging bad memories, bad
tastes in their wakes. He switched the transistor to news to
keep awake: "Former Attorney General Mitchell impli-
cated in Watergate raid scandal. Nixon's press secretary
says: 'Whole thing blown out of proportion.' "

Honk! Honk! Honk! The foghorns out on the islands in
the Sound started going off. Then the fog itself appeared,
rolling in from the tule beds on Paradise Cove. The moon

came out above the fog and lit up the prison like an abandoned stage set. Fast-Walking got scared. He always got scared at night up on the wall post. The fog could hide a break. An escapee could climb the wall and shoot you in the back of the neck with a zipgun. Zap! He turned around. More fog, shining double white: the moon, and the fluorescent light in the Isolation Yard. The truth of the matter was that Fast-Walking wasn't really scared at all. *I'm not scared.* It was just his old trick. He encouraged it. He took the natural uneasiness that any healthy human being would feel up in an exposed and naked position like that, above a prison teeming with enemies, with dangerous and criminoid men, alone, in the middle of the night, and he escalated it into full-fledged fear, fright, terror, without declaring it outright, just to kill the boredom.

When he was a kid of eight and nine he had rheumatic fever and had to spend a year in bed. That's when he got the habit. He'd get so bored all alone in his large blue room in the Associate Warden's Mansion with the small round nautical-type window that looked out across Quintana Sound to the Alvarez Straits Bridge and the city, the same old seascape, and on the other side the same old wallscape in penitentiary yellow and gray, day in and day out, that he'd invent monsters, witches, dragons, giant two-headed tortoises, tarantulas as big as cars, coming up the freeway from Mission Santa Bonita, just to kill the time.

Fast-Walking brought his Mickey Spillane out and tried reading by the flashlight under his overcoat. But that bored him too. Couldn't even get a hard-on. Couldn't even get a rise thinking about his long ago seventeen-year-old French maiden in the golden summer fields of Poitou. He unloaded his .38 Police Special and put the six cartridges in his pocket: one . . . two . . . three . . . four . . . five . . . six. . . . He counted them again to make double sure, fail-safe. Then he opened the window and aimed at running targets, ghosts, and imaginary electrical blips, gliding by in the dense tule fog. Then he picked them off, squeezing off shots just like at the Insititution Firing Range. POW! Every half hour on the dot Fast-Walking called Control. If he didn't they'd call him and ask him what he was dreaming about.

Pretty soon Barry came back from supervising chow

time and shower time in the East Block. Fast-Walking let
down the key.

"What's happening, man, after all that excitement this
afternoon?"

"Zero."

"Don't know if that's good or bad," Fast-Walking said,
"action passes the time, at least."

"Take it easy, fellah, you don't wish that on anybody.
Way things're going, Galliot and these here niggers gonna
give you some excitement you don't want!"

Barry went walking on down to the Pig Pen, where the
Control Point sergeant and the two reserve men and the
swing shift runner had a cozy little scene going, sitting
there before the pot-bellied stove, bullshitting and playing
cards and censoring inmate mail for entertainment, laughing at all the spelling errors, and the funny places, getting
a big bang out of the sexy parts, crossing them out, along
with all the swear words, all derogatory remarks about the
Joint, or its officers, or the State or the United States government or its President, or its foreign or domestic poli-
cies. Their nightly camaraderie made Fast-Walking shiver
with envy.

He phoned Control and asked Harry to get him the Pig
Pen. The Control Point sergeant answered:

"Yeah?"

"Say, Sarge, this is Miniver. Listen, I know this is irregular. But, just to keep me going, can you send me up a
couple of letters to censor?"

"You getting drowsy?"

"No . . . I just . . ."

"That was quite some little scene out here this afternoon, huh?"

"Oh shit!"

"You looked like a real killer up there."

"Had him right between the pecs."

"We knew that, man, and we appreciated it down here.
You gave Big Arv room to operate. I watched the whole
thing from in here. Didn't want to move cause I was
scared I'd get in your line of fire."

"Next time!"

"Right!"

"You handled it beautiful, Sarge. What'd he say when
they got him in his cell?"

"Nothing. But Big Arv let him know where it was at."

'I figured he would. What the black motherfucker say then?"

"Nothing. Just got smart-ass. Laughed like it wasn't nothing new to him."

"Well, it ain't."

"No sir!"

"He'll be laughing out of the other side of his mouth pretty soon."

"Oh boy!"

The sarge and Fast-Walking laughed together over the phone. Fast-Walking's heart wasn't really in it. He didn't especially want to see that nigger dead. He was just going along with the sarge, knowing he had to, if he wanted to get anything out of him.

"Okay! I'll send Barry over with some letters."

"Thanks, Sarge!"

In a few minutes Barry came over and laid three censor letters on him. Fast-Walking let the bucket down, thanked him, and wound it back into the wall post shanty.

(NSCC-34265) 660 Name	Ignazio F. Mendoza
Number	455321

New Sonora Maximum Security Facility
Mission Santa Bonita, N.S. 86611
Date   18 December   , 1972

Mr. Robert Adelphi
67543 Cook Blvd.
New Sonora City, N.S.
86614

DEAR MISTER ATTORNEY ADELPHI I WISHING ON RECEIVED THIS LETTER YOU ARE IN THE BEST OF HEALTHY AND HAPPINESS I HOPE YOU GOING HAVE GOOD EASTER HOLIDAY WELL AS FOR ME IT IS NOT THAT GOOD BECAUSE I BEEN IN PRISON SENSE NOVEMBER 1963 I HOPE YOU WONT BE ANGRY WITH ME MY CASE IS THE SAME CASE THAT YOU HAVE BEFORE IN 1961 ARMED ROBBERY I NEED YOU MORE NOW THAN EVER CAUSE THEY GOT ME HERE IN ISOLATION WITH NO HOPE. I WILL LIKE TO ESPLEAN YOU BY WRITEING YOU BUT I DONT KNOW TO WRITE TO GOOD SO WILL

YOU PLEASE COME AND SEE ME AS SOON AS POSIBLE I
NEED YOU I NEED YOU PLEASE DONT WORY BOUT
MONEY I WILL SEE THAT YOU GET PAY AS YOUR JOB
SOON AS I GET OUT AND WORK A SCAM I NEED HELP I
THINK THEY USEING TO MANY CRIME AGAINST ME BUT
I DON'T UNDERSTAND LAW. THAT IS PITTYFUL. WILL
YOU PLEASE SEE ME SOON AS POSIBLE YOUR TRULEY

IGNAZIO MENDOZA

(NSCC-34265) 660	Name Robert A. Davis, Jr.
Number   987678
New Sonora Maximum Security Facility
Mission   Santa   Bonita,   N.S. 86611
Date   18 Dec.   , 1972

Ms. Sandra Kelly
Attorney at Law
27 Harper Court
New Sonora City, N.S.
86614

Dear Ms. Kelly:
Hey Lady, is it Miss or Mrs., or Ms.? . . -. for future
references only . . . At any rate, Greetings from the
Inferno, the eighth wonder of the world. It is here
also, that in lieu of my problems I can find no visible
solution. Maybe after you have surveyed this your in-
sight for remedying circumstances may shed some
light on the saturation of this problem at hand . . .
Are you interested? Well, just in case you are—it's a
legal matter. You see, on the 20th day of March
1972, an incident took place at Brown Maximum Security Facility in the "Adjustment Center" section
where very little adjustment and a lot of maladjust-
ment goes on. Anyway, on the above name date one
officer was stabbed to death and consequently I'm
writing to you. I am confront with trumped up
charges that reads: "Complicity with inmate William
R. Galliot in the fatal stabbing of Correctional Officer
B. Y. Pritchard." Yea! And I agree with you—
"Trouble!" What makes it ridiculous is the fact that,
even if I sympathize with the high aims of Brother

Galliot and his movement 100%, I am not at present a member, nor never have been. However, the prison authorities have knowledge that I belong to another movement for the liberation of black people (the name of which I cannot report here) and they have taken this opportunity to make a clean sweep of the AC, mopping up the last black militants left alive, and figuring to dispose of us permanent that way. I know that your schedule keeps you busy, but if you could devote a few minutes to listening to my problems I sho would appreciate it. If you don't stand for something, girl, remember, you'll fall for little or nothing.

Sincerely yours,
Bob Davis

(NSCC-34265) 660	Name	Franklin Pierce Harley
	Number	897654

New Sonora Maximum Security Facility
Mission   Santa   Bonita,   N.S. 86611
Date   18 December   , 1972

Howard Wilson
Attorney at Law
4456 Madison Street
New Sonora City, N.S.
86613

DEAR MR WILSON I USE MY RIGHTEOUS NAME: FRANK-LIN PIERCE HARLEY ON THE BACK OF THE CHECK WITH MY DRIVER LICENCE VAILETDATED OF STATE CALIF. THE PARTY WHO WRITTEN THE CHECK OUT TO MY NAME AND HE WAS TAKEN INTO CUSTODY WITH ME BUT RELEASE FROM CUSTODY UNDER FORGED NAME AND IDENTITY BEFORE I WENT TO PRETRIAL THE DISTRICT ATTORNEY OVER PRIOR ME SET MY BAIL TO 25,000 DOLLARS?

YOU WILL NOT HELP ME CUASE IM BLACKMAN BUT I NEED YOUR ASST. FORM YOU OFFICE, WILL LIKE YOU TO COME AND SEE ME BECOUSE I NEED HELP AND RE-SPED YOUR AUTHORITY PRETAINING TO LAW AND OR-DER COURT DATE IS SET FOR FEB 73. DEPT #3, HONOR-

ABLE JUDGE JONES IM IN CUSTODY NEW SONORA MAX
ISOLATION THE END OF THE WORLD AND NEED DESPER-
ATE HELP YOUR TRULY

HARLEY

By the time Fast-Walking finished reading the letters he
was getting very sleepy. He couldn't follow the convicts'
line of thinking. He couldn't read their writing. Like all
prisoners' letters, they just bored the hell out of him. He'd
read probably literally a million since he started work at
the Joint, and they all sounded exactly the same: whiney.
They were all emotional cripples, every last one of them,
no matter how well-educated or literate they might be. All
they could do was just piss and moan like animals in a
cage.

Fast-Walking farted around, censoring the word "Inferno," and the phrase "ISOLATION THE END OF THE
WORLD," as derogatory references to state institutions, and
censoring "I THINK THEY USEING TO MANY CRIME AGAINST
ME," as a libelous allegation in reference to the State Department of Justice.

But his heart wasn't in it.

Fast-Walking was falling asleep. Just before he dropped
off he wondered *why do they waste all their time hating
the white man? Galliot too. He's smart. Why does he hate
me? Why?* Then he set the alarm clock for 10:30, and fell
directly into a strange and fitful sleep in which he
dreamed that he was Galliot, locked in a cell in Isolation,
dreaming of a cushy job in the Pig Pen. RIIIING! The
alarm went off. He checked with Control, reset the clock,
and went back to the same dream without missing even an
episode. Galliot, he found, was dreaming too, dared
dream of even more too, dreamed of rejoining his family
too, went beyond the Pig Pen and the Isolation Yard and
beyond the Joint and, trailing all his big family of wife
and kids behind him, riding the moonbeams above the
fog, rode across the night, across the state, across the
world to a remote and marvelous arid southeastern corner
of Oregon, never to return . . .

And in that way both Fast-Walking and Galliot were
able to get through the night.

Ten

"Shakedown!" Sergeant Weed said in a hawking cigarette whisper, and you could hear it echo all over the East Block.

"Shakedown!"

The word went up and down the five tiers like scatter shot and, thirty seconds later, Arv knew the entire cell-block from top to bottom, Yardside to Soundside, would be light as a dime and clean as a whistle.

"Lighten up! Clean up, motherfuckers, here come the Pig!"

You could hear eighty-five toilets flush in unison while Big and Little Arvin Weed clanged up the spiral metal staircase, up the corrugated metal steps two at a time, all the way to the fifth tier, the celebrated segregated special tier where they kept the baddest of all the bad-ass niggers.

The Weeds strolled along the barred cells looking for a likely search. It was dead-balls but pregnant quiet. You could hear the sparrows twittering in the rafters . . . only the pigsfeet on the walkway.

Little Arv, absolved of all moral responsibility by the letter he carried, swaggered loose and evil as his old man down the walkway, delighted to play the role of Pig . . . as long as it was only an act.

At Galliot's cell Big Arv paused meaningfully and glared in through the bars.

"Well, look who's here!" Big Arv said, oafish as usual, "if it ain't our old friend *Mister* Galliot! Fancy meeting *you* here, boy!"

"Oh-oh!" somebody said down the tier; you couldn't tell where it came from.

"Shut up!" Big Arv yelled.

"Fuck you, Pig!"

"Ice the Man!"

"Dust Chuck!"

Big Arv paid them no mind, 'cause he was one pissed-off Pig. He glowered in at Galliot, who was lying on the cold cement floor doing sit-ups, counting it out . . . thirty-one, thirty-two, thirty-three . . . pointedly not noticing them . . . thirty-four, thirty-five . . . cocoa-colored stomach muscles bulging with the effort . . . thirty-six, thirty-seven. Face composed and calm. Bright eyes, brow unfurrowed, not showing the strain. Like he went through this kind of thing every day . . . which he probably did.

All he had on was his shorts. Naked you could see he was built like a small solid white man. Buttocks not humped and rounded. Feet not flat and wide and spread at the toes. Heels not curving out behind the ankle. Not hung like a blood either, Arv reflected. Ordinary hardware. Just like anybody else.

"Hey kid! Run down to the end and pull the bar!"

Arv ran down and pulled it and CLANG! the bar slid into open position. Then he came strolling back along the gauntlet of hateful black eyes with bloodshot whites, eyes that followed him with murderous intent, with hatred and maledictions, with desire, infinite desire for his life. He whistled a little, a Neil Young number, *Alabama,* ironically, since this was the fifth tier, infamous tier, the place of the black "incorrigibles," the "unregenerates," the "criminoids," the "murderers," the "agitators," the "militants," and the "unrehabilitatives," the third lowest pit in hell. Compared to this, Death Row, where the condemned had unlimited supplies of candy bars and Juicy Fruit chewing gum and a TV in every cell, was heaven. Only the "Adjustment Center" and Isolation were down closer to hellfire.

Needless to say, the men of the fifth tier did not appreciate Arv's nervous whistling irony.

The shouts and screams of the damned pierced the iron-enclosed air.

"Die Honkey!"

"Shank Charlie!"

Arv pretended to look up at the sparrows flying around frightened in the rafters.

Soon these desperate motherfuckers are gonna find out where I'm at.

Galliot was still counting it out like he didn't know . . .

fifty-one . . . fifty-two . . . fifty-three . . .

Arv bopped up, slow time, and Big Arv stuck the big brass key into the lock. Smiling. Just like they taught him in Inmate Psychology at the In-Service-Training Center. And his sick "friendly" smile sent the fear of God into Arv's scared little asshole, his tight sphincter tightened up still harder.

"Sorry about this," Big Arv said, real polite, as if they'd never met, as if they didn't both know this was the inevitable result of what went on down in the Isolation Yard this rainy afternoon. Big Arv's breath was shaking with desire to hurt. It sounded something like a guy you'd walked in on and caught playing with himself.

"Shakedown?" Galliot asked, pausing in his exercises, polite, smiling back.

"Yeah," Big Arv said, maintaining his smile, "you know the rules, I guess." Little Arv was struck by the modulation in his father's voice. It seemed now that his father was not intent on what Arv'd thought he was. It looked now like he had something other than violence on his mind, something that might hurt Galliot even more . . . and anyway there were too many witnesses here.

"Actually I don't," Galliot said, in extremely civilized tones, breathing hard and sweating from his exercise, "I'm new here."

"Oh, yeah? Does seem like I ain't seen you around much," Big Arv responded, attempting his own brand of feeble humor, and all the time his shifty little eyes, lizard's eyes, darting around the cell furtively. "Alright," Big Arv said.

Galliot was still sitting on the floor, looking frankly and innocently up, his brown eyes open wide, a pleasant but tense grin on his face.

"Alright," Big Arv repeated, flustered by the unexpectedly friendly and nonviolent attitude of the prisoner. "Listen," he said, "here's what you do. You just go out on the tier and have a cigarette while we search the cell . . . it's the rules."

"So soon?"

"You never you mind and get along out there, goddamnit!" Big Arv said, hulking over the smaller black man.

"Okay," Galliot said calmly, looking out at Arv who

was shuffling around embarrassedly on the tier.

"Wait a minute!" Big Arv shouted, far too loud for the tiny cell.

"Yes?"

"You got to take your scivvies off."

"Pray, what do you intend to do with me, Sarge?" Galliot said archly, "huh?"

Arv heard sniggers and guffaws down the tier. You can hear everything in a cellblock. There are no secrets, not even whispered ones, not even silent ones in the dark of night or under covers.

"Shut up, damnit, or I'm going to . . ."

"Yes? What are you gonna do, Sarge?" Galliot asked.

"Arv?"

"Yeah!"

"Call that gunman over here! Where's he been, anyway?"

"He's down on the third tier."

"Call him!"

"Hey Billy! The Sarge wants you up here!"

"BOOOOOOOOOOOOOOOOOOOO!" went a hundred black voices, young voices, for the most part, but ragged from screaming up and down the tiers, ragged from too many cigarettes and bad food and acid coffee and drafty ill-heated cells. "BOOOOOOO!"

Billy, the East Block gunman, came running up the corrugated iron gunwalk that ran along the outside wall of the cellblock, out of reach of prisoners hands, but not out of reach of their missiles. He was pelted with bars of hard soap, pieces of leather, shoes and belts. His Winchester Rim-Fire banged against the safety railing. He was a fat elderly man, with popping blue capillaries on his forehead and temples, and huffed and puffed as he bumped quickly along, ducking to avoid the missiles. All the inmates laughed.

"Billy?"

"Yeah!"

"Will you cover us while we search this . . . this boy's cell?"

"Sure, Sarge!"

"And shoot the first sonofabitch you see throw anything at you, you hear?"

"I'd love to, Sarge! Just love to!" said Billy, showing his

chaw-stained teeth behind his long stubbly pointed chin.

"Now, goddamnit," Big Arv said, breathing hard, as he turned again to Galliot, "are you gonna take those fucking scivvies off?"

"Of course, Sergeant, but I'm really beginning to wonder about you fellows in the Joint. This is the fifth time today someone's tried to get my britches off!" he said, as he slid his black bikini-style jockey shorts down over his brown muscled legs, smiling politely. Everyone in the building heard the exchange. The convicts laughed and jeered.

"Oohie!"

"Fucking hacks all the same!"

"Right on, brother!"

Big Arv watched Galliot careful, real close: "Now, Mister Galliot, I want you to go out there and spread your cheeks for the officer and then I want you to go twenty feet down the tier and wait . . . And Billy?"

"Yeah!"

"Kill him if he looks crosswise!"

"With pleasure!"

Galliot stepped gingerly out in his bare feet like he wasn't used to it, and looked straight into Arv's wavering eyes. *Hey man, I'm on your side!* He just stood there looking at him for quite a while, making him say the words he didn't want to say, making him, forcing it out of him, having no mercy. It took Arv a long time to get them out. And when he was finally made to by the fleeing moments, and his acute embarrassment, he had to do it harder than he wanted to, just like his father had *so this is what he wanted?*

"Okay wonder boy," Arv shouted in his rapping voice, his prison stage voice, for all the block to hear, "bend them knees and spread that moon, hands up against the rail, and we'll see what you got up there besides what's supposed to be!"

Galliot bent over and spread his cheeks just like he was told and his smile was still there. It said: *for this you will die, punk.*

Arv went through the motions of checking his asshole *why do I have to be the villain?* and then sent him up the tier.

Slow, dick swinging, Galliot swaggered up past the long

line of cells to the tune of cheers, a thunderous ovation, "Yeah!" "Do it!" "Go 'head with yo bad self, brother!," graceful as a dancer, lithe as a panther, Black Panther, but kind of affected. Yet it was perfect, and you could see that it had captured every inmate on the tier: black magic: black faces squeezed between the bars watching, applauding with their hands and with metal cups on the bars, hanging onto the crossbars loose and menacing.

"Okay, Arv, get in here and search this cell. And I want to see you do it right!" Big Arv said, as he stooped low and put something under Galliot's mattress. It looked like a . . . knife? Then Big Arv stood guard out on the tier, watching Galliot and the cellblock for trouble, writing down names and cell numbers. The inmates passed the word that he was writing disciplinary reports.

"Boooooo!"

"You think we give a shit?"

"You start hasslin' Black Fence, motherfucker, you be a sorry hack!"

"Yeah!"

"Blow Black Fence!"

"Go for soul, man, go for the fucking hack with you body and you mind!"

Little Arv went through the black man's meager possessions, according to regulations.

William S. Galliot, Number 240976 possessed only:

1. 13 sheets prison stationery
2. 1 metal mirror
3. 1 blanket
4. 1 mattress
5. 1 pair trousers
6. 1 shirt
7. 1 pair shorts
8. 1 pair socks
9. 1 pair of shoes
10. 1 ball point pen

Arv stood on tiptoe and opened the ventilation duct with his pen-knife, running his hand over the lip, looking for weapons or dope. Nothing. He checked the color of the toilet water for the telltale marijuana green. Nothing. He looked under the bed . . . and found something re-

markable. Under the bed he found a tiny bird cage, hand
carved apparently by secret prison craftsmen from a single block of plastic. It was ornate and beautiful, and told
a story. On one side were ships and black men waiting on
a sandy palm-fringed shore. On another they arrived at a
dock in a more civilized land. On another they were put
into chains and set upon an auction block. And on the
fourth side they burst their chains, flinging them into the
air. Inside the cage a tiny pale brown sparrow with a broken wing pecked uninterestedly at a few bread crumbs. A
small neat white card tied to the top with red ribbon said
something about "Welcome to the Hellfire Club, Brother
. . . You Fellow Sufferers in the East Block." Arv left it
off his list, despite the fact that it was an unauthorized
personal possession. Big Arv wasn't looking. Arv waited
until he was looking and then peeked theatrically under
the mattress. There was the knife. He picked it up and put
it in his pocket, right next to the letter he was carrying
there.

"What's that? . . . I said what's that?"

"It's the knife you put there," Arv said, playing dumb,
just loud enough for the man in the next cell to hear.

"They planted a knife!" the black man in the next cell
yelled. "I heard them talking! I heard! They made a plant!
They made a plant!"

"What?"

"Kill the motherfuckers!"

"Off the Pig!"

"We'll tear this fucking place down!"

The whole cellblock went up in smoke. The gunman
got pelted with so many missiles he couldn't tell who to
shoot at. The sparrows that had drifted back into the
building took off again in fright, banging up against the
walls, braining themselves and falling to the polished cement floor, filling the cellblock with feathers.

"Kill!"

"Murder the hack!"

"All power to the people!"

"Rebel!"

Big Arv got real nervous. He got scared and pissed off
at Arv, furious, steam coming out his red little piggy ears,
but he couldn't say anything. He walked over to Arv and
Arv quick reached into his pocket next to the letter and

whipped the knife out handle first and laid it snappily into his old man's palm, making him suspect that maybe Arv'd done it on purpose.

"You stupid little gunsel," he hissed under his breath, Arv's father did, to his only begotten son, he did! The sonofabitch took notice of his little shrimpy son one time. He did! He said it, and then he turned around and went out the door again.

"What you talking about?" he hollered to the cellblock at large. "Who said anything about a knife? This dude must be crazy! We ain't found no knife!"

"Oohie!"

"Caught the peckerwood redhanded!"

"Yea!"

They continued yelling and futzing around for a while, but soon they quieted down. You could hear them chattering low and happy between cells: even the diversion of potential violence and death is welcome in the Joint.

Arv carefully scanned the corners of the cell, the ceiling; he ran his hand above the cell door, following regulations. Nothing. He ran his pocketknife along the seams in the cement floor, checking for hiding places. Nothing. He ran his knive under the bottom bar of the cell door. Nothing. He looked under the neatly folded blanket and found two unauthorized books: the 1972 Winter edition of *Tri-Quarterly Review,* a special number entitled "Literature in Revolution." And the late George Jackson's book *Blood in My Eye* with the following quotations underlined:

> Right now we can be placing our soldiers inside the various police and military prison staffs.

and:

> The fascists believe that one guard with a machine-gun can control a thousand men, but I know that this guard cannot watch all one thousand at once. While his attention and gun are trained on a gathering of ten who whisper freedom—closing on his blind side, my knife will claim his life.

Arv figured he must have borrowed them from somebody in the next cell. He did not mark them down in his infractions book either. Arv looked up. His old man was looking down the tier at something. Arv went quickly into his pocket and brought out the slightly crumpled letter with the Free Galliot Committee letterhead that he'd been carrying around all day, and stuck it in *Blood in My Eye* on page 86. Then he picked up Galliot's rumpled bundle of blue denim clothing. Squeamishly, as always, he went through the pockets, the bottom seam and the pant legs of the jeans, the sleeve rolls of the denim shirt, feeling the man's body oils on his fingers, the stale nervous sweat. The smell on Arv's fingers, the smell of another man, the invisible alien oils under his nails, wouldn't scrub away tonight at home, no matter how he washed. Arv shook each item of clothing carefully over the floor, shaking even Galliot's bikini jockey shorts while his father watched him again *what I know about Galliot is not very much: I know he wipes his ass clean. But that is very important. Would I trust even my own brownless when checked by a nonobjective stranger?*

Through all his diligent searching Arvin found:

1. 1 pencil
2. 1 comb
3. 2 snapshots

which he noted down, showed to his father. But Big Arv was no longer interested, now that his stupid vicious plan, whatever it might have been, was foiled, and merely waved his hand angrily at his son.

The woman in one of the color photos was big-eyed and black, about twenty-seven years old. She sat on the white wooden stoop of a gray rundown Victorian house in a West Coast city. She was wearing a suede midi skirt and a red Indian cotton blouse and thick-heeled lace-up boots. It must have been taken a couple of years before. Her kinky reddish hair she kept very short, Miriam Makeba-style. She was smiling. It was a nice smile. She was pretty and bright and wholesome and lively looking. Her dark eyes sparkled in the sunlight. She might have been a graduate student in English or Philosophy. Arv stared at that foxy lady for long moments, until the old man said, "Come on! Let's go!"

But still he hesitated, peeking quickly at the other snapshot. It was Elaine in that picture, Arv's instructor at City College, which didn't surprise him a bit, in light of the rumors of their former "intimacy" that had been circulating at City College for a couple of years, in light also of the fact that Arv was certain that the contraband letter he now carried had originated with Elaine . . .

"I said finish up, goddamnit!" Big Arv yelled, "and let's get outa here!"

Arv replaced the photos and came slowly out of Galliot's cell.

"Alright, Mr. Galliot!" Big Arv shouted down the tier, "looks like you come away clean this time. But don't let that fool you. Believe me, you ain't gonna wanna allow yourself a mistake around Big Arv. Or you'll regret it, I can tell you. Till your dying day . . . which won't be too long coming . . ."

But Galliot wouldn't answer.

After the shakedown (two more shakedowns, one on each tier to make it look like they weren't just after Galliot) Arv and his father went down to the main floor and locked themselves in the guard shanty with the East Block sergeant. The other officers, and the tier men, were all busy with shower time out on the floor. Big Arv sent the night runner over for their lunch pails. He decided it was time for a lunch break. He sent the second runner over across the Yard to the Main Kitchen to raid the pantry for milk and cake, the only two items on the cons' diet which they found palatable. He stuck the coiled electric stinger into a jar of water and it jerked and sputtered and finally boiled. Then he dropped some Nescafé into it, and they all settled back on the guard shanty counter, their legs dangling over the edge, swinging lazily, having a nice cup of coffee, a nibble, and a long chat.

That is, the two sergeants had a chat. Big Arv ignored his son, after his insolence this afternoon. The East Block sergeant did the same. Arv, silent, kept his own counsel. Anyway, he knew what his father and Sergeant Byrnes, a ruddy-faced Southerner, were going to talk about probably even before they knew themselves. He listed the topics in his head:

1. Galliot

2. what he wants
3. what he will do if he gets it
4. what will be done to stop him
5. what public opinion will say once he's been stopped

And sure enough, his guess was right. At the end of the conversation that ensued, Big Arv said, "Well sir, I'll tell you, Byrnes, our old buddy-boy ain't long for this here world," and, lowering his voice to the merest gravelly whisper, intoned: "They say they already got a *contract* out on him," Arv's presentiment was confirmed in all its details.

After lunch break Big Arv sent his son up to the little-used fifth tier guard post, where he locked himself in and checked with the Control Office by telephone every half hour. Big Arv thought he was sending the kid to hunger, to a place of the vilest disgrace, where he'd be out of "mischief." But Little Arv was delighted. He switched on one of the prison station's three radio channels, "Soul Music," put the earphones on tight over his ears and, for the next two hours, until the Last Count, he acted just according to the regulations, he "maintained surveillance of area of responsibility and censored inmate mail." There were only three inmate letters awaiting censorship. They lay before him on his desk. After finishing the first two Arv read with great relish Galliot's outgoing letter to:

> Ms. Elaine Mourutsos
> Department of English
> New Sonora City College
> New Sonora City, N.S. 86617

which when he first came into the guard post he'd perceived lying on his desk unsealed as prescribed by institution rules.

(NSCC-34265) 660 Name William S. Galliot

Number 240976

New Sonora Maximum Security Facility

Mission Santa Bonita, N.S. 86611

Date 18 December , 1972

Dear Elaine:

Hopefully now this evening I'll be able to fix up and send to you this almost unreadably crumpled letter I've had finished for days, and have smuggled with me hidden in the soles of my shoes through three prisons and innumerable shakedowns.

You ask about my life, my "background of experience" for dissemination to the various chapters of your Free Galliot Committee. This query, from my devoted and beloved and much-appreciated editor, agent, one-woman booster club, literary executor (if the need regretfully arises), dear friend and dynamite waterbed partner of yore, can only provoke immediate response. Also, it's been a good while since I've gone over the events of my past. I've been too busy living. How I've changed through the years! I see my progress through these forty-three years as often rough going, but a continuous movement upward toward the light, toward truth, understanding, freedom and justice, though this might be hard to believe about certain periods in my life.

The important thing about me is that, as a young man, I didn't share in the usual black ghetto experience, or the southern cotton fields. My mother died when I was born. I never knew her. I grew up with my father in the small California town of Chino, located in the Pomona Valley near Los Angeles. *"Chino, Where Everything Grows,"* the sign on the edge of town proclaimed proudly. The earth was indeed very fertile there: they grew oranges, walnuts, alfalfa, cows, green beans, tomatoes, corn, but mostly walnuts and oranges. The nights there I remember with pleasure: Mount Baldy and Mount San Gregorio high above me in the moonlight, and the ghostly Valencians, the orange trees, and the tall straight eucalyptus, the whispering junipers. And the winters, clear and warm and windless, except once or twice a year when it would freeze and they'd set out the smudge pots to save the fruit trees, smudge pots that smudged up everything, smogging your room and your clothes and your clean white shirts, anticipating by several years that curious "smog" that came along, permanently discoloring the Los Angeles Basin, spoiling the view, and your lungs, wrapping it all up in the twentieth century's special deadly package. But in the '30's, when I was growing up, in spite of the movies and Hollywood, the "Southland," as the newspapers called that part of California, was still deeply, safely parochial. Any strangers were looked upon with raised eyebrows. Black people were virtually unknown. Okies did not "deluge" California. It was the booming World War II defense industry that did that. Within fifteen years the Okies were totally assimilated. And in twenty years you couldn't tell an Okie from a native. But in the '30's, yes, it was definitely not very nice to be an Okie; it was almost as bad as being a Mexican native born in California, but not quite. There was great animosity between the Okie and the Mexican, natural competitors. And when the local landowners dumped their oranges into the Santa Ana River bed rather than sell at deflated prices, it was the Mexicans and the Okies who fought over the rotting remains. The irony of it all was that the Okies never saw who their proper class enemy was, never. They simply concentrated with their hard dirt Mid-Western resolution and endurance to *become* the enemy, the Pig, which they did in very short order. Ninety percent of the guards in West Coast prisons are of lower-class southern Cracker or Mid-Western dirt farmer origins. As George Jackson says, in *Blood in My Eye,* ". . . it can be said that this right-oriented sector of the working class is a new class, a new pig class." But anyway, let's pass on to this story of my life. I'll try to keep politics out of the early years, as you have suggested, but you know how difficult it is for me! Also, I'll be reiterating some information that you probably already know, but since this is intended for publication you'll understand.

Oh shit! The Santa Ana River! Sad little creek flattered beyond its means, rising in the heart of the San Bernardino Mountains at Big Bear Lake at 8,000 feet and descending in trickles through the boulder-strewn dry foothills through Riverside and Corona and Chino, going into the sea past Santa Ana at Terminal Island (fitting name, somehow) in Long Beach. Generations have wasted time swimming in its meager waters. I did, and it was only a foot deep and ten feet wide in its brimmingest years. And yet it is the only stream of any size in all of Southern California. Essential to understanding me is the fact that I grew up in an arid land. It makes for a special kind of human being. I am a seeker. I always have been. People from places with little water, and dry hot air, are often like that.

My father and I lived near that river, in one of those typical stucco and wood frame one-story houses with the windows shaped like rainbows. This window shape had a great vogue in the Los Angeles area in the teens and twenties. You often see them in old Keystone Cops, or Laurel and Hardy movies as a backdrop for chase scenes, behind small grass yards rimmed with built-up concrete, two feet above a street which is concrete too, with black tar lacing the cracks in the pavement.

My father was first a caddy at a private country club, and then he was a caddymaster, ran the pro-shop, and eventually bought out the pro-shop concession, emerging as a member of the homeopathic and minuscule black middle class of the time. I grew up on the golf course, caddying from my earliest years, listening to the rich white folks talking, picking their heads for ideas, for intimations, of how to survive in this albescent world. I largely succeeded. It never occurred to me to rebel at that time. In a way, believe this or not, I am glad I didn't. I hadn't enough experience of the world. I would have gone under, dying uselessly, like so many of my young brethren, in a liquor store holdup or police chase at the tender age of nineteen.

I grew up like a white man, acting like him. I had his values, his hopes, his *Weltanschauung;* I was completely separated, in terms of experience, from my black brothers. We were the only black family in town. My mother, the "matriarch" in whom the black family's soul, its nigrescence, almost infallibly resided, was long dead. My father had become a white man, a mimic man, a soaphead, right-thinking and inoffensive. My friends were without exception white. In short, I lived in the same blank-white world as the majority of the citizens of this capitalist republic.

By the way, if my style changes perceptibly now—fewer polysyllabic words—it is because my cell has just been searched and the southern cracker East Block sergeant has taken away *Soule's Dictionary of English Synonyms*. I luckily managed to pass my other books down to the guy two cells away. *Soule's*, it seems, is not on my "authorized" reading list. This may be fortunate, however, in that it compels me to discard this last vestige of my inferiority complex.

To continue: there were, of course, scars, the inevitable scars that every black brother or sister in Amerika suffers. But I would not permit myself to see them, feel them, nor the blows, the hits, and bruises, the slashes and cuts and wounds that made them. I *was white only in my eyes*. The remainder of the world saw me as a coal black nigger, and responded toward me accordingly with condescension, hidden animosity, love-hate, etc. No need cataloguing all that for you. My white friends only pretended that my light color, and my white man's manners and way, made me "okay," acceptable, presentable. They kidded themselves about me; it pleased them. Even as president of the student body of my high school I was a house nigger to them. Even more a nigger for my success. They used to fight over me! Trying to sort out whose friend I was going to be. Just under the surface of their consciousness I was their pet chimpanzee. Listen to me! I was a racist myself! In 1935, when it was time to enter kindergarten, they put me in the Mexican school on First Street in Mexican Town. Since there were no other blacks in Chino they didn't know what else to do with me. Mexicans were segregated at the time, so it seemed to them the only logical choice. By the time I reached the fourth grade I was utterly miserable, ostracized, beaten up, my bike stolen and wrecked and abandoned in a dirt Mexican yard overgrown with cactus and spikey Spicky rose bushes. I was cursed and made fun of daily in a language I couldn't understand. How I hated those greasers! How they hated this nigger! In a racist society the sickness does not abide only at the top, its evil runs through the fiber of all races, all classes and castes.

My father finally got me out of the segregated Mexican school with pull. Yes, he did have influence in that little town. As a businessman, as a country-club "personality" (oh, you know of course how funny he was—had to be—how he made those high-class white folks laugh and slap their knees with delight at his antics!), my father had some real connections in Chino. There was no black community, so there was no "nigger problem." They could afford to tolerate him, be generous, even offer him a kind of grudging, condescending respect for his "sense of humor," and his knowledge of golf.

And so it went with me. In the white school I was a great success, on a superficial level. I was strange. I was different, exotic even, at that time in California. The notorious Watts, for example, was still a solidly, stolidly Russian and Jewish neighborhood. By the time I reached high school I was remarkably popular, a student leader, athlete, the life of every party. Oh those "Rastus" jokes I told! And damn how they all laughed! But you know what? Never once did I dare ask a white girl out on a date. All the way through high school and college.

When I was a senior in high school I was offered several athletic scholarships. "So are a lot of niggers," I thought, and turned down all the baseball and track offers for a golf scholarship at USC. Golfing, you see, is not only a white sport, but a gentlemanly white sport as well. I had pretensions, you see. I was despicable. But now I look back on it all with equanimity. It's almost as if it was necessary for me to become the Pig, the white man, lactescent, soul-bleached, to achieve the objective understanding I later needed for my revolutionary struggles.

I was a great success in college, just as I had been in high school: gentleman golfer, president of Senior Class, Phi Beta Kappa, Valedictorian, Cadet Colonel of ROTC. Do you know what I majored in? You'll never believe it! Criminology. I determined that my only hope of a secure future was in government em-

ploy. The L.A. Police Department was at that time
thinking of creating a "Department of Criminology
Theory" for long-range planning for, and instruction
of, its police cadres. My aim was to join that group,
and go all the way to the top! I had plans, Sister!
Dreams of success. Driving ambition. All the qualities of Mister Charley. But in reality I was nothing
more than a wart, a grown-over scar, a human sore.
None of my wounds were open. I denied they existed. I loved a lie, and found happiness with it. True
happiness? Well, what is happiness after all? I
laughed a lot. I had fun playing golf and studying. I
enjoyed reading. I liked driving my car, a beautiful
little 1948 MG "TC." Sure, I had fun at college, as
much fun as anybody else, I suppose. It's just that I
wasn't really *alive*. When the sailors and marines
came down on the Chicanos of East Los Angeles, for
example, in 1943, blasting their way into the ghetto
and killing the hard-fighting but outnumbered
Pachucos by the score, burning, raping, murdering,
emasculating the Chicano brothers, do you know
what I was doing? Listening to the radio reports of
the incident like all the white folks, cheering on the
jarheads and gyrenes. That's where I was at during
this first authentic race war of modern West Coast
history.

I had no self-definition, no awareness of my real
possibility of being as a black man, a brother, a
blood, under all that whiteface, that covering, that
layer upon layer of soundproofing, weatherproofing, I
had stuck together around myself. Perhaps one of the
reasons I didn't find it odd being reasonably happy,
and content, in spite of my callousness was that most
other people, white, brown, yellow, black, that I saw
around me were the same way. They weren't alive to
themselves either. They had constructed insulating
fabrics around themselves too, just like me, albeit for
differing reasons, different traumas.

One of the truly important things to remember
about the black experience is that it is a human
shock, a trauma that a black man or woman suffers
like anyone else when he is put to extreme psychological duress or peril. The only difference, in fact,

between ordinary traumatized people and black people (and what keeps *us* alive) is that *we all suffer together*. Our common traumatic experience is precisely what gives us that indefinable quality *soul*, what makes us a community. The unfortunate thing about me is that, removed as I was from my black brothers, I suffered alone my dead soul . . . just like the Honkey.

Upon graduation I was commissioned a second lieutenant and, along with many of my white college buddies, went away to Asia with the 40th (California National Guard) Division to fight in the Korean War.

I was a virgin, a willing casualty of the Color Bar, till the day I landed in Pusan.

I won't bore you with the details of my combat experience. Suffice it to say that I was seriously wounded in the Inchon invasion and sent to a pleasant hospital in the woods near Kyoto to recuperate. At this time the first of many changes or reversals in my life took place. At least I thought of it at the time as a "reversal." From my vantage point now I see clearly that it was merely another layer of scar tissue I grew around myself: I rejected all my past, emotional and material, all my antecedents, black and white. It happened one day on a train going along a rainy windy rice paddy between Misumi and Kumamoto, on the island of Kyushu. I viewed the destruction of a pond of water fronds in the rain; they lay there perfectly, I thought, perfectly cold, perfectly crushed, perfectly abandoned. They were like me, I thought. I was like them. My reversal was complete.

I arranged soon after to be discharged from the army in Kyoto. I studied Buddhism there for two years, meditating, living very frugally on my mustering-out pay, looking for the way, the path to my personal enlightenment or, as I was thinking in those days: "to let go, no seeking, no striving, no stewing in my own juice . . . to open up and welcome the peace that comes natural, the peace that passeth understanding."

Eventually a woman changed my mind, engendered my next "reversal," taught me in one glance across the garden of Ryoanji that it was impossible to leave the world behind. And then came striding across the snowy winter grass of the park in hiking boots and blue jeans and her green eyes sparkling and her cheeks rosy red and blowing huge clouds of steamy cold healthy breath. She asked:

"What is it you're looking for?"

"You look like you already know," I answered.

"You're looking for nothing."

"What is nothing?" I asked.

"Beauty . . . and the truth," she said.

"What is beauty?" I demanded.

"Earth and dung."

"What is the truth?"

"Little things in nature . . . a little bird."

"What are you?"

"Earth and dung."

"What am I?"

"A little bird."

"And what will we be," I asked, "if we come together?"

"A little bird perched on a hill of steaming dung!" she said.

She was a strange and wonderful woman, a beggar woman, a beautiful young road woman, a proud wandering Belgian Jew. She loved me, changed me profoundly, and then left me behind quite suddenly one day to ponder her lesson. She was white, of course, my first white woman, and it became apparent to me that I had loved her with all my love of White. . . . Even her leaving had taught me a lesson. That is why she had to go.

I rode the train to Tokyo that night with not a yen in my pocket. I simply leapt aboard a departing express train and when the conductor came around I said, "Lost my ticket." The Japanese are so polite, especially to the *"gaijin,"* as they call foreigners, and they have so few dishonest or disorderly citizens among them that they never dream of questioning you. First class all the way: Nagoya, Toyohashi, Hamamatsu, Shizuoka, Yokohama . . . It was snowing. It was a year to the day since we had met in the

winter rock garden at Ryoanji. Suddenly I felt exhilarated, inspired. "What a wonderful woman!" I
thought.

The profound truth I had learned through her departure, the exquisite sadness it gave me, the discovery of her powerful magic, the realization that she
was the kind of person men used to call "goddesses,"
the fact that she had deigned to select me as her tyro,
all of this set my head spinning, my heart skittering
with an overwhelming joy at being alive.

I got a room in Shinjuku, a kind of Tokyo Green-
wich Village, hung out at the Check jazz club, the
Don-zoko bar, and the Fugetsu-do coffee house with
a lot of beatniks and coffee house *cognoscenti* and
expatriates. I worked as an English conversation
teacher for a penny-pinching German in Shimokita-
zawa, a model for the men's fashion magazines, a
bit-part player on television and in the movies (I was
probably the only black actor around Tokyo at the
time, so any time the role called for a spook, I was
it!). I did a lot of porno flicks too. Hungry one day
and flush the next. Smoking a lot of dope, a lot of
opium, fornicating casually with every kind of
woman from Korean whores to white Embassy wives.

In three years I had a little bankroll and left
Japan, traveling East: Hong Kong, Singapore,
Bangkok, Phnom Penh, Saigon, India, Afghanistan,
Turkey, the Arab countries, scrounging, conning,
begging, borrowing, running out on hotel bills, smuggling gold and jewels and contraband cameras and
dope to make a buck. I was good-looking, young, intelligent, and utterly without scruples.

Funny thing: one of the things I have found out in
the Joint is that everyone in here is guilty. The only
trouble is that they're often not guilty of what they
are charged with. Almost nobody in this world hasn't
been a thief of one kind or another. I am guilty of
having been a petty international criminal. For that I
never spent a day in jail. It took something I definitely *was not* guilty of to send me to prison.

In another couple of years I wound up in Europe
where I lived for a long time as a con-man, road-
man, a gigolo in London, a car thief in Germany, a

forger on the Costa del Sol, a café philosopher on
the Piazza Navona in Rome, a street singer in the me-
tros and show queues of Paris, a dancer with a troup
of expatriate American blacks. The dance gig lasted
longest. We got together a reasonably good modern
dance group, not good enough for the States, but
quite fine enough to trade on our black faces and the
international preconception (and probable fact, I
unconventionally believe) that black people are
somehow endowed with magic qualities of movement. We played in second-rate night clubs from
Naples to Lucerne to Kiel to Gothenburg and across
the Atlantic in the West Indies, Brazil, Nicaragua.
The incredible thing was that this was the first time I
had ever really got to know black men and women.
And I was an utter failure. There was no way in the
world I could relate to them except on a superficial
level. I was never one of them, and preferred it that
way. My woman at the time was Italian; we had our
own white friends.

Finally, after many adventures, certainly more
than I have time to outline here, I returned to California. It had been fifteen years but I took up just
like I'd left the week before. I got a job as a traveling
salesman, selling hope chest items to single black
working girls for their wedding day. I did very well,
soon becoming a team manager, putting together a
very successful sales team of black high-pressure
salesmen who traveled all over, up and down the
West Coast making a fortune off the unobtainable
dreams of young black girls. It was about this time
that I began affecting a kind of exaggerated Negro
dialect, jive talk, but I don't think I fooled anyone,
certainly not myself, probably not even the poor
working creatures we daily cheated of their hard-
earned cash. I was still lily-white at heart. As a matter of fact, I had become the very essence of The
Man. I was the oinkingest, snortingest, jive-ass Pig
you ever did see! A veritable walking talking broad-
sheet for the American Dream, the Free Enterprise
System, and damn the torpedoes!

Meanwhile I was drinking and gambling heavily,
playing poker in little back room parlors in small

towns up and down the San Joaquin and Sacramento
and Imperial valleys, winning, winning like crazy,
cheating the Crackers and wetbacks and niggers out
of everything they owned, then blowing it on booze
and bawdy ladies.

About this time the government's "Black Capitalism" campaign was fully under way. I obtained funds
from the government through some highly placed
friends in black political circles, and a little Mau-
Mauing in the proper places, and began manufactur-
ing my own hope chest items and selling them from
coast to coast. Labor costs were nil because all my
workers assumed they were in on the ground floor of
a great communal black effort. Bursting with enthusiasm, they worked for virtually nothing. That's where
they were mistaken. All the real remuneration went
into the Swiss bank accounts of a tight coterie of me
and my friends.

A true American success story! My picture was in
the paper. I was pointed to by the administration as
an example of black business acumen, looked up to,
fawned over in the black community, the Tom black
community, that is, and suddenly found myself,
through some quirk of fate, as a "spokesman" for the
blacks in New Sonora City, where I had located the
national headquarters for my booming business.

Then, when the great spate of black riots swept the
country, in the mid-sixties, I found myself in a very
difficult position. As the white man's pet "responsible
spokesman" for the black race, I was more and more
often the butt of jokes in the radical and cool black
worlds, laughed at, made fun of, and finally roughed
up, shot at, almost assassinated. When the inevitable
riot came to New Sonora, and the city began to burn,
I took a cautious approach, allowing my rhetoric to
go only far enough to keep the blacks happy, and the
whites at bay (or the other way around). I succeeded
in juggling the two worlds like this to an almost unbelievable extent. Then one night, drunk, as I was
more and more often lately, I went out into the burning streets to watch and listen, and got more and
more and more pissed-off, angry, het up, furious, to

discover that *we*, that's right, *we* black brothers were the ones getting hurt by that riot. We were the ones getting blown off, we were the ones whose property was destroyed, whose homes burned down, we were the ones hurting! Not the white man!

In the morning I woke, battered and numb, and another of those fundamental changes in my life took place. But this time it seemed different somehow. And it was. It was not just another sea change. The fires of the riot had burnt away my scar tissue just at a time when it was about to harden into grizzly callus and cover me over forever. It is a miracle of the first order for which I do not thank the white Christian God but the great human deity within my poor blackman's broken soul which has finally come home. I knew, for the first time in my life, a profound consciousness of my own negritude. I felt it. It ran through me suddenly flooding me with a powerful and wondrous black light, filling me, filling me right up to my nappy brim with pride and potential and power, and it has never left me to this day. It is my sole sustenance . . . now in my days of adversity.

I liquidated my assets immediately, including my recently acquired Jamaican "Octoroon" wife, who did not consider herself "a shit-eating nigger" and left me in a fit of pique when she found out my intentions.

From the nucleus of a black street gang, into which I rapidly pumped funds, energy and organizational skills, I created almost overnight the Black Fence.

Though my thoughts have changed perhaps in recent months on many things, and though I've renounced nonviolence as an effective deterrent to Pig aggression and oppression, and renounced also peaceful neighborhood self-help and organization as a practicable revolutionary tool, I am still quite proud that the Black Fence was at its inception and continues to be today a movement like *no other black movement in all of history*. I combined elements of mysticism (I had always been devout, one way or another . . . a devout Missionary Baptist, Zen Buddhist, cynic, beatnik, con man, and capitalist pig),

Communism, Socialism, Black Nationalism, Black Power, Black Pride, Neighborhood Self-Government, Communal Capitalism, Kibbutzism and myth. I borrowed, plagiarized and stole freely from black thinkers from Saint Augustine to Marcus Garvey to Huey Newton to Leroi (Baraka) Jones. But the basic nucleus of my plan was all me, a conscious manifestation of my metamorphoses from me-thinker to we-thinker. I had been to Jamaica, to Haiti, to Rio de Janeiro, to Liberia. I knew the marvel of Voodoo, of the Ras Tafarians, of black religious fervor, of black song and dance, its hypnotic powers. I knew and loved the Jamaican Reggae. I'd read about the Ghost Dance of the American Indians in the late nineteenth century, dances of magic, trancelike dances of pride in one's race, one's own songs and myths and origins. Dances of communion with one's brothers, dances of a power so majestic that they nearly brought the U.S. government tumbling down from terror. A song came into my head, as if by magic. It stuck there. "That's right!" I thought. "You goddamn fucking A right, Jim, we sure can dance!" letting the song run out in my head, dancing around my living room, creating on the spot a dance, a kind of shuffling street walk, a funeral march, or a carnival samba step, that would enchant the brothers, bring them out into the streets of this jive-ass land like the Ghost Dance, bring the black men out like old-time red men, shake the Pig in his jackboots!

The first thing I did with my street gang was teach. Don't ask me where I got the words. They just came to me. I taught them that the white man had always been right. Them niggers sure *could* dance! And they could sing too! Ain't that beautiful! We could dance and sing better than Whitey, and we could do anything else better too. We got rhythm. Sure we got rhythm. And what is rhythm but the pulse of life?

The black man had used his myths, his gods, his songs and ritual dances for four hundred years as a place of retreat and evasion, a secret terrible place of defense where Chuck couldn't come, a magic fortress as real to him as Machu Picchu to the Incas, a fortified fairyland where no one but soul brothers could follow. I proposed to retain that defensive aspect of our black magic, but turn it to *active* ends.

I brought my black street gang out the first time I had a chance. We Black Fenced to the main square. It was magic, all the brothers caught on fast, started following us, dancing it in the middle of the street, just like I'd seen in Rio. It worked! I felt like a magician, a shaman, a witch doctor! I felt beautiful. I shivered with my own power.

Within a month the Black Fence was a national rage. Everyone was doing it. Reporters came to me, interviewed me. They wanted to know what my platform was, what did the Black Fence mean, in political terms, what were my intentions? The fact was, I didn't know yet. I really didn't. My first problem had been to mobilize souls. Now I'd have to give my Black Fence cadres a *raison d'être,* goals, a political philosophy. Quickly I set about writing it up. I stole from everyone, as I've stated, but the synthesis was all me. It was simple, it was direct, it was practical, and practicable and most important: it was attainable, I felt. I concentrated on what I thought was really possible now.

First I had to mobilize a great following of black poor people, the ghetto dwellers, through myth and dance. Then I had to put the emotional impetus of the dance to work. I had to create a solid cohesive bloc, a powerful pressure group, which would capitalize on white fears, perhaps, but only utilize lawful means: lawful protest, dissent, the vote, skillful bargaining, existing laws, economic pressure, boycotts, the Constitution, to effect certain changes in the status of black people, concrete changes. Nothing more audacious than that. We would be incorporated legally as cities, using existing laws. We would have our own separate school system, district laws, police, courts, jails, draft boards. We would, in short, become lawful municipalities with all the rights and obligations thereof. This, at the time, I was sure I could do, was sure I could achieve. I knew I had to concentrate on the probable, rather than the possible. I knew that I must make no promises that I couldn't deliver. I knew that success was essential. Success *now*, not in the distant revolutionary future.

I set about working on my first success right in New Sonora City. Once I'd won there, well, then I could concentrate on the rest of the nation. I wrote up our manifesto; the Black Fence, a much larger organization now, led by some of my bright young streetwise former gang members, endorsed it unanimously. Then, with rallies, marches, boycotts, dances, voter registration campaigns, we began our drive. We began acquiring property in the ghetto, a solid block of property which we fenced in and policed. We began building houses, apartments, stores, shops. We began collecting and disposing of our own garbage. We started a fire department, a citizens' volunteer militia.

The white community, the newspapers, politicians, law-enforcement officers, law-abiding citizens, voters, completely misunderstood the significance of the Black Fence (or understood it only too well: they knew it would really change things). They misapprehended its original peaceful intentions. They didn't listen to its demands, did not reply to its lawful queries, did not read its manifesto.

All they saw, felt, heard, was the dance, the song, the Black Fence.

Shoom-chooga-chooga, shoom-chooga-chooga,
Black Fence
Blaack Feence
Blaaaack Feeence
Blaaaaaaaaaaaaaaaaack!

"The New Ghost Dance," the newsmagazines called it. Its great mystical power over our people frightened the whities. It scared them silly. It was *irrational*, uncontrollable. That's what got them. Its emotional effect on the brothers gave birth to a contrary emotion in whites. All their immemorial terrors of the black man reemerged, stronger than ever. The whites too held rallies, condemning Black Fence, vilifying and slandering it. Legally, of course, there was nothing they could do. As a matter of fact, if the Man had obeyed his own laws, I would have continued doing so too. The only one who broke the law in my case was the law itself. It is not I who am the criminal here, but Amerikan "justice" itself. Daily, almost, the police harassed me, searched my office, stopped me in my car on the freeway. Any time a Black Fence member was arrested the newspapers blew it up into a major case. Informers were everywhere in the organization, police spies, *agents provocateurs.* Eventually they busted me (as you know only too well) on a pathetic phony dope beef and sent me to prison. I got out after six months, my parole officer violated me on another phony beef and I wound up in the Joint again. And I've been here ever since. It is two years now. Two interminable years. They gave me this open-ended sentence, "one to life," thinking they could keep me on ice indefinitely that way. By the time I got out, they figured, the Black Fence and everything it represented would be "as dead as the dodo." They miscalculated in this matter, however. The Black Fence, essentially a mystical entity from the beginning, now had its saint, its prophet, its martyr. Yes, I dare say to you now that I am a saint to my people in the Black Fence. I say it with only the slightest trace of vanity (and yet I *did* earn their adulation, didn't I? And my own self-respect? This can't be taken away from me. Never!). Our movement burgeoned and spread after my first incarceration, and during my second it has grown like never before, creating a wave of reprisals against black people, indiscriminate reprisals against blacks of all political persuasions. I don't have to enumerate the ways in which the Pig can hurt his captive slaves. There are a million ways, and he's tried them all, ranging from welfare cutoffs to congressional slashing of such pathetic New Frontier and Great Society programs as Head Start and free lunches at school . . . to much heavier stuff like (I do not exaggerate!) political assassination, false imprisonment, job layoffs, and so on.

But this program of government intimidation has backfired. It has brought about an unheard-of closing of our ranks, a new cohesion, a heterogeneity in our movement, a tremendous solidarity in our black community in New Sonora, and in all the other Black Fence communities across this Amerikan land. For every leader the Pig assassinates or locks up indefinitely in the Jam, another quickly springs up, proud and unafraid to fill his place, no matter what the consequences. They have taken recently to calling me "The Last Militant," in the newspapers. I find this laughable. Old Sylvester only wishes that were so. There are a thousand fine young black brothers on the streets of Amerika right now, ready willing and able to jump into my shoes if the need arises.

In the prisons of Amerika, and especially this state, the Pigs believe they've effectively put a stop to our movement. Through persuasion, intimidation, bribery, removal, parole, isolation, physical threats (I assure you it's true) and through torture, lobotomization and even murder, the Man has definitely made some large and painful slashes in our ranks. But to state, as our "liberal" Warden, showing his true colors, stated on television only last week, that "the Black Fence movement has been contained within the penal institutions of this state" is the sheerest nonsense. It's absolute bullshit. If anything, their program of torture and intimidation has helped the movement. It has created more saints and more martyrs for our brothers on the Outside to emulate: Gerald Baker, Leroy Baker, Moe DeCamp murdered in cold blood on the Main Yard at Brown Max (where they just missed offing me), John French, Carleton Willis, Willy Lee Charles locked away in the hole at Harbor Max for three years on "diet loaf" and water, no exercise, with barely enough air to breath . . . an environment of total terrorization.

Because of this kind of barbarism our movement on the Street is growing, and with its new ideological impetus (my renunciation of nonviolence, and my public espousal of militant revolutionary Marxism), it is growing like never before, "like wildfire," as the New Sonora Times has it. "Free Galliot" has become a powerful national force, a force to be reckoned with, including many white liberal and radical organizations. This, of course, I welcome, and without the least false modesty. If my deification serves the cause, I don't care. I only wish the radicals on the Street would raise up John, Carleton and Willy, and thousands of other political prisoners like them who languish and die in the prisons of the archfascist, to my "Olympian" heights.

Well Elaine, as you can see, though I've single-spaced it nearly to death, and written on both sides in a microscopic hand, and left out all the margins, we are drawing to the permitted 12-page end of this all too brief epistle which is, as it turns out, *my life*.

To close quickly: this is where I'm at now: the prison and state authorities are in a quandary (it will be the sheerest chance if this passes the censors; I can only count on the proverbial illiteracy of the Cracker Pigs). If they let me out, parole me, as is my legal due at this point, the body will have its head back, its soul. That's the sole reason why they've saddled me with this absurd "murder" beef.

If they arrange to "dispose of the problem administratively," to have me blown off in the Joint, the movement will have a Jesus. Recently, however, the grapevine has it that the authorities have come to a decision, a "final solution." The lesser evil, it seems, lies in my mortal discharge, my "severance with extreme prejudice," my "custodial disposal," and other such nightmarish, Kafkaesque euphemisms translating into plain English as *murder*. They have put a contract out on me already, it is whispered. For all I know the hit man is with me now in this cellblock, a few cells down, or on the next tier. I can't let it deter me, can't let it bother me, can't!

Love to you, dear friend, from the depths of the Inferno.

ALL THE POWER TO THE PEOPLE
William Galliot

Arvin, still locked in his minuscule guard post on the fifth tier, had several choices in regard to the letter which he finished reading now five minutes before the Last Count. He could:

1. throw it away
2. keep it myself

    3. send it as is
    4. censor it according to regulations

However, in spite of Galliot's derogatory references to officers of the state, and his piggish simile that Arv detested, and his criminally irresponsible accusations, Arv elected to seal the letter (licking it and pressing it closed with nervous tongue and quivering fingers), rubber-stamp it CERTIFIED with an official state seal, sign it, and send it off to its addressee exactly as he had read it. The basis for this illegal action, for which he would receive no remuneration, which would cost him his job if it was discovered, was a two-part evaluation of Galliot's character:

FOR	AGAINST
1. honesty	1. hubris
2. sincerity	2. prejudice
3. intelligence	3. flawed perception
4. courage	4. inconsistency
5. perseverance	5. short-sightedness
6. imagination	6. irresponsibility
7. ex-caddy like me	7. violent intentions

When writing his lists to himself, Arvin put his reasoning down just as it came to him. It was a point of honor not to change a word. In this way he honestly examined his true motivations and attitudes.

He concluded, therefore—as he unlocked the door and slipped out onto the fifth tier, as he flashed his light on the sleeping figures (including Galliot's, curled up on the mattress in fetal position . . . one eye open), as he clicked his mechanical clicker counter at his belt, click-click, one, two, three, making his last count of the night—that his natural and spontaneous feeling toward Galliot was one of surprising partiality, in view of the exact numerical balance in his assessment of the positive and negative elements in Galliot's character, in view, additionally, of the fact that the seventy-five dollars he had collected that afternoon was for the delivery of only one letter, and not this special favor.

When Arv came walking back down the fifth tier there was a note sticking out of the crack in the lock mechanism of Galliot's cell door:

FRIENDS COME IN THE FUNNIEST COLORS

Arvin took the note, raised his knee as a backboard and scribbled a response:

> RIGHT ON, BROTHER! SORRY ABOUT THIS
> AFTERNOON BUT YOU DIG WAS NECESSARY
> TO THROW OFF SUSPICION—DESTROY THIS
> WHEN READ, LOVE AND PEACE, A FRIEND

feeling as if he'd misrepresented himself somehow.

But his lonely prison guard's heart beat wildly to think of the sudden and wonderful exciting change in his situation, the sudden infusion of glamour into his life, his frightened, unhappy, surpriseless, imprisoned life.

Wow! Galliot, of the Black Fence!

Eleven

The bulls gave everyone a little green Orientation Handbook and Uncle Big Arv marched them out into the Isolation Yard and after a little racial disturbance out there, a few minutes of niggeration, typical coontail white-eyeball pissing and moaning and complaining on the part of whiney diddly-ass chickenshit Galliot & Company the bulls marched them all into the East Block real easy. No problems. Cause it was cold-balls with that rain blowing in flat over the walls stinging like bullets. Got them through the Block Gate and through the Control Point fast. Unlocked their handcuffs and ankle bracelets, unchained Wasco finally from the junkie. Leaned them up against their cells, feet wide apart, thirty-degree angle, holding onto the bars. When everyone was inside they yelled, "Turn around and strip!" The convicts pulled down their cold wet denims and their shorts, shivering and shaking, hopping up and down on one foot getting free of their shoes and socks. Then the shirts and T-shirts. "Bend over! Spread them cheeks! Wider! Come on boys, don't be shy!" Fifty-five Spic, Honkey and Jigaboo moons, mooners, bad-smelling brownouts. The junkie hadn't wiped his ass.

"Pee-you!" Wasco yelled, pretending he didn't like it. Actually, there was very few things in this fucking world that old Wasco liked more than ass. He spent probably half his time thinking about it, thinking about the prettiness of young dudes' asses, their size and shape and color and their soft touch. *Ooh them pretty asses*, Wasco was thinking, and repeated it:

"Pee-you! You make me want to cop!" he hollered, and everybody laughed. Only in the Joint would you laugh. Only in the Joint would you figure it out. Only in the goddamn Slam would a man equate dirty unwiped asshole with sweet pussy . . .

"Shut up! Keep in line!" the bulls yelled.

One of them going through their pathetic bundles of clothes on the freezing stone floor. The other one flashing a light up their cold assholes. Into your ears and your mouth. Under your shriveled joint and your dry-frozen ballbag. Checking for contraband for the fourth or fifth time today. By now you don't feel no humiliation. You just forget on purpose to think about it. Let your mind wander. Like second nature to you by now. Like a little pain that you ain't going to worry about. It was the bulls themselves that was nervous now. Shuffling around awkward and not knowing what to do with their big hands. When they finished they said, "Alright, pick up your clothes and get in them fucking cells!"

"Which cell?"

"Which one's mine?"

"The one right in front of your nose, idiot!"

"Yes sir!"

The screw down at the end pulled the pin on the tier lock, the long iron bar that ran all the way down the row. One of them grabbed hold of the heavy iron lever, put his foot up against the end cell, and yanked back with all his might, grunting.

"Oink!"

The bar sprang open and Wasco pulled the cell door and went in. The squeeze followed close at his heels but Wasco took his time.

"What's your rush, sweetie?"

CLANG! The bull let it fly back into lock position. ZANG! Almost getting the little junkie's fingers.

"What's the matter, honey, they hurt you?"

Naked, cold as the day they was born, two of them to a cell, the prisoners, the white ones, were all locked up. The blacks got herded up and locked in on the fifth tier with the other bloods.

"Alright now!" the screw yelled out, "read that there handbook good, you hear?"

Wasco put his clothes up on the crossbar to dry. The squeeze asked him if he had any preference in the way of bunks.

"Top or bottom?" he asked real tense and troubled around the itchy eyes and trembling pale fingers.

"Well," Wasco said, slow, like he was thinking hard,

rubbing his chin, "I'll tell you what . . . which one you want?"

"I'd prefer to have the bottom."

"Oh yeah? Well, look; that's the one I want."

The junkie shut his face and went up on top and lay down without another fucking word. Wasco could feel him quivering in fear of his life, or at least his dirty little hole. But he ignored the punk's measly existence.

Heat, lots of good prison heat piped direct from the Central Heating Plant blowing in through the big ventilator at the back of the cell. Wow! Thanks to Jesus for that!

It was a strip cell, a holding cell that would hold them for only one night, till they got their permanent booking tomorrow. It was empty. Bunks, mattresses, toilet, wash basin, and that's all. But it was furnished, baby, fully furnished. Stocked full up. It smelled of a thousand sweating squirming bodies, a million nervous depressions, a billion impossible comey daydreams. It was the same smell as at the Haley Reception Center. The same sweet laid on top of bitter-sweet smell of the New Sonora County Hospital. It was a good smell. A nice familiar old smell.

Wasco lay down on his bare mattress and lit up his thirty-third cigarette of the day. Not to mention the ceegars. Blowing smoke rings up at the ceiling. Perfect circles. You get good at smoke rings in the Joint.

"Say there, Squeeze, what you doing?"

"Reading."

"What?"

"The Handbook."

"Oh yeah? Well listen, I'm going to ask you to read it to me. Is that alright with you, honey?"

"Uh . . ."

"Just go right ahead, man, you never know, it might behoove you . . ."

The junkie still hesitated. Wasco said real low, murderous, spitting it out between the wide gaps in his sharp teeth, "Read it, punk!"

And he read. He read it good. The squeeze even had a little education the way he read it. Wasco would remember that. Wasco would remember the information in the Handbook too. Once, someone a few cells down to the left objected to the punk's loud voice. "Shut up, motherfucker!" he yelled. But Wasco wouldn't let him stop. "Keep on reading," he said, "you can handle that cat, can't you?"

The dude down the tier kept hollering, "Shut up!" and Wasco kept making the kid keep on reading. After a while the other dude stopped yelling, muttering threats to get the punk in the morning. His small loud voice tooted on and on, fragile and reedy as a penny whistle, but shrill and abrasive and loud.

When the kid finished Wasco didn't say anything. He just lay back and relaxed, making plans, feeling the top bunk trembling above him . . . Let's see . . . so how will we fix up the permanent cell? Amazing what you can do . . .

"Say, Squeeze, can you draw?"

". . . uh . . . Yeah, a little."

"Oh yeah, well listen, if you clean up your stinking ass I might pull a few strings, get you in my cell. Turn you out, man, initiate you in this here Jam. You can draw us up some fine jailhouse murals, real sexy, make the time pass. What you think?"

The punk was too scared to answer. Wasco just let him fret, planning out the next year or so, real careful. Let's make use of it. Time is money, man, got to remember that! Maybe a few night school courses. Correspondence courses too. Well-known Writers' School, maybe. There ain't no losing when your will is strong. Ain't nothing you can't do if you got the balls. Most of these punks come in here and go to sleep. Shit! You can make your fortune in here! Maybe we'll crack a few books this time, aside from everyday business. Get into a little math. Maybe even learn a trade. You never can tell, that's what old Evie always said, old Mom, every man got to get himself a good trade he can fall back on in case of need or in case of he's hiding out or laying low. Get into journalism even, or article writing. Wasco Weed, prison novelist! Or get into the Drama Club again, like at Prill Reformatory. Write a play. He sure had a lot to write about, Wasco did. The experiences! Wasco Weed, playwright, director, actor of the first category. Offered jobs on Broadway. Wasco Weed, originator of Drama 73, revolutionary new prison drama! Author of *Weed, The Joint, Shooting Gravy* and many other fierce and original tours de force.

But he was just shucking, old Wasco. He was really just
a businessman by nature, and only flirted with the arts. A
dilettante, that's what he was. Actually he had his entire
Joint career planned out in minute detail. Especially these
first eventful action-packed six days when he would rapidly consolidate his power inside and outside the walls.
The results of his clever planning already had a name in
Wasco's clever mind: "The Grand Design." A work of
art. A thing of perfection. Something to be proud of. The
Grand Design had begun to assemble quickly in Wasco's
head as soon as the nice gray-haired D.A. of New Sonora
County brought up his kind offer. And the process
speeded up tremendously when, just as Wasco was on the
point of leaving the sweet old guy's office, he very help-
fully suggested that Wasco avail himself "of all the fruits
of our considerable investigation into the life of this dangerous and radical black man . . . this . . . ah . . . this
Mr. Galliot . . ." he said, mentioning the hit's name for
the first time in their long interview, "I want you to study
his case thoroughly. I'm making all our records available
to you. You won't be able to remove any material from
the office, of course. You'll have to work right here," the
old fellow said, "and I needn't remind you that your very
life depends upon your total discretion and . . . I might
add . . . upon the speedy success of your endeavor. . . .
So, work fast and efficiently, Wasco, practicing the
greatest caution. Nothing in the case will be kept back
from you, and that includes tapes from our wire-tapping
activities, and full records of our careful and lengthy surveillance of all individuals involved, including the
prisoner's family, friends, ex-wives, lovers, political associates, et cetera. I want you to be perfectly prepared for
any eventuality. I want a flawless covert operation from
you . . . no slip-ups! Is that understood? I'm sure you
know what the penalty would be for . . . well, never
mind!" he said, removing his sunglasses for a moment,
stroking the little red crease they had made on the bridge
of his nose. "I'll tell my secretary I'm allowing you in
here to prepare your defense. . . . She'll believe I'm letting you plead guilty to lesser charges in exchange for
your information on underworld activities . . . a fairly
common practice here, as I'm sure you are aware."

"Oh, you bet, sir!" Wasco exclaimed, permitting a

slight, sharky grin to glide across his red face, "I know *all* about that! Har har har!"

"Now," the polite dapperly dressed old man continued, regarding his perfectly manicured hands, long and slender and tanned, above the stacked indictments on his desk, "in your examination of our confidential records here, I want you to pay especially close attention to a certain . . . Elaine Mourutsos . . . a college teacher, Communist or fellow-traveler, and ex-lover of the prisoner. Although their former intimate relationship was terminated when another woman, a colored woman, entered the picture, this Elaine Mourutsos has remained his closest confidante and most trusted associate. I'm sure you'll find her quite interesting in the context of your planning activities. It is through women, Wasco, that men invariably fall. Remember that. And good-bye," the D.A. said, and Wasco walked out of the office and down the stairs to the County Jail in a state of such euphoria that he forgot the first three steps and almost broke his fucking neck, and the neck of his burly accompanying guard, tumbling down the clanging iron stairway. . . . Cause, by then, shit! That old Grand Design, it was already total and under control, right inside Wasco's wiggy gourd!

And by the next week, after Wasco'd had a chance to go over those important and highly informative confidential records in the D.A.'s private file room, and after he'd sent Moke out to Bert's Beanery, where Aunt May worked, to answer a waitressing ad, and after Moke'd gone over to City College to sign up for Creative Writing I for next semester, and after she came back next visiting hours reporting that not only had she gotten the job, and gotten into Elaine's class handily, but Wasco's little college-going cousin Arv happened to have signed up for the same fucking course, Wasco's joyfulness was so complete that he became almost irretrievably convinced that God was on his and the old D.A.'s side. Cause the only flaw in the Grand Design up to that time had been: *how the fuck do we get that caca-liberal cuz of mine who is also our one indispensable talent in on the deal?* Now, Wasco'd known pretty well that it'd have to be real round-about, getting that Little Arv to help out. Knew the little fairy was a Commie-leaning, radic-lib, Joe College asshole type who would resist all efforts to enlist him in any real patriotic endeavors. And Wasco'd racked his damn brains trying to figure out how to do it. And then, bam! It'd just been laid upon him like that, on a magic platter!

We'll start him out slow, Wasco had planned to himself, before the big news, *we'll corrupt him first for what he figures is "a good cause," and then at our leisure, we'll nail the little motherfucker holding the goods, and blackmail his ass into anything we want! It's gonna be ticklish, working the Slow Shuck on him. It's gonna be rough as winning a mustang with canned carrots.*

And then, shit! It got laid right in their lap like that. They didn't even have to work for it!

Yes, sir, Wasco thought, somewhat more subdued, after he'd calmed down a bit, *that old Arv. But he ain't dumb. Might be chicken, but he ain't that stupid. What if he don't go for that old Slow Shuck birdshit? Well,* Wasco figured, *maybe he won't go for the shit, but he'll sure fall for the bird! Har har. Cause he ain't never seen anything like Moke. Never! and never will again. Cause he just ain't got enough class for a woman like her, ordinarily. And she could charm the gold outa old Getty himself, by Christ, I'd bet on it!*

Then Wasco considered old Arv's ancient challenge out on the dirt football field at the Joint, back when they was just itty-bitty kids . . . "Just you wait!" Little Arv said, crying real hard, looking up at Wasco, shaking his little curled-up white fists, "I'll get even someday! I swear I will! I swear!" And Wasco thought now, *Well, so what? Even if the kid figures the whole scam, there's a chance he might bite anyways . . . as a kinda personal way to lay it down that he ain't scared of his big old cuz no more. . . .*

The slight risk that Arv might not fall totally for the Slow Shuck that Wasco had planned out, as part of his Grand Design, or that he might go along with it only till he could shuck Wasco in return . . . with English . . . only made the whole proposition more attractive and exciting to Wasco . . . *more kinky that way,* he thought, as he often thought of a lot of negative possibilities in his life . . . even the most negative of all . . . getting zeroed out . . . death . . . by freakish accident, terrible disfiguring disease, treachery . . . How kinky! Woo!

The Slow Shuck routine that Wasco was pulling on Arv, it was an old scam, one of the oldest in the Joint.

Wasco was using a little variation on it with Arv, but in its classical formula it went like this: first you got a foxy lady on the Street. Then you got some prison guard to start bringing in and taking out little things, crystals, rainbows maybe, cart-wheels, yellow-jackets, reds, nickel and dime bags of coke, paying him real well, spicing it up with "sexual favors" from the chick. Now, up to this point, it wasn't a very serious proposition at all. At least a third of the cons were hooked legal anyway. The shrinks in the Joint handed out Darvon and Valium and codeine and a hundred other pain killers and tranqs and uppers and downers by the bottleful to keep the gunsels quiet.

Anyway, then the convict starts asking for heavier and heavier things, tools for escape, guns, Communist literature, smack, crank, grass . . . whatever he was into. Blackmailing the hack when he hesitates. Threatening him with exposure, murder. Threatening his baby's ass. Meanwhile he's paying the screw less and less. Putting him into a funk. Terrifying him and browbeating him till he's a virtual slave. Then he gets the guard to run a very heavy caper. A twenty-piece smack deal, for instance. The convict makes his fortune, because another third of the dudes inside got an illegal habit they brought in from the Street, and smack in the Joint costs just like Outside.

So after the hack does this one last number, the con lets him off the hook with a big tip. He's so goddamned relieved that he ain't dead, and so happy for the money (considering his lousy little pittance of a state salary) that he never says boo-coo shit to the authorities. Then the con just sits back and does his time, hiring the best lawyers that money can buy to make his time as short and sweet as possible, sure that when he gets out he'll have enough bread to last for a good long while. . . .

So after all Wasco's fretting and planning, that's more or less just how it happened. Except that Moke shucked Arv without even having to do it slow. Got him to agree to everything without any fuss at all. Shucked that teacher chick, that Elaine Mourutsos, even before she shucked Arv. . . .

Moke went up to see her after class one time, after a couple of months, after she'd gotten to know the Commie bitch real good, after Moke'd let it be known on several occasions that she was the one rabid Pig-eating New Lefty girl. Approached her with what Moke knew she'd jump

at: the golden opportunity to send secret letters in to Mr.
J-Boo in the Joint. Moke said, "I wanna help out against
them fucking Pigs," or something like that, "I hate 'em!
Got gang-banged, raped by three off-duty prison hacks
when I was hitchhiking out on the freeway one time," she
said, or something better than that. That's what Wasco
suggested she say. But Moke was smoother than Wasco in
a lot of ways, so he gave her plenty of rein. Sometimes
you just couldn't figure out how she achieved such fan-
fucking-tastic results. But one thing you could always
count on: she came through, that Kanaka! She came
through! So, Moke says, "I know a guard who I think will
carry stuff in to your man, when he gets sent up here to
the Joint."

"Who's that?" the chick asks.

"Arvin Weed," Moke says, "he's in your class."

"Shit," the chick says, "he won't do it! I already asked
him. He's as piggish as the rest of 'em!"

"Maybe so," Moke says, "but I'm betting he's just a little piglet, at heart," real sentimental, she said it, like she
was hot for the cat.

"I bet he won't do it," the chick says.

"I bet he will!" says Moke.

"Alright," this Elaine says, "go ahead and try, but I'm
telling you, it won't get you nowhere."

Blew her fucking mind when Moke comes up to her
next day after class and says, "Okay, Elaine, he says he'll
do it."

"What?" she says, "I don't believe it!"

"Ask him," says Moke.

"How'd you do it?" she asks.

"That's my secret, honey," Moke says.

So, anyway, that's how Wasco's Grand Design got
transformed into a work of total perfection, a work of the
highest patriotic art, and the most flawless criminality . . .
just like the old D.A. ordered. . . .

Wasco was a natural-born unrepentant ferocious criminoid motherfucker, and admitted it. Why not? Nothing to
be ashamed of. He engaged in business just like anybody
else. It's a dog eat dog world, out in the world of affairs.
Anybody'd tell you that. There had to be hanky-panky or
you wouldn't win. And business only respects a winner.
Wasco couldn't see how he was any worse than, say, ITT
down in Chile, inciting rebellion against the forces of evil,

the counterbusiness, counterprogress elements . . . people'd get killed in that kind of operation too . . . but that
was part of the game.

But well, not that Wasco was all that hardnosed either.
Wasco was a dreamer too. Always had been. Just to pass
the time away. On the bus from Haley today he'd
dreamed a whole long cycle of love and betrayal and revenge and sex and murder. It was better than going to the
movies, and he didn't mean no harm by it. It was just like
a movie, real violent, with a lot of fucking in it, that you
might watch. Now he dreamed again, dreaming his new
original drama, waiting for them to unlock the squeeze
and him to go to chow. He dreamed the Great Escape this
time. Even though, in real life, he was too smart for that.
Knew the grounds like the back of his hand from the time
he was five and knew the Joint was escapeproof. If the
guns didn't get you the sharks or the treacherous currents
would. Even though Wasco knew he'd pull his whole
time, the whole bit, the entire slat (because he *wanted*
to), even though he knew escape was impossible, an un-
makable caper, even so, he dreamed of the institution garbage dump and the abandoned World War II airfield with
the rusting C-46 still crouching there, squatting in fog and
rain, winter in and winter out, dreaming too, like Wasco,
of the impossible flight, not even really wanting it, maybe,
just teasing itself, its piston engines quivering with simulated desire, its propellers slow and waiting, its sagging
wings and fatigued metal fuselage dreaming the sound of
wind slapping, the weight of air, the slow climb, the
banked turn, the slough and the Sound far below. Wasco,
for a moment, became the old C-46 in person and then,
shortly before the crash, he abandoned the rusty old thing
to its fate, erased its flight, expunged it from history, left
it sitting there on the weeded-up runway for the entire remainder of eternity. . . . Instead, he hid out after he went
over the Laundry Wall, hid among the piles of prison refuse, tin cans, soggy cardboard boxes and rotting food in
the garbage dump, dreamed of running through the tule
beds just after the twelve o'clock count, and then out
along the long wharf that ran out into Paradise Cove,
where they used to tie the prison ships in the old days,
bullets from Gun Towers #3, #4, #5, #6, and #7
pattering all around him on the wood, chipping at it,
reaching a powerful speedboat with honest Moke warming

it up. Bullets fleeing after them, burrowing into the wood
and the mud, kicking up spray in the water, stinging, hitting at them, striking his thigh, his shoulder. OOh! They
got me! Then they spun that plastic yellow monster of a
blown Jimmy-engined power cruiser and split, swooped
out, roared across the Cove, tracers whizzing orange-col-
ored all around, smacking into them, piercing the plastic
shell, stitching it through, finally, just off Holly Island,
sinking them, getting their ship. But it turned out to be
lucky, see, cause there was this Coast Guard launch waiting for them off the Santa Caterina Peninsula with
a thirty-caliber machine gun. Swam to shore under cover
of darkness with that strong-swimming mermaid, that fish-
woman, that Moke-bitch, slippery as eels, their cold-
blooded sharky blood staining the inky oil-smelling water.
Washed up on a deserted beer-can beach. Searchlights
playing the sound and the shore. Dragging the bottom for
them between island and beach. 'Hey! They must have
drowned! Nobody can swim in them Straits!" He fucked
her then. He fucked her a great Honkey victory fuck and
she hollered out in her Hawaiian pidgin English: "OOH!
You da kine! You da stud! Fuck 'em up, big Haole!" And
he didn't. Not at first. He tickled her brown Kanaka
quiver, her baby pineapple dork, her Primo Warrior, her
Moke mound, ran the tip of his bleeding tongue over it
till it grew like a kitty dick. Noisy. Wet and dribbles.
Went down on it like a hungry rat, ignoring her cunt,
squeaking at her hard little clit, her pussy whipping up a
froth like a heavy sea, dilating like labor, like baby coming home. Sucking crazy, man, sucking goofy fucking
wild! Wait till she's just a taste away from island paradise.
Then stop. Tease it. Tickle it. Now drive home, motherfucker, assbackwards! Drive it on downtown!

Goddamn, Wasco was thinking, *you know what? I'm a
poet, And my feet show it. They're Longfellows. Har har
har har! I am, though. I'm the man of the rap. The poet
of the scam. The king of the stony wailers. Ain't nobody
beats old Mister Wasco P. Fucking Weed!*

Now that Moke, Wasco was thinking too, *that girl, she
has accomplished all and more than her daddy has
deemed. My my my my! But that girl loves her old man,
don't she? Ain't nothing she wouldn't do! Cause he gives
her what she wants and needs and got to have: money.
Cause it sure as shit ain't sex or love. Money, so she can*

*get the best. The best that money can buy in everything
from dope to fucking candelabras. Cause she wants class,
that little Moke. She thinks her old daddy don't know.
Shit! If I hadn't of seen that in her eyes when I met her in
the first place I'd a never tied up with that chick. She
thinks like I think. Like a businesswoman. Only one thing
in this world that keeps things straight: money. U.S.
Mint. You got bread out in front, there's never complications. Without it you got chaos. It's the greatest equalizer,
justice-maker, honesty-inducer in the world today. Money
is a form of trust. Trust is a form of love. Love is the finest emotion in man's experience. That's what I feel for
that little slant. Affection and trust and love for all that
good scratch she brings in. And there ain't nothing, baby,
nothing in this here fucking universe that could induce old
Wasco to forsake his one and only true friend, his love,
his sweetmeat, his moneymaker, Miss Moke! And the
same goes for her man. Ain't nothing could make her give
up on her big daddy! Oh, no? What about Little Arvie?
Sheeeeit! The little fellah just ain't a real dude yet. When
he is we'll get him all set up. Ain't got nothing against
him. Him being family and all. Nothing but the best for
the old Stinkweeds! Not that he can't make his little con-
tribution to the family coffers. Him being the most fan-
fucking-tastic sharpshooter this Joint's ever seen! No reason not to put the little pip-squeak jerk to work, is there?
Why, hell no!*

Later on the bull opened up the tier and let Wasco and
the squeeze out for chow.

"Listen, Squeeze, you stick close behind me but not too
close, you dig? Don't press me and I'll see you don't get
shanked."

The squeeze didn't say nothing and did like Wasco told
him. He was the first private in Wasco's army. If he
obeyed orders Wasco would see he was promoted up the
ranks in the future. And if he carried out his orders faith-
fully, no telling how high he could go in the organization
before he became expendable.

The screw herded them into the foyer of the East Block
and around through the Control Point Rotunda and out
across the Main Yard to the Dining Hall. Wasco bopping
along happy as could be. Relaxed. Comfortable sticky in
the jockey shorts. Pubes pressed together like a wire-

haired terrier. *Glued with my own juice I am, cause
prison is my home.*

Wasco looked close at the floors smooth and shiny as
dry ice from a billion sweepings and moppings and wax-
ings. He smelled the good pine oil antiseptic smell. He
checked those pretty institution-green pastel walls and
ceilings. Within a week he'd know every crack, every
flaw, every blemish and hump in the chow hall, would
create maps and worlds and universes joyfully from their
contours.

They waited a long quiet time in the chow line. The
other cons stared, the old studs. Everybody looking at the
fish, the newcomers, very interested. With interest but no
love. With hatred and laziness. With evil intent but no
out-front reaction. Like a mean old curse that cancels itself out. Wasco thought of it as a kind of warm welcome,
under the circumstances. It was familiar too. All at once
all the fish, feeling just like Wasco, started talking to each
other in spurts. Even the squeeze tried to get in a word
and Wasco had to cut him short. All the fish seemed to
feel like, wow! at least somebody recognizes us! Look!
We're alive after all. Feel, baby, gimme pain, gimme skin,
I don't care. Cause I'm real, I'm a human fucking bean
too standing here in a room full of other human beans
who would, sure, who would hate my guts, who would
love me . . . would love my butt, my body and my balls,
who would even pay me the ace-high, the king of compli-
ments: *who would murder me if they could.* If they were
sure they could get away with it. Rip me up the gizzard.
With no regrets. A very warm welcome! That's what
Wasco liked about the Joint. It was concrete, neat, and
complete! You always knew where you were at. On the
Street, you don't know what's going to happen. Here everything is sure. Just like his old man used to say when
Wasco was a kid, the *only* thing the old sonofabitch ever
said, he said, "Shitfire! I'd rather be a goddamned bull in
the Joint any day than a cop on a beat on the Street; out
there you don't know when some loco might mow you
down. Here, if they're gonna do it, you know it, so you're
waiting for it . . ." And he was right. It's the only thing
the old fart said, and he was right. He had a hundred per
cent record of rectitude, and that ain't bad! Very few
dudes can say that about themselves. Sure, the old man
was right, Wasco felt it all the way down to his motorcy-

cle boots, which, as he looked around, seemed to have already put a sparkle of cutthroat envy in some dudes' eyes. He'd have to fight to keep them. He'd have to use his wits, scheme and plot, sleep with one eye open. Hell, he'd get by. *I'm me!* We are all brothers under the skin. We are deadly enemies. I hate you, you motherfuckers. I love you. Look at me! I'm jealous and sexy and alive! That's the way all of them were thinking.

A fat mess sergeant dressed up all in white was standing to the side of the Food Service Rack supervising an officer who was supervising a white trusty who was supervising a black man who was dishing out the cake. The cake was the only part of the meal that needed any supervision cause that's the only thing anybody would conceivably ever fight over. The rest was just Shit on a Shingle. Toast and creamed corn beef, and a portion of canned peas. If the black man gave out a little too much cake, the screw would call to the trusty who would call to the black man who would call the con back and tell him to cut some off. "No favoritism," the screw would say, loud enough for the porky mess sergeant to hear. He was a tall yellow-skinned Okie, the screw, with a receding chin and a big Adam's apple. Wasco was sure he was one of the Baptist Seminary students from Mission Santa Bonita who swing-shifted it, working their way through seminary. Just like Little Arv, probably. That's what he does. Goes to City College, marking up them points, rapping with them hippy chicks, *and another one.* Oh . . . I bet she got that cat going! Got him down to business already, I bet, under control. If I done it before I can do it again. Shit, old Wasco, he'd had that clean-cut Mr. Arvin at fingertip, dancing to the beat of *his* tom-tom, for seventeen fucking years, for most of the little chickenshit's life. "Sure, Wasco! Whatever you say, Wasco." Maybe he could get Arv to get the squeeze a job as server on the food line till they got the other business going full blast. Food is money. Money is love. Love is power. Power is time. Time is immortal. You buy time, you live forever. . . . Wasco made a mental note to write that down as soon as he got back to his cell. He made another mental note to buy himself a pen and notebook as soon as he got some bread together. Every time he was in the joint he filled a little green notebook. Pearls of philosophical wisdom. Word games. Puzzles. Aphorisms. He always spent his

time productive. Learning things. Looking things up in the
dictionary. When he hit the Street he was always ready to
lay down a barrage of words, words that would spook
them. A fretful forgetful fog of words, a low-lying tule
fog of poetry, devil's verse, that would mystify them, send
them up the wall in wonder at his absolute heaviness, his
powerful and original jailhouse brilliance. He'd hit frat
parties, maybe, this time, City College, professors' cocktail
hours, scientific soirees, faculty teas . . . stagger them
fucking fairies with his audacious perceptions: "Yeah!
Food is love. Love is money. Money is power. Power is
time. You got enough to eat, you got love. You got
enough love, you got money. You got enough money, you
got power. You got enough power, you got time. You got
enough time, you've won eternity! The happiest man in
the world is a sloppy fat rich powerful loving Kike. He's
got all the time in the universe. He can even buy time
from God, the Temple, and the County Hospital . . ."

The black man slopped the Shit on a Shingle onto
Wasco's metal tray and he set off across the chow hall to
find an empty table. Above him, on the gunwalk, a squat
black Pig paced up and down, swinging his sawed-off
shotgun. Wasco paid him no mind.

In the Joint you never sit down unless you been asked.
Wasco wasn't asked. In the Joint you don't make waves.
Or, if you do, you soon find your gills slit up to your
ears, sliced down the center like a carp, or your pee-wee
peeled off, unraveled, packed into your cut-off and empty
ballbag like mutton in grape leaves in A-rab land and festooned on the bars of your cell.

Wasco spotted a four-place table on the other side of
the room and raced for it, almost upsetting his coffee in
his haste to evade the skinny junkie kid who was still on
his tail. But not too fast to watch out for "accidentally"
stuck-out feet in his path. He dodged one little Wop's
tripping high-tops and catalogued his face, while behind
him he heard the squeeze go down, heard the food tray
hit the floor, and a face splattered on the cement, and
loud raucous laughter, and Wasco just kept motating. File
that tripper's face away. Photographic memory for the
punks who are the enemy. Strike first when you know.
Never let 'em know what hit 'em. Or else it's you out
there laying offed in the mud puddles of the Yard.

Wasco reached the table at the same moment as an el-

derly white man who looked like he was alright. Looked
like he minded his own business, did his time. He right
away started slopping down the Shit as fast as he could.
Didn't say a word. Then he slipped off. Con-wise. Do
your time. After he was gone two Mexicans sat down
when Wasco gave a nod and started chattering in Chicano bop talk very rapido, sliding their slippery tongues
real sensual over the usual hard "ch" sound of ordinary
Spic: "Ay shingao," they said, "era una shamacaaaaaaa!"
They didn't pay him no mind either. He appreciated that.
He liked to hear them rap. He liked hearing something
suave and slippery that you couldn't understand. Quick he
did in the Shit and then looked around the room for old
friends, checking the action. He saw a few dudes from
Dewayne Vocational Institution and one from the old
days at Prill Reformatory, a little Puerto Rican with a
bright red hennaed Afro and cat-green eyes. They recognized each other but pretended like it didn't happen. Bugger brothers, they were; *amigos.* Oh, them nights up in the
mountains at Prill. The "Mother Load Country," they
used to call it. Locking themselves into the broom closet
off the TV room. As good as any mama. Sweet and soft
sucking. Real gentle. Never bit. Didn't mind if you did.
But this time the dude wasn't buying. Had a new sugar.
Some black-ass Muslim, probably, with a sixteen-inch
prison-made shank waiting in somebody's dark. *In my
dark. In my dark future there's a long one.*

Nothing of interest. Wasco took his head elsewhere,
over the wall to the employees' housing area, where his
old house was, and school, and Cousin Arv, out to the
ball diamond, the dirt basketball court with the basketless
hoop, the sandy football field, out on the brown summer
hills where they rode the donkey, the green winter hills
where they shot their BB guns, their .22's, used to sleep
out in summer, and the tree houses they made, the fort
they built, underground, timbered with illegally felled
pine, fashioned with their Boy Scout hatchets, their Boy
Scout knives:

"Let me stick it in, come on you little weenie, turn
over, over! Now open up, or I'll shear your fucking head
like a log . . ."

*And then he liked it. Did he really like it? Sure, he
liked it alright. But every time he imagined I'd done something against him the little chickenshit would run home*

*and take it out on Canary, just cause the donkey and me
got along. He'd hit it with a big stick and choke it with a
chain . . . I seen him once . . . and figured it was just
me he was working on . . .*

The squeeze had gone all the way through the line
again, almost crying, got his food together, avoiding the
glances, the mean looks, the laughter, of the assembled
bulls and cons, who all knew a squeeze when they saw
one, and he had gone all the way around the other side of
the chow hall, trying to avoid the Wop, the tripper, trying
to make it to his only hope, meager as it was, his only
buoy in this storm, Wasco . . . just the way old Wasco
figured it. And the little punk of course got tripped again,
and went sailing, but managed to get his footing, and save
his Shit, and tiptoe lightly, not listening to the threats and
evil giggles, through a veritable gauntlet of stuck-out feet,
and made it to Wasco's table, where he sat down, with
tears in his weak Irish punk junkie eyes. And then, and
only then, did crafty old Wasco, Ma, Ma Wasco, did she
take pity on the poor little fellah, put her big arm around
his skinny shoulders, giving him pity, shelter . . . for all
the chow hall to see, for all of them cons to see . . . just
whose squeezy the little quivering punk was!

"Now, Squeezy, don't worry," Wasco said, "them cats
who did that. You remember their faces. Old Ma going to
pay them back for you, dig it?"

And through his tears the punk smiled and nodded, just
like a kid.

When he finished chow Wasco got up and left the punk
and strolled over and lined up behind the swing-shift runner who was waiting at the iron plate door to lead all the
new men back to their holding cells. He got there early on
purpose to chat with the hack.

"Say there, Officer, I'd like to introduce myself."

"Why sure," the screw said in a Tex-Arkana accent,
very polite, just like they taught him in In-Service-Training. The place was loaded with Okies. Look out for them
Crackers. They're cold.

"My name's Wasco, Wasco G. Weed."

"Well, I'm mighty pleased to meet you, Wasco."

"Yeah, I bet you don't know something, sir. I'm related
to a lot of people around here."

"Oh yeah?"

"Sure, let's see, do you know Sergeant Big Arv Weed?"

"Listen, buddy-boy, don't gimme none of that shit!"

"It's true, ask him!"

"Lookie here, hombre, you looking for trouble, or what? You looking for special treatment?"

Wasco knew he had him. Something about old Wasco's red hair under his baldy. Something about his kewpie-doll face, the face simultaneously of a mean old woman and a willful little girl. Something in the fat Weed lips and wide Mexican Indian nose, something about the illogical cold English blue of his little slanted mongrel eyes told the hack that he was dealing with a real Weed. There was no denying it. And it struck the fear of God into his quaking cowardly Jesus-loving Okie soul, his redneck heart, his poverty-born dirt farming bowels and bones. He was up against a Weed! Yes sir! There was no missing it!

"Why, no sir!" Wasco said, threatening, mocking the Okie accent, saying with his small mean eyes just the opposite of what he was speaking with his lips.

"Listen, Officer, I just do my time. Ain't no cause to get all het up a-tall!"

And it worked. The Cracker shut his thin Scotch-Irish peasant mouth firm, clamped down on it so sudden that it trapped his scared little white tongue for a second, held it wet-tipped at the center of his long face like a dog dick a little bit aroused but uncertain and retreating back into safe foreskin. And he never said another word all the way to the holding cell.

A poet! A poet of the rap! And my feet show it . . . Har har har har!

When they were locked up Wasco made the squeeze strip and wash his ass.

"I'm being frank, man, you stink!"

"How am I going to do it with no water? They've cut the water off in the tap!"

"Do I even have to wipe your ass for you? I'm going to get pissed off at you in a minute. Take your T-shirt and wipe, see? And if it don't come up brown then call me a liar. Then throw it out on the tier, a long way down, dig?"

The squeeze bent over and set to work with his T-shirt, coy as a young girl. He was skinny and junkie-yellow, unhealthy, pop-veined, needle tracks carved up and down the inside of his arms, swollen hands, but his legs and buttocks were clean. He was still left with the remains of what was at one time a lithe strong young body. His legs were long and well-formed, his pec muscles well-defined, his fingers long and tapered, his buttocks hairless and pretty as any Greek statue; he was even hung substantial enough . . . and his face, his face was almost pretty. He looked kind of like a Greek statue, a magic faun, a young satyr. What he looked most like to Wasco was Joey Dallesandro in the movie *Heat*.

The squeeze did his business quick and shy, getting Wasco an enormous stiff blood-pounding hard-on, a hard-on he had to release, had to unzip and free from the confines where it lay trapped and hurting against the blue denim, and let it grow red, let it grow up to its full eight-inch height, let it go up to its full pride, towering at an oblique angle above his supine body like a blue-veined Pisa.

The squeeze saw it and knew in his trembling coward's heart the fear of Jesus, and Abraham and Moses, the fear of the burning Weed, the close red eyeballs, the sinister gaps between the Weedy teeth. And hopped tight-ass back up to his bunk.

Wasco let him lay there till the lights went off at 10:30. Then he let him lay there while he jacked it off twice, spurting up and hitting the springs of his mattress with an audible *schplaaaaat!* Let the punk lay there while the Okie hack came clanking along up the tiers from bottom to third, clicking his counter . . . sixty-seven, sixty-eight, sixty-nine . . . calling the numbers out loud, shining his brilliant flashlight into the always surprised and angry eyes of the convicts, owl eyes, shining in on Wasco's cold blues, his cat-eyes, that could see in the dark, illuminating his enormous renewed and redoubled erection, which seemed almost to give off a light of its own power, like a great pulsing red lighthouse on a dangerous point of land, with rocks and sirens below. . . . And Wasco still waited. His huge cock stopped the hack right in his unimaginative tracks. Jaw hanging open in amazement. His eyes all round and scared. Then the poor hack even forgot where he was, forgot even his number, and the counter at his belt that kept it for him. Forgot everything, hypnotized by that gigantic behemoth that glowed vermilion in the darkness of the cell. . . . And Wasco had to whisper, had to remind it to him through his crooked pointed wide-gapped teeth across his stiff-growing rod:

"Sixty-nine, punk, sixty-nine . . ."

And he scurried off like the rat he was down the tier, clicking frantic . . . seventy, seventy-one, seventy-two, seventy-three . . .

Then Wasco let all the block go quiet and dark, let it go all to stillness and stale warmth and the smell of farts, listening to the squeeze's short quick scared-ass junkie breathing, and then said low and sweet, talking to him, as only he could:

"Now you listen, baby, why don't you come down here and sleep with Ma."

"I don't . . ."

"Come on, honey. It's cold and lonely in here. We got to have some humanity, man, a little quiet conversation in the dark, human warmth . . ." Wasco said, picking his warm asshole and sniffing it on the end of his fingers, the right fingers, index and thumb, rolling it, like a booger, rolling and sniffing, talking to the squeeze . . .

"I . . ."

"Never mind, kid, I'm going to be your Ma. I'm going to treat you nice, get you what you need, keep you straight, dig it? All the way through your bit. With me, honey, you'll get off, you'll cop . . . every day . . ."

And as soon as Wasco mentioned sending him off with a little schmack the junkie was in his arms within ten seconds and Wasco was gentle with him that night. Talked to him real low. Broke him in slow for size (he wasn't no novice, as far as that went, but it was the size of Wasco's loaf that had to be taken into consideration).

And said: "my love, my baby, oh your skin, don't ever fix on your legs, man, or your sweet ass . . . never! Or you'll lose your trade, no lie! Oh you're so beautiful! So fair and pretty . . . like . . . like a movie star . . . like Joey Dallesandro, man, I'm not kidding!"

And the squeeze cried and Wasco kissed his thin lips, his eyes, his sniveling Irish nose, his tiny ears, out of love, out of hatred, out of pity, out of evilness and deviltry, ran his fingers through the punk's hair and the poor little guy cried all night long, telling his sad story, cradled in Wasco's huge hairy loving, hating, hurting, squeezing, nut-cracking, head-knocking tender arms. . . . His name was Arthur Hearne. But nobody ever called him Art. They called him (Wasco had guessed right . . . Wasco was always right) "Squeeze," and "Dog," and "Punk." His old man was an Irish cop who beat him. His mother suckled him till he was almost five. He grew up in a tough neighborhood in the Mission District of San Francisco, on Sanchez Street, but he was weak. He wasn't weak in his body, but he didn't have any guts, no balls, no nerve. All the kids made fun of him, made him cry. He was always the last to be chosen when they chose up sides for football. He joined the navy at seventeen, to get away. He became a medical corpsman, got a habit from dipping into the refrigerator on the aircraft carrier late at night. Got caught, was flown from the patrol area in the South China Sea to Long Binh Jail. Tried to escape, got caught, tried to commit suicide by slicing his wrists with a razor. A *typical loser's story,* Wasco was thinking. Finally he got out with a dishonorable discharge. Boosted cabs to feed his habit, cracked shorts all over the city. Did time on several real cheap beefs. Became a squeeze in order to survive in the prison environment of total terror. Was finally busted on a heavy beef, an eleven five hundred, possession of opiates, and an eleven five o one, sales . . . and so here the punk was in the flesh . . .

"Don't cry, little Squeezy," Wasco crooned, "Ma will keep you, Ma will hold you good and tight and safe; never take your Ma off, your man, or you will regret, darling; Wasco's your daddy; Wasco's in control, sweetheart, remember, and nothing can harm you . . . you just do like your Ma says . . ."

And what does junkie taste like?

A bitter pill. But real. As real as the number of your cell.

And all through the hours of darkness, with the punk cuddled up beside him, Wasco dreamed the night along, deliriously, madly, listening to the hot sweet bitter-sweet Penitentiary air blow through the ventilation duct, smelling that good Mission Santa Bonita smell of the New Sonora County Hospital where Sergeant Weed's daddy, Wasco's granddaddy, died in his own urine, soaked through his chewing tobacco-stained pajamas, "county issue," dreaming like Wasco of the future and the past, the present total and under control. . . .

Twelve

Driving home from work that night with Fast-Walking conked out beside him on the front seat, sleeping his naïve prison guard's sleep, the sleep of the innocent and the unjust, and the rain and the wind and the clouds gone far away off south to California and Mexico, and the moon coming in low over the Alverez Straits like a bomber, like a night fighter, a spy plane, Arv thought of sweet Moke, his island girl, his love from across the sea . . .

When she first showed up at the Weed house, a few days before, Arv had right away figured it was perhaps just a bit too much of a coincidence that she just happened to be in his English class at City College and just happened to work waitressing at Bert's Beanery with his mother May, and just happened to get herself invited to supper at the Weeds' on the day that he just happened to be coming to dinner. He was suspicious. And well he might have been. All prison hacks got suspicious of people after a while. They had to, for self-protection. Every guard got approached at least once in his career, by either a con or one of his outside contacts. They usually tried to seduce you into bringing contraband into the Joint. It was the oldest con game in the world. And yet, amazingly enough, a lot of guards fell for it. Started bringing in crank or smack or weapons. And then when the convict got all his money out of the deal he finked, snitched on the guard, got him fired, prosecuted. And then the poor hack ended up in the Joint himself, where the convicts harassed and browbeat him for being an ex-Pig. That's what happened to old Muffin. A black officer. A good old buddy. Got conned into doing favors for a black militant and his old lady, bringing weapons and illegal literature in for them. Muffin used to go to school with Arv. Star guard for the City College basketball team. Now he was

scoring points for the Brown Max squad. They were leading the State Prison league. Muffin high point man. As if
those fucking points did him any good at the Parole
Board.

So Arv was a little suspicious, but pleasantly suspicious,
not at all scared. Whatever she had in mind, it would be
interesting. And the way Arv's life was going, down,
down, down, with an inevitable future working at the
Joint for the rest of his life, and no hope of escape, any
change was welcome, even a change in the direction of
danger. Danger was at least adventure. And, for a man
without hope, adventure holds many imaginary marvels.

Well, anyway, that evening, Arv's day off, a week or so
back, Moke came roaring up onto the Weed front lawn
all in a black leather jump suit with a red zipper going all
the way up the front. Riding her hot red little Honda 250.
Went right up over the little hedge, leaning back and pulling hard on the handlebars and bringing the front wheel
over and then finding a tiny break for the back wheel and
doing a neat little Christy stem-turn, skidding and biting
into the inmate-trimmed lawn. "Vroom! Vroom! Vroom!"
she went, revving her fired-up little engine. And the sound
was solid glamour to old Arv. And he knew that she had
to be on the Slow Shuck. Because nobody like this would
ever come into his life otherwise. It was too good to be
true. And you know what? He didn't give a diddlyshit. *I
dreamed you up! You're unreal.*

Arv watched her from the Weed bay window, not
knowing who it was yet. She swung wide-legged off the
bike like a boy and clomped up the walkway in her heavy
black motorcycle boots, pulling her goggles up onto the
forehead of her black helmet with the red lightning streak
running down the sides. Swaggering, like a fighter pilot,
jet jockey, after an ace-making run over Hanoi, after getting three MIG's and a flotilla of sampans, stomping,
swaggering . . . CLOMP CLOMP CLOMP . . . winning Arv
before he even saw her dark face.

He couldn't see what she looked like till she got up on
the front porch and removed her helmet entirely, pulling
it off backwards over her thick black hair. He couldn't see
what she looked like, but he knew for sure she had to be
fucking gorgeous. There was no mistaking that physical
self-confidence. It came only with years of watching other

people watch you with adoring eyes. She shook her elegant head like a dark swan, freed her smoky locks that shook out all the way down to her perky little well-turned bottom. . . . She was absofuckinglutely beautiful!

Arv let his mom go to the door; she was *her* guest.

"Hi, Mokie!"

"Eh, howa you?" Moke said, brushing past Arv. And that's when he recognized her for sure. And got suspicious. And his suspicions set his heart pounding wildly. Because the thought of receiving "sexual favors" from Moke was the most tempting notion in the world. Never, never, never would he have a woman like that. Never could he attract anything like that, never, not if he lived a hundred years. And yet, for just a little run or two into the Joint, she'd be his, for a time, for a week or a month. Before he ever said a word to her, Arv, the fucked-up prison hack, in his loneliness and despair, was already seduced and lost, his fate sealed, stamped and duly signed as surely as if some great Notary Public in the sky had done the whole thing up real proper.

Yes sir! Before little Arv even got fucked, he'd been fucked over . . . royally!

He smelled her, as she went stomping past. She smelled like rain and leather and two-stroke engine oil and fragrant hair.

"Leesten," she said, "ah wunnah, can ah fina batroom to geed ouda dees ting," spinning suddenly, on parade, with the entire Weed family standing up humbly before her like an audience in their own living room, tiny bedraggly-haired Mom, fat Dad, dull normal Libby with her triple chin, and squat Arv, gawking their heads off. She was the most outrageous thing that had ever entered their prison living room. She was a fucking savage! An impossible visitor from another century, a barbaric century of fishing spears and dug-out outrigger canoes and waterless atolls and relentless suns. A flat wide Kanaka nose, a savage's nose, and thick beautiful protruding pouting lips, sexy exciting lips the color of loganberry juice or Welch-Aid, wild unblinking feline eyes that slanted up at an unhuman angle on their trailing edges . . . and *gray* gray eyes! Eyes so impossibly gray and glistening they looked almost silver. *Jesus H. Christ! I made you up!*

"Eh! You een mah class!" she squealed, playing her game out, walking up to Arv and looking him in the eye.

"Yuh, yeah," he stammered, intimidated, befuddled by the Hawaiian patois she affected (in class she spoke perfect American, was one of the very best. students, and very articulate, quite as articulate as Arv himself, if not more).

"Say, dat someting!" she said, wiggling in front of him, going almost too far with her play, her game, but not quite.

Finally he laughed. It broke the ice. The rest of the family realized that the accent was a joke, and laughed too. Now Moke apparently thought she could shut it off, since she'd had her little joke, and she said in perfectly clear Standard American, "So, the bathroom's in there?"

"Right," May said, and showed her the way.

Standing there in the little green Weed living room, with the ragged sofa and the imitation leather armchair and the Sears Roebuck TV blaring the Six O'Clock News: "Chances Dim at Paris Peace Talks," Arv and his old man just shuffled around on their big feet, not saying anything, looking uncomfortably alike (for Arv's taste). When that scrumptious little island thing came back into the room it was like a foreign torpedo breaking into their sealed hull. Neither one of them could utter a word. Even Mom and Libby, they couldn't say anything either. Moke was wearing a red low-cut minidress. That's all. No shoes, stockings, earrings, lipstick. Nothing but that mini that cut her shapely nut-colored thighs just this side of wonder. Big Arv just about dropped his teeth. She was such an exotic curvaceous little thing. Not much taller than Arv's tiny red-nosed mom. Her luscious edible little body literally brought water to Arv's mouth, as it did daily in their class at City College when, hypnotized, Arv followed her perfect small tits when she moved at her desk, tits as round and sweet and juicy looking as mandarin oranges. Or at least, that's the way Arv told it to himself every time he saw her.

Big Arv finally got up the gumption to talk. "Say there, honey," he said, "how's about a beer before supper?"

"Shu," she said, resuming her pidgin, "eev you cut da foam weed a knife."

Big Arv laughed uncertainly, probably what she wanted, and left the room with May and Libby, all of them heading out to the kitchen to hasten supper . . . and to get away from this bigger-than-life thing, this something from another world who had entered their stale-smelling lives.

Arv gathered up the courage when they were gone and, summoning all his strength of will, attempted to sound cool and offhand. Conspiratorially, one young hip City College student to another, he said, with painful attempted brightness, "Wow, if I'd known who was on after my old lady I'd've been over there every night!"

"I wish you had," she said, real friendly, laughing, thrilling him, aiding him nicely in forming his earnestly and obviously and tentatively sought conspiracy of youth and learning and hipness in a land of squares and boors, "you don't know how boring it gets with that old lush Bert!"

"Oh Jesus, I can imagine. And I know how my old lady can bend your ear . . . I hope she . . ."

"Oh, no! Lookit, she's beautiful, really. I mean, she *will* tipple now and again," Moke said sincerely, accurately, and yet smiling and kind and very hip, letting Arv know where it was at with her culturally and intellectually, "but she's one of these ladies from my mother's scene, the World War II long bar scene, the Carmen Miranda and Betty Grable scene, the . . ." She searched for an additional phrase. It was Arv's cue. She was trying to find out where he was at . . .

". . . The . . . right! . . . the high-piled ratted hair scene, the bonnets piled up with fruit, and front room pillows made of shiny silk with pictures of Manila Bay and aircraft carriers with 'Bring the Fleet Home' written on it," he offered, desperately trying. As if it had really been that way. As if he'd really been trying to really win her. As if he'd had a real chance without falling, or having to fall for the Slow Shuck . . . the pack-mule scam, without becoming the muleback man . . .

"Right!" she said, and Arv, refusing to believe he was being used, honestly felt he'd passed her first test, the first test that a chick who's interested in you always throws out, when she's genuine, and wants to know who you are.

Moke continued as if her train of thought had not been interrupted. ". . . They're honest, those ladies, I've found. And even though they got a few minor flaws like overimbibing occasionally and nagging and bending your mind and ear with their loneliness, they are, I've really found, especially working as a waitress, in general pretty good-natured, trustworthy and . . . they come through when they're needed. And, well, like that's more than I can say for a lot of people *our* age!"

"Hey! You're right!" Arv exclaimed, absolutely overwhelmed by her, gamely attempting not to choke on her, trying not to sound too uncool, trying not to sound like just another prison hack, "uh . . . I think she's like that. Yeah, and I agree with you about our generation . . . Can't trust 'em!"

Before Arv could make a total fool of himself Big Arv came in and saved him.

"Here's your beer, honey. Cut the head clean off!"

"Thanks," she said, raising her face up to him, regarding his mountainous belly that hung over his wide belt just inches from her nose. "May tells me just about everyone in your family works at the prison . . ."

"That's right," Big Arv said, shuffling around on his triple E's, squinting up his eyes the way he always did around threatening, that is to say, pretty, women.

And that's just about all there was to be said . . . nobody could think of anything to offer the conversation. The three of them would have just sat there on the sofa and the artificial leather chair till the end of time, Arv felt, with nothing but shit to talk, if it hadn't been for May's cheery dinner call:

"Okay! Come and get it, you guys!"

Arv rose quickly and showed Moke to the seat May directed him to, next to him, opposite sister Libby, who sat alone, poor fat thing, sucking her gums like always. They all sat down and Moke wet her thick lips with an upward motion of her rough catty little tongue, displaying its erotic purple bottom. And Arv's heart was won. He let her know it. He looked at her and he raised his eyebrows ironically and stared openly, letting her know that he knew her scam too, knew it well, and didn't care, didn't give a damn! *Go ahead! Take advantage of me! Stomp me! Beat me! Break my balls! Nothing could be worse than where I'm at now. Look at this scum! This shoddy scummy dining room. These freaks, these dull normal obscene freaks who are my own . . . who are me . . . Look at them! Do you think I'd spend even an instant making my choice! I'll take romance and the road of crime and*

an early death. Anything but this! Anything! That's the
way Arv was thinking. That's what he was sending out to
her. That's what he let her read in his sad bleary orbs.
And she dug it. He saw her dig it. She smiled . . .

And then they all fell to, eating away at the normal
Weed speed, like crazed locusts, eating the normal Weed
fare, the invariable Weed repast of wilted lettuce and
mealy tomato salad soaked in inferior stale supermarket
vinegar and oil, and the soggy overcooked carrots and
tasteless canned peas, the greasy fried potatoes, rotten
cut-rate chuck steak, a canned fruit dessert.

"Say, couldn't we have something better for dessert?"
Libby foolishly complained when they were finishing up,
holding her fat tummy, not succeeding at restraining her
heavy rumbling belch.

"What you complaining about," Big Arv demanded angrily, "in front of guests! Most people around here don't
even get dessert!"

And it was true. Most of the Okie, Arkie and Texas-
born WASPS around there, and the shanty Irish, never had
dessert, as far as Arv knew, never got past the doughy instant dumplings and mashed potatoes, the frozen pre-
cooked fries, the canned Mulligan stew, Dinty Moore
brand, considering dessert ("deezert," they called it) a
rather lewd and Latin extravagance that "them Spanish"
were always indulging themselves in, going to needless expense over supper.

"Well, guess who's getting transferred into the Joint?"
Little Arv asked the table at large, breaking an unwritten
prison guard's law to change the subject: *never bring the
Joint home with you.*

"Galliot!" chorused May and her tubby daughter, oblivious of Arv's indecorous breech of Joint etiquette. May
was spry as ever now, after her afterwork hours' furious
chug-a-lugging, if you expected the bright pinky color of
her alcoholic's unanonymous nose. It was amazing how
she did it. A two-hour nap and she was raring to go again,
anticipating the warm hidden six-pack she cached under
her bed.

"Who told you?" Big Arv wanted to know, picking his
nose absent-mindedly, the way that indicated "curiosity"
in his extraordinary lexicon of personal mannerisms, mannerisms so defined and vulgar and perfect they should

have been invented by a brilliant cartoonist, an Al Capp
or an R. Crum.

"Why, everybody knows that," Libby said, "ain't
nothin' a secret in the Joint."

"Don't say 'Joint,' honey, that's vulgar," May corrected,
"say 'institution.' Anyways, it ain't no surprise, is it? Mrs.
Blankenship seen him over there in the city when he was
doing that dance of his with all them . . . all them . . ."

May, glancing around, not sure of her ground, with
Moke in the room, had been about to say "them niggers,"
or at least "them colored," but thought better of it and
changed the subject unembarrassedly in mid-sentence,
confident that the normal frequency with which she lost
the thread of her thoughts would hide her error.

"It's that there war that's to blame," she continued
without a falter, "stirring them all up. What we doing
over there anyway? Better tend to business right here at
home. Like I tell your dad. Just like with your damn old
Aunt Evie. She's bad seed. Let that kid Wasco run wild
and now he's gone bad too. Run off on him when he was
just a little bitty fellah. Now *some people* think up all
kinds of excuses . . . hanging out over there at her place
in Mexican Town all the time. When they got plenty better to do right here at home . . . for the little money that
comes out of it . . ." May said, trying to get a rise out of
Big Arv.

"Well," Little Arv said, endeavoring to change the subject again fast, so May wouldn't start going on about Aunt
Evie again, of whom she was insanely jealous, "I tell you
what. Them 'peace talks' over there in Paris, France . . .
you been keeping up with them on TV? They ain't worth
a good goddamn, it seems like to me. I know, cause I
been over in the Nam. What that Nixon's got to do is either shit or get off the damn pot, don't you think? Either
'bomb 'em back to the Stone Age,' like the man says, or
pick up and come on back home."

Arv, as he always did around his old man and his old
lady, employed a vocabulary and inflection he no longer
used anywhere else. And, to save time and trouble, he always tried to agree with them about everything, always
tried to tell them exactly the kind of thing they'd want to
hear. He knew from bitter years of experience that it was
the only way to avoid endless complications. His parents

were far too ignorant and opinionated and set in their
narrow ways to change now. All argument with them was
pointless. Arv winked now quickly at Moke and was grati-
fied by her secret smiling response. She dug what he was
up to. Probably had to do the same thing at home . . .

"Honey," May said, grinning indulgently, "now you
stop using language like that at the dinner table, hear? We
got company tonight!"

"Well I don't know," Big Arv said, leaning back on his
food-splattered chair at the head of the table and picking
his teeth with his unclean thumbnail, answering Arv but
looking at May as if she'd made that statement about
Vietnam. "When Little Arv left for Vietnam down at Burney Field that time, he looked kind of white-faced to me.
Kind of like the blood just drained right out of his damn
head. And that time during that Tet thing, don't you all
remember? Wrote home that he was sure to get killed
. . . scared the living daylights out of him."

The Weed family habitually changed subjects at the
dinner table as rapidly and capriciously as they changed
their volatile moods. Their talk never had much to do
with "conversation" as an exchange or exposition of ideas.
It served as simply a kind of release mechanism for their
petty pent-up hates and peeves, their emotions, raw emotions, dumb, inchoate, animal, but charged up with a dy-
namo-sized load of unachieved, unachievable human desires and needs.

The fact that Big Arv's talk now had nothing to do with
the conversation made no difference to Arv—he cringed.
He didn't know what to say back to him. He was in a
quandary, a quandary of his father's cunning design. If
Little Arv defended himself, having to lie to do it (he *had*
been scared during Tet, scared nearly to death), him and
his father would get into it again, starting a great big
family fight. If he let it go, Moke would think him a coward. Arv therefore took the extraordinary measure of ad-
mitting the truth, hoping to evoke her sympathy . . .

"Yeah, that's right. I was scared."

"Sure, honey, anybody with any sense'd be scared,"
May said, taking her son's part, as she always did.

Big Arv, of course, always did the opposite, disagreed
with whatever Arv said on principle.

"Sheeeeeit!" he said, "what you mean, May? That Little

Arv, he's tough, ain't he? When I think about it I don't
believe anything could scare that kid. Why, I can't think
of a man in the Joint who's tougher and meaner than old
Arvie. 'Marvie-Arvie' the kids used to call him. Right,
May? Remember that time he licked the whole housing
area out in that boxing ring I rigged up? Har har har
har!"

"Stop it!" May said, rising to her feet. "Goddamnit
Arv, you quit tormenting that kid!"

"Aw, sit down! And he ain't no kid. He's a grown man
with a kid of his own. Even though you'd never know it
. . . hiding behind his ma's apron strings all his life." Big
Arv was positively unable to address his son in the second
person in company.

"Who's gonna make me sit down?"

"*I* am, if you don't stuff something in that there
blowhole of yours!"

Libby began to cry. Arv Junior rose to his feet and offered Moke his arm. It was the daily ritual, starting up as
usual. Arv's parents hated each other so much they
couldn't even hold it in for company. This scene tonight
represented a real effort on both their parts to "be nice"
for their guest. There was nothing they could do about it
anymore. Actually they loved it, couldn't live without its
daily revivifying effects; it was the only drama in their
surpriseless lives, the only constant renewal of emotion.

"Now ain't you ashamed of yourselves?" Arv asked,
feeling a little guilty that he hadn't come to the defense of
his mom, who had come to his defense unselfishly, and
suffered for it, more times than he could count. But he
couldn't. He blamed them both, solely because he couldn't
put the entire blame where it lay, was afraid to . . .
still . . .

"You two just gotta stop this!" he said mildly.

"Right!" Libby said, tossing her kinky dun-brown hair,
"really! I never heard of such a thing!" As if she didn't
hear it every day of her life. "You haven't let our guest
get a word in edgewise!"

"Come on out to the living room," Arv said, leading
Moke by her bare brown elbow, hairless elbow, warm
dry-skin elbow that beat against his fingers, that thrust
into his sweaty white palm, exciting him.

It turned out to be worth the hassle. Arv was really a

very shy person, unsure of himself around women. But something about his profound shame of his family, and the horrid depressing plebeian supper, and the stupid pointless family squabbling, made him ask Moke if she wouldn't like to go to the movies in Mission Santa Bonita. In his mind Moke had already become associated with the possibility, elusive, less than tentative, of escape from this claustral environment, this prison of his heredity, these bonds of chance that held him.

"I'd love to," she said, smiling at him. Her bright white teeth, teeth so perfect and tiny and pearly and sharp as to have almost been honed one by one by a small careful leprechaun with a minuscule file, gleamed in the yellow light of the stand-up lamp behind the sofa.

Libby, fat and ugly and grittily Weed but always a good sport, said, "Sure, that's a great idea. I wish I could come but I got homework. Have a good time!"

Moke got her things together and said good-bye to May, who ran out from the kitchen apologizing profusely.

Big Arv lumbered out behind her.

"Don't worry about it none, honey. That's just the way we are around here," he said, perceiving Arv's success with the beautiful Hawaiian, trying to fuck him up with her, as he always did when he saw Arv with a groovy chick.

"Come on, let's go," Arv said, and hustled her out the door before the old man tried to screw his act up some more.

"Whew!" he said, as soon as they were out the door, "neurotic, huh?"

"Are you kidding?" She laughed. "Sounds just like home! Sounds just like my folks before they died."

"I guess you're right," he said, "American as cherry pie and hollow-headed bullets!"

"Sure!" she said, "American as Agnew!"

"American as overkill!" Arv shouted, laughing heartily, as they ran in the rain across the lawn toward the waiting Merc.

"I think we're gonna get it on," she said, as soon as they were in the car, as if she were surprised by that notion, as if she hadn't already designed it that way, as if she hadn't already spun her web . . .

"Yeah, hey! I think maybe you're right," he said, fully

cognizant of that design, that web, his heart racing with the starting motor as he cranked the Merc over.

"Hey! What about my bike?" she asked.

"We'll pick it up on the way back," he said, confident now, cheered on by her friendliness, however affected, and their sudden rapport.

"On our way back from where?" she asked, blinking her long black lashes rapidly, doing a ham coquette number to make him laugh.

"From devouring your mandarin oranges."

"Mandarin oranges? Me no got no mandarin oranges!"

"Oh, but you *do,* my pet!" he said, tweaking his moustaches, rolling them, ogling her like a villain in a cartoon melodrama.

"I'm a night owl," she said irrelevantly, as they drove out past the institution firing range toward the freeway.

"Oh yeah? I'm the same way," he lied, "but I got to pick up my friend at the Joint tonight. He's staying with me over in the city. Gets off at twelve."

"Who's that?"

"My friend, Frank Miniver. 'Fast-Walking,' we call him."

"How come you call him that?"

"You'll see."

"No, tell me!" she insisted, pouting, leaning up against him while he swung the Merc out onto the fast lane of the freeway, in heavy traffic, picking up speed.

"Weeeeeell, old Fast-Walking . . ." he began, and started laughing, "well, I tell you. We call him Fast-Walking cause he's the fastest walker in the entire state pen. He moves like a Watusi warrior or a Martian prince, like a man from another world. Fast-Walking is the aristocrat of the Joint, the Warden's son. When he walks, it looks like he's going real slow, but he's actually going very very fast, faster than an ordinary man can run. He's long and lanky with these skinny impossibly limber legs like rubberized stilts that cover great distances, great gulps of ground without trying, without looking like even moving. And he's got huge flappy feet like a clown's. His knees get to knocking, feet get to stomping, little arms get to waving, hips start to swaying, legs get to flaying, toes get to splaying, and he starts to trucking on down the line! And the funniest thing of all about Fast-Walking is that, in the end, he never gets anywhere anyway! With all the chances in the world, all the advantages, a head start and all, with his old man the Warden and all, Fast-Walking's never gotten anywhere in his whole life, and never will. He's a total wreck, total failure, bound for worse, bound for the fucking dregs, and anyone in the Joint, con or hack, will tell you the same. He's just a good-for-nothing, that's all. Though I do love him dearly," Arv finished, with a flourish, nudging her.

"Yeah!" she said, approving his rap, urging it on, "keep going!"

"Yeah, well," Arv said, stroking his moustache, thinking it over, "Fast-Walking's over at my pad now cause his wife's kicked him out. And he's working this extra job so he can save up enough money to pay off his debts so his wife'll let him back in the house so he can rest happy again. But, it's obvious to everyone in the Joint that, without the direct intervention of a benevolent god, no matter how hard Fast-Walking works, no matter how fast he gets going while looking like slow, he will in fact never get anywhere, never save enough money to get his salary disattached, never get back into the happy home he loves so much. Cause poor old Fast-Walking just can't get anywhere in life. He's constitutionally unable. Therefore, if you look at it that way, it's the mirage that's true in Fast-Walking's case, the illusion that's realer and truer. Even though he's in fact going fast, what it looks like he's doing, what it *appears* he's doing is the truth of the matter. Dig?"

"Yeah!" she said, digging it, liking it, watching him.

"So, anyway, Fast-Walking lives with me now and works this extra job with my Aunt Evie over in Nueva Ronda. She's got this store, over in Mexican Town, for the labor camp boys, the Mexican Nationals, wetbacks, the *braceros,* we call them. And it's celery season now, so business is good. The labor camps are full up. So every morning Fast-Walking and my old man drive over to Evie's and get into a little blue VW minibus and drive all around Nueva Ronda through the little muddy pot-holed roads and around the broken-down cactusy neighborhoods yelling out *'Vamos a la tienda! Vamos a la tienda!'* through the loudspeaker on the roof."

"What's that mean?"

"It's something they've learned will always bring them. It means, 'let's go to the store, let's go to the store!' The *braceros* can't resist an invitation for a free ride, like that. Who knows? They seem to think it might take them somewhere wonderful, somewhere full of marvels, or something. So they hop on. They come running from every labor camp, as if it were like some great adventure. And my old man and Fast-Walking load them up and drive them over to Evie's little store where they buy vulgar trinkets and cheap imitation leather belts and inferior flashlight batteries and plastic sandals and reject blue jeans and shopworn Fruit of the Loom underwear and glass-studded cowboy gloves and presents like that to send to the folks back in Chihuahua and Jalisco and Michoacán, and also, some of them . . ."

"What?" she asked, in a tone that indicated that she already suspected something lewd.

"And also to visit Evie's back room, where a skinny Spic woman with buck teeth and tits like deflated rubber tires, and a big fat black mammy with platinum blond hair will accommodate them for ten bucks a throw . . ."

"You know what?" she asked, laughing deliciously, throwing her head back on the plastic-covered seat.

"No, what?" he responded, swinging the Merc skidding too fast around a semitrailer, sending rainwater spraying over the windshield of a little MG, his pulse pounding with excitement, with joy and sureness now *I ain't such a fucking cluff after all, am I?*

"You're alright, Arv," she said. "You're okay for a fucking *Haole.*"

Driving out on the freeway with this beautiful woman next to him, this Oriental woman, with slanted eyes and smoky hair and nut-colored skin, took Little Arv straight back to Vietnam. It was a good feeling. He had loved those slant women, those exotic ladies, those dark foreign females he associated with fucking. And when she turned to look at him out of the side of her wonderful upturned Eastern eyes that were yet as silver gray as Norwegian fjords, Arv for the first time relaxed. It felt like home to him. He had known several women like her, and he had fucked every one of them.

He switched on the radio. Bob Dylan was singing *Lay Lady Lay.*

Moke slid over and sat beside him. "I love that song," she said.

"I do too," he said, "but let's not say anything."

"Good idea," she said, laughing, snuggling, looking up at him over his shoulder.

He put his hand on her bare thigh below the hem of her mini. He just left it there as they rode over an overpass on the freeway with all the lights of the small hill towns and city suburbs around them, and with the lights of the Joint behind them, and the city across the Sound, and the yellow and green and blue lights of the suspension bridges far off in the night. The texture of the skin on her leg was soft and yet amazingly firm, it reminded him of something. It reminded him of Southeast Asia.

While Bob Dylan and Johnny Cash slid into their beautifully carefully offhanded funky rendition of *North Country Fair,* Arv slid his hand up higher on her thigh, under the mini a smidgen. She didn't stop him. He left it there, driving, happy, listening to the radio. He turned and looked at her, laughing. Or rather he breathed out in one hard breath like a short laugh, but what it really was was more a kind of conspiring with her. He was sure of her now, and let out that breath again. And she responded, this woman who would use him, as he would use her, this woman with whom he already had a contract, unwritten perhaps, unspoken, but solid and binding nonetheless. She crept closer. Instead of playing out his temporary advantage, however, he rubbed his shoulder up against her too, her small-boned fragile shoulder, like a little playmate, a little boy, a conspirator. It seemed to charm her, as she charmed him. Arv, content, relaxed, slid his hand up to the edge now of her frilly panties while *For she was once a true love of mine* Johnny and Bob sang it, singing it, lost and lonely in the North Country, while Arv slid and slid, deeper into the country, into the north, the woods, the bramble, right to the place where her upper thigh became body, and left it there, resting, panting, lost for a moment, getting his bearings.

As Arv always did when trying to find his bearings, he drifted back into the past, looking the way he had come, to find the way he might go . . .

She reminded him of Southeast Asia.

It was Christmas. Him and Freddy got a five-day R and R to Phan Tiet, a small beachside resort on the South

China Sea. Arrived in time for the slopehead Catholic cel-
ebration. It was wild and drunken. Soldiers shooting off rifles in the park. Lots of music, firecrackers, free drinks,
smiling faces, pretty girls, loudspeakers strung up in the
palm trees, blaring:

> We got to get outa this place
> If it's the last thing we ever do

a rock song born in the American ghetto which had become the theme song of the Vietnam War, beloved by
even the young Yé Yé slopeheads who could never even
dream of getting out, even if it was the last thing they
ever did. Anyway, there was lots of music, firecrackers,
smiling faces, pretty girls. Phan Tiet has a reputation for
good-looking and relatively untouched women. That's why
they went there, hitching up along the coast in a C-130
Specter gunship that sprayed the jungle and the fields and
rivers with gatling-gun fire, banking, idling, slowing, turning, spewing out that random fireworks display into the
empty trees on the off-chance that a VC or two might be
lurking there. Arv and Freddy paid a few piastres and
danced with the taxi girls on the bandstand amid banyan
and palm trees in the central park. All the local people
laughed to see the whitemen trying to do the native dances.
They got very drunk and went to a brothel, a walled estab-
lishment on the beach, surrounded by enormous bamboo
trees and sharp cactus plants. Inside there were thirty-five
or forty tiny huts, or cells, arranged around the inner edge
of the bamboo wall. It was like no other whorehouse
Arv'd ever visited. Very smiley and friendly. Amazingly
beautiful girls. Girls as lovely and exotic as this one beside him now in the Merc, motating down this freeway on
the West Coast of the United States of America. Driving
now off the freeway on the Molina Valley off-ramp and
going through the business district of the tiny woodsy
town toward the dark misty hills and the redwood forest,
with the rain starting up again, smudging the street lights,
obscuring the trees and houses, not saying anything, and
Bob still singing away with his frail lonely American
voice. And Moke and Arv happy together, or pretending
to be, their breath coming faster, his hand now upon her
firm little brown belly. . . .

Arv took a pretty little sixteen-year-old to her cell. He chose her because she was the softest looking. Her eyes were like Moke's, but jet instead of silver. He'd never kissed a hooker before. He kissed her tiny copper tits, her tiny slits, her slopey eyes. She liked it. Maybe she'd never been kissed by a customer before, at least not *there*, right on her racial trademark. He wasn't rough or brusque or anything with her, not at all. Nor was he now with Moke as he slid his hand into her panties, lower, lower, reaching finally her bristly little Oriental bush, her burning hot tree. She didn't say anything. She started to, but he shushed her. "Shush!" And she did, while he drove the Merc up the curvy road into the hills with one hand and sent his other hand slowly down lower. She felt dry and warm still. He hesitated to go any further, it was so nice. He rubbed shoulders with her, friendly, conspiratorial. She snuggled her head on his shoulder then, with her eyes open, watching the rain dash against the wrap-around windshield, blinking only rarely, while they listened, not listening, to the radio.

In Phan Tiet he kissed the little girl's soft wide lips, very gently, and he fondled her small breasts with no nipples and her scentless cunt for the longest time, as a lover would do. None of it was at all like the horrible stony-ass hardness, the vulgarity and cheap nasty thrills of Western-style bought fucks. It made him happy to be with her. It seemed to make her happy. And yet he couldn't know. She might have been a fucking VC for all he knew. Could he now know? Was it all an elaborate act? He never knew. When he got up from the mat with her, brushing the straw off him, and the tiny sand crabs that crawled over his naked flesh, itching him, he started to leave and she said, pointing at him quaintly, "I like you. You like me?" in English. She had no reason to say this, no ulterior motive. She'd already been paid. She thought she'd never see him again. It was the most flattering thing that had ever been said to him in his entire life of twenty years' duration. He remembered her with such great pleasure. Especially her tiny even white animal teeth, her firm brown breasts and buttocks that looked so much more natural when they were bared naked than when they were covered, her strong lusty rice-paddy good health, the sport of fucking her, the downright athleticism of doing it all

over the floor of the cubicle frontwards and backwards
and upside down and her on top squatting over him
revolving like a rotor, like a rotor-motor . . . rotah-motah! Rotah-motah! Rotah-motah! his rock and roll imagination had gone, digging it, wailing, thinking even then
while she did it, rotah-motah, about where, impossibly, he
was, mythologizing his adventure while it happened to
him, telling the story for friends in his mind while she
worked over him, absorbed his spurting healthy yellow-
white come, his curds and whey and . . . for a moment,
with her, his own slope, he ceased to be at the mercy of
the American inside him, the hairy white beast. He was
brown too, or felt like he was, nut brown or copper
brown and hairless and scentless, a handsome brown clean
animal like her. That's what Arv felt now, as he slid his
hand down over Moke's lips, the lips of her smiling little
Oriental hole, and felt what he was ready to feel now:
wet. Betal-wet, toothless wet tube: hole. Black and gaping
and opening wider. Again he snuggled his shoulder against
her head, friendlylike, kidlike, it felt good. *Don't go too
fucking fast, man!* She smiled again. The radio went on
and on. Neil Young sang:

> It's only love can break your heart
> Try to be sure right from the start
> Laaa la la la la Laa Laa Laa la la la la Laaa . . .

The next afternoon in Phan Tiet Arv and Freddy were
lying on the beach in front of their little bamboo hotel.
Sun lit the clear green water of the cove. Red- and yellow-
and blue-painted fishing sampans bobbed in the waves.
High, heavy and tropically blue-black thunderheads
heaved and climbed the jungle mountains behind them.
Fine white sand shimmered in the sun. A hot breeze blew,
ruffling the trees, bending the thin cactus plants, transpar-
ent cactus plants that you could see pale yellow suns
through, and sea green clouds. Little waves lapped foamy
and sloppy at the brown rocks at the sea's edge. And Arv,
fresh from the waters of the South China Sea, glistened
tan and sunny as the afternoon itself.

The beach was long and white and wide. A group of
naked brown boys cavorted in the swells, throwing water
up and letting the wind catch it, scrambling over two an-

chored sampans, throwing stones at little dogs. Two slope fishermen cast their little round nets in the surf. Several horsemen were wetting their tiny mounts out on the mud-bank. . . .

Here it was the same in the car with Moke: all was peaceful and quiet and sweet. The radio and the motor droned on, without meaning *You got to do the rotah-mo-tah, do the rotah-motah, Bomp-Bomp-Bomp!* The lovers-to-be breathed in and out, the rain fell against the wind-shield, the dripping redwoods fled by, the mountains rose in the heaving purple mist, and no one said a word, no more than the beach had said in Phan Tiet. Arv turned off the narrow winding road and followed a dirt track through the black needly forest of pines and redwoods and firs, with cones and rocks and pine needles crackling under their tires, water splashing. Raindrops from the branches fell on the roof of the Merc, banging on it. But Arv didn't care. He didn't even worry about getting stuck. His hand crept into the folds of her skin, his finger into her wet pussy. His fingernail got sticky, got cotton debris stuck to it. Arv didn't worry about getting stuck in the mud on this road because he'd worked here with the State Forestry as a kid and knew that its base was solid gravel, under the mud. He'd laid it himself. He'd laid it himself. He'd even laid another woman, many, some, several women, got stuck there, even Deanna and he had come here and got stuck there, like doggies, stretched out on the front seat, got stuck with it, and little Wendy fused then, became mortal, with rain then beating on the metal roof of his car, another one, another Mercury that time, a blue one with Tijuana "Tuck and Roll" upholstery and a mad raked front end and magnesium racing hubs and cut-out pipes. . . .

Arv stopped the car. All was quiet except the rain. Still he said nothing. Nor did Moke, the Hawaiian, the mixed-breed, the slant, the slopehead. His style pleased her, in spite of her game, her prostitution to whatever cause she represented, whatever criminal illegal venture she had in mind. She liked him genuinely, he was almost sure. She was relaxed. They got along. They'd already established an easy rapport with each other. They had the same inter-ests: they even had the same instructor, the same course at City College. They were perfectly suited for each other, if you thought about it. A computer would have picked them for each other. Even to the fact that he loved exotic foreign women.

When the car was silent and only the rain fell off the trees onto the roof of the Merc—Bong Bong Bong—Arv went in and he went in and out with his right middle finger, scraping the inside stuff with his fingernail just the slightest bit, feeling the stuff slide up under his fingernail, feeling it, knowing it would stay there a long time, and that even when he went home eventually and tried to wash it out it would still stay there, a secret smell, for days, this he knew. Saying nothing, listening to her breathing faster, genuinely faster, not faking, digging it! Breathing faster. And just as Arv was thinking of laying her . . .

. . . Just as Freddy and Arv were thinking of laying their beach towels in a sunnier spot, suddenly sixteen busloads of city kids from Saigon came running toward them . . . kicking soccer balls, throwing coconuts at each other, playing catch with volleyballs, shouting and waving at each other. They were all boys, between ten and fourteen, having a groovy time at the seaside. Arv and Freddy laughed, watching them tumble and wrestle in the sand. One or two of them caught sight of the two white men and came over to get acquainted. They spoke in sign language with each other, smiling and giggling and making friends. Then a few more boys came over. And a few more. And a few more. And more. When the group got larger it became more difficult to communicate in sign language. Arv and Freddy were still lying on their beach towels, catching the rays. The slope kids looked at them like they'd never seen anything so weird. They couldn't figure out why anyone would want to lie down voluntarily in the hot sun baking his skin. Arv and Freddy tried to make them understand the notion "suntan" but it was beyond their experience. When the other kids saw the little circle on the beach they came running to find out what was happening. The circle got bigger . . . and bigger . . . and bigger. All the kids were laughing and having fun and staring. Arv and Freddy stared back, and tried to keep laughing and smiling. Somebody way in back of the circle threw a candy wrapper and it sailed in the sunlight, shimmering, and landed in the center of the circle, just at

Arv's feet. Everyone laughed. That was real funny. Arv
laughed too. Then somebody threw a volleyball. Arv
caught it and threw it back. The white men stopped laughing. Somebody threw a sharp-edged seashell. It hit Arv on
his bare thigh. He threw it back as hard as he could and it
hit a little kid above the eye, splitting it open. It began to
bleed. He started crying. Nobody got particularly mad
about it. The sight of blood didn't seem to bother them
very much, no more than it did the other kids in Vietnam.
Arv was very sorry and went over to the kid and tried to
pet him on the head, to pet him . . . He pet her . . . she
began to pet him . . .

Petting, he was lost and he didn't know where for a
moment. Where was he? In Vietnam? In Moke's brown
arms? Or going home from work, with Fast-Walking's
loud slumber in his ear, and the Alvarez Straits Bridge
coming up on the freeway, shining bright orange in the
moonlight that shone through the mountainous Pacific
cloud mass . . . He petted her head, her buttocks rose
. . . where was her head? Her buttocks now were firm
and round. He pulled her panties over her hips that had
risen on the plastic seat covers and he pulled them down
her slim brown legs and round her little wiggling toes and
he pushed her then, he pushed her down the other way
away from the wheel and pulled up on her mini *her toenails were painted metallic silver!* pulling it up around her
hips and then she moaned like the other one, like . . .
which one? The other one. Where was it? "Kiss me!" she
whispered, urgently, like in fifty-cent porno novels.

"Where?" he asked, honestly not sure.

"Anywhere," she said, and he kissed her with true passion on her moist cunt. He kissed her with all the passion
he had saved for her lips, hugging her hips and buttocks
as if they were her back and shoulders, hugging her to
him in a loving passionate embrace he kissed this Hawaiian woman as he would kiss her mouth, with his tongue
going in and out and in and out and the juices going over
his moustache and his chin and tasting her good taste and
up and down and up and down he moved himself against
her metallic-silver painted toes and howled as she howled
and moaned too and he was lost in time and space and
only after the longest time did he, still kissing her, did he
remember where they were. Where were they? He and

Deanna, he and Freddy were on a beach in Phan
Tiet . . .

He and Freddy were on the beach and they'd hit a little
boy. Arv tried to pet a hurt little boy on the head, saying,
"I'm sorry," over and over again in English and in
French, *"Je m'excuse, je m'excuse,"* and then, just as he
was about to pet the boy again another little kid with a
broomstick hit Arv a glancing blow on the shoulder and
the neck. Arv saw red! He forgot himself, chased the boy
through the crowd, through the cactus and brambles and
bamboo trees, caught him, got him down on the ground,
took his broomstick away. The boy got up and started
running. Arv, fucking Moke, kissing her, loving her
mouth, the mouth of her body and her body kissing back,
could still see him running and running. Running and running, Arv, driving up the incline of the Alvarez Straits
Bridge, could see him. All the other kids too were running, running after Arv. He couldn't catch the boy he was
chasing. He was too fast. But another one, just behind
Arv, was laughing and making fun of him. Arv turned
quickly and the boy darted into the water but Arv got
close enough to jam the end of the broomstick hard about
three inches up his asshole. "Aiiiiiie!" he yelled, like a
comic-book Gook in an E.C. war comic. "Aiiiiie!" as Arv
jammed, as he . . . jammed . . .

Arv jammed his cock into her wet and throbbing
Hawaiian cunt and came immediately and she undulated
against him as if her life depended on it but his load was
gone as surely as shit. And you could see her little sloping
slanting eyes bulge. Her . . . yes . . . bulged too . . .
slanted eyes bulging out of their slanting sockets . . .

He howled. She howled. Aiiiiiie! Like a Jap in a movie.
Aiiiie! Moke yelled, coming. Aiiiie! yelled that yellow-
faced boy.

Deanna pretended to yell, and moan, but she was only
jiving, already knocked up.

The boy too was hurt bad. He lay in the shallow water
floating in a little curled-up ball, howling and swallowing
water, the sea around him, the South China Sea, beginning to turn a yellow-brown color, turning, turning
around him . . .

Arv began to feel his cock stirring again, already, she
was so beautiful under him, her eyes bulging, it stirred, it
moved, she smiled, she brought her arms up, brought him

down on her, kissed his swollen stuck-together eyelids, his lips of bitter-sweet cunt, kissed him again and again, wiggling her hips under him, opening her legs, and he plunged deeper, and did not come, and deeper, and did not think of coming, and fucked her like a real dude, fucking her and fucking her, thinking of missiles and rocks and paper wrappers and seashells and beer cans coming sailing after him and Freddy from every direction while the kids attacked and while the other poor little guy lay in the water curled up like a dead shotdown duck in his own shit.

"That's enough," Moke gasped.

"Wait," he lied, "I haven't come yet."

While he and Freddy fought for their lives, fought their way back together to the hotel skirmishing with angry murderous slopeheaded children all the way. Finally, bleeding from many wounds, they reached their bamboo hotel. All afternoon there was a huge crowd outside, clamoring for their blood. Finally an army truck pulled up and an ARVN officer and some soldiers got out and chased them away.

Arv and Freddy felt like their whole R and R was spoiled.

That night, with a police escort, they went again to the little walled whorehouse on the beach. Arv found his little sixteen-year-old girl and asked her how much. She said she didn't want to fuckie-fuckie with him because his breath was bad . . . "Whiskey smell, whiskey smell," she kept saying.

Then we got a hop on an OV-10 observation plane and went back to Saigon where the people appreciated us more and the whores weren't so sensitive, Arv thought, fucking his slant-eyed Moke, with her smiling under him. Fucking slowly and powerfully Arv got it up again, not coming, Arv fucked, fucking he did not come, not coming he fucked on and on, hurting her. "Please, please stop!" she cried, "I love it, I love it, but it hurts!" And quickly he hurried and undulated rapidly and simulated the ecstasy of coming.

"That that that!" she sighed, happily, and he believed her. And softened toward her in his heart, and came back to her, flying back in over the trees from Nam, and became tender and loving, his heart beating with joy.

"I guess you know why I . . ." she said, rubbing happily against him.

"I guess so," he said, "I mean, I knew it wouldn't be
just for . . ."

"It wasn't," she said, "but it turned out a way I didn't
know it would."

"You don't have to bullshit me."

"No, it's true. If I was smart I'd have waited longer,
teased you, made sure I got what I wanted first, and then
given in."

"Okay," he sighed, as a man sighs who's already spent
the loan money and now must start paying off the debt,
"what is it?"

"Aw, come on!" she said, "it's not that bad! I just want
you to take a letter to Galliot when he arrives. I can give
you seventy-five dollars every time you take one."

Arv laughed. Laughing, his chest heaved up against her
perfect breasts. They were still lying entwined together,
stuck together, on the front seat of the Merc. It struck
him funny, all this talk. It struck him funny that she
wanted him to take a letter to Galliot and that they were
discussing it precisely at this moment. He'd had it figured
as a dope deal, a money deal. Moke didn't look like the
ideological type. It made him feel good, somehow, that
she'd done it for moral, ethical, or political considerations
rather than for money. It relieved him. She was someone
he could believe in, whether he agreed with her politics or
not. But actually, he did sort of believe in her politics. After all, everyone in the Joint knew Galliot was innocent,
had been pushed up against the wall by the Man.

"Elaine must have put you up to it," he said, still laughing, thinking of his fiery, comic New Left instructor.
Somehow those New Left types seemed as irrelevant as
the Neanderthal in the solid seventies. "Yeah," he said, "I
know it was her! She tried to get me to do it a couple of
weeks ago and I turned her down flat. She's gonna be jealous that you succeeded where she failed! Even if she does
get her way in the end . . ."

"I can't tell you about it," Moke said, tight-lipped.

"Anyway," Arv said, lying, "you won't have to do this
with me anymore. I'll do it without that. I don't mind,
and I need the money. And I'm trapped here working at
the Joint. I'm desperate enough to take any chance, on the

chance that it'll get me out of here. I've got to get out of this place," he said, and the refrain from Vietnam, the famous one, ran through his mind like M-60 machine-gun fire: *if it's the last thing I ever do* . . . "And anyway," he said, "I haven't got any moral objections to helping out Galliot. He's not a bad dude. And he's been framed. Everyone in the Joint knows that. And what'd he do in the first place, anyway? Just smoking a joint. And they never even proved that."

"But you don't understand!" she said, smiling under him, nuzzling up to his neck, "I've discovered that I *want* to be with you, at least for a while!"

"Aw, come on!"

"Honest!"

Arvin, a natural sheep, already a love slave, or feeling like one, trembled to hear those words, true or false, and would have done anything in the world to prolong that moment, to prolong it beyond history and their separate deaths. He was already in love. With the first fine lady he'd ever met. And it was all a shuck. It was, therefore, an allegory of his life, the life of a perpetual loser. *No,* he thought, *goddamnit, destiny's in my hands!* And at that very moment, Arv determined to use all his wiles, all his considerable intelligence and art to win her.

"I'm going to win you," he said, "even though you think you're using me, you'll see! In the end I'll win you and you'll really be mine. You'll see! It'll take you by surprise. You'll see, goddamnit! I'm gonna win you! Yeah!"

"Oh no you won't," she said, shaking her head against the plastic back rest.

But to Arv, the charm of her smile, flashing white against her dark skin, belied her words. He would not, did not hear them.

And the big Merc rumbled backwards out of the dark panting redwood forest.

He took her home. She lived in a strange old Spanish-style mansion under the freeway bridge in Molina Valley. She had a small apartment on the second floor, she said. It was pitch black as Arv drove up the winding driveway through the huge overgrown grounds: the garden had run all to weed. No light in the house. "Just let me run in and change, and then you can drop me off at my bike," she

said, and started to get out. Then, as if it had just occurred to her, she said, "Say, you wouldn't like to go
swimming, by any chance?"

Now, anybody else would have been shocked, or put
off, or would have thought she was nuts. But not old Arv.
He was a hard surfing West Coast boy, and knew that Pacific Ocean and her moods as well as he knew his own
mother and her capricious moods. Yes sir! He could
bodysurf, and surf with a board. He could swim for miles
in mountainous seas. He'd won the trans-Sound paddle-
board race two years in a row, Junior Division. So this
Moke, huh? this Hawaiian chick thought she'd scare the
mainland boy off, huh? Uh-uh, honey!

"I'd love to!" he said, "I dig swimming at night, although, I must admit, I'm not exactly used to going out in
late December, in the middle of a storm!"

She seemed surprised and delighted.

"Wait here!" she said breathlessly, "I'll run in and find
us some dry-suits!" and raced across the wet crabgrass
lawn into the tumbledown old house. Arv saw her room
light up and then the place looked a little more friendly.

Afterwards she took him out to China Cove. She had a
man's rubber dry-suit for him. It was a little big on him
but it worked.

"I'm going out to Iguana Rock," she said, "but you
can't follow me."

The sky was pitch black. Rain drove against them.
Waves crashed on the gravelly shore. Arv figured he
could handle the small chop of the Cove, and the water
temperature. What bothered him was the heavy crashing
waves in the Sound, and the fact that there were no lights
to be seen now, anywhere.

"How we going to find it?" he asked.

"I told you," she shouted into the black rain and the
wind, "you can't follow me."

"The fuck if I can't!" he insisted.

"Can you?" she asked, incredulous.

"Sure," he said, spitting it into the wind, zipping himself into the dry-suit, "I can swim miles!"

"You won't be able to follow me," she repeated. And
she was right.

In the middle of the icy Sound, on the way to an invisible Iguana Rock, with mountainous seas battering him,

dunking him, driving salty spray into his mouth and nose and lungs, blinding him, Arv gave up hope. And the funniest thing was that, he figured, if he couldn't follow that fucking Moke, that Hawaiian, then he'd just give up. Even if she was the best swimmer he'd ever seen in his life. Sliced the water like a fish, like a sea snake. Thinking of his small beloved sea snake, his competitor, his conspirator, his secret sharer, Arv was just about to give up and slide down to the seaweed, the muddy heaving bottom, when he saw lights! The Standard Oil Refinery at West Hazelton. He got his bearings, but had no time to think back upon the way he'd come. He had to strike out again quickly into the blackness, with what little of his strength remained, making for where he imagined the rock would be. He swam and swam. But no rock. He must have gone the wrong way. Maybe those weren't the Standard Oil lights, after all. Maybe they were the lights from the Pony Island Submarine Base, or the Naval Air Station. He swam and swam. But nothing but blackness and the driving punishing sea. He must have gone the wrong way. He turned right and swam for a half hour. He was lost. He saw lights again, but they were ten miles away. He didn't know what lights they were.

Finally he heard her calling.

"Over here!" she called, and it sounded like her voice calling from every point of the compass. "Over here!" she called again, and he followed where he guessed it came from, from the left. "Okay!" he yelled, "here I come!"

When he reached the rock she was laughing wildly. The rain drove against her black rubber suit, the wind shot rain and salt water into her mouth, against her laughing teeth. She pulled him up on the rock.

"Ha ha ha ha!" she screamed into the tempest, "you old sonofabitch, Arv! You made it! Nobody could make it, and you made it! You're superhuman, man! Superhuman! You made it! *You!*

And Arv, for a single half instant, was convinced that he was in the presence of the angel of death.

She was so glad to see him, though. She hugged him and jumped up and down on the slippery mussel-covered rock. "Yippee, you did it! Not bad for a fucking *Haole!* Fucking *Haole!* Whoopie!" she shouted, truly delighted that he'd made it alive. It was sort of like they were two

good friends, two buddies who'd just made a really difficult swim together. It was like there had been none of
that kissing and fucking just an hour before, as if all that
had just been erased. Now it was just camaraderie. Arv
liked it. Entered into its spirit too. And she dug it. Appreciated how fast he picked up, matched her moods. And
they both began jumping up and down in the wind and
rain like kids, patting each other on the back and running
round in circles.

They spent a long time on Iguana Rock in the rain.
Very long. Arv never knew how long exactly, but when
they were finished with their fun and games in the
darkness, and she'd showed him how to pick fresh mussels
off the rocks and eat them raw, and after they'd swum all
the long way back to shore together, with Moke leading
the way, it was almost dawn.

"You all right, *Haole!*" she kept saying all the way to
the Joint, "damn if you not all fucking right for a fucking
Haole!"

Part II

Part II.

Thirteen

Honk! Honk! Honk! The six A.M. whistle over in the prison laundry went off. RIIIIIIIING! The alarm on the bed table went off beside May Weed's graying head. She sat up in bed, with the alarm still going, and tried to get her sleep- and mascara-glued eyelids open. She tried and tried, even prying at them with her shivering shaking fingers. But they wouldn't open, not for the longest time . . . long enough, in fact, to give her a clear and exact vision of inferno in all its details: her unhappy life passed unsummoned and unwanted before her imprisoned eyes. . . .

Mother Weed had been married in old clothes in the unlucky month of her namesake. Lula May was her name, but all her friends they mostly called her just May. She was a spidery, dark-haired little thing, only fifteen, but looked older. And it rained all the way through the ceremony. She was a May bride and her maiden name was Mayhew, married in the greatest cloudburst the state had ever seen. All the guests were trapped in the church. The inundation followed them even up the aisles to the altar platform where on their bony hard-dirt Okie knees and their soft round Mexican-Indian knees they huddled and prayed with the Baptist preacher while the waters crept higher. It occurred to no one that it might be an omen. They rejoiced when the storm abated and the waters retreated, and gave God his due.

It was planting time when May was married, boom time, spring of 1946, baby boom. And she honeymooned, four and a half months pregnant but not showing it, at Maiden Rock. And all the time it rained. Her young groom was a prison guard just back from the wars. They coupled in their room at the Maiden Rock Hotel for three days and three nights without cease. The bride's family: mother, grandmother, father, and six sisters, was planting

a late Victory Garden at the time, in the auspicious late
springtime damp, and phoned the lovers daily to inform
them how the sowing went. This was the only intrusion
little May permitted.

Immediately upon arriving at the hotel, May asked the
desk clerk why the rock with the face of a woman, on the
loaf-shaped mountain above the parking lot, was called
"Maiden." The desk clerk said, "An Indian girl, unhappy
in love, jumped to her death from its pinnacle in the time
of the Spanish."

Though May didn't believe the clerk (he uttered the
sentence as if he'd learned it by rote), she forever associated herself with this tragedy, and with the rains that fell
every winter of her married life: "In December, when the
rains come/and seafogs ride like streetcars through the
dark tunneled hills," her son Arv's first poem had
begun. . . .

There was a fire at the hotel one night during the honeymoon and everyone ran into the scrub oak and mesquite
woods to escape the flames. May became separated from
her husband and came upon him later copulating in the
darkness with an older woman in a patch of corn. And
that was not the last time May, May Maiden, was made to
cry. . . .

She started smoking on her wedding day. And all the
rest of her life she had the habit of lighting up ciggies (as
she called them), snuffing them out half unsmoked, and
relighting them later.

On her wedding day too she was offered her first drink.
And that problem was never resolved either.

To her children, a boy and two girls and a younger girl,
she was associated with black hair, the cat, the snake,
rain, the heel of the palm (where she had a crescent-
shaped birthmark), wrinkles, ineffectual anger, death, divorce, divination, drunkenness, and the sewing machine.

To her boy Arvin's way of thinking she was by turns
lovely and cruel, ugly and beautiful, stingy and generous,
self-centered and self-abasing. If he were asked to pin-
point a memory that summed her up to him, it would
probably be a certain August day (in the colors of Renoir:
flies buzzing, yellow hay, yellow day, and the snorting of
goats) when she drunkenly but justly dispensed justice under the scraggly weeping willow in her back yard: a Sat-

urday picnic in the shade, the air filled with humid heat and electricity and the threat of imminent flashfloods, Daddy gone off fishing in Paradise Cove, a naughty boy punished (Wasco) with a slap, a shy nice little boy rewarded (Arvin, three years old) with candy and beery caresses.

When her children's baby teeth fell out May put them under their pillows carefully, made no pretense about "The Good Fairy." She very seriously believed that dead teeth had divinatory powers and left the nasty things in bed for weeks, taking them out every few hours and worrying them like beads. She never got discouraged, and once in a while one of her predictions would actually come true. Like the time she said, "Arv's going to break his arm but he'll be okay." And he did. And he was. And everybody said, "Oh hey now, May old gal, you really are a witch, ain't you?"

Arv alone believed in her magical powers.

She had a penny pocket mirror that she flashed at her son to call him home. She was only four feet eleven and a half inches tall in high heels, so she'd stand up on the safety rail on their front porch, balancing herself precariously, but never falling, and she'd shine her mirror way down to the prison ball diamond or the football field when she wanted him. Whenever he felt that strong bright light on his face, be it half a mile up in the hills, he'd hie back to the house, knowing she was capable of striking him momentarily blind if he didn't. That's how he figured she could be cruel too, if she had to be, in spite of her basic goodness. You knew there was something in her, in those crazy yellow eyes, in that inscrutable pointed little sharp-chinned face, that would go beyond safe, beyond insurance, would follow a thing all the way out, wherever it led. There was something in her that didn't have any brakes or safety railings or Band-Aids ready, something in her that was mad, anarchic and foreign and not . . . white. "That's the Indian in me," she'd say. And it was true. Her mother was a quarter Osage, from Gray Horse, Oklahoma. And like an Indian, nothing could defeat her. Battered, buffeted by winds of outrageous fortune: a brutal husband, a dead-ended marriage, alcoholism, poverty, debts, ignorance, inexperience, ungrateful children, failing health, early old age, there

was yet something remaining in May, The May Maiden,
even now in the September of her years, that stood up on
its hind legs and kept fighting, kept plugging away, trying,
always trying.

In the kitchen May was queen. No one, not Dad himself, dared enter her domain uninvited. The refrigerator
was especially sacrosanct. She pasted a picture of herself
on the frig door when Little Arv was two years old. She
drew a cartoon speech cloud above the picture with an arrow pointing to her mouth. In black wax crayon these ancient and time-honored words were inscribed:

> DONT TOUCH KIDS
> AND YOU TOO DADDY
> LESS MOM SAYS OK

The picture remained there on the white enamel
through all the years, yellowing, food-splattered, till it no
longer bore any resemblance to the aging May of present
time, till the pink chubby cheeks of eighteen-year-old May
Maiden in the photo mocked her, mocked Dad, mocked
them all, and triumphed. . . . The day before Little Arv
left for Vietnam she tore it down and threw it at her husband in a drunken fury when he alluded, in his typical
originality, to the fact that "the old gray mare ain't what
she used to be."

The picture still existed, however, in the collective
memory of the family, exactly as it always had been.

May, long before the daily hangovers of her mature
years, had always been a hellion in the mornings, rising
like a supernova and bursting into flame at the first contact with any form of matter. WHAM! CRASH! BLAM! You'd
hear her kicking out at her night stand, the bedroom door,
the toilet seat. And everyone in the house would hunch
his shoulders in terror, huddling silent, eyes lowered, over
the Kellogg's Corn Flakes as she reeled out to the kitchen,
her eyes crazy as a cornered lynx, hair wild and matted as
Medusa's, trailing flame and smoke, smoking ciggies and
putting them out, drinking cup after cup of coffee. Then
Big Arv would start the day off, per ritual: he'd say
something to provoke her on purpose. They'd all be waiting for it. Big Arv would say, "Say there, May old gal,
you're looking real chipper this morning, never seen you

looking better!" And she'd yell, "Aw, shut up and get out
of here and get to work you lazy ass-breath S.O.B.!" And
he'd shout, "Aw, blow it out that shithole you call a
mouth, you fucking old hag!" And so every day began.

That is not to say that the emotion of love was unknown to them. There was a time, at least one time, when
they had loved one another. It was from their example, as
a matter of fact, that Little Arv had first discovered the
true nature of love. It happened this way: one day after
Big Arv had been called up for the Korean War, May got
Grandma Dora Lee and the kids, piled them into the '42
Buick Special, drove them down to the Northwestern Pacific Depot in Mission Santa Bonita, and parked in the
trackside parking lot so they could all wave to Big Arv
when he came through in the troop train on his way overseas. At two o'clock in the afternoon precisely the train
came whistling past the station house. They saw Big Arv,
waved, he waved back, the train zoomed by in a cloud of
steam and coal dust, and that would have been that if
some bug, some crazy Indian beetle-bug hadn't gotten into
Mom. She went wacky, lit out after that streamliner steam
engine barreling the old Buick in overdrive down along
the Sound and over the hills and out onto the salt flats.
Driving sixty, seventy, eighty miles an hour. Dora Lee
screaming, "Stop, stop, you nut! You're gonna kill us all!"
Little Arv and Carol and Judy, crying and yelling,
jumping up and down in the back seat. But May wouldn't
stop. She just wouldn't. There was something in her eye.
They all sensed that they were going to catch Big Arv, a
seemingly impossible feat, or die trying. By the time they
hit the Mission Valley turnoff they were doing ninety
miles an hour. They'd run three cars off the road, gone
through nine stoplights, and had two Highway Patrol cars
chasing them, sirens blaring.

Then, fortunately for their lives, they could see way up
ahead that the train had stopped and gone off on a siding
to let another train go by. Old May brodied broadside off
the road, turned the wheel hard right, hurdled an irrigation ditch, and shot fifty yards out into a tomato patch before the car stopped, sunk up to its axles in thick black
lowland mud. She bailed out fast, with the cops right on
her tail, whipped off her shoes, threw them at the cops to
slow them down, and raced barefoot through the black

mud toward the train. By then all the soldiers on board had seen her. Big Arv had seen her. Little Arv could see them all from the car. The GI's were hanging out the windows of the train, shouting, cheering her on. The whole troop train went up in a mighty, slow-rising roar. "Yeeeea!" And the cops got bogged down in the mud and fell behind. May's thin little spider legs churning up that black mud, grassy clumps of it flying out behind her swift flying heels. Then three MP's came out of the train, figuring she was some kind of crazy bombthrower or something. And she dodged around one guy, and then another, and it looked like the last guy, a big black man, was going to get her. Then he looked at what she was running for, Big Arv with his arms outstretched in the window of the train, and just sat down in the mud, took his overseas cap off, and started laughing. The whole train exploded in a thunderous cheer: "Hooray! Hooray! Hooray!" It looked like it might lift right up off the track. "Come on honey! Come on! Come to me!" the soldiers all yelled, "Here! Here!" Four hundred burly GI arms reached out of the train to catch her up. Then she spotted Big Arv. She raced toward him, leaving the cops far behind. Oh, but she was fast then, that May, still only nineteen years old! She ran and ran and reached Big Arv's arms just as the train started to pull out. The soldiers went wild with delight. "Yippee! Yea!" they all shouted. The police and the MP's ran alongside the moving train laughing and clapping each other on the back. Big Arv held her tight in his arms, kissing her eyes while she cried. He held her hard for perhaps thirty seconds, with her dress hiked up over her pink panties, and her feet hanging down muddy and green with tomato, kissing her hair, eyes, cheek, mouth, ears, neck, and then the train started going too fast, so he had to drop her into the arms of the Highway Patrol.

Back in the mud-stuck Buick Special Little Arv turned to his tearful Grandma Dora Lee and said, *"That's* what love is, ain't it Grandma?" He'd never known what it was, and had always been asking everybody what it meant, until that moment.

"That's it, ain't it? Ain't it, Grandma?"

And she said, in her fancy phony voice she saved for important occassions, she said, "Yes, my child. Yes, that's what love is!"

This "love," this lifetime of misery and squalor and torture, this one instant of rapture above the railroad tracks, all came about because May had been a friend of Grandma Dora Lee's daughter Coalinga.

May lived with her family in an unpainted old Victorian place two doors down from Dora Lee's Scotch husband's inherited home in Mission Santa Bonita. May was very poor. She'd quit high school at fourteen to go to work. At least, that's what she always told her kids. At least part of the truth was that she was no good in school and didn't like it at all. Besides, she was embarrassed to wear her torn and raggedy old clothes. Nobody spoke to her at school. She knew no one. All the kids made fun of her stupid answers in class. She never got a chance to show her personality, she once told Little Arv, because her family moved around so much she never got to meet anyone. They'd lived in Texas, New Mexico, Arizona, Utah, Oregon, all over the place. Her father was a sometime plumbing contractor, then a plumber with the WPA, then a defense plant assembly-line worker.

May started her career as a waitress at eight dollars a week. She was a waitress all her life. She was a staunch Culinary Workers' Union member, paying her monthly dues as regular and natural as she had her period. As a result of the efforts of her well-heeled union president, an Italo-American ex-convict, she had seen her wages rise from a lowly eight to a full thirty-five dollars per week in her own lifetime. She was a pleasant waitress, with a friendly smile, and always had a whole big group of steady customers who asked for her table every time they came in, and treated her to all the gossip of the town, and their problems and endless worries and hopes and dreams. She was never too busy to lend them her ear. May was a gum chewer, her mouth never still, stuffed to the gills with a pack and a half of spearmint at all times of the day and night. But she always kept herself neat as a pin and clean as a whistle, and made up real careful in front of her mirror every morning, applying her thick pancake makeup and her ruby red lipstick, the same color and brand she'd been wearing since the year 1943. She wore a hair net always, and a crisp white uniform that she washed, starched, and ironed daily, and white polished wedgie shoes with a nice pair of stockings. When the children were grown she was sometimes pulling in as high as twenty to twenty-five dollars a week in tips on top of her regular salary.

By the time May was thirty-five, most of her memories from the years before her marriage had escaped her. It seemed almost like her life began on that rainy day when she got tied up with Big Arv. After her kids were raised she often tried to remember, but she'd lost all but the very tip end of the iceberg of her consciousness in the dreamy, murky, hungry waters before the year of the baby boom.

She remembered only:

Her twin sister Maggie burning up in front of the gas heater in 1935. Her little back-flapped bunnysuit pajamas caught fire and she just went up like a torch, right before her eyes.

Walking with her sister Peggy and her brother Bob to see Johnny Mack Brown at the Roxie on Baseline Avenue in San Bernadino, California. Walking across the streetcar tracks and the Lytle Creek Bridge in the winter rain, snow to be seen through the orange groves and misty desert foothills on Mount San Antonio in the distance.

Breakfast at home: gravy and biscuits and hominy grits and bacon and eggs and pancakes and Postum or coffee and honey and butter and jam in the halcyon year of 1944 when everybody had a job in defense. Everyone around the table. The big pot-bellied iron woodstove red hot in the corner. Bob coming sliding down the daily polished bannister, a tall, gangly, smiling seventeen-year-old with a shock of white-blond hair.

Her mother telling the story of her elopement: "I run off with a traveling man, the first one I ever seen, just to get away from Pa, run off across the Arkansas River in the moonlight in Pa's old wagon we taken, a big pair of white-butt Oklahoma mules leading on . . . got stuck in the quicksand on the Pawnee side, coyotes ahowling, your daddy and them mules pulling us out, and that there prairie moon shining down on all three of them bare-ass behinds . . ."

Her father picking up brother Bob by the ears (Bob later killed on the 38th Parallel at the age of twenty-three) and shaking him up and down because he'd been naughty. He was always mean like that with Bob. That's why the kid always had such big floppy ears, she said.

May was her daddy's favorite, though. "Maysie!" he'd
call from his big old straw rocking chair, and take her up
on his knee and play with her legs. She loved her daddy,
even though he drank too much and his Mississippi accent
was hard to understand and he beat her brother and lived
alone out in the garage for the last twenty-five years of his
life and didn't have much to do with the kids, and nothing
to do with Ma. They called him "Boomer Mayhew" down
at the barroom. He'd been a traveling man all his life, a
man with a highly speckled career as a carpenter, railroad
man, plumber, bootlegger, and gambler. He'd lived all
over the West, and in Mexico and Guatemala too. He'd
served time in a hundred city jails and three years in the
West Texas Prison Farm. He smelled of chewing tobacco
and whiskey and male sweat and woodshavings. He
smelled good.

That's all May remembered except for the time she met
Arv. She was going strolling down Mission Avenue one
day and it was an early Sunday morning in autumn. Clear
and bright with black cold shadows. She went down to see
her friend, Coalinga. Coalinga's whole family, Grandma
Dora Lee, Arvin and the two girls, Coalinga and Manteca,
and Wasco and younger Sanger (every one of them
named for a small town in California), was lying around
on the living-room floor after breakfast reading the funny
papers in the *New Sonora Times*. They were fighting
about who got which section next. Sanger liked Prince
Valiant. Arvin liked the Katzenjammer Kids. Grandma
liked Blondie. That's all May remembered, except that
somebody said there was a dance that night down at the
20-30 Club. Big Arv offered to treat them all. He'd just
got paid at the Joint. So they all went to the dance and
May drank too much, and Arvin was persistent, noticed
her, talked to her, danced her, romanced her to the beat
of the *Balboa*, that was popular then, and jitterbugged
with her, everyone clapping at how good they were together, and took her for a ride in his 36 Ford Coupe
alone afterwards out along the Rio Hondo levee, and . . .
that's where her bondage began.

During the middle '50's sometime May heard that Arv
was gallivanting around with that tramp Evie, his own
brother's wife, mother of his favorite nephew, whenever
she passed through town on her fruit tramping circuit.

May began making plans for a divorce. Through the entire remainder of her married life she would be actively making plans to leave her husband over his indeterminate but highly suspect relationship with Evie. To summon up the nerve, she took to drinking a few beers a day after work at the restaurant. She tried to get up the nerve for seventeen years, drinking more and more beers every day to help her along. It didn't work, but she had one compensation: she was afforded the deeply rewarding pleasure of souring her husband's existence every day of his life, hounding him toward the grave with her endless nagging, her plans for immediate separation, immediate divorce.

"Go ahead!" he'd yell, "I don't care, leave!" and then she'd break down in tears and say, as if it were some kind of major surprise:

"You don't love me!"

"That's right! You goddamn right I don't love you! I don't even *like* you, you whory old bitch!" he'd holler, going sickly-blotchy red and blue in the face.

"Aw, eat shit, you frijole-eating Spic bastard!" she'd scream, fouling the air with her morning beer breath, and the kids would duck for cover. It was a twice or thrice weekly show that got more and more serious through the years. Small as she was, May's aim improved with every dish she threw. She'd sent Big Arv to the hospital at least twice with serious cuts and abrasions. He'd given her innumerable black eyes that had to be explained to the skeptical neighbors as "bruised" from running into a door.

This married couple did not "mellow" with the passing years. (Few do.) There was none of that largely mythical "companionship" of later years. With each and every year their mutual hatred and antagonism grew. With every year they regretted more ephemeral lost "love," their empty lives, the deadening sameness of existence on the grounds of the Joint. . . .

And so it was on this glorious December morn after a fine rain, and Christmas only five more shopping days away: May had been lying blissfully abed dreaming of her youth, her handsome soldier home from the wars, her fleeting moments of youthful rapture, the minute or two in the year 1946 and the instant above the railroad tracks in the year 1950, which were all she was ever to know of happiness, when the alarm went off.

RIIIIIING! It was excruciating.

"Shut that goddamn thing off!" Big Arv shouted from his side of the bed, red-faced and raging, even at this impossible hour of the dawn.

May still couldn't get her eyes open. The alarm and her husband's raw angry voice and her blindness and her sordid hopeless life, and life that still passed unasked, unloved before her eyes, drove her to despair. "Ahhhhhhhhhhhh!" she screamed, not sure yet at what or whom, "Ahhhhhhhhh!" she yelled again, and her eyes burst open and saw her fat ugly piglike husband, displacing much weight, sagging the bed beside her, and she screamed again, "Ahhhhhhhhh!" and the thought of why and at whom she was screaming, whom she blamed and hated for her vision, made her sure why she'd been screaming and she screamed again, "Ahhhhhhhhhhhhhhhhhhhh!"

"What the fuck's going on?"

"Ahhhhhh! Shut your mouth you no-good spendthrift greaser bastard!"

"Aw, eat shit, you ugly old witch!"

And the day began.

After breakfast: Kellogg's Corn Flakes and coffee, after making their daughter Libby cry bitter tears with their hatred and anger and murderous dangerous words, they all piled into Big Arv's beat-out old white '61 Chevy Impala and drove out the Front Gate. May cried and complained all the way, trying to sour her husband's corn flakes and coffee in his voluminous overacidic belly.

Driving down the freeway, later, taking May to work and Libby to high school, May in her hair net and white waitress' uniform, Libby in her J. C. Penney's fake peasant blouse and red corduroy bellbottoms and brown suede boots. Big Arv pissed and moaned all the way, trying to get May to stop her ceaseless nagging.

"Nag, nag, nag, that's all you do!"

"You goddamned right, you S.O.B., if you'd get some money in this house to pay off that useless freezer and that screwed-up TV and them dumb-ass uneatable rabbits you bought, maybe I'd shut up!"

"You're gonna shut up right now!" Big Arv said, speeding up in the heavy workbound morning traffic, jack-rabbiting through lines of cars irresponsibly, trying to get the old bag to work before he killed them all.

"Oh no I ain't!" she said, turning toward him fiercely, not afraid of him in the least, looking forward to whatever the sonofabitch would deliver, welcoming it, as the only passionate and tearful diversion in her drab existence.

"Oh yes you are!" he said threateningly, his voice registering the no-no mark, the highwater mark where one went but did not go beyond on pain of bodily injury.

"Please, please, please!" Libby squealed in the torn and stained plastic back seat, patting her mother on the shoulder, "please, Mom! Please!"

"Who says I . . ." May started, gritting her teeth like a Mongol warrior, fearless, free, unafraid, opening her arms to adventure.

PLOW! BAM! WHAM! ZAP! Big Arv struck her shoulder, her face, her ear, her side, flapping away with his right hand while with his left he valiantly attempted to keep them out of an accident. The Chevy weaved dangerously, skidding, skidding.

ZAM! WAK! CRASH! May hit back with all her strength, swinging her heavy handbag weighted down with her wedgies that she wore at work. She got him on the arm, the elbow, wrist, and shoulder, and . . . she didn't mean to, but she got him right dab in the eye . . .

"Goddamn you!" he shouted, losing all self-control in his fury, his face contorting, going beyond red into blue and then deep purple . . . his heavy meaty pink fist doubling up, pulling back, poised, all attention on where it was aiming . . . right smack into her harridan's sharp-pointed nose or chin . . .

"Stop!" Libby hollered, "look out! A wet spot!"

Big Arv grabbed the wheel with both hands but it was too late. They hit the slick rain water and spun neatly around in a half circle and when the car came to the end of the puddle and hit dry cement again it went up on its left wheels and hovered that way for an instant, eternal instant, teetering, trying to make up its mind whether it was going to make one roll or settle back down like normal. Meanwhile the heavy rush-hour traffic was screeching and twisting and banging into the guardrails trying to avoid them. Giant semitrailer trucks blared their horns. HONK! HONK! Passenger cars honked too, and skidded and banged into each other, scraping metal, sending chrome and glass flying. WHAM! WHAM! Two wrecks. A Greyhound hot out of the mountains on its way from Denver gave them the closest call, brushing the rear end and bashing in the taillight. WHAM! WHAM! Two more wrecks. They were beginning to pile up on the lanes. Traffic was halting. Miraculously the Chevy was still unhurt, still teetering just on the edge of disaster.

The Weeds' eyeballs: ZONK! Looking out at that big-ass Greyhound motating by. "Ahhhhhhhhhhh!" May wailed, realizing the end of ends of her nightmare.

"Oh nooooooooo!" cried poor Libby, convinced that this was already where her sweet fat young life came to its early doom, Weed-like, imprisoned in the twisted metal of a wrecked automobile with the twisted wreck of her family.

"Oh fuuuuuck!" said Big Arv and, quick-thinking for once, leaned in such a way that the Chevy was impelled downward onto its natural rubber and landed with a THWONK! looking back the wrong way with three thousand screaming machines, cruisers and destroyers and rocket ships bearing down on them, riding from the end of the night to run them down, flatten them into iron ore dust.

"Ahhhhhhh!" the women yelled, throwing their hands back in anticipation of an immediate extinction in eight lanes of heavy traffic.

Inches away from an ignoble and meaningless death on the freeway, but still American to the core, Big Arv dropped that fucking little Chevy Impala into low drive and brodied around and dug out fast, spinning rubber, and split down that long wide stretch of reinforced concrete highway at ninety miles an hour and whipped off at the Molina Valley off-ramp, leaving a trail of broken parts, broken bodies, broken metal and strained steel, strained nerves, strained reality, littering the endless interstate roadway, and a traffic jam sixteen miles long that wound all the way over the hills and into the ground fog of Mission Santa Bonita, blending finally, amalgamating itself with the next traffic jam, caused by low visibility, in the tule beds and swamp lands by the Quintana Sound. . . .

Fourteen

The croaker, the six A.M. buzzer, went off over all the huge gray echoing block, setting the sparrows to chirping and winging crazily around in the rafters. Four hundred radios turned on simultaneously to get the morning news from Outside: "Nixon mines Haiphong. Bombing resumed above DMZ."

And then the racking cigarette coughs, the hawking lungers, green and purple wake-up phlegm, laughter, pissing and moaning, the sound of two hundred piddles of peepee bubbling in the open commodes . . . and then a thunderous flush as it went down, the water pipes banging all the way to Quintana Sound, and then curses, knocking heads and knees, feet slapping the hard concrete, electric shavers, cold-water taps running . . .

Someone in a cell on the next tier shouted:

"Nope! I ain't gettin' up! Pig got to come *drag* this nigger out!"

"Oohie! Run it down, brother!"

"Shut up, niggers!"

"Eat shit, peckerwood!"

"Shut off that ass-breath you call talk, raghead!"

"Die, Honkey!"

"Bugger you, Jigaboo!"

"Fuck you, Chuck!"

"Kill the coons!"

"Off the Kelts!"

"Viva la Raza!"

"Aw, y'all stop yo pitchin' the bitch!"

"Right on, *negrito!* Stop them nappyblacks and paddies from hasslin'! 'Member who you real *enemigo* got to be!"

"Who the enemy?"

"The Pig!"

"Absofuckinglutely, babies!"

"The Hack!"

"The Main Cop!"

"Aiiiii Chihuahua!"

"The Man!"

A tremendous cheer went up, sending the sparrows flapping and fluttering for the barred windows for the first time that day, relieving the air, air so tainted and stale and daily lived in, yet so fraught with electric shock that, with another escalation of this rhetoric of the Rap, it might have carried them all Lord knows where, might have caused everybody a whole fucking shitload of trouble, and cracked black heads, and popped blue eyes too, and it was too early, Wasco figured, far too cold and damp and early for that kind of caca, no matter how the black cocksuckers begged for wrath.

At six o'clock in the morning, Wasco thought, as he lay in his warm three-blanket fart sack in his brand new East Block holding cell, *at six o'clock in the morning all men are brothers . . .*

"You want to get up first?" the squeeze asked from the top bunk.

"Naw, sweetbuns, you go ahead."

So the kid threw off the covers, releasing a whiff, a good human sniff, and jumped down naked, his piss hard-on hitting against his thigh with a loud SMACK! And went over and had a tinkle.

The cell was only eight by ten, and with a bunkbed, a commode, a cold-water wash basin, there was only room for one man to move around at a time.

The punk, shivering in the cold, threw water on his face, brushed his teeth furiously, combed his pale hair, put on his skivvies, got down and did a surprising twenty (considering his tracked arms, swollen hands—these fucking junkies are amazing!), twenty official rulebook push-ups, dressed, and jumped back up on the top bunk like somebody'd just hit him with a whole bindle of speed.

The second buzzer went off. CROAK! CROAK! CROAK!

Fifteen minutes to chow time.

Wasco's uncle, Officer Sanger Weed, yelled into the block loudspeaker, "First Tier to chow!" His voice was like the croaker, rasping, discordant, the result of a broken windpipe suffered in a Golden Gloves match twenty years before.

But Wasco stayed abed, relaxed, fart-happy, sniffing under the covers, thinking things over for another couple of minutes. Then he unfolded the blankets and swung his feet to the floor.

"Pee you!"

"Shut up, Squeeze, or I'll make you call it perfume," Wasco said, laughing good-naturedly. The squeeze beamed in his top bunk, basking in this Wasco-style benediction.

"Goddamn, this floor's cold! We got to get us some bread together. Get some shower shoes at the canteen."

"Right on, man, got to get us some Moo!"

"Don't you ever talk nigger jive around me. Understand?"

"What?"

"You heard me. Now listen," Wasco said, going for the pail of hot water the inmate "key man" had hung over the crossbars on the cell door, "I got it figured how we're gonna get us a few boxes."

"Boxes?"

"Money, man. Cigarette cartons. That's money in here."

Wasco lathered up with the greasy prison soap and shaved quick, scraping the skin on his neck.

"Fuck! And we're gonna get some English Leather shave lotion too!"

The key man came around unlocking the cells. Click, click, click . . . forty-one, forty-two, forty-three, forty-four . . .

Officer Weed yelled, "Third Tier! Chow time!"

The bull at the end of the line of cells pulled the heavy release pin—CLANG!—and eighty-seven fresh-shaved, steamy-faced convicts stepped fast out into the fluorescent white light of the tier, closed the cell doors behind them—BANG!—staying well clear of the big lock bar—ZANG!—as it came sliding back like a firing piston.

They made their way in a gang down the spiral metal staircase, silent, grumpy, grinding their teeth, and out onto the cement floor (Wasco could see his punchy old Uncle Sanger sitting inside the guard shanty talking to the tier man over a hot cup of stinger-made coffee) and through the huge steel doors to the Big Yard.

Wasco and the squeeze put their hands in their pockets, like everyone else, and looked around. The Yard was full of convicts, sea gulls, and pigeons, milling and queuing in

the bright early winter morning after a storm, splashing in
the shiny puddles of rainwater on the blacktop.

Wasco was thinking about his old Uncle Sanger, whom
he'd always kind of dug, even though he was punch-drunk
and stupid, even though he couldn't stand his nagging
bitch of a foul-mouthed wife, Betty. Him and old
Sanger'd always got along just fine, even used to spar
around together from time to time. Sanger'd taught him
quite a few boxing tricks that'd come in real handy later
on in life. In fact, you could just about say that Sanger
was part of the secret of Wasco's enormous pugilistic success in life, and was partly responsible for his ascendance
over all the rest of them hardnosed motherfuckers in the
Motopsychos. Wasco always liked to give credit where
credit is due, so he had to admit, Old Sanger had really
helped him out in life, which is, after all, just what an uncle's supposed to do, ain't it? But Little Arv, that was another story. Even though Sanger had tried his best to
teach the little sonofabitch a few things, how to defend
himself like a man, he hated Sanger's guts. Ever since the
time when he was only about sixteen and they went over
to Sanger's place on the prison grounds with May and
they all got drunk together on cheap white port and
lemon juice and Sanger tried to carry on Arv's boxing
lessons out on the front lawn. Old Sanger, what with the
drinking and all, and the fact that he was so punchy he
didn't know his asshole from a hole in the ground, beat
the hell out of Arv, smashed his nose, cut his eye so the
lid drooped always after that. Changed his looks for life.
But it didn't make him any uglier. Nothing could have
done that. Arv never would forgive old Uncle Sanger.
And Sanger, the crazy bastard, never seemed to forgive
Arv either. As if it was Arv's fault for sticking his face
out in his way, setting himself up for the swift left jabs,
the solid six-inch right hooks and, later, when they were
even drunker and rowdier, and at Wasco's admitted instigation, wild full-force bolos and haymakers that split his
lip, broke his teeth, cut his ears. Little Arv crying, "Go
ahead, you sonofabitch, go ahead, hit me, hit me! I got to
be a man! I got to be a man!" and Wasco yelling, "Yeah,
hit the little bastard, just like he says, he's got to be a man
someday, got to be a man someday! Hit him, Sanger! Hit
him!" and May yelling, "Stop, you'll kill the boy, you'll

kill him, stop!" and Arv just going on and on screaming
and bawling, "I got to be a man! I got to be a man!" and
old Sanger just quietly slugging away, working at his belly
and his nose and eyes, saying, real quiet and sure, drunk
sure, "Shit, you little fruit, you ain't never gonna be a
man, not ever!" POW! POW! POW!

Wasco, out in the yard with his punk, squinting at the
sun that was just rising over the eastern hills, just coming
up over the prison walls, reflected now that Sanger'd probably, sadly, been right, the little guy probably never would
grow up, never would be a man, unless Wasco himself,
his Big Cuz Wasco, helped him along a bit, just for his
own good, just to make a real fucking man out of him, a
real dude . . . a stud with bones behind him . . .

After chow in the Joint everyone came out with a little
bread for the birds. Nobody paid any mind to the yellowing notice posted on the Big Yard bulletin board, most
people didn't even know it was there:

NOTICE

The habit of tossing bread to the pigeons and sea gulls
in the Main Yard or sparrows in the cellblocks will cease
forthwith.

Hereafter, any inmate seen scattering crumbs or littering the premises will receive a NSCC 114. Unsanitary littering will not be tolerated.

B. F. Bischoff
Yard Lieutenant

Wasco gave his crumbs to the squeeze and he threw
them at the birds, which flapped and fought over them for
a long time. Then a fat sea gull with a crooked beak got
away with the biggest morsel and flew over the wall with
it, the whole white and gray flock of them wheeling after
him into the mist.

"Easy for them, ain't it?" the squeeze said.

"Don't be so obvious, man," Wasco replied.

They went back to their cell to wait for the eight
o'clock bell. Neither one of them had applied for a job,
school or vocational training at the Sign-in Desk the day
before. Wasco said, "We ain't working for no thirty-five
cents a fucking day!" And, since there weren't enough

jobs or places in school to go around anyway, the bulls wouldn't bother them, Wasco figured. He figured he'd be able to get them both a tier man job, a gravy slot, or they'd be free to just stand around all day out on the Yard, hands in pockets, cigarettes dangling, pitching horseshoes, playing dominoes, and dealing with the operators, the high-rollers, the pros, the nonworking aristocracy of the Joint, their crime partners.

On the way up to the cell Uncle Sanger yelled out, "Hey Wasco, how you doing?" He was smiling real friendly and Wasco remembered again that he'd always dug his punchy old unckus and smiled back and said, "Hey, Uncle Sanger, aside from the Jam, things couldn't be more Kopasetic!" pointing to the squeeze behind him, affecting an obsolete slang that he knew would please Sanger. And Sanger, who knew after all that Wasco was no fucking skippy, no queen, was just covering his physical needs the best way he could, under the circumstances, yelled out, "Good boy! Just be sure you have his front teeth out!"

"Don't worry, Unck, if he gives me any trouble, I'll have 'em out myself!" Wasco said, brandishing his big thick fist.

And old ring-worn Uncle Sanger, he just cracked up at that, and waved them on up the tier, and went back to talking to his graveyard shift tier man, laughing to beat all git out, and Wasco heard him say, with great pride in his voice, "Yeah, that criminoid sonofabitch is my nephew! Ain't that something?" And Wasco like to just about bust his denim shirt with glee cause this here block, he knew, would now have the skinny on exactly who Mr. Wasco G. Weed was!

Even the squeeze kept bright eyes, took nothing amiss, and wasn't hurt by the ribbing and all, knowing that his future was tied up with a winner. He held himself high, in a way, the punk, to be the one and only squeeze of a man who was definitely going places in this here fucking hole, destined for big things, destined for the tops!

At the eight o'clock whistle, when every buzzer and steam horn and toot-toot in the Joint went off, when the laundry and the jute factory and the auto license plant and the central heating plant and the dairy all blew shrill and long, signaling the faithful to work, Wasco just stayed put in the cell.

"Look," he told the squeeze, "I want you to make your way out to the Yard and try to cop a couple of nickel bags of boy and maybe a cap of crank on credit. Maybe a whole fit if you can get ahold of it."

"I don't want to start chipping in here," the punk said. "I don't want to start up a habit I can't feed, man."

"Who said you had to start using? Did I say anything about that?"

"Well . . ."

"Alright. You just keep cool. Let your old Ma do the thinking. Now, actually, if you did want to start up, I mean like maybe just snorting, don't worry. I'm gonna be able to keep more than just your little four bag habit fed."

"What you mean? I had a fifteen bag a day habit when I come into the Slam!"

"Get your fucking ass out on that Yard!"

It wasn't but about an hour before the kid come back up and laid the whole unit on him, everything he'd asked for.

"Leave that cell door open a hair. I want you to go back out in a while. Hey, Squeezy! Damned if you might not work out after all!"

"It was easy," he said.

"Yeah? What'd the cat look like who sold it to you? Let's see what we got here . . ."

Wasco hung his shirt up on the bunkbed so it hid him from the tier. He spread the speed cap, the bags of heroin, and the works, the fit, the dropper, point and cooker out on the blanket.

"He was a white dude with a cross tattooed on the web of his left hand, a Pachuco number."

Wasco didn't listen. He very carefully examined the bags of smack, paying special attention to the exact way they'd been bagged, packed and folded. Then he said, "You want a little wake-up, man?"

"Sure," the squeeze said, and his junkie's eyes went the way Wasco knew they'd go, they went like moons, lit and round and already pinned at the thought of a fix. And, very serious all of a sudden, real efficient, he went for the smack, unfolded it, poured a bagful into the bottle-cap cooker.

"You want to get off too?" he asked.

"Never touch the stuff," Wasco said, "it's a filthy habit."

The kid went to the tap, took some water into the eyedropper, released it into the powder in the bottlecap and cooked up: heated it up with a match, drew the dissolved heroin solution through a cotton ball into the eyedropper with the hypodermic point on the end, swung his left arm around violently like a softball pitcher warming up, unbuckled his belt with one hand, looped it expertly around his upper left arm in a tourniquet, traded the point to his right hand, found a big pouting vein near the crook of the forearm, held it pinched between his middle finger and his thumb, and delicately, with great skill and style, tap tap tapped the needle slowly through the skin and deep into his bloodstream. He held it in a long time, sitting on the bed behind the hanging shirt, enjoying the operation, the ritual of a junkie, almost as much as he would enjoy the later rush. Face red, intent, lost in pleasure, the squeeze jerked off until the dropper was nearly full of his own backed-up blood. Then he pulled the point and wiped it on some toilet paper, wiped too his bleeding arm, waiting, savoring the moment of waiting for the jolt, waiting . . .

After a moment Wasco impatiently asked, "What's happening?"

The squeeze sat for another moment, twitching with disappointment, and finally said, "We been dealt a fucking blank, man. Fucking lemonade! Feels like about ninety-nine per cent mannita and quinine. You'd have to fix six bags of this garbage to even get straight!"

"Bullet."

"Huh?"

"It's a dude named Bullet who's the connection. Here, man, sterilize that point and dropper if you don't want us all down with hep. And clean that cooker! I knew there was four pushers in here now with the capability to deal within the Joint itself. And only Bullet packs his skag in writing paper around here anymore, and folds it envelope-shape. And he never did deal good smack. He's never held anything that would take the eight in his whole fucking life.

"Now, here's what we're gonna do. Let me run it down for you. After lunch you're going back out to the Yard

and find old Bullet. Tell him his old buddy Wasco wants
to talk to him."

"Will he come?"

"Shit, he'll come. I known that cat for years. He's
scared not to. We been through it all before. He used to
call himself a take-off artist. Tried to beat me and the
Motopsychos. We got him and his crime partner at their
stash pad. Tied them up and gagged their fucking satchels
and rolled them into the trunk of a little '55 Chevy.
Drove them out to the boonies, man, to the Motopsycho
Burial Ground. Like Tarzan's old Elephant Graveyard,
Squeezy, full of graves and bones and snuffed punks.

"But out in the National Forest, see, a goddamn State
Park Ranger stopped us cause he thought we was
poaching deer. He saw the trunk weighing the car down
in the rear and got suspicious. Pulled his gun and had his
partner cover us. Taking no chances. Cause he recognized
me. Smart-ass. Said, 'Lemme see what you got in that
there trunk, son.' What could we say? I went around, already starting to crack up, it was so funny, and I turned
the key, and man, old Bullet, him and his crime partner
thought they was going to meet their maker. Their eyes
was like they'd already been blowed off, man. And the
ranger, wow! You can figure how surprised that cat was.
So they take us all in and book us on a one eighty-six,
see? Attempted Murder. But we was just laughing. Cause
we knew Bullet wouldn't fink. He was too scared, see?
That this time we wouldn't just dust him, we'd double-
dust him! So he said, 'No, listen Your Honor! You got
this all wrong. We're in this motorcycle club, see? Motopsycho M.C. See our club jackets?' And we all showed
him the cut-offs. And he says, 'So look, me and my partner here are new members, just being initiated into the
club. This is what you call a form of "hazing," Your
Honor, just like in a frat, or something. And they was just
going out to maybe pants us and put us up in a tree and
make us go through the club initiation, see?' Well, the
Man didn't go for it, but what could he say? No witnesses.
So they let us go. We all copped to the cheaper beef. Mis-
demeanor. 'Malicious Mischief,' and walked out on
probation. And when we stepped out onto the courthouse
steps on Eleventh Street, I says, 'Hey Bullet, you a lucky
motherfucker!'"

"And he says, 'How come?' only he was smiling real happy, see, cause he knew. And I says, 'Looks like you might remain with us on the planet a while longer.'

"And he says, he just laughs, see, and says, 'Okay man, I'll call you God if you call us even!' And he laughed again, see? And it looked like maybe he thought I wanted to shake on it, and he waved an open hand around in the sky like a spook and came down at me for skin and got nothing out of it but air. And you should of seen his face, man, it fucking fell out of his head and lay down and quivered on the ground like a boot-licking dog. And I said, 'I don't shake hands with niggers.' And that's the last I seen of him till now. . . ."

That afternoon the squeeze went out to the Yard and, sure enough, came a-trailing the Bullet behind him. He was a tall shifty-eyed Polack of about thirty-seven or -eight with an acne-scarred satchel face. He was the dirtiest man in the Joint. He took great pride in the fact that he never showered, and that he always got a cell by himself because no one could stand his smell. Beneath and in between his heavy big-boned frame he gave the impression of being completely soft and empty, like a spider web on a strong limb.

"Hey man, what's shakin'?" Wasco said while he was still out on the tier.

"Same ole same ole," Bullet answered, smiling painfully through the horrid pimples, his grease- and dirt-caked face shining in the white light.

"Hey, Squeeze," Wasco said, "do your number!" and the squeeze split downstairs. Then Wasco said, "Listen, Bullet, I told you not to ever use nigger talk around me, do you hear? Don't ever give me that 'same ole same ole' shit again. Seems like some dudes get into the Joint and want to copy them big-lipped watermelon eaters. They're backing the wrong fucking horse, if you ask me. Now come in here, I got something to discuss."

"Is it okay?" Bullet asked, hesitating in the cellway.

"Okay? What do you mean? I got one uncle the graveyard shift block officer and another one swing shift sergeant and you're asking me is it alright to come in?"

The Polack stepped inside and Wasco laid the whole trip on him immediately.

"Listen, man, I'm buying you out," Wasco said real low, making Bullet strain to hear, making him ask.

"What?"

"You heard me," Wasco said, breathing through his mouth so he wouldn't get a whiff of the foul-smelling bastard, "I'm gonna be frank with you, Bullet old baby. I'm gonna make you an honorable proposal of a business nature that you're gonna find it impossible to turn down. . . . Here's where it's at. You're no match for me, and you know it. Number one, you're a junkie. You can't retain the objectivity needed in an operation like this. Number two, you don't have my organizational and supply skills and connections. Your action here is a weak, small-profit, nickel and dime bag scene, man. Your supply is erratic, your goods are inferior. You deal nothing but trash and garbage. I can offer this market area dynamite smack, man, the best that money can buy. Strong enough so you can get off beautiful just snorting. Save a lot of people the hassle of carrying a fit around all the time. They can just chip like that till they get out. I got a guaranteed daily supply coming in six days a week by the half load and bundle already cut and bagged. And not in cheap prison writing paper, man. Glassine, pure glassine folded up nice in perfect little stamp collectors' bags! And number three, I can offer total protection to everyone in the business from top to bottom."

"But listen, man," the Polack said, "your uncle is . . ."

"Who said anything about my uncle? You think I'd lay a trip like this on my own family?"

"So who's made?"

"Never mind. Now listen to me. I'm offering a totally smooth operation, with enormous growth potential and a guaranteed seller's market," Wasco said, very seriously, with only the slightest edge of irony, an edge that Bullet would not detect. "Available, in terms of the supply question, I got any kind of thrill in any kind of quality or quantity the customer desires. I sell by the cap, the bag, the bindle, the bundle, the half load, the nickel, dime, quarter or trey bag, the piece or the pill . . . under any name you want . . . I got tranqs, speed, bombitas, coke, bam, black beauties, cartwheels, yellow jackets, reds, long greens, rainbows, beans, STP, DMT, LSD, mescaline, psilocybin, synthetic cannabis, amphetamine, meth, Biphetamine, phenobarbital, Dexedrine, Benzedrine, Librium, Miltown, Dilaudid, methadone, morphine, Seconal, Demerol, goofballs, truck drivers, yellow stripes, Tuinal, Desoxyn, carbon tetrachloride, strychnine and arsenic. I'll even have a hole drilled in your head, man, for the ultimate kick . . . everything but grass or hash, which I refuse to sell in the Joint, cause I don't like the smell. I can even offer dollies, man the best Dolophine that money can buy, for anybody who wants to kick his habit sweet and easy a day at a time. I ain't jealous. As you know, I ain't a junkie. And I ain't in favor of any kind of dope. The way I look at it, it's just another market area. If you got people who want to buy, you might as well sell what they want. Otherwise they're going to buy it from the next guy. There's a lot of dudes brought their habit in with them. They got to have that wake-up, that nooner, that matinee and that sleepy-time daily, four times a day, seven days a week, like clockwork. Well, every man to his own poison. And I'm prepared to offer this here Jam the best fucking hard-ass poison available on the market today, and at competitive prices too. I'll undersell anyone in the Joint, even Roundo and Yuba, your heaviest competitors with the black trade.

"Moreover, my man," Wasco went on, hardselling, while Bullet scowled but didn't dare say anything, "I'm offering room for attractive diversification of industry. Many potential growth areas remain uncapitalized in this place. There's room for operations not only in dope, but in cigarettes, prostitution, banking facilities, loan services, organized gambling, liquor, clothing sales, uncensored postal service, stud service, underground courier service direct to the Street, not to mention direct telephone service to the Outside. Shit, man, our growth area can even encompass diversification to the extent of selling processed hair accoutrements to the raghead nigger konks, and smuggling contraband hot sauce for the Spics' cellblock snacks direct from the Tio Pico chile factory in Tijuana! There's a world of profit to be made, old man, a whole world of capital gain!

"Now here's the package I'm prepared to offer you: you're going to deliver your operation over to me intact, as is, the moment that I prove to you, this very afternoon, the superiority of my supply system and products. I will give you a full silent partnership in my much-expanded business, and you just set back with no risk and collect half the profits of the new business, making more money than you ever did before."

Bullet winced and stood up tall, moving the muscles in his jaw. "Oh yeah?" he said, "and what if I say no?"

Wasco smiled, real slow, real cold. "If you say no, then I just angel off your customers with my superior products, man."

"And what if I decide to engage in a trade war?" Bullet said, standing above Wasco in what he hoped would pass as a threatening manner, but it was no good, his fear of Wasco showed all over.

"I will defeat you through my greater objectivity, my superior experience in these affairs," Wasco said, very confident, looking him right in the eye, like a businessman over the desk at a difficult client, "and through my flawless organization, supply, products, sales team, protection, reserve funds, and my quick native business acumen."

"And what," Bullet asked, hesitant, afraid, but still determined to spar with him, as long as he still wasn't hurt for real, "and what if I still refuse?"

"I'll kill you, man, right now, right here, right where you stand. I'll throw you off the fucking tier and run for the door around the other side and when the sergeant comes up, Day Sergeant Byrnes, a man I've known all my life, a man whose kids I grew up with, whose daughter I used to go out on dates with, a man whose dog I used to walk, whose American Legion football team I used to star for, I'll slip out and when I come back in, if the sarge asks me if I did it, I'll look him right in the eyes, man to man, just the way I used to when he caught me goosing his daughter or shooting my BB gun in his back yard as a kid, and I'll say, 'Nope, truthfully, George, I didn't.' And he'll believe me, man, cause I'm home folks, local boy, and he'll file an 'accidental death' report and that will be that."

"Hey man," Bullet said, smiling heartily, advancing toward Wasco with his right hand extended, "I'm just kidding. Actually I was thinking about taking on a partner anyway to fight the competition in here. It *is* pretty stiff, especially, like you say, Roundo and Yuba and that good-looking wife of Yuba's from the city that brings it to him deep-throat style a half-piece at a time with a stuffed Trojan down her fucking black gullet. . . . Sure, man! You got yourself a deal. Let's shake on it. I'd be crazy not to accept . . .

"And anyway," Bullet said after they'd shook on it, exhaling deeply, as if a heavy weight had been lifted from his shoulders, but overdoing it a bit, making it a little too theatrical to suit Wasco, "anyway, you know what? This takes a great responsibility off my back, man!"

"Sure," Wasco said, "look at it this way. You're the dynamic self-made tycoon who, when he's got it made, retires to the board of directors and lets the business run itself through a manager, dig it?"

"Great!" Bullet said, beaming, "listen, let's go on out to the Yard and I'll introduce you to my organization and we'll start the transfer and inform the troops about our new partnership."

"Okay . . ." Wasco said warily, "let's go."

"You first."

"No, after you!"

"No, no, no, you go first, since you're the boss now."

"No! I insist!"

"Absolutely not, I insist, you first!"

"Alright," Wasco said, "if you put it that way," and headed out the cell door expecting the violent shove which did in fact come as soon as he was on the tier. But Wasco was ready for it. He'd already dropped to his knees by the time the Polack's heavy rapidly moving body reached him. Bullet tripped over him and flew full tilt into the iron railing. THWUNK! He fell all in a heap to the tier walkway, bleeding from a cut above his eye, moaning, moaning, expecting no mercy, no mercy at all from Wasco. Wasco stood above him in the white fluorescent light, looking down calmly into Bullet's fear-glazed hopeless eyes . . . but that isn't what Wasco had in mind, not yet, not ever what a man expected, never, that was Wasco's motto.

"Get on your fucking feet before I kill you," Wasco snarled. "You know what? You're so stupid I wonder why they haven't put you in the nuthouse instead of the Joint. Fucking with Wasco G. Weed . . . and two different times! What's wrong with you? Now get this straight, motherfucker! I'm not going to kill you right now. Don't ask me why not. It must be a soft spot in my heart. But another move like that and you'll find your balls stuck in your mouth some morning, and your own cock sticking out of your asshole. I'm going to give you one more chance. Now, I want you to stroll out to the Yard with me arm and arm, and we'll talk with your boys, and when they determine that my supply system and products are superior, which will take place this very afternoon, as I've already told you, then we'll effect the transfer. Now get up on your feet, goddamnit, like I told you!" Wasco shouted, slapping the smelly Polack around his sick green gills. "Get up, goddamnit!"

"You'll kill me," he whimpered.

"I'll what?"

"You'll kill me . . ."

"I'll kill you if you don't, you candy-ass. Get up!"

"Help me," the Polack whined.

"Oh, alright," Wasco said, aware of the game, playing it too, and reached a hand to help him up and the dumb fucking Polack pulled at his arm trying to pull off some stupid plan to get Wasco over the side, figuring he'd trip him up or something, but too stupid to figure the leverage of the situation, too dumb to see that a man lying the way he was could never do it and Wasco kicked him hard in the face, crunching a couple of teeth, and kicked again, and the pathetic sonofabitch, knowing he had to fight, knowing that if he didn't Wasco would let him live only long enough to effect the change, and would snuff him like a fly, the mindless fucking dolt got hold of Wasco's heavily muscled calf and weakly jerked at it. Wasco just let it fall hard against the Polack's belly, knocking air right out. "WHOOF!"

"You had enough?"

"Yeah . . ."

"Now lookit!" Wasco said, real sincere, "I know what you think. But you're wrong. I firmly intend to keep you on, as long as you stop fucking around. Really! You can count on me. Listen, I got a reputation to keep up. If I start double-crossing business associates, people will no longer have any trust in me, you see? Now pull yourself together and get on your feet and let's go on outside and do our number."

Bullet, with no other choice, chose hope, and forced

himself against his better judgment to believe Wasco's smoothly uttered words of assurance. "Alright man," he said, surprisingly spry, as if nothing had happened between them, "I guess you're right. No hard feelings. You know what I thought, I figure, but if you say . . ."

"Of course, man," Wasco said, "I know what you thought. But let's forget all about it now. Let bygones be bygones. Come on!"

And Wasco took his old buddy Bullet by his smelly arm and the two of them did just what Wasco wanted them to do, they marched out to the Yard arm and arm, buddy buddy, beaming with wide-ass smiles for the population of the Joint, and concluded their deal in real style.

You had to hand it to old Bullet, in the end. Knowing what he knew, about his future and all, it showed a lot of class what he did, and how he did it.

He did everything Wasco told him to.

Fifteen

"Whew!"

"Wow!"

"Oh my Lord!"

"Jesus H. Fucking Christ!" said the Weeds, "that was a close one!"

"Oh yeah!" they said.

"It sure was!" they all said, as the luckily only slightly damaged Chevy Impala, guided by Big Arv's now-steadier hand, hurtled off the wreck-littered freeway and speedily, intrepidly, into the real world on the Molina Valley off-ramp.

"We sure were lucky, weren't we?" the Weeds said, congratulating each other on the incredible fortune that granted them back their lives for a few more months or years. And then, full-blooded Yankees all, they went about their business as usual: May went to work at the restaurant, Libby went to high school, as if nothing had happened, happy almost, in a way, that something had taken place that got their minds off the perennial battle between Big Foot Arv and Mama May.

Big Arv even kissed little May on the cheek, perkily almost, out in front of Bert's Beanery, and said, "Boy! Huh?"

And she smiled quite happily at the attention and said, "Whew! Yeah!" and went whistling contentedly off to her job.

Libby too. She was even laughing. "Oh boy, Dad! See you!"

"Okay, honey," he said, he who never ever under ordinary circumstances deigned even to notice his plump unhappy young daughter, who went weeks without addressing her except in tones of command.

And Big Arv, judiciously avoiding the freeway, whistled

and sang (his radio was on the blink) *I've Got You Under My Skin,* over and over again all the way out across the hills and over the humpback bridge that crossed the Sound.

It was a bright sparkling warm West Coast winter morning after rain. Mist rose off the greenish-brown waters under the bridge. There were dark splotches of blackish mud in the frothy water, brought down in torrents from the mountains, let out into the Sound in a thousand bubbling brown little rivulets and streams and rivers. Across the huge gray-painted suspension bridge, seven miles away, Big Arv could see the tankers tied up at the refinery, silver ones, black ones, Exxon, New Jersey Standard, Shell, Mobil, reflecting the brilliant early morning sunlight. Sage-clad islands slid by under him, driftwooded up underneath the bridge, as Big Arv's old Impala stretched its legs and revved out, soaring across the giant double-arched bridge, the sunlight coming in through the green-tinted windshield, shining on Big Arv's dark glasses, warming him up on his khaki shirt, down on his overall legs, reflecting off the pencils and pens in his bib pocket, and reflecting too, gloriously, he saw, way off sixty miles off east, to his left, reflecting too off the virgin snow on the highest peaks of the New Sonora Alps, those wonder-filled mountains that cut the horizon, cut the West Coast of the old U.S.A. off entirely from the rest of the continent, cut them! Cut them off!

Cut us right off! Big Arv was thinking, *cut us off from them fucking assholes back east!*

Sergeant Weed could say this, disdainfully even, though he himself had been born across those mountains, born prematurely in a hot Rio Grande tomato field that had once been an Indian battleground. His father cut the umbilical cord himself and buried it among the vines. Big Arv was born red-faced and slightly pop-eyed and fat and would remain that way till the day he died. He had a bad heart. The doctor said he drank too much beer, smoked too much, ate too many starchy foods, put too much salt on them.

He was deeply in debt all his adult life, and no matter how hard he worked, no matter how many extra jobs he took on, he always seemed to get into it deeper. A fortuneteller at the New Sonora County Fair once remarked that the initial *M* was formed by the principal lines in the middle of his hand. It was supposed to indicate either that he would die with "Money" or die in "Middle-age," which to the Sarge seemed "a damn good set of odds, as good as anybody gets." That is not to say, however, that he would not curse his fate when he died that premature middle-aged death, bemoaning his early passing, his meaningless years on earth, and in the Joint, his uncompleted life. On the other hand, even if he died at ninety-nine, he'd probably end up bemoaning the same damn set of things. . . .

Big Arv was an easy-going fellow by nature, but terrible when provoked. His fellow guards, and the inmates in his charge, found they often provoked him, as did his wife and children, whom he beat vengefully, with a grave sense of justice.

When the mood struck him he could be kind, patient, funny, sparing neither his time, energy, nor his extremely limited powers of imagination to entertain his kids. He took them into the dry yellow hills above the Joint, and the cow pastures and the sage brush, dragging his beloved nephew Wasco along, and he took them into the oak forest in winter, out to the fog-bound Pacific Ocean beaches in the summertime. He cut holly, mistletoe and illegal Christmas trees for them in season, taught them the names of trees, plants, grasses, birds, and wild animals. He spent hours of his time teaching them games, how to pitch, shoot a free-throw, straight-arm, whether they wanted to learn or not.

As it turned out, his kid Arv never wanted to learn. Wasco always.

The only thing he could teach Little Arv was how to shoot. He started him out with a .22 Bolt Action at the institution firing range when he was twelve, and by the time Arv was eighteen, and going into the army, he was the most famous marksman in the Joint. This was one of his few redeeming qualities, as far as Big Arv was concerned.

Big Arv was jealous of his authority in the family. Every time it thundered he said, "Look out kids! Here I come walking!" This activity he described to his wife as "puttin' the fear of God into the little bastards!"

The things Sergeant Weed liked were what he thought he was good at: hunting, fishing, gambling, playing baseball, animal husbandry, jitterbugging, chasing strange pussy, and working at the Joint. He got his buck a year hunting in the New Sonora Alps, brought home strings of salmon each run, won scads of money on poker night at the prison fire house, belonged to an Industrial League baseball team till he was well up in his forties, till his heart specialist made him quit. He was a fantastic dancer who knew all the latest steps and never forgot an old one, tangoing across the floor with some broad heedless of the folds of unhealthy fat that flapped around his belt and over his collar and between his obese legs. And, rather astoundingly, Big Arv always had some divorcee in Mission Santa Bonita he could go to for sport, even though no one in the Joint could figure out what she saw in him.

The things Big Arv hated were what he wasn't good at, or didn't understand. He wasn't good at and hated tennis, reading, figuring out income tax and helping his wife around the house. He didn't understand and hated mostly the usual: niggers, Jews, convicts (excluding his nephew Wasco), hippies, and "agitators." He didn't much care for his archrival either, Fast-Walking Miniver. And then, after that, in descending order of importance, he hated his wife. His son Little Arv was the only exception to this rule of nonunderstanding: Big Arv didn't understand his son and he hated him; but, utilizing all the strength of his flabby will, he loved him. His wife he hated cause she was a lush. She said she took to drink cause he hated her in the first place. He never sorted out which came first.

Big Arv loved birds and animals and always had a donkey and two or three dogs and cats around the place. He kept chickens and rabbits in the back yard despite the complaints of the neighbors. He enjoyed caring for his animals, feeding and watering them diligently every night and morning. And yet it was with great pleasure that he killed them too, whacking their heads off heartily with a hatchet and draining their blood on the ground. . . .

Once a week Big Arv used to come home from work at the Joint and cook up a big pot of piping hot chile beans. It was his greatest pleasure of the home, and a great event for all the kids, who came from all over the prison housing area and lined up at the back door (along with the burro, the dogs and even cats) to get a whiff and maybe a little handout. They were absolutely the best chile beans anyone had ever tasted, and the most powerful. Wasco called them the "original musical fruit," and that they were . . . relatives coming over days later would remark the terrible gaseous odor around the place and say, "Guess you had your cooking day recently, Big Arv. Smells like some kind of secret Russian weapon in there."

The reason why Sergeant Weed made such excellent and high-powered chile beans was entirely cultural: he was raised on them, along with corn tortillas, tacos, chile peppers, enchiladas, frijoles, guacamole, refried beans, pollo mole, menudo, hot tamales, Spanish rice and hot sauce, and learned how to cook Mexican style at his family hearth.

It's quite a story how it all happened, an American success story, actually, and not at all untypical:

Great-grandma Miller was born of a half-breed Cree mama from Indian Territory and a teetotaling Ozark pa in a covered wagon on the way out to McAllen, Texas. Like many women out in south Texas at the time, she grew up a rough and independent spirit, riding, shooting, and brawling like a man. She was married six times. Her last husband bequeathed her a boardinghouse on "D" Street in McAllen, across the street from the Missouri Pacific railroad yard. During the '20's, high times, the place turned a real good living for her. One of her tenants there was a gandy dancer by the name of Alfonso Encina, a squat, light-colored, green-eyed Mexican from Cuidad Camargo, Chihuahua. Fate decreed that Grandma Miller's daughter Dora Lee, a real west Texas frontier beauty, with raven hair and a bosom that set the engineers in the roundhouse to tooting off every locomotive under the shed whenever she walked down "D" Street, fall madly rapturously in love with the pudgy slant-eyed fellow and, at the mere age of sixteen, form a scandalous liaison with him, right before her mama's eyes. Eventually, despite Grandma Miller's (and the entire town of McAllen's) objections as to the interracial and interdenominational (if not ecumenical) nature of their attachment, they were married in the Catholic Church and moved into a little weathered, unpainted wooden shack in Spic Town. A bleak little place it was, with a dirt yard, cactus plants in back, the inevitable bitter scraggly rose tree, chickens and a mule in front, tied up to a rotting wood fence, sage brush and the limitless Rio Grande country across the sandy unpaved road.

During the Depression Alfonso lost his job on the Missouri Pacific, and took to drink, coming home nightly beating up on poor Dora Lee and the kids, blaming all his woes on her.

One day Dora Lee made her escape. It was not an ingenious escape, but simple and direct, like an animal escapes trouble. As she explained it many years later: "You run water in the coyote's hole and he's gonna hightail it!" She stole the family Model T while Alfonso was out on a binge at the Cantina Tamaulipas and lit out with all their worldly goods and their five kids for the promised land of New Sonora. They worked their way slowly along with a party of Okies and Arkies and Kansas people. It took them a year to make it through west Texas and New Mexico and Arizona and California to New Sonora, picking tomatoes, beans, prunes, grapes, melons, knocking almonds and walnuts, trying to assimilate as West Coast gringos a little more each day along the way. In Brawley, California, a steaming Imperial Valley town near the Colorado River, they shed their Catholic faith. In Arvin, California, a middle-sized oil and earthquake town near Bakersfield, she changed the name of her eldest boy from Alfonso Segundo to Arvin. In Wasco, California, a dry hot San Joaquin Valley town, she changed the name of her second son, Hernan Maria, to Wasco. In Coalinga and Manteca she changed the names of her two daughters. In Sanger, near Fresno, she changed the name of her baby boy. And finally, in Weed, California, a small town near Mount Shasta, Dora Lee applied for a legal change of the family name, "in honor of this fair city," as she marked down on the official form at the city hall. The local judge, highly flattered, acceded to her demand with the greatest alacrity. And by the time the new Weed family settled down in Mission Santa Bonita, New Sonora, and Dora Lee got herself safely married up with an elderly prison guard of Welsh and Scottish ancestry, they had become perfectly acceptable white Anglo-Saxon Protestants, with all the potential upward mobility of that favored race. In other words, like the majority of immigrants to the New World, they created a new identity for themselves as they went along. And who could blame the Weeds? What with the times, and Mexicans and Indians being just the yellow side of nigger out on the West Coast in those days, who could really blame them? As Grandma Dora Lee, alive and kicking at seventy, told it, "Shitfire! If I ain't a done it y'all'd still be squattin' on the ground, stoop-pickin' tomaters down yonder on the Rio Grande, just a-squeezin' that river-bottom black mud 'tween your toes!"

Out in New Sonora no one knew about their déclassé origins. But they never really learned how to rest easy as Anglos; there was always this vague feeling that they were teetering just on the edge of disaster. And prejudice against Mexicans was so strong in New Sonora at that time, and they were so afraid that someone from Texas might show up and expose them as impostors, that they rapidly conditioned themselves into believing that they had always been WASPS, and even tried to forget the Spanish language, their Catholic heritage, and their Mexican father, who lived all his life in that family shack in the Rio Grande Valley, until he became mortally ill and they let him come out to the "bosom" of his family, where he died unloved and unvisited in the New Sonora County Hospital in Mission Santa Bonita, smelling bad, smelling of beer breath and bean farts, but happy, with a smile on his Spic face, a face that had gone darker and more Indian-Mexican with age, undisguisable as a WASP. Lying on starched white sheets for the first time in his long poor life, in a clean well-lighted pine-oil-smelling green and eggshell room in official county issue pajamas . . . Alfonso thought he'd already entered the pearly gates, and he had . . . he'd already entered Weed heaven. . . .

Big Arv, therefore, grew up with a profound sense of the fragility of his self-image, of the vulnerability of his position in his chosen world, the world of Anglos. His reflex was, not surprisingly, to conform, to never rock the boat, never. Big Arv had become so much a product of Weeddom that one time he caught himself yelling over the intercom at the Joint, "Put that fucking greaser on ice!" when an officer rang him up complaining about "a Spic named Encina acting up." After he'd hung up Big Arv thought, *Hey, shit! That Spic might be related to me!*

Now, driving out across the bridge, over the Sound, Big Arv was one-hundred-per-cent All-American from his triple-E work boots to his milk-fed but hard buttocks to his high protein belly to his hanging carbohydrate-surfeited pectoral muscles to his peeled naked army sergeant eyeballs to his close-cropped balding dark-rimmed pate. Yessirree! Full-blooded western American to the core, to his very "one-sixteenth Cree Indian" roots . . . all of his roots he admitted to, but enough of the truth, enough, quite enough.

Big Arv kept driving. The bridge rose up before him. With that powerful automobile under his ass, under his hand, under his total control, rising, going faster, that big-ass American automobile, invented and constructed there, in that wonderful new land, America, like the bridge he crossed, like the clothes he wore, like Big Arv himself. . . .

Big Arv was heading for work. He always had himself a second job. He'd been on this one over at his ex-sister-in-law's place in Nueva Ronda for three years now.

The reason he was working the extra job was that he dreamed of someday owning his own little home off the grounds of the Joint and he also needed a new car. In order to achieve his dreams Big Arv had worked at second jobs as a milk man, night janitor, cannery employee, parking lot attendant, shoe salesman, bartender, Bible salesman, and service station attendant over the years. But somehow the extra money never seemed to get him any nearer to that dream house and dream car. Any money he made, or that May made, simply disappeared into the mouth of the hungry family, swallowed whole by years of poverty and need. There was always something that one of the little bastards had to have. Big Arv felt suddenly, as he went through the toll gate on the other side of the bridge, looking up at the giant oil storage tanks with STANDARD OIL written around their fat middles, depressingly, that he'd spent all his years working for nothing. He was angry at this thought, angry as he would have been at an inmate who insulted him inside the Joint. It was a horrible nasty thought, a thought that cut into his bright good mood like a black cloud on a clear Pacific day.

"Here we are, got all the kids but Libby raised up, and Judy and Carol happily married, and I feel, shit, like I been working all these years for nothing!" he said out loud, after he'd dropped the seventy-five cents into the green-uniformed toll taker's fresh pink hand . . . and responded to himself, "You know what, Big Arv? You're fucking A John right! All for nothing! All for nothing!"

And for the briefest little instant Big Arv, debt-ridden, hag-ridden, was overwhelmed with a desire to turn his beat-out Chevy off the freeway at the East Hazelton Exit and follow around the Pearl Valley Interchange cloverleaf and reemerge upon the freeway by way of the East Hazelton Entrance going exactly in the opposite direction and pull up at the toll booth again and pay his seventy-five cents again and drive fast out to the middle of the giant swayback suspension bridge and stop in the middle right between the dromedary humps and get out of the fucking car and bail out just bail out of this world hurling himself down through the sweet morning, the salt-tinged air, to the brown rain-swollen waters of the Sound 343 feet below.

And when that tantalizing East Hazelton Exit rose up before his eyes on the right, as he accelerated, Big Arv even went so far as to let the Chevy drift over into the right lane, behind a lineup of big trucks and trailers, even went so far as to allow the car to slow down to a snail's pace, truck-pace, going up the steep grade, and then . . . slowly . . . teasing himself . . . went past his last chance, and stepped on the gas, heading toward continued destiny, continued living, convinced that if he'd really turned off, that would have been it, really it, the end!

The acceleration of the Chevrolet, however, did not relieve his depression.

Big Arv had always been all his life up to his ears in debt, ever since the day he bought his first automobile. And with a wife and four kids and a minuscule prison guard's salary you couldn't get out of it. Debt was a necessity of life. It was as natural as cars and freeways and TV sets. But now, in the last week or so, poor old Big Arv, he'd gotten himself almost to the point where his fucking poor little hard-breathing blowhole itself was inundated.

It was all Evie's fault but he didn't blame her. She'd lost quite a sum herself, though she could sure as shit afford it more than Big Arv.

Two weeks before she'd come to him and Fast-Walking on the job at her place and showed them a "foolproof" way to win at roulette. It was a very complicated system but it basically involved doubling your bet after each turn of the wheel, and leaving your money always on red. The "doubling" recouped your losses, theoretically, and made

it impossible not to win eventually. It was just a matter of
gutting it out until red came up again. Evie talked him
and Fast-Walking, neither one of whom could afford it,
into investing their "talents" in the gamble, and drove
them down to the Nueva Ronda Building and Loan Company where she had a big account. And, at the early hour
of ten o'clock in the morning, she got each of them a
$750 loan at a usurious interest rate, got them both to call
in sick at the Joint, and they all caught a Greyhound for
Stateline, Nevada. The trip was free-of-charge, two drinks
included, courtesy of the Stateline Casinos Association. It
being right after Social Security and welfare check time,
the bus was loaded to the fucking gunnels with old age
pensioners and welfare high-rollers on their way up to
make the fortune that'd give them the break they'd always
missed, put them on Easy Street for good.

In Nevada Big Arv and Fast-Walking sat down at the
roulette wheel with Evie and started betting according to
the new system ("Weed's Law" as Yuba later dubbed it in
the Joint's barber shop: "If you can't win, keep losing.
Sooner or later the scales will tip around full-circle to
winnings through the sheer weight of losses"). Big Arv
and Fast-Walking insisted on pooling their money, figuring they'd have more "cushion" that way. They forgot
their fierce rivalry this one time in the interests of mutual
benefit. Evie decided she'd play it out alone. The two
prison guards lost three hundred dollars within two minutes, playing very cautiously. Evie won three hundred.
Then Big Arv and Fast-Walking painfully won back their
starting money, surpassed it and, when red came up seven
times in a row, won four thousand two hundred dollars.
Evie just kept plugging away winning small sums steadily,
nothing spectacular. A crowd gathered around them. A
blonde jumped up and did a jig, tossing her long hair out
behind her, shaking her flabby middle-aged breasts. "Say!"
the people said, "those two guys are prison guards on
their day off!" And even more gamblers gathered round.
The two boys yelled over at Evie, praising her. All eyes
followed.

"Hey Evie, how you doing? Jesus, you're the smartest
goddamn woman I ever *did* know! Whoopie!"

"Whoopie," echoed the surrounding crowd of middle-
age, middle-class, middle-Americans.

But the boys knew they couldn't buy all their dreams

with just four thousand two hundred dollars split two ways. That wouldn't even get Fast-Walking back in the door of his wife's house. And it wouldn't even get Big Arv a sniff of that private home he desired so much. So they kept playing. They won another five hundred and fifty dollars. The crowd grew up around them until it seemed they were the only two people playing in the Casino. It wasn't that they were the biggest or most daring gamblers in the place. They weren't. What moved the crowd, what captured its always elusive attention, was the fact that they were poor low-paid prison guards going for their last chance at success. Something of Fast-Walking's and Big Arv's extreme desperation, their all-or-nothing risk, was communicated to the growing crowd, that's what won them.

The boys forgot all about Evie, even lost sight of her. They won another thousand dollars. Cheers went up. "Come on boys! Keep it up! Keep it up!" The blonde did another rapid shuffle, a quick buck and wing with her breasts and her enormously fat "riding breeches" thighs flapping like mad, raising howls of laughter. But it did not distract the boys from business. Business was as usual. They were close to fortune, ultimate fortune, *that* close! And nothing, nothing would deter them. The croupier spun the wheel. Black! He spun again. Black! Again: Black! Black! Black! Black! Black! Black! Black! Blaaaaaaaaaaaaaack! Black came up an incredible fifteen times in a row and cleaned them out. Big Arv broke down and bawled. It was the only time anyone except May'd seen the big fellow cry. And she'd seen him only once: when she ran and jumped into his arms on his train overseas.

Fast-Walking looked like he'd been gassed, or shell-shocked. He figured it'd take him ninety-nine years to get back into his happy home now, ninety-nine years before he ever slept in the arms of his sweet French wife again.

Evie came over and said, "There, there, now, fellahs! It'll be alright, don't worry, don't worry."

"How'd you do?" Big Arv asked through his tears.

"Me? Shit!" she said, "I got cleaned out too!"

She lent them her last ten dollars and they promptly lost it too when black came up again two more times in a row.

The crowd drifted away to another table where an Armenian farmer from Modesto, California, had just made six straight passes.

Fast-Walking and Big Arv and Evie dropped their last bits of change in the slot machines. Dead broke, they still had about six hours before the bus went back to New Sonora. It was snowing outside. Out over the lake, up on the High Sierra peaks, outside the Casino on the fir trees and pines and mountain cedar, on overturned Lake Tahoe rowboats and motorboats and sailboats, on ski rental shacks and on parking lots and motels and milk shake stands and real estate agencies and on neon signs hanging out over the highway and on curbing and asphalt, it was piling up. Billowing, swirling, hiding things, the snow came down, slow and easy, but steadily, falling and falling.

The three unhappy gamblers sat inside in the modernistic green lounge staring at each other for the whole six hours. Evie tried to make small talk about the store. But Big Arv and Fast-Walking wouldn't listen, or couldn't hear. The sound of the Gaylords' singing bar act, and the slot machines, the crap shooting, the shouts of winners, the cries of losers, the bartender stirring exotic drinks, tinkle tinkle tinkle, drowned out Evie's high soprano voice.

Even when you could hear her good, when there was no distraction, Evie's voice, coming from behind the folds of fat at her neck, turkey-fat, seemed like it was coming from another room, even though she might be a foot from your face. Well, that day, her voice sounded like it was even farther away than usual, and there wasn't any way you could hear her. No way at all.

After that Big Arv and Fast-Walking swore to Jesus they'd never gamble again. And asked Evie for more hours of work at the store and driving her bus, and a raise to two dollars an hour. She generously agreed. But it looked like neither one of the boys would ever pay off his debt to the Nueva Ronda Building and Loan. They were going to try to pay off as much as they could, five or ten dollars a month, without letting their wives find out. But with the tremendous interest rate it became rapidly apparent that the loan was going to get bigger instead of smaller every month.

The day of payment came and went and the loan com-

pany sent threatening letters and attached Big Arv's salary
and double-attached Fast-Walking's, which had already
been previously attached by another loan company. Fast-
Walking's wife found out about it and went to see a lawyer about a divorce. May ranted and raved and stomped
up and down the living room, fuming, breathing fire and
ciggie smoke and, in an hour-long orgy of self-righteous
indignation, created the greatest knock-down-and-drag-out
scene of a married life replete with such scenes. Eventually Big Arv regretfully had to cool her with an easy left
jab to the kisser. And that got Little Arv, who was just
stopping in before work, pissed off, and the two of them
got into it, and Big Arv, besieged from all sides, with even
Libby jumping up and down and slapping him across the
shoulders, had to cop a sunday on his kid, his son, a sunday so fucking powerpacked that it sent him flying over
the table like a gull and into the glass panels of the Sears
Roebuck blond sideboard, which fell on his head with a
clatter of shattering glass, fortunately without doing any
permanent damage to either him or the sideboard.

Big Arv had lost his temper. His face went redder and
redder. He started breaking furniture, cracking dishes and
glasses and pots. He kicked over all the chairs, tore every
picture off the wall, and sprained his toe kicking at May's
bedroom door. Then his heart, his poor cardiac-racked
heart, started a-palpitating. Just a one potater, two potater, palpitater! . . . like Wasco was always saying about
the Weed males' hereditary tendency toward heart trouble: heart spasms, heart stroke, hard heart, and a predict-
able early death through heart attack. . . . His heart started palping heavy and hard. That was the only thing that
stopped him. He cried out, "Oh! My heart! My heart!"
and everyone in the family suddenly stopped yelling at
him, ran to his side, helped him to the sofa, laid him
down. And when the doctor arrived a little later May and
Libby and Little Arv were all crying and patting Big Arv
and each other on the back, saying, "You'll be alright,
Daddy, you'll be alright!" They'd never felt more like a
family. They told each other how much they all loved
each other, Big and Little Arv too, and how much they'd
all pull together and get out of this hole, and so on. And
they all laughed and patted him on the back when the
doctor pronounced that what he was feeling was only minor palpitations, he'd not had anything like an attack.

Within a week it'd all been forgotten, and everything was the same. The salary was still attached. And neither Little Arv, nor May, nor anyone but Evie said another word about helping to pay the loan back so he could eventually get his salary disattached. May even began saying the "heart attack" was a fake. "Why, all he had was them palp . . . palpit . . . palpitaters," she told the neighbors and the relatives, "I get them all the time. Men can't stand up to pain the way a woman can, and that's a fact."

Big Arv motated fast along the Soundside Parkway that went by the mudflats, smelly mudflats with spare tires and driftwood sticking out of the oil and gunky black bottom. Past the racetrack where he used to place a two-dollar bet a couple of times a week, back when he was younger and had a dime or two to call his own. Then he went lickety-split down the Nueva Ronda off-ramp. Out through the flat-top housing developments of the suburbs. Over the West Hazelton Hills to Nueva Ronda, Spic Town, Tortilla Flats, Grease Gulch, Little T. J., Enchilada-by-the-Sea, where he drove up an unpaved and rutted muddy road to Evie's place.

Evie had herself a nice little setup. She had a small store with a Pepsi-Cola tin poster proclaiming it "Montoya's Market" (Montoya was her deceased husband). Besides that, right next door she had a nice older wooden home, with a screen porch that went all the way across the front, a patch of grass in front, and out in back a huge cluttered yard that went back almost two hundred feet.

Big Arv drove the Chevy up on the lawn (sparkling dewy warm winter lawn, with sunshine coming through the large date palm tree by the side of the road), got out, and was just having a look at his bashed-in taillight when Fast-Walking pulled up alongside on the grass in his big old '59 Buick Roadmaster.

"Hey, baby, what's the haps?" Fast-Walking said, sitting in the Buick, leaning back on the headrest.

"Listen, Mister, you ain't going to start up the day with that nigger talk, are you? I got enough to think about without hassling with no goddamn niggers!"

"What's wrong, Arv?"

"Shit! What ain't?"

"Who climbed up on your taillight there?" Fast-Walking asked, laughing, rising up out of that low-slung two-toned red and green Buick on his long stork legs, wobbling a little, but covering the ground over to Big Arv fast. "Looks like we got ourselves into a little accident this morning."

"Well, I'm still alive, goddamnit."

"Sho. Let's go see what old Evie's got cooking for us," Fast-Walking said, leading the way through the screen door, across the porch, and into the front room, "get your mind off your troubles, man."

They went across the dark living room, wending their way through the shabby brown felt armchairs and old-fashioned couches and love seats, and into the yellow kitchen. It was yellow everywhere, piss-yellow, on all sides. The ceiling and walls were yellow, the floor was covered with yellow asphalt tile, and the table was yellow plastic. Even the refrigerator was bright modern yellow, out of place here in this old wood frame and paperboard room. On the table the keys to the minibus were laid out with the day's instructions:

> *Dear Boys* Here is what I want you all to do first go on over to Soundside Hardware get me a claw hammer and a case of number nine nails then run out to the feed store in West Hazelton you will have time cause things are slow except at the packing shed I want four bags of rabbit feed they are fat enough but I want them fatter then stop at Vargas, Martinez, Garcia, Abelar, Cienfuegos, and Mendez labor camps it will take only one trip I think then clean out the girls houses and the back yard including the animal pens I will be up then and we can see how it is going.   *Evie.*

The boys didn't do exactly like she told them. They had better ideas. They knew from what the labor boss had told them the day before that there'd be no one at all at the camps. Everyone would either be at the celery-packing shed or out in the muddy fields chopping celery. So they drove to the hardware store and the feed store and then out onto the low marshy flatlands where the celery grew. They stopped, turned off the main road, and drove across

the muddy, misty fields to where the wetbacks toiled on a
huge one thousand acre tract, bent over double, chopping
at the celery with long machetelike knives, standing up to
their knees in the soggy mud of yesterday's rain. The sun
was glorious, shining down on that rich bottomland mud,
on the green plants, on the colorfully dressed Mexican laborers in serapes and sandals or bare feet, in wide sombreros or straw cowboy hats.

"Oye! Miguel!" Big Arv yelled out in greeting.

"Ese! Cómo estas, hombre?" said the Mexican strawboss, standing up to the ankles of his U.S. Army jump
boots in slop and green mashed celery.

"Listen," Big Arv said, leaning out of the cab of the
minibus, still speaking Spanish, "I got ten dollars says you
give these boys a whole hour off for lunch!"

"Cómo no?" said Miguel, shrugging his fleshy shoulders, blinking his dark eyes in the brilliant light.

Big Arv laughed, reached out of the bus, and slipped a
folded ten-dollar bill into Miguel's tanker-jacket side
pocket.

"We'll be over at twelve and pick them up. Have them
ready, okay?"

"Por supuesto, Señor!" said Miguel, showing his
cracked yellow teeth.

Over at the Wright-Bayard packing shed it was the
same. Mud, sun, slippery squashed celery underfoot.
Forklifts spinning their wheels in the slime. Pallets piled
thirty feet high with packing crates of vegetables. Railroad
cars, refrigerated yellow-painted "reefers," lined up on the
Southern Pacific siding, awaiting loading. The shed had no
walls. It was just a tin roof suspended over a cement floor,
supported by metal braces. A long conveyor belt ran
down the whole length of it. At one end fenderless mud-
splattered war surplus Dodge trucks from the fields lined
up with their stacked dirty boxes of fresh-cut celery. A
Mexican unloaded them onto the conveyor belt, along
with a procession of fast-working, fast-chopping, slicing,
cutting, boxing, packing, stacking Mexicans tamed the
wild growing vegetable for the salad bowl of America. At
the other end another *bracero* stacked the neatly packed
boxes of fresh-smelling celery eight high and eight square
on a pallet. Another one came along in a forklift with
special mud tires, lifted it off, and carried it to the siding

where another gang of dark sweating laborers stacked them in the icebox cars. The noise in the place was deafening: the loud motor of the conveyor belt, the revving, knobby-tired, mud-squishing forklifts, the shouts of the workers who, like all Latins, could not endure work without some kind of self-entertainment. There were screams and curses and jokes and field-calls and double-entendres in Spanish so the American foreman couldn't understand. And then there were just random shouts, simple expletives to relieve the monotony:

"*Aiiiiiiiii Chihuahua!*"

"*Poco más arriba!*"

"*Ai! Llévate a la despacio!*"

"*Pinchibato, cabrón!*"

"*Pélame la berga!*"

Several of the men in the long line at work on the conveyor belt wore bright new yellow raincoats and sou'wester-type peaked rain hats. Big Arv remarked this and, halting the VW bus by the belt, called the Nicaraguan strawboss over to the car. Big Arv, in his dealing in the field, always tried to handle everything from within the car. This, he felt, gave him a certain psychological advantage. He was relaxed sitting up in the cab. Sort of like a bossman. The other dude was forced to stand down in the mud and, unconsciously, he was bound to pay Big Arv more respect.

"Hey, Octavio, listen man," Big Arv said in Spanish, "we got some more of those yellow raincoats in. Here's a fiver, and let me pick these *coños* up at twelve-fifteen. They could use some slickers in this kind of weather. Also, a lot of them ain't got laid since two weeks ago, okay?"

"*Pues . . .*" said Octavio, accepting the five-dollar bill as if it were some kind of dead small animal, "*pero . . .*" and Big Arv hit him with another fiver and he lit up. "*Pues claro que sí, hombre!*" he said, waving at them as they spun off through the mud.

When Big Arv spoke Spanish, he affected an atrocious gringo accent. But Fast-Walking didn't hear it. He thought Big Arv spoke it beautiful.

"Hey, where'd you learn such good Spanish?" he'd asked when they first went on their "route" together.

"In high school," Big Arv had answered, looking at him quite sincerely.

Sixteen

Moke rose, reluctant, from the tatami mat in one distracted motion, not bothering to unfold her shapely brown
legs till she'd risen to her full five feet two. She'd just
come home from Little Arv's place in the city and rustled
up a quick rice and fruit breakfast for herself and already
it was time to get ready to go out again. But still she put-
tered about, dawdling, clearing the low round table, washing dishes, tidying up. *Just wallowing in cleanliness like
always.*

Alone among junkies, if she kept herself straight with
her cutter's stash, Moke maintained herself and her pad
spic and span.

More than anything she hated going out into the bright
morning light. It wouldn't be so bad when summer came,
when the heavy North Pacific fog kept it dark and dismal
till noon at least. In New Sonora, August, not April, was
the cruelest month, the coldest and dreariest month. At
three o'clock in the afternoon the cold gray fog would
suck in off the icy waters from Alaska and come stealing
in through the Alvarez Straits under the huge arched
bridge and would flood the whole large valley of the
Quintana Sound to its yellow brim, creeping up the hilly
flanks of Holly Island, slipping into Paradise Cove,
around the Santa Caterina Peninsula, licking at the forty-
foot like-colored walls of the Joint. At twelve noon the
fog would retreat every day for an hour or two, hanging
threateningly in the air above the ocean a few hundred
yards west of the Alvarez Straits bridge, before it rushed
in again, obscuring the world.

August was riot season in the Joint and in the city.

August was Moke's favorite month.

But now, unfortunately, it was merely December, a
clear winter's morning. Even the rush hour traffic noise

above her on the freeway was worse, unmuffled by August's delightful gray drizzle.

Moke cast a practiced eye around the neat little room, the "living," as she called it, of her three-room apartment. It was an inimitably Moke room. Nothing of Wasco's former presence remained. And even when he'd been around, on one of his rare visits, he'd left it her way. Their mainland friends, *"da Haole,"* as she called them, Motopsycho freaks and junkies and pushers and heavy connections mostly, found it the most exotic of pads: floors overlaid in three layers of soft tatami, walls covered with tapa fiber, ceiling lowered to six feet with Hawaiian fishing net, a low-hanging lamp fashioned from a discarded lobster trap. A chairless room designed for barefoot floor living, bright-colored pillows and mats lying around on the straw, cushions for *Haole* visitors' unhabituated elbows and asses. No posters, no prints, no pictures. The inked design on the vegetable tapa cloth was her own. Emblem: water lily and flame tree entwined. Fess: spouting volcano and five fishes marshaling, on a field, purpure. The fishes were drawn front, back, and side view, swimming together and alone, free, through kelpish weed, and around the submerged base of the gigantic volcano. The shark, the whale, the barracuda, the albacore and the mahi mahi. The shark smiled, the whale looked somber, the barracuda laughed his wicked laugh, the albacore looked flatly content, and the mahi mahi pursed his lips in a puckish cynical whistle. Rabbit Island, low and white, with its solitary coconut palm, rode the near background like a sleek outrigger. And beyond that, a tiny swirling smear of red and gray and yellow on the horizon marked the other volcanoes: Mauna Kea and Mauna Loa, and their foul-breathed daughter, Pele. A curious motto in Moke's childlike scrawl adorned the lower right-hand corner of the western wall:

13 = M = Moke = Money
Honey eev ya wanna
Geeda long weed me!

No, nobody but Moke herself had ever really dug this pad until Little Arv came along. One night last week she'd cleared off her cutter's table and stashed all her works and invited him over for din-din. He could barely eat his food, staring all around him like he was "reading the walls," as he said. Moke got into it too. Tried reading herself through her walls like Arv was trying to do. And realized that more of her than she strictly would have liked was revealed. And rushed him with his dinner and forced him to hasten off to a late movie in the city. And never let him come back anymore. Just always arranged to meet in class at City College or at his place or outside the gates of the Joint. That Little Arv! She found herself seeing him much more often than was really necessary for business reasons. He asked her: "How come you're hanging around me so much? You don't have to! I'll do it anyway!" Though he didn't know the half of it yet. Still, was it really necessary to be calling him all the time? She had him wound right around her little finger, didn't she? Sure. Then why? *How dumb to fall for the first dude who fucks you right.* Why not?

Alone among junkies, if she was kept up with her wake-up, nooner, matinee and bedtime fixes, Moke had a hardy healthy young girl's appetite for fucking. Just like a normal person. Wasco never fucked her right. The only way he could get it off was from the rear. The only way she could get it off was by sitting on top. It became apparent from the very inception of their relationship that they were effectively unsexed together. After a while they'd given up even experimenting and just hugged like brother and sister in her wide bed when Wasco decided to stay the night. "You are the only one," he said, and she believed him, "you are the only one I trust, honey . . . never take your Daddy off and he will always treat you solid" . . . and she believed him. He considered himself her only protector and adviser: "Why don't you cut your hair short like them Frog chicks, baby? You look so tacky-ass Hawaiian the way you let it hang down to your asshole" . . . *So I cut it all off that time. . . . It fell and fell . . . on the tiles of the bathroom floor . . . and . . .* "you gotta cut down on them bright nigger colors you're always wearing, honey. A little fucking Brownie like you . . . gotta wear tans and grays and real subtle colors, with a complexion like yours, dig it? Give you more *Haole* class that way, see what I mean?" *And I did it. I threw all my pretty bright muumuus away. Gave them to the Salvation Army man. He took them away down the stairs in a great big colorful Island bundle. . . .*

How dumb to fall for the first one who fucks you right, though. So you don't have to sit on top. How dumb!

They are from the same family, Moke thought, while she swept and mopped her little kitchen.

They are from the same family . . . even look alike except Wasco is bigger all over, and he's got red hair, she thought, as she carefully cleaned her fit, her heroin works, over the sink, and sterilized it in boiling water.

She'd got off good. She felt real good all over. She felt like fucking. Alone among junkies . . .

Am I really alone?

What's the diff between them?

Moke had forgotten her plants! She went into the tiny kitchen again, filled a sprinkler pot with lukewarm water, returned quickly to the living, and watered her plants: miniature palms and rubber trees, big-leafed ferns. Then she remembered Alii. She got the bird feed and some more water. Alii she kept in her bedroom, next to her low-canopied queen-sized bed and her cutter's table where she worked every day cutting and packing smack. A huge ugly black mynah he was, that Alii. Wasco had bought him for her at an old-fashioned Chinese pet shop in the city. She liked him when he was quiet and she was alone and knew he was just quietly being with her. But she detested the animal when he spouted the one-line vocabulary Wasco had taught him. He was talkative this morning and she hated the stinking moth-eaten thing while she poured his feed, filled his water dish. "Black powa muthafucka black powa!" the mynah repeated over and over again while Moke dressed, "Black powa muthafucka black powa!" But soon she shut him from her mind. And strangely, once she'd closed him out, he stopped. Didn't say a word. And only when she was making up in front of her mirror did she suddenly realize it. She kept him in a cage that was really quite small for a bird his size. But when she'd closed him in a bigger one he'd had a tendency to flap his wings violently and hurt himself. He seemed happy enough in this new one, however, and was now busily pecking away at the seed, ignoring her.

Moke looked at herself in the mirror. She imagined the two Weed boys on either side of her. What's the difference between them? Wasco, who was a powerful masculine figure, and her closest friend and crime partner in the whole world, and yet not a man in the full sense of the word. Arv, who was riddled with self-doubts and inferiority complexes, was a man to Moke. And this one unforeseen ingredient in Wasco's beautifully ugly brew threatened now to upset its perfect balance, and . . . destroy it? No chance! The saving factor, Moke thought, watching herself in the mirror, watching the Weeds beside her, the saving factor was an innocent child. Flo . . . conceived four years before with no pleasure. Flo, conceived by fluke. "A rectal child," she said out loud, laughing. Conceived by dreadful chance. Will I ever tell her someday? "Honey, you're the result of a fleck of come that dribbled out of my asshole and sparked in my hungry unloved womb out of pure wishfulness!"

Moke regarded herself closely in the mirror while she did her eye makeup, the only beauty aid she employed. She abolished the Weeds beside her and looked closely at herself, narrowing in sharply, narrowing in . . . with the aid of her drug . . . Except for her nose, Moke had the kind of regular prettiness that would have been rather boring on a *Haole* woman. That is what her mirror told her. But her wide Kanaka nose and her rich brown skin and her large upward-slanting gray eyes made her different, and interesting, she assured herself. Though Moke was vain, in a lazy, cocksure sort of way, she was too positive about her looks to bother much about them. It pleased her now, as she finished doing her eyelids (powdery gold eyeshadow), to ignore completely the squat toady Weeds abiding invisibly beside her, and contemplate the origin of her shockingly silver-colored eyes, inherited through some remote genealogical possibility from a shipwrecked English-German great-great-grandfather: a certain Hiram F. Todd, who washed up on the lepers' island of Molokai in the mid-nineteenth century, living only long enough to conceive a son (in the proper hole, hopefully), bequeath Moke his name and his extraordinarily pale gray eyes, and expire in a squalid sugarcane shack among rotting taro and fish guts on the Halawa Side. He left only one testament to his existence in the Islands, one cracking yellowed page of the journal he kept. Moke had committed it to memory as a small child, without really even understanding the sense of the words:

Hot Kona weather hath come down upon us from the south end of the Pacific Basin. The visitation of an evil heathen god. Doldrums and the Volcano Coast. Lightning flashes in broad daylight with no clouds above. Rainbows in the middle of the night. Artillery shells and aerial flares in the strangely shaped cerulean mountains above the jungle. The island is alive and dripping blood. One minute in the mango trees and my poor mortal flesh is hotly soaked and sweet with living leeches. The rain forest will devour my body. There is naught but to pray for my soul. They will never know I was alive. The flies descend upon the dog, Kaaava, and flay her alive with their tiny flagellations. They have eaten all her hair. She sits, parked on her hunkers, woefully afflicted, lacrimae rerum, *stripped of her canine swanker, sweeny as some kind of Mexican Hairless, her pink skin gone all black with wriggling knots of horseflies, gnats, mosquitoes, ticks and fleas and mites. She lies perishing now in her own excrement, in the humid fishbowl shade of the monkeypod tree in my woman's yard, a yard that has now gone to rotten green, blackgreen, horror green, and has begun to creep into the rooms of her nasty shack. Her bed sprouts strange plants. Insects control the cookhouse and the outhouse. I am the front line of defense, and my flanks have withered away beneath the fury of this oozing bombardment. The wind blows skinny insubstantial spiders from the Marquesas Islands four thousand miles further south; they land in our jungle back yard, breed themselves, hatch out fat white little eggs, attach themselves to our wretched yelping bitch, and to me! And her howls, just outside my paper window, in the primeval funk and heat and rot, are my howls. Help me dear God to endure and play out this my mortal coil . . .*

And it was precisely that Kona weather, Moke thought now, stepping out of yeasty yesterday's panties and into frilly white today's, that made her miss her home islands terribly, on occasion.

Moke thought of herself as a mystic. What this really meant was that she sought verification for the fact that her pursuit of money and her heroin habit had absorbed all her other volitions, that she no longer possessed a free will. She got out her book and threw the *I Ching*, and when it came out in favor of a short journey she pretended to be delighted.

Oh yes, more than almost anything, Moke hated leaving her dark apartment for the bright daylight, hated leaving shadows for sun. It was a strange mock-Spanish old house, the building Moke lived in, a mansion really, the last one in this industrial-zoned section of town. In the '40's it had been willed to her landlord, the City of Molina Valley, by an eccentric old lady, on the condition that it keep the grounds, including a large duck pond, a park, and a small vineyard which produced extraordinarily good wines, in good repair in perpetuity. The City of Molina Valley had regretted its acceptance of that request almost from the beginning. It set aside the pond as a bird refuge but after a few years it became so polluted from surreptitious night garbage dumping that no self-respecting duck or decent goose or swan would be caught dead there and even the sea gulls avoided the place. The park they let go all to wild weed and creeping underbrush. Hoboes took up residence there in cardboard and tin shacks. The palatial old house went slowly to ruin over the years. The windows broke in the wind and were left unrepaired. The elegant spirals of the staircase crumbled away to white ants and sawdust. Moke loved it. Except for the deaf old caretaker, she was the last renter who remained. That suited her fine. Since she lived on city property there was very little chance of the police bothering her. She almost never saw the old man. It was, therefore, with utter confidence that she had set up her cutter's table in the bedroom with only the raucous black mynah to watch over it. And, as Moke often said to him in her lighter moods:

"An you only a mynah mattah!"

Moke's cutting room/bedroom was large and queenly. But all the big old-fashioned French windows she'd had to cover with blankets to keep the sun, light, and curious eyes out. Next to the bird cage she'd fixed up a huge oak table, spreading it over completely with black cloth covered with a sheet of glass. At one end of the table she always had a big pile of packed glassine bags the size of her fist. Every day Moke, working in a surgical mask under brilliant white fluorescent light, emptied those glassine bags onto the table and cut them with mannita and quinine: four parts mannita, four parts quinine to one part heroin. She always packed only the best smack, shit that would always without fail "take the eight," could always be cut eight to one with no sweat and lots of good profit. When she was working at cutting the smack she got one of her coathangers and covered it with nylon stocking material. She poured one part heroin and eight parts mannita and quinine onto the sifter and shook it carefully over the table, scraping the little drifts careful careful with a razor blade, keeping the pile nice and even. She then scooped it up and sifted it again and again. She went through this process six times, making sure she got a clean good mixture, with zero chance of impurities. Then she took a tiny measuring spoon and dipped it into the cut stuff, leveling it off with a razor blade. She shoveled it into a bag: a tiny glassine stamp collector's bag. Then she folded the bag neatly, professionally, and sealed it up tight with a special highly adhesive tape. She always did a beautiful job, a pro job, rubber banding all her bags in bundles of twenty-five each, and stacking them on the table with great care. She took real pride in the perfection and tightness of her bags. For a lot of the Joint trade she would be packing Sheik prophylactics with an ounce of cut stuff. She didn't like that idea, really, It didn't leave room for a neat pro job. It was just sloppy shit, not fit work for a girl who really knew her number. But she meant to do her best even with those sloppy old rubbers, folding them square and neat, stuffing them clean to the top with superbly cut smooth snow. Just like Wasco always said, "A crazy pack of smack and you win the lazy hack . . . a mad fad is a bad ad." "Bad," in Wasco talk, as Moke learned as soon as she met him, meant "good." Just like good meant bad, as in, "Shit, that dude's nothin' but *good!*"

Sure, that old Wasco, he was a tough-talking sonofabitch, but Moke knew him for what he really was, under all the swagger. Underneath it all there was a quivering scared little chicken's soul, just like in everybody else. Only Moke in all the world knew this. Wasco was utterly successful in convincing the rest of humanity that he was bad-ass and unrepentant and scared of nothing. Only Moke knew the truth. But there was one tiny particle of her very perceptive little head that had entertained for two or three scary seconds, on two or three scary occasions in the past, the notion that Wasco's "confessions" to her, and his tearful admissions of murderous guilt, and his oft-admitted fear of death, were only ploys too, schemes,

shows put on to win her to his way, soften her up, win
her trust and her love. "I never had no real friend till you,
honey," he said, over and over, whispering it in her ear.
And she believed him. Did she really? Sure, she did. "No,
I never had any kind of real friend. Only punks and lack-
eys. I don't know how to make friends. Never did. All I
got is just enemies and inferiors."

Wasco had even made a shocking admission about his
cousin Little Arv, one evening lying beside Moke on her
queen-sized bed, with the mynah sounding off in the background, "Black powa, black powa!" He admitted that he
was a little bit jealous of Arv, in a way. Tearfully, Wasco
admitted it, confessing, with his thick lips in her ears.
Crying real tears, he revealed it. "Why?" she asked, genuinely surprised. Why would Wasco be jealous of someone
he'd so often ridiculed to her, poked fun at, asking her to
laugh with him, though she'd never met him? "Why?" she
asked again. But he wouldn't answer. Never did he answer. Now that she was with Little Arv, and knew him,
Moke had formed a suspicion: Wasco was jealous because
Little Arv had something he didn't: a capacity to give and
receive love, real honest-to-God man and woman love.

Of course, Little Arv was jealous of Wasco too. She'd
seen through that the first night they really talked. He
couldn't do anything but talk about his big cousin. Just
like Wasco was always talking about him. As far as Moke
could see, the two cousins were fixated on each other, for
some reason. One as much as the other. The way Moke
figured it, each of them saw in the other something he admired and desired but knew he could never achieve: Arv
force, and Wasco love. . . .

Finally Moke had herself all ready. Safeguarded against
the dazzling sunlight with thick dark sunglasses, she
locked the door to her flat, and the outside door to the old
mansion, and trod gingerly across the weedy wild yard to
the broken-down garage. She rolled her Honda out, sat
down, cranked it over, warmed it up for a few minutes,
and rode down the winding driveway past the old caretaker who was watering the nonexistent lawn in front of
his tiny gatekeeper's place. She waved a breezy good
morning to him, accelerated around the bend, out the
gate, and up the freeway ramp.

Punched the 250 full out, dodging in and out of traffic,

jackrabbiting at seventy miles an hour, seventy-five, un-
mindful of the ever-watchful Highway Patrol, thinking
okay Haole heah she come!

She shot like a small red bomb down along the pale
waters of the phlegmatic Sound, over the greening hills,
past a grove of poplar trees in a narrow canyon—her
grove (she wandered there often in the middle of the
night)—and within fifteen minutes she was waiting in a
long line of visitors' cars in front of the Joint's long gray
wall, revving her engine at the Back Gate. When her turn
came a paunchy young guard checked her identification,
verified it on a list, and waved her on. "And watch the
speed limit, twenty miles an hour!" he called out after
her. But she had already accelerated to fifty, and kept it
there past the Employees' Dependents' School, and the
guards' uniformly gray housing project, and past Arv's
parents' house. At the Second Gate they warned her
again. "Keep that machine quiet and slow or we'll revoke
your visitor's privileges!" So she idled it over the hill to
the dairy farm and the Industrial Area and the Ad Building Parking Lot. She shut off the motor on the bike and
went into the Ad Building where they gave her a card
with a number on it and conducted her to a waiting room.
A busty butch matron with a crew cut told her to turn her
handbag in until she'd finished with her visit. She said,
"Can I go to the lavatory first?" She affected an English
accent, pronouncing lavatory as "lavatree." She often did
that kind of thing when she felt nervous, guilty, playful,
or under the thumb of authority. She even did it with
Wasco from time to time, either the English accent or an
outrageous pidgin Hawaiian, when she was perfectly capable of speaking good Standard American. The matron
looked at her knowingly, woman to woman, and said,
"Sure, honey, it's right over there." Something about the
woman's vulgar assumption that she was menstruating
made Moke want to puke. She hadn't menstruated in ages,
in such a long time she could barely remember when she
had last, since her habit topped ten dollars a day at
wholesale prices, she thought.

In the bathroom she climbed out of her jumpsuit, took
a leak, wiped herself thoroughly, and removed her panties, placing them in the coin purse of her bag, thinking
Didn't you know, ma'am, that junkies never bleed? . . .

She spent a moment brushing her windblown hair, tucking her blouse into her miniskirt, went out to the matron and handed her the bag and folded suit.

"You got any gifts for the inmate?" the matron asked.

"Oh yes, actually, I'd rather fancy leaving a small token of my esteem."

"Yeah? What is it?"

"Well, a little money, perhaps?"

"How much?"

"Would twenty dollars be too much?"

"The limit is ten a visit. Here, take it out and I'll give you some vouchers. You can give them to the inmate inside. Money isn't allowed in the institution."

Moke took the vouchers and sat down in a large hall full of folding chairs. It looked like a State Unemployment Bureau on payday. Everybody but Moke was low rent: Spic, Okie, or nigger. The air was stale and smelled of sweat and chitterling breath and bean farts and tobacco juice. Every three chairs there was a brown-splattered spittoon.

They called a name every few minutes. "Brown. Gonzalez. Moore. Shandy. Mendez." She tried passing the time by guessing who was who by name alone. She was amazingly accurate, divining ten faces and names out of ten. It was easy. Each ethnic group, black, brown and white, was so different from the others, with its own walk, talk, smell, gestures, way of dressing, with even its own way of wearing sideburns and hair and moustaches and wigs . . . that there was absolutely no problem in distinguishing between them, none at all. They might as well have been Earthlings, Mercureans and Martians, for all their dissimilarities. It made Moke feel great that nobody would be able to figure her out, that she belonged to none of these degenerate American races.

Finally the matron called her name: "Weed, Prosperity F.!" And she hastened off with the guard out the door, along a carefully manicured lawn, under a tall metal gun tower that gleamed in the sunlight, across an old-fashioned brass suspension bridge that traversed a deep moat filled with chemical-colored water, and up to the Third Fence Gate. An ugly tough-looking old sergeant sitting in the gatehouse stared at her legs as she approached. When he came to open the wire mesh gate he brought a ferocious Doberman Pinscher along with him.

"Hello there, mate," Moke said to the dog, in her English accent. Both men frowned. The dog growled.

"Visitor for Wasco Weed," the guard said.

"Relation?" the sergeant asked.

"Who?" Moke inquired with wide-eyed innocence, "him, you, or me?"

"You . . . er . . . him!" the sergeant barked, angered at having been tripped up so easily.

"Husband!" Moke shouted back, just as loud, and he opened the gate, keeping the Doberman firmly in check with a leash. Still, the beast pointed his nose right where Moke thought he might point it. And, when the sergeant slammed the gate, loosening his hold for a moment, the animal made a sharp-nosed thrust for it. Moke turned around quickly, however, fast-thinking, and gave him a sniff of her bottom instead. He didn't seem to like that as much. Nor did the sergeant, who pointed brusquely with his grizzled hand up to the Wall Gate. "You go in there," he said, and dragged the dog into the gatehouse. Moke strolled up the clean stone rockway cautiously, holding her mini and her light coat down in the stiff breeze off the Straits. A young guard with a fresh handsome face and a ready smile opened the Wall Gate and allowed her into the Lock Chamber. He pointed to a small green door on the left. She went over and knocked. Another guard opened up and let her in. "You got any vouchers? Leave them with me," he said, "I'll see that the inmate gets them."

Moke could see Wasco down at the end of a long line of visitors and inmates leaning over closely and looking at each other through a reinforced glass window. She walked down and took a phone off a small hook on the long table and looked up at Wasco, who had no hair on his head, but seemed as cocky as ever.

"Hey, what's truckin', foxy lady?" he said. It sounded like he was in the Islands rather than right across the table; the static on the line was terrible. His voice came across as small and distant.

"Eh, *Haole*, not too much. Why you no write mo', eh?"

"Busy, getting it all together in here. You wear what I told you?"

"Sure," she said, glancing out of the corners of her eyes at the guards at either end of the room, and the two women seated on either side of her, and the two convicts on either side of Wasco.

"Yeah?" he said. "Well you just go ahead and flash, sweetlumps, and keep on flashing!"

Moke obediently complied, as she did with everything Wasco asked of her, as he in his turn unfailingly did when she asked anything of him. They never let each other down. Never. Not in any way. Their loyalty had been tested and proved a hundred different ways in times of the most dire and desperate stress. It had been tested by fire and money, and come out clean as gold, again and again. Each of them accepted the other's most capricious demand, and carried it out without question, without hesitation, as a matter of faith. This was their beauty, their truth, and they held it dear, kept it, guarded it jealously, never allowing a crack or gap or flaw in its perfection. Never allowed a blink, a shifty self-serving glance, a moment's hesitation, or even a raised eyebrow to mar its beauty. The inviolability of this mutual trust, tempered with gold, was the only thing in the world that either of them really believed in, believed to be real and true and lasting. All else was either merely temporary, or illusory, or corrupt: prey.

Moke complied, therefore, quite easily, as an article of faith, as others go through the stations of the cross: slipped her mini hem up high, watching the guard, higher, higher, higher, slowly, sexily, till Wasco and the two scalped convicts on either side of him could see what they wanted to see, what Wasco had probably charged them three or four cartons of cigarettes apiece to see: Moke's sweet Hawaiian fern, her perfect black curly little Island forest, unmatted, combed and cared-for and perfumed like the kitschy crotch of a *Playboy* cover girl, like a porno queen.

Smiling, paying her dirty dues, as others crawl toward Calvary on bloodied knees, as Wasco'd always paid his to her with no fail or falter, Moke flashed the pop-eyed cons, unobserved by old lady or officer, thinking: *shit what hasn't the sonofabitch done for me? Stuck by me through thick and thin with no regrets and no looking back. He is consistent, which is more than you can say for the rest of the world. And once he makes a decision, he sticks to it, to the bitter end. Could have thrown me over, abandoned me and the kid a hundred times and never did, never, in*

spite of better offers, prettier merchandise both male and
female, and richer and hipper ones too, could have left us
alone without bread or roof over our heads, could have
run off when times were bad, real bad, could have thrown
fits when he caught me in bed with other dudes, could
have cut off my supply of boy, stuff, smack, could have
snuffed me, could have dusted me with a hotshot when he
had doubts, many times, could have . . . could have . . .
might have . . . but he didn't! The old sonofabitch.
Never! Never even considered it. Stuck with us, goddamn-
it, through everything! And how many straight and hon-
est and decent law-abiding folks can you say that about?
None I ever met. Not my own Tutu, not my own Mom
and Dad would, not through everything, asking no ques-
tions when you're strung out, depressed, trying to cut
down on the size of your habit, asking no questions, leav-
ing you free to do your own thing, suffer when you had
to, never there to bug you, only there when needed. Shit!
How many? How many of the finest? None I ever met ex-
cept good old Wasco, the evil old bastard. Not one of the
self-righteous, self-congratulatory sonsofbitches, not one!
None but Wasco she thought, flashing, long and loud,
paying her dues, driving them all up the wall with the
sexy vehemence with which she paid, distracting all three
cons from their conversations, their wives, their homosexual predilections, distracting them all with the sheer magical mystical power of her mad Moke mound, her wondrous fold of Kanaka quiver, Hawaiian pineapple, her
Manoa mango, Pacific pie, Honolulu hairy, her powerful
medicine, her home, hole of the world, whirlpool, spore,
plant, place, peewee, her bounteous beauteous box, her
prickly sweet snatch that she loved and cared for with as
much attention as her face, her hair and skin . . . thinking: *get into it, Moke! Yeah! Get into it!* moving in her
hard seat, wetting it, widening, *get into it! Yeah! Flash!*
Flash 'em! Flash! thinking: *never are you so alive as*
when you're pulling a scam, never do you feel the life
beating inside so hard as when you're shucking them,
driving them wild, never do you feel so alive as when you
feel your own power and watch it working, working mira-
cles before your very eyes, making alien flesh and matter
move before your very eyes. . . . That's what poetry is. I
am a poet.

The power of Moke's positive thinking, her purposeful

sexual magic, her mental orgasm, done without a word, had got all three of the horny-ass convicts off, dropped their loads for them . . . their faces relaxed, they were able to resume their conversations . . . "Say, darling, what was wrong?" . . . "Oh, I just had a pain in my stomach, but it's gone now . . ."

Even Wasco was able to speak again.

"Hey! So how are you, honey?"

"Oh, fine, baby, how're you? Looks like the Joint agrees with you alright, you sly old dog."

"Sure! Like always," he said, and that was the end of the foreplay, the friendly comradely marital formalities. That wasn't where it was at with them: romance, and all that stuff, it never had been.

"So what's up?" Moke asked, getting it right on down to business, where it was *definitely* at with them, onto the firm ground that held them and steadied and nutured their elemental and durable relationship.

"Okay!" Wasco said, delighted at her timing, and their solidly re-established rapport, "here's where it's at on this end . . ." and proceeded to relate to her exactly what he'd accomplished inside the Joint, exactly what was done, and what was left to be done. He did it all in their personal code, a crime code, a thieves' cant, an argot of innuendo and double-talk and baby-talk and parody of martial small talk that had grown up over their danger-filled, larceny-laced five years together on the Street and on the Road and in the Dope World and the Underworld, the world of the Shuck, the Scam, the Caper and Number, that no one in the outside world could pierce, *the world outside just him and me* . . . not only couldn't pierce but wouldn't even know it was being employed, would on the contrary believe that they were carrying on an ordinary hubby and wifie crowing clucking conversation about the mundanities of Home and Joint life. . . .

What Moke was given to understand by Wasco's coded speech was that within the walls of the prison all was not only going according to his meticulously worked out plan, but, aided by Wasco's extraordinary criminal intuition, his guts, his ability to capitalize on the breaks of random chance, things were going better than he'd ever dreamed possible.

On the dope front, his private business, Wasco had ev-

ery reason to believe that the existent organization within
the Joint would be turned over to his control this very day
. . . as soon, in fact, as he received this first shipment
that Moke and Evie were at present busily arranging.

On the other front, the State business, things were also
going smoothly. Wasco had already succeeded in making
an appointment with the Warden and would see him this
afternoon. The haste with which the Warden granted the
interview boded well for the outcome. Since it usually
took months to see the Warden, if one had the great luck
to secure an appointment, pressure from higher quarters
had obviously been applied upon him, and it seemed it
would be no time before he was brought around.

When he finished recounting his unbroken record of
speedy successes in the last twenty-four hours, Wasco
said, "And how's things on the Outside, honey?" And that
was her clue. And she told him. She laid it down for him
in a coded message so obscure that her own Tutu couldn't
have broken it. All was well, she conveyed to him, better
than well, everything was perfectly according to plan. All
the pieces were in place. Everybody who was to be made
was either made already or just about to be made. Everyone who was to be shucked was either shucked now or
would be by this very afternoon. Everyone who had to be
got out of town would be seduced clean out of the state,
by tomorrow morning at the latest. Everyone who was to
be used was in exactly the right place to be used to the
very best advantage, when the time was ripe. The people
who were to be placed were being placed right now, in
just the right position to make the complex mechanism of
Wasco's Grand Design wind and run and work, just like a
fucking Swiss clock.

Evie, Elaine, Fast-Walking, Big and Little Arv, even
May and Sanger. All of them, whether they knew it or
not, were right now at this very moment in rehearsal for
the greatest show ever written, *The Grand Design*, by
Wasco G. Weed, Moke's very own Daddyman! Moke often did this kind of thing, flattered Wasco to the heavens,
just to feed his voracious ego. She kept him happy that
way.

"And your mom, Evie, she'll be in here to visit you today," Moke said, "I just talked to her on the phone . . .
and you can run it down for her, what you want her to do
today. Or I can tell her myself . . ."

"Naw, honey, that's alright," Wasco said, "I can tell her. But . . . I know it's a little rough on you, cause you two don't get along too good . . . but, I would like you to spend a little time with her today, if you don't mind too much. Go on out to her place after her visit this afternoon and keep her company . . . while she handles them . . . employees . . . of hers. You don't even have to say nothing . . . just by *being* there you'll help her out in . . . *selling* . . . them boys, dig?"

"Sure, Wasco," she said, cringing inwardly at the thought of having to spend even a half hour alone with Evie. Her and old Evie, they'd hated each other's guts always, from the day they first met five years ago. Moke knew Evie called her "nigger" and a "little uppity picka-ninny" behind her back while she smiled drippy-sweetly to her face. Knew she'd always tried to come between Wasco and her from the beginning, always bringing up other women in conversation, trying to line him up on the sly with "nice neighborhood girls," always telling him, "Hey, son, what you doing with that little black thing? Can't you do no better? One of these here days you're gonna be a big enough boy to step up to White, don't you think?" Evie's hatred even extended to their child, poor little three-year-old Flo. One time when Moke and Wasco had to disappear for a couple of months, for legal reasons, and asked Evie if she'd watch the kid, she told Wasco, "Shit! You must be fooling, big boy, if you think your old Texas ma's gonna allow any little semolia-head to come in and grease up her clean beds! Sheeeit, kid, you gotta be jokin'!"

Moke hated Evie with her whole heart. Never could understand what Wasco saw in her. He took shit from her he'd never take from anyone else in the world, and always came back for more. Worse! He required Moke to take her shit too! Required her to pretend she liked her mother-in-law, for "the sake of form." Forced her to fawn over her, compliment the fat red-eyed bitch on her looks, her cooking, her house, car, even her sordid "business," forced Moke to play the role of dutiful daughter-in-law to the dirty bigot, the self-centered stingy old whore. . . . And worst of all, Moke complied! Not knowing why, hating herself, Moke went along with Wasco's wishes, acted just like he wanted around her, "just as nice as pie." Never complained, never let him know how it rankled,

how it itched her skin to be with Evie, how very happy
she would be to see her smashed and dead . . .

. . . Anyway . . . "Say, that's real good, honey, real
fine!" Wasco responded to her rather hesitant assent, affecting the tones of a happy complacent husband, signaling the end of their interview, though there were still
ten minutes to go on the time limit, and the guard wasn't
looking their way, "just . . . uh . . . just fine, dear, well,
I sure hope that little Flo's got over her cold. You'd never
figure a kid'd catch cold so much out in Hawaii, would
you? Don't old Tutu take care of her right?"

"No, don't worry, baby," Moke said, in the tones of a
loyal wife, concerned mama, "it's just that Manoa Valley.
So damned damp up there. As soon as we can I'll have to
get her back over here to this drier climate. And Tutu's
getting so old . . ."

"Yeah, well, it's been real nice, honey. And take care,
huh?"

"Sure, sweetheart, see you."

Only as she rose to leave did he reveal his true character for her. Only that once during the whole interview did
he offer her a glimpse . . .

She'd turned, and was starting out.

"Hold it!" he said.

"What?"

"Say it!" he commanded.

"Say what?"

"You know what . . . say it!"

"Aw, come on, baby, it's so stupid!"

"Say it, goddamnit!"

"Oh, alright . . ."

"Good, say it!"

"*Aloha,* you sonofabitch!" she said, laughing openly, revealing her real personality too, her ironic self, just that
once, for the road, and Wasco dug it. He dug it and he
dug her, for exactly what she was. In all her immense
complexity, a complexity as deep and slippery as the sea.
She could tell he did. She could see him laughing about
her ironically to himself all the way out of the visiting
room, laughing while the guard at the other end shook
him down, laughing, waving at her and laughing through
the wide gaps in his ugly Weed teeth till the huge iron
door slammed BANG! and shut him from her sight. . . .

And all the way to City College, all the way along the mudflats by the Sound, and over the toll bridge, and down the long 18th Avenue of white stucco houses, Moke ran it back in her helmet: Wasco laughing, his teeth showing, the big iron door crushing closed, BANG! cutting off the flashing laughter of her man, Daddy, bad-ass Dad, just like someone pulled the socket right out of the wall, on a very dark night. . . .

Seventeen

On the way back over to Evie's place in the VW bus Fast-Walking started up on that damn southeastern Oregon again. Big Arv was sick of this latest obsession, so he told him to shut up. Then, just to be funny, he started up a-teasing Big Arv again. He loved to do it. Always did, for one fucking reason or another. Used to tease him about Arv and Deanna, cause he knew Big Arv felt it was a real feather in his cap, being tied up with such a big 4-O outfit as Warden Miniver's family. Then when, to Big Arv's great and everlasting displeasure, they got a divorce after only two years, he started teasing him again. "Say, you must be all broke up, Big Arv," he said one time in the Briefing Room. "Why's that?" Big Arv asked, like a damn sucker. "Well," he said, "looks like your future in the old C of C might've gone the same way as that there marriage, huh?" And everyone on the swing shift got a fat laugh at Big Arv's expense.

Now, Big Arv figured that Fast-Walking'd begun teasing him just to kill time on the job. Took his mind off his financial problems and his family troubles. Or maybe he did it cause he blamed Big Arv for all his new worries. It was Evie, after all, Big Arv's ex-kin, who'd gotten Fast-Walking in debt up over his head, got his salary double-attached, got him into such a state that he'd never be able to hold his head up high again. Big Arv watched it all, the whole complex process of thought and blame, as it ran across Fast-Walking's handsome tanned WASP face while they drove in brilliant morning light across the soggy fields of celery: *It's all Big Arv's fault. And that fat-ass Evie. They're like twins. Just like that together. I know he wants in her pants. Evie, it looks like, just plays the co-quette and don't let him get away with nothing. She just plays him for what she can get. Big Arv's always fawning*

over her, and kissing her butt. Fast-Walking wondered as
they drove out of the fields and out onto the freeway,
with the sun reflecting off the gray submarines drydocked
at Pony Island, off the shiny jet fighter planes lined up on
the runway of the Naval Air Station. And Big Arv
watched him wonder, wondering whether Big Arv'd ever
got into Evie's size forty knickers. Wondering, and hating
them both with all his ungrateful heart, and resenting Big
Arv, and envying Evie all her money, Fast-Walking
turned to Big Arv, raised his sunglasses up onto his high
blond forehead, and said—Big Arv knew what he'd say,
he'd say something to get at him—he said, "Yes sir, Arv,
you sure do speak Spanish good. Where'd you say you
learned it?"

"In high school."

"Oh yeah? You know what?"

"No, what?"

"I believe you got a little greaser blood in you."

"Oh yeah? Well you believe what you want," Big Arv
responded, but rather uncertainly, off his step, as he always was when somebody asked him this difficult question.

"Where'd you say you was from?"

"I was born in Texas."

"What part?"

"McAllen."

"Why, that's right across the border from Matamoros,
ain't it? Lot of Spics around there, I bet. Where'd you say
your old man was from?"

"My old man?" Big Arv said. "Uh . . ." he said awkwardly, and then slipped with years of practice into the
smooth story he'd developed while he was still a teenager,
"my old man, he was from Minnesota, originally, Lake of
the Woods, up in the northern part, lumber country.
Came out to Texas as a kid. Met my old lady in McAllen.
Her mother ran a boardinghouse down there."

"Oh yeah?" Fast-Walking said. "Well, all you Weeds
got something funny-looking about you, you got something in the eyes. You all got these little-bitty slanted
eyes."

"Oh well, that's Indian blood. Ain't you ever seen an
Indian? They got these same little eyes. Ugly as hell, ain't
it?"

"Yah, I got to agree with you there. But, you know what? I think maybe you might have an old touch of the tar brush somewheres way back that you don't know about . . ."

"You do, huh?" Big Arv said, realizing that his guilt in covering up his past left him vulnerable to all sorts of attacks. "Uh . . . well . . ." and began again, "uh . . ." and, totally confused, took refuge in affected anger. "You know what? If you keep on needling me, kid, you and me are gonna have to get into it, right out here on the fucking freeway!" Now Big Arv was alright. Now he was on solid familiar ground. Violence. Threats. That's what he was good at. Now his voice was strong and forceful. All his uncertainty and embarrassment disappeared in the blink of an eye. Fast-Walking saw it and deferred to Big Arv: "Naw, no use getting into it with each other, man. Ain't worth it. Shit, we're just two of a kind, two fucking old broke-ass, debt-ridden, unloved old struggling overworked prison guards." Big Arv understood that this sudden sympathy for their plight was an unconscious design of Fast-Walking's to rationalize away his sudden fear of the stronger, more violent man. He understood it and accepted it, but didn't let Fast-Walking know that for a few moments, just to make him dangle awhile . . .

"Hey!" Fast-Walking said, looking right in Big Arv's mean little eyes, "I was just kidding, baby. Really!"

"Yeah?" Big Arv said, on top of things again, feeling good, "well, if you want to stay on good terms with me, kid, you better stop talking like a fucking coon."

"Sure, Big Arv . . . Hey!" and Fast-Walking, looking out the window as they drove up onto Evie's dew-drenched front lawn under the date palm tree, "lookie here!"

Two young black girls in low-cut minidresses and red knee boots were turning into Evie's driveway. Fast-Walking clambered out of the van and went fast but looking like cool and slow across the driveway. Big Arv stayed behind in the bus, watching.

"Say there, girls, can I help you?" he said, smiling, bowing low on his long spindly legs, his loose basketball player's body very attractive the way it moved oily-jointed and easy. The girls giggled, crossing and uncrossing their legs uneasily. One was very pretty, with a brown long wig

and huge black eyes. The other one both men dismissed.
A bush-nigger-looking thing, with thick Ubangi lips and a
flat wide baboon nose; it looked to Big Arv that she understood this real well, and shyly retired behind the cute
little one to her proper place.

"You workin heah?"

"Yeah."

"We lookin fo' Miz Mount-oya."

"Oh, I see," Fast-Walking said politely, "well, I handle
that facet of the operation here. Listen, let's talk. Why not
step over to the Frosty Freeze with me for a moment?
Can I offer you a milk shake, or something?"

The girls, who obviously weren't used to this kind of
courtesy, especially from a white man, agreed readily,
"Sho!" and with happy smiles accompanied him across the
road. Big Arv watched them going down the dirt road till
they went into the parking lot of the Frosty Freeze on the
corner, and then he went into the house to see if Evie was
up yet. If she was, he was going to tell her that Fast-
Walking was just getting to be too much. She was going
to have to let him go. There he was gallivanting around,
fucking around with them niggers, lying to them, using
Evie's good name to further his filthy desires, trying to get
into their black pussies, when there was work to be done
in the back yard.

Big Arv went into the house. He walked into the living
room and opened up the shades, letting the sun stream in
on the brown felt furniture, the faded "Persian" carpet.
Then he stepped in to see if Evie was up.

The room was dark and sweet-smelling. It smelled like
Evie. It smelled of a fattish older woman, like sweet sickly
cactus candy that you could buy in Evie's store. Arv liked
the smell. It reminded him of his childhood home on the
Rio Grande, and his ma, who was always making cactus
candy in a big iron pot, stirring in the rich honey that the
Yaqui boy brought around once a week.

It was almost pitch black in the room. All the shutters
and shades and drapes were drawn. Evie couldn't get to
sleep except in total darkness. She breathed deeply now,
snoring every fifth or sixth breath, snorting, and then letting it out slow. Big Arv stood in the room for a long
time, listening to her beloved breath, remembering, smelling, barely breathing, unmoving, remembering.

Big Arv loved his Evie, just like his wife had always suspected, though he'd never admitted it to anyone. Not to anyone except to Evie herself, whom he'd pursued unsuccessfully for more than thirty years, since they were kids growing up in the same neighborhood in Mission Santa Bonita, in the depths of the Depression. She was older than Big Arv, but he'd always gone for the older ones. As a young man he'd come real near to marrying a widow of fifty. Big Arv remembered, standing there alone in the dark. he remembered the time when she married Big Wasco, and how he used to go over to their place as a kid, only sixteen, and Evie twenty or twenty-one. He used to make it a point to go over to her prison row house and listen while she practiced on her piano, practiced up on her gospel singing. She wasn't too good, but she had a lot of energy, and a loud voice, and belted out the songs in such a lusty full-bodied way that everyone loved to hear her. One time while he was standing beside her at the piano, watching her close, she suddenly stopped playing and kissed him on the lips. Right smack on his lips. It was in March of 1939. He'd never forget it. She just turned around and kind of melted her body up against his. He sprang an enormous hard-on immediately. She put her hand on his cock. He was trembling with desire. He put his hand on her big tits. She rubbed up against him. They kissed again. He dropped down on his knees and she hugged him to her tits and kissed him a long long time, all the time reaching down and rubbing his joint firmly and smoothly. He reached down and unbuttoned his dirty white corduroys and let his prick move out slow like a snake into her plump red hand. She rubbed it, rubbed its fleshy hanging goat's beard, rubbed it up and down, while they kissed again and again. Then he couldn't stop. He undulated in her palm, back and forth faster and faster, came came came crushed honeysuckle-colored jizz bubbling into her hand, her red palm, between her pink fingers. The come ran over her hand and through her knuckles and dripped on the floor, on the red rug. The stain remained there for three decades. Until after Evie'd long gone, till after Big Wasco, her first hubby, was long dead. Big Arv always looked for it when he went by there. Now the Brownes, the family of Sergeant Browne, lived there. They'd finally got rid of the rug.

And Big Arv remembered even before, when he was nine and she was thirteen, out in the chicken house behind her daddy's place, under the big old-pepper tree that smelled so good. She'd just developed tits, but already they were busting out of her brassiere. She took him out into the hen house and tried to get him to whip his cock out. He was just a little guy, and afraid of her. She said, "Okay then, you got to look at my twat." So she pulled up her pinafore and sure enough, she hadn't worn any panties. Big Arv looked at that thing for the longest time. He'd never seen one before. It didn't turn him on, at the time. He was too young. It was just kind of . . . interesting . . . to him. He was, after all, just a little-bitty old kid. It looked like the mouth of a big fish, to him, bald and gray as a fishface, with dry scaly skin and a dripping mouth, dripping liquidy substance onto the cracked chapped lips, making them drier and redder, making them raw.

"Touch me," she said, and he did. It felt like melted butter in a hairy tray. "Now sniff it!" she commanded.

"Ugh!"

"Sniff it!" she repeated, urgently, breathing heavy, like a bitchdog with her tongue hanging out, rubbing herself up against his little chest. So he brought his finger to his nose and sniffed. It smelled like what it looked like. It smelled like fish. Big Arv didn't mind fish. Always loved it. So it didn't taste bad. Tasted like fresh trout.

Those were the only times Evie'd ever let him get near her. Just here recently she'd told him how it was, very frankly. "Listen, you know how I am, Big Arv. I always stick with the winners. Now we had this thing between us for years. And you know as well as I that it's love and always has been from the beginning. But like I say, I always been and I always will be nothing but a betting woman, a woman who only goes for the sure things, the good horses, the big winners. So you ain't got a chance, and you might as well get used to it. Cause I ain't got no time for losers, Big Arv, no time for nags. Now if you ever . . ." she said, hesitating, and then let it drop. Big Arv knew what she meant, though. She was a strong-willed independent woman. Always had been. No man could expect to keep her if he couldn't stay even with her, couldn't equal her in all ways. And Big Arv, there weren't no two

ways about it, he was just a goddamn failure, a goddamn
hack sergeant at the Joint, with no prospects for the future, and a bad ticker to boot. He wasn't worth it. She
knew it. Arv had to agree with her and, agreeing with her,
loved her and wanted her more than ever, and dreamed of
her like a teenage boy, a teenage boy who once wanted to
be a dancer, and won the Mission Santa Bonita High
School Jitterbug championship two years in a row: 1940
and 1941. Big Arv placed all his dreams in Evie, regressed
to childhood through these dreams, and possessed her
there in the dreamlike chicken house of his desire.

Slowly the sun came around the side of the house. A
gray light shone in through the closed blinds. Slowly Big
Arv began to pick out objects in this room, a room he
dwelt in too, in his imagination. First he saw the new
Singer sewing machine. Then he picked out all her religious accoutrements, things from every American religion
(she wasn't choosy—"I ain't taking no chances," she said,
"I want a little grease with everybody's Jesus"), a statue
of the Virgin Mary that lit up from inside and shone blue
out the eyes, a stack of *Awake* magazines, a plain wooden
cross above her bed, an ornate Catholic picture of Christ-
on-the-cross hanging on her western wall with a pierced
bleeding heart and thorns sticking out of his tortured
flesh. Then, turning his head in wonder, as he always did
when he came here, like a small boy, Big Arv watched the
gray light illuminate the dirty machine-made lace curtains,
the souvenir serapes from Tijuana, the plastic statue of a
knocked-up teenage girl with pigtails and tears in her eyes,
knock-kneed and pigeon-toed, with "Kilroy was here" inscribed on the plastic base. He saw the metallic pistol cigarette lighter on her bed stand, the cigarillos she smoked,
her golden filthy bedspread that fell away abandoned on
the dusty green and gold linoleum floor. He watched the
light change slowly from gray to yellow, watched it light
up her Mexican sombrero hanging on the wall, and then
he began to make out the separate pieces of her collection
of years, her collection of kewpie dolls from carnivals and
fairs and boardwalks of the '30's and '40's and '50's
and '60's and '70's, kewpie dolls of every size and shape
and color and material, blond kewpie dolls, black ones,
kewpie dolls made of plastic, rubber, pottery, china, glass,
and fake human skin, kewpie dolls of the finest crystal,

kewpie dolls of metal and vegetable and solidified animal fat, kewpie dolls in Jarhead suits and GI and Flyboy and Gy-rene suits, kewpie dolls demure and kewpie dolls just saucy baggage, kewpie dolls in pinafores and chicken feathers and donkey fur and burnt human skin, kewpie dolls laughing and kewpie dolls crying, kewpie dolls that cried real tears and kewpie dolls that had a laughing machine inside, kewpie dolls that walked, talked, and wiggled and giggled and bumped and ground, kewpie dolls dressed up like cops and firemen and prison guards, kewpie dolls in widow's weeds, and kewpie dolls in the virginal white of brides, kewpie dolls with the long snouts of piggies, and curly tails, and kewpie dolls with the faces of many differ-ent kinds of dogs, each conveying a corresponding type of human character, kewpie dolls kewpie dolls kewpie dolls, that's all Big Arv saw, standing unmoving, moved, loving, in the broadening light, light that now entered the deepest shadows near Evie's private domain, her yellow bed, and revealed her in all her beloved glory and beauty, beauty that only Big Arv in all the world saw, beauty that he treasured for its secret, and the fact that he was the only one who could see it, beauty that was real, beauty that would always last, the beauty of a thirteen-year-old gray-faced fish, a true and wondering beauty that he would never free himself from, a captivity he had always known. And he shivered now, shivered with the power of her un-conscious drag on him, the incredible magnetism about her that drew him, drew him even while she dreamed. And he watched the light play on her, reveal her. It was hot in the room. Evie always set the thermostat at eighty degrees, winter and summer. She got cold very easy and preferred to sweat and smell of prespiration than "get a case of chills and die young." She'd thrown the bed clothes off during the night. She now slept half turned on her side, like a child, her mouth clamped down tight over her toothless gums. She was beautiful.

What did Evie look like?

She was gorgeous.

Evie was a double for her son. She looked like Wasco in drag. Exactly. She had the same high forehead and balding crown and the same tiny squinty Indian eyes and the same low hard squat short-legged body. She looked like Big Arv. She looked like a Weed. She was. Grandma

Dora Lee was her first cousin on her daddy's side. Almost a Weed, Evie had the same red hair as her son, the same pouting willful mouth and wide-gapped teeth, the same rosy healthy cheeks, the same powerful thick limbs, the same smashed nose and wide flaring nostrils, the same tiny slothlike ears, the same glittering tiny points of eyes. And yet, somehow, Evie was all female, as intensely female as Wasco was male. Like her son, however, she retained certain very definite physical aspects of both sexes: in spite of the peach-fuzzy red moustache on her upper lip she had a rather pretty lady's face, a face she pampered and patted and powdered and mascaraed and painted daily. Now her lipstick was smeared over her lips and chin; her mascara had run down beneath her eyes. Her strawberry blond hair was done up in large curlers for the night, an unruly strand or two hanging free. Her white face powder and pink rouge remained though, only slightly less conspicuous than usual.

She looked like Wasco. She looked like one of her own kewpie dolls. She looked like a little girl. She looked like the devil.

Her breasts spilled out of her pale tobacco-stained nightgown like pierced balloons. They seemed to have a separate and copious life of their own. They rose and fell and bubbled and bellowed and flowed. They were absolutely the biggest tits that Big Arv had ever seen. You could build a house on them and live there, it seemed to him, if you wanted. You could build a dam between them and water a thirsty nation; you could put a TV antenna on top of the peak of her nips and beam the Six O'Clock News to a waiting world. You could go up in there between them like a starving old dog and die there, die content as could be, pillowed to death in their mammouth folds as some are rocked to sleep in their mama's pillowy scented lap.

Big Arv would have done that. He would have if he could have gone right up in there like a goddamn dog and died if she'd let him. Even if you had to die to get up there between them big monsters, it'd be well worth it. Cause, up there, on that stufuckingpendous breathing mountain of meat, that's where love was, up there on them big red-tipped nips, them freckled boobs. That's where all of love lived, as far as Big Arv could see. . . .

Eighteen

Arv and Moke sat together with ears cocked in their Creative Writing class, listening to their favorite teacher, Elaine of the crazy eyes, do her inimitable act. They loved the way she did it. She was a genius, a true performing artist. Her students watched her goggle-eyed. She'd held them enthralled with her antics all semester, tickling them till they doubled up with stomach cramps. She leapt on chairs and tables, waved her hands madly, pouted her lips, stuck her ass out and walked like a duck, lay down across half a dozen desks at a run, scattering books and pencils; she hung out the windows till the gardeners yelled "Another suicide! Third floor!" She screamed, shrieked, stamped, danced, whirled, laughed hysterically, cried real tears, held forth histrionically, declaimed, descanted, denounced, renounced, announced, all to make her points, her precious inspired and telling points which, in the end, were really rather subtle and intelligent, but of a kind that you couldn't figure out rationally. She used everything to advantage in class, to make her points: her acting ability, her apparent training as a dancer and mime artist, her native comic talents, her body, her training as an existentialist and short story writer, her training as a Marxist and New Left revolutionary, everything!

" 'Every authentic writer discovers not only a new style but a narrative form which is his alone, and which in most cases he uses up, exhausting its effects for his own purposes,' " she quoted, "does anyone know who said that?" sitting up on the teacher's table, swinging her tanned shapely legs. She was a remarkably pretty woman, midthirtyish, with the red fleshy lips of a sensualist, the straight high-bridged nose of a classic Mediterranean, lush black hair, golden eyes, long dark lashes that curved up, heavy black lids, eyebrows that met Persian-like over her "third eye" and an infectious smile, a friendly wonderful smile that had tempted Arv from the start. Voluptuous, slightly used, with a couple of marriages and divorces and a kid in her past, short and tough and olive-skinned, Elaine attracted her student Little Arvin Weed most powerfully precisely because she was just a trifle, a mere delectable taste, overweight and overripe.

"No! Not you, Moke!" she admonished, laughing with pleasure at her star pupil, "you always know . . . someone else, for a change . . . Arv?"

"Uh . . . Jean Genet?" he offered rather timidly, embarrassed as always in front of a large gathering.

"Right!" she said, pointing her long narrow finger at him, leaping off the table and sliding in a stylized slithering snakewalk (that set them laughing wildly) to the blackboard.

"The reason I asked," she began, standing at the board, chalk poised, serious again, or mostly serious, you never knew . . . "is because he said it about someone who didn't start out as a writer but ended up one through the force of circumstance, and because the circumstances themselves created his writing, dictated it, were its forge and fuel, its necessity, and his personal spiritual salvation . . ."

"George Jackson?" Moke asked, cutting in, knowing she was right, spoiling Elaine's moment. Ever since Arv'd starting going with Moke, ever since he'd delighted them both by agreeing to take Galliot's letters into the Joint, it had been love-hate and constant bickering and public making-up between the two volatile women. Arv felt very flattered, flattered beyond anything he'd ever imagined, though he wasn't at all sure their warfare had anything to do with him. It seemed to go beyond that, beyond success or failure, desire and its achievement, beyond ideology, into the realm of the feminine and unfathomable.

"Yeah, how'd you know?" Elaine asked sarcastically, pointing the chalk at her defensively, letting it become well known that, good sport though she might be, she did not like interruptions.

Moke often liked to spoil Elaine's moments even though, or precisely because, she was her best student, her best writer next to Arv.

"It's obvious," Moke returned, just as sarcastically.

"How so?" Elaine wanted to know, pretending genuine curiosity.

The class started murmuring and poking ribs at the extreme cattiness of the exchange.

Moke wouldn't respond. She just went, "Tsk, tsk," poking Arv, making him embarrassed, as if he were some kind of conspirator with her. Moke enjoyed trying to break Elaine's pace, her timing, her beautiful act, and sometimes succeeded, to Elaine's immense chagrin. It was possible to knock Elaine off her pace. But it was such a wild and wonderful pace, such a hollow victory, that Arv would never dream of trying. It was like shooting down pretty winter ducks: even though Arv loved shooting, and was the best shot in the Joint, he never went hunting birds anymore. Why spoil their smooth and lovely flight?

Anyway, Moke had succeeded, as she did sometimes; she'd gotten Elaine uptight.

"Oh, stop being a drag, Moke, I'm getting a little tired of it," she said.

"Oh really?" Moke rejoined. "Well I don't appreciate being called a 'drag' either, especially by someone who prides herself on her enlightened 'feminism' and the 'sisterhood of womankind.'"

"I don't see what sisterhood has to do . . ."

"You don't see a lot of things, unfortunately . . ." Moke said.

"Aw, come off it, I begin to wonder about . . ."

"You begin to wonder whether it was worth it with all these freaks . . . right?"

"Not at all! That isn't what I was going to say at all! As a matter of fact, I was leading up to an explanation of why I submitted this course idea to the English Department last year. I was tired of middle-class milk-fed students. I wanted people like you! People who weren't like other college students, who weren't from the 'privileged' classes. People from minority groups, from the working classes, people from the drug and counter cultures, the underground, people with different backgrounds, different interests, different insights into the problems of today's urban environment, people with more experience of the real nitty-gritty street world out there. . . . **And** . . . so far . . . I thought we'd succeeded beyond my wildest dreams! We've got an ex-prize-fighter in here, a former drug addict, two ex-convicts, people from every minority group in New Sonora including an American Indian, and even . . . believe this or not, we even have a . . . prison guard in here!"

Elaine's dark eyes were clouding over with her passion, her hope, her dream. Moke had succeeded at breaking her cool, but even broken, breaking down, tearful, Elaine was triumphant . . . she had a way of always ending up triumphant.

Arv finally spoke up. "I think it's a success!"

"So do I!"

"Me too!"

The whole class, with Moke's exception, responded favorably. Finally she had to apologize. "I'm sorry," she said, "I don't know what's gotten into me today."

"No! That's okay!" shouted Elaine, prancing around before the blackboard, getting back into her stride, "I expected the going to get tough at times, and it has, but I think it's been worth it, don't you?"

"Sure," Moke said, and smiled sweetly up at Elaine.

"Anyway," Elaine said, offering them her brilliant beautiful smile, "let me read something by our prison guard that has just the kind of thing I've been after in this class. It's entitled 'Wall Post #8,' and I think it has a few problems of construction, and a slight tendency toward sentimentality, but on the whole I think it's very good, very good indeed. Let's see what you think . . ."

Elaine stood up before the class and began to read Arv's story, the first story he'd been able to write about his prison experience, a story about pigeons and sea gulls in the deserted Big Yard, and the loneliness of the guard in the gun tower, and about how being locked up in that tower was no different from being locked up in a cell, except you were able to come down for sixteen hours every day . . . come down to your dismal gray guard's cottage on the prison grounds. He'd written it as a kind of refutation of her statement of a few days before when she'd said, ". . . but you, Arvin, you're not *in* prison! You're the oppressor, not the oppressed!"

Arv let his mind wander while Elaine read. He loved to hear his own stuff read, and it was good, just like she said, and he was delighted to see how jealous its quality made the other students . . . even a slight tinge of it he saw now reflected in Moke's Oriental eyes as she sat beside him, listening intently. Nevertheless, Arv let his mind go, he let Elaine's superb reading voice take him off to the time three weeks before when she called him to her table after class, after reading his first work, a fictionalized biography of his mother and father and their horrid unhappy marriage. She found it "extraordinary," and "full of pathos"; his work was proof of a "unique and original though, as yet, unformed and unfulfilled talent." She complimented him this way, sending his heart singing toward the sky, even though his paper had little or nothing to do with the assignment she'd given, a critique of V.S. Naipaul's *A House of Mr. Biswas.*

After class she asked if he had time to come down to her office for a conference.

"Sure," he said, "but I don't have much time. I got to get to work."

"I just wanted to tell you how happy I am to have you in the class," she began, as they eased out of the crowded classroom together. "I've heard of you before, of course. I don't know whether you know it or not, but you've got quite a reputation around the English Department, ever since you published that short story last year in the *City College Review*. 'The prison guard who can write,' they call you."

Arv could never figure out why it was so unusual or strange for a prison guard to be a writer. There'd been longshoremen, truck drivers, brakemen, farmers, gandy dancers, even cops, who could write . . . and every gunsel convict in the Joint who could sign his name thought of himself as a "great prison novelist." Why not a prison guard, then? But he said nothing.

"I think you're a writer," she said, but Arv felt no thrill of happiness. It seemed like her compliment was given absentmindedly. Arv had the feeling that somehow, even though she was very interested in him, she wasn't really interested in him at all . . . not in *him*, himself . . . but in something else which she believed she saw in him . . . which, he was almost sure, didn't exist at all. She had asked him especially to enroll in her class, she'd come up to him during registration and asked him personally. He'd been highly flattered that she'd heard about him and his work in the Poetry Workshop.

So him and Elaine, they went clickety-click down the brown asphalt tile floor of the City College modern hallway smoking and talking and pushing their way through the throngs of shabby, unkempt, bleary-eyed students. She was trying hard to make him relax, make him laugh, but it wasn't working out because all the students passing by them in the hall were staring strangely at him. Arv wasn't the kind of guy she was usually seen around with. It was usually just bearded intellectual types and long-haired Philosophy Department freaks. Arv felt like his hair was too short, his sideburns too high-clipped, his moustache too well-trimmed, his jodhpurs too shiny cordovan.

"You know, you and Moke are my best writers. And yet, the two of you are so different in styles. She's from Hawaii, you know. But between you and me, you're the one with the really formidable talent. And the greatest thing," she said, seeming to divine his thoughts, "is that you don't look the part! Thank God you don't look like a 'writer'!"

Nervously he laughed, smoked his Kent with rigid fingers. Then he just shook his head, trying to smile pleasantly, not succeeding, trying hard not to look at her as a "sexual object," something she roundly condemned in class on many occasions. Though Elaine had no "shame," no pride, no care for her "dignity" as a "lady" in the old-fashioned sense, Arv found her very dignified in her own way. She seemed to have a true sense of her own worth, but it had more to do with being a writer and an intellectual than with being a good-looking young woman.

"No, I'm not kidding!" she said, smiling her warm genuine smile at him, her smile that Arv did not altogether trust as yet, "thank God you're not 'literary'!"

At the time, Arv's attitude toward her was wholly ambiguous, even to himself. He admired her, but he didn't like her or understand her. She was very "funky" and "real," all the students said admiringly of her, especially the hip and hairy ones. Arv had often thought she might be as phony as her smile which was, sure, beautiful, but you could tell she thought about it first, before she decided when and where and how to beam it at you.

But then, on the other hand, he had thought, you just couldn't trust your own motives when dealing with 4-O's, individuals of the upper-middle and educated classes. He had a native antipathy for them, inherited directly from his Grandma Dora Lee and Big Arv, and considered them untrustworthy by nature.

The truth of the matter was that he was absolutely in awe of her, and all intellectuals, and aspired with all his heart to be like her, like them, someday, to be as different as possible from all his grimy mindless antecedents. But the ambiguity, the low-class suspicion was still working at him too . . . *Why couldn't she just do what she really wanted to do in life?* Arv was thinking, *why is she always pretending that what she's worried about is the welfare and happiness of other people?* She was on dozens of Leftist committees, anti-Vietnam War committees, Free Galliot committees, Fair Shake for Black Fence committees, abortion legislation committees, women's lib committees, and so on. But Arv, in a way, distrusted her motives. He perceived in her an egoist, and that didn't put him off. What put him off was the fact that she didn't freely indulge her egoism. Why didn't she just live for herself? he wondered, why didn't she just do nothing but write? She was a good writer. He'd read one of her short stories in the library. "Nominated for the O. Henry Award," it said on the flyleaf of the book. Why didn't she just live for writing, for herself?

Little Arv, on the very eve of throwing the full weight of his ambition onto the side of the intelligentsia, still gave very little credence to the vaunted "social conscience" of the American intellectual class. But he was smart enough to apprehend thoroughly the power of its myth. That is why he at least halfway understood Elaine's impulse when, finding him impossible to "relate" to as a human being, finding him opaque as ironwood, and wanting something out of him, she crazily, agitatedly, as if it meant everything, attempted to bridge the enormous gap that Arv in his native paranoia had widened between them as they walked down the hallway.

Arv realized that she had something in mind for him, saw him in some role that he might not himself care for at all, foresaw the possibility of the Slow Shuck, the possibility that she might want to use him for political purposes inside the Joint. He knew that she'd never use him out of malice. He knew that she romanticized him outrageously . . . as she did all members of the lower classes. In him, Arv was sure, she saw her "great hope for America" she spoke of so often in class. Here was a "middle American" who was open-minded, rational, sensitive, and talented. Here was her long-hoped-for "opening to the middle sector" that would turn American politics upside down. Here before her was the personification of all her beliefs, living vindication of all those summers spent fruitlessly depressingly registering voters, leafleting, working in recruitment drives, indoctrination campaigns, picketing, lying down in front of ammunition trucks, shouting down politicians. . . .

In this way Arv knew she was fair game for him. If he wanted. If he played his cards right he might even get something off her. At the least a good grade in her class. And that was nothing to be sniffed at: with his lousy grades in everything but writing courses it would be a miracle if they let him graduate. But there was something of him that she would want in return, that was sure.

It was at that point that his male ego flattered him with the thought that what she wanted from him might be altogether pleasurable . . . even sexual . . . in nature.

"The reason I concern myself with students," she said, apropos of nothing, the minute they were inside the door of her tiny office, "and the reason for my activities in the radical resistance, and the reason I've always been an activist, and the reason I write, for that matter, is that I'm really sort of fucked up in the head."

While she explained in frank detail the meaning of "logotherapy" and its relation to her life, confessing the gist of Arv's speculation ("What motivates me is self-interest," she said, "but there's room for a lot to be done in this world with a little constructive self-interest"), Arv was thinking that either she was trying to trick him some way, hoping to gain his trust by a personal confidence, or that she was surprisingly inconsistent in her thinking: her motivation and her "constructive self-interest" sounded to him suspiciously like warmed-over Ayn Rand, whom he'd read and believed at sixteen, and dismissed entirely at eighteen.

"I'm subject to uncontrollable compulsions," she said, changing the subject of her monologue for no apparent reason, "but don't let that worry you. It happens only very infrequently. No!" she said too loudly, wild-eyed,

"I'm just kidding. You won't report me to the Dean, will you?" She managed a laugh, but Arv could see that she was extremely distracted about him . . . about something . . . and could not at all contain her nervousness. She was very frank about her personal life in class, and she encouraged them to be, but this was getting to be a bit much.

"But I'm really capable of the most sudden and incredible caprices, the wildest changes you can imagine," she went on, forgetting all about Arv's "talent," and his "extraordinary paper," forgetting indeed, it seemed, that he was even in the room with her. Arv found himself unconsciously backing away from her across the little office, peering out the window as if he were really interested in the gardeners working on the rose trees in the Quad.

"I get into the most ridiculous setups. But I like to keep it all in perspective by laughing at myself as often as possible," she said, and laughed heartily to punctuate her statement. And yet she was deadly serious, her eyes flashing, her finger jabbing him in the back, whipping him around from the window with a flick, buttonholing him up against her Free Galliot calendar. He let her handle him like an overgrown child.

"If you make fun of your own foibles," she continued, "once in a while then you're sane. It's people who take themselves seriously who're really loco, don't you think?" she asked, and went racing on.

Then he thought: *she likes me. She's trying to impress me in her way. She's nervous and afraid around me and wants to get close.*

And when he thought that way, instantaneously he became nervous and self-conscious too.

And they stood up in her little cubicle bobbing and weaving like boxers, shuffling papers in their hands all the time, dancing like fighters in the ring, like mating birds.

"Currently I'm having an affair with Harris Mills, Minister of War for the Black Fence . . ." she went on without a break or breath, "crazy, isn't it? someone so filled with hatred and violence? . . . Understandable and even . . . just as it may be. But it's typical of me. Before him it was William Galliot himself. But he wasn't violent at all. The sweetest man I've ever known, ever loved, and I've loved a lot. I was mad about him! Probably most of all because I knew our affair was doomed from the beginning. Sexual harmony and ideological agreement aside, I *am* white, after all! So, after two of the best years of my life . . . phhhhhht! It was because he had to get out of the old mold. Had to think black. It was a conscious effort on his part . . . which I subscribed to . . . on an intellectual level, at least. And then he found Harriet, who is black . . . and beautiful . . . and I understood. I really did! I mean, like, you've got your big countries and they're always lording it over the little ones, and your rich over your poor, white over black, male over female . . . and there's no one in the whole political universe lower on the totem pole than the poor black woman! . . . So, as I say . . . William's decision was completely rational as far as I was concerned, and . . . we've remained friends . . . probably even tighter friends now that the sex . . . thing . . . is gone, and anyway, well, he's so much *older* than I am . . . and, that's really nothing, but in a way I see my love for him as a part of a very sick syndrome in me . . . I still have a thing for my father, you see . . ." Elaine said, rambling farther and farther and farther afield, "even though I detest everything he represents. He's an army officer, you see . . . like my second husband. The shrink tells me my dad was 'overseductive' to me. If that's so I was never aware of it. All I remember is a nice warm lap. But I always hated him, I think. I grew up on army bases all over the world. I'm one of your typical screwed-up army brats, I guess . . . and I did marry men much older than I . . ."

By now it was apparent to Arv that this was her frantic way of coming on to him. There could be no mistake. She was in a state of extreme emotional turmoil and agitation. She was spouting out anything that came into her head, madly, trying to hold him, lasso him, tie him down with her whirling, tripping, binding words. It was a free-association seduction! With that realization, Arv got scared, got jittery and young, pursued by the older woman, the vampire, the man-eater, dragging snakes in her hair.

"You know," she went on, touching his arm and shoulder whenever she made a point, "you know," she said, chewing gum violently, her head empty of new devices for a moment, her brain racing for new free-associations, anything! "You know," she repeated, her eyes still frantic, empty of ideas, "you know," she said for the fourth time, desperately casting out for a subject, even the most mundane, just to keep the words flowing, "you know . . . I chew gum all the time, even though I consider it vulgar and I feel very ashamed of myself and laugh just like the English at Americans abroad when I see them doing it . . ."

And Arv then fully appreciated her desperate fix, and gave up all idea of allowing himself to be seduced, or even of hearing her eventual critique of his story (which seemed to be completely forgotten now anyway), and now only hoped to get out of her office that morning with his life.

And it was then, in that instant, as Elaine fully revealed her powerful anxiety, that she unknowingly lost her sexual hold on Little Arv, lost any possible help, any favor she wanted from him. And the pity of it was, she might have won him to her side, the side of right, the side of conscience, as Moke later did, if it weren't for her fatal, terrible, honest, nervous sense of guilt . . .

"I was engaged seven times before I actually got married," Elaine said, coming right out in front now, holding his hand, rubbing up against him "inadvertently," looking suggestively (but unconvincingly so) over at the army surplus sleeping mat spread out in the corner, "two times I left them waiting right at the altar with the whole retinue and all . . . My father just said, 'Well here we go again!'

"Oh, that thing!" she shouted, responding to a question he did not ask, "that's for my naps. I take one here every afternoon. I work so late at night, you see, with this Free Galliot thing . . ."

She looked up at him. She was actually able to focus on his face. But her expression was still distracted, her golden-flecked eyes turned inward, busy, absent. Elaine wanted him, but somehow not him. Maybe she wanted someone like him, or someone she imagined him to be, or someone she'd dreamed up who bore no relation to any living being, or maybe, he thought, maybe all she wants to do is just feel herself look at herself in the mirror of my eyes, or maybe she wants . . .

"I was a virgin till I was twenty-four," she said, leading him toward the army mat like a sheep to the slaughter, like a captured Cong, a tortured slopehead, his legs going weak . . . she led him to the sacrifice, the bed of torture . . . "and then I became insatiable," she said, laughing wackily.

"I . . . I . . . don't believe you," he finally managed, although he actually did believe, sitting on the mat with her, leaning up against the green drapes, listening to the gardeners' conversation outside the window on the tree-lined campus walkway.

"He nothin' but a jive-ass Jew . . ."

"I've never achieved orgasm," she said, not having heard him, or the two black groundsmen outside her window, not concerned with them or with Arv's belief or dis-belief.

What is she concerned with? Arv thought, *is it only to trap me into something? Or is it only to ultimately touch herself? And she's a writer. There's got to be something else. What is it?*

"What is it?" he shouted into her face, spitting at her.

"What?" she asked, finally brought out of herself, out of her nervous state.

"What the fuck is it?"

"Uh . . . uh . . ." she began hesitantly, ". . . uh . . . will you . . . ? Oh, I give up! I'm not any good at this . . . will you take a letter to Galliot when he arrives at your prison?"

Now he pitied her, and her pitiful desire to help the condemned man. In winning Little Arv's pity, she lost his aid.

"Are you Jewish?" he asked, Okie, Cracker, racist; he asked it very low. Now it was his turn to be evasive.

"Yes," she said, giggling anxiously, "how did you know?"

And in an instant it all became like the proverbial crystal ball to Arv, who lost all respect for this Jewess, this Kike, who wanted something out of him, and didn't have the guts to pay for it, and wouldn't get it, this Yid, and her Israelite eyes as yellow as the salt pools of Gaza.

Her achievements as a short story writer diminished in the blink of an eye . . . Jews are good at that kind of thing . . . just like making money or playing the violin . . . and somehow, in a way he couldn't put his finger on exactly, her talent no longer interested him.

And with the demolition of each brick in the cracking

wall of her attainments, Arv's erection retreated, till it was just a tiny useless fold of skin at the bottom of his belly.

"Look," she said, "I was going to try to . . . I just can't take advantage of you. I'd just appreciate it, and I believe it would be the moral thing to do, if you'd take a letter in to that poor guy, that's all . . ."

Arv, who might have done, finally did do it, under other circumstances, was lost to her, and said kindly, "I'm sorry," rising to leave, "not that I wouldn't like to, but . . ."

"Right! Well, fuck off then!" she said angrily, rising up too, pursuing him to the door, barring him with her miniskirted body . . . all her nervous effort gone for naught . . .

"Listen," he said strongly, but still not going beyond the bounds of proper respect, still mindful that she was his teacher, and that she had the power to fail him, delay his graduation for another year, "all you want to do is just use me. That's the only interest you've got in me. I can't trust anything you've said about me . . . about my writing . . . or anything."

"No!" she said, "that's not true! Maybe I was using you, for a good cause, but about your writing talent . . . I was surprised by it, knowing your background. But it was a pleasant surprise, believe me! You are a writer. You are! Why, I'd even be willing to try and get some of your stuff published . . ."

"I'm sorry," he said politely, and gently removed her from his way.

"You'll be sorry!" she yelled after him.

But he kept going, down the hall, out into the parking lot to his car, pretty sure, somehow, that he wouldn't be too sorry, pretty sure that Elaine, nice and attractive and Jewish as she was, just didn't have the power to make him sorry about anything.

After Moke won him over, probably at Elaine's instigation, a week or so later, and now even more after last night when he'd delivered his first illegal letter, Arv wondered what Elaine's reaction would be. He imagined it would be highly ambivalent. Part of her (the egotist part) would be jealous that Moke had won him over when she could not, and part of her (the moral part) would be delighted that he'd come to the defense of truth and justice.

And though Arv felt sure he'd detected a strong jealousy between the two women, he still wondered about it now, waiting, seated by pretty Moke, listening to Elaine read his story.

Elaine finished up and said, "What do you think about this story?" to the class at large.

"It's great!" Moke said.

"It's fabulous!" another kid, the American Indian, shouted.

"Yeah!"

"Wild!" all the other students said.

"I agree," Elaine said, beaming at him, with every indication of complete sincerity. "This person is a writer already. Someday we'll all read his work in books. I'm sure of it!"

And Arv believed her. Did he really believe her? Sure, he believed her. Believed he was a writer. Trusted her word implicitly, in spite of the favor, even felt good about it, now that it'd been done once, because . . . despite his base and dirty and self-serving original impulses, he'd now done something of which he could be truly proud. He was proud of his courage, and the strength of his conscience (something for which the Weeds were not at all renowned), and his willpower, resourcefulness, and his power to do good. And suddenly he liked very much the way it had all turned out, this grand decision of his that was replete with the possibility of grand consequences, would greatly influence the entire course of his life, would perhaps even influence the course of *history*. It was done! And now that it was done he was glad and would keep on doing it. Because, the die was cast, motherfucker! He'd chosen his side, the side of truth and light and social equality and justice for all, the other side, the opposite side from where he came from, vulgarsville, funktown, the side diametrically opposed to his family, friends and all the ignorant illiterate low-rent people he knew *they're losers and losers can't be right.*

And Little Arvin Weed, seated there in that City College classroom in the Humanities Building, Room HU-364, seated before his pretty, radical, Jewish English Department teacher, with his beautiful exotic foreign girl friend beside him, listening to their praise, their adulation, even, knew finally and forever where his fucking bread was buttered, knew where his destiny lay, goddamnit, and it sure as shit wasn't back there with them no-account, racist, sadist, piggy prison guards and Weeds and know-nothing low-class assholes back home. No sir!

At that instant in the classroom, surrounded by his young peers, aspiring intellectuals and artists all (who apparently knew where their fucking bread was buttered too, seeing as they came from the same funky place as Arv), Little Arv chose his future, embarked, and set out on his predestined course into the great world beyond the prison walls. At that very instant he became in his own mind a part of the great radical-liberal intelligentsia of America and the world, aspired in his most vivid dreams to its utmost heights, selected his fate, his new world, determined then and there to accomplish all the practical things necessary to make his dream come to pass: determined to persevere till he got his B.A. and then go abroad for his M.A. to St. Andrews or Edinburgh or the Sorbonne and then his Ph.D. somewhere else (he had only the vaguest idea what a Ph.D. was), and then go on to to become a writer, professor, scholar, braintruster, world-traveler, on and on into the rosy place that he imagined in his utter naïveté existed in the comfortable circle of academic, artistic and intellectual eminence . . . Yes! Arv determined to leave Joint, family and former life far behind, to travel, receive scholarships and literary awards and the patronage of rich and famous philanthropists, go to Europe, learn foreign languages and customs, publish novels, works of criticism, works of literary theory and biography, articles for literary journals, book reviews in *The New York Times*. Yes! He would go on and on! He would be famous and respected and rich. He would eat good food, drink excellent wines, learn which fork to pick up first, how to pour and slice and serve properly. He would break away for good. Break away clean. He would never allow himself to get into debt. He would marry a woman who was an intellectual or artist too, his peer. He would finish graduate school with honors. He would have money, a home, a car. He would see all the world. It would take years. He would have to reach up out of his caste. He would leap up out of the ignorant stinking pit the Weeds had always been in and raise that hereditarily degenerate

Weed-Encino blood (a bloodline that had not in all its years of history produced a single man or woman of even the smallest wealth or power or respect or intelligence, a bloodline that before Little Arv had never produced even a high school graduate), raise that weak regressive blood to full rights as human beings, independent souls, thinking, rational human beings. Arv's dark sons and daughters, aided by reason, imagination, hope, ambition, wealth, love, conscience, would conquer the universe! Arv saw his task before him. He would do it. With his mind, his talent, his intellect. There was no other way. His gift for writing prose was God's gift, luck, and this stroke of luck, coupled with the points he now planned to chalk up in the world of the intellectual Left, the world that he considered to be his fated world, and his ticket out of the morass, would see him through. This was his chance, his day. He must seize the day, "seize the time!" Or stay behind, behind those tall gray walls forever.

Little Arv, swallowing in his utter ignorance the propaganda of his native Middle America, actually believed that the groves of Academe sheltered a solid radic-lib race of men, believed that he must strike out for that grove, seek shelter there amongst them, those "fellow-travelers," those "fairies" and "Com-Symps," those powerful bogeymen of his boyhood myths, myths nurtured on his daddy's knee, in the single classroom of the prison school, over the evening meal, during the Six O'Clock News.

After class Elaine wished everyone a "Happy Holiday!" and asked Arv to come down to her office for a moment. This time when they walked down the hallway Arv held his head up high, unembarrassed, unintimidated. And Elaine and he, aware that the favor'd been done and they were now allies, laughed out loud together just for fun. And when they reached her office there was no awkwardness, no anxiety, no suspicion this time. They were easy together, friends, co-conspirators, equals. Moke had to wait outside in the hallway.

"It's private," Elaine said a little spitefully, closing the door on her. Then she turned to Arv and said, "I want to thank you very much."

"For what?"

"You know."

"Oh, that!" he said. "Moke still pretends it's got nothing to do with you."

"That's ridiculous! I mean, after all, she came to me suggesting she might be able to make contact with Galliot through you. She wanted to do something for the cause, she said. But I told her I'd approached you about it before. She insisted though . . . and she turned out to be right! . . . surely she hasn't forgotten . . . anyway, thanks so much! You don't know how much this means to Galliot. He's been isolated so long. He was afraid he'd go crazy in there without real correspondence. This might save his life, literally."

"I wish I didn't have to ask for money," Arv said, "but I'd never get out of the Joint if I didn't. You see? This money might save my life too. I'm not kidding."

"Oh, don't worry! I understand, really."

"Well, I just wanted to say that I'm glad I did it. My conscience feels better now."

"Does it? . . . Oh? By the way . . . I was only kidding the other day . . . when you asked if I was Jewish . . ."

"What?"

"The other day . . . I'm not Jewish at all," she said, sort of smiling, but something else, righteous indignation perhaps, Arv thought, hiding out in her yellow eyes, the eyes he'd been so sure were from Gaza, "actually I'm purebred second generation Peloponnesian Greek-American."

"Oh yeah?" Arv answered, noncommittal, suspicious.

"Yeah," she said, smiling aggressively, "but I said I was Jewish just to teach you a lesson . . ."

"Okay, I'll bite. What lesson?" Arv asked, annoyed with her again, like he'd been the other time.

"I wanted to poke a little fun," she said, pronouncing every word very carefully, "at your atavistic white-trashy anti-Semitism."

"I see," Arv said, starting out to sneer but at the last instant, the very last instant before the words came out of his mouth, making it sound humble instead, "yeah, well, I know, I've got a lot to learn. I don't mean to be that way but . . ."

"Oh stop it, Arv! I know you're still a racist Pig at heart! What I hope to do is trap you somehow into becoming something else . . . something much more noble

. . . because, I sense somehow, it can be done, but only if you're *trapped*. You see?"

"Well," he said insincerely, "maybe you can . . ."

"Stop it, I said, I don't want you to say easy things like that just to please me!"

"I'm sorry," he said, totally self-conscious again around her, just like he was the last time. "See you next letter-time!" he said, a little to loudly, backing out her door.

"Wait a minute!" she said, and handed him today's letter and seventy-five dollars in cash. "We won't have to go through Moke as intermediary anymore. Okay?"

Outside Moke said, "What'd she want?"

"Aw," he said, "first she thanked me for pulling the number in the Joint and then she called me a racist Pig."

Moke laughed in a way that was delightful to Arv. She laughed in a way that indicated she thought Elaine's eccentricity could often be tedious. "What'd she say about the story?" she asked.

"She forgot about that."

"Typical."

"Yeah?"

"Typical of those fucking 4-O's," she said viciously, and then laughed suddenly, showing her pretty and sharp Polynesian teeth, gripped him tightly by the arm, and changed the subject.

"Let's meet tonight," she said, "I'll wait on my bike outside the Joint."

"How come?" he asked, teasing her.

"I wanna gobble you up!" she said playfully, nipping at his shoulder, at his neck and ear, "I'm gonna eat you up alive cause you are such a sweet sweet bitter sweet thing!"

Nineteen

"Say, you girls are gonna need some spending money," Fast-Walking said, sucking on his root beer freeze through a red plastic straw. "Here it is only four more shopping days to Christmas and you ain't got a job," he added, waving his short little skinny arms like a mating ostrich waves its ineffectual wings.

"Now lookie here, I'm presently employed with Evie in the capacity of recruiter for her ranks of girls. And we're seriously considering an expansion of our operation, and quite frankly, we need talent," he said, in the tones of a legitimate prospective employer, looking them over real careful out of the corner of his eye. They were just dumb little pickaninnies from the ghetto across the Santa Fe Railroad tracks, fifteen or sixteen and probably out on the street for the first time, probably playing hookey from junior high school looking for a score to buy some bubble gum or something. But Fast-Walking didn't feel like *paying* for anything, that spoiled the fun. . . . The ugly little niggeress was real scraggy, fat-assed and pimply, with some kind of skin disease that ate into her black skin pigment in spots, making her look like a fucking pinto. Her hair was all greased up and icky looking, like you'd never want to touch it. But the other one, Corvette, she wasn't bad at all. Good body. Big tits. Pretty face with a white woman's thin nose and lips, and luscious milk chocolate skin. So they believed him.

"Oh yeah?" they said.

And he said, "Yeah. So, listen, let me ask you frankly. You in the market?"

"Sho!" they said.

"Now, remember, ain't no bed of roses, you dig? It's them wetbacks from the labor camps. And they ain't exactly noted for their cleans."

"We don't care. We don't care!" they hollered . . .
"Mama two week overdue on the rent and we ain't got no
moo . . . We just down here right now hustling for a
damn little hamburger and a milk shake."

"Alright. So look. I want you to answer me a question."
He looked straight at the cute one. He could tell she knew
what he was going to say. She giggled coyly, in the cutest
way, crossing her long black-brown legs and rocking back
and forth on the Frosty Freeze's asphalt, under the pep-
permint-striped awning, eating her strawberry sundae with
a plastic spoon, getting a little on her upper lip . . .
"Now, would you girls buy a car without trying it out
first?"

"Nope," they said. The cute one was smiling, showing
her strawberry and vanilla tongue against her dark skin.
"Shit no!"

"Well, dig it. This is a very important expansion that
Evie is contemplating, and she's got to make sure everything's just right. So look, honey," he said to the fat ugly
one, "you just stay right here and have another ice cream
on me, huh? While we go over to Evie's and give Corvette
here a little trial run."

"But what about me?" the fat one asked, pouting, sticking out her big fat lips, real pathetic.

"Get this," Fast-Walking said, real tough, "and remember it, honey. You try out a piece of merchandise from a
first-class dealer, and it works good, why, then you know
all his stock got to be right. Right?"

"Yeah, I guess so," she said, kind of sad, and Fast-
Walking and the groovy-looking little chick split down the
road and sneaked into Evie's back yard through the big
wooden gate.

Evie's back yard, surrounded on all sides by a six-foot
cinder block wall, was like a little world of its own. It was
huge. Half of it was high with green winter grass, and the
other half was cemented over. On the cement part she
kept her new Cadillac and her shiny streamliner house
trailer. She kept them there all nice and pretty, making
Big Arv and Fast-Walking wash and polish and vacuum
them out once a month just in case she ever got "light-
foot" again, "itchy on the soles" of her big feet. A large
fish pond had been shaped out of the cement section of
the yard in a perfect figure-eight shape. It was filled with

fat red carp. Concrete pedestals dotted the yard, on which
Evie had placed her outside bric-a-brac: plaster jockeys
and niggerboys and elephants and herons, mermaids,
whales, donkey carts, rearing stallions. Out in the wild
back part of the yard, overgrown with deep grass and
weeds and grapevines gone free, Evie kept her animals:
chickens, ducks, a small loud-mouthed calf, two goats,
twenty or thirty rabbits in two large hutches, and a small
yellow donkey. The donkey was actually Big Arv's, and
had been in the family for years, but he'd asked Evie to
keep it in her yard when the residents of the prison housing area got up a petition for him to remove his "smelly
dirty animals" from state property. They were "giving a
bad name," they said, to their neighborhood. . . . At the
very rear of the yard Evie had constructed three large
chicken coops out of redwood lumber mill scraps. In one
of these she had all her big old Rhode Island Red hens
roosting. They laid good there, she said. The other two
coops she'd had Big Arv and Fast-Walking remodel. Now
they were real nice inside. They'd laid a cement floor, put
up some white plasterboard inside, sealed the tarpaper
roof with fresh black tar, and they'd put in big king-size
mattresses that completely covered the floor. In each coop
they'd covered the mattresses with unzipped spread-out
sleeping bags. These two chicken coops were now called
"houses" by everyone around Evie's property. Privately,
however, among themselves, Big Arv and Fast-Walking
called them "chickie pens," or more graphically, "cunt
coops."

Fast-Walking guided his Corvette, his beautiful young
pickaninny, across the cement and weeded-up yard fast,
not seeming to move, neither of them, seeming not even
to touch the tips of the blades of dewy grass with the bot-
toms of their slow-moving but racing heels.

"Where you taking me?" she said, tittering in the cutest
way. "Seem just like when I was a kid, heading out in the
back yard with my cousin."

"That's right!" he said, panting with desire for her
brown body, "just like playing Doctor and Nurse."

"Just like playing the Dirty Dozens with you ole Uncle
Cousins!" she said, but he missed her ethnic allusion.

When they got out to the coop Fast-Walking closed the
door and locked it and turned on the little portable radio

that each coop was equipped with and said, "Now, honey, let's see how good you're going to work out. Remember, your whole employment opportunity rests on your try-out performance here today!"

And they went round and round on the come-stained sleeping bags, dirtying them with their muddy boots, whirling for a whole minute, getting into it, dipping, bowing, spider legs, spade legs, wailing, but never touching till the end when Santana on the local FM rock station went up high yelling *Black Magic Woman* and Fast-Walking grabbed her and they rubbed it out together crazy in the half dark of the coop. And he pawed at her young black buns. Sucked her long strawberry nigger tongue, her sweet young African spit, unspoiled spit, as yet. Dry fucked her against her mini skirt till he came into his jockey shorts and dry fucked her till he got it up again. Pulled her into a corner and put his hands on her bare soft brown butt under her bikini panties and she rocked against him and moaned her strange nigger girl's moan from the depths of the jungle so he backed up onto the bed with her straddling him and he got her panties off while she clutched and groped at his fly. And she got it down, got her long-fingered narrow black hand on his erect white joint, his fountain of snowy flesh, with its blue veins popping fit to bust, then she got both black hands with pink bright palms around it, went down on it, blew it, talked to it with her brown wig flying, sucked it, stroked it, played like it was a telephone, a microphone . . . "Helloooo! Who's there?" . . . Got one of his balls in her mouth, sang to it, hummed to it, vibrating it with the sound while he switched and ate her bright red good-smelling pussy raw, feeding at it, biting it, pulling at the little wiry hairs with his front teeth. Getting lost, lost like he was living up inside her Zambezi hole, an animal inside its nest, its burrow, its den, a manatee in its cozy damp home under the black banks of the Congo. And then he came. He came a gigantic white sudsy mellow yellow load into her mouth again, nearly blowing the nappy back of her black head off, blowing her wig right off her noggin. Then she came to him. Got him down on the Mex-smelling, sex-smelling mattress and brought her beautiful come-filled mouth up to his top, his front, him, Fast-Walking himself, right up to his face, his pale lips, with the come running out the corners of her mouth, down her chin. And she kissed him, with passion, he was sure, on the mouth, and rubbed against his body with her wet used black muff, her Swahili snatch hot as an East African afternoon. And old Fast-Walking, he did the humanly impossible. He got it up again. Got it right up again and sucked his own snot-colored come right back out of her black nigger life, out of her mouth. And she stayed on top this time, and she fucked him. She fucked that Fast-Walking sonofabitch like he'd never been fucked in his entire fucking life. He lay there in wonder, unable to move, too dumbfounded by the unsurpassed size of his own erection, the grandiosity of his own pleasure, to even consider undulating back. She did it all, panting and grunting and moaning and screaming with joy, trying with all her young fifteen-year-old black might to get herself that job she so desperately needed . . . "Oh! Oh! Oh!" she yelled, trying to get a lit-tle money in her purse. "Oh! Oh!" she yelled, he yelled, he came, she came, they came, and came again, and lay finally exhausted together on the mattress.

Then she turned to him and looked at him question-ingly with her soft brown plaintive pickaninny eyes. And Fast-Walking said, "Honey, quite frankly, I don't think you measure up."

"What?" she said, disbelieving him, tears of bitter dis-appointment and exhaustion welling up in her eyes.

"Now we got these two big old women out here now, honey," Fast-Walking said, trying to be as sincere sound-ing as possible, and even believing the story himself, in a way, "and they're built like trucks. They can handle the trade. Them wetbacks are rough. And you're quite frankly a little bit too small and inexperienced for what we got in mind."

Escorting her out across the grown-over portion of the yard, and out the wooden fence in the wall to the front yard where her friend awaited them, Fast-Walking said, "Oh look, honey, don't cry! I'll tell you what! I'll give you another tryout this afternoon if you want. Come around about two o'clock. We're busy with the Mexicans at lunch hour but I'll have a few minutes about, yeah, about two o'clock.

"Thanks a lot, Mister," she said, smiling through her

tears, wiping them away, "you're real kind." And then she reached over and grabbed her friend's bag, like she was going for a handkerchief, and she looked at her and said, "Gimme the speaker!" And her friend tensed up. And Corvette came out of that black fake-alligator purse with a cheap long-barreled Japanese Saturday Night Special and aimed it right into his face, and braced her strong brown legs wide apart and closed her mouth down firm, and her friend ran around to Fast-Walking's other side, and Corvette said, in a trembling angry nervous murderous but still young voice, "Alright, motherfucker, now you gon' get splaped!"

It was all so unreal. There they were standing out on the lawn beside the cars, near the date palm tree, under the warm winter sun, and people were walking by, Mexicans, on the sidewalk under the eucalyptus trees on the other side of the street, and nobody seemed to notice.

Fast-Walking smiled, he didn't know what else to do.

"Hey, wait a minute!" he pleaded.

"Shut up, Paddy! I'm gon' blansh you, X you right out! Throw you wallet on the grass!"

He pulled it out awkwardly, unhappily, it had his whole freshly cashed paycheck from the Joint in there, or what remained of it after the loan attachment money'd been deducted. He hesitated, and then dropped it on the grass. The other black girl picked it up and yelled, "Come on Ellie, let's swoop outa here!"

"Gimme a second. I'm gon' blow this ofay semolia-brain Honkey away! Blow him off! Ice this Chuck right now!" she screamed, frenziedly, trying to work herself up to do it.

"Stop it, Ellie!" her friend begged. "Come on!"

Corvette, or Ellie, was shaking. She wanted to kill Fast-Walking. More than anything else. He could see that, and felt not fear, not terror, not even the approach of nothingness. A terrible and overwhelming sense of guilt and self-hatred is what he felt, is what made him nauseous now, for what he'd done to her, what he'd done to make her hate him so much. It had all started out as a sort of joke. He never even thought he'd get away with it. And now . . . *she hates me,* he thought, truly surprised by that notion.

Suddenly he felt no fear. He was emptied of fear . . .

if this is the way it is going to end. He took a step forward, and said, "Aw, shit, I don't blame you. I don't even know why I . . ."

Fast-Walking let his words drift off. Still she stayed there before him on the grass, aiming at his head, her gun hand shaking. Her girl friend was all the way down the street, running like hell with the money.

"I want to kill you," she said calmly, and he knew he was going to die. "I want to kill you, to kill you," she said, chanting it, starting to weep, trembling like a passionate child, "Kill you! Kill you!" she screamed, still wanting it with all her black heart. Only her rational scared mind *her white mind,* Fast-Walking thought, and her experience probably of State Juvie Halls prevented her. Only her reasonable defensive angry intelligent head prevented her from the sweet revenge her black heart demanded, deserved.

She turned and started off, then stopped, turned, took aim again. Fast-Walking stood there transfixed and white in the sun under the date palm tree. *Now she gets me.* Mexicans walked leisurely across the street, heading for the supermarket three blocks down toward the Sound.

Corvette began to sob, to cry in despair, as if she'd lost something very precious to her. "Oh I could kill you, you dirty stone cold Whitey motherfucker bastard, I could kill you, I could kill you!" she cried out in her hatred and frustration and bewilderment, bewilderment, Fast-Walking believed, almost of a kind with his own. . . . And then she turned and ran off. Fast-Walking stood there for five minutes without moving, getting the feeling of living again, letting the blood run again out through his long limbs. Then he jerked, ran to his Buick, jumped in and raced off down the road after the two girls. But he couldn't find them. Couldn't find his wallet with all his money in it.

Couldn't he find them?

Nope, he couldn't find them anywhere. And that was the only money he possessed in the whole world, and even that didn't belong to him, and it was all his fault. And that great big thirty-four-year-old man, Fast-Walking, he just broke down on the West Sound Freeway and cried too, just like the little pickaninny had, he cried long and loud and hard, beating his head against the plastic fake-

wood steering wheel of the Buick, crying, "God's punished you, God's punished you, God's punished you!" just
like he'd done as a little boy when he'd killed a little bird
with his sling shot and then fell down and skinned his
knee. "God's punished you!" he cried, thinking of that
poor little nigger girl, and what he did, taking advantage
of her like that, and her just a kid with no money, just a
ghetto kid. "Got what you deserved! Got what you
deserved!" he cried, all alone in the automobile, with the
traffic whizzing by, and the sea gulls off to the left, over
the mudflats, settling down on the half-sunk rubber tires
and rusted tin cans, "Got what you fucking deserved,
Honkey!"

Twenty

The sun had crept around the side of the house and now shone through the pulled yellow shades and lit Evie's room. Big Arv tiptoed over and sat on the bed. Evie did not awaken. Slowly he lifted his big celery-mud covered boots up and laid them on the bottom bedboard. Cracked pieces of rich dried black bottomland soil broke off and fell on the linoleum but Big Arv, normally neat, couldn't bother.

Big Arv lay beside her now, his beloved, barely breathing, his heart pounding, threatening attack. Her heavy pendulous right breast, just a hair's breadth from his left hand, quivered with every shudder of her expansive lungs. Big Arv's fingers quivered too, wanting, wanting, as he wanted his youth back, his healthy heart. . . . Her boob had fallen out of her nightgown and now lay limp against the stained sheet. Its large bulbous veins showed purple and blue just under her goose-pimpled skin. Big Arv's fingers shook, reached out, dared not. Evie slept, and then, aware of a human presence beside her, allowed her pale blue eye to flicker open, peep sideways at him, at his creepy crawly hand. Let the hand crawl and get there, where it wanted, let it rub her warm sleepy skin.

"Oh Evie!" he said aloud, and rolled toward her, his dirty boots falling on the exposed sheets, soiling them.

She opened her heavy flippy arms, arms with rolls of honest fat hanging down under her pits, and held him to her. He hid his face in her beloved breasts, speaking, the sound muffled in her startling cleft . . . "Oomph . . . oomph . . . I can't stand it nomore! Can't stand it! Want you! Want you!"

Evie's voice seemed, as it traversed the voluminous folds of billowing fat, her five chins, her six necks, as if it came from a long way off, a long long way off. It was a

remarkable voice, a tiny quavering other-worldly voice
that had chilled Big Arv to the marrow, and thrilled him,
from the time he was five years old. He loved that voice
so much that he could almost *smell* it, he sometimes believed. It smelled childhood, to him, like childhood's
immemorial pepper tree and the chicken house it sheltered . . . "I know! I know, my love, I know," she said,
low into his ear, breathing into it, "I know, but there's
no way, unless . . ."

"Unless what?" he asked, urgently, ready to do anything for her, anything to get into that pink nightie, into
those terrible wavelike folds of white flesh, into the
warmth of her magical bed-smelling sleep-smelling embrace.

BANG! BANG! BANG! Fast-Walking knocked frantically
on the door of Evie's bedroom. "Help, I been robbed!
Been robbed!"

Big Arv, afraid Evie's store'd been knocked over, leapt
out of bed, ready to do battle for his lady. Evie hastily attempted to cover her exposed breasts.

"What happened?"

"I been robbed. They took my whole fucking paycheck!" Fast-Walking cried.

"Oh . . ." Evie said with undisguised relief, "you guys
are just the bad luck boys, ain't you?"

"That's all the money I got in the world!" Fast-Walking
moaned.

"Now, lookie here," Evie said, taking charge, "there
was something I wanted to discuss with you all today . . .
who dirtied up my bed like that? Was that you, Arv?
Damn! You oughta know better than that . . . anyway
. . . yeah, we got to get you fellows some money, and
that's all there is to it. This here clinches it. Just about the
last damn hair in the pie, don't you think? We got to get
poor Fast-Walking here back home with his cute little
French wife where he belongs, keep him out of mischief.
And we got to help Big Arv out too, get him out of debt
finally, at his age! And get him . . ." she said, pausing
significantly, lewdly, "that little *sumpin'* he's always
wanted which only I can give . . . but that's between just
us two. . . . Yes sir! You boys just seem to get deeper
and deeper in a pickle, no matter what you do. Ain't that
right? Now, listen, I'm going out on business for a spell. I

want you, Big Arv, to clean out that back yard and the house trailer. And Fast-Walking, you watch the store. Open up, sweep it out, dust up. Then you all run out and get them wetbacks, bring 'em back, make sure Honey and Lola get set up in their houses, and run through business. By then I should be back with some real news about getting us some cash."

"Say, thanks a lot, Evie," Fast-Walking said, too shaken to remember the last time she'd offered to help them out.

"Yeah, thanks," Big Arv dittoed, forgetting too . . . lost to the world thinking about that "little sumpin' " she'd hinted at . . .

"Nothing to it," Evie said, and rose like a queen out of her bed and allowed Big Arv to enfold her in her bathrobe. "Some people," she said, gesturing grandly, "all they got is, like the man says, 'a handful of gimme and a mouthful of much obliged,' but I know you boys will know how to thank me . . . won't y'all?"

Two hours later Big Arv and Fast-Walking drove the VW minibus lurching down the celery fields yelling out, *"Vamos a la tienda!"* It wasn't a minute before all the *braceros* who wanted a new yellow raincoat or a good piece of ass were loaded into the bus beside and behind and around and on top of the boys. Some of them even clung to the roof and hung onto the bumpers. Fast-Walking headed out fast over the dirt road to the packing shed, loaded even more Spics on board, and drove for home. Dirty bare flat-footed Mexican peasant feet, tomato green between their scarred black toes. Rubber tire sandals tied on with leather thongs. Ropes for belts. Thick dirty greasy tomato-stained blue-black Indian hair. Oriental eyes. Eyes like a Weed. Gold teeth for the incisors, and stainless steel, flashing at you metallic when they smiled. They smiled a lot. The boys liked the wetbacks generally, except for a few smart-ass young ones, ones who'd got rid of their sandals and bought pointy-toed shoes and fluorescent shirts and tight black pants at Evie's store. They gave the boys a little trouble, sometimes, even today, a little bit, as they headed out the freeway toward the store, whispering *cabrones* and *chingados* and *gringos* under their breath. But Big Arv, who understood their lingo, shut them up fast.

"Qué te cayes, peón!" he yelled at one smart-ass kid, and then *"Silencio, animáles!"* to the company at large.

When they got back to the place everything was ready. Honey, the great six-foot platinum-blond black whore, was all set up in her "house." So was Lola, the skinny Mexican one. They were lying strip-ass nekkid on the come-stained sleeping bags, with legs in position, widespread and ready. They always like to take off all their clothes before going at it with those wetbacks, cause they were so muddy and dirty and smelly and unscrubbed. So the old whores, they just carefully took off their skirts and sweaters and hung them up on the special wires that Big Arv had installed, on nice little wooden hangers. And the whores took their panties and bras and slips and put them over the wire too. Then they just laid down and waited, with their legs spread, knees up, for all the world like they were laying up in a gynecologist's office waiting to be examined.

When they finished up every day, those whores, they were filthy dirty, covered from head to foot with green celery stains and mud and spit and dirt and tobacco juice and wetback come. It was a sight to behold. But, no problem. Big Arv'd solved that one a long while back. He talked Evie into letting him run the two old whores into her garage after work. Then they stood in there naked on the cement, jumping up and down with cold, flopping their tits up and down with every jump, and Big Arv squirted them down like after-work elephants with a special high pressure hose he'd hooked up to a hot-water outlet. He just hosed them down real good, from head to foot, mouth to crotch, and they took some Lifebuoy soap to themselves, rinsed, with Big Arv's help, and dried off. Then they just put their fresh unwrinkled clothes on, walked out into the street to catch the bus, and looked as respectable as you please.

First Big Arv let his load of wetbacks off at the store. He unlocked it and sold seven of those yellow rain slickers and three pairs of shoes and fourteen Sheik rubbers and a case of whiskey and a bottle of T-Bird. Then they all wanted to get out in back. So Big Arv sent Fast-Walking back to try to round up another load of Spics at the packing shed, and he escorted the other Mexicans back to the two chickie coops.

It wasn't for no reason that Evie had wanted a "security-conscious man" for this job. Big Arv knew how to handle crowds. "Movement supervision" was right up his alley. It wouldn't do to cause a disturbance with the neighborhood people, who were Mexicans too, it's true, but respectable home-owning people, nonetheless. Even though Evie paid off the local sheriffs real well, it still wasn't good business practice, she said, to anger your neighbors. So Arv lined them all up single file, every day, out in the walled-in back yard, and shut them up real quiet and orderly, while they waited their turn in the chickie coops.

The whores in the coops just lay in there the whole time, Mex in and Mex out, blinking, listening to the radio. Big Arv always switched it to Mexican *ranchero* music, the wetbacks' favorite. The whores lay in there naked, with their legs spread wide to diminish the friction of ten to twenty men, and the braceros, kept in line by Big Arv, came in real orderly and quiet, one at a time, single file, and did their thing: fell on them with muddy horned feet and green-stained knees and dusty unshaven faces.

Rain, shine, wind or hail, the rest of the Mexicans, carefully supervised by security-conscious Big Arv, just usually stood out in the yard, not saying much, not worried or even seeming like they were thinking much, just waiting their turn with Lola and Honey, real peaceable.

When Evie came home Big Arv was out in the garage spraying down the whores after work. Honey had taken the opportunity to wash her hair with an old tube of Prell that Evie kept on a cobwebby shelf above her washing machine. She was jumping up and down in the spray yelling, "Too strong, too strong, turn it down!" So Big Arv turned it down a bit while they worked their lather off.

"Hey, Big Arv!" Evie hollered from her kitchen, "come in here! I got some good news!"

Moke, the little Hawaiian gal who worked with May at Bert's Beanery, was with her, looking cute as hell in a pair of navy surplus bell-bottom pants and a big bulky white fisherman's sweater.

Big Arv rinsed the whores down good and shut off the water, trying to figure out what the hell she was doing around here . . . getting even a bit suspicious . . . *What the fuck is goin' on around here?* Big Arv thought, *last*

*time I seen her was over home with May and Little Arv
. . . What's she doing hanging around over here? And
with Evie?* And he chuckled now to himself remembering
certain things that he'd heard from Evie over the years,
certain things that maybe she didn't even know she'd let
out, certain overheard phone conversations with Wasco
before he got put in the Joint, and certain inadvertent
references by Evie to her "little nigger gal" daughter-in-
law who she hated like poison for getting her boy all tied
up through her "sneaky pickaninny ways." Evie might've
thought that Big Arv was dumb. But he could add up two
and two. He remembered other things too, from the past,
veiled threats, curses, accusations . . . "If you give a
damn nigger bitch an inch she'll take a fucking mile!" Big
Arv had heard that one distinctly several times. And other
things too, other things which conveyed to him quite
clearly . . . something that he wasn't supposed to
know . . .

Evie's jealous of that little thing, Big Arv thought now,
*and, shit! You know what? I think she'd be jealous of any
woman with her boy, nigger or not! Har har har!* No sir,
Big Arv, damnit, he wasn't *that* stupid! He had fucking
ears, by God! And, like all guards, because of the ever-
present possibility of the Slow Shuck, he was suspicious
by nature. And doubly suspicious now because he knew
his boy Little Arv was some way mixed up with that gal
Moke . . . who was . . . at the same time . . . mixed up
with Wasco and Evie. . . . He didn't have it all figured
out yet, but, as he coiled the rubber hose up neatly and
placed it on a nail in the tool shed, he figured he wasn't
going to let himself get too worried about the whole thing
. . . cause . . . some way, Big Arv sniffed money in this
suspicious situation . . . yeah . . . and sniffed something
else too . . . if he wasn't mistaken . . . sniffed Evie . . .
and the possibility of gaining what he'd always
wanted. . . .

"I sniff pussy!" he shouted, splashing Lola and Honey
as they toweled themselves off in the garage.

"Wouldn't be a bit surprised!"

"Ain't poke chop, dat fo' sho'!"

"Har har. Well, see you gals tomorrow," he called out
cheerfully as he went in through the kitchen door.

Inside Big Arv sat down with Evie and pretty little

Moke at the yellow kitchen table. Then Evie, she did what he figured she'd do: she went right into a long and suspicious rap about how Big Arv and Fast-Walking was gonna "get it all back together again," and so on. All the time looking over at Moke and petting her on the head or shoulder real phonylike, saying, "this here little gal's the one who's gonna make it all possible, yep!" Evie kept saying that. But you could tell she didn't mean it. She even meant you to know that she didn't mean it. It was just business form, that's all. That's what she meant you to know by her tone of voice. She kept saying, "yep, this gal's as good as gold," but you could tell she hated her guts. You could tell right off that neither one of them gave a rat's ass for the other. Moke smiled in the nicest way, and nodded, and said, "Oh, yes! Evie's too sweet to me. But she's right! We're going to be able to really help you guys out." And you could tell she was real insincere too, at least when she was talking about how sweet and nice Evie was. But Big Arv, he just let them rattle right on. Let them wind their whole damn long rap out.

"We're gonna get you boys outa debt. Get Fast-Walking into his happy home. Get you both back into a position where you can call yourselves whitemen again," Evie said, as if Moke wasn't sitting right there alongside her.

And Moke, she smiled at Evie just as kind as you please, but her smile looked to Big Arv sort of like a knife slash running right across her little face. And them gray-ass eyes of hers, they was *cold*. Just as cold as Evie's.

"Now," Evie said, "you listen to me, Big Arv, and I don't want no backtalk . . ."

"You ain't gonna get no backtalk if you promise me right here and now, Evie, that I'm gonna get that little sumpin' we was talking about . . ."

"Oh," Evie said, fluttering her big doll-like eyes in the cutest way, making Moke wince with a disgust she couldn't hide, "damn you, honey, but you're just a big silly . . . anyway, if you really insist . . ." she said, leaving it unfinished, teasing, shaking her strawberry blond curls like a real prima donna . . . making Big Arv blush with pleasure. . . .

But anyway, by then the war of wills was over. At least on Big Arv's part it was. He surrendered completely to Evie's charm, and her unfinished promise, and the winning smile of young Moke beside her at the table, and their captivating female competition with each other, and their irrefutable logic, a logic so powerful that it even finally overpowered most of their mutual hatred, made them as one, for the moment, like "A" and "B" in an algebra problem in high school. . . . The only thing is, Big Arv, neither in high school nor now, ever figured out what the whole of the "X" thing was at the end . . .

"Now, you know, Big Arv . . . and Fast-Walking, he knows too . . . I ain't overpartial to that there damn son of mine. Even if he is my own flesh and blood. He's bad seed. And there's no denying it. Tried to put the knife to his own daddy, who, you know, I never had much love for neither . . . but still . . . see? Wasco's no-good and he always has been. But, right now, he's got a scam worked out with this here little gal, and I think it might make us enough quick money to retire us all on a tropical island somewheres . . . ain't that right, honey?"

"Ooooooh, yes, ma'am!" Moke said, smiling the prettiest white-toothed little smile up at Big Arv. "Wasco's truly got this planned out to perfection. I can promise you that. And, he asked me to tell you especially, Mr. Weed, that there's absolutely no chance of any flub-up because he's got 'wall-to-wall protection from the powers that be.' Those are his exact words. He said you'd understand that and he'd discuss it with you further inside the prison. He said to tell you that this dope scam is merely a 'diversionary exercise,' to divert attention from his real efforts in the prison which are of a confidential nature but, he's instructed me to tell you, are 'officially inspired and condoned by our highest state government officials toward the goal of racial tranquillity in this state.' He said you'd understand . . . in view of all the rumors going around about Mr. Galliot. He also told me to tell you that, because of his state 'security blanket,' covering all his activities, there would be no danger involved for you or Fast-Walking. On the contrary, he said that you will be reimbursed 'beyond your wildest reckoning' for your aid, which he further characterized as your 'patriotic duty.' "

"Well," Big Arv said with sudden decision, placing his life in their hands, "I tell you, I don't know about no 'patriotic duty.' But I do know one thing. That Wasco, he always did have a good head for business!"

When Fast-Walking came back from hauling the Mexicans out to the packing shed Evie made Moke run and hide in one of the chickie houses. "Don't ask me why," she said when Big Arv raised an eyebrow, "Wasco said they wasn't supposed to meet. And I'm just doing like he says, since he's the feller running the show. . . . He said something about he didn't want Little Arv mixed up in this, and he figured Fast-Walking might tell, since they're living together over in the city now."

"Good idea! I don't want that boy tied up in any of this, Evie, and I mean it," Big Arv said, and then a wrinkle of sincere worry crossed his lowish brow. "And listen! About this Moke. She's been running around with him lately. I seen them. Now, I don't want him involved in this in any way, goddamnit. Understand? He's got enough worries as it is!"

"Now, don't you go worrying about nothing, Big Arv," Evie said, "I've made her swear to Jesus on her mama's grave that she won't divulge nothing about this here operation to Little Arv. Anyway, if you ask me, I think she's sweet on Wasco and only running around with your boy to kill time while Wasco's in the pen. Though . . . between you and me, I wisht somebody'd do us a favor and run off with the bitch for good. . . . Anyway, don't you worry none. I promise everything'll be alright, honey," she finished hastily, preparing a smile for Fast-Walking as he glided like a toothpick phantom across the front lawn under the date palm tree and up the wooden steps of Montoya's house.

Fast-Walking didn't resist Evie's pitch for even a minute. Never even put up a fight. "Whoopie!" he hollered when Evie showed him the neat stacks of plasticine bags in the trunk of her Caddie. "Here's where we all make our fucking fortunes, you guys! Whoopie! . . . Marie-Claude, goddamnit, you don't know it yet, baby, but your daddy's coming home!" he said, and didn't even bat a eye when Evie opened up one of the bags and poured an ounce of snowy white six-cut heroine into his lunch pail Thermos bottle. . . .

Twenty-One

May phoned Little Arv at his place in the city when he came back from school and asked if he couldn't stop and pick her up at Bert's on his way to the Joint. "Big Arv and Fast-Walking been held up over at Evie's and only got time to just barely make it to work."

"Sure, Mom!" he said cheerfully, still cheerful he was then, before his lone drive across the Alverez Straits, before he had time to think of work at the horrible fucking Joint. And drove in the Merc across the toll bridge and over Brando Grade on the freeway thinking about Elaine and Moke and his story and the new letter he had in his pocket and Galliot and finally, just as he swung off the freeway at the Santa Caterina Peninsula Interchange, of his Uncle Sanger and a wild fight they once had on his front lawn when Sanger beat him to a pulp, broke his nose, cauliflowered his ears, scarred his eyelids for good, yelling, "You ain't ever gonna be a man! Never! Ya little fruit, never!"

Part of Little Arv, deep in his imprisoned soul, believed what Sanger had said. Believed it . . . in spite of his recently manly decision to dedicate his life to the fight for right, the just battle . . . Believed Sanger. Arv knew he wasn't a man yet. He was afraid he'd never be one. He couldn't tell what a man was. A real man. He didn't think he'd ever met one.

Arv drove down the Molina Valley off-ramp past stinking oil sumps and salt flats and shabby shacks on stilts above the black water and broken-down houseboats and sewer bogs and garbage dumps and supermarkets and parking lots and service stations and shopping centers painted like candy bars, like ice cream cones and peppermint sticks, thinking: *what the fuck is a man?*

He pulled up in front of Bert's Beanery in the artsy-

craftsy older part of Molina Valley. It was a small frame
building, with timbered redwood walls and a huge stone
fireplace and a sunny terrace that overlooked a distant
forest, somebody's nearer trashy back yard garden, and a
long row of unpainted cabins where a bunch of hippies,
refugees from the city, from the halcyon days of summer
'67, lived and bred and ran small handicraft shops: making boots and belts and jewelry and gay long hippy chicks'
dresses and skirts and shawls. Arv liked that kind of stuff,
liked to see it on people; it made the world so much more
colorful, he thought. Arv had nothing against hippies, or
hippy clothes. He liked to think of himself as a person
with none of the prejudices of his class . . . unlike the
rest of his family, who looked down on hippies . . . unlike the hippies themselves, who looked down on him.

Bert's Beanery was the hangout of the local hip and literate. The owner was a boozy old painter of some repute
in the area. His burning electric eclectic pictures, brilliant
reds and yellows and oranges, pictures that looked to Arv
like the nightmares of a man with the DT's, hung all
around the wooden walls.

Arv went in the front door of the place, very conscious
of the effect his Commission of Corrections uniform
would make, getting a bang out of watching the hip long-
haired heads jerk around . . . and the inevitable word, the
word he'd long grown to love . . . as a kind of symbol of
his own individuality. They all looked alike. Exactly alike
with their beards and beads and long matted hair. He,
with his uniform, was different. Arv liked being different,
and he let this predisposition overrule for the moment his
resolution of that morning. . . . Anyway, in his new
metamorphosis he wouldn't be like them. He'd have long
hair and a beard, maybe; but he'd be the other kind, not
the druggie, scaggy type. He'd be more the pipe-smoking
type, maybe, the art colony type, wearing a Mexican
Toluca sweater over his denim work shirts and bell-bot-
tomed Levis and boots . . . that would be more his
type . . .

"Oink!" somebody said, the beloved word. And another
one took it up . . . "Oink! Oink!"

And again, "Oink!" said a sandy-haired little hippy
twirp of seventeen as Arvin passed by him. "A Pig, you
guys! Look! A Pig!"

"That's right," Arv said, "smell!" and he raised his thick Weed leg and farted the fart he'd been saving carefully all the way over the Alvarez Straits and Brando Grade directly into the boy's incredulous and brightly pimpled face. Everyone laughed, even Bert, even Arv's waitress mother, for some reason. Arv was a little embarrassed by his success.

Mom and Bert were sitting at the bar sharing an after-work boiler-maker. Arv realized, with a sinking heart, that this drink wasn't the first of the evening.

"Ready, Mom?"

"Just a minute, Arv," she said, waving her arm vaguely, "how 'bout a drink?"

"Aw, you know I can't drink in uniform, Mom. It's against the law," he said, feeling his neck getting itchy, the blood going to his cheeks, the snickers of the boys behind him.

"Oh, alright. Listen, Bert," May said, rising to her full four feet eleven and a half inches in her wedgies, patting her hair net, "can I take a couple of six-packs home from the freezer? Just take it off my check."

"Sure, May. Hey, why don't you get your boy here to quit that goddamn prison? Look at him! He's not a bad-looking kid. Much better than that bunch of sadists, don't you think? He's still got a chance to get out of there."

"Well now," May said, screwing up her little freckled nose, squinting her Okie-Indian eyes, "my husband's been with the Commission now for twenty-five years and I don't think he's done so bad. Nothing to be ashamed of," she loyally continued, even though at home she spent her whole time nagging at Big Arv about his horrible job, the lack of money, a future, advancement, "and anyway," she went on, pointing over at the embarrassed Little Arvin, "Arv's got no intention of making a trade out of it. Ain't that right, Arv? He's going to college, studying . . . studying . . . what's that you're studying, Arv?"

"Say, let's go, Mom," Arv said, trying to edge her out of the door, guiding her by the arm, afraid some of the long-haired dudes lounging around might go to City College too, and bug him if they saw him at school, or gang up on him in the hallway, beating up on him and yelling "PIG!" in his ear. . . . Arv forgot for the moment that he'd determined only hours before to become one of them. It would be hard making the change. *It just don't come natural. It's gonna be hard . . .*

Arv got her out to the car just as the hippy chorus, inevitable frog-song, "Oink! Oink! Oink!" started up again, this time with the drunken, green-faced Bert leading, spreading his huge arms wide in a parody of a classical music conductor. . . .

All the way to the Joint she, his mother, May, yesterday's May Maiden, who was still young and dark and freckled and Okie-Osage pretty, and only forty-one years old, and bright and cheerful, most of the time, except the mornings, and friendly and kind, and had family galore, and a few friends, and no more worries than all the rest of the people she knew, May kept hitting those canned suds, cracking those big twelve-ounce cans of New Sonora Lager, popping those hookers, chug-a-lugging it, burping and belching fit to kill, looking straight out over the padded dashboard of the Merc. One can, two cans, three, four, five, rolling down the window every once in a while for air, letting the wind blow in her face, and then cracking another aluminum self-opening can, setting the empty ones neatly back in the six-pack, trying all the while to maintain a normal clucking motherly conversation:

"Well! My lands! Oh this weather's bad. Clouding up again. And it was so nice this morning. Well, like I always say, 'December, when the rains come,' . . . honey, you taking care of yourself over there in the city? That there apartment of yours . . . and all them Colored . . . you got to watch out for yourself. Used to be they was much nicer. . . . And now this Galliot fellah . . . But old Mrs. Handy, you remember her, honey, when you all was little. . . . Well, you know, I saw your little daughter yesterday. Kept her at the place all afternoon. My, I spoil that child. Feeding her cake and ice cream all afternoon! But I just don't get to see her much anymore, what with the job, and all. She's getting so big people don't recognize her anymore. And it seems like only yesterday . . . Deanna ain't looking so good, though. You seen her lately? Lost a little weight. I think she's studying too hard, don't you, honey? Well, like I always say . . ."

And then gurgling down another twelve-ounce hooker. By the time they got past the Front Gate and past the schoolhouse and arrived in front of the Weed family's small gray institution row home, Arv's poor Mom, May, May's Maiden, May's Mother, that sweet kind lady who always thought about others before herself, always served the family first and then ate alone, after working eight hours as a waitress, serving other people food, May who always saved the best slice, the biggest richest fattest helping for someone else, Arv's dear little midget mother May had passed out cold as a fish in the front seat of the Merc, her hair-netted head lolling lank and empty against Arv's brake leg, like a big rag doll, abandoned, like a cat that got hit by a car, like a kid with a broken head, her mouth hanging open, her breath fogging up the Merc's window, befouling the air. . . .

After he put his mom to bed for her daily after-work nap, Arv drove down the hill to the employees' service station and pulled up in front of the ethyl pump. He looked at his watch. Still an hour before work. He figured he had just enough time to run over and see Wendy at the Warden's Mansion.

Two inmates, white men, happy to have this cushy outside job, jumped out and washed the windows and the sideview mirror and checked the oil, battery, tires, and filled it up. The officer-in-charge, an old white-haired guard about ready to retire, came out and took the money and waved him on. Arv whipped the Merc out of the station and past the In-Service-Training Building and into the Warden's Mansion driveway. He drove up in front of the three-car garage. Deanna's little red Austin-Healy and Lobo's new Buick were both home.

Arv got out and rang the doorbell. He tapped his foot while he waited. No one came for the longest time, but that was to be expected. Deanna and the Warden were obviously on the grounds of the Joint somewhere, and Patsy, the Warden's wife, was forever "indisposed," forever languishing in front of the TV set on her bedside table, sipping orange juice and gin in her soiled nightgown.

It started raining suddenly, came down hard, blew in almost horizontally off the Sound. Arv crept closer and closer to the door. The Warden's Mansion was a kind of pseudo-antebellum pad, with white porticoes and a tall elegant front veranda that kept some of the wet off. Finally Ignazio, the Warden's haughty inmate servant, opened the door.

"Yes?"

"I wonder if I could see Wendy?"

"She not home."

"Oh? Do you know if she'll be back soon?"

"No."

"Well, do you know where she's at? Is she on the grounds?"

"No."

"No what?"

"Don't know."

"Oh . . . okay, thanks," Arv said, and ran back out to his car across the already soaking lawn. *That goddamned little Flip!* he thought. But that's the way Ignazio'd always been. Arv had always hated his guts. He was so fucking supercilious, always acting like he was in on some secret that you weren't. . . .

Arv, disconsolate for some reason, something he really couldn't even put his finger on, drove down Front Street to the Southside parking lot, locked his car, and walked up the asphalt hill toward the barber shop, very conscious of the sky above him, low and gray as his mood, like the ceiling of an unhappy room.

In the barber shop all the talk was of Wasco. Not only had he been granted an interview with the Warden on his very first day in the Joint, an unprecedented occurrence, but, Yuba said, the vine had it that he'd already been made tier boss in the East Block! And, as if that weren't enough, Roundo reported that he'd heard that Wasco'd already had two visits: one of them from the foxiest little colored gal (or half-breed Filipino, depending on which story you heard) that anybody'd seen at the Slam in years!

But Little Arv, depressed as hell about something, something he couldn't really even name, ignored all the talk, let it run on right over his head, like the words of a song you don't like, kept his eyes out on the rainclouds squeezing fatly through the high pillars of the Alvarez Straits Bridge.

Roundo tried. So did Yuba. So did Fast-Walking when he waltzed in happily late with Big Arv. But nobody could get through to Little Arv. Nobody.

Twenty-Two

At the top of a bounce, practicing on the trampoline in the empty prison grounds schoolhouse, Deanna saw Arvin's Mercury flash by outside and remembered, with that extraordinary clarity bitterness brings to womankind, another trampoline, another bounce, years before . . . her first time around at Santa Bonita J.C. The incomplete, unsuccessful time.

In gym class at Santa Bonita Y.W.C.A., at the top of a bounce on the trampo, upside down coming down on a back flip, it had occurred to her that it was no longer possible to deceive herself. She was two months pregnant at least. She hit the taut white canvas hard and went up again, higher, did a one and a half with a full twist and landed on her belly, belly, belly, belly, three times going round and round and round and then tucked under and bounced again and flipped harder than she should have into the unsteady arms of the other girls who stood around the trampoline to catch you if you fell. Everyone clapped for her performance. But actually they were all jealous. She was the star of the Y.W.C.A. gymnastics team.

That afternoon she avoided Mary and didn't meet her at Bert's Beanery. They were supposed to be working on their singing act together, their rock duet.

Instead, Deanna caught the commuter Greyhound over to the city and went up to Doctor Murray's office and got the results on her rabbit test: *marriage didn't interest me. I was tired of working for men, as a secretary, slave to men's whims. What I was looking for was not a man but freedom, a profession of my own.*

Results of her rabbit test: Positive.

She didn't create a scene. She just said, "Positive, eh? Well, thank you, Doctor," and left. There was nothing that old fuddy-dud could do for her anyway.

Unpanicked, numb, laughing even, a little, sort of ironically, as she remembered it now, Deanna rode the elevator to the ground floor of the Marines Memorial Building with a smiling black woman who seemed to *know*.

She stepped heavy across the shined marble floor of the enormous uptown building, her high thick heels clicking outrageously, a rich modish sound which, by the time she reached the air of Fuller Street, made her giddy, sick with disappointment, and her erased future, her cruel fate, her killed prerogatives, her now-finite possibilities. *Just when I finally had the attainment of my hopes and dreams within my grasp, just about to break away, go to college, I was got with child by a man I definitely do not want to spend the rest of my life with, a man who is the absolute personification of everything in my childhood prison-grounds milieu I so desperately want to get away from.*

On the way down Fuller Street to the Greyhound depot she decided she'd have to phone the daddy, Private Arvin Weed, Jr. She hadn't seen him since that night in his car under the redwood trees *the rain coming down on the roof like skeletons dancing.* She hated to call him now. She was embarrassed because he'd think she was chasing after him. Then she realized that she *was;* she *was* after him. She had no one else to turn to. That's how men had it all over women. Men never got trapped like that. *I told him to pull it out before.*

Cursing her womanhood, cursing the deceitfully planted seed within her, *he didn't want me to know he came as soon as he went inside,* and its deceitful father, she went into the depot on 3rd Street, her mind buzzing and racing ahead with plans for the embryo's immediate and violent extirpation.

It's bull that women are beautiful when they're pregnant, she thought, dialing the number of the Control Operator at Fort Ord, Monterey, California.

"Hi," she said when she finally got him, "I just thought I'd give you a ring."

"I was going to call you too," he said, "but this damned Advanced Clerks' School shit . . ." He made his excuses without conviction. The injustice of it! Having to make him think she couldn't live without him! When all she wanted was to borrow some money to exterminate the residue of his regressive Weed sperm, the vile germ, the trash he had deposited within her body.

She hung up on him. She was mortified that her voice had betrayed emotion. She was furious with herself for permitting him to believe that the emotion was for him. She vowed she'd never see him again, and directly began phoning her friends in search of an abortionist. She didn't beat around the bush . . . "I'm pregnant," she said, "do you know a doctor who'll do the deed?"

But no one seemed to know a doctor, off hand.

She caught the Greyhound back across the Sound to the Joint. All the way over the Alverez Straits Bridge and through the Brando Tunnel and down along the Sound *here's what he did. I know what he did. I haven't forgiven him to this day and I never will. He came inside me as soon as his excitable little thing touched wet. Then he went through an act. Pretended to continue enjoying it. Went faster, moaned, suddenly pulled it as if he were diligently carrying out my orders in regard to* coitus interruptus, *and pretended to have a highly enjoyable orgasm outside* she was thinking how generous women were. After Arv's indiscreet slip-up in the front seat of his car she had forgiven him silently, telling herself: *Oh, well, the chances are rather remote at this time of month.*

She got off the bus outside the Front Gate and waited her turn at the phone booth. She waited in a long line of frowsy and dumpy black and Mexican prisoners' wives, visitors, and went into the phone booth and regretfully called her best friend.

"Mary, I'm pregnant."

"Who did it?"

"Never mind."

"You want to have it?"

"No," she said, she most certainly did not. But Mary didn't know any doctors either.

Up, up, up, bouncing on the schoolroom trampoline, with the three-year-old result of that unachieved but earnestly sought abortion lying out in the teacher's empty office taking a nap, Deanna asked herself frankly whether she still felt the same way. . . . However . . . because she loved Wendy, she wouldn't answer that, not even to herself.

* * *

After sweating it out for a whole month, and not coming up with any money, or any other alternatives, or even decent advice, she went to her mother in desperation and, after swearing her to secrecy, confessed.

"An abortion is out of the question," she said, not taking her eyes off the Bert Parks show on TV, "think of your dad's position."

Marriage was the only answer.

Deanna adamantly refused. Even the family doctor and the prison chaplain, Chaplain Edwards, failed to convince her.

Mrs. Miniver went over and had a chat with Mrs. Weed. Over beer, cheese and saltine crackers, on Mrs. Weed's day off from the restaurant, they agreed that the two kids ought to get married as soon as possible. After all, it wasn't like they were strangers, or anything. They'd grown up together, almost.

When Deanna found out their plans she made her own plans for immediate escape. She figured that if she could borrow three hundred dollars it would be enough to go down to California and try to get a shrink to sign the necessary papers to have the abortion "legally" performed. Otherwise, if that failed, she'd have enough to hitchhike down to Tijuana. She called every friend she had. She called again from the phone booth outside the Front Gate. She used her last five dollars making all the calls, standing the whole hour in the booth while the visitors and prisoners' wives banged on the glass. She went through every name in her address book. She even phoned her old boyfriend Sun King, the leader of a rock band in Santa Barbara, California.

"Hey, Sun King! Can you lend me three hundred dollars?"

"Are you serious?"

"Listen, this is an extreme emergency."

"Say, you know I'd do anything."

"Sure," she said.

In desperation she phoned her brother Fast-Walking in the Joint.

"Say, Frankie, can you let me have three hundred for a month or two?"

"Three hundred what?"

"Dollars?"

"Gee, honey, you know I would but . . . well you know what kind of debts . . ."

"Yeah. Okay, sorry for bothering you."

When she came out of the phone booth she hated herself because she couldn't stop crying. Her brother's refusal hadn't bothered her much. He never came through for her when he was needed. It wasn't that he was mean, or anything. He was just weak . . . or, something else . . . insubstantial, like he was made out of cotton candy or something. What hurt her though was old Sun King. She had loved old Sun King, when he was a senior and she was a junior in high school: she had given him her whole heart. In a way she would never give it again. She'd believed him when he said he loved her. Maybe he had. They'd achieved a rapport that was almost magical, especially when they sang together. They sang great together with his band in high school, at the Junior Prom and the Sophomore Hop. He was the one who'd discovered her talent. "Sing me some more of that fifties shit," he'd say, laughing. And she'd go:

O O O O Gee
My O O me
O hear my plea
How I love that boy . . .

But then the Sun King went away. And he no longer remembered what it was like before. How could it be that he didn't remember? He didn't. That's all. *Only we ourselves alone exist in our memory of the past. I am better than other people. I can feel them. They cannot feel me. I am a human being of good will. I am rare, and alone.*

Poor Deanna, crying hard, real tears, went right past those hard lower-class black and Okie and Mexican eyes of the prisoners' wives and back into the Joint. Sanger Weed, who was Front Gate man at the time, smiled and waved her in. Sanger asked her if anything was wrong. He was a sweet burly old ex-boxer and he'd been kind to her when she was a child, always giving her lollypops and bubble gum when she rode her bike or her horse around the gate house.

"No, no, nothing wrong," she said, and hurried up the black asphalt roadway along the prison Front Street, past

the neat inmate-trimmed lawns of the Joint's upper-offi-
cialdom, past the Employees' Service Station and the fire
house and the In-Service-Training Building and everyone,
cons and cops, waved at her and said, "Howdy, Miss
Miniver!" and she just looked straight ahead, thinking,
this is my home, everyone will know.

Even if nobody found out, she hated getting a reputation as a "temperamental young girl."

When she got home Arv was on the phone. His mother
had called him at Fort Ord, and told him Deanna's sad
tale.

"What's all this?" he asked, resentfully, suspiciously,
unpardonably arrogant.

"It's true. But I didn't want . . ."

"You didn't want shit!" he said cruelly, and that
stopped her tears of self-pity halfway down her cheek, got
her English up:

"To hell with you! It's your fault. You're not a man. A
real man has control. I'm going to tell everyone in the
Joint that you're not a real man!" She slammed down the
receiver, thinking *oh now dear Lord the poop's going to
hit the fan because I tweaked him where it hurts, got him
in his tweaky little male ego* . . . and picked up the
phone again and called him back at Fort Ord.

"Alright," he said, a little calmer now, "I'm sorry too. I
realize what a state you must be in. We'll get married."

"No!" she insisted, "I don't want to get married. Lend
me some money, or borrow me some money and I'll run
away from home. I'll go down to San Francisco and get
rid of it before they catch me."

"How do I know it's mine?"

"Who else would be so weak on control? It's yours alright, unfortunately for the child."

"I don't know that."

"Listen, can't you just help me as a friend? You're a
real weakling, aren't you?"

"Who said you were a friend? You were nothing but a
piece of ass to me."

Deanna hung up then with the distinct feeling that,
despite the vehemence of their exchange, they would be
married. Because there was no other way out. She had
also detected something despicable in Little Arv's voice:
his male pride was all tickled and swelling up thinking
that he was a real daddy, a real stud, as if his nervous

quick dribbling had been the rarest and most remarkable feat. Her hatred for him knew no bounds. She would have murdered him at that moment without a qualm, would have loved to see his blood bubble, his early death in Vietnam. And though he changed toward her the next time she saw him, and changed a great deal during the two years of their marriage, and he apologized sincerely for his behavior, calling it the result of "panic," and though he became later kind enough, and gentle with her and even, with time and help and encouragement, a competent lover, even so, in her heart, Deanna hated Arvin, for spoiling her, socking it to her before she had a chance, ruining a young life that she'd only just begun to enjoy. Worst of all, and what she'd never ever forgive, was that he'd trapped her in the Joint! From which still she had not escaped, after all these years. There she was, still practicing trampoline in the schoolhouse where she and Arv and Wasco and Fast-Walking had all gone to *kindergarten*, for Christ's sake! And there she was still, steady Deanna, bouncing away, up, up, up, but never going anywhere. Trapped, just like her brother. Just like Arv and everyone she knew . . .

. . . After Deanna hung up on Arv that last time she went out to the glassed-in veranda that overlooked the garden and the swimming pool and the summer house of the Warden's Mansion and did what she always did in moments of extreme anxiety, she lay down for a nap on her favorite couch, a delightful old straw thing that had been in the family since the Victorian era. Before she went to sleep she thought *what if your sins are visited upon your child?*

Sleeping her sleep of distress, Deanna had dreamed then, had dreamed of her girlhood that was not over. And her white mare that she used to ride. Then she dreamed that she was the white mare herself. And that she could conceive merely by turning her tail and raising it to the north wind. It occurred to her that in the Joint the north wind was known in convict slang as "Mr. Hawkins," and then she woke up. She was awakened by the loud vacuuming of Ignazio, the inmate houseboy, an intrepid Filipino about four feet ten in height, who was always peeking at her from behind the potted plants and watching her dress through keyholes. She realized that he had been going over and over the same five square

feet of rug for a very long time, and that's what
brought her eyes suddenly open. They met his, which
were muddy and enigmatic. He smiled and said, "Good
afternoon, Missie," and she knew from the way he said
it that her skirt had crept up the back of her thighs. He
giggled lasciviously. She felt for her hem. Sure enough
. . . And as she rolled over, a bright Sunkist orange fell
to the floor from where it had been carefully arranged
in the middle of her rear crotch.

It was such an astounding audacity that she hadn't the
heart to tell her father. Instead she dismissed the little
brown fellow, turned on the tape recorder, and practiced
singing rapid jazz-rock riffs, skatting along with the girl
lead singer:

> Get down
> A little closer
> To the ground
>
> Ooh!
>
> You gotta get do-o-own
> A little closer
> To the grou-ou-ou-nd . . .

until she realized that the name of the group she was
copying was "The Joy of Cooking."

She shut it off.

Remember what little Mia Farrow cooked up, she
thought, in Polanski's daydream, his movie, and remember
her waddling pregnant down the street and remember how
obscene her panic was. *There's no dignity in a swollen
belly,* she thought, *with Rosemary's fortune in the womb.*

And all that evening, at dinner, in front of the ever-
playing family TV, Deanna suffered the extreme anguish
of her unique and private brain affliction, a condition she
had long ago defined as "Futurity," meaning that she suffered in the present her coming vicissitudes: *we will be
married, divorced, and the child will be mine till it is
grown. But someday I will get away. Someday!*

Someday, Deanna thought, going up, up, up, on the
trampoline, as Wendy now bawled at being alone in the
teacher's office, *someday soon I'm going to get away!*

Twenty-Three

Wasco laid up in his new Chief Tier Tender's day bed in the East Block guard shanty practicing bird calls and clipping his nails with a pair of State scissors. Stinger-boiled coffee water sizzled behind him in a Mason jar. The squeeze snored above him contentedly in the Assistant Tier Man's bunk. Wasco gathered up the fingernails where they'd dropped on the concrete floor, slid them carefully together in a neat little pile, pinched them up, and stuck them in the squeeze's pant cuff as a joke. *No telling how long he'll carry them around. Ha, ha, ha.*

"Tweet, tweet, tweet!" went Wasco, imitating the sparrows that fluttered and called in the rafters. Afternoon raindrops splashed in through the cellblock bars. Water dripped from the shanty tap. Otherwise not a sight or sound in the whole huge empty block. Outside in the Big Yard you could hear the loud raucous voices of four thousand raw-nerved convicts as they milled and coughed and farted on the blacktop, upwind, waiting to be locked up for the prechow count.

Wasco was thinking. He liked being left alone to think. He was pretty happy about the way everything in his plan of operations seemed to be turning out. Not that it was any big surprise. Wasco didn't like surprises. In fact, Wasco denied the very existence of surprise in his life. Surprises were what he sprung on others. Beware the man who pulled one on *him!*

Wasco held all the cards. But that was nothing new. He never moved unless he did. In business matters, Wasco made it a point never to accept a risk. Risky ventures were for amateurs and gamblers, not for pros like him. Wasco only bet on sure-fire things. Solid Gold. Blue Chip. *Yes sir! Shitfire! How the hell can I complain? Huh? Ain't no more risks this time than any other! What more could you fucking ask? One day in the Joint and I got me a hon-*

*eypie, a profit-making business, a rewarding commission
of service to my State and Race and Nation, a good cell,
and a good job. . . .* This very morning the East Block
tier man, a crusty old con who'd been on the job for five
years, had received a surprise promotion, a transfer to a
cushy unsupervised trusty's job in the Pump House, and
Wasco'd been appointed in his place by executive decree.
Yes sirree! Got that fastidi-ass old Warden to hopping!
And then Wasco'd immediately appointed Squeeze to be
his assistant, and taken possession of the tier man's keys,
his locker and desk in the guard's shanty, and set the
squeeze to brewing the astonished day sergeant some fresh
Nescafé.

And the asshole never said a word to Wasco, never got
up the nerve all day long: cause he knew he was in the
presence of real class, and clamped his purple Portagee
lips down tight, and only hoped to stay on good terms
with Wasco . . . who was destined to be, as any idiot
could see, Kingpin, Con-Boss, Queen of the Block!

"Tier man" was the most coveted job in any Slam. The
tier man was in fact a kind of unofficial guard, with keys
to all the cells, free run of the entire cellblock and yard, a
special card to allow him out later at night than anyone
else. He was the last to go to bed at night, and last to be
locked up, and the first to be unlocked in the morning.
Tier man was a hard job. It entailed a lot of running and
climbing stairs. It was coveted not because of the heavy
work and movement (in the Joint normally a job where
you're occupied all day is optimum: it makes the days
pass quicker), but because its unlimited freedom gave the
tier man unlimited opportunities to "do business." Tier
men were traditionally the Joint dealers, pushers, traders,
contrabandists. Prison authorities recognized this, and permitted them their freedom to sell a little dope and liquor
and laundry favors, pimp, pass things from cell to cell,
and so on, as long as they kept them informed of any
serious illegal activities they heard about on their rounds.
The authorities were naturally interested particularly in
political agitation, escape attempts and murder conspir-
acies. It was not an easy job, and not without danger either. Many white tier men especially had been iced. Some
said it was by the black militants, the Black Fence boys,
paying them back for snitching. . . .

The fact that Wasco had been appointed to this coveted

post in such short order, through special executive decree, was absolutely without precedent in the history of the New Sonora Commission of Corrections, and sure proof that the State had utmost confidence in Wasco, utmost faith and trust. As soon as the word got out, the entire Joint would be alerted that Wasco was the Man's man, would know for sure that something very very heavy was coming down, and soon. Otherwise there wouldn't have been such an all-fired rush to promote him. Wasco viewed this eventuality with complete equanimity. *Put the fear of BeJesus into the Joint, the fear of the loco-weed.* That way, when they knew who you was, and where your power lay, then you could lay down the word to them. And what was the word? The word was derring-do: murder. That was the fucking word! Wasco wasn't afraid to say it. Let's not pussy-foot around. Race war! Murder from the lowest scummiest convict to the very upper heights of Jointdom. Just to stir up the shit.

Wasco sat there thinking, sipping at his coffee while the squeeze snored away, waiting for the big doors to open, waiting for the count. He turned his attention to Lobo the Warden again. He knew that Lobo's "wishy-washy liberal" image was nothing more than a cover, a coat he had put on when it was in style, and would take off now that it was out. Wasco'd been too cagey to let that out to the old D.A., who still believed Lobo was a goddamned radical New Frontiersman. That way Wasco figured he had one up on the wily old prosecutor. And, also, more respect would accrue to Wasco when he finally achieved the conversion, and obtained the active participation of Lobo Miniver, the famous liberal reformer of the Joint.

Yes, that was all a plus in Wasco's favor. Still, he'd thought all along that if there was going to be any crink in his scam, his Grand Design, that crink would be the Warden. And that impression had been confirmed in their meeting in the Warden's office today, just after lunch, when Wasco had frankly come right out with the truth, figuring a frontal assault was the best way to sound Lobo out . . . since Wasco knew he wasn't nearly the goody-goody all them bigwigs up in the state capital thought he was.

"Warden," Wasco began, "I'm here on a special assignment as undercover agent for the State . . ."

He paused then, and when Lobo didn't say nothing, just kept looking at him across the big old oak desk with them steel-blue eyes (eyes that didn't scare Wasco one bit, cause he knew there was nothing but mush under the hard appearance of them Anglo-Saxon eyes), Wasco continued audaciously, "and because of my highly special and technical operation here in the prison, I'd like to ask for your cooperation . . ."

When the Warden still didn't say nothing Wasco became certain that he must've got some kind of word from On High, word from the Big Boys. He didn't think they'd let Lobo know the whole gig. But, Wasco figured, they probably just said, "Now look here, Warden, we want you to do this and do that, place this sergeant in this cellblock and that officer in this one and we want that colored man here and that inmate there . . . and, this boy Wasco Weed, we want you to go along with his minor requests for us, won't you Warden?" Wasco figured them Big Boys said something like that to the Warden. No rough stuff. No secrets. Just a little subtle pressure, just like Wasco himself would've done it, if he'd had their power.

"So, I tell you, sir," Wasco said, encouraged by Lobo's response (or lack of response) to make bold, "I wonder if you'd be kind enough to appoint me Chief Tier Man in the East Block, effective today, if you don't mind . . ."

"Why, that's unheard of!" Lobo exclaimed, and Wasco had his first indication that the Warden might prove a bit difficult *though, shit! I ain't dumb! Already got that contingency covered!*

"I mean, really!" Lobo went on. "What will the other inmates say? It'll create an intolerable situation . . . jealousy . . . accusations of favoritism . . . even nepotism, considering the fact that you grew up here on the grounds . . ."

"Warden Miniver," Wasco said, taking the tack he knew best, the direct one, the rough one, looking him right in the eye, "I don't think you believe me. . . . Now, that's real understandable. Why should you? I'm sure a lotta guys come in here with stories. I tell you what. I want you to pick up that there phone of yours and call the state capital. I want you to call Mr. Muller himself, the Commissioner of Corrections, and . . ."

"Oh, no, no, no! That won't be necessary, Wasco," he said, and Wasco knew he had the bastard bluffed out, "I was simply concerned that . . . but never mind! I think we can handle your request. . . . Now! Will there be anything else?"

"No, sir," Wasco said, "that'll be all, thanks," and left the room triumphant and walked through the Third Fence Gate and all the way through the Main Gate and the Isolation Yard and the Big Yard to his own East Block feeling like his old feet wasn't even hitting the ground, was just a-stepping on a cushion of pure soft marshmallow about an inch above the blacktop, feeling so incredibly dynamite good that when the squeezy come running up happily accosting him with impertinent questions Wasco couldn't resist a sweet and enigmatic cruelty:

"Never shit where you eat!" he growled at the squeezy, thrusting him away, *just to watch him squirm* . . .

But still, Wasco thought now, *I still don't trust that Lobo.* Cause the Warden had a grudge of long years' standing against Wasco. Had no love for him at all. And Lobo was also the kind of dude who'd let a fellow do a dirty number for him, reap its benefits, and then blame it all on you, pretending to the world (and maybe even to himself) that he'd never known what was going on. That's what Wasco figured. But that didn't worry him in the least. He had the shifty-eyed sonofabitch figured, knew what would make him the most rabid nigger-hating hack, the most dutiful co-conspirator in the history of Joint warfare, knew what would bring him around faster than anything in the world. A *thing of value.* That's how it worked. A powerful man's belongings. What was closest. And then once you got ahold of that something, why then you just snuffed it, destroyed it, and pointed the blame right where you wanted it pointed, at the enemy. And whoever got the blame for blowing off a thing of value, that motherfucker would be a sorry sonofabitch. Cause *a thing of value* would send a man to the limit. That's the way Wasco looked at it. He looked at it real businesslike. Nothing personal in it at all. Though he hated the Warden, and the Warden's thing of greatest value, with all his heart, for private reasons dating back to childhood, *things that most people would think of as minor . . . but old Wasco, he never forgives and never forgets, unless it's necessary*, that didn't have nothing to do with his present plans. Wasco never liked to let emotions get in the way of financial affairs.

The squeeze opened a red-webbed eyeball and looked down at him. Wasco felt the gaze on his neck and looked up and smiled, whispered in his coarse, rasping, yet high little voice, "Hey, honeybuns, how you doing?"

"Beautiful, man, thanks to you."

"You just stick with your Ma, sonny."

"You bet," the squeeze said, and Wasco's heart beat faster. He was growing to truly care for this little pretty-assed punk. Wasco spent many a moment daydreaming of their sweet midnight, their sweet-smelling fart sack, and the punk's beautiful little buns. Wasco would slowly take the squeeze more and more into his confidence. He was actually a godsend to Wasco, who'd figured originally he'd have to pull the whole scam off by himself, wouldn't be able to trust nobody here in the Joint. But the squeeze, Wasco had begun to believe, might be his boy, his lovie-pie. Wasco was almost sure now, almost . . . Wasco carried on, whispering real low. The squeeze leaned down to hear better, but still couldn't understand all of what Wasco was laying down. Cause Wasco didn't want him to; he never put all his cards on the table till he was sure. He laid down a hint, maybe, a sniffle or two, give a man a whiff and looked at him real sharp to see how he reacted. Wasco worked in innuendos, watching. Only when he was sure, from mighty watching, mighty checking, probing of a dude's ideas, thoughts, reactions, attitudes, desires, ambitions, interests, aims, values, morality, loyalty, trustworthiness, did Wasco lay a job on him, only then. He was one of the most careful employers, old Wasco, more careful than even IBM, and he prided himself on it. That was one of the secrets of his success in the business world, the total check-out. He was even thinking of employing a polygraph, a lie detector, in his outside personnel screening, just like he'd read some of the big companies did. Only the most modern methods for Wasco! Anyway . . . "Now, Squeezy," Wasco whispered, handing him up a hot cup of coffee, glancing over at the snoring day man, "everything is going according to my complex plan of attack. My attack is two-fold, two-pronged," Wasco said, winding his thoughts out, using

the squeeze as a kind of sounding board. The squeeze
was getting wiser and wiser by the minute. But he still
didn't have the whole scam down. Wasco let it ravel out
for him, let him dingle-dangle, testing. The squeeze was
surely getting wise. He let Wasco lead out, let Wasco
dangle it for him, and didn't ask questions. The little
cocksucker was learning fast. Wasco appreciated that in
a young stud. "You'll go far, Squeezy, if you stick with
your Ma, and keep your fucking satchel shut tight, and
don't ask too many questions, and listen good, and do it,
dig?"

"Yeah!" the squeeze said enthusiastically, sure where
his destiny was now. Knew it was locked in with Wasco's,
and that Wasco was going places, Wasco was going back
to the very top of the heap, and even farther this time
. . . beyond!

"Now," Wasco said, whispering in the squeeze's ear, "as
soon as the swing shift comes in I'm going to have more
skinny to digest. I got total confidence in my help on the
Street, and Inside. I'll make a prediction for you. Guess
who's going to be East Block sergeant on the swing shift?"

"One of your goddamn uncks?"

"How'd you guess? And who do you figure will be his
help?"

"Some more of your fucking relatives."

"Right again! You're catching on fast, kid. Now, look
here, time is of the essence. Everything's got to be done
within the next few days. I mean, everything on one side
of our two-sided business thrust, dig? You always insure
yourself, Squeezy, always. Never accept a contract without backup, some kind of insurance to go along with it,
see? Now, I got my contract, my official state business,
and we got ourselves a sweet little dope scam too." Wasco
then apparently decided against revealing any more to the
squeeze. "By the by, baby," he said, jumping to another
subject, "we're gonna receive our first supplies today, exactly as directed, at 4:15 P.M. sharp. Then after that I
want you to run up and get the con accountant to draw
the transferral-of-ownership contract up and then I want
you to bring Bullet to my cell as agreed upon, so he can
look at the quality of my shit, and sign the final papers,
and we'll conclude our deal. . . . And then after that our
need of Mr. Bullet's services will be terminated . . ."

Wasco said, very slowly, very carefully, testing. . . . The
squeeze, quick as ever, picked up.

"Oh, yeah? Well, I'll handle that myself. You never
know. It's dangerous around here, with them niggers all
fired up and looking for Honkey blood."

"Oh yeah! You never know when one of the bastards is
gonna throw you right off the tier with a little note pinned
to your pantleg: 'Die Whitey,' or something like that."

"You're right there. You never know . . ."

"Right, Squeeze! You know what?"

"No, what?"

"I really do declare, I think you're gonna work out. I
think you're gonna be my main man, I really do! So look.
We want the dope half of the caper completely set up
right away. Then we can run it out long term, secure and
happy and hauling in the bread. But the other half of our
dual thrust, our two-headed dragon, baby, got to be tied
up and accomplished within the next five days. As I said,
time is of the primal essence, man. Public opinion is still
stirring up against the enemies of America. And it'll be
stirred up a little more, before we're done with things in
here. But it ain't gonna stay stirred up forever. Dig? The
American public is fickle as hell. They never remember
who their true enemies are. They're forgetful. That's why
we gotta work fast, see? And the fact that we got help,
'conspirators,' within the walls of the Slam, dictates immediate action. Iiiiimmediate! Nothing stays a secret in the
Joint. Before our little secret gets out, we got to move, secure on our rear and on our flanks, pull off number one,
and our *two* will be covered. What I mean is, if I do my
little favor for the State, the State ain't going to be bothering me about no little dope scam on the side, even though
that wasn't part of the understanding, dig? That's how I
mean I cover my trail always, how I always cover myself
with insurance. If we pull off our *one,* nobody's going to
worry about a few niggers relaxing with a little junk. In
fact, they'll probably give me a medal for keeping the jungle bunnies quiet."

"Something I never figured out," the squeeze said,
"where do them niggers get the money for smack here in
the Joint?"

"Shit, man, just like Outside! They beat their brothers
for it, rip 'em off, beg it from their old lady's welfare

money, pull scams, rob, pimp, murder, just like they always done. You got to learn something, kid. Nothing's different in here. Nothing! It's just like Outside, except it's just more concentrated. You can see it all better, more clear. You can see its outlines and meaning better in here. That's why I call the Joint a real education, man. In here you really learn the truth about man and society and this American nation and what it's made of and what it's made for and what it means. You can see it in all its beauty. And I love this nation just the way I love this Joint, Squeezy, and I'm not gonna let no fucking niggers take it over. Cause I got a soft spot for the old Joint, just like I got for America. It's where I was born and bred and brought up. The Joint, just like America, is my home."

"Oh yeah," the squeeze asked, skeptical again, "well what's it mean, then?"

"What's what mean?"

"The Joint."

"Nothing."

"What?"

"It don't mean nothing, man. That's the secret you learn in here. And it's a big fucking secret. Takes most people a whole lifetime to learn it. Some never do. Very few people on the Street know it. But the answer to your question is, again, 'nothing'! It don't mean nothing. Nothing at all. And it's the biggest lesson of your life. So listen good. You want to learn it real good. And figure it this way: the Joint is like a little Outside, a little Outside World. And if the world don't mean nothing, then you better carve out a little nothing for yourself alone, dig? Not worrying about the next dude. In a fucking world without meaning, son, in a null and void and nebbish universe, antireal, you better just take care of your own nullified ass . . ."

"Wow!" the squeeze said, like he was listening to the word of the Lord, and Wasco, hearing those tones of wonder, laughed even a bit self-consciously, and then concluded that maybe the squeeze was right. If there was a God, an avenging angel in this here Joint, a meaningless angel, avenging nothing for the sake of nothing, giving meaning the meaning of nothing in the meaningless fucking nothing Joint world, then Wasco himself was the Lord of Nothing in person! Yeah man!

".Anyway, before our secret gets out, we got to move with number one," Wasco continued, still testing the squeeze, "then we can concentrate on getting rich. Now, you, sweetheart, you're working out so good that I'm even contemplating at the ~moment requesting a transfer for myself," he said craftily, testing, "to a Minimum Security Facility after our first project, and leaving you here to run this end. That way we'll open up a new branch and double our profits. They got even more dope heads and junkies down at Burnes Minimum than they got here . . ."

"No!" the squeeze said, protesting, wisely, "can't we stay together? Maybe we can break another dude in? Maybe . . ."

"Well . . ." Wasco said, and his heart beat for joy, "well, you really do dig your Ma, don't you, honey?"

"Oh," said the squeeze in a light airy little nigger boy's voice, "you know ah does, big mama!" And Wasco just about split his britches laughing.

BUZZ! The 4:10 P.M. buzzer went off. The noise in the Big Yard got louder. Everybody was off work now. The yard was full. Wasco could hear the convicts lining up outside the massive steel door of the East Block, waiting to go into their cells for the First Count.

"But there's only one thing," the squeeze whispered, as the day sergeant yawned and began to awaken.

"What's that, baby?"

"How we gonna get public opinion on our side?"

"Listen, I hear tell the niggers are brewing up a race war, man."

"Race war? There ain't no race war!"

"No?" Wasco began, and then a light bulb appeared above the squeeze's head, an almost visible light bulb that warmed old Wasco's larcenous murderous heart, "well, I'll tell you what then . . . we'll just have to have one of our *own!*"

And the squeeze got to laughing. His knees got to jerking on the bed, hands started up to shaking, feet got to jumping, head got to rocking, hands got to clapping, belly got to heaving, and the old squeeze. he just about laughed himself up into a fit, and Wasco had to run him down to the shower room and give him a triple fix of Bullet's inferior shit to shut him up. . . .

When they got back from the head the day sergeant, a

slight, curly-headed almost totally incompetent old Portagee named Boa, roused himself sleepily, anticipating the
end of his shift. Day shift hacks worked an hour longer
than swing shift people. The shifts overlapped between
four and five o'clock. So the old man was bleary and tired
at the end of the workday.

BUZZ! BUZZ! BUZZ! The 4:15 P.M. buzzer went off.

"Go open up that door!" Boa ordered.

"Squeezy! Go open up!" Wasco ordered in turn.

The squeeze, last man on the chain of command, said
"Yes sir!" and bustled to the steel door, clanging his keys
around self-importantly. He turned the lock and swung
the heavy door open. Convicts immediately flooded into
the cellblock like so many rats, smelling like rats (sour
and pissy), chattering together like rats, ratlike too in the
face. Fifteen hundred of them came in within ten minutes.
Each one of them was quickly and perfunctorily shook
down by the swing shift officers in the yard. Wasco could
see Little Arv, Big Arv, Fast-Walking, and rejoiced in his
heart that with the Lord's and the State's gracious and
kind help everything was . . . he walked over to the
squeeze and said it out loud . . . "Everything's according
to plan." And the squeeze, sweet kid, winked knowingly,
though he didn't dig the totality of their mission yet. Confident though, the squeeze was, as if to say, "But I *will*
know soon, won't I, Ma?"

"Almost looks like I'm running the Joint myself, don't
it, man?" Wasco asked, standing alongside Hearne
watching the inmates running in, watching them watch
him and the squeeze with surprise, anger, vexation, horror, trepidation, hatred, love, with envy in their prison
hearts at Wasco's sudden and unprecedented ascension in
the prison's ordinarily rusty hierarchy.

"Right on, man!" the squeeze said. There he was again,
going into that nigger talk. You could never learn some
people.

"Shut up!" Wasco said, watching the last stragglers
come in through the gaping steel door.

Then the officers came in, locked the door behind them,
and headed for the guard shanty.

"Hey, Wasco," Big Arv said, looping his fat red hand
into his wide belt, "looks like you're doing alright for
yourself!"

"Got to, Unck," Wasco said, gesturing toward the squeeze, "nobody else's gonna get it for me."

"That's right, kid. But how'd you get tier man so fast?"

"Merit," said Wasco, "what else?"

BUZZ! The third buzzer went off.

"Let's go, boys!" Big Arv yelled.

Fast-Walking, Little Arv and the two tier men ran up the tiers, Little Arv and Wasco to the fifth, and Fast-Walking and Hearne to the third. The cellblock was rocking with noise. Fifteen hundred convicts standing outside their cells in the cold drafty winter air, leaning on the safety railings, on the cell bars, slapping their hands, dancing on one foot two foot, whacking each other on the back, blowing into their palms, shucking and jiving, shuffling, dealing, soft-shoeing it, laughing, belching, yelling, arguing, bitching, pissing and moaning, killing time till the cells were opened. Hunger pangs and pangs of depression, the depression of the end of the day, gnawed at their tight bellies, bellies sour and acidic with too much cold coffee and too many cigarettes.

"*Aiiiii! Cabrones!* Let us in them fucking cells!"

"Oohie! Come on Pig! Ah wanna go home!"

"Lock us up, *chingados!*"

Wasco led Arv up to the fifth tier, their heels banging on the corrugated metal spiral staircase.

BUZZ! The fourth buzzer went off just as they got into position at the end of the tier. Wasco pulled up his keys on his key chain, unlocked the bar mechanism, and, tensing his heavy muscled legs, his tight massive stomach tendons, heaved back pushing with his right foot on the metal cage wall.

WHAM! The bar came firing open. Eighty-five stinking tired convicts stepped quickstep into their cells. ZANG! Wasco let the bar go home, locking them all in.

Then he and Arv went along double locking everyone in by key. CHANK! CHANK! CHANK! All the way down along the line of cells.

Down below on the floor somewhere a tremendous cheer went up.

"Hey!"

"Whooie!"

"Yeah!"

"Blow it Black Fence!"

"Galliot!"

Little Arv and Wasco looked down over the metal safety bar and saw guess who but old Brother Galliot himself bopping along down on the main floor coming into the block late, nigger-arrogant, trying to show everyone who was boss, with a big office typewriter in his arms. All the blacks slapped him on the back, called his name, cheered him on. Others took his burden. The Mexicans and the whites just turned their backs on him. They didn't like him. He meant trouble.

"Hey man," the blacks said, "when they let you pick up the typewriter?"

"Just now!"

"Right on!"

Everyone assumed he'd won his court case in the State Supreme Court, and that's why he had all his privileges back. He'd sued to be allowed his "free speech" and his "freedom of the press," while he was still down at Brown Max, on the grounds that he was being held incommunicado for nothing more than "vague political reasons."

Wasco was the only dude in the entire East Block who had reason to believe that the black motherfucker had not won his case. Wasco had reason to believe the Warden had been ordered by higher state authority to release him to the general population, to give the silly sonofabitch anything he wanted. Just like a dude on Death Row. Anything he wants! Wasco looked upon that typewriter now as a kind of Last Supper for the nigger.

Arv and Wasco moved down to the fourth tier and performed the lockup without a hitch, not saying a word to each other. Wasco kept twittering like the sparrows, practicing his bird calls. Tweet! Tweet! Tweet!

He didn't know why Arv had to be so surly with him, like a coon. Wasco was always looking out for his little cousin, and his welfare, and his best interests. He should of had more fucking gratitude, the way Wasco figured it . . .

Then Arv locked him and Hearne in their cell on the third tier. Nobody, not even a tier man, was permitted out of his cell during the First Count.

The squeeze, a little out of breath, lay on his back on the top bunk. Wasco was breathing hard too.

"Lot of work, this tier gig, ain't it?"

"You ain't just a-shitting there," the squeeze said, letting his hand hang out over the bunk bed. Wasco began flicking at it playfully with the flat of his hand. The squeeze liked it. He let his arm swing back and forth in the air.

"You see Galliot?"

"Yeah, funny, a militant like that getting out of the hole so easy."

"No suprise to your Ma."

"You know a lot," the squeeze said, giggling, letting his hand drag, "I'm getting a little suspicious . . ."

"You and the whole Joint. That's why we got to work fast."

CLICK, CLICK, CLICK, sixty-five, sixty-six, sixty-seven, sixty-eight . . . Fast-Walking came along clicking his metal counter, clanging his metal flying jodhpur heels on the walkway, doing his First Count.

When he went by the cell he tossed something inside and it landed with a messy wet FLOMP on the stone floor. The squeeze like to jumped out of his fucking needle-riddled skin. Wasco reached over real casual and picked it up without changing his supine position on the bunk. It was a slippery wet Sheik prophylactic stuffed to the rubber rim with white packed snowy boy.

"Wow!"

"Don't get all worked up, man."

"What is it?"

"What the fuck you think?"

"Wow!"

"I told you to let your Ma handle things."

"How'd you get it in?"

"Smell!"

The squeeze sniffed. "Say! Smells like coffee!"

"No shit?"

"Brought it in in his Thermos bottle!"

"Now you're thinking, sweetbutt. When we go down to chow I want you to lay this on Bullet as a gift. Tell him it's merely a token of my esteem. Once he gets a snort of this dynamite scag he'll be over here post-fucking-haste rattling my bars for more. He'll turn that organization over quicker than you say rat. And then . . ." Wasco hesitated, testing, waiting. The squeeze did not disappoint him . . .

"And then, don't worry, man, your sugar will handle the remainder. . . . But you know," the squeeze said, "you're beautiful, man," catching at Wasco's hand that was catching at his where it swung limp below the bunk-bed, holding it, "you've earned yourself a little kiss, big boy, big cock, suckface, lovieshit, shitprick, caca cock . . ."

"Sometimes," said Wasco, shifting over to the mattress to make room, "you are the sweetest thing. . . ."

The squeeze came down and they kissed passionately and petted, rubbing heavy beards SCRITCH SCRATCH SCRATCH together, and when Fast-Walking came around again, doing a recount cause he'd fucked up the first count, Wasco, who was on the bottom this time, and dig-ging it, caught his eye (wide eye, outraged: "It's alright to fuck, but to let yourself get fucked . . . !"). And Wasco, unafraid, unashamed, caught his eye, held it . . . he often employed shock as a device. He'd early discovered that certain weak people, people with pathetic little pip-squeak imaginations, feared the unnatural. And, rather than dis-daining those who dared the unnatural, these weak people . . . they feared them, feared brave men like Wasco who would go all the way, do anything, try anything. Wasco wanted to put the fear of the Weed into him, make him prance. Pay him back for the times when they were kids, and Fast-Walking, years older, would come around and break up Wasco and Arv, who were always getting into it, like healthy boys of the same age, more or less, would come around and break it up and beat shit out of Wasco at Arv's chickenshit instigation. . . . Wasco was paying back, like he always paid off his dues, with interest! So Wasco didn't give a shit that Fast-Walking halted, tripped, lost his count, his recount, hovered outside the cell door, embarrassed, red to the roots of his pale yellow hair, while him and the squeeze loudly fucked. SCHMUCK! SCHMUCK! SCHMUCK! went the squeeze's little cock as it went in and out of Wasco's poopoo-lubricated asshole. Fast-Walking just about dropped his eyeballs in surprise and hatred and fear. And Wasco didn't give the tiniest lit-tle damn. Cause, like, he wasn't shy. And cause old Fast-Walking, well, he just didn't *count* anymore. After he'd brought in the dope he was fated for, just one more load. Fast-Walking, the way Wasco figured it, was one of them spiritual cats . . . he was destined for more spiritual and eternal things . . . SCHMUCK!

Later, selling cigarettes to stake out his turf, Wasco made his way to Galliot's cell.

"I'm gonna be frank with you, man. I'm into dope," Wasco said, handing over a free pack of Camels, "but if you don't hassle me I won't cramp you either."

"Oh yeah?" the nigger replied, tossing back the pack of cigs like it was a bomb or something. Real cocky, real crafty-ass, sitting up on his bunk with his legs hanging over.

"Yeah," Wasco said, just as hardnosed.

"Well . . ." the nigger began.

"Well nothing!" Wasco cut in, "I come over here to make friends. Come over to lay some skinny on you that I picked up off the vine: they got a contract out on you, I hear. They say the hit man's already in the Jam."

"I don't go in for rumors," the jigaboo said, awful fucking tough for an old nigger like that, with gray hair already sprouting out on his sideburns.

"Look, man!" Wasco said, real sincere, "I wanna propose a truce. I won't fuck with your militant number if you don't fuck with my dope number. It's that simple. *Détente,* like you read in the papers. Dig it?"

"I'll tell you what," the nigger said, real calm and deliberate, deliberately not getting irked by Wasco's insolence. "I'm not going to have anything to do with you," he said in a deep resounding voice, the kind that white actors always try to get when they do a black man, like Sir Laurence Olivier in the movie *Othello,* but real educated and smooth, real clear, like some kind of CIA agent or 4-O whiteman or something. "I'm an extremist," the nigger continued, "that means I've earned myself a certain amount of freedom of choice. It's wild, you ought to try it sometime. It's really liberating. When your back's up against the wall and you're fighting for your life, you suddenly discover that you don't have to compromise anymore. Everything's cut and dry."

And Wasco retorted quickly, "Shit, man, I *been* there, all my life. I been alone, fighting for my life, fighting the whole rest of the world, with my back against the wall."

"But I'm not alone," the nigger said, "that's where we're different. I used to be like you, in a lot of ways.

Now it's not just me I'm looking out for, like an animal just looking out for itself. My life doesn't mean so much anymore. It's my Brothers that count, my whole nation. When you don't have to worry about yourself anymore, only about your Brothers, it liberates you. Look man! Think of all the little men who spend their whole miserable small lives squatting over their pathetic little nickels and dimes, wasting all their time husbanding it, guarding it, squandering their freedom of action for the sake of money. They're slaves. So are you. And I've got no sympathy for slaves, even black ones. My sympathy is given only to the dude who breaks his bonds and fights back at the Pig. And you ain't fighting back. You're just the Man in a different guise, that's all."

"You know what, nigger . . ." Wasco began, and Galliot, who'd probably been expecting something like this, threw a metal soap container at Wasco through the bars. But it hit the bars and bounced back into the cell, breaking into two pieces, THWACK! spraying them both with soapy water.

"Get out of here, Honkey, or I'll strangle you on the bars!" the nigger hissed between his yellow nigger teeth, pissed off that he'd missed.

But old Wasco, he never flinched or faltered, Hitler's Little Helper, he just laughed at the brown man and swaggered away down the tier, wiggling his ass.

Never let a spook know that he's scared you. Otherwise, just like with a spooky horse, you'll never get the motherfucker under control again.

Down in the guard's shanty everyone was listening to the radio. Wasco felt kind of frisky so he said, "Hello, sweetmeat, howya doin'?" to Little Arv as soon as he walked in the door.

Arv just ignored him, so Wasco sat down on the wooden pass counter and said, "Come on, Arvie, why don't you come over here and sit with me, huh?"

"I don't want to!" Arv said, his voice cracking, like Wasco'd planned it to do, making Arv say it coy like a girl who was afraid to sit down with a great big pricky smelly man.

"Say, come on, man! Pleeeeesie! Come on over and sit down with me, cuz, I got a few private little matters I

want to talk over with you . . . wanna . . . har har har
. . . wanna get somethin' straight between you and me
. . . har har har!"

"You got nothing to say to me."

"Oh no? You'd be surprised, little buddy!"

"I don't want to hear it."

"What's wrong, pussycat? You shy? Aw, come on! You
scared of your old cuz? A great big prison bull like you?
Now you just come right on over and sit down next here
to Ma," Wasco said, patting the counter next to him,
camping it, wriggling his big heavily muscled buttocks.

Big Arv and the squeeze got to snickering at Arv. Fast-
Walking looked sympathetic, but didn't say anything.
They all had one thing in common, as far as old Wasco
was concerned: they all figured Wasco had him running
again, just like he always used to. He used to get Arv
going sometimes so bad that the tears would come into his
eyes. It seemed like he never knew what to say back to
Wasco. But . . . really! What could you say when a
grown man asked you to sit down on his lap? If you did,
you were gay. If you didn't, you were chicken. That's how
Wasco'd designed their little game, years ago.

"Come on, sweetiepie, sit over here with me and let me
babble sweet nothings in your ear."

"Shut up! Leave me alone!" Arv said, tortured again,
just like he used to be.

"Well, honeylumps, if you're gonna be so shy about it
. . ." Wasco said, and left him alone for a minute. He
turned to Big Arv, who sat there with a great big stupid
lumbering grin on his face.

"Hey Unckus, you seen my ma lately? How's she
doin'?"

"Oh, she's doing alright," Big Arv said, a bit cautiously,
now that it was his turn.

"Oh yeah?"

"Sure, her store's doing a good little business and . . ."

". . . And . . . yeah! I know about that other, them
hookers, that's your end, ain't it, Unck?"

"Now, Wasco, I wisht you wouldn't talk about that
around here, private business and all, you . . ."

"Oh sure, Unck, anything you say! Won't let it happen
again! Say, what do you make of this here Galliot thing,
huh?"

"I think he's a fucking goner," Big Arv said, with obvious relief that the subject had been changed.

"Oh yeah? Why's that?"

"I hear there's a contract out on him."

"Wow! I wonder who the hit man could be . . ." Wasco said, leading them on, leading it out, letting the air clear for a moment with the idea, the perfectly logical and plausible idea that Wasco *might*, just might, be the hitsy boy . . . letting them sift it through their dense fucking sifters for a minute, sift the considerable extent of Wasco's power in the Joint, and in the State, let them, in other words, speculate on whether or not Wasco was in charge now, in this here fucking cellblock, with the entire majesty of the State behind him, and the entire sentiment of the populace of that State, who'd very recently voted the death penalty back into being . . . with just specifically this here particular wise-ass uppity dangerous Communist nigger in mind, this last fucking radical militant bomb-throwing killer of all . . . let them dumb prison hacks rattle that notion around in their empty gourds for a moment. And then Wasco took it by brute force, took by audacity what he'd only had to hint he might have . . .

"Big Arv," Wasco said, full of meaning, "I want you to step out here for a sec. We got some business to discuss . . ."

And Wasco led the Sarge out on the floor and held him at rigid attention while he delivered to him his strict orders of the day.

Twenty-Four

Arv went down the tier clicking his counter . . . fifty-six, fifty-seven, fifty-eight, fifty-nine . . . making his First Count. The last man down at the end of the tier turned out to be Galliot, ensconced in his brand new cell. An empty cell stood gaping on either side of him. Arv paused, looked in, and smiled, saying nothing. Galliot seemed puzzled for a moment, looking around from where he was one-finger tapping at his typewriter. And then, remembering Arv's face, understanding, he smiled back. He had a nice smile, the smile of a nice middle-aged black professor. Arv put his finger to his lip, reached into his pocket, and handed him the letter that Elaine had given him that morning at City College. Galliot smiled, crinkling up the corners of his eyes good-humoredly, shaking his head and raising his thick curly black brows as if to say, "Hey! Don't know why you're doing this for me, but thanks!" Arv flipped him the V sign and started off down the tier. Galliot stopped him with a hiss, waved an envelop, and smiled again, asking silently if he'd take a letter out that night. Arv thought a moment and then nodded yes.

Continuing down the tier on his rounds . . . sixty, sixty-one, sixty-two . . . Arv felt good. Felt like he was on his way . . .

Down in the guard shanty Big Arv and Boa and Little Arv waited for Fast-Walking to recount.

Big Arv cursed, "That sonofabitch never could count straight. We're gonna be the last block done. Now, I don't appreciate that kind of black eye."

Finally Fast-Walking came sliding and breezing back down taking three steps at a time coming fast down the spiral staircase but looking like slow, without a sound, like a long-legged ghost floating off the tiers. "Okay, okay, try this one," he said skeptically, as if he still wasn't sure it was a good count, "eighty-six on the third."

Big Arv phoned the count into Control.

"Good count!" he repeated after the Control man, and everyone relaxed and waited for the All Clear.

HONK! HONK! HONK! It went off immediately, indicating that they'd been the last block to phone in the count. "Goddamn stupid fucking incompetents!" Big Arv yelled, ranting at all of them but meaning only Fast-Walking, "you really wanna gimme a black eye around here, don't ya? Huh? Don't ya?"

Little Arv and Fast-Walking went up and let the tier men out. Wasco came down into the shanty after a few minutes and started giving Arv a whole lot of shit, barbing at him, teasing, trying to embarrass him and make him uptight and scared, just like he always did. Arv, with a clinched hating heart, realized the cocksucking queen could still do it. Could still do it! But he'd get his, some-day, the bastard. Just like Arv had sworn he would, when he was still a little kid, out on the Joint's football field. He'd get him back! Hated the motherfucker worse than anything in the world . . . *And silently I challenged him to the death.* . . .

Then Arv and Fast-Walking had to run up with the tier men and get into position to open the cells when the din-ner whistle went off.

TOOT! TOOT! TOOT! Chow time! Wasco went down the line unlocking cells. CHANG! CHANG! CHANG! When he got to the end and started down to the fourth tier, Arv waited for his father's yell, "Fifth tier, *chow* time!" and then he heaved back with all his might on the lock bar. It wouldn't come. He heaved again, straining his back. It was so hard! Yet Wasco did it without even hardly trying. Heeeeeeeave! It came finally CLANG! WHOMF! . . . hitting Arv in the breadbasket, knocking the wind out of him. It clanged open and eighty-six ugly convicts stepped out of their cells and headed quickstep for chow, hungry-eyed, shaky, bellies rumbling with disturbing dreams of T-bones and top sirloins. BAM! They slammed the cell doors in unison, yelling up and down the tiers to friends:

"Hey, Pinky! Sit with me!"

"Table sixty-two, near the trays!"

"Meet me before the movie, Harv!"

"I'm gonna get you in the yard, Punk!"

Arv let the bar slide back, ZING! Locked the mechanism and followed Wasco down to the fourth tier. CHANG! CHANG! CHANG! Wasco went along unlocking cell doors. When he reached the last one Arv pulled the bar. WHAM! It came easier this time. He locked up and headed down the spiral metal staircase to the guard shanty again. On the way down, surrounded by quickly moving shouting laughing cons, right in the middle, Wasco punched Arv on the shoulder and said, "Hey, baby! We work pretty good together, huh?"

What could Arv do but just smile and wanly nod his head? Wasco was perfectly capable of pushing him down the stairs, humiliating him in front of the other cons. And none of them would ever snitch. And if they did, well Big Arv would just laugh. So Arv had to let his convict cousin's unseemly familiarity pass.

After everyone went off to chow, Arv and Fast-Walking locked Big Arv into the block according to regulations and followed the convicts out to the Yard chow lineup to supervise movement. Up above them on the rain shed gunwalk a lonely guard paced up and down, Winchester in hand, making sure nobody crowded in.

"Sure glad I ain't up there no more," Fast-Walking said to no one in particular.

"Worst job in the Joint," Arv said, almost wishing he were up there again, as he'd been a few months ago. Anything to get away from Wasco's ribbing!

Fast-Walking and Arv stood out in the Yard for thirty-five minutes exactly, keeping the line straight, making sure there were no fights, no gambling, no soliciting, no drug vending. Actually, they more or less let the line take care of itself, bullshitting about one thing and another, once in a while shouting a perfunctory "Get back in line!" or a "Quit the roughhousing, goddamnit!" Every time they yelled the sea gulls and pigeons in the Yard would fly up all in a swarm, whirring around, sometimes almost hitting people when they wheeled down low, dropping pellets, splatting on denim jackets and khaki too, and then settling back down on the wall.

When the East Block finished eating, Fast-Walking and Arv escorted the inmates back across the Yard, performing a symbolic shakedown at the door (pat on the ribs, pat on the thighs; guards hated getting up into the nasty sweaty genital area, it made their hands sticky), and let the fifteen hundred men back into their cells.

WHAM! WHAM! WHAM! They went pounding up the metal stairs, and got locked up again. The crash of metal doors again. The sound of steel sliding on steel. Loud masculine shouts. Queeny calls.

"Goddamn!"

"Oh, you silly fellahs!"

"Fuck!"

"Pinchibato, cabrón!"

Prison routine. When Arv got into it, going up and down the tiers, running full blast, locking, unlocking, counting, opening up for night school, TV time, movie time, club night, shower time, each unlock and lockup a separate and complicated maneuver, requiring a five-story running climb, the sheer physical effort of it put his mind to sleep, gave him the peace that labor brings, made the hours pass. That's why most guards preferred working the cellblocks to tower duty. Time never dragged among the convicts. There was action, the possibility of surprises, of danger (no telling when one of the cons would take it into his head to throw you off the fifth tier, splattering you on the concrete like a squished bug). But the danger, Arv and most of the guards figured, was a risk they were perfectly willing to take. Anything rather than that horrible eight hours trapped up in that tiny tower above the empty yard. Up in the tower there was no one but yourself. And that got stale fast.

At shower time Arv stood alone up on the third tier and supervised inmate bathing. He let out half a tier at a time and they went down and crawled in, forty-five at a time, under the six showers in the rancid peeling shower area, and Arv turned the water on. The cons stayed in as long as possible, standing up in their Jap thongs trying to avoid the live athlete's foot that crawled in the filthy water, scrubbing themselves three and four times over, trying to get that prison grit off, the black evil stink that got into your pores and stayed there, the stench of guilt. Just like Arv did when he went home, the convicts scrubbed and scrubbed, endeavoring with all their might to wipe away that filth, their pasts, their indefinable sep-

arate and collective guilt. Arv understood their impulse
to stay in the shower very well. He spent hours under
his shower at home, ran the hot water out every night,
and yet never felt like he truly got the dirt of the Joint
out of his pores, out of his ears and nose and hair. He
felt like he'd smelled like Joint all his life, longer than
all these fucking cons he watched now. By God, he had!
He'd spent much more time in here than ninety-nine per
cent of these dudes before him, much more! The thought
made him physically ill. Think of it! *How many years
have I been locked up? How many? Every year of my
life!*

When the black tier's turn came Arv watched Galliot
real close. He went down and showered quickly and then
he clambered up the stairs to talk with Arv. There was
still a lot of life in old Galliot, even if he was already in
his forties. He took those stairs three at a time and wasn't
even breathing hard. Nobody down in the shower paid
much attention to Arv and Galliot. It didn't look suspicious. There was always some convict up there bullshitting
with the hack, trying to get something out of him, some
extra privilege, some extra favor, even a cigarette. Nobody even looked twice.

Arv checked the surrounding cells. No one was around.
They were alone above the steaming shower area. It was
hard for the bathers even to see them through the vapor.
Galliot came bopping along the walkway fast.

"How's your sparrow coming along?" Arv asked.

"Fine. He'll be ready to set free soon. I just wanted to
thank you," the black man said, in his well-modulated, educated white man's voice, the voice of a man who reads
and writes more than he talks.

"Nothing to it," Arv said, a little bit proud, a little bit
awed to be in the presence of this well-known personality,
a bit dazzled by this man with a worldwide reputation, a
man he'd seen on TV news reports for years.

"I can't figure out why you'd do it . . ." Galliot said,
puzzled.

"How about . . . money . . . for openers," Arv said,
affecting a toughness he didn't feel.

"Sure, but . . . your career . . ."

Arv laughed. "My what? You think I look like a career
Pig, do you?" he said, dangling the possibility that he was

perhaps a paid spy, or an undercover agent for the underground, or something equally exotic and romantic.

"No, but, well, I've got to admit I had no idea people like you worked in the Joint," Galliot said, accepting the cigarette that Arv offered, leaning up against the tier railing, one foot on the first bar, cupping his hands when Arv lit it up.

"Well, what did you think? That we were all fat middle-aged sadists?" Arv said, finding himself speaking rougher than he really wanted. "You must be reading too much of your own propaganda. The average guard in here, if you didn't know, is just about like me: young, with a little college behind him, a wife and one or two kids. Shit! The swing shift is thirty per cent college students working nights and going to school in the daytime! Personally, I'm a student at City College. I think you know one of my teachers there . . . Elaine Mourutsos. . . ."

"Oh," Galliot said, noncommittal, frowning a little, realizing that Arv knew the origin of the letters he received. But then he went on with the conversation as if that didn't matter. "No, I haven't been deceived about the Pigs in here," he said, calmly still, but you could see his eyes narrowing, "I know the statistics. But you could say the same thing about the U.S. Air Force that Nixon's put back to work in Vietnam again. They even smoke dope in there, all those college boys flying Phantoms—drop LSD, and bomb defenseless yellow people to death."

"Look," Arv said, gesturing with his cigarette, saying things he wasn't sure of, but saying them as if he were very sure. The important thing to him at the moment, with this formidable presence before him, was to impress him with his flow of words, with his command of the Rap, and the Rap comes easier very often if you disagree. "Look, you can't make everything black and white like that. I was over in the Nam. And I'm no fucking sadistic killer. I was just there, because I wasn't rich enough or smart enough to buy my way out. I just got trapped, like I got trapped in here. You gotta see that a lotta cops," Arv said, warming to his subject, believing in what he said more and more with every flowing word, "a lotta cops are human too, and honest and generous and kind. You can't condemn all of them as merely 'Pigs.' When you call a man an animal, when you deny him humanity," Arv continued, forgetting that only moments before he had bristled when Galliot mistook him for a career Pig, "you absolve him of responsibility for his actions. It's the wrong strategy, if you ask me. Maybe if you treated the Pigs more like humans, they'd respond to you in a more humane way."

"Bullshit!" Galliot exploded. "Ninety-nine per cent of you motherfuckers deserve the appellation 'Pig.' You *are* Pigs. You don't belong to the human race. If I told you what you nice white boys did to me down at Brown Max . . ."

When Galliot got pissed off he bounced on the balls of his feet. He had extraordinarily shaped feet, a ballet dancer's feet. . . .

"But, did you ever consider how a guard feels," Arv said, getting carried away with his own rhetoric, his rap, sure of himself now, now that he sensed that Galliot wasn't capable of killing him, "did you? Did you ever mull it over? Ever consider how guards feel? Locked up in here with four thousand bloodthirsty convicts? Taught by their leaders that they'll be murdered the first time they're careless? Look, I'm helping you out, but you know what? I wish you'd learn a little something about tolerance, man. It's people with your kind of unbending hatred for the opposite side that's the cause of all our troubles in this country. Why not try understanding the other side? You're a reading man! Think of the humanity of Thucydides," Arv said, repeating almost verbatim a sentence he'd heard his Humanities II teacher recount, "when he praised the virtues of the opposite side in battle; think of how civilized that is! Modern man has split up into camps. Americans are all polarized, man. We got to avoid that, or we'll all end up iced!"

"You can't be fucking serious!" Galliot said, getting pissed off now, springing from the tier railing. " 'Understand,' you say! Understand what? We understand already, man, too well . . . that you want to kill us! That's what we understand. I don't know why you're helping us out, man! With that kind of mentality. I really don't. Unless you jiving! You shucking us, man, or what? Maybe you ain't," Galliot said, speaking ungrammatically for emphasis and flavor, but letting you know it was a rhetorical device, saying it like it was in quotes, "but if you think you doing it to help, then let me lay this one on you: we sick and tired of trying to understand Chuck! We had four hundred years of patience, waiting out back, trying to understand the beast. And we done, peckerwood, we finished! You dig? We sick. Now we gon' ask no quarter. We gon' declare a moratorium on giving and receiving or accepting or understanding, in regard to the white man . . ."

"I really want you to understand my point of view," Arv said conciliatorily, "to me, you're just not being rational. Don't you see? The Main Cop's got the power; you want the power. Frontal assault, man, is not the way to attain it. You're going to have to devise a hell of a lot more subtle methods than that. Look," Arv said, employing Galliot's rhetorical device with vigor, as if it were his own, "ain't you guys sick of dying yet? They've just about blown you all off. You're just about the last one left, ain't you? Why not kiss a little bit of ass and lie and tell them you love them and get out of the Joint quick and . . ."

"You're a nice kid," Galliot said, "but you know what? I tell you, you're naïve, man. And naïveté of your kind is dangerous. You better watch out for yourself."

"What's that mean?" Arv asked pugnaciously.

"Just what I said."

"Is that some kind of threat, or something?"

"Play it like you find it," Galliot said, spinning and starting for his cell.

And Galliot's golf term, though uttered in defiance, reminded Arv of their one single tie in experience. "You know what?" Arv asked, asking the perennial meaningless question that prefaced every statement in the Joint.

"No, what?" Galliot responded per ritual, spinning back, on his guard, with all the cons in the shower staring up at their exchange, unable to hear them over the sound of the high pressure hot water, but picking up their heavy vibes . . .

"You must've been a caddy too," Arv said, breaking into a grin, "when you were a kid, just like me."

Galliot smiled too, finally. His face muscles relaxed and he rewarded Arv with a wide yellow-toothed grin. It was, after all, a kind of little bond between them, small and tenuous as it might have been: it was their only link. Absolutely their only one.

"But, you're too much!" Arv went on, still smiling, and with real confidence, "you've got an arrogance that's gonna lose you some friends. I think it's kind of dumb to bite the hand that feeds you," Arv said, and hastened to add, when he saw Galliot's face fall, "seems to me it might be smarter to kiss it while trying to sneak around in back and get at the food's source."

Arv judged that Galliot would respond violently to this statement, but that the violence would be only vocal. He judged that Galliot was, after all, just what he said he was, a rational man, up against the wall, fighting for his life. This certitude did not, however, dispose Arv to make peace, at least not for the moment. On the contrary, it made him want to test the black man even more, take him as far as he'd go. After all, he couldn't do much to Arv, and he owed him a favor. And Arv was a ball-passing man. He liked to throw the ball real sharp and see if the other dude could catch it with as much style as him and then whip it back at him with a style of his own. It was good to rap, to toss the ball back and forth, with a famous dude, a celebrated personality, like this one, this black man. Arv had known very few black men in his life. Only one, as a matter of fact, only the guard Muffin, who was now in the Joint too, playing basketball down at Brown Max.

"Let me tell *you!* White boy!" Galliot raged, striding back up to Arv, but a tiny bit theatrical now, getting into what Arv was into, realizing that at least some of Arv's rap was theater. And one thing you learn in the Joint fast: life is theater. Life is killing time, playing roles, and it oftentimes doesn't matter which. Arv had the feeling that if they'd been locked up in a cell together, they might have even switched roles, Arv playing the nigger, Galliot the Pig, and had a lot of fun. Galliot dug this notion now, it looked like, it showed on his dark face, there was irony written there now. After all, they both knew the rules of the Joint. They both knew the main rule: THERE AIN'T NO RULES.

"I had enough feeding at the hands of Peckerwood!" Galliot said. "I think it's about time I fed that motherfucker a little something, about time I stuffed something up his beehine for a change!"

"I'm disappointed in you," Arv said, when in truth he wasn't at all, was highly impressed by Galliot's quick pickup of the game. "I expected you to be a more rational leader, to tell the truth." Arv was actually betraying a slight crooked little smile; it just cracked the corner of his mouth. Galliot picked up on it.

"Rational?" he loudly demanded. "My old man down in California, he rational! Kissin' the whiteman's ass fo' seventy years and dyin' like a black eunuch! Only way Chuck gon' let go is through the fear of the black irrational bangin' at his fuckin' do'!"

"That's where I think you're really mistaken," Arv said. "You start banging like mad on a dude's door in the middle of the night, shouting violent gibberish, and his first impulse is to fight you to the end. He's certainly not going to hand over his home to what he considers to be the forces of darkness."

Galliot burst out laughing. He slapped his knee, bent over, cracked up on the metal walkway of the tier. And Arv, who had perhaps acquired an ideological enemy, felt that he'd acquired a "soul brother" at the same time.

"Aw, sheeeeeeit!" Galliot ranted. "You make me laugh, man! I mean, like, no offense, but I never expect this kind of argument from no turncoat guard," he said, watching Arv's eyes blink with traitorous guilt. "What motivate you, anyway?" Galliot asked, in the tone of voice with which you ask someone how old he is. "That the only thing I can't figure out. I think you an old-fashioned idealist, man. Either that or some kind of clever-ass opportunist. But I tell you somethin'. You surround a guy's house in the middle of the darkest night with a hundred howlin' dancin' black dervishes carryin' burnin' firebrands, and you tell the motherfucker, you tell him, 'Gimme my money! Gimme freedon from yo corrupt rule, or I'm gon burn yo house down!' . . . Well, he just naturally gon throw in the fuckin' towel. Cause he like you, man. He rational and white. And what more reasonable? Relinquishin' a few privileges, or gettin' yo house burnt down?"

"You're wrong," Arv said, sincere for once, seeing the error, sincerely believing Galliot was either in error . . . or . . . had Arv detected a note of conscious falsehood in Galliot's voice? . . . Could it be that Galliot had made these stupid inflammatory statements for reasons of policy rather than conviction? Was this the new line he was now laying down for his cadres? Or had he simply got caught up in their rap too, like Arv, and didn't really mean it at all? Arv didn't know. All he knew was that, for whatever reason, Galliot was truly in error. "You're wrong," he said again. But Galliot, you could see, he couldn't tell for the first time, couldn't tell where Arv was at exactly, where the theater went, what was the meaning of their confrontation, their quintessentially American rap. "You're wrong," Arv honestly repeated once more, "goddamnit you're wrong if you think the white man is that kind of rational. He's got a thing about home and hearth, and all that bullshit. Surely you know that, for Christ's sake! He won't be threatened in that regard, I can tell you that!"

"You're the one who's wrong," Galliot said, trying to be as sincere as Arv, switching back out of the dialect as if he were attempting to underline that sincerity. And then he laughed . . . "Well, sheeeeit!" He laughed long and loud, showing his teeth, showing his sense of true irony. The darker blacker wrinkles of experience under his eyes crinkled up in a most attractive way while he laughed. "Now, look! I'm right," he said, "but this won't get us anywhere. And I recognize you as a man of good will. And so I'll therefore modify my opinion about the solid monolithic structure and nature of Pigdom to allow for one single small state prison Pig who goes to college, and has ideas and, at considerable risk, does me a great favor, a favor that may end up saving my life. How's that?" he asked, smiling real friendly, sticking out his hand, exactly as if he'd secretly taken Arv's earnest advice about toadying up to the Pig. Arv half expected him to kiss his hand. But he smiled back, and they shook. They'd both enjoyed the exchange, though neither was exactly sure of its meaning. *But,* Arv reflected, *is anyone ever sure of any exchange?*

Arv remembered suddenly the time he spent a whole late evening practicing his college French with a Québecois child molester in the West Block.

Starting to turn back to his work, his area of responsibility, figuring those fucking cons in the shower might be killing or buggering each other by now, Arv paused a last second. He wanted to say something, he wanted to convey something—he said what came right off the top of his head, he said, "You're a good writer."

"Why, thank you!"

"Yeah, you're honest and you got guts."

"Oh, yeah?"

"I'm a writer too. I mean, I'm trying to be a writer. I admire your sincerity."

"You do?"

"Yes, I believe in sincerity."

"Well, so do I!" Galliot said, "so do I! Say! Bring some of your stuff around some time on the night shift. I'll have a look at it. Maybe we can criticize each other's work. There're so few good critics in the Joint!"

"There ain't *any!*" Arv said, guffawing. "If there was anybody capable of any degree of critical objectivity—con or bull—he wouldn't be in the Joint!"

"I disagree with you entirely," Galliot said, "but we'll fight about that another time. . . . Listen," he said, bending close to Arvin on the tier, cupping his hand, whispering low, "you still going to take that letter for me?"

"Sure."

"Good! I'll have it ready for you after the Last Count. Please convey it direct to the party it's addressed to, and no one else. It's vitally important. Almost, you might say, a matter of life and death, okay?"

"It's done!" said Arv, turning back to his work finally, swelled with pleasure, and a sense of destiny. Here was a published writer of two blockbusting books, an intellectual, revolutionary, theorist, activist, militant and charismatic leader of his people, who actually deigned to have truck with a poor prison hack like Little Arvin Weed. . . .

Twenty-Five

Fast-Walking sat in a folding chair on the second tier, leaning on the guard rail, a Chesterfield stuck in the corner of his mouth, surreptitiously clipping news items out of today's paper. Ostensibly he was supervising TV time. The Tuesday night fights were on and, since the fighters were both black, there wasn't much trouble. Blacks, whites and Mexicans chose their boxers tonight on merit rather than race, and were now yelling away happily, cheering them on: "Get him, Harmon!" "Kill him, Blackey!" socking at their open palms, "Knock that motherfucker out!" jumping up and down on their folding chairs. On nights when there was an interracial fight they had to call the gunman to stand up on the inside gunwalk brandishing a sawed-off shotgun to keep them from killing each other.

Tonight was heaven in comparison. Fast-Walking barely heard the inmates cheering, and busily snip-snip-snipped at the newspaper, thinking about his lovely French wife, Marie-Claude. Tomorrow he was going to pay a call on her, tell her he had his salary disattached now, and the loan was gonna be paid off too. They were once more financially solvent. He'd tell her he'd won the money gambling, but that he'd never gamble again, as long as he lived. He'd tell her he loved her. Did he? Yes! More than anything in the world! Needed her so much that everything else in the world paled in comparison. He'd have done anything for her, would have . . . Fast-Walking paused for a moment in his reverie, put the newspaper down, stuck the scissors in his back pocket. He'd heard something behind him . . . steps . . . barefoot, creeping along the tier . . . he turned around fast! Nothing. What had it been? He got up, searched the tier. Nothing. *Must be your imagination. With this dope deal and all, you're getting all het up over nothing. Shit! Don't worry, baby, who would dare harm you with the protection you got?*

. . . Fast-Walking started thinking about Marie-Claude again. What would he do for her? He'd do anything. Anything! He'd beg, borrow, steal, even . . . murder, to get her back, her and the kids. He really would. Therefore, this little muleback courier work he was doing, piddly-ass dope stuff for a few weeks, bothered him not at all. If that was what he had to do to get back into her graces, back into her safe home, then so be it! And he already had an ideal alibi figured out in case they caught him . . . creep creep creep. He heard something behind him again. Looked around. Nothing. Easy, man. Easy down, now, big fellah . . . His alibi was . . . in case somebody accidentally caught him holding, and the chances were extremely remote . . . he would say that someone switched Thermoses on him on the Outside. He could prove that his Thermos was blue. This one was red. All his friends knew that. Anyway, they weren't going to catch him. No way. Wasco, it was clear, had the most powerful protection in the Joint, in the entire State of New Sonora, probably, certainly extending through and beyond Fast-Walking's own father the Warden. . . .

And what would him and Marie-Claude and the kids do when they got it together? They'd take the money and buy a self-sustaining place of their own, maybe up in southeastern Oregon, maybe in Idaho, somewhere a long fucking way from this here pine oil-smelling, piss-smelling, horrible, ugly . . . He heard it again! A sound . . . creep creep creep . . . twisted in his chair above the TV area floor . . . Nothing. He rose . . . creep creep . . . again . . .

AAAAAAAAAAAAAAAAAAAAH! A body hurtled through the air and passed not a foot from Fast-Walking's head, landed SCHPLAAAAAT! on the TV area floor. The fights on TV kept going. You could hear the announcer calling the punches . . . "A right to the jaw, a left jab to the stomach, right cross, solid left hook to the solar plexus . . ." Nobody said a word. Someone turned off the TV. The Sarge came running down the concrete floor from the guard shanty.

"What's going on here?" he yelled.

Fast-Walking had trouble reacting. He didn't feel anything. It was a guy down there splattered over the cement, blood sprayed over the concrete, splashed on the backs of foldup chairs, blood coming out of his mouth, and Fast-Walking couldn't feel anything. He just sat there leaning over the railing, staring, staring, just like all the convicts.

Big Arv came up and said, "Who is it?" to the crowd at large. Someone said, "Bullet."

"Who?"

"A dude named Bullet."

"Come on, goddamnit, what's his real name?"

"He's got a real weirdo name . . . Polack," someone said.

"Yeah? Well what the fuck is it?"

"I think it's something like . . . like . . . Roman Paskiewicsz . . . or something like that."

"Alright. Fast-Walking!"

"Yeah, Sarge!"

"Get off your ass and run down and ring the lockup bell!"

"Right!"

Fast-Walking, delighted to have something to do, ran down the tier as fast as he could to the end. All the way down he could hear someone above him, someone light on his feet, on the fourth tier, two tiers up, running along with him. But he had no desire to investigate . . . he's the murderer . . . He had no desire to know his name. He glided down the spiral staircase without touching, like a wraith, and reached the telephone in the guard's shanty just as Little Arv and Wasco did.

"What happened?"

"Somebody got thrown off the fourth tier."

"Jesus!"

"Hello, Control? There's been a homicide in the East Block. Send the ambulance and the lieutenant, please!" Fast-Walking yelled into the receiver. Then he hung up, and pressed the lockup buzzer . . . BLAP BLAP BLAP BLAP! All the cons, for once happy to get off the TV floor, rushed up the stairs to their cells, happy to leave that poor man, that Bullet, where he lay snuffed and squished on the pavement. Arv, Wasco, Hearne and Fast-Walking followed the cons on the double, locking them in quickly and efficiently, with the convicts' heartfelt cooperation.

Last ones in were Wasco and Hearne. Just as Fast-Walking clicked the lock to their cell, Wasco caught his eye
and said, "Too bad about old Bullet, ain't it?" and a tendril of anxiety, vague, uncertain, ran through Fast-Walking's tired body before he shut them in . . . *a tendril, like
a beanshoot*, before Fast-Walking decided to get rid of the
notion, to disappear it, as something not to be mulled, not
to be worried, not to be belabored, something to bury and
forget forever. Which, hurrying down the iron staircase
to let the lieutenant in, is exactly what the prudent officer
did, he forgot it.

BLAM BLAM BLAM! The loot wanted in the steel door.

Fast-Walking opened.

"What the fuck's going on in here?" said the bald-
headed old lieutenant, Lieutenant Marty Boudin, who'd
been on the swing shift for thirty years, and got mad at
everything, everything equally. An untidy cellblock floor
pissed him off as much as a knifing or a rape—sometimes
even more, depending on his mood.

"A murder!" Fast-Walking exclaimed.

"Oh! I thought we had an escape!" the lieutenant said,
with genuine relief registering in his foghorn voice.
"Racial?" he then inquired, with worry furrows starting up
on his pasty white forehead.

"I dunno."

Big Arv came up. "Yeah, it's racial, alright."

"Yeah?" the loot said. "How do you know?"

"How about this, for a starter?" Big Arv said, relishing
the suspense while he searched through the pockets of his
Ike jacket. He brought out a rough note written on a dirty
Kleenex. It was scrawled out in an awkward childlike
script. All three men, and Arv too, when he joined them,
read it over the loot's shoulder; read it over and over for
five minutes as if it'd been a lengthy epistle of philosophical or theological exegesis:

DIE FUCKING HONKEY

Twenty-Six

Dear Elaine:

This letter, I have every faith, will be conveyed to you direct. No other eyes will see it.

I've taken my time deciding about our courier, testing him out, and now I'm happy to report that in my opinion he's okay, and won't betray us. Tonight, when I spoke to him, and determined that he was honest and trustworthy, I relaxed for the first time in weeks. "Now," I thought, "now I've finally got a fighting chance, now I can let poor Elaine know the truth, ease her mind. Now, goddamnit," I thought, breathing a sigh of profound relief, "we can go ahead with our plan!"

I have hesitated till this very minute to reveal to you that there is a plan for my self-liberation from this concentration camp, a good one, an excellent . . . almost foolproof plan. And, let me hasten to tell you that, in view of the current extremely perilous situation here in the Joint, I would have to make an attempt at self-liberation *no matter what*. My life is in immediate danger of extinction. The hit man is definitely now within the walls, in this very cellblock. I even have a very good hunch as to his exact identity, though in the byzantine complexity of this prison world, this labyrinth, one can never be sure about anything.

The salient point is quite clear, however: there is a conspiracy, involving prisoners, guards, prison officials, and state authorities at the very highest level, to murder me as soon as safely practicable.

From closely examining the tactics of the enemy to this date, I and my friends and advisers within the Joint have arrived at a fairly educated guess as to exactly how the fascist oppressor plans to achieve his

aims. Within these walls, one's options are greatly
limited, so limited, in truth, that it was an advantage
to us in this case. Here is the Pig's probable outline
for my destruction, from past through present to future:

1. High state officials *recruit killer*
2. *place him* within striking range
3. create through *agents provocateurs* a state of
   racial conflict in order to:
   a. alienate white *public opinion*
   b. stir up dormant *racial hatred*
   c. *hide the act* of murder in the melee
   d. make the *cover-up* easier
4. commit act of *murder*
5. *conceal true identity* of murderer, through:
   a. *hiding it* in larger context of prison riot and
      racial violence
   b. making murder seem like *accident,* a result
      of:
      1. *self-defense,* or:
      2. ordinary prison *argument,* or:
      3. *anonymous* result of general battle

This, it seems quite safe to say, is broadly the Pig's
strategy. This is his plan of attack. From the way
things have been escalating around here . . .

You will find this difficult to believe. I've just left
off writing for an hour. As I sat here writing these
words to you a white man was thrown off the fourth
tier. He died instantly. These words were written on
a note pinned to his shirt: DIE FUCKING HON-
KEY. I, who am in *the* position to know, can assure
you that *no black man* has done this deed. We can
therefore deduce that phase number three of the Pig's
plot is now in operation. Need I explain more in regard to our desperate necessity for speedy defensive
action? Need I justify the terrible risk I take in conveying the following *exact details* of our self-liberation plan to you by hand? I have no other choice, as
you will readily perceive. If I do send this to you
there is a chance, however slim, that I will be betrayed. If I don't send it, I'll be dead in a matter of a

very few days. There is almost *no time* to act.

Therefore, with love and fervent hopes for ultimate success in our endeavor, here is our plan,
which, I needn't remind you, must be burnt immediately after its first reading:

1. We are in possession of an official Commission
of Corrections guard's uniform. It is hand made by
prison tailors and, though not exact in all its details,
might pass a slack muster.

2. There is a black man employed as a guard here
who looks something like me. That is to say, since
Officer Jackson is black, approximately my size,
weight, and color, and has a skull shape of the
roundish rather than the elongated negroid type, the
proverbial Honkey inability to tell one nigger from
another renders us effectively doubles. At least, this is
the hopeful assumption all our plans rest upon. Other
details of Officer Jackson's appearance, like the fact
that he wears longer sideburns and a slim moustache,
can be readily duplicated in here with the aid of our
prison disguise experts. We even possess forged
documents proving that I am he, i.e., driver's license,
social security card, C of C badge, etc. Enough said
about the credibility of the disguise. Suffice it to say
that we are pretty confident it'll get by. The brothers
in here have been beautiful. They had this all set up
even before I *arrived!*

3. Officer Jackson works the day shift as Honor
Block officer. He's a most ambitious and diligent little
Pig Lackey, this house nigger, and every day spends
from twenty minutes to a half hour helping the dull
white Swing Shift man do his paper work. On a day
very soon the day shift Control officer will receive an
urgent phone call. *You will make this call.* A city
woman doctor will demand that Officer Jackson be
released from his duties early to rush off to the hospital. His wife is lying there in critical condition after
having been struck by a bus at the corner of Division
and Mercado streets in the city. The Control man
will send the reserve man over to take Jackson's
place and convey the tragic news.

4. The moment the reserve man passes through
the yard and into the Honor Block, a crowd of un-

ruly black inmates will collect around the doorway. A second later, they will suddenly break up their circle, prodded by Officer Jackson, who is apparently in such a hurry that he's come out through the Honor Block gate at the same moment that the reserve man has gone in. The wall post gunmen, who will have been forewarned by telephone of Jackson's emergency departure, will think nothing amiss. "Alright, break it up! Goddamnit, I'm in a hurry! Break it up!" Officer Jackson will yell, pushing his way through the black men, hastening across the yard. The wall post #8 man will let down the key for him, he'll pass quickly through the Big Yard wall, across the Isolation Yard, through the Lock, across the outer lawn, through the Third Fence Gate, and out to his car in the Soundside parking lot. He will produce a set of keys (our keymakers in the Honor Block have managed to borrow the originals for five minutes, long enough to make a good wax imprint from which a perfectly matched set of keys were cut) and rush away toward the city hospital and his poor dying wife, driving swiftly through the open Second Fence Gate and the rapidly opening Back Gate, whose officer operators have been alerted to the emergency.

5. Meanwhile in the Honor Block the real Officer Jackson's key man, an old black lifer who's been with him for years and handles the office and takes all Jackson's phone calls, will suddenly have second thoughts as to the authenticity of the lady doctor's call. Jackson's wife works as a nursing assistant in the city and should have been at work in the Pacific Hill district rather than at the corner of Division and Mercado streets. The key man will suggest (a fact that will later indubitably earn him an early, and highly ironic, parole) that something's fishy, in his opinion, that they'd best phone the nursing home and check and see whether Jackson's wife isn't where she belongs after all. They will debate this question for a minute or two, eventually deciding that perhaps it is best to check the veracity of the call. When they dial Control they'll find that something indeed is very fishy: the line's been cut! No—after all, if the line had been cut the alarm would have gone off. But

nonetheless someone has rendered the telephone in-operative, perhaps within its receiver mechanism. Jackson will send the reserve man all the way out of the Honor Block and across the full length of the Big Yard to the Yard sergeant, who will attempt to utilize the Yard telephone to call Control and inform the Control officer that something fishy's going on (something triple-fishy, since he probably saw the other Officer Jackson walking by). At this moment, however, a great heaving wave of black men will swing around between the sergeant and the Yard tel-ephone, not harming him in any way but, seemingly, just gathering outside the East Block to be let in for the First Count. By the time the Sarge weaves his way through this polite but ungiving mob to the phone and calls the Control man, who calls the wall posts and the Lock and the Third Fence Gate and the Second Fence Gate and the Back Gate to verify that someone purported to be Officer Jackson has in fact passed through, and by the time he sounds the General Alarm siren and calls the State Highway Pa-trol and the County Sheriff's Department, old Inmate Galliot, No. 240976, should be long gone.

6. Harris Mills and Harriet must meet me *without fail* with a speedy car and a female disguise at the Richfield Station at the prison freeway entrance. They must drive into the parking lot there and park in front of the Men's Room at precisely 3:39 P.M. We'll abandon Officer Jackson's Ford, and rapidly drive to Molina Valley, where we shall meet you. You'll be parked in the parking lot of the Safeway Supermar-ket at the corner of 10th and B streets, *in the far southeast corner*. I'll take it from there. And don't worry. I've made arrangements already to remove myself with all haste from this chill and perilous land to a place of much palmier clime for a certain period—a certain period of necessary revolutionary exile. And don't waste a minute of worry or concern about me. I've never felt so ready, so alive and real. With only a slim chance of life, the life pulse, the will-to-live flows strongest through my veins. *We will triumph in the end!*

ALL POWER TO THE PEOPLE!
William Galliot, Revolutionary

Twenty-Seven

Arv and Fast-Walking drove out of the Joint and into the darkness of after midnight. Both men avoided talk of the murder in the East Block. Once they cleared the walls they always tried very hard to leave the Joint and its problems far behind, like a bad dream, till the next night, sixteen hours away. Now Fast-Walking seemed more worried about his car, his Buick Roadmaster that was on the blink out at Evie's, than about any murders in the Jam.

"Shit! How'm I gonna get to work tomorrow morning?"

"Take the bus," Arv said, who had a day off tomorrow, from both work and school, and had no intention of waking up at six in the morning just to give him a lift across the estuary.

Just before the Merc reached the freeway entrance, its high beams struck a red Honda. Seated upon it, far back, leaning forward like a motorcycle racer, they spotted a pretty little nut-brown chick dressed in black leather.

"Hey, wow! Who's that?" Fast-Walking hollered, peering deeply into the tinted windshield. "Say! Might be Wasco's 'foxy brown lady' that Yuba was talking about!"

"Bullshit," Arv said, "she's waiting for me."

"Wow! Aw, you're shucking, man. It can't be true."

Arv slammed on his brakes happily in reply to Fast-Walking's incredulity. The girl jumped off her bike and ran over and kised him through the car window, breathing fresh steamy sweet-smelling puffs of air in on them, and Fast-Walking had to believe.

"Ooh!" she said, in her lilting Island accent, "there he is!" clapping her hands in delight, "let me get a look at him! Oh! He's just like you said, Arv, exactly! Oh he's lovely!" she shouted, and laughed, and her laughter sounded clear and bell-like and welcome in the stale Merc.

"What you been telling the lady about me?" Fast-Walking asked, pretending like he was angry, turning toward Arv with his fist clinched. But, in reality, he was charmed, and surprised, as much by her color as her sex. He smiled his straight-toothed Miniver grin at her, a grin aided by legions of childhood dentists and orthodontists, and Arv's dirt-eating low-class poverty-stricken heart began to sink.

"Come on, honey!" Fast-Walking yelled, "jump in! You're gonna catch newwwwwwmonia out there! Say, I know you," he said, surprised, "you work down at Bert's on the night shift!"

"Let's put her bike in the trunk," Arv interrupted, as Moke got in.

"That's right," Moke said, replying to Fast-Walking's question, "but he let me off early tonight, just so I could meet you!"

"Oh yeah?" Fast-Walking said, easily, certainly, as if that kind of thing happened to him all the time.

The boys lifted the Honda and put it in the trunk. It wouldn't close all the way, so Arv had to reach in and find some twine to tie it down. He picked the bike up by the front wheel, the lightest one, so he wouldn't strain his slippery slipping disc. He'd had a lower vertebral problem since childhood, only one of many indications of his inferior heredity, his weak Weed blood.

"Hey, watch out for your sacroiliac there, buddy!" Fast-Walking teased.

They drove out the freeway to the city. Arv went real slow on purpose. He wanted to delay their arrival as long as possible. He was jealous of Fast-Walking's renowned success with women. In Joint circles, his exploits were often discussed with envy. That was one of the reasons his wife had found out about his philanderings. Nothing's a secret in the Joint. But Arv thought Fast-Walking'd be at a disadvantage in the Merc. Arv could talk better than Fast-Walking, could rap better, more lucidly. And then there was the possibility, probability, that Fast-Walking would fuck himself up, show his nuttiness, his monomania, and lose all his attractiveness in comedy. Arv, intensely competitive once he had a girl friend, comforted himself with the notion, patently self-deceptive, that "women don't fuck comedians . . ."

When Fast-Walking started up again on his obsession

about southeastern Oregon, Arv's jealous skipping heart calmed down, relaxed again, certain as it was that old Fast-Walking would screw himself up.

But Moke dug it! She actually liked it! It was so boring, so stupid. But she ate it up!

Fast-Walking lit them up a prerolled joint (from where it came Arv didn't know) and proceeded to drop right into his Oregon rap without a hitch or a pause.

"So like I was saying," Fast-Walking began, very reasonable and calm and sure of himself, "that unpopulated corner of Oregon . . ." and Moke listened to his drivel in rapt attention, barely even bothering to puff at the joint when it was passed her way.

Because Fast-Walking was crazy and didn't know any better, he always went unembarrassed among women, unself-conscious, never betraying a single second's hesitation or unsureness. And women adored it. No matter what bullshit he laid down. Arv always suffered around dudes like that. He figured he was smart and sensitive enough to feel every single vibration or scent of change or feeling in the woman he dug. Consequently, he got uptight, nervous, around her. And when he got nervous, he felt with his acute perception that she was turning off on him. And the more she turned off, the more he got nervous. Finally he got just tongue-tied, shame-faced, pink with humiliation, and escalated their common discomfiture to an unendurable extreme, to a point where he just wanted to fall down on his knees and roll over like a dog and shit and piss his pants and kick his feet like a baby.

Arv's problem was this: he found and lost women with amazing frequency. At first they liked him, generally, attracted by his off-beat fashionably bashed-in ugliness. Then, when they got to know him, and saw how scared and lonely he was, and how uptight around women he was, they dropped him like a hotcake, again and again.

But, he comforted himself: *if and when I was ever really sure of a chick, sure that she dug me, only me, then I knew I'd be able to rap, to wail, to send her wiggy with laughter and delight.* He used to be able to do that with Deanna. And then, after a while, she had pulled away from him. Even though he'd never loved her, really, it kind of hurt him when she finally pulled away completely. He lost confidence in himself around her, and ended up as scared and nervous around her as if she'd been a stranger, a strange woman. Once there was a slight crack in Arv's self-confidence, he was lost. Women, as far as Arv could see, detested men who weren't absolutely sure of themselves, even if they were sure of themselves for insipid and spurious reasons. Women had no patience with the sensitive or weak-hearted man, no understanding of a sensitive man's problems, his fears and woes. Women always picked the irrational man, the man of fierce and violent temperament over the man with sensible, soulful temperament. . . . Anyway, that's the way Arv was thinking now, feeling sorry for himself, driving the Merc at forty miles an hour over the Alvarez Straits Bridge. What chicks really wanted, Arv thought, was a big-ass daddycat, to keep them in line, someone with no self-doubts. Even though a man who never doubted himself had to be stupid almost by definition. Arv hated men like that because only very rarely and for extremely short periods of time could he maintain the fiction that he wasn't, just like all the women he'd ever met, lost and scared too, a kid who'd lost his direction in the woods.

"So, Maleure County is where I've figured we'll build our commune," Fast-Walking was saying, talking to Arv, but you could tell he was really talking to Moke, trying to impress her, get into her pretty pants. And you could never tell when Fast-Walking was excited. When he got that way, sometimes, he could wail. He too became a poet of the rap, like Galliot, like Arv himself, in the right circumstances, the right time. Fast-Walking, when he was on, was formidable, if you thought about it. His words came out low and reasonable-sounding, but so fast that they flowed like an endless stream, like Fast-Walking's energy itself, and its source . . . flowing *out*, but never ending or resolving anything or building anything. . . .

"Now I've recently acquired a substantial cash sum," Fast-Walking went on, though Arv couldn't imagine where it came from, unless . . . unless . . . "soon, I'm gonna have enough to buy some property," Fast-Walking said, "and up there in Oregon, in that one little corner, land's dead cheap because it's mostly desert. Up along the South Fork of the Owyhee River. But they do get precipitation, in the winter, in the form of snow. Now, I'd like to get some groovy-looking ladies up there, two or three to a

man, and Indian it out," he said, laughing at his own turn
of phrase, turning to Moke, who found it funny too, "like
to take my gorgeous French wife up there and a few
outasight chicks like you, young lady," he said, patting
her leather-clad leg, leering, "and squaw it right through
the winter, collecting precipitation in these special giant
earthenware pots I've invented especially for the purpose.
Now, the first year we'll all live in a giant communal Nez
Percé Indian dwelling that'll keep us all warm. Lot of
bear up in there. We'll shoot bear and eat pussy and howl
at the moon up there! We'll cover the floors with furs,
cover the floors and walls and beds and roll around in
there strip nekkid on wolf and bear fur humping everything in sight. We'll get into a little incest too in the winter when there ain't nothing to do. Keep our spirits and
bods in good shape for spring planting when you got to
work your ass off in the fields . . ." Fast-Walking said,
giggling at the unknown places his talk was taking him,
surprised as Moke was at his own ramblings. He did not
surprise Arv at all, of course. Arv knew that Fast-Walking lived out many of his most stupid and silly fantasies
orally, at his friends' expense. But Moke, sucking on the
weed, the joint of Fast-Walking's fresh Happy Grass, feeling it, eyes sparkling, was digging it all greatly, digging
Fast-Walking too. Arv watched her. She sat up straight on
the seat between them, her mini peeping out of her black
leather jump suit where she'd unzipped it for air. She
didn't look at Arv. She only had eyes for Fast-Walking as
he wailed on and on, rocking his long-necked body, his
handsome blond head back and forth with the telling, all
the way across the bridge and through the tunnels to the
city.

"Now, the Fort McDermitt Indian Reservation is right
nearby there and they got a trading post, so we can get a
lot of our supplies there. The country is rolling sage
brush and wide vistas that go forever, all the way to
Idaho and Nevada. The valleys up there are gray, kind
of, with this short swordlike buffalo grass. It's bleak and
ugly and cold and empty and infertile and lonely. Just
what a guy needs nowadays! None of this soft modern
life for us! Why, that country's made-to-order for the
man who really wants to combat nature. The Indians
who used to live up there was so poor and cold and
miserable they let the buffalo eat *them!*"

Moke shrieked delightedly, like a small brown foreign child, like a little slopehead, jumping up and down in her seat. "You're beautiful, man! Beautiful!" she kept yelling.

And so the evening went. All of a sudden, to Arv's immense chagrin, they were a threesome. They went to a bar Moke knew in the hippy section of the city, Miguel Park, and listened to drunken bearded "New York" poets spout their self-conscious middle-aged piddle. Then Moke, and then Fast-Walking, and finally even solemn old Arv, got drunk on boilermakers and ran out of the place together and bounded around the late night streets of the foggy city, singing and yelling and spouting their own poetry into the clouds of yellow mist, making up their own poems, their own songs, which Arv, feeling looser now, better, happier, proclaimed "Fifty million times hipper than all that shit the 'real' poets sling!"

Moke, paraphrasing a slack-key song of Gaby Puhanui and Atta Isaacs in her own inimitable way, changing the words to suit her mood and story, sang:

> I'm a leevin on-a-easy
> On a bottle of wheeskey
> I got some money
> To suit my honey
>
> Please sock it to me Haole!
>
> I don't see M no mo'
> He is so . . . so-so-so
> He got no personaleetee
> To suit my geeneeologee . . .

Fast-Walking sang a limerick that he made up on the spot:

> There once was a hack from the Joint
> Had a weenie so smart it could oink
> When asked how he came
> He replied with an aim
> "Son, all you got to do is just point!"

Arv made up a strange poem which he called a "Racial Memory," claiming that it had come to him in a dream just the night before. He recited it with tragic countenance and serious mien, much to the amusement of Moke and Fast-Walking, who lay before him on the gentle incline of the Miguel Park hill, wetting their clothes in the foggy dew:

THE SILVER MOUNTAIN

In the *cañon* the claywater lay. Under the metal ramp. The dam bursting. The choke. The pond. The white trees and the sun shining.

Manola came down the ramp to the woods. The silver sliding.
The white dust. The scrap. The settle. The waste-day . .ʾ. In the pepper trees there are secrets, Manola. Between only you and me.

Antonio Cienfuegos has a black moustache. "Zamba!" he said.
"The mother of the rogue a Zamba nigger off the Mosquito Coast!"

. . . And by now my jaw would be stuck open for air. The white dust in my hair. The dam bursting. The chute. The break. The stay. The whistle in the mine blowing.

At half past four in the afternoon the miners came down in donkey carts from the hill. The silver mountain shining. Broadswords. Fire-locks. Truncheons. And me halfway to Guerrero! Antonio Cienfuegos will call me *cobarde,* my mother a great black whore. And me halfway to Guerrero! Zamba!

After much laughter, and fun and games, and rolling on the grass, getting green all over their clothes, Moke insisted that each of them show the others something about the city that the others didn't know, some secret place nobody else had been to.

Fast-Walking showed them an ancient cracked Chinese bell lying in the grown-over back lot of the Southern Pacific yardmaster's office, hidden in a maze of railroad tracks and rusting abandoned railway steam engines near

Soundshore Yard. They stood there in the boiling red-lit
fog, down there in the warehouse and dockyard section of
the city, sniffing Pacific and sniffing coffee from the coffee
warehouse across the tracks, and looking at the ancient
Chinese bell for a long time, in utter silence. Then Arv,
getting into it now, into their trip, with the booze and
dope and all, screamed, "I know one! I know one too!"
And they ran to the car, tripping over dark railroad tracks
and switches and piles of old coal. They reached the
Merc and leapt in and Arv skidded out of the yard
parking lot and drove them at breakneck speeds across
town and over several steep hills (hills that bred tall
wooden Victorian houses that climbed one upon the roof
of another) to the corner of 23rd and Valenzuela where
23rd Street went straight up the steepest hill in the city,
straight up the blacktop at an impossible forty-five-degree
incline. Arv raced the Merc rumbling in low drive up
the Victorian street. The tires skidded, the nose of the
car pointed straight up to the stars above. The tall old
houses whizzed by, falling away beneath them, propel-
ling the Merc toward the heavens. When they reached
the peak, going sixty miles an hour, they couldn't see
the ground in front of them. All they could see was air,
and sky, and black worlds above, and the fog shining in
the headlights. And then the hood of the Merc, in slow
motion, turned down, like a diving bomber, like a jet
peeling off over Vinh or Phnom Penh, and they came
hurtling back to reality with a loud THWUNK! as the car
hit and headed down fast, crash-diving. And they could
see the lights of the entire city laid out beneath them
. . . yellow and white and red and blue, and the white
lights of the West Hazelton Bridge and the green lights
of the Alverez Straits Bridge and the colored lights
of the Naval Air Station across the Sound and the strung
pearl of lights that came down the West Sound Freeway
across the black waters of the estuary and, as they went
down down down, until their stomachs leaped into their
mouths, it felt like the Merc was just falling away beneath them, like someone had pulled the world out from
under them, like they were going over the falls with no
barrel, and then, after the longest time, they felt the sea-
level land heave up and grip their stomach muscles and
they went Whee! Whee! Whee! over and over again. And
stopped the car, and flung the doors wide, and fell out

onto the dark pavement of the sidewalk where their too
rapid fall, too great trajectory, had taken them, laughing
and laughing, finding it impossible to get their breath
back. And then, when they had their courage back up,
they did it again and again, each one taking a turn at
driving. "Whee! Whee! Yours is the best place, Arv!
Really the best!" they yelled, until they were all exhausted, tired and bored and not scared of heights anymore, not scared of the world falling away . . .

"Now my place!" Moke shouted, "Now mine! Now
mine!" like a delighted child, like a birthday girl. And she
drove them down 20th Street to the corner of 20th and
Sonora in the Mission Nueva Sonora district to an after-
hours Mexican place she knew of and parked in front just
as a Mariachi band walked in. They were all clad in black
and silver charro outfits, with big black sombreros. Each
man wore a black pencil-thin moustache and was slightly
overweight.

"Hooray!" the gringos yelled at them.

The Mexicans, for the sake of business, turned around
and smiled. Then they went in, followed by Arv, Fast-
Walking and Moke.

And all the time Fast-Walking had not stopped his insane monologue, only giving it up to laugh or sing, and
then whipping right back into it without missing a syllable. "Now the way I figure Oregon," he said, as they
stepped into the bright fluorescent-lit restaurant, and
Moke finally had enough.

"Aw, shut up! Will you?" she said.

And he shut up. All the Mariachis laughed. Arv was
delighted too, and ordered Carta Blanca beer and a thick
menudo.

"And bring lots of tortillas and butter and refried
beans!" Moke said.

The Mariachis came over and asked them if they
wanted to hear something. They were the only gringos in
the place, and felt rather self-conscious for the stares they
were getting. Especially Moke. They couldn't figure her
out. "Sure," she said, "please start out with *Mira Bartola.*"

"That ain't Mariachi," the fattish charro who played the
guitarrón said.

"Okay," Arv said, "how 'bout *Guadalajara?*"

The *guitarrón* didn't even wait to respond but started it

up immediately. The trumpet player was belting it out
right into Arv's ear. But Arv loved it. Moke got into it
too, and laughed and patted them both on the back. "Ooh
yeah!" she said. The beer came, and they all downed a
bottle fast and ordered more. The Mariachis kept playing
on their own: *Cielito Lindo, Las Mañanitas, Rancho
Grande,* all the shit they figured the gringos would dig.
And they were right. They loved it, and ordered beer after
beer, and slurped up the dregs of their tripe soup and ordered more, and after that tacos and pollo mole and enchiladas, eating and eating, but still feeling like they were
starving to death, starving as only pot smokers do. Im-
bibing, indulging heavily, slurping and sucking at the beer
to quench their dried-out throats, their fierce thirst, laughing and punching each other in the ribs and on the shoulders, they all had a fantastic time. Moke was playful as a
kitten. Arv had his self-confidence back. Fast-Walking
was busy eating. "Whoopie!" Moke hollered. Arv stroked
her arm. She dug it, the innocence of it, the genuine
friendliness of it, you could tell. Played with his hand.
They kept eating. The band kept playing. Moke bought
beers for an hour straight. The trumpeter blasted his way
directly into Arv's mind. He stood playing six inches from
his right ear and the noise went in and did not come out
the other . . . it stayed, echoing around in his hollow-feel-
ing gourd. Arv was in Mexico. Following his dead
grandpa down across the Rio Grande back to Chihuahua.
And he felt it. He smelled it and heard it, Mexico, all
around him. Guitars and chile and Carta Blanca beer and
beans and trumpets and moustaches and slanted Indian
eyes.

   "Ai, Chihuahua!" he yelled, the cry he'd learned to imitate at a very early age from Chicano cons. *"Aiiiiii Chihuahua!"* Everyone in the restaurant cheered. He did it
again, standing, arching back like a little bantam fighting
cock, crowing it, flapping his elbows, wiggling his ears,
"Aiiiiii Chihuahua!" Eyes popping, lungs bursting, Arv
did it again and again, his grandpa's yell, the one he sang
out just before he passed on, the one Little Arv heard
from the lobby of the New Sonora County Hospital in
Mission Santa Bonita, or imagined that he heard, the defi-
ant one, the final cry of an old dying Spic, *"Aiiiiii ha! Ai
ai ai ai ai ha ha ha ha ha ai ai ha ha ha ai aiiiiii Chahua*

hua!" Everyone in the place started laughing. They'd never heard a gringo who could yell like a real *norteño.* The little cat on the trumpet started to laugh so hard Arv thought he might swallow his instrument. He started laughing into his mouthpiece and then he just couldn't play anymore. The trumpet made one last sound, a kind of POOP, and that set everybody to laughing all the harder. Finally the whole band broke down, slapping their knees, cracking up. Then the entire clientele starting yelling *"Ai Chihuahua!"* Moke nearly fell off her chair. She'd never heard anything like it. She loved it. She loved Arv for doing it, it was clear. She let him know with her eyes. She tried it too, *"Ai ai ai, Chihuahua!"* And Fast-Walking too kind of croaked it out, like he'd learned it in the Joint. *"Chihuahua!"*

The place was in a terrible uproar until the door burst open and two big white cops yelled, "What the hell is going on here? You want us to revoke your license?" And everyone shut up fast.

They stayed on another half-hour but it wasn't the same. Everybody seemed intimidated, even the musicians, who stood at the bar drinking tequila and whispering to each other.

"Let's split," Arv said, and they got up to go. When they paid and started for the door the landlady of the place, a pleasant dark-faced woman of late middle age, with a massive belly only partially hidden in the flouncy folds of her peasant skirt, yelled out, real friendly, *"Donde vas?"* to Moke, mistaking her for some kind of Mexican. Without a moment's hesitation, Moke yelled out, "Mexico!"

"Sí, Mexico!" Arv seconded. *"Aiiiii ai ai ai ha ha ha ai Chihuahua!"*

"Ai!"

"Ai Chihuahua!"

And waving, with the suddenly revitalized cantina waking up behind them, they slipped through the red and green bead curtain and into the street, surprised, almost, to see this big West Coast American city all around them, lit up like a fireproof plastic Christmas tree.

"Yeah, Mexico!" Moke yelled to the world at large.

Across the street in their black-and-white prowl car, the two cops scowled.

"Yeah, let's go!" Arv said.

"Not me," said Fast-Walking, "I got to see my wife to-morrow."

"That's alright," Moke said, taking Arv's arm, "we wanted to be alone anyway, didn't we, Arv?"

"You bet," Arv said, and let his heart run out where it wanted. "*Ai!*"

Down the block the Merc wouldn't start up. They pushed the sonofabitch a hundred yards but it just wouldn't crank over.

"I ain't letting them omens get me!" Arv said, shoving on the door while he guided the car.

"Me neither," Moke said.

"You better think twice about that," Fast-Walking said, out of breath, "this beast is trying to tell you something."

"Bullshit!" said Arv straining with all his might.

"Yeah, bullshit!" Moke said, setting her thin shoulders up against the Merc's rear end . . . and lo and behold . . . RUMP . . . RUMP . . . it seemed like it wanted to start all of a sudden. RUMP RUMP RUMP RUMPRUMPRUMP WHAM! BANG! ARRRRRACHOOKAPALOW! With a fiery smoky cough and a ferocious almost human wail the big Merc turned over and started and off they went, heading down 20th Street, Arv driving, Moke and Fast-Walking hanging on the rear bumper for dear life.

"*Aiiiii!* Let's go! Let's swoop! Let's wail away to Mexico!" Moke shouted into the flying yellow city fog.

"Yeah! Let's go!" Arv shouted into the wet wind through the car window, not really believing they would, not really caring, caught up in the excitement of the moment, the excitement of his first great success with her, with Moke, thinking about their emerging, slippery, uncertain . . . tie . . . or whatever . . . that seemed to be building, twisting between them, in spite of her resistance.

"Yeah!" Arv shouted when the car got going good. "Yeah!" he yelled again, and stopped it in the middle of Slate Avenue, while cars whizzed by them on both sides, honking and blinking their lights . . .

"Hey buddy! Where you think you're goin?"

"Jump for it, Fast-Walking!" Arv shouted, "we can't take you back home. The car'll stall! Jump off and get a taxi home, okay?"

ROOOM ROOOM ROOOM! Arv kept the old Merc wound

up so it wouldn't die. Moke ran around and jumped in the front seat.

"Let's do it, baby!"

"*Ai ai ai*, let's wail!"

Fast-Walking got down slow and dejected from the back bumper, head hanging, left out, left out of all the fun, and only thirty-four years old, and you could tell he was debating whether or not to come along . . . so Arv dropped that motherfucking Mercury into low drive and burnt rubber right out of there, waving his hand at Fast-Walking who was just standing there in the middle of Slate Avenue looking kind of hang-dog, like he'd lost his best friend.

"Poor old Fast-Walking," Moke whispered, as she crept to Arv's side and kissed his ear neck hair mouth moustache forehead arm . . . *Ai!*

Arv went up Slate Avenue to Bird Street, down Bird to 18th Avenue.

"Hey, this isn't the way to Mexico!"

"I got to drop something off and we'll be on our way."

"I know what it is!"

"Oh, yeah?"

"Yeah, it's a letter. Am I right?" she asked, wheedling.

"Right," Arv said.

"It's a letter from Galliot to Elaine, isn't it? Lemme see it!"

"I didn't even look at it myself."

"Why not?"

"He said it was private."

"Come on, let's peek!"

"Nope."

"Come on . . ." she pleaded, wiggling up close, licking his lobe, touching his thigh, blowing at the corner of his mouth.

"I can't do it."

"You too fucking honest, *Haole!*" she said, sulking, and sulked like that all the way to Elaine's stucco tract home on 18th Avenue.

Arv jumped out of the Merc and ran across her lawn, hurdling the low hedge, and knocked loudly at her front door, under her lit porchlight. The living room light was on too, so she was probably up.

"Arv! What're you doing here?" she asked, surprised

and delighted and a little bit embarrassed by her torn bathrobe and her hair up in curlers.

"Listen," he said, breathless from his run, "I got an important letter for you. But I can't stay. I'm in a big hurry. Moke's waiting out in the car. Bye bye!" he yelled, running back across the lawn, leaving her open-mouthed under her yellow porch light, holding the letter in her opened hand.

"Hi, Moke!" she yelled, waving out to the Merc. But Moke didn't wave back.

"How much money you got?" Moke asked, as Arv spun out on the southbound Soundside Freeway in light night traffic, long-range traffic, owls and nighttime bandits like themselves, heavy semitrailers and night freighters and refrigerated reefers and traveling salesmen and bank robbers and escaped prisoners and con men going cross country.

"Almost nothing. Ten dollars."

"That's okay," she said, friendly again, suddenly, close to his ear, grooving behind him, and the show in the cantina, and the rapidity of his decision, and his spontaneity, and even his refusal, the strength of his resolution not to show her the letter . . . *women dig men who know how to say no,* Arv was thinking.

"Don't worry about it," Moke said, "in fact . . . shit! Money no problem at all, little *Haole.* I got enough fo' da two of us!"

And on that remarkable night Arv's real and unreal, invented and uninvented, dead and eternal grandpa sent them down that long foggy freeway for Mexico. And the yellow wind drove Alfonso, *abuelo,* past them and down the long boulevards of eucalyptus trees of New Sonora, down down down on the journey to the south, fateful journey, down the cold alfalfa fields of Central Valley California, the shrieking cactus of the Imperial Valley. Going back, he sent them, *back on Weed,* back on Arv's gnarled and twisted roots, the weedy transformations before he was born. He sent them home, the old man did, down and down home. And the Merc followed Grandpa Encina valiantly, home to his final resting place of spirit. Arv saw him out ahead. He beckoned, the old sonofabitch did, the ancient Spic, flying out ahead of them, billowing through the coastal fog, streaking through the clear desert night. Flying and flying. Out front. Leading them on home to the root of all Weeds, the *encina* tree, the live oak, that grew somewhere south of the border . . . "And never come back, never!" he called, time and time again through the long night, hovering out front, just over the Merc's hood ornament, *"Nunca vuelves! Nunca vuelves!"*

Arv started them off along the Sound at a steady seventy-five miles an hour following the water down the long string of freeway-side commuter-train suburbs. Then they crossed over the slim muddy end of the Sound on a gray-painted drawbridge and then they wound their way over the low Coast Range in the darkness, the moonless blackness above the fog, high beams in their eyes, Johnny Cash singing on the radio, a whole long album about Folsom Prison, of all things, that sent them into the pitch black Central Valley of California where they were stopped at the stateline and asked if they possessed any out-of-state vegetables or fruits . . .

"Theah's owny jutht meeeeee," Moke lisped to the officer. But he didn't even crack a grin.

They followed the freeway down the west side of the valley past sleeping little dusty one-horse towns like Patterson and Crow's Landing . . . Arv listed them in his head while he drove, Moke asleep on his shoulder. He listed his family's slow and painful way north, only in reverse, going back on them at eighty-five mph:

1. Los Banos
2. Dos Palos
3. Firebaugh
4. Mendota
5. Coalinga
6. Avenal
7. Kettleman City
8. Alpaugh
9. Wasco

Twenty-Eight

Fast-Walking took a taxi over to Arv's place on Orchard Street. He sat hunched over in the back seat, drunk and sick and feeling sorry for himself.

"Sonofabitching little Spic abandoned me left me in the middle of the street . . ." When he got out on Orchard Street he couldn't find the key to the apartment. He searched his pockets, couldn't find it. Bent down and looked under the welcome mat. Nothing! "Sonofabitch!"

Fast-Walking, abandoned in the middle of the fog-bound city, in the middle of the night, with not a place to hang his hat or lay his weary head, no family, no home, hung his head and cried on the steps of Arv's ghetto apartment for a long time. Hung his head, in fact, crying his eyes out, until three young spade cats began half-circling him in the darkness like sleek black wolves. Then, looking like slow, moving fast as lightning, he slipped off the porch and trucked down Orchard Street to the boulevard and hailed a taxi which, disregarding the immense cost, he took down Bird Street and down 18th Avenue, through the tunnel, over the bridge, over Brando Grade and right up to the Back Gate of the Joint.

There he stopped and chatted with the night man for quite a while, discussing the murder in the East Block . . . "Shit, man! Never seen anything like it! The dude whizzed by me not six inches from my ear. I could've reached out and touched him . . . Racial killing," he said, speculating, now that he was back in the Joint.

Gathering up the nerve to go see his wife, to beg shelter for the night.

At first he felt terrible about it, having to go mendicant to her door like this. But then he felt better. He had *good news* for her, after all. He had the means now to pay off all his debts. He'd tell her. "Marie-Claude, I won some

. . ." How should he start it? How to explain his sudden
riches? First things first. Should he call her up from the
gate house? Or should he just knock and wake her up? He
thought it best if she could see him in person. He slipped
some Juicy Fruit into his mouth to kill the liquor smell,
said good-bye to the night man, and walked down the
blacktop road past the schoolhouse to prison residence
#71. He stopped out in front and paced up and down on
the sidewalk. He was in luck! Her bedroom light was still
on. She'd had a little trouble sleeping lately. Maybe she
was still up, reading one of them French magazines her
aunt sent her, *Elle*, or *Paris-Match*, or *Jour de France*. He
stood outside in the boiling fog for ten minutes, with his
uniform collar up, hands in pockets, trying to summon up
the nerve. The car patrol came around and shone the
spotlight on him.

"I guess I do look pretty fucking suspicious!" he managed.

The two guards laughed behind their spotlight.

"What'sa matter, Fast-Walking, afraid of your old
lady?"

He waved and forced a smile and, to show them that
all was well, walked up his sidewalk between the short
trim hedges, and rang the bell.

"Who is it?" she asked in her throaty French voice behind the door. The car patrol boys watched from the
road, under the white street light.

Fast-Walking was thrilled to hear her voice, her accent.
She was so different from other men's wives at the Joint.
He was proud of her foreignness, delighted that she was
so unique in his world. She was a stranger. He loved her.

"It's me," he whispered.

To his immense surprise, she opened the door. He expected her to be cold and formal . . . but . . .

"Tsk tsk," she said, clucking her tongue like a mother
to a naughty boy, a tall gangling teenage boy who is
Mom's favorite. "So *zer* you are! Well come in zen . . ."

He followed her into their pink kitchen, watching the
lights of the car patrol run across the living room walls as
it rolled away toward the Back Gate.

Marie-Claude busied herself making them a pot of tea.
Fast-Walking sat down at his old place at the pink formica table. In spite of the insomnia, Marie-Claude looked

great. The bags had disappeared from beneath her eyes, her skin looked fresh and rosy. Her step was bouncy and energetic. She looked better than she'd looked in years, since before the ill-fated "accident twins" were born. Fast-Walking, who realized that his absence had created this new health in his wife, trembled with fear . . . "Uh . . . I'm real sorry I came over so late . . ."

"Don' worree 'bout eet, *chéri*, I cannot sleep . . ." she said, folding her lacy negligee around her thin sagging breasts. It was the same negligee that her aunt had sent from France three years before. It was lovely, Fast-Walking thought. He eyed it, and what showed underneath, ravenously. Tired and worn and aged beyond her years, his wife was yet beautiful to poor old Fast-Walking. Each of Marie-Claude's multiplying imperfections Fast-Walking read to his own advantage, and rejoiced. *Nobody going to run off with my girl,* he reassured himself, loving her with all his soul.

Fast-Walking wasn't capable of conversation yet. He thought his heart would break open and flood out over the kitchen floor. She seemed to understand, and to like it that way. She always seemed to understand him. But she was hard on him when he fell. When Fast-Walking fell, victim of the weakness of his flesh or his hunger or greed, she had no mercy. She was the hardest of taskmasters, and brooked no weakness, none at all. When Fast-Walking lost money, or stayed out late, or came home drunk or with lipstick on his collar, she turned him flat out, with no hesitation, no second chance, and it was the very devil getting back in. Marie-Claude let Fast-Walking sweat in his chair at the pink formica table, as she heated up the water, poured the tea, let it brew. . . .

Finally she said, "So . . ."

"Honey," he began, scared to death, "I've worked my ass off . . . I couldn't sleep either . . . I love you . . . now I got enough money and . . ."

"You 'ave enough to pay ze debts?" she said doubtfully.

"I got enough to get my salary disattached and enough to start . . ."

"And you won' talk no more of ze pipe dreams, no more of Oreegon?"

"Uh . . ."

"And you promeeze not to gamble and . . ."

She went on and on, doing what he wanted her to do, making him bow his head humbly (bowing humbly to his mother was something he'd dreamed of constantly as a boy . . . and yet his mother, crazy as a loon, had never required it of him, to his everlasting regret), making him beg forgiveness, swear repentance, vow total obedience . . . "I swear, honey, anything you say . . . anything you say . . . !"

When it was bedtime Marie-Claude made him sleep on the couch. The chasteness of the arrangement fit perfectly with his mood. When he started to kiss her goodnight she said, *"Mais non!* Only on ze sheek tonight. We most wait till we see 'ow you be'ave . . ."

She made up the rollaway couch for him. He sat on the rocking chair watching her, trembling in the last throes of a pleasure so sublime as to make him think for an instant that he'd prefer his life to end right there and then. She made it up the French way, rolling the sheet over the long round French pillow she'd brought all the way from Poitiers in her trousseau. Fast-Walking loved to watch her do that. The sheets were white and starched and she made it up expertly, her hands flying over the folds, her breasts sagging in the light when she bent over. . . .

When he was tucked in and had been kissed goodnight on his innocent brow, Fast-Walking dreamed he was in a sanitary Paradise of starched clean-smelling French nursing sisters.

He awakened once, in the blackest hours of the night, and giggled, remembering where he was, and thrust his feet back and forth in the white fresh-smelling sheets in ecstacy, just like he'd done as a boy when his mom's linen was fresh back from the Joint laundry. . . .

Twenty-Nine

"They on their way yet?" the squeeze asked, lying in Wasco's horny arms.

"Sure," he answered, and the single word echoed sharp and little from the commode to the bunk, in their night-cell, nightsong, nightsecret, nightshit . . .

"How do you know?"

"I'd trust that chick with my life."

"A cunt?"

"Don't gimme that queenie shit, punk! We been through it all together. She's proved herself a hundred fucking times. She comes through, man, like nobody else. Better than my own mother. She coulda done me in a hundred times. Coulda took me off, abandoned me in the Joint to rot, midnighted it out with my fucking bank account, sold me to the cops, the Mafia, the niggers, iced me a million different ways. She stayed tight, man, tight-ass and clean and steady, never blinking. She's brought dope across fifty different borders, icy, cold, not batting an eye while the man went through her bags. She's a real lady, punk, a real fucking Wahini, and don't you ever talk nasty about her around Wasco. Cause she's solid stuff, motherfucker. She's the honey we depend on. Without her, man, we are . . . nothing. I'd put my beating heart right in her hand. Put my balls in her mouth and she'd never bite, no matter what they offered. She's solid gold, ninety-leven karat, man, pure crystal, she'd take ten, man, she's Snow, Brown Beauty, she's the angel of the under-world, the marquess of thieves, the queen of the scam, the princess, baby, and ain't nobody ever going to lay a hand on her as long Wasco's alive, nobody!"

"Never trust a cunt," said the squeeze, spitefully, spitting it out. And Wasco could hear his little ass tighten up—SCHMOCK!—with anger. Daring, the little punk had become in the last twenty-four hours, daring as a woman secure in her sexual power. And Wasco, lying back on the bunk like an indulgent husband, with his hands behind his back, indulging his little honeypie's caprices, Wasco simply repeated himself dutifully, "Listen, man, I told you. She's had the power to do me in. But she's always, always, without fail, always come through. Just like I done for her. She's like a sister to me, man, a blood sister."

The squeeze, wishing to guide the conversation away from his chief rival, said, "Why you want them out of town, anyway?"

"I got my reasons."

"What's that?"

"You're pretty fucking curious. What are you, a cop?"

"I think you want the kid out of the way for a couple of days so he don't cramp your style in the Joint. Then you got something planned for him. You got some more monkey business brewing."

"Oh yeah? You think you know a lot," Wasco said, teasing, thinking it out, touching the squeeze's penis a bit timidly, titillating himself, like a happily pussy-whipped hubby with a willful wife.

"No, honey," the squeeze said, wiggling peevishly away, "I don't feeeeeeeel like it right now, damn it!" and continued . . . "no, not a lot. But I'm beginning to put P and Q together. I'm not as dumb as you might think, you big old . . ."

"Now stop it!" said Wasco, "you little silly! You know I dig you. You know you got me," he said, wondering whether it might be true, feeling at his own big red-nosed hard-on, twisting it till it touched with its warm blue-veined head the punk's cold pink flank.

"Oh no you don't!" the squeeze said, squirming deftly, wifelike, away, "not till I figure things out. I'm jealous of that bitch! You tell her things you don't tell me! Let's see. I figure you want that hack cousin of yours out of the way so he won't be around to help his friend if he gets in . . . trouble . . . like Bullet . . ."

"Into what?" Wasco asked, kissing the corners of his eyes, not listening, kissing too his high Irish forehead, his tender boyish ears, nuzzling his huge throbbing leaking loaf against the squeeze's thigh and hip.

"If you don't want to tell me . . ." the squeeze said,

pouting in the darkness, moving away. But it was a symbolic gesture only, considering the narrowness of the prison bunk, considering the high degree of their growing intimacy . . .

"What do you think, Squeezy?" Wasco teased.

"It looks like race war, to me."

"So . . . if you got it all figured out, what do you want?"

"I want to know. Why're you going to start your race war? You really the hit man?"

"Who ever gave you that idea?" Wasco asked, breathing heavily, kissing and kissing, sliding his lips down the squeezy's tight little tummy, rubbing his mouth eyes ears in the squeezy's short limp pubes, licking his erect little peepee, sliding his thoughtful tongue over it, and his mouth and eyes and ears over it, letting it leak into his lobes, slits, choppers, sucking slow, sucking easy, running his mouth over the chubby head, then swallowing it whole to the hilt, honking it, like a goose, like a gander, like a Cadillac car, HONK HONK HONK he went, saying it, HONK deep throat, gargling it, GURGLE GURGLE GURGLE making the punk laugh and heave and thrust and undulate, controlling him, sucking him, honking it, easy and good . . .

"I'll pull it out if you don't tell me . . . I'll pull it out . . ."

Wasco didn't even stop.

"You'll be making a mistake," the squeeze said, while Wasco just kept on a-honking HONK HONK, "you'll be making a big fucking error if you don't cut me in on some more of the action . . . Listen to me!"

But Wasco wouldn't stop. With his mouth stuffed full of taste he said:

"Wumph, wumph, thit! Oo wittle thtinky! Awright, awright! Ah'll wet oo thnuff a couple of niggerth in vee morning, okay? An' if vat ain't enough oo can continoo vee wathe war wif a hack in vee evening!"

"Outasight! Groovy! I'm your man! Okay, I know who the hack is, that we're gonna hit, but who're the niggers?"

Wasco ignored him . . . HONK HONK!

"Who're the niggers, goddamnit, in this race war? Or I'll pull it out!"

"Oh . . . wumph wumph . . . Damn oo! Awright . . . vee haiwcut boys!"

"Who? Who'd you say?"

"Vee haiwcut boys, Woundo and Ooba!"

"Who? Roundo and Yuba? Why them?"

"Cauth evewybody 'ikes vem, thtoopid!"

"What? What's that? . . . cause everybody likes them?"

"Thath wight! Thtirth up mo' thit vat way."

"Stirs up more . . . shit? Yeah . . . you know what, Wasco? You're a fucking genius, a genius!"

"Yeah? Good! Now thut up! O ah'll bite it off!"

"No, you won't," the smart-ass punk said, "no you won't bite."

Later on he shit on Wasco's cock and said he didn't mean to. Quick he ran Wasco over to the cold water faucet and cleaned it up, saying, "Oh gee, I'm sorry, honey, didn't mean to. You socked it too far all at once . . ." and like that, but Wasco knew. Now that he'd made his bones the punk was testing. And Wasco, who needed him, loved him, if he did admit it, in his own way, was falling for the skinny little prick, Wasco, let him get away with it.

Thirty

While Galliot, sleepless, locked in his cell on the fifth tier, scribbled and doodled in his journal in the light from the arc lamp on the Soundside wall:

I wish this hour was over. I wish it would end. What does "end" mean? Stop. I wish this hour would stop. If the world stopped, if the end came and I was left a barbarian, how much of civilization could I re-create? I wonder if I could make this pen, this ink, bind this notebook? I would get a quill and sharpen it and that would be my pen. Where does ink come from? The cuttlefish, says the dictionary. I would use animal blood for ink. I would use parchment for paper. Parchment: animal skin prepared without tanning and used for writing and painting. I could paint too. I've never tried my hand at painting and I've always wanted to. Brushes: I would use animal fur. Why does man have no fur? Did he design clothes even before he became a man? Then did he go bald under his clothing like a gentleman who's worn his hat too long? The black man has less hair than the white man. Has he therefore worn clothes longer? I wish this hour was over. I wish that it would end. I wonder how I'd make pencils, pens, paper, brushes, and ink if the world went aground. . . . And I solve the problem with the answer that pops most readily to mind: I would use the blood, skin and hair of an animal . . . a thin-skinned, white, hairy animal . . . I wish this hour would hurry up and end. I wish the world would hurry up too, and give me chance to try my hand at a craft. . . .

Thirty-One

And Sister Libby, ample and warm as a dumpling, did her high school homework late into the night, on the dining room table, under yellow lamp light. It came hard for her. Fifth time that she'd written this essay, sitting there motionless at the table for hours, her expansive teenage buttocks hanging over the hard wooden chair, and still she couldn't figure out what the English teacher meant by a "dangling participle." But she would work till she got it right. It came hard for her, but she wouldn't ever give up. *No, I ain't never going to give up till I get married.*

And Sergeant Big Arvin Weed, lying restless in his marriage bed, dreamed he was making the Last Count and at the last cell on the tier he flashed his light inside and Evie was sitting there naked on the bunk, beckoning him in . . .

While in the living room, on the sagging patched davenport, May, Mama, May Maiden, sipped the last dregs of her New Sonora Lager from the bottom of the big twelve-ounce can, shut off the Late Late Show, and vomited soundlessly onto her green Sears and Roebuck rug, trying real hard not to disturb her poor overweight daughter's study.

The TV flickers for a moment before going out, the sound remains for another two or three seconds:

"Why have you come to Casablanca?"
"For the waters."
"What water? This is the desert."
"I was misinformed . . ."

Part III

Thirty-Two

Moke rose sleepy-eyed now from Arv's lap where she'd been zeeezing it just in time to see the great golden orb rise up westward in his fiery chariot out of the snow-capped Sierra Nevada, just in time too to hear the high siren wail of a California Highway Patrol hopped-up black and white Olds as it brought them over to a dust-raising, fish-tailing halt right outside the city limits of the town that gave Little Arv his name: Arvin, California, nestled on a dry plateau between the earthquake-prone Tehachapi Range and the white-capped High Sierras.

The burly brown-clad cop, wearing the inevitable gold-rimmed teardrop-shaped sunglasses, sauntered around the Merc's back fender, glanced at Arv's NEW SONORA STATE PEACE OFFICERS' ASSOCIATION sticker, and leaned inside the car window, checking Moke out thoroughly, checking out Arv's uniform and his NSCC cap real careful.

"Good morning, sir," he said, smiling politely.

"Good morning, Officer."

"Do you mind if I ask where you're coming from, sir?"

"New Sonora. My wife picked me up after work at the Commission of Corrections and now we're headed to Mexico for a couple of days."

Arv showed him his driver's license and his badge and the speed cop waved them on.

"Always glad to oblige an officer of the law. But take it easy, huh?"

"Sure," Arv said, smiling, elbowing Moke in the ribs so she'd smile too, "thanks, Officer!"

And he sped back out on the bright freeway in bright early morning light and punched it right back up to eighty-five, realizing that these California boys respected truly other worthy members of their profession, other Piggies, and had real heart.

t whizzing by. All the way
way the road followed the line
cut along the first rise of the
farming land on its eastern side
dried-out hills, unirrigatable hills.
way it was yellow and dead on the
nd green and lush on the left, the val-

behind them toward the great green
valley, . . . , "The miracle of irrigation!" but Moke,
still sleep, ded and a bit dithery, the way she always
was when she first got up, hadn't the vaguest idea what he
was talking about.

A few minutes later he stopped for gas and coffee. She
ran into the ladies' room, stayed for at least a half hour,
but when she came out she looked great.

"Ooh!" she said, "now I'm ready to roll!"

Arv knew that Moke was some kind of dope head. Every time they got up together in the morning she'd be nervous and cranky till she excused herself and went to the
toilet, staying always a suspiciously long time. Then, when
she came out and hopped back into bed, she was always
bright-eyed and bushy-tailed as ever, and looking like a
million bucks. It was the same at night. Like last night
coming down the freeway into California. She got all
frantic all of a sudden. Made him stop at a service station.
Ran into the bathroom. Was gone a long time. When she
came back she was all relaxed and curled up and went
right to sleep, saying she'd taken a "sleeping pill." The
possibility that Moke was even a junkie had crossed Arv's
mind. But he dismissed the notion, choosing to believe her
story that she was "a real pill freak." *She likes to swim;
junkies hate water. She likes to fuck; junkies hate to be
touched,* he thought, remembering something he'd read in
his Hygiene course in high school. He chose to ignore his
own experience of the matter in Vietnam when, entwined
with dark brown Cham in her cinderblock apartment
above the Saigon River in Cholon, snorting skag and
smoking opium-tipped joints, he fucked with great feeling
all night and all morning, not even hearing what the papers later called "a Viet Cong rocket attack on riverside
Saigon."

At the moment Arv felt great. Never felt better. He

loved long stretches of night and early morning road with
no traffic, loved his headful of Moke's crank pills and the
long black asphalt road ahead of him, and brown hills and
great distances and dry western air, and the excitement of
Mexico just a few hours away. In other words, Arv wasn't
questioning things very much, like whether or not someone was a junkie, like whether or not she was telling the
truth when she told him that all those little red spots on
her pretty ass were merely "a harmless rash." Right now
Arv felt like he was in more of an accepting mood, than a
questioning one. He felt right now like he could accept
about anything in the world. He felt groovy.

It was strange. It was marvelous. None of his extreme
and desperate happiness and excitement of last night had
dissipated. None at all. WHAM WHAM WHAM! Arv's heart,
speed-spiked, beat out the rhythm without fear. He suddenly knew that he'd never have a heart attack. Knew that
the familial cardiac weakness hadn't touched him, and
never would, knew that he'd live a long long life, as the
fortunetellers say, and die in bed. Knew it for sure!

"Goddamn!" Arv yelled out, "you know, shit! I'm only
twenty-six years old!"

Moke laughed. She understood just what he meant.

"You fucking A John," she said, "and I'm only twenty-
five!"

"Yow!"

"Whoopie!"

"Let's do it!" Arv shouted, and punched the Merc, and
the Merc, happy to be moving out, going long range,
happy to be blowing out its cylinders, getting a breath of
air, the Merc responded with a surge of power that left
them breathless.

"Who said this sweetheart wouldn't make it?"

"Yeah!" Moke loudly affirmed, "Christ, that Fast-Walking, he wouldn't know an omen if one came up and
tapped him on the shoulder!"

"Yeah!" Arv said, "you know, that cat's so unconscious
that Yuba, the institution barber, presented him one
Christmas with a special machine he called a 'Head Puller' that he designed and had made up over at the machine shop. It was a fantastically complicated machine
with all kinds of chains and levers and pulleys. Fast-Walking accepted the gift very graciously and then he got a

real puzzled look on his face. 'Gee, Yuba,' he says, 'thanks a lot for the present. But what is it?'

" 'It's a Head Puller,' Yuba said.

"What's it for? Fast-Walking asked. And that was the line we were all waiting for. Everyone in the barber shop, cons and bulls, yelled out in unison: 'TO PULL YOUR HEAD OUT OF YOUR ASS!' "

Moke started laughing. She was digging his rap. Digging what they were getting into. Digging where their talk, their rap, was taking them.

After they finished laughing, she said, "Last night in the car I had a dream."

"Oh yeah?" Arv said, "what was it about?"

"I'll tell you," she said. "I guess it's because I ride a bike that I had this dream. I dreamed of a motorized unicycle. You know, a one-wheeled bike. You would start it by going down a long embankment. The pedals would be stationary. It would be propelled by a tiny turbine engine at the axle. And the faster you went, the farther you'd have to lean forward. Otherwise the wind would blow you over backwards. And then I thought that when you got really good you could have a jet-propelled one made up with the engine tied to your belly around your waist with a tube running inside your leather jumpsuit to a special opening in the sphincter area. And you would have a special cape like Batman's that would catch the wind. And at a hundred and fifty miles an hour with the wind whistling and your jet engine shrieking and your body extended forward till you were leaning almost prone into the wind you could actually take off the earth and fly for long seconds, the flames just spouting out the ass back of your clothes and the unicycle wheel going around so fast as to be invisible. And then I dreamed that somehow all of this was occurring on Balticoast . . ."

"Where?"

"Don't ask me where. All I remember is from the dream, 'Balticoast,' it said in the dream. Anyway, I saw a long white Baltic-like beach with a long line of low chalk-white cliffs behind, and a grassy field, with a white lane running straight through it, and an enormous crowd of Teutonic-looking individuals in overcoats and fur mufflers and their breath all steamy on both sides of the lane. And then I saw me come racing down the lane on my motorized unicycle. And somewhere a loudspeaker announced me. 'Ladies and Gentlemen,' he said, 'let me intro-duce you to Moke Todd, The One and Only Motorized Red and Yellow Chickenshit Fastest Unicycle Alive!' And I started off down the white lane with white chalk flying out behind me. And the faster I went, the farther I leaned forward until I could see the chalk of the road just an inch from my speeding nose. And then I soared out over the cliff and felt the cold wintertime Norddeutsch wind on my face and I saw the white waves far below me and at the highest point of the arch of my glide I closed my Batman's wings and let myself fall. I fell and fell, scaring myself on purpose. Because I didn't really want to die. I was just teasing myself. At the last moment, I pushed a little button in my belt which released a tiny parachute. It opened. I descended to the Baltic Sea where a little rowboat was waiting. All the way down to the boat I could hear the Teutons shouting, 'WUNDERBAR! WUNDERBAR! WUNDERBAR! and then I woke up."

"Beautiful!" Arv cried.

"It's just a dream," she said.

"You're a dream," he replied, "I dreamed you," and his heart leapt out fast ahead of the Merc like her dream, like his grandpa, dancing just beyond the hood ornament, flying through the white morning, riding on south at an easy road-eating ninety miles an hour going along the high white mountains above Bakersfield. Driving with one hand, grinding his jaw with the effects of the amphetamine, Arv pulled and twisted at his hair, working himself up, listening to the THWONK THWONK THWONK of the bass in the rock record on the radio. With the speed and the sound and the white peculiar light and beautiful Moke beside him, Moke the rapper, Moke the poet too, with her trippy imagination, Arv got wild and frantic, tuned the music and the voice out and just listened to that solid bass beat on the radio, twisting his hair into balls, grinding his teeth down to nerve, preparing, getting ready.

"Yeah!" he shouted, taking courage from the sound of his own excited voice, "lemme tell you, Moke, this trip reminds me . . ." he began, ready for his test, the rap test, the road rap; women don't give a fuck for the dude who can't rap, and now was Arv's chance; he could do it; he knew it. "Yeah!" he repeated, louder, stoking himself up.

Moke, he could see, wasn't impressed. She knew what he was preparing but wasn't impressed. Didn't figure he could pass the road rap test. He'd show her.

But then when he wanted to rap, just rap . . . the truth of what was under the rap came out instead. Arv cursed himself because there was just no way he could play it cool.

"I'm gonna win you on this trip," he said, slowly, carefully, meaning it, blowing his cool entirely.

"Maybe you are," she said, just as careful, just as heavy and meaningful, looking gloomily out the window at the huge mountain of silver-colored granite on the Ridgeroute above them, "but you won't like it."

"Jesus, is it that bad?"

"Worse."

"Why?"

"I already been won."

"Who's the winner?"

"The winner you wouldn't like."

"Who's he?"

"The *devil*," she said melodramatically, and burst out laughing.

"Oh shit, you ain't so bad," Arv said, laughing too, listening to the THWONK THWONK THWONK of his own ticker going along with the bass on the radio, "you know what? I think you're just flattering yourself. Christ! The devil's too busy to worry about a little chick like you. He's got more important things to think about."

And Moke laid her head back on the seat and laughed all the harder. And Arv, encouraged by the success of his patter, felt like the was now ready, ready for the rap that would win her. "Lemme lay this one on you," he began, confidence surging through him as he gunned the Mercury along the six-mile-long avenue of sand and wind-blasted eucalyptus trees that led up to the Ridgeroute. "Moke, roll us another joint, will you? Lemme lay it on you," he repeated, not at all sure what he was going to say, waiting for the pure unknown words to bubble up clear and untouched from his source, ready for the rap. "Yeah!" he said, "you know," he said, still not sure, "you know . . . when I got out of the army I lost my plane fare home in a crap game at Fort Monmouth, New Jersey. Stuck in New

York City and three thousand miles from home and not a fucking dime in my pocket. But I ran into this old Vietnam buddy of mine in the East Village. Went out to his pad on West 28th Street, Puerto Rican neighborhood, right next to the city swimming pool. Crummy place, with the street full of slung garbage and broken bottles. His girl friend Lise, a black chick, needed a ride out to New Sonora too. She was a sculpture student and wanted to go out and study with old man Alatri who, as it happens, runs the art school which is right across the street from my present pad. Anyway . . . yeah, gimme a drag." Arv took a long deep drag on the joint and immediately went into his rap again . . . "so we went down to the docks and met all the liners for two days. Finally we ran into these two dudes with bread, an English rock musician and a French fruit. They wanted to go out to the West Coast too . . ." Arv hesitated, not satisfied with the flow, stoking his driving beating rapidly palpitating Weed heart up to unexplored velocities . . . "Yeah!" he said, offering the expletive up to his own encouragement, "so we told them foreigners, we said, 'Look, we'll get you to the West Coast if you pay for gas.' They said, 'Sure.' We went down to one of these driveaway places, places that offer a service to drive certain dudes' cars across the country for a special fee. They fly across the country and their car is waiting for them at the other end. You can get a car that way any time you want. But . . . so . . . see . . . this Englishman would forget he was in the Colonies, see, in the land of the right-hand drive, and end up driving on the left side of the road. He almost killed us three times. We'd be wailing along in Nebraska somewheres and we'd hear this horn in the middle of the night and wake up to see a giant truck and semitrailer heading directly at us, and one of us would grab the wheel at the last second and pull us over and get the motherfucker out from behind the wheel. He just wouldn't learn. Every time we let him drive it was the same thing. The Frog was just as bad. He thought he was Barney Oldfield. Only me and the chick could drive. But we preferred balling in the back seat, much to the dismay of the Europeans on the trip. They wanted a piece of the action . . . the Limey with Lise . . . the Frog with me . . . but we only had eyes for each other. So it was like that all through those sixty mad afterburning methadrined

red-trailed eyeball hours across this monstrosity of a tur-
tle-shell of a green and yellow Howard Johnson land in
the heat of August to . . ." Arv hesitated again, looking
over at Moke. She was watching him now, digging it,
watching the rap pick up, lift off, Arv knew it would lift,
it would! The car sped along the freeway through the long
tunnel of tall eucalyptus trees. He twisted his hair, ground
his jaw, driving with one hand. Punched the Merc up to a
hundred miles an hour. He was wailing! Felt the juices
flow. Felt the dope go to his head. The Merc held the
road. The engine purred. The land stretched away clean to
the white mountains of the Ridgeroute . . . "And death,"
said Arv, "and death I felt following us out of New York
City and death came running behind us on the Pennsyl-
vania Turnpike and Interstate 80 and Highway 40, death
done up like a black sixty-eight Caddie El Dorado came
chasing us through New Jersey and Illinois and Wyoming
and Nevada and death I finally found too in Lise's
deep dark cavern, her black hole of Haiti, death when I
plucked the hairy strings of her guitar-shaped gash, death
in her slippery lips her wringing red mouth and death too
always behind us in the shiny El Dorado with its sixteen-
year-old red-headed hillbilly girl driver from Pearl River,
Mississippi, death, nothing but death everywhere on the
raw swath of freeways cut across landscapes and in all the
cars that, following the El Dorado, wheeled by us at seventy-five and eighty miles an hour like bright-painted racing toads. And death too I found in the abandoned cars
rusting by the side of the road. . . . And then, I found
myself, unaccountably, listening to the electric rock on the
radio, getting sucked into it too, liking it all, the devasta-
tion on every side, seeing it with new eyes, the eyes of
those two foreign cats who were digging it supremely.
'Wow! Look at that! Look at that! *Regarde ça! Regarde
ça!*' they kept yelling, pointing. And my eyes, they followed, they were seduced by their excitement and dug it
too, just like them, seeing it through their foreign eyes,
and my heart set to skipping and jumping wildly out on
that wide-ass two- and three-lane strip of black concrete that thundered over everything in our way, and all
those big red and yellow and brightly painted monsters,
those racing toads, racing along with us, and the black
El Dorado always just behind . . .

"And it was funny cause I wasn't used to so many cars, having just got back from the Nam . . . and nobody in America walks, nobody! All I saw was just cars and mobile homes and dying abandoned farms with the wood front porch rotting away and weeds growing in the farmyards and new drive-in restaurants and drive-in movies, laundries, banks, stores, and enormous parking lots made of black asphalt, miles square in area, and old discarded newspapers blowing across, pasting themselves to the windows of broken abandoned automobiles, broken houses, abandoned and boarded-up filling stations, roadhouses, markets, and I got so fucking depressed that I wanted to back out, wanted to go back even to the Nam . . . well . . . no, not the Nam, but even to corrupt Thailand or lovely tragic Cambodia yes . . . and in the car, wailing across the Nevada desert, I screamed out to Lise and the Englishman and the Frog, I screamed, to an advertising jingle on the radio, I screamed:

> Service station yellow
> Supermarket sackpaper brown
> This motherfucker
> Howard Johnson
> Jive ass
> Superhighway nation
> Is got me down!

And they all yelled, 'Yeah!' and 'Right on!' and *'Tu as raison!'* laughing crazily. And that's when I realized what everyone loves about this place: death, and its evidence all around, everywhere you look . . . and . . . and . . ."

"No!" Moke said, with passion, as the Merc rose up the long straight steep rise to the Ridgeroute that went over Frazier Peak and Gorman to L.A., "hey, no!" she said, grabbing his arm, holding it. "Don't stop, baby!" and Arv was as incapable of disobeying her command as he was incapable of taking his foot off that swift rising Mercury as it rode at ninety-two miles an hour swooping like a mallard down a long dip and then taking off the flat Central Valley, soaring up and over the peaks on the back of the long-legged beast, the freeway, whose legs spanned enormous chasms, whose burrowing molelike head churned and twisted through mountains of solid rock . . . "Yeah!" he shouted again, for encouragement, and then went on with it, went on and on and on till finally she had to say:

"Slow down, Arv."

"What?"

"Slow down, you're going over a hundred miles an hour and there're curves up ahead."

"Oh, yeah," Arv said, looking around himself again, still twisting his hair, driving the Merc with his good right hand.

"Why do you play with your hair?" she asked, obviously trying to guide him away from where he'd been going with his furious talk, his furious driving. . . . It seemed he *had* gone too far, too fast, after all . . . it seemed there *was* a limit, of some kind, after all, with her . . .

"Yeah," she said, "you're always pulling at it, messing it up and then smoothing it out, twisting it up into knots."

"I guess because my mother always did it. I used to try to imitate her as a little boy and got the habit."

"How come? Was she special some way?"

"I don't know. It pleased me as a kid to imitate my folks. I still squint my eyes up the way my old man does. And I notice that since I started smoking I imitate his mannerisms when he smokes.".

"So you just like it? That's why you do it?"

"No, I wish I didn't. The thing that's so disquieting about it is that when I start playing with my hair I usually get real nervous and can't concentrate. And yet, I start doing it in the first place because I'm nervous."

"You're an exhausting person, you know?"

Hurt to the quick, Arv struck back at her:

"Why do you always avert your eyes when I ask you personal questions? Are you lying?"

"I don't always tell the truth."

"Not even to me?"

"No."

"Then I can't trust you, can I?"

"I don't know."

Then they really started trying to hurt each other. Arv had begun it. Now as the Ridgeroute grew up around them, high dry-down yellow hills and white granite peaks, Frazier Mountain snowy in the distance, Moke retaliated:

"You're starting to go bald, aren't you?"

"You're starting to get wrinkles around the eyes, at only twenty-five. What'll you look like at thirty?"

"By the time you're thirty you'll be bald as a dome."

"You'll be withered as a cracked leather bag."

"No I won't," she said suddenly, with tears welling up in her slants, putting an end to their game, their vicious but somehow *necessary* game, "no I won't. I won't live that long!"

"Don't say that," Arv said, believing her in some inscrutable way, "don't!" he said, and they were friends again, just as suddenly as they'd become enemies. The basis of their new and greater friendship was a certitude they shared, that had been brought out in the fire of their battle: Moke was right. She'd never see thirty. It was written into her forehead, showed right in her eyes. And Arv could now see that, because of death, and its certainty in her near future, Moke was quite mature enough, despite her youth, to see him for exactly what he was. No better, no worse. And, since Arv believed himself to be fundamentally good, and kind, and decent, sensitive, intelligent, imaginative, he *wanted* her to see him fully, was very glad she saw him for what he was.

She, on the other hand, was still hiding a great deal from him, more than she showed. That he knew for sure. Nope, old Arv didn't know her at all. And, knowing her secret was destructive to their relationship, sensing it, remembering something, suspecting something, he did not press to know her . . . *I seen her one time before I met her, where was that? I don't remember.*

Did Arv really not remember?

No, he was sure he didn't remember.

"Let's have another joint," he said.

She rolled them another and they sat there unspeaking all the way into Hollywood past the Capital Record Dome and out the San Bernardino Freeway to Redlands. It was a bright southern California winter morning, smogless, with snow shining on Mount Baldy, Mount San Jacinto, and Mount San Gregorio. The orange trees of Redlands shone too, bright and green and resplendently golden in the brilliant sunlight.

At Banning, on the ridge between the San Bernardino Valley and the Imperial Valley, Arv pulled over for gas.

Moke rolled them another joint, gave Arv another amphetamine, and by the time they rolled back out onto the
freeway, gliding down into Palm Springs, they were
zonked out of their minds.

"Ooh ooh ooh ooh, *Haole!*" she yelled.

And leaned toward him while he drove, feeling what he
felt . . . their violent impetus toward one another, the
friction, and the electricity, as their spirits met.

"Oooh ooh ooh Zing!" she said.

"Oh, VARRRROOOOOM!" he shouted back at her.

"Wham wham wham!"

"Crash blam boom!"

"Plow ping poo!"

"*Aiiiiiiiie!*"

"*Ai ai ai ai ha ha ai Chihuahua!*" he cried. And yet
they were still apart. "*Aiiiiii!*" he yelled, touching her,
touching her small breast, wanting it, wanting to love her,
wanting her not to die. "Oh!" he shouted, trying to love
her, trying to summon her back from the jaws of death.
. . . "Oh oh oh oh oh!" he hollered, seriously, half-seri-
ously, clowning, meaning it, not meaning it, laughing desperately, for no reason, till he was laughing so hysterically
he could barely guide the car.

Moke was laughing too, she was laughing at him and
then she came close to him and started kissing him on the
ear neck cheek hair eyes and he had to stop the car. But
soon he evaded her pursed lips, pawing hands, and his
own despair, and drove out onto the road again. He
couldn't stop now. His grandpa Alfonso beckoned, still
just beyond the hood ornament. "Come on, kid, you almost there! It's you only chance, you two! Come on!
Véngase! Véngase!" And Arv followed, foot to the
floorboard, following that old Spic sonofabitch on down
home to Mexico, hightailing it down that highway going
through Indio and Coachella heading for the border at
ninety miles an hour. Moke was kissing and kissing. But
she couldn't make him stop.

"And never come back!" his grandpa cried.

And Moke unzipped his fly, groped for his cock where
it lay sweating and throbbing in his uniform pants,
brought it out till it stood up straight against the steering
wheel in his lap, kissed it lovingly, kissed and kissed it
with all her heart as if it had been his lips, as he had

kissed her cunt before, in the dark panting redwood forest in the rain. And, as the Salton Sea, locked in its salty yellow desert basin, fled by them, Arv sensed to the roots of his gnarled Weed-like dick, that she loved him, truly. The rapture of this little brown woman, this girl with the sloping head and slanted eyes, could not be faked. It was real. There was no mistaking it. She loved him. And her love, just as he rounded the turn coming into El Centro, California, brought him sudsing, spouting into her open mouth, and while he drove off the freeway through the flat neon desolation of central El Centro, she drank him, drank him down, while he stroked her beautiful long black hair, and loved her and was lost to her forever, stroking her long shiny little girl's hair. And, as he spun the Merc down Main Street and out of town southbound passing warm truck stops, Giant Orange stands, Frosty Freezes, Mobil Oil stations, Holiday Inns, Moke loved him, the little slant, as he loved her, with her face in his crotch, loving his legs and his thighs and his stomach and his tool again, while Arv smiled at pedestrians in crosswalks and traffic cops and startled truck drivers, loved him and loved him, kissing him for all the world as if it would be the last time she'd ever kiss a man she loved.

They sped through border customs and raced out of Mexicali on the San Felipe road. Arv drove five kilometers out of town, out onto the Colorado River Delta salt flats, and stopped the car. She was in his arms before he could switch off the engine. And Arv had the extreme narcissistic pleasure of kissing kissing himself, tasting himself . . . and it was good . . .

She pulled away. Reached down and slipped her panties off under her miniskirt. Came to him again. They fell to the front seat *And I pricked her dulcet embouchure*. They lost themselves, kissing, swapping spit, talking while they fucked. Arv couldn't think of anything else. Only of talking to her, fucking her.

"Oh."

"Oh!"

"Oh oh oh!"

"Oh."

"Ooooh!"

"Ooooh! I dig you!"

"I dig you I dig you I dig you, uumm beautiful beautiful."

"Umm kiss kiss kiss I dig you too never before umm before."

And when they finally awakened their heads were lying on the floorboards, their bodies were entwined on the seat and their legs went up into the air into the back seat all mixed up one with the other like fucking octopi and an entire family of Indians was standing around the Merc, just outside Arv's window, pointing and laughing . . . and Arv's grandpa, old Alfonso, stood just in front of the Merc's grille, in the white dust, laughing too.

Arv jammed it into reverse and spun out. Moke laughed and said it again, as if she were surprised about it herself, and had to get used to the idea, "I dig you," she said, "I really dig you. . . ."

Arv, in control of the situation now, cock hanging out, a powerful Merc under his power, and a dark slant-eyed foreign woman, a woman he dug who dug him who lay naked in an abandoned position on the seat kissing his hip and his ribs through his U.S. Army shirt, old Arv said, "What's so strange about that?"

Thirty-Three

Croak! Croak! Croak! Yuba heard it. Wrapped up tight with big Roundo in their love-bunk, Yuba heard it, hated it bitterly as he hated it every morning, that horrible old six A.M. croaker worse almost than death itself which, blinking his eyes open suddenly, blinking at the bright morning sunlight shining directly into the eastern windows of the East Block, Yuba felt approaching now immediately. Yuba did not awaken Roundo, his Ma, his love and friend and crime partner of twenty good and bad years, five state prisons, two federal, innumerable city and county jails. Yuba let him go right on snoring, the morning sun warming his relaxed black face. Let him snore right into Paradise. And considered for a second or two what ole Death himself, White Folks, Mister Hawkins, felt like—coming—creep creep creep—coming creeping down the tier in the sunlight, listening like Yuba to the shouts and calls, the electric razors and radios switching on, the stale saved-up nighttime farts exploding all around . . .

Well, the ole hack, he creeping up the staircase and no-body gon' to know who he is cause we in the last cell— creep creep creeping up and he hear and feel what I does. He hear the radio saying words he don't understand. What that radio saying?

"Two B-52's and an F-111 lost over Hanoi in resumption of fullscale bombing" creep creep creep creep "Perfect Apollo splashdown ends era of moon flights" creep creep creep "16 Attica inmates indicted for role in prison revolt" creep creep "NYC police find new discrepancy in heroin seizure" creep "Newsman faces jail in refusal to cede Watergate scandal data" creep "Murder in New Sonora State Prison—Warden sees danger of 'race war' " . . .

"White Folks?" Yuba said, just lying there in bed creep creep creep hearing that light-ass white man's step outside the cell door, knowing that he had gas or cleaning fluid . . . "White Folks?" he said, sniffing the fumes just outside, knowing there was no defense, no way to stop him from pitching it in, tossing a match or a lit rag after it, lighting up the oven . . . no way the hack could make it from the guard shanty in time to unlock the cell and get them out . . . "White Folks?" he said again, lifting his voice.

And he talked, by Jesus, the ole grim reaper did! He spoke right up.

"Yeah?"

"YOU THE MAN GON' BURN IN HELLFIRE, NOT ME!!!" Yuba hollered out, unafraid, with all the soul of his great black lungs, waking up poor ole Roundo, his only crime partner, waking the whole fucking cellblock to what was coming down.

"Guess again, nigger!" White Folks whispered, and then yelled, "Race War!"

WHOOOOOOOOOOOOOOOOOOOM!

Thirty-Four

Moke, curled up like a tawny brown cobra, hissed words of something (words of love? She did not know) into his ear. "It's you! It's you!" she found herself saying, not knowing really what it meant, "it's sure! Cause you nice, *Haole,* will be sweet to me, and who cares about money?"

Enamored for the moment, but still sharp-eyed, she spotted a gas station out across the sagebrush, on an abandoned airstrip overgrown with mesquite. The huge gray desert peaks of the Sierra San Pedro Martir glowed pink and rose under the sun that was now going down behind them.

"Hey! Stop here!" she yelled, and Arv bounced the Merc over the sandy white road between the low gray-green sagebrush and pale yellow-green tumbleweed and parked at a rusted gasoline pump. Moke jumped out, bag in hand. . . .

Come, she felt then, running down her bare thigh. Running, she ran around to the back of the filling station. The low sun hovering just over the high westward mountains made her shadow long . . . as she leapt over the rock pile, her long slender shadow leapt too . . . and followed her onto the gravel . . . CRUNCH CRUNCH CRUNCH . . . then found the wooden door stuck, pushed against it hard, beat at it with her small fists . . . WHAM WHAM WHAM! Opened, she rushed into the incredibly dirty, fly-specked, cockroach-crawling, shit-splattered toilet, *the warm at the mouth,* opened up and then cold and wet *running down my leg* . . . she let it, however, let it run, forgot about the smell of the toilet, ran trembling fingers through her black leather handbag, Indian-crafted, silver buckles and studs, and turquoise trimming, bought in Gallup with Wasco after a successful dope run from Culiacán, running down her hand down, looking for her cotton swabs, got it, got it, began to cry, remembering her lost brother, remembering Wasco, lost love, who was her Daddy, crying, bawling now like a kid, hysterical till she could find her works, her fit, *where the fuck is it?* trying not to fall in the pee-splotched muddy tile floor. Fell, onto her knees, splashing in piss and shit, dabbing at her . . . eyes with the cotton, fretful, forgetful of what she was about, *what am I about to do?* dabbed at her dripping good-feeling cunt, bad-feeling, her face, *oh oh oh oh love going . . . love going to do me in and I didn't even ask . . .* cooked up . . . skin-popped . . . *relaxez-vous, MothaJew,* like Wasco always said . . .

Got herself together, cleaned up, straightened out, looking in the dirty cracked mirror. Heard Arv honking. And ran out.

I'm as fresh as a daisy!

Running out, the sun almost gone down behind the towering Santa Catalina Peak, a thin shaft of it striking her eyes. Avoiding it, turning, raising her bare copper-colored arm, and ran to the car over the rocks and crunching gravel crunch crunch crunch.

Inside the Merc it was warm and smelled of travel. Moke felt she had traveled. A very long way. Does love travel well? No. Love does not travel well at all. And still she didn't know where they were going. They were going to San Felipe, where she had known they were going all the time. It was she, in fact, full knowing why, who'd suggested it: "It's on the Sea of Cortez," she had said brightly, cunningly, "cut off from the winter Pacific weather by the summit of the highest mountains in Baja California. The sea's warm enough for swimming all year round. It's a little fishing village on the desert shore. Dry air, warm days, brilliant cold stars at night. You'll really dig it, I promise!"

Inside the Merc, Moke looked at his face, her new lover, her new mark, and kept her silence. His face was ugly. She could not stop. She kissed his ugly face she could not stop she kissed his moustache.

What is his face like? Not like his cousin's, though they look like cousins.

"I don't know where we're going," she said out loud, bitterly, as he wheeled the Mercury in a cloud of dust out onto the long blacktop road that, Moke knew well, ran

straight as an arrow one hundred and twenty miles from
Mexicali across the gigantic white alkali flats of the Colorado River Delta to San Felipe, ran on a high levee above
the stinking salt sink, like a Great Wall of China without
stopping for anything.

Eighty, ninety, one hundred, one hundred twenty miles
an hour, Arv punched it out, the Merc purring, wanting
it. Moke wanted it. *What do I want?*

"I want to go fast! Go fast! I don't care!"

"I'm stoned too," Arv said, smiling idiotically, beautifully, as innocent as only the zonked can smile, misappre-
hending too, naïve, as only they can be.

One hundred twenty-five. The Merc missed a beat. Arv
turned, laughing stupidly, like a hippy, like a dope head,
and said to her softly, lulling her, digging her, her too,
*digging the little sonofabitching asshole prick Haole
bastard*, he said, low-voiced close to her ear, he said,
"That's as fast as she wants."

"Her too," she said, giggling wackily, pointing at her
round little right breast.

The Mexican desert—red and gold, dust settling, wind
ceasing, tumbleweeds lying unmoving and piled up in the
white alkali at the base of the roadfill, sun sinking, birds
going home, rabbits in their nests, mice tucked in—the
desert closed up for the night. . . .

"Why do you like me?" he asked, smiling shyly, twisting his hair, guiding the Merc over a dip and a little
bridge at 120 miles an hour.

"What do you look like?" she responded, purposefully
irrelevant.

"I'm ugly."

"You're beautiful."

"What do I look like?" she got him to ask, getting him
to abolish his sudden shyness, getting him to admit by his
question that in his heart he was not perhaps *all* ugly . . .

What is it I want with him? she asked herself, as the
white desert, the iron-red Sierras fled by her eyes too fast
to pick out single objects smaller than a mountain range, *I
don't want to hurt him. I want to* . . .

"You're neck isn't right," she said, starting up their
vengeful hurting game of the Bakersfield and Ridgeroute
morning, a million miles before, and yet she didn't find it
inappropriate, now that they had fucked themselves into

this situation . . . "You got dark curly hair that grows obscenely down low on your neck, like a Wop," she said, and he wouldn't answer. But watched the darkening road ahead, watched the Punta San Felipe still one hundred miles away, with its ancient purple volcanic peak guarding its approaches, looming up larger and larger every minute . . . he ground his jaw, twisted his hair into knots . . . Moke watched.

Moke saw her Tutu, flying out in front of them. Tutu was born in a sugarcane shack at Keoneoio, Maui, on the dry desert side. It looked like this. The extinct volcano at San Felipe Point looked like Haleakala from the Kanaio side. The air was dry and clear like this. Tutu would've liked it here. Always said she couldn't wait to get out of that wet old Manoa Valley, but never got around to it. Moke saw Tutu, flying out in front, hovering just over the hood of the speeding Mercury . . .

"You noteeng boy. You weak. You not da macho kine," she said, striking his thigh with her tiny fists. "You noteeng but da kine *Haole,* da kine jail hack, an dat all you evah be! You got da big eahs dey steek out," she said, and then, as if she had rapidly tired of the pidgin game, continued in plain American, "you got a chin that threatens to point and then rounds out at the tip, like a simpering baby girl. What are you like? I'll tell you what you're like, you motherfucker! You got acne scars all over your cheeks and neck, fat lips, your arms are thin and underdeveloped, your chest has no hair but your back is covered, your stomach muscles are undefined. Someday you'll go to fat, go to slack nervous fat. You got a tendency to bad breath because you're always so fucking nervous, unsure of yourself as a man. You suck your gums, grind your jaw, and you blink too often . . . makes you look like you got no character. And you clatter your teeth, and suck your gums till they bleed and the blood goes sour and stinks up your mouth. You're a fucking neurotic. Your breath smells of raw meat gone bad. Your prick is smaller than a normal man's," she said, clenching her teeth, going too far on purpose, "your prick's small when it's soft," she said, modifying her aggressive stance, somewhat . . . "it's small in repose, like a marble 'Hermes Resting,'" she said, softening toward him, "but it gets hard for me," she said, feeling herself run down like melting butter, not knowing where she was going, her emotions taking her down untrodden paths, where her head would never take her. Her head had taken her on this trip. And then her passions had stolen the wheel, and were now winning, conveying her she knew not where, in spite of everything she could do . . . "But when it gets hard," she said, trying again, "it slithers forward like a worm growing and becomes, if not formidable, at least very long and slim like the penis of a fox. After we did it that first time, after we went for the swim and I was home alone, for me there was much more pleasure in thinking about the act than the actual fucking itself which, after you went inside me, left me cold and ill and stupid. Toweling myself off," she said, watching him, watching him to see what he would make of it *what's he supposed to make of it? What am I to make of it?* "toweling myself off in the bathroom I thought: 'He didn't even know where my clitoris was. He was scared and too fast, like a rabbit, like a little boy shaking his thing. He is self-conscious and afraid. He talked little boy talk with me when he put it in, like I was his little friend and we were playing nasty under the house. I didn't want a little playmate. You came too fast and you were afraid to admit it. You turned me cold as a trout!" she screamed, lying through her clenched teeth, hitting at his khaki shoulder, hitting and hitting at him.

The Merc crossed over the double line and drifted. Drifting drifting drifting slowly left. It hit the soft beginning of the soft shoulder and the left rear wheel dragged them toward the deep abyss, the alkali, the white dirt, the dust, the settle, the wasteday, their clean salty graves, the white dust in their hair, their jaws stuck open for air, white alkali dust settling down on them, on their eyes and teeth and ears, like lovers in Hiroshima, Los Alamos, Vietnam. . . . Arv spun the wheel, never taking his foot off the gas. Moke kept hitting. The left rear wheel went back on the blacktop. Arv let up. The speedometer went down down down 120, 110, 100, 90, 80. It felt like they were standing still. Arv let it drift back over to the right-hand side of the road. Moke could see that it had all been very slow for him, because of the grass. He wasn't scared.

Moke had done it. Why had she done it? *To give the lie*

to my words, she thought, *to tell him, to tell him,* she thought, and kept talking, talked herself right back into this world, out of the other . . . "You are built low and strong, with thick strong legs and wide strong shoulders, large perfect hands with long tapering fingers, the fingers of a sculptor. Your nose is high-bridged and goes in a humping little off-kilter line from your brow to its tip. Your ears are pointed. You have black curly hair. You have, perhaps, hidden away, a little fluffy tail. You look like a satyr. I love satyrs."

"You're insane," he said, with the great volcanic peak of the Punta San Felipe looming above them like Haleakala, and the end of the banked roadway in sight ahead.

He took his foot off the gas and let the Merc slow down on its own. It had taken them one hour to go a hundred and twenty miles, a lifetime, an eternity.

"You're not afraid, are you?" she asked him very seriously.

"Yes, I am," he said, and all of his answers that day were right for Moke.

Thirty-Five

That morning in New Sonora Fast-Walking had awakened in bliss, in the bosom of family. His kids, tall eleven-year-old Ralph, and his tiny dancing princess, three-year-old Margie, had gathered around him while he still slept.

"Daddy, Daddy!" they hollered as soon as his bleary eyes flickered open.

"Hey Daddy! You gonna stay home?"

". . . If ee's a good boy!" Marie-Claude called cheerily from the pink sun-lit kitchen.

"He'll be a good boy! He'll be a good boy! the children yelled, jumping up and down, "won't you, Daddy?"

"Sure," said Fast-Walking, wobbling up to his full unsteady height, receiving his children into his short little outstretched arms, his loving small arms, "you bet!"

In the kitchen Marie-Claude was working over the gas range, heating some *croissants* in the oven, making Cream of Wheat for the kids, coffee for the adults. Fast-Walking glided ghostlike up behind her, smooth and fast. The sun came shining in the eastern kitchen window, lighting up her honey-colored hair, the outline of her thin worn body under her robe, the body that he had worn out with his children and his troubles and his running around. He touched her shoulders lightly, tentatively. Nuzzled her neck. She didn't stop him.

"I love you, *chérie*," he said.

"Too soon for zat kind of talk . . ." she said, but she didn't stop him.

After breakfast, the happiest breakfast of his life, Fast-Walking called Big Arv over at Prison Residence #64.

"Say, Big Arv! Listen, I'm back over home now. So you can pick me up here on your way to Evie's, okay?"

"Sure enough! Hey boy! You sure are making up for lost time!"

"Got to," said Fast-Walking, "ain't getting any younger."

"That's for sure," Big Arv said, "don't know anybody round here who's been doing *that* lately . . ."

"What do you mean?"

"You heard the TV?"

"No. Why?"

"Race war."

"What?"

"Race war in the Joint. Roundo and Yuba got fried in their cell this morning."

"Shit, man, you gonna start up with that goddamn Joint talk so early in the morning, and me just home for the first time in a month?"

"I just thought . . ."

"Well, save it, for Christ's sake! You'll spoil my breakfast," Fast-Walking said, and hung up.

Thirty-Six

Arv hit the steep hump at the top of the ridge just north of San Felipe still doing ninety, with old Grandpa Alfonso still flying out in front. The front end of the Merc left the earth like it had done a lifetime ago, on 20th Street in the city, went clean over the old ghostly Spic, and came down hard on the rutted road on the other side, skidding in the soft sand, fishtailing dangerously. Arv idled the Merc, letting the dual pipes rap out, slowing down to twenty. When he got the car back under control they could see the few lights of the little town two miles off across the sagebrush and dry creek beds that cut their way down from the Sierra. The sky had darkened to that peculiar blue-black hue of early evening on the desert. Mars, still alone in the heavens, twinkled bright red above them. The weak yellow lights of San Felipe blinked happily in the twilight. San Felipe occupied the mouth of three small dry creeks that ran into the Sea of Cortez. It nestled just under the extinct volcano that formed the point which distinguished this part of the Gulf of California coast. The one little dirt main street of the town ran down along the edge of the beach. The tiny minority of its residents who could afford finished stucco houses lived there, alongside fifteen garish cantinas with loudspeakers spouting *ranchero* music into the still night air. The other people of the town, poor Indians and mestizos, lived in mud hovels and in overturned hulks of fishing boats along the creek beds and on the beach.

What had got Arv excited, what had made him think that the whole trip might turn out to be perfect, was the fact that, just as the Merc leapt into the air, he had spotted a fiery red and yellow rocket go up high into the clear arid sky and explode into the appearance of a million scattering stars, blue ones, silver and gold ones, green ones too, showering upon the sandy countryside, starting several little brush fires.

"Ooh! Did you see that?" Moke had said.

"Yeah. What is it?"

"I don't know. What's the date today?"

"December twentieth."

"Too early for Christmas, isn't it?"

"You'd think so. But there's sure as hell something going on!"

"Wow! A fiesta! Are we in luck?"

"Yeah, wow!" Arv said happily, wheeling the Merc skidding in the soft sand out onto the main drag, riding it slow down the line of scraggly juniper trees and cactus plants and adobe walls. The central plaza was packed with Mexicans. Hundreds of them, dressed in everything from pirate costumes to bicycle racers' outfits to cowboy and charro regalia. Another rocket went up. *"Ai!"* the crowd yelled. Little Arv and Moke yelled too, *"Ai Chihuahua!"* and parked the Merc on a dirt sidestreet, got out, and joined the action. Nobody paid them any mind. In the darkness they were taken as Mexicans. When they got out of the car they were shocked at how very warm the air was, and realized that they hadn't felt the air, really, not really felt it to walk around in, since they left New Sonora sixteen hours before.

"Hey! It's warm!" Moke said, dancing around in her black leather pants and red minidress top.

"Yeah!" Arv said. "Let's get into it."

BANG! A gun went off. Fifteen bicycle racers took off down the main drag in a kilometer sprint. The crowd roared. *"Ai ai ai!"* Horses reared. Charros waved their broad black sombreros. Motors revved in brokendown old pickup trucks. Indians with straw American cowboy hats shuffled in their sandals or cheap leather boots. Arv and Moke spotted their first gringos: two yellow-haired South Bay or La Jolla surfy types standing outside a cantina in bleached Levis and bare feet.

Arv went up to them and tried to find out what all the commotion was about. They looked him up and down, staring very hard at his uniform. Finally they responded, "We don't know."

"How about a cheap hotel? You know where I can find one?"

"There's one across the street, over there behind that windmill," they said, and then padded off down the dirt street, avoiding him as if he had the plague.

Arv hustled Moke across the white dusty road and through a cactus garden and across somebody's dirt yard to a long low adobe dwelling with a tarred gravel roof. An old woman sat under the arches sewing by the light of a Coleman lantern.

"*Hay lugar para dos personas?*"

"*Que sí!*" the old woman said, looking up nearsightedly from her needlework. "*Blanca, ven p'aca!*"

A fat old brown Indian woman came around the side of the house, out into the light.

"*Vete monstrar el matrimonio. Esto Señorito tienne prisa, no?*"

"*Pues, claro, con una negracita así!*"

"*Ai! Es en verdad un pedazito de melón!*"

The old woman and the Indian laughed about something that Arv didn't understand and then the Indian took them across a white sand yard, under young eucalyptus trees, to a small ground-floor room with a large cracked cement shower. It was clean enough, though a fat cockroach ran out from under Arv's foot as soon as he stepped in. The bed was large and the sheets were white and pressed and dry. The shower leaked and the water tap dripped and there was a wide crack under the door that let the sand blow in, but Arv thought it would do.

"*Cuánto?*" he asked.

"*Cinco dólares al día.*"

"*De acuerdo.*"

She left them alone under the pathetically weak yellow light of the bare overhead bulb. The sound of music and rockets and happy shouting came in through the half-opened window.

"Well, it ain't the Ritz . . ."

"I like it!" Moke said, bouncing on the bed, "I really do. It's so, so, Baja California!"

"Yeah," Arv said, glancing at the sand drifting under the door, considering the possibility of scorpions coming in the same way. "Listen, what do you say we clean up and then whip out and get me some threads? I feel like a freak in these Joint clothes."

"Sure," she said happily, running into the shower . . . "Ooh! . . . Cockroaches!"

When they went back outside everyone in town was
eating supper. The ones with enough money were eating
in one of the fifteen cantinas. The others went home for
tortillas and refried beans or bought a hot buttered and
chilied ear of corn from a man with a big tin scrub-tub
and a fire of mesquite wood. And others rifled garbage
cans. Others went hungry.

Arv found a dry goods store open. It was run by a Chinaman. Several of the shops in San Felipe were run by
Cantonese businessmen who'd come down from San Francisco during the Depression and opened up shop and assimilated, as much as a Chinaman can ever assimilate.
The Chinaman didn't speak a word of English. Even his
father, born in San Francisco, whom he summoned in
from the back screen porch, couldn't manage to communicate in his native tongue. But Arv and Moke, between
them, with their high school and Tijuana and travelers'
Spanish, made him understand that Arv wanted a pair of
boots, some corduroy pants, a Levi denim cowboy shirt,
and two pairs of socks. Moke insisted that he get the
boots even though they cost twenty dollars. They were a
beautiful pair of yellowish charro boots made in Ciudad
Camargo, Chihuahua. *"Ai Chihuahua!"* she yelled as soon
as she saw the label, while the younger Chinaman looked
on glumly, not digging the reference. He must have
thought they were nuts, and never cracked even the suggestion of a smile, even though Arv and Moke laughed
and capered around his shop for half an hour, trying everything on. They emerged finally in holiday finery: Arv
in his black cords and boots and denim shirt, and a straw
cowboy hat. Moke in a long red and green and yellow
fiesta skirt with wide petticoats and a white embroidered
wedding blouse, a black flat-brimmed Andalusian hat, and
a pair of red Flamenco sandals. They looked, in their
brand-new store-bought finery, their shop-worn, moth-
ball-smelling, crinkled-up outfits, like a couple of dudes
just in from Jersey City, and created a great commotion
as soon as they got out into the street light.

"Oye, mira, dos gringos de Nueva York!"

"No, Julio, que vengan de Chicago."

*"Que no! Una negrita de la Habana y un rico de Lon-
dres!"*

"Ai, que chupa la berga!"

"Con estos labios? Claro!"

"Ai ai ai aiiiiiiiii Chihuahua!"

Moke and Arv stepped smartly down the street, trucking it in the white dust, ignoring the good-natured calls of the loitering vaqueros and drugstore cowboys.

Moke made Arv stop at a peso arcade and shoot a .22 at a long line of rubber balloons.

Pow! Pow! Pow! Pow! Pow! Pow! he went down the long line blasting each and every one of them, and the spinning and revolving and jumping targets too, Pow! Pow! Pow! till a large crowd collected around them, cheering him on, and Arv got nervous, and missed winning the kewpie doll, fat, cherubic, red-headed, that Moke had wanted so much.

"Aw shit! Ya fucking *Haole*, you mees da doll fo' me!"

"Don't worry about it, honey, I can win it for you any time."

"You really dat good?"

"Fuck! I'm the greatest. U.S. Army Sharpshooter, First Class, Marksman Number One, New Sonora Commission of Corrections! That's why I didn't have to go out humping the boonies, getting zapped with all them grunts in the Nam."

"How's that?"

"Shit! I wanted a cushy desk job in Saigon with easy access to the ladies. I figured you could count on the army to place you in exactly the opposite MOS your talents dictated. So I won the Fort Ord Sharpshooter Award and landed at G-2 in a Saigon Headquarters Company clipping war news from foreign English-language newspapers and pasting them in a notebook marked FOR GENERAL WESTMORELAND'S EYES ONLY. It was a Fast-Walking paradise. He would've gone wacky there, with all that beautiful paper to clip and paste. When I told him about it he nearly died of envy."

Farther on down the street they stepped into a little cinderblock cantina called El Barco Negro that advertised the best tamales in the world . . . *Los tamales mejores en el mundo entiero!* Two bands were competing with each other for the noisy drunken clientele, who lined the walls and spilled out the door and hung out the open windows and clambered over the tables. One of the bands was *norteño*, dressed in northern Mexican cowboy style, with

blue jeans and boots and rodeo shirts and pearl buttons
and wide-brimmed straw hats like Arv's. They played guitar and a big bass and a fiddle. The man on the bass beat
it like a drum. It was funky, homely range music, with
piercing whistles and raw frontier harmonizing. The other
band was *veracruzano*, from the State of Veracruz on the
Gulf of Mexico side. Its three members were much
darker, with obvious African blood, and dressed all in
white, with red kerchiefs and leather *huaraches* and small
Cuban-style straw hats. They were much more sophisti-
cated. Their music was smooth and rhythmic and very
Caribbean. It made you want to get up and truck and
wing and wiggle your ass, made you wanna do the cha-
cha-cha or the rhumba or the Mambo Rock. A great big
fat black man with a Charlie Chaplin moustache played a
tiny ukulele-type instrument. A teeny fellow, no more
than a dark brown wisp, played a huge portable harp.
And a middle-sized dude, very ordinary-looking Spic with
a thin moustache, played a normal-sized guitar. Their
rhythm was very complicated, unlike the *norteños'*. And
they sang in high rapid voices, skatting it, almost, going
around the room making up rhyming verses on the spot
about various characters they stopped in front of. After
they'd run through their verse everyone would laugh.
They were obviously poking fun at some of the customers,
who were supposed to take it in good humor. But several
times Arv saw some of them get pissed off, some of them
even had to be restrained by friends from pulling knives
or *pistolas*. The Barco Negro was a good Mexican bar, a
vibrant and exciting bar, a bar with that eternal Western
Hemisphere vitality: the threat of violence, the possibility
of sudden death. . . .

"*La Bamba!*" Arv yelled, when the *veracruzanos* paused
for a moment. *La Bamba* was the only Veracruz song he
knew. They started it up immediately, and the whole
crowd started yelling as soon as it heard the song's infectious beat, it's unforgettable melody and rhymey catchy
verses:

> To dance the Bamba
> You need a horn of plenty
> A horn of plenty
> Bamba, and higher and higher
> And higher and higher . . .

The *veracruzanos,* singing and playing and swaying like Mexicans in a black and white MGM production of the late '40's, slid around to where Arv and Moke had sat down at a table by the door, chug-a-lugging Carta Blanca beer, good hopsy Mexican beer with a wet but bitter taste, to get rid of their road thirst.

> Para bailar la Bamba
> Necesita una boca de gracia
> Una boca de gracia
> Bamba y arriba y arriba
> Y arriba y arriba . . .

Moke asked them to play it again. They did. Arv ordered *huevos rancheros* when the waitress came around. And more Carta Blanca. And tequila for the *veracruzanos. Salud!* They tossed it off and broke into *Negracita de mi Corazón,* a Cuban song, singing it to Moke:

> Negracita negra mia
> Pedazito de melón
> Negracita encantita
> Dueña de mi corazón . . .

they sang: "Little nigger girl, little nigger mine, little piece of melon, little nigger, little enchantress, governess of my heart" . . . they sang, and the whole place broke into wild applause and laughter. Arv and Moke loved it. "Geev it! Geev it!" Moke shouted in pidgin, not at all put off by the racial overtones of the song, since it was sung in such good humor. More beer! *Más cerveza por favor!* Tequila! After a while the band took a break and they sat down with Moke and Arv. The middle-sized guy spoke a little *Angleesh.*

"Deez is ma frens: Manuel, Miguel, and me, Martín."

"M, M, and M!" Moke shrieked, jumping up and down in her chair.

"Seguro! You lak de musica?"

"Oh yeah! Very much!"

"You wan mo'? You paga tweenty-fi' pesos, we play all the night!"

"Okay," Moke said, "Ah geev it," in pidgin, handing it over, and they understood her perfectly.

And so for the rest of the evening, wherever they went,

Moke and Arv brought their own band along with them, the best band in town. Throngs of people followed them. Even the two surfy blond gringos got hip, and came along. They went to every bar on the main street, creating a grand stir wherever they entered, making friends and adding to their entourage everywhere. They walked singing and dancing and playing *La Bamba* over and over again, right down the middle of the street. They sang for the fat dark cops sitting on their Harley-Davidson motorcycles in the central square. They played for the priest, three Tijuana whores, a family of mysterious Czech refugees and Johnny Domingues, the most famous sportfishing captain on the Gulf. They played for Michael X, an American fugitive from justice who ran a little beachside bar. They played for his gorgeous Andalusian wife Mari-Carmen, and her beautiful little twenty-year-old sister Conchi. And it was there that they ended the night, lying around on straw mats and low wicker stools in the open-air bar, drinking tequila and smoking joints of beautiful mellow local grass.

They all had a marvelous time till, at four o'clock in the morning, Michael X whipped out the .45 he kept under the bar and fired it into the air to celebrate the success of their party. The discharge brought his palm frond roof down on his head, and on Mari-Carmen's too, knocking her out cold. The sizzling fat in the tortilla pan got into the palm leaves and caught fire. The roof went up in flames. They dragged Mari-Carmen's delicate, pale-white figure out and revived her by dunking her in the black muddy waters of the Gulf. Michael laughed hysterically as his bar, his only possession in the world, burnt to the ground.

"Goddamnit, I had a bar in Ibiza, one in Puerto Vallarta, and now this one!" he cried, tweaking his thin black moustache, stamping his black boots in the wet sand, "and they all burnt up!"

"Well, fuck it!" Moke yelled. "Let's take up a collection!"

They did, and came out with a hundred dollars. The *veracruzanos* gave their whole night's profits. Two friendly tradespeople from the town offered him unlimited credit. Everyone volunteered to help in the rebuilding *mañana*. Michael broke down in tears at everyone's beneficence

and offered free hot beer all around, a gift that was grate-
fully accepted. Moke and Arv loved the world, loved
Michael X and Mari-Carmen and Conchi and the
veracruzanos and each other. As dawn was cracking over
the mountains of Sonora Moke yelled, "Let's all go swimming!" But everyone looked glum. This was going too far.
They'd been game for anything all night long, and were
terribly sad that they had to chicken out now, but as
Martín said, "Eet too focking *frío!*"

Arv and Moke stripped down to their underwear and
ran full speed to the water and dove in, stroking swiftly
toward a fishing boat two hundred yards out, feeling the
icy night water numb their bodies.

They raced, the water bubbling up white around their
thrusting legs, their swift-stroking arms. The physical effort brought the dope and the alcohol to their brains.
They experienced that wonderful scary feeling you get
when you go in deep and long into night water when
you're drugged. They experienced bliss, and not caring,
and a communion of the physical and spiritual that nearly
exceeded their sexual adventures. Moke glided ahead of
Arv like a slim minnow in the dark water. Halfway out to
the boat, they saw the first sliver of sun come out of the
Sierra del Pinacate on the Sonora side of the Gulf. It was
just a needle of light at first, that struck them on their
heads with the force of a bullet. Moke went out ahead of
Arv. He tried and tried and almost cramped his legs
trying to keep up, but he just couldn't get that little
Hawaiian. Only two thirds of the way there, with the sun
beaming in his face, he saw Moke up on the deck talking
to the captain, who turned out to be Johnny Domingues.
He'd left the party at three in the morning, grabbed three
hours of zees, and was now preparing to sail.

By the time Arv splashed up to the side Moke had arranged to hire the boat for the day. Johnny, who wore
long sideburns, a scraggy goatee, and a bandanna around
his head, looked like some kind of corsair off the Spanish
Main. He was supposed to go around to the trailer camp
on the other side of the point to pick up some gringo fishermen from Des Moines, Iowa, for the day. But when
Moke put it to him he said, "Aw, fock eet!" with amazing
alacrity, "we gonna have de bes time *en el mundo entiero,*
no?" and cracked them all another ice cold bottle of Carta

Blanca. When Arv struggled up on board he said, "Hey, Moke! I thought you didn't like sunshine!" And she said, "Wow! Hey, I forgot. Maybe I'm going through some kind of change, or something."

"*Ai ai ai aiiiii chihuahua!*" they all yelled as they set out southeast toward the Cabo Tepoca, watching the drunkards and partygoers on the land following them tripping and rolling in the sand all the way down to the end of the beach.

All day Moke and Arv lolled in the sun, dragging their hands in the waters of the Sea of Cortez.

"You no wan feesh?" Johnny kept asking.

"No Johnny," they always said, "all we want is some more of that fine grass of yours!"

They had a delicious lunch on the other side, at a little desert place called Puerto Pañasco. They had fresh barbecued whole hake fish with lemon under a palm frond shack in the fishing port. And lots more of that good Carta Blanca beer. The sun was hot but not too hot. Arv got nicely burnt.

Swigging at her beer bottle, tilting it up in the brilliant sunlight, while the ragged Indian fish-stand proprietor looked on, Moke laughed and said, "Hey! You know what? I like it!"

"What, the sun?"

"Yeah! It's outasight!"

On the way back across the Gulf to San Felipe Johnny put on the radio and they listened to more *veracruzano* and Cuban music from the Mexicali station. Arv and Moke flaked out in the late afternoon in the sleeping quarters under the heaving bow of the boat, heaving together briefly, lustfully, and then fell asleep, feeling well-stuffed, well-fucked, well-sucked, sunburnt, windburnt, beer high, a bit stoned, and very very mellow, listening to the waves patter on the wooden prow, feeling it heave and rise up and slap down on every swell, as they had swelled and slapped and heaved wetly and risen, only minutes before. Arv kissed her when they awakened. Her lips were dry and tasted of fish oil and charcoal and lemon and salt water and come. They tasted good. He kissed them again. She licked his face.

"Ummmmmm . . . you taste good too!"

When they went up on deck Johnny was just anchoring

the boat off Michael X's brand new palm frond bar. He
lowered the boat and rowed them to the beach. Moke hit
him with the money for the trip.

"Eh! Dat too much!"

"Don't worry about it," Moke said.

"Say, you're rich!" Arv shouted.

"Not nearly rich enough for my taste!" she yelled back
through the wind-driven spray.

On the beach they could see Michael and Mari-Carmen
and little Conchi waving. The two surfers and the
veracruzano band and everyone from the night before was
sitting on the beach and sipping tequila out of a common
bottle and licking salt and lemon off their wrists, waiting
for them.

"Say, what a far-out bar you got here!" Arv said, as
they ran out onto the beach.

"Verdad?" Michael asked.

"Faaaaaaaantastickooooooo!" Moke interjected, in a
heavy affected Gringo accent, grabbing the tequila bottle
from Martín, tilting it up in the last rays of the sun.

They all sat down in the still warm sand and drank and
talked about nothing much in two languages. The
veracruzanos started up again.

"Guantanamera!" all the gringos yelled.

So they sang it:

> Guantanamera
> Guajira Guantanamera
> Guantanameeeeeeeeera
> Guajira Guantanamera . . .

And that's the way it went all night until eight o'clock
the next morning when Moke and Arv returned to their
room for the first time in two days. The Señora was sitting
out in her dirt patio taking the first sun. Her husband,
a squat, gray-headed, moustachioed old vaquero who
chewed tobacco, was sitting beside her.

"Jou espik Ingles?" he asked.

"Yeah," Arv said, not wanting to be sucked into a long
conversation at the moment, but hesitating, anyway.

"I leev in Texas turty-tree years," he said, showing his
stained teeth in a big wide grin, a Texas grin.

"You look like my grandpa," Arv said, telling the truth.

"He was from McAllen, Texas. His name was Alfonso Encina, you know him?"

"I wok een McAllen one year," he said, ". . . Alfonso Encina . . . Encina . . . Sure, I know heem!" the old man lied, blinking his eyes rapidly. "Where he at now?"

"Oh," Arv began, glancing at Moke, who stood there in the shadow of the archway, and knew nothing of his grandfather, and waited patiently, listening to the exchange, "oh," Arv said, "he's up in L.A. now, doing real good. Made a fortune up in Las Vegas in construction. Went to the casino and hit red fifteen times in a row on the roulette wheel and made himself a millionaire. He's retired now."

"Yeah?" the old man asked warily, "no sheet?"

"No shit," Arv said, in the sincerest tones he could muster, "really, no shit!"

"Weeeeel," the old guy said, chewing real slow on his Bull Durham, "you tell de old sonofabeetch dat hees ole fren Hector Gaticas in San Felipe, Baja California, he ain't doin' so good, eh? Tell heem send a leetle money sout o' de border fas', eh?"

"Sure," Arv said, easing in toward the room, "well, so long, we're going in for a little siesta, okay?" He felt a little guilty, for some reason, like he'd done something wrong, or something.

Inside their little dark room with the sand drifted up under the door, and the weak yellow light, their room with dusty curtains and crumbling cinderblock walls and cockroaches on the cement floor and dried carcasses of last year's scorpions under the bed, their room with a rusty mossy cold-water shower, Arv and Moke bathed happily together like children and jumped into the sheets and kept each other warm.

And slept, dreaming their separate dreams, till late afternoon.

Thirty-Seven

Meanwhile, back in the Joint, would you believe it? Fast-Walking was in a hurry! He ran up the corrugated iron staircase in the East Block doing a flying prechow count on a cold Friday evening . . . and only one more shopping day till Christmas. He had new leather heels on his flying jodhpurs and his keyes were going jingle-jangle and his metal counter banging against his big belt buckle but he didn't dig what a fearful clatter he was making, he was so hot to get out from behind them gray walls and down to meet the sweet Marie-Claude, his only love, his only little wife, who'd promised just this morning, she'd do it finally, after two months without, would do it any way he wanted it, this very night after work!

So then some dude, someone unknown above him up on the fourth or fifth tier, some young gunsel nigger, or someone affecting to be, yelled out, "Hey Pig! Stop yo mutha-fuggin' jingle-jangle!"

"Aw, blow it out yo white ass!" Fast-Walking hollered back, setting the whole East Block from tier to echoing tier . . . white tiers, black tiers, Spic tiers . . . laughing fit to split a gut . . . setting the sparrows to flying wackily about in the rafters, beaning themselves on the walls. . . . The same thing had happened before, the same dude yelling out. It had, in fact, become almost a ritual with them in the past few days. And Fast-Walking had yelled back a new funny line to him every night, making the whole block crack up with laughter. It was the only thing he could do to fight back, he figured, with these evil-ass cats in the East Block. The block echoed so much that you could never pin the cat down. He could call you any name he wanted. Was there only one? Or more? He didn't have a clue. It sounded like the same voice. But you could never tell. So old Fast-Walking, he just made a joke out of it. That's the only way he figured he could handle the matter.

As he strode down the metal walkway he flashed in on the napping bodies with his flashlight and they all looked like they were sleeping like babies. But Fast-Walking knew better. Convicts never sleep. They catnap, for good reason. You learn to keep one eye open at all times at the Joint . . . your good one. Else in the dark you get stuck in the ribs, the heart. Yet, as he went striding down the fifth tier, trying to figure out which one of them mothers yelled at him, his leather heels clanging on the metal, clicking his counter . . . one . . . two . . . three . . . four . . . five . . . flashing his flashlight in on the reclining forms in their bunk beds (two nappy heads to each three-by-eleven cell) they might have all been counting sheep, for all Fast-Walking could tell. Not a peep was heard.

Eighty-seven on the fifth tier.

He wrote it down as he flashed his light in on Galliot, sleeping by himself in the last cell. Was it him that did the hollering? The holler, this time, you see, it wasn't just for fun . . . and what with the "race war," as the newspapers were beginning to call it . . . and everything . . . no, this holler wasn't strictly for kicks. There was another sound in it. It was a warning, or a threat, wasn't it? Or maybe not. Maybe he was just getting a little uptight lately, working for that goddamn Evie, and that fucking bad-ass Wasco, and the dope, and all that shit. Yeah, maybe he was just a little nervous. Or maybe not. That's the thing. You could never tell in the Joint. Even when you were under the King pin's umbrella. Maybe just because of that. But how would you ever know? Nothing was clear, nothing was real in the Joint. Anything could happen. Was it Galliot, then? He held the light steadily on his heaving chest. "Make sure them cons are *breathing* for the count," Big Arv always said, "you never know. It might be a dummy, or it might be dead . . ." But old Galliot, he was breathing alright, taking his evening nap. His heavy well-developed pecs going up and down, up and down. But he was shucking. *No more sleeping than I am. Was it you hollering? Naw. You too big a dude, motherfucker. Wouldn't waste yo time, would you, Jim?"*

When Fast-Walking hit the fourth tier and started

counting again the same voice yelled out, "Shut up, punk!" And there was something else in that voice again, something not for play. But it wasn't worth the bother to answer this time. Even for a laugh. Fast-Walking was in a hurry.

Click-click-click . . . one . . . two . . . three . . . four . . .

Eighty on the fourth tier.

The seventh cell down was Wasco's. Sweet-ass Hearne was squatting in there now, over the toilet; Wasco was still probably down in the guard shanty.

"Jez douchin', Doc," the squeeze said, winking lewdly.

Seventy-nine on the third tier.

Eighty-five on the second.

Down in the guard shanty Wasco had the stinger stuck in a glass of water, warming it for instant coffee. *Tonight,* Fast-Walking was thinking, *tonight Wasco's got the puss of an aging Irish gypsy princess, the satchel of a carny queen past her prime, the face of a little girl gone bad, the face of evil.* As soon as Wasco spotted Sanger, who was the new East Block swing shift officer, and spotted Fast-Walking as they headed in from the count, he put four teaspoons of Nescafé into the water. The electrified water sizzled, the hot wire jerked and danced, the coffee brewed, right off the 250-volt line, a process that always held Fast-Walking transfixed in wonder . . . he watched it now; the coffee brewed. It smelled good.

Big Arv was in there too, tilting his chair back on the cardboard wall, his feet on the sarge's desk, waiting for the count. Fast-Walking gave him a piece of paper on which he'd marked the number of inmates on each tier. He did it with the sinking heart he always had when he knew for sure he'd miscounted and would have to run all the way five stories back up for the recount. Had to do that more and more the past few days. Losing the old touch, that's what he was doing. *Got to get it together. Or you'll blow it, baby. Keep on top of it, man. Easy-breezy.*

Big Arv took a long time looking at the count, enjoying Fast-Walking's anxious suspense. Then, with a self-satisfied smirk on his fat greasy Spic face, he said, "Miscount!" And Fast-Walking's heart fell.

"That's alright, partner, I'll run up and help you out," Sanger, doing a little ring dance, said, shadowboxing around the shanty, his slack pectoral muscles and slack fat beer belly flipping up and down, "keeps me in shape!"

Then Big Arv laughed. "You forgot to mark old Wasco down, Fast-Walking, you must be slipping, boy!" he said, happy for a chance to display his pathetic sense of humor.

Fast-Walking sighed, too genuinely relieved to be angry at his fat rival. "Oh! Okay! Let's see, then. That makes eighty on the third, right?"

"Hey! You're thinking real fast here lately, Fast-Walkin'!" Big Arv exclaimed, heavily ironic, sipping loud and vulgar at his dirty plastic cup, looking sleepy like he always did, but under his heavy lids his little green eyes darting, darting. . . .

After running the convicts to chow and shaking them down coming back, Fast-Walking went in, pulled his lunch pail out of his locker, and sat down with Sanger for a little coffee break and a snack. When they were finished they reached again into their lunch pails, laughing and poking each other like naughty boys . . . "Har har har har!" as they leaned forward over their plastic-baggied, wifie-packed sandwiches and supermarket apples and oranges and picked out their extra-large Thermos bottles . . . "Har har har! Remember how old Evie packed 'em?" Sanger guffawed, socking Fast-Walking perhaps just a trifle too hard on the shoulder. . . . Yesterday Sanger'd accepted "employment" at Evie's seedy store too. . . .

"I sure do!" Fast-Walking laughed, rather labored . . . "Ha ha" . . . fishing with his long index finger for what he was looking to find in the slime: cold coffee, a quarter pint of pure cream for opacity and, floating spermy and rubbery in the froth . . . a Sheik prophylactic stuffed to the roll with a full piece of five-cut boy. . . .

After a while Wasco said, "Hey man, can you just hike up to the tier and lock me in for an hour or so?" winking broadly, "I want to do a little exercise . . ."

"Sure," Fast-Walking said, smiling nervously, and started up. But Big Arv wanted to play, it seems.

"Wait a minute," he said, "how you getting along lately with your punk, Wasco? I hear she's a real Lulu in bed, eh? That junkie-butt's pretty good stuff, I hear!"

"Aw, come on, Sarge, you know me better than that," Wasco said coyly, cute, kewpie doll, blinking his little red eyes, letting Big Arv pretend that he still had a little power around the East Block, at least enough power to crack a joke once in a while, "why, the squeeze's a real nice young serious business apprentice," Wasco said, strutting around the wooden pass counter, "I'm thinking of breaking him into my commercial affairs, quite frankly speaking. He's coming along great. I believe in youth. And helping young folks on their journey through life."

He poked Big Arv as he went out onto the cellblock floor. "Dig it?" he said, and Fast-Walking could hear Big Arv laughing about it salaciously all the way up to the second tier.

Fast-Walking unlocked the huge steel lever that barred all the cells. He put his foot up against the wall of the end cell and pushed against it with his foot, leaning backwards and jerking hard. He tugged twice but it wouldn't come. He felt like he just didn't have any power left in his little skinny arms anymore. He heaved again, panting. Wasco left his cell door, where he'd been waiting, jiving with the squeeze, and swaggered back down to Fast-Walking.

"Here! Let me do it, goddamnit!" he said viciously, and with one mighty heave his heavy-built brick shithouse Weed body snapped back and brought the cells crashing open. "Now, gimme the shit!" Wasco said, and Fast-Walking was obliged to reach down into his sweaty shorts and bring out the wet sloppy stuffed rubber and give it to him. "Now, get the fuck out of here! And don't let me see your ugly satchel till shower time!" Wasco said, and then walked slow and easy over to his cell and went in. Fast-Walking let the steel lever slide back into place, locking all the cells, and everything was quiet as he tiptoed down the spiral metal staircase.

Later, at TV time, Big Arv sent them up to supervise movement on the tiers and keep a watch on the floor. Sanger covered the first three tiers and Fast-Walking had to go all the way up again and cover the top.

Fast-Walking was still in his uncharacteristic futile hurry. Today, instead of going fast but looking like slow, he went fast and looked it. Looked rushed. Harried. Nervous. Shifty-eyed. Scared-ass. Today, instead of going along smoothly unsteady, unsteadily steady, sure-foot wobbles, he was going just flat-ass shaky and jerky-kneed. He felt like a strong wind could blow him over. The tap of a sapling branch. A baby's fist. A grasshopper kick. All

he wanted to do was just get back home to Prison Residence #71 and his sweet wife's wifely French caresses
where he could feel safe again, safe and strong and unsteadily steady again, sure and shaky. . . . Two more
hours to go. He skipped up the stairs, rubber-legging it,
taking two at a time. On the fifth tier he went halfway
down and lit a cigarette, leaning on the iron railing, looking down at the TV on the floor, listening to the nine
o'clock news summary: "B-52's in 4th day of bombing"
creep creep "U.S. border guards accused of 'improprieties'
in drug traffic" creep creep creep "Astronauts rejoin
families" creep "Philip Berrigan paroled after three years
in jail" creep creep "Evidence of government 'collusion' in
Watergate wire tap case" creep creep creep creep.

Fast-Walking heard something. It was creep creep like
he heard the other night when Bullet creep creep . . .
there it went again . . . creep.

The floor was full of convicts coming in from the
movie, night school, milling around. Whites on one side,
blacks on the other. Spics in between. Shucking and
jiving, conspiring, staring across at each other, threatening each other, laughing at the tube . . . creep creep
. . . There it was again. What? . . . creep . . . What was
it? Fast-Walking surveyed the scene below him without
seeing it creep creep creep his head was gone off some-
place else, over the walls to Marie-Claude, to Ralphie and
Margie and his happy home at #71, or beyond, out of the
Joint and New Sonora altogether, all the way to Oregon,
the faraway arid elusive unobtainable tantalizing
southeastern empty corner of Oregon . . . where the Indians were so poor the buffalo ate *them*, that Fast-Walking
. . . creep creep creep . . . would have . . . creep . . .
could have . . . creep creep . . . one day, if only, might
have transformed into a wonderland of his own . . .
creep . . . invention, with the honest sweat of his honest
labor . . .

He knew he was going to die.

Creep creep creep.

He would not turn around.

Someone swung at his head. Fast-Walking ducked. The
blow glanced off his shoulder and struck him on the back
of the neck. The next one caught him on top of the head.
The bill of his military cap slammed down and smashed

his nose and bloodied it and he couldn't see or breathe. His cap was over his eyes and the blood came and stopped his nose and his mouth. He couldn't push the cap aside. He couldn't move. He was dead. But he could still feel everything, hear everything. But there was no more inside to him. He wasn't Miniver anymore. And that came as a kind of relief. As did the thought that, in all his troubles and debts and loans, he'd never let his life insurance run out, for old Marie-Claude and the kids. Oh Jesus, that poor old fool Fast-Walking, he sure used to have problems! Already he wasn't Fast-Walking. He was outside of him now, watching him on the tier. Not one special thing now. He was everything. He was nothing. Nothing basic had changed. He was dead.

Relaxed, stoned, beaned, sentient, supreme, dead, but still waiting, Fast-Walking felt someone go through his pockets, empty things out. Felt him pin a note to his khaki shirtfront, lift him off the cold corrugated metal, heard him grunting with his weight, felt his breath upon his long narrow . . . narrowing . . . face . . . knew him . . . forgave him . . . it was all so far behind him now. . . .

Blessing his murderer, at peace, dreaming of life everlasting, Fast-Walking flew down through the stale air of the East Block and a cry involuntarily escaped his lips. Who would have known that his own jaw'd turn traitor on him, lock open for air, suck blood till his lungs burst, kill his afternoon food violently? Who would have known he'd shriek and scream till he thought his ears themselves would call him back to life . . . "AAAAAAAAAAAAAAAAAAAA-AAAAAAAAAGGGGGGGGGGGGGHHHHHHHHHH!"

But nobody heard him. Didn't anybody hear him over the sound of the TV? Nope. Nobody heard him. Not a soul. Not a living soul. Not until he hit. SCHPPPPPLLLLL-LLAAAAAAAAAAAT!

"Despite bombing, life as usual in Hanoi."

There was a one-word note pinned to Fast-Walking's chest when Big Arv found him on the floor:

PIG

Thirty-Eight

Moke awakened from a dream that she was falling. She was. She was falling off the bed. Arv was tickling her, laughing and blowing and slurping comically at her round brown belly with his mouth, showering spit around the covers when he shook his head, woofing like a dog WOOF! and driving her right off the bed onto the sandy cement floor. She grabbed him by the hair, shouting and laughing, "Ow, ya *Haole* sonofabitch! What you trying to do to me? Goddamnit!" and pulled him up to her face and kissed his nose chin mouth teeth and he went inside of her and she liked it.

Then they lay back exhausted on the dusty bedspread, silent, not touching, getting their breath back. Then they started up again, without saying anything, no longer laughing or playing, kissing themselves into seriousness, into a lover's self-indulgent and serious oblivion, into a hypnotic state induced by their own sensuality, their own maddening desire of and pleasure in the other's body, the other's essence and deep true being. They made love gently then, and slowly, all without saying a solitary word. Their bodies were warm and salty and sunburnt. They crawled up into each other's bodies, the nest of the passions, the seat of the soul, and indulged themselves more times than they could count, scattering the tidy webs and feathers that had lain there undisturbed since childhood. They entered into the very most profound level of the other's existence, without thinking, without trying, aided only by the joints of solid Baja grass that they lit up every hour or so. Time disappeared. They slept again. Awakened. Moke couldn't think. When she slept she dreamed of Wasco and forced herself awake again. Wasco was angry. Arv went places in her where his cousin had never been. Moke suffered a moment of guilt. But only a moment. This, as Moke had reflected rather often in the last few days, this was the one unlooked-for ingredient in Wasco's plan, his plot, his pot, his human stew, this was the spice that could spoil the broth, the fallible human spice, if she let it, tried it, shook it over the mixture herself. Wasco never had been much for experimental cooking, she thought now, remembering his disinclination for anything more exotic than potatoes and steak. Neither Moke nor Wasco had dreamed of this spicy possibility, this impossible possibility of love and affection and companionship and sexual gratification between Moke and Little Arv, Wasco's "shrimpy little twirpy square-ass cuz." Moke now perceived that what Wasco knew of his cousin, what he'd conveyed to her over the years, was the façade in Arv's makeup that had taken her only minutes to pierce. What was underneath, what she had come to love and cherish and admire, Wasco obviously had no inkling of. Though she knew Wasco was not unintelligent about most things, his failure to comprehend his own cousin put him in a quite different light. Moke had trusted Wasco always to see clearly, brutally right, unemotional, correct, to bore through appearance and get immediately to the cold reality underneath. It was a street-born talent he had perfected to its highest state, a talent that all first-rate criminals possessed. "Never let bullshit sentiment get in the way of business," Wasco always said. The only way to explain Wasco's present lapse in Arv's regard was . . . jealousy? . . . anyway, Wasco had some kind of ax to grind with Arv, that was sure. . . .

The truth was that Wasco's castle had just fallen in Moke's rigid scale of "class," now that his perception was proved to be flawed. Arv consequently rose on the scales.

Moke knew that this was true: Arv had little experience of women, real women. And in the normal course of events, as a prison hack, he'd probably go through his entire life without meeting one, not a real one, a beautiful free one, an independent road woman of the highest hippest evolution, not a woman like Moke. But, and this was the one little ingredient that changed the whole chemistry of the thing, when a woman like Moke gave herself to him freely, Arv's emergent self-confidence brought with it many great and unexpected gifts: he was a sensitive and excellent lover, an intelligent and imaginative companion;

he had a capacity to put down his guard and give of himself without thinking, to receive the same; he had a pleasing desire to evoke the greatest pleasure in his partner; he could enter another's deepest being too, if he was allowed; he was a daring and courageous lover, therefore, a lover one could believe in, touch, surrender to, without fear.

All this was of course different with Wasco. He was her big-ass Daddycat, father of her only child, Flo, her anal angel, her baby girl. He was evil Daddy who gave Moke only this child, and dreams of money, dreams of glory. But she had no regrets.

Had she really none?

No, she had no regrets, none at all.

Wasco had hurt her many times in the past, in many different ways, testing her out, training her, like a man trains a dog cruelly. But she had trained him too, and over the years they had grown to rely on one another as the only two in the world in whom they could place total confidence. There was no longer any kind of physical element in their relationship. It had evolved over the years into something very precious to Moke, the relationship of two excellent business partners with total trust in each other's judgment and honesty. And in the perilous world where they lived, the world of dope and murder and prison, this was the absolute highest form of human relation that existed.

What bothered Moke now, nettled her, made her feel nervous and edgy and guilty, was the fact that she saw in Wasco's cousin something far beyond what she had been led to expect. Far, far beyond! And her loyalty to Wasco was now beginning to be torn, beginning to go out equally toward Arv *a situation I must not permit!* She was beginning to feel like Arv's lover, his "soul-mate," as she picturesquely phrased it in her mind. She had seen in their creative writing class with Elaine and later when they fucked together with love that he was far more than even he knew himself yet, more than he dared dream. Moke saw this now, in great clarity, was certain of it, and of the depth of his compassion for humanity under the prison hack's uniform, saw too that he was going surely to escape, had to, no way out, would because of the poet's spirit within him that would break the prison's hold. Moke assured herself, perhaps a bit romantically, that Arv would go on and on to achieve great things in the world. Farther in his world than even his cousin, the power-hungry Wasco, would in his world: the underworld. Wasco was unbeatable in the West Coast dope world, the champ. He would someday, if he didn't get blown off in a dope war or executed for murder, become the absolute top man among the non-Italians, kingpin, boss of all operations outside of the Cosa Nostra. That was sure. His talents in that vein were formidable, far out in front of any conceivable competitor. Everyone in the dope world recognized it. Even the Wops, who would probably eventually arrange some kind of laissez-faire tribute-paying truce with him if his long string of successes continued. He would grow rich and famous, probably, old Wasco, and would retire to do legitimate business in Vegas or London or Amsterdam or the Bahamas, running a gambling house, or restaurant or bar, holding court, receiving gifts of tribute, oaths of fealty, noblesse oblige. All this, of course, if he wasn't blown off first. But those were the breaks, the chances, the risks of the game, and Moke had long ago firmly decided to follow his star, his black star that didn't shine and never set, just went up and up, ascending to the top of the top of the heap of all the other black and shiny stars. Because, goddamnit, she'd always been looking for her Daddy, Daddy-man of the world. And, by Christ, she'd found the motherfucker. No one could compare with Wasco. He could *handle* people. There wasn't anybody he couldn't handle. People did what he said. Look at the way he took over that mangy motorcycle club and whipped them into the spiffiest fifty-man army of dope smugglers, cutters, baggers, wholesale dealers, retail pushers, bankers, soldiers and big-time thieves on the West Coast! Look how he made a virtue out of every flaw, created victory out of adversity . . . look how he took over the entire Joint every time he got sent up . . . look how, every day, in every way, he made the world bend to his will! Look at Wasco, how could he be beat? He was the man Moke had always sought, "M," the man other men didn't dare stand up to. And it wasn't for submission . . . a form of masochism . . . Moke assured herself . . . that she had looked for this man, waited for him, found him . . . it was to . . . what? . . . to see if she could surmount him, reign as victorious queen of the empire he would win? Or follow his dark star to fortune? She wasn't clear about this herself, but she was pretty certain she'd never dare challenge him; she knew the appalling odds against anyone daring to go against the power of Wasco . . . his almost unusurpable sovereignty.

But with Arv . . . it would take longer for Arv's genius to grow into maturity, because the discipline he sought, literature, required a greater perspective of years and experience and physical distance before he could act. Moke saw that Arv was still initiating himself, in the way of geniuses everywhere . . . without knowing he was doing it, not aware of his own genius. The genius itself was leading him on now, had him in rigorous training. . . . Even his prison job had a meaning for him, now. Soon he'd go on, following his genius, which would lead him, rewarding him, beating and torturing him, feeding him, starving him, for the day when he would stop, would sit down at the end of his training and his journeys of discovery and, like Joyce, "forge the consciousness of his race" or whatever (she forgot the exact quotation, wasn't sure she had it right), forge the consciousness of his own race and blood, the shit-eating New World breed, Okie-Mexican-Indian, paradoxical American breed—dead and alive, vital and violent, farmer and hunter, eupeptic and dyspeptic, compost: a rose on a dunghill—a breed the knowledge of which would set the pale-faced old Mick, James, to quivering fearfully in his faraway grave! "Roll over Beethoven!" the Beatles, those other poets of his generation, had sung. . . .

And Moke, in her deepest being, in a separate but equal part of that being, in a compartment deep as the one where lived her Daddyman Wasco, wanted to go with Arv, Little Arv, till he grew up finally to become Big Arv, Bigger Arv, Great Arvin, poet of his generation! Wanted to be with the ex-hack when he sat down to do it . . . when he sat down to carry out his given mission upon this earth, the task he'd been sent to fulfill . . .

Oh yes she did want to be with Arv then . . . because . . . she knew that there was a poet in her too! Of a race that had never ever in modern times produced one, not a real one, except for maybe Tutu Cereza dn Gaby Puhanui and Atta Isaacs the slack-key artists. She was a poet too, Moke was, if she wanted to be. Her talent, her own genius, is what permitted her to see Arv for what he was, when no one else in the whole Joint, in all of New Sonora could. . . . And she knew she could follow him, follow Arv, if she wanted. She could follow either man out all the way, even Wasco, if she wanted, *or I could even lead them, if I wanted, being cleverer and greater in my hard heart than either.* . . . Yes, Moke was an artist too, if she wanted. It was sure! And this was the danger for her, the dreadful tragic danger. She let her mind wander. She saw her and Arv in the impossible future, twenty years hence, alive and happy together, minds healthy and working, living together freely, lovingly, but independently, each with his and her own place to go and be alone . . . but each with the other as a shoulder, a support, in case of need, each with the other for worth and warmth and sin and skin, for fucking and dreaming, for swimming late at night and for backrubs and for honest critiques without rancor of the other's private work . . . what a dream! But . . . this she really saw! Dreaming, she dreamed of enlightenment, of art and love, freedom and perfection and liberation, dreamed of an Okie-Mexican Jean-Paul Sartre, poor thing, and a Kanaka Simone de Beauvoir . . . poor Moke! She knew it would never be. Could have! But now too late. Moke had long ago made her choice, and her speculation now was merely wishful thinking, daydreams, whiling her hours wastefully away upon the Mexican bed waiting for Arv to wake up. . . .

Wasco, the sonofabitch, called again from the depths of her consciousness, all the way from New Sonora, from the Joint, angrily. What angered Wasco, all the way from Slam, was that Moke was bothered about something, wavering. What bothered Moke was that Wasco wanted to break him, break poor Little Arv to his will, his heretofore invincible will. "I don't wanna hurt the little asshole," Wasco had assured her, long before it even mattered to her, "all I wanna do is get him hip, turn the dude out in the world." And Wasco, Moke was positive, could do it, could do anything he wanted with Arv. He'd broken stronger ones before. She'd seen him do it. He would break poor Arv, before he was ready to resist, spoiling what his genius had in store for him. Helping him out maybe, sure, with a little money. But killing the growing poet for good . . . because . . . Wasco could do it because . . . he had Moke's expert and promised aid in this endeavor. Aid that was irresistible, that could call a ship upon the rocks with no effort, aid that had been proven before with a hundred Johns, a hundred marks, a true underworld talent that could sing such a song, spin such a web, that no man could resist it.

Her problem had now become amazingly complex, obscured in puzzling darkness and ambivalence, ambiguities, uncertain motives, enigmas. . . . She cried out in her half-sleep, perceiving for the first time the enormity of her quandary, the vertiginous depths and interminable complexity of its labyrinths. She perceived for the first time the inevitable tragedy it would sow. Her heart quaked in terror, and, simultaneously, thrilled to its core, for Moke was a child of darkness, a child of chance and risk and blind black fortune. Found life most heightened, most exalted and crisply real when the risks were greatest. *Never is life more intense and . . . never does mere existence* zoom *like when you're up against the wall!* Thinking of these two men in her life, both men of genius, and her coming choice, a choice without hope for her personally, Moke exulted in her power, *zoomed* at the notion of her almost surely coming tragedy. . . .

This one unforeseen, unpredictable human element, then, had upset the balance that Wasco'd so carefully calculated and weighed in his Grand Design, had upset the perfect harmony of Moke's and Wasco's good scene together for the first time. Their great mutual love and respect and trust had been built upon the greatest and steadiest and most reliable element in human character: greed. Moke believed in it sincerely. But now another large gaping frightening world, a world with different risks, different possibilities, beckoned for the first time: a world with the possibility of chaos, no money, loss of the dignity that money gives, and the terrifying probability of total financial failure. Not the failure of Arv's genius. That was infallible if left alone, left to its own devices. But failure of dignity. To Moke, money bought dignity. There was no dignity with an empty belly. No dignity in the mendicant's bowl. And Moke saw clearly in Arv's future precisely that bowl, in a street in Paris or Yokohama or Cairo, standing out in the rain filling with only water, while Arv futilely begged for enough to get a hot meal.

That is what tilted her. *Nothing else,* she thought, *when you get down to basics.* That certain and necessary but undignified begging bowl did it!

Arv had awakened now. He was watching her, watching the wheels turning in her head. He didn't completely trust her, maybe.

Moke surprised hell out of herself sometimes. She volunteered information about herself now for the first time since they'd met . . .

"I'm married, you know."

"Yeah, well, I figured something like that."

Moke continued now, astounding herself, letting it come out all in a great rapid flood of words. As she was wont to do (she was a naturally histrionic type, was always dramatizing her own life, and the lives of those around her, dramatizing sometimes even the act of love, moaning and writhing so that she never knew how much was her and how much was drama, even when she was sincerely aroused), she dramatized the information, but did not lie. Didn't she lie at all? Nope, she didn't once lie to Arv . . . she just left a few things out . . .

"Moke," she began, "small and comely and brown, unfolded like an amphibious bat at the first sign of dark. She came out only at dusk. She loved night and black water and U.S. dollars. They were her lovers and her prey . . ."

And then she told it . . . "I never had anything in my life, nothing to call my own . . ." she said, and wound it out . . .

Getting stroked, getting stoked, wrapped up lightly in Little Arvin's coarse-haired weedy arms, entwined in stony abandon on that come-stained rose-colored bedspread on that high squeaky Mexican bed in that small dirty room with raw cement floors in that cheap cinderblock motel in San Felipe, Baja California, a room they would grow to love and would always remember, would remember till the day they were dead, with an orange like Jacques Prévert's poetical orange on the table and her dress on the floor *and you in my bed, sweet present of the present,* singing the poem to each other one line apiece faultlessly and with perfect timing to the tune of *An Affair of the Heart,* a kind of Alicante of their minds, and the white wind of winter whipping off the sand desert and the Sierra

Pedro Martir, sweeping far out into the Sea of Cortez, turning the cove to milk sperm, and blowing soundlessly under their plywood door, flicking against their one scarred and scratched window like tiny pieces of corrosive glass, Moke told it. . . . "To this day," she told, "I can't endure my Tutu, because she wouldn't leave me my privacy, my peace, my possessions, something of my own with my label on it, something in the world that proves I exist, with my stamp and smell and feel on it, something of me, something of value. Tutu was always clutching and grabbing at me, trying to get hold of me, keep me, own me. I wanted to belong to myself! Jesus, she'd even follow me into the outhouse, she loved me so much. So I started locking the door, spending hours and hours in there, sniffing my own stink. By God, at least my shit was my own! I'd spend half the day in the toilet, reading newspapers, books, figuring things. I still got the habit. It takes me an hour to take a shit. I do my accounts there, figure out my budget. I know, I'm crazy, but you see why . . . to never have your own things, when you're a kid, it's terrible! It's a wonder I didn't go nuts . . ." she said, telling it. Higher than a kite, a Kraut, a lead-headed blimp, a fiery zepp, toking away at that good Mexicali-pressed hash, rapping without fail or falter, spinning a spider's web, she rapped it, queen of the rap, laid it down for that zonked prison guard, telling it, surprising herself, telling it almost truly . . . Moke told it. . . .

"You don't sound like much of a radical Leftist to me!" Arv exclaimed when first she paused.

"Who said I was?"

"Well, I assumed, since you were so hot to get me to bring those letters into the Joint . . ."

"What? Are you kidding? I'm doing it for money, just like you! Anyway, listen! Let me finish! So . . . my life isn't what I husbanded with such care, that was nothing! It was my goods that were important . . . so . . ." she hesitated, puzzling it out, "so I left the Islands as soon as I could, looking for money, pure and simple, and everything money buys . . . buy you know what?" she said, brilliant-eyed at her own dream of riches, "when I left the Islands, I found out it wasn't so easy to acquire that stuff I wanted so much . . . that green stuff . . . Then

. . . this man came along and saved me. . . . A lot of people would call him ugly. Others might call him evil. But I was smitten the first time I smelled him. He smelled good. He smelled like filthy lucre. If I'd ever seen long green walking, he was it! And we've been together now for over five years. Through thick and thin. And we've been rewarded for our loyalty to each other, rewarded greatly, beyond our wildest dreams, and now, especially now, we are about to be rewarded to the extent that we'll be able to retire for the rest of our lives as rich and respectable gentlefolk, if we want. . . . It has something to do with those letters you're bringing into the Joint. That seventy-five you're earning is just a drop in the bucket to what we're into . . . But . . . don't ask me any more questions. I won't be able to answer them . . ." she said, shushing him with her index finger, "shush! I gotta let this all come out . . .

"Anyway, neither this man nor myself had ever had anyone we could really trust before. No one! And it was so beautiful when we found each other. Even Tutu, my own aunt, who loved me, would betray me. She often did. If I ripped off something at the five and dime store, as a kid, something I needed and couldn't get any other way, she'd take me down and shame me right in front of the people. Call me a thief, ask the manager to punish me. She was a fucking colonial subject. Just like all those Hawaiians. Why didn't she pat me on the back, taking money from the *Haoles*, those thieving *Haoles* who took our whole island away from us? Oh, I hated her, with her muumuu mentality, and her devout whiteman's religion, Congregationalist, that'd been imported by the *Haole* along with disease and racism and his primitive morality in the nineteenth century.

"So," she continued, sighing, calming herself, allowing Arv to pet her now, again, pet her ass and her pretty flanks and her black shiny long hair, allowing him to begin arousing her again, arousing her to moist and messy passion . . . she went on, "so you see, I couldn't trust my Tutu, who loved me. I couldn't trust 'love.' Love is what made Tutu betray me. I didn't want any part of it. Love is what was evil. I wanted something solid and real that I could hold on to. Something I could trust. Money builds trust, like in the Banks and Trusts, like on Wall Street.

Money *is* trust. Trust is respect. Respect is flattery. Flattery is fuel to the ego. The ego is greed. Greed is need. Need is a form of love. Money, therefore, if you follow me, is love," she said, and turned her delighted smile to him, her white smile framed in dark skin and hair, and laughed ironically, and kept it up, her rap, entranced with her own story, with the danger that Arv would detect the thread of other stories, another person, that she carefully wove into the fabric of her rap . . . Moke told it . . . "So we always kept receipts with each other. We always paid our debts to each other on time, with interest, without fail. We still do. It became a code with us, a point of honor. We could do what we wanted with the rest of the human race. But our relationship was . . . inviolable."

Arv, who'd risen up on one elbow, and left off the necessary stroking of Moke's lithe loins, was regarding her nervously now, excited, agitated by her words.

"But what about . . . ?"

"Sexual love? That isn't it at all," she volunteered, for reasons obscure even to herself. "He's sort of really uninterested in women, I suppose, all except me . . . he's kind of . . ."

"Gay?"

"Yes . . . sort of . . ." she said, a bit ashamed of what she was revealing, and maliciously pleased too, in a way, to be revealing it. . . . Was this the way betrayal began?

But Arvin apparently didn't pick up on it. He got more and more jealous with every word.

"So, I was wrong about you?" he asked.

"About what? The letters? Oh Christ, you're not going into that again, are you?"

"When I first met you," he said, "you can't imagine how happy I was that it seemed honest conviction rather than greed that . . ."

". . . That made me corrupt you?"

"No . . . I'm just kidding. I . . ."

"I don't think you're kidding! Deep down you're loyal to that Joint, aren't you? Loyal to everything it represents."

"That's not true! I hate that place worse than anything in the world!"

"Is that why you decided to bring the letters in?"

"Well," he began, very careful, reasoning it out slowly as usual, "number one: I'm trapped at the Joint. Number two: without bread I can't get out. Number three: I got a certain sympathy for old Galliot . . ."

"Come off it! What you're saying is that you did it for greed. Money! Just like me! Don't gimme that 'holier than thou' shit!"

"Number four . . ." Arv persisted.

"Shut up!"

"Number four . . ."

"Stop!" she yelled, and when he still persisted, gave up, rolled over and looked the other way, vanquished by his unyielding stubbornness.

"Number four," he said, "is that I loved you, loved you the first time I saw you in your waitress uniform at Bert's, the first time I heard you speak up in class, arguing with Elaine, the moment you walked in our door at the Joint . . ."

"Stop it!" she shouted from the other side of the bed, staring at the sand drifting under the door. But he wouldn't stop.

"I swore I'd get you!" he staunchly continued, not to be deflected from his set course. "I knew you probably had a man. It didn't matter. I swore I'd win you, swore I'd beat him or die trying. I had nothing to lose, baby. My life was impossible, dead end. . . . I swore . . . and you were kind of familiar to me . . . I'd seen you before somewhere . . ."

"Stop it, damnit!" she yelled, twisting around to him again, putting her finger to his lips. To hide her terror she intended to ask some kind of insipid question of Arv. She even began, "Let's change the subject . . ." But then instead she did something outrageously dumb, something very dangerous, something that might have been fatal. "Let's change the subject," she said. "Say! I wanted to ask you the other day! That cousin of yours that you're always talking about, that motorcycle guy . . . is he really as bad as they say?"

"He's worse," Arv said, "he's antisocial, inhuman. He's like a meat-eating animal. He's paranoid the way an animal is, amoral, takes it for granted that the rest of the world is as hostile as he is, and strikes first with no remorse, no second thoughts, like a snake . . ."

"Wow!" Moke exclaimed, facetiously. "Really, like a snake?"

"Stop being funny," Arv said, "I'm serious."

"I can see you are."

". . . like a snake," Arv continued, refusing to be swayed from his purpose, "like a snake he never got the connection between hitting and hitting back. Never figured out that if you struck, you might get struck back."

"Who says that has to be true?"

"Wasco's a moral idiot, is what he is," the stolid Arv said. "When we were kids I used to watch him. He never figured out you could lead a happier life by being nice to people."

"Say!" Moke said, "I never figured that out either. In fact, some of the very happiest people I know have never done a good deed in their lives!"

"Shut up! I'm talking!"

"You're talking shit!"

"No, I'm not. You wanted to know about my cousin, now let me tell you."

"Alright, for God's sake, go ahead. But make it short, huh? I had no idea what I was getting into when I asked you a simple question about the guy."

"Wasco was born bigger and tougher than other people," Arv went on, "he was born also with elemental desires, elemental drives. Because he was strong, these desires were always granted. He learned to take, only take. He did this with the encouragement of my father, and his other elders in the Joint. They called it 'feistiness,' and said 'boys will be boys' when he drowned a cat or a bird or painted a dog with turpentine or scalped a little girl or stole my favorite toy or ruined a new bike . . ."

"This is too funny for words!"

"Shut up! Let me tell you!" he said, and finally she had to give up and let him run it down. She had to listen to him tell the whole long story of his unhappy childhood with Wasco. He told it in minute detail, going on and on about Wasco's "evil ways," and about how all the kids hero-worshiped him, how Arv kowtowed to him every time he beat him up, trying to get back into his graces, about how he had to set up a "complex system of allies" to help him resist Wasco's power, how he ultimately became a "good student, a nice boy, an Eagle Scout, a guard in the Joint, and even a soldier in Vietnam," to protect himself from Wasco's seemingly all-consuming power over him.

During all the telling of this horrendously long and sad tale, Moke kept up a rapid patter of ridicule, calling him "sanctimonious," and "preachy," and a "pompous ass." Finally she got him to laugh at himself when he referred to Wasco's "brutish desires."

"His what?" she asked, incredulous.

"His . . ." Arv began, and cracked up with laughter.

"Hey! I tell you what," Moke said, "you're always making those lists. Why don't you just make a list of all the evil this cat has done you and save us both a lot of time and trouble? Okay?"

Then, camping it, ranting, making her laugh, but not quite succeeding in abolishing the seriousness of the matter, Arv ran down his list of evil for her:

1. pantsed me and rolled me in spunglass
2. fucked my sister and told
3. tied me up on the sand hill and left me with no water
4. broke my wrist and
5. my nose a second time
6. made me let him bugger me in our play fort
7. stole my first girl friend
8. got me drunk and tried to run over me
9. abandoned me ten miles from home naked and penniless
10. made me jack him off
11. laughed at the size of my prick
12. stole my record player
13. wrecked my bike
14. wrecked my first car
15. alienated the affections of my pet donkey
16. lied to my father about me
17. called me a queer

Moke began to laugh, laughing, her mouth stuck open for air, gulping it down, almost choking, her eyes filled with tears of glee, she twisted and turned and rolled herself into the sheets and blankets, hugging her pillow, laughing and laughing, kicking her feet, hiccuping, choking, spitting, thinking of poor Little Arv growing up with that big mean cousin of his!

"Tell me the truth!" she said when she could finally contain herself.

"What?"

"You actually wrote that list once, didn't you?"

"Yeah," he said sheepishly, giggling, "when I was seventeen years old."

And Moke just about laughed herself into a shit-fit, thinking about Arv at sixteen or seventeen sitting down at his high school desk and writing down seriously this long list of grievances against his bad-ass cousin Wasco, this tragicomic list written out and numbered like some kind of Declaration of Independence . . .

Soon he hushed her . . . "Shut up! Lemme finish!" But he was laughing too. She'd succeeded in getting him to do that. He was laughing like he'd just learned to laugh about this thing, this largest thing in his life, like it was the first time he'd ever been able to laugh about it, like even his attitude toward the subject wasn't clear within himself yet, like he wasn't sure whether to laugh or cry about it. His laughter was loud, hilarious even, but there was more than a tinge of wonder about it, more than a tinge of self-doubt too, and not a little real pain remaining. . . .

Arv's story got Moke a little paranoid, finally. Got her wondering. Could Arv know about her and Wasco? Had he seen them somewhere together? Was the prey now tracking the hunter? Was his game to win her, destroying his cousin, vanquishing in that way his childhood torturer? Is it *he* who's merely using *me?* Moke wondered, tightening with loyalty to Wasco. Then, just as she started to explore her own motives, and the possibility that she'd laid down a hint, a scent for Arv on purpose, that he might follow *if he wanted* right to Wasco . . . just as she was about to do that she said "Aw bullshit!" to herself and dismissed the whole thing from her mind. Realizing that her new doubts, doubts influenced by Arv, and his new hold upon her emotions, were extremely dangerous for her, dangerous for Arv too, Moke just pushed the whole problem right out of her mind. For, if there was anything that would bring out the ruthless unblinking murderer in Wasco, it was an even suspected or imaginary betrayal on Moke's part. She was his only sustenance, the only rock upon which he anchored his transient life, his thief's life. . . .

But that pernicious thought, that evil spark of doubt about Arv, it came back . . . *Now,* she thought, *if some-*

*one really wanted to get at Wasco, and knew about our
relationship, how would he go about it? Like Arv is
doing?* And chaos for a moment reigned supreme. Could
Arv be that diabolical? Moke trembled beside him in the
Mexican bed, in her sunburnt copper skin . . . and . . .
if the truth be known . . . she . . . she . . . thrilled . . .
positively thrilled to her marrow at the immense possibilities before her, at the huge gaping mouth of fortune
and chance and risk and danger and adventure that lay
open in front of her, and drew up her knees into Arv's
hard breadbasket, knocking the wind out of him, and
pulled his hair, bit his lip, scratched his back till he
cried out . . . and he didn't hit back. Didn't he hit back
just a little? No, he didn't hit back at all. . . .

And Moke thought about smack for the first time in a
long while. And realized that for the first time in the entire course of her habit she'd missed her wake-up and her
matinee fix and didn't even feel it, barely itched or missed
it, and decided to cook up right then in the bathroom, under the pretext of a quick shower . . . and thought too
. . . of the Merc, parked out on the main street. Wondered if Michael X had borrowed it like she told him,
stuffed the panels like he'd done three times before with
other cars, other men, stuffed it with brown Culiacán
heroin that Johnny Domingues weekly carried across
the Sea of Cortez in his fast fishing cruiser.

And only then, on the way to the toilet for her fix,
crawling off the Mexican bed, ruffling Arv's tousled hair
on her way, did Moke get herself to relax and push the
evil paranoid thoughts from her mind and enjoy sweet
Little Arv for just what he was . . . a boy, unachieved,
inconclusive, going places, sure! But not there yet, not
there yet, like her Daddyman was . . . she thought . . .
she thought . . . she was almost sure. . . .

Thirty-Nine

"Say!" Wasco said, stepping casually out through the iron doorway of the East Block and into the tense and nippy Big Yard, "you get your nooner, honey?"

"Yeah."

"Didn't notice you cook up," Wasco said, just to make talk, letting his eyes rove quick around the gray stone yard. Unnatural quiet. Niggers on one side. Whities on the other. Spics on another. It was icy cold out on the blacktop, yet the tension out there, since poor old Fast-Walking's unfortunate accident, you could almost hear it, it crackled in the air like a hot summer night. *The nigger figgers the last one was white so the next'll be nig. It's a race war after all.* . . .

"Sure, baby, of course I did!" the squeeze said, looking up at him in a daze of junkie bliss, "couldn't live with*out* it. Check the pins."

Wasco looked at his pinned round eyes with their long boyish lashes.

"Shit, you're getting fast, kid."

"Naw. Got off right in the guard shanty when the hack was out. Figured he'd never know the diff."

Wasco laughed, picking his nose, rolling what he found there, flicking it into an ice-over mud-puddle. "Sock it to 'em! We'll show them screws who's boss, eh sweet-ass?" he said, stoking his fire, splashing over the primed and charged yard. "Them fucking punk-ass bulls, chickenshit cops, slimy cuntlicking screws," he went on, though actually he approved of the law and order of the land, and its officially appointed and elected servants. *Sometimes,* he thought, working himself up on purpose, stoking his boiler up higher, inflating himself up into red-faced anger and power, working himself up for his meeting with his new crew, Bullet's crew, *sometimes,* he thought, *stoking your boiler up to full blast, stoking it up to hugeness and mean-*

*ness and conflagration, all by yourself, working yourself
up is sometimes half the fun.*

"Alright goddamnit!" he yelled, still stoking himself,
stroking it, building, growing in this tense climate like a
tornado grows in the rich land of the Mississippi Basin,
"alright," he said, motioning to the hunched-over, shivering circle of white cons, Bullet's ex-boys, or ex-Bullet's
boys, or whatever, a bedraggled and bullied bunch, while
he was still coming up ten feet away across the wet cold
yard, "alright you sonsofbitches, stand up straight and tall
and tighten up them assholes and satchels, goddamnit,
cause here he comes in person, in the flesh, here comes
your kingpin, the bossman, Mister Wasco P. Weed, Hitler's little helper!"

They started laughing, and he let them, Wasco did, let
them get away with that. "Straighten up, babies!" he
shouted, frowning gloriously, "you ain't under the Bullet
no more! Got to show a little class now! Straighten out!"
he repeated, as the squeeze hurried to catch up.

And then the slack circle of stinking frozen convicts
opened without a sound and received him into its midst,
him, Wasco, Big Dick, like powerful sperm, and burst
into life as soon as he came inside. He, Wasco, brought it
to life. Without him they would have just stood around
out there in the cold yard with their hands in their pockets, backs to the wind, like cattle in the rain, for the rest
of eternity. But old Wasco, him, with his powerful sex, his
heavy breath, blew life into them weak-ass motherfuckers,
blew survival and fitness and action into their tired cowardly penny-ante souls. He did it! Him alone! With just
the little squeeze running behind, squeezing into the circle,
waiting, alert, listening for word from the leader, the
Maximum, El Maximo himself, who was now measuring
his army narrowly, how many of them? . . . seventeen
here . . . measuring his army narrowly, looking close.
Weed out the bads. Cull them fast. Get rid of them, or
frighten them into better use. Let's see. Then, waiting.
Letting them sweat it, even in the cold, the rain. Let them
wonder what'd be coming down next. . . .

"What's your name, son?" Wasco asked, smiling his
smile that chilled men to the balls *this cat's got the jacket
of being a rat* speaking to a little greasy Wop kid not
much bigger than the squeeze.

"Uh . . . uh . . ."

"Never mind," Wasco said, impatient.

"Uh . . . Tony!" the rat said, just as Wasco was dismissing him with a wave of his huge arm.

"What'd you say?" Wasco asked, letting the arm stay up there where it had risen high above the quaking callow crowd of inferiors like the vengeful arm of Jehovah.

"T-T-Tony," the rat stuttered, his eyeballs fixed on that raised and poised arm of destruction.

"Tony what?" Wasco said, still holding it high, flexing, like it might strike him dead on the spot.

"T-T-T-Tony P-P-Parenti," he sputtered, eyes closed.

"Tony, boy, I want you to . . . Say! Ain't you the dude that I saw the first day I come into the Slam? Over in the Mess Hall. That was you, wasn't it?"

"I wanted to talk to you about that . . ."

"Yeah! That was you. Say, I'm glad I've met up with you. You're a pretty tough customer," Wasco said, and turning to the circle at large, went on, "Yeah! This stud is the guy that tripped me. Tripped *me*."

"I didn't mean . . ." the rat said, caching his ratlike Wop nose in the upturned collar of his denim jacket, hiding his freezing hands in his pockets, wishing he could hide as easily.

"Like, hey, don't worry, man!" Wasco said, smiling, "I like a young fellow that stands up to authority. Real initiative. I'm going to remember you, don't worry, for some real special assignment," he finished, letting his toothy grin freeze on his face, letting the corners of his mouth fall like the two ends of a speared fish that breathed its last, letting the light dim and grow cold and red in his eyes . . . so blue they went purple, so purple they went fire red, and the rat read it, he read his own enslavement there. . . .

Wasco ignored him then, turned his attention to other matters, matters of business, while the squeeze, beside him now, where he'd been motioned, took rapid mental notes.

"Okay. Where's the bank?" Wasco asked. A fat middle-aged Irishman with a little puggy dog nose came forward. "As of now, what we holding?" Wasco asked, staring out over the Irishman's head at the windy winter yard, at the pigeons and sea gulls wheeling and settling on the mud puddles, at the scared nervous guards up on the gunwalk, fingering their weapons, at the thousands of shaky inmates waiting for lunch call, looking over their shoulders all the time, on their toes, at the prisoners sitting on the cold ground playing dominoes, at those standing pitching horseshoes, at the single dudes, the loners walking up and down the yard, close-lipped, scared, intimidated, trying to keep away from the fearful "blocs." The blocs stood in solid crowds. You could tell what they were from a hundred yards off. There was the Mexican Mafia bloc, which was the Right Spic block. And the Brown Berets, which was the Left Spic bloc. Then there was the Aryan Brotherhood, which was the White Right bloc, and the CDS, which was the Left White bloc. And then you had the Muslims, which was the Right Black, and the Black Fence, which was the Left Black, which Wasco paid special attention to now, scanning them carefully where they practiced their flowering Black Fence dance steps in the southeast corner of the yard, just outside the Honor Block. Wasco watched them while the fat Irishman ran it down for him, the whole business of the day: assets, deficits, accountability, projects, investments, interest, supply, sales, merchandising, packaging, protection, security. Wasco watched them. They were dancing. Playing around. Flowering it, that vile Black Fence, that black devil dance, playing around, Galliot in the middle of them, trying to keep them cool, cooling them with the dance, Galliot, in the middle of them all, guarded, double-guarded, protected with big black bodyguards.

Wasco thought: *it'll be very fucking difficult to get him in the Yard because of that bodyguard of his.* . . . Galliot stood in the center, Wasco saw him. He was a soulful dude, you had to admit. A real leader. Knew how to retain control of his operation. You had to hand it to the nigger. While them young niggers danced around him, and he talked real serious with his lieutenants, them nigger bucks dancing, young sweet-assed ones, *I'd like to cop a nigger's boyish ass,* niggers dancing, Black Fencing, the other blackboys trying to knock them off their step, trying to knock them off the rhythm just for fun. But it didn't work, they kept right on dancing. They double-stepped if they lost it, got it right back, or quadruple-timed it if they had to, never losing it, never losing it. . . .

When the Irishman got finished running it all down for the bossman he said, "There's something you dudes got to learn from the niggers. Just one thing you can learn from them, and that's timing, and rhythm. If there's one thing those black bastards got, that's rhythm."

"Oh yeah!" they all laughed, the boys, Wasco's new crew, "them niggers sure can dance!" they yelled, delighted with the simplicity of Wasco's cliché.

But old Wasco himself, he was gone off again, gone off from that smelly shivering group, letting them rap on their own, letting the squeeze mediate for him. Wasco was trying to figure out them niggers. That Galliot. There hadn't been any rioting. Even though everyone expected it, what with the niggers' claims that the "race war" was nothing more than a Pig plot. Why not? Why hadn't they burnt the place down? There was tension in the air you could slice with a shank. But no rioting. Why not? Two of them blackboys dead. Burnt right up in their cell. Screaming like bloody hell. Disturbing everyone's dreams. That was enough for anybody's vengeance. Thinking: *he's got a twenty-four-hour watch, niggers taking turns peeking out of their cells with hand mirrors. . . .* Sure, that's enough for anybody's vengeance. What was old Galliot waiting for? That Galliot, he's cagey, Wasco thought, while the squeeze ran down a few important business items for the boys . . . "You do this and you do that and you go here and you go there . . ." Just business. Wasco let him run it down. He was his man.

That Galliot, though, he sure was playing it smooth. Holding them niggers in check like that. Had a mystic power over their black asses. They were just itching to tear this Slam apart from one end to another. Take some hostages. Get their boy off on the first hijack flight to Algeria. But he's holding them in line, quiet, holding their righteous anger and wrath right down in check. What for? What for? Why don't he want to bug the Man right now? Put him uptight. What would Wasco do in the nigger's place? That ain't the way I'd do it. Unless, unless . . . what? Yeah, old Galliot, he's got something going on in that nappy head of his, behind them wet brown limp eyes. What is it? We got to work fast cause if we don't he's gonna fly the coop before we make our move. *Can't reach him through a Judas in his ranks because, in the Joint at least, they're still resisting all efforts to influence them into the way of law and justice according to the State. . . .*

HOOT! HOOT! HOOT! The lunchtime whistle blew loud and long, blew steam up in the gray freezing air, made the pigeons and the sea gulls hop in the ice of the yard, got the convicts moving toward the mess hall *should I take him here in the Yard or in the block?* Wasco was thinking, as all the blocks, including Wasco's own Dope Block, started moving across the yard toward lunch, none of them touching, none of them talking or approaching, none of them even sending emissaries back and forth like they usually did. As neatly self-segregated as the Main Cop could ever wish. *And now, what with poor old Fast-Walking and all, public opinion is highly inflamed.*

A world of separate organizations is most advantageous to a man of Wasco's mettle and ilk. They are not obstacles but aids in his rise to ultimate power. *You crack an organization like, say, the Mexican Mafia, and you don't have to work Spic by Spic, subverting them to righteousness under the law. The entire one hundred chili-eaters are delivered to you on a bean platter. Har har. That is a ploy of power. Power is God. God is Right. Right is Good. Therefore, God's little messenger here on earth, God's little helper, Mr. Wasco G. Fucking Weed, by the power of strength which is truth, by the force of winning, the winner's always right! Wasco was the ever-infallible Right and Good upon this Joint. That must be considered. And I am the man to do it. I am the man to consider many things at once. Here I am. I listen to the squeeze, check the bulls, the boos, and stretch out into theory and long-range planning, never forgetting the nitty-gritty practical problems of every day at hand, common sense, and down to earth. Yeah! That's me. I am the man! I can operate six scams at one time right in my gourd! The head of a genius and a poet of the hard trade! That's me! On this cold day on the eve of Xmas Eve. Yep, since the death of the Warden's only begotten son, Prince of the Jam, that old American public has become con-fucking-flagrant! Whoopie!*

"Hey Squeezy! You know what, man? It's already zero shopping days to Xmas! What'd you get your Ma?" Wasco asked, camping it right out in front of the boys, cowing them with the strength of his daring, the will of his inverted flesh, the out-fucking-rageousness of his perversion, and the utter frankness of its telling! Scaring the

shit out of them, Wasco repeated it, in his little girl devil
voice:

"Aw, come on, tweety, tell your Mumsy . . ."

"That's a sur*prise!*" the squeezy said, shaking his little
white head primly, admonishing him, while the crew,
scared to their marrows, tightbuns, shivered together on
the cold blacktop, goose pimples running up and down
their cold-dried scalps. And Wasco, Ma, the world's
largest little girlsie, hulked red-headed and invulnerable
above them . . . above them . . . her dollies, her dollies,
dollies, dollies. . . .

The Joint is my dollhouse, Wasco thought, and felt like
a happy man, almost. Everything felt like it was just turning up roses, almost. Everything smelled so sweet it made
him want to cop. Walking across the stormy yard toward
the dining hall in a mass of untouching stormy evil-ass inmates thinking *they want to blow, them nigs, they want to
fight and die, but he won't let 'em yet* Wasco got a big
hard-on for the wiggle of the squeeze's well-turned little
*culo. I want to cop. I want to cop. That's what my
jacket's all about. Doing time behind an ass-jacket,
poopoo beef. That's me. Har har.* He poked the squeeze
while they lined up outside the mess hall, the freezing
wind whipping at their collars, blowing the sea gulls and
pigeons off course as they wheeled, waiting for after-lunch
crumbs, banging some of them into the walls, scattering
feathers. . . . The squeeze didn't understand what he was
getting poked for, didn't understand Wasco's giggle.
Which was good. Never let them understand. If they
understand they'll see how easy it is, and get uppity. Get
uppity and they'll take you off. Never let the punks
understand. Wasco was good at that, usually. The only
thing that worried him now was old Galliot. What was
he up to? It was nice to be kind of worried about something. Just a little. *By now the whole thing must be out
in the open with him.* Wasco figured Galliot knew the
scene. Knew who his man was by now. And how he was
going to do it, more or less. Old Galliot, he wasn't
stupid. You could tell. Wasco seen that the first day he
watched him on the streamliner bus riding into the Joint
across the salt flats. No, he wasn't dumb, that nigger.
Had contingency plans of his own. Wasco saw their battle as a conflict of greater minds, far from the field,
generalissimos, field marshals, out in neutral space—

and tears almost came to Wasco's red eyes, tears of admiration for himself and his heroic black opponent, locked in mortal combat far above the place of normal men. Wasco, though he could already see Galliot's blood splattered across the clean floor of the block, or running into a frozen mud puddle in the yard, could not see that blood as other than an abstract quantity. Wasco even figured that, just like a football game or an Olympic wrestling match, if the blackman Galliot was the loser, as it was planned in God's greater scheme of things, that at the end Galliot would understand in a way, and tip his hat to the better man. Wasco hoped that Galliot dug that all this nigger-baiting shit was only part of the sport as far as he was concerned, and nothing from the heart, nothing personal at all.

Wasco never enjoyed a game unless it was fixed. Now that this one was wired, he began to enjoy it. Began to form a true affection for his valiant and worthy adversary, began to take pleasure in the artificial excitement of his minimal risks. . . . *Warden came right to the East Block and saw him . . . his only begotten son . . . squished like a bug on the concrete floor . . . and didn't bat a fucking eye. . . . Then let the newspaper cats in and shed a tear or two for the cameras.* SNAP SNAP POP POP *Oh them sweet headlines!*

Stepping across the cold stiff yard, with that low billowing sky up above, a sky that was the color and texture of brain matter, a sky as walled-in and narrow and gray as the top of the inside of your skull . . . and that cold wave sweeping down upon the Joint, cold wave that broke through an Alaskan high-pressure front and came down straight off the Arctic Ocean, the Noonday Night, hurling itself on the West Coast like a gigantic Arctic wolf, laying British Columbia and Washington and Oregon to waste, dumping neck-deep snow like wolfspore, wolfsbane, and now threatening to freeze over even temperate Quintana Sound . . . stepping across that yard Wasco toyed with the tense black man. He toyed with him now, that jittery nervous intelligent black Galliot, warm climate man, African, tropical jungle man. Toyed with him, like a cold wave wolf, though he didn't exactly have him yet, almost, but not all the way yet. Toyed with him, like an imaginary bug, a firefly, a captured warm climate insect in a refrigerated jar . . . toyed with him . . . daydreamed even

. . . for him . . . daydreamed the Great Escape for him, for old Galliot. Gave the nigger a running chance. A head start. Let him get all the way to Arv's back yard where he hid out in the rabbit hutches and then, flushed out by the forces of law and order, leapt upon the canary yellow donkey and split for the abandoned World War II airfield and rode for the saggy wing of the C-46 and got it started, propellers turning, took off into the cold heady air, lumbered out over Paradise Cove, lumbered through the billowing clouds of brain matter, motors failing, wings cracking, spitting fire, till Wasco shot him down with his fifty-caliber machine gun mounted on Tower #2, shot him right out of the sky in flames, while him and his copilot, the helmeted and goggled little smiling donkey, fought for control. Down down down, nailed by the hand of the Mighty Man, Wasco, down he went, the black motherfucker, down he went and crashed into the shitwater Sound. *Shit! You can't get away you crazy little firefly!* Wasco thought, just like when he was a kid with a Mason jar.

And Wasco carried it out, he was never a man to limit the paths of his wonderful wandering imagination. *Go ahead, man! Carry it out!* Thinking: *sure, this is my home. Let's postulate it. This is my home: the Joint. A man's joint . . . har har har . . . a man's home is his castle. Every man is number one in his own home. It's only natural. And walls breathe. And the Joint is alive. Therefore, he shoulda figgered—how do ya figger, nigger?—that the Joint would love its own. Ain't nothing like mother-love. And an angry Ma looking out for her own spawn, why, she's something to watch out for. He shoulda figgered, the nigger. The trouble with old Galliot is that he ain't a mystic soul like me. He's nothing but a Commie, a rank fucking materialist. And they lack the finer spiritual qualities. They lack an appreciation of the more romantic things. Like the poor Joint's hurt feelings, Galliot would never understand that. And the Joint's inordinate love for its only true son. He'd never believe that, the nigger, being an atheistic Communist from the start. That kind of thing is going to prove his undoing. He ought to know, he really ought to know, shoulda read the Bible as a kid and drawn the proper parallels, like Wasco did, with the help of that great believer, Mama Evie. The nigger really oughta figger. Yes sir.*

But anyway, after all that'd settled down, after Galliot was gone and buried with his black daddy and things quieted down a bit, and racial and political tranquillity returned to this chosen land after many years of rank dissent, Wasco figured he'd lay back and enjoy the fruits of his labor for a while. Squeeze the fruit of his labor. Har har. No use rushing back out into the freeworld. Shit, it's dangerous out there! A cat could get hurt out there! Wasco figured he might do a little writing, with the squeeze maybe ghostwriting for him. Getting the correct English down, and all that shit. He, Wasco, couldn't be bothered with that kind of stuff. He was the artist, the poet. Let the fucking underlings of the world, the hacks of the world, do the shitwork like spelling and scribbling stuff out. He was an idea man, old Wasco was, not a fucking scribe. So, anyway, Wasco figured he might start writing his (abridged) autobiography. Dealing with his years as the fiercely independent and misunderstood rebel, the hard-riding Robin Hood of the West, the leader of that misinterpreted bunch of solid rough-and-tumble good fellows, the Motopsycho M.C. Har har har.

When they all got to the Rotunda outside the dining hall, Wasco ran into the same Tex-Arkana Cracker officer he'd talked to his first day in the Joint.

"Howdy there, Officer! How y'all doin' today?" he called out, imitating his hard-scrabble accent, letting the squeeze and his boys pass him into the dining hall. Letting Galliot and his boys go by too, watching them, checking them out real good. Galliot was talking to them slow and calm. Settling them down, like a cowboy settles jumpy cattle on the night of an electrical storm. Wasco saw it all. Wily, that Galliot was, a real foxy nigger, cooling them off, figgering, hairtriggering, jiggering, the niggering bastard, figgering that he'd have more options without violence as yet. Real smart! Yeah, a real brainy dude, that Galliot. . . .

Wasco kept talking Okie shit to the Cracker all the while, and the Cracker tried to ignore him, but Wasco wouldn't let him. Wasco went right up to him and pressed it out, squeezed at him. Got him running right away. Got him uptight and nervous . . .

"Cain't y'all hear me, Officer?" he said. "Don't y'all remember me?"

"Nope. Ah don't believe ah do," he returned, shifty-footed, flicky-fingered, looking for a way out of it.

"Well sir, let me refresh your memory, I'm inmate Wasco G. Weed."

And the fucking weak-chinned Okie asshole took it this time. Took it without a word. Didn't let out a peep. Cause he had the word. He knew who the kingpin was. Yes sir. Now Wasco was People. Real Human People now. And no little piss-ant hacks was going to bug him in any way whatsoever. That's the message the pimply peasant got.

Wasco delivered it, his message of fear and fealty, scaring the shit-talking Okie right out of the Rotunda, and then went in and joined the squeeze for their luncheon date.

"Where you been?" the squeeze asked, as soon as Wasco slid his tray onto the table.

"None of your fucking business," Wasco said, laughing, slugging him playfully on his frail shoulder. And the squeeze just about shit his pants with pride to be seen by the entire mess hall as the punk and emerging buddy of Wasco Weed, King of the Slam. And he said, "Well, Squeezy, I think we're just about ready to cut you into a major pie, just about to lay the entire number upon you. You are truly shaping up, you little motherfucker, I must say. Faster than any junkie faggot I ever knew! You better watch out or my old lady's gonna sue you for alienation of affections!"

"I'll take my chances," the squeeze said, real serious, and Wasco wondered laughingly if the squeezy was still carrying them clipped fingernails around in his pant cuff, them old dirty fingernails Wasco'd put in there days before. . . .

And then, catching Galliot's eye from way across the room, just as he plunged his spoon into his delicious stewed prune dessert, Wasco thought: *can we take him in here? A possibility. Four men to a table. Three big spooks with Galliot. Screw gunman is stationed directly above his table. I walk by. "Hey, niggerboy, you trying to trip me?" Pandemonium. Or, no! Maybe he holds the niggers back. Says, "Hold it boys, he's just trying to provoke us into getting shot!" So I hit him.* WHAM! *He hits . . . no! His bodyguard hits me.* WHAM! *I go down. Get up. Jump on him or one of the other niggers. The rifleman . . . the marksman . . . fires into the mass to break up the fight. Now pandemonium. Everyone runs for cover. The guard*

keeps shooting. Riot. When the smoke clears, there lies
Galliot, the leader of his people, the last militant, deader
than a gull, in a pool of his own African blood. No! Too
fucking dangerous. I could even get hurt!

And then Wasco, overcome with emotion at the greatness of his charge in the vital interests of his state and
race, overcome with his own mighty responsibility, turned
to the squeeze and motioned to the huge mural that covered the entire southern wall of the dining hall. It was a
remarkable mural, done in the WPA Post Office style of
the 1930's.

"You see the mural, Squeezy? That mural took a great
convict artist the entire ten years of the Great Depression
to finish. He worked night and day, hanging upside down
like a bat from a series of ropes and pulleys, since lad-
ders, as you undoubtedly know, are not allowed in the
Joint. He worked hard, and he worked well, year in and
year out, through winter and summer, heat and icy cold.
And when he was finished, his work was acclaimed far
and wide. The Warden and the Governor even came
down for the night of commemoration. Four thousand
convicts stood for three hours in driving rain and wind in
the yard to listen, to join in convoking and commemorating this great work of native New Sonora art. Now, let
me show you something! The mural tells a story. You see?
A story of the greatness of this state, this land, this people, this great Joint. Look, Squeezy! Over there on the left
you see them miserable blackbottom Mud-Hen Indians,
huddling naked in the storm, tearing down their tule
shacks for firewood, eating nothing but worms and toads
and sea snails, squatting in the mud of the promontory
where the Joint would one day rise, the most unhappy and
degenerate heathens known to man, the only race that
habitually befouled its own nest, shit the bed and was too
dumb to cover it.

"And then, Squeezy, over there, a little farther to the
right, you see the time of the Spics, with their wooden
prison ship tied up where Indians used to dig worms on
the banks of the promontory. And then farther on again,
you see the Mex's coming in, with their fat brown gener-
als with greasy moustaches. And then, you see, in the
middle of the mural, at the very focal point of the entire
shebang, here come them courageous white covered wag-
ons across the continent bringing your great free and

equal white ancestors and mine, bringing them to the far
benighted Western shores with their great manifest destiny, their great racial charge and duty in the interests of
freedom and progress and pride to grind them filthy
bean-eating Mexicans into the East L.A. and South of
Market San Francisco and Westside New Sonora dirt
where they belong and will remain forever through the
immutable will of Yahweh, who is, after all, like the Bible
says, white as you and me. . . .

"And then, kid, on the right you see the heavenly
promised land come true, settled and built up here on the
shores of the Western Ocean by God-fearing, clean-living
pioneers of the ancient Anglo-Saxon race. And you see,
later on, their cars and highways and skyscrapers and
smiling faces, and there—see?—at the far right-hand corner, you see the walls of the Joint! Great gray and yellow
stone walls that grew up out of the primeval slime of the
Mud-Hen Indians, ascended out of the squalid beansmell
of the Spic's and Mex's, rose up out of the clean but poor
cabins of the honest white settlers, and finally, in our
great day, a day better and beyond all other possible days
and ages, a day of glory and power forever, a day of perfection, with this great American land from sea to shining
sea residing at the absolute pinnacle of its majesty, noble,
heroic, imperishable . . . in our great day rose earth-shak-
ing the walls of the gigantic Joint, the great and promised
walls of Jerusalem! Jerusalem! Which we have raised up
here! Jerusalem! And not a Kike in the entire C of C!
Jerusalem!" Wasco exulted.

And the squeeze, sitting across the table sipping his rancid coffee, following Wasco's arm as he gestured toward
the mural, following his rap, got to laughing, got to heaving and hooping and stamping the asphalt tile floor. . . .

"Ha ha ha!" the squeeze said, "you gotta be shucking,
man!"

"I'm dead-ass serous," Wasco said, with only the
vaguest of twinkles in his ruddy cheery eyes.

"Then," the squeeze said, "you know what?"

"No, what?"

"You oughta been a preacher."

"Like, you know, kid, I've often felt I had the calling,"
Wasco said, "just like my old mom!"

On the way back out into the yard everyone stopped at

the bulletin board. The Yard lieutenant had just put up a
new notice:

---

23 December 1972

CROWD CONTROL

As of this date it is strictly forbidden by authority of the
Warden to gather in groups of over three inmates in the
Main Yard. This ruling will remain in effect for two weeks
minimum. Any group, crowd or gathering of men which
refuses to disband will be warned three times and fired
upon by the yard gunwalk officer.

B. F. Bischoff
Yard Lieutenant

"Sensible course of action!" Wasco said, "as far as I
can see. Break these here 'blocs' of inmates up. There
oughta be a lot more intimate relating in here, oughta be
more human relations, more contact, more relating, more
genuine human touch and relevance among these here
cold-ass convicts. Don't you think so, Squeezy?"

"Right!" said the squeeze.

While over in the southwest corner of the Yard you
could see old Galliot trying with all his black might to
cool down them stirred-up nigger-boos, them restless
Afro-Americans, trying to keep them straight, forcing
them to obey the Warden's latest intelligent provocation.
Wasco could see him, grabbing them three at a time,
trying to hold them off, for just a little while longer:
what's he got up his sleeve? Wasco wondered, like a chess
master who, even though he's confident as hell, and
known he's unbeatable on the board, he still takes a real
great pleasure in trying to figger the smart-ass moves of
his fine but inferior nigger opponent. . . .

On the way into the East Block to resume their constituted duties as duly appointed tier men, Squeezy threw
some bread crumbs to the birds, just like he did on their
honeymoon morning. And, just like on that bright morning, the big old fat sea gull swooped down and stole all
the bread from the other birds.

"Sock it to 'em, Fatty!" the squeeze hollered.

"Now you're talking!" Wasco said.

Forty

On the way back from San Felipe Moke made Arv pull
over at the same gas station they'd stopped at before.
Stepping over the same gravel pile, crunch crunch crunch,
pushing on the door, cooking up over the same shit-splattered sink, fixing in the same filthy toilet stall, crying for
no reason, just like the last time, while she jerked off,
watching the blood back up, Moke for a moment had the
terrible wonderful feeling that the whole trip to San Felipe
had not occurred yet. That it had all been merely a junk
dream. That she was still there in the toilet skin-popping,
on her way south, with Arv impatiently waiting in the car.
And that none of it had happened yet. And it was all to
be done just as she now imagined it, with her knees giving
way, sinking to the stinking piss-stained floor . . . or . . .

Maybe that afternoon, before leaving San Felipe, when
they'd fallen asleep on the beach, wrapped up together in
two blankets. A big wind had sprung up, sweeping down
off the Sierra San Pedro Martir. When they awakened
they were covered with sand, almost suffocating together,
with tiny itchy grating grains of sand in their eyes and
ears and hair and genitals, pinching, stuck together with
sweat. They'd risen then, shaking the sand, bent against
the shrieking wind, and they'd run for the car, so acutely
uncomfortable to be still in San Felipe that they'd rushed
straight to the motel, paid their bill, and split. . . . But on
the other hand, maybe they hadn't . . . Moke dreamed
. . . feeling the rush of goodness from the smack as it
curled around her pissy shitty bare toes in their sandals on
the horrid floor . . . maybe the sandstorm hadn't even
come up. Maybe she was still dreaming on the beach,
dreaming . . . an unfortunate but soon-over bad dream,
nightmare, and she'd awaken in a moment still wrapped
up in Arv's sweet loving weedy arms . . . or maybe . . .
poor Moke, lost, in love with one and owned by another,

poor Moke she gave way almost to the butt-end of despair, dizzy, dopey, crunch crunch crunch, and the gray desert mountains looming high above her. She ran over the gravel to the car.

"Hey, what're you crying for, baby?" he asked her, concerned, as the car barreled across the white flat desert at ninety miles an hour . . . ten miles to Mexicali . . . *I have five minutes* . . . "What're you crying about?" . . . Moke hit him then, that fucking prison hack, she struck him hard, like she'd done the first time *which time?* going the other way *which way?* . . . "Hey, goddamnit, what're you trying to do?" . . . struck him on the shoulder on the arm and hand, grabbed the wheel . . . "Let go!" . . . grabbed her bag, hit hit him with it, hit his arm, hit him before the salt wash bridge . . . kicked his gas pedal leg, crying, "I'll kill us! I'll kill us!"

The Merc, bouncing over the bumps and dips of the high-banked desert road over the salt flats at ninety miles an hour, drifted right. A bridge was coming up. Coming up fast and narrow ahead in the dusty haze. Moke kicked. Hit. Hit him, bit him, that fucking hack, and the Merc drifted. Curved slow right. Arv wouldn't look at her. Kept his fucking eyes pasted to the white line ahead. And the blacktop. The bumps and curves and dips and road signs. Pushed her away with his right hand, right arm . . . fucking *Haole!* The bridge was metal, painted gunmetal gray. Just in front of it a sign said: PASADO DE GANADO. The Merc crept right. Arv hit Moke hard on the ear. She grabbed his hand. "Ouch! You sonofabitch!" The Merc touched metal at eighty miles an hour. SCREECH. The side scraped on the iron bridge. The door knob came off and clattered behind them. The chrome strip on Moke's side of the car came off and flew into the air. SCREEEECH. The sound went directly to Moke's central nervous system. Like the sound of Miss Kapalani's long red-painted fingernails on the blackboard at the Kamehameha School. And Moke let go then. She dissolved like junk in a watered cooker. And the Merc, slowly, surely, under Arv's steadying hand, edged back left, onto the road, straddled the white line. picked up speed again.

"You're insane!" he yelled, like he'd said it that other time *which time?*

Moke just lay back across the seat, tingling with pleasure and despair.

"You're a junkie," he said.

"So what?" she said, letting her head loll like a rag doll against the plastic back of the seat.

"Don't take me with you," he said, rather sadly, like a little boy.

"Oh no, Arv, I won't, my darling!" she cried, touching his sleeve softly, crazily, where she'd just been beating at him, hitting . . . "I won't! I won't! I don't know what's . . . Arv," she said, squeezing his arm, "listen, baby, let's split!" she said, surprising herself, smiling stupidly at him through her tears *what am I saying?*

"What?"

"Listen . . ." she said, with big Wasco looking right over her shoulder, growling at her, pounding his massive chest like an ape, "listen, baby, I got a habit. But I can kick it if you help me . . ."

On the right ahead a sign was coming up, with an arrow pointing east and south:

HERMOSILLO
CIUDAD OBREGÓN
CULIACÁN
MAZATLÁN
GUADALAJARA

"Let's just do it," she repeated, urging him to turn right and follow the signs, "let's just split. I got enough money for both of us."

"Okay," he said simply, smiling at her as much as if to say, "I'll make this sacrifice for you . . ." clucking *tch tch tch* like an indulgent daddy, smiling at her and saying it like he'd done it that night in the Mexican restaurant in New Sonora . . . how long before? . . . *three nights ago? Four? How many?*

"Let's just go away," she said, "we'll follow the border road east to Sonoita. Then we'll get out visas and head straight south to Mazatlán. There's a beautiful beach there. And then we'll ride up to Guanajuato. It's marvelous, with an open covered market made of steel struts and stained glass that's an Art Nouveau masterpiece. You'll really dig it! We'll avoid Puerto Vallarta and Juliapa. Too many druggies. Oh yes! Let's go!" she said, smiling up at him desperately. "Listen! I never mainlined it, Arv. I

swear! All I did was just chip at it, really. I wasn't really
any kind of pro, honest! Always made sure I just skin-
popped. Cut down, eased back down a bag or two every
month . . ."

"Sure, I'll help you," he said, as the Merc sped across
the black and silver *Gran Desierto* toward Sonoita, Sonora, Sinaloa, Nayarit, toward the real old Mexico far
away to the east and south.

They didn't say anything for a whole hour. The dusty
desert raced by. Different kinds of desert. Alkali flats by
the Colorado River. Tumbleweed desert on the hills above
it. Organ cactus and saguaro desert on the higher plateaus.
Moke watched the desert flying by, watched the wind
blow, dust hieing, tumbleweeds rolling. Watched and
watched. Each yucca plant. Each cactus. Each boulder
and rock and adobe house. Every hill and hillock and
mountain range. She read each road sign along the way.
In this manner she was able to keep Wasco out of her
mind.

Then, out in the bone-dry brittle hills above San Luis,
Arv turned off the main highway and went left, went
north at a sign that read:

GADSDEN ARIZONA
FRONTERA INTERNACIONAL
11 KILOMETERS

"Why you turning?" she asked, secretly relieved, and
terrified at the same time.

"Listen baby, you know what?" he began, very kindly,
sensing rightly that this was the way she wanted to be
turning, trying very hard to explain it to her reasonably
and right, "I got too many things to clear up back in New
Sonora. I'd like to finish the semester out at least. It's only
three more weeks. And we've both worked so hard, at
least in Elaine's . . ."

"You're just chickenshit!" she yelled, spitting it at him,
indulging herself in an angry reaction she didn't really feel
from the heart *who am I pissed off at?*

"No, it's not that, really! I just can't leave like that
without . . . I'd like to say good-bye to my daughter, and
. . . I'd like to get my own bread out of the bank
and . . ."

"I told you I'd pay," she said.

"I know, but I got a lot of things to do first . . . I promised to bring a letter into the Joint for Elaine, for instance, and I'm already late. And then, after we clear things up, if we still want to go . . ."

"Coward!"

"No! Listen, damnit. I want to split as much as you. And I will. But we just can't take off like that. Not if we want to stay away a long time. It just can't be done. It might be romantic, and all that, but it won't work. I want to resign properly from my job, for example. They're already gonna be pissed off at me for not phoning in, taking an extra day off, or two days . . . which is it?"

"Bert's going to fire me!" she shouted, "and I don't give a shit!"

"Sure but, like you say, you got bread! I want to resign formally instead of just splitting on them this way. You never know . . ."

"You're joking!"

"No. I'll want to get another job someday. I'll need a recommendation. I don't want to fuck up my work record."

"Weakling!" she said, still indulging herself in that wondrous anger, "you're in love with that bloody Joint, just like your old man and all your relatives!"

"That's not true! I'm just more reasonable than you are. I see what's got to be done. And then when we go, we'll be able to stay."

"You're going to be sorry, Arvin. You are going to be sorry."

"Baby! Listen, I'll help you kick the habit . . ."

"Forget it. I was wrong about you. I don't want your help. I don't love you. I don't want your slimy fingers touching me anymore," she said, and continued in the same vein all the way to the United States border, though if he'd turned around she would have begged him just as vehemently to return to the States. All the way she was thinking how delighted she was that it has been he and not she who'd given in first *I would've told him to turn around myself in another ten minutes I couldn't have run away either. . . .*

A mile or two before the border Arv made her throw out her personal stash of smack. She threw it far out over an irrigation canal and watched the shining plastic bag fall, watched that highly ironic and irrelevant tenth of an ounce of white powder spread like froth upon the brown water, thinking of that other more relevant stash of five kilos of Culiacán brown heroin, of whose existence Arv was totally unaware, packed to the windows in the panels of the Merc. . . .

At the International Line the U.S. Customs Service man took one look at Arv's NEW SONORA STATE PEACE OFFICERS' ASSOCIATION sticker, and the badge in his outstretched hand, and smilingly waved them on.

"Have a good trip, sir?"

"You bet!" Arv yelled, and punched the Merc, blissfully unaware, out onto the highway for California.

When they crossed the Colorado River again, at Yuma, Moke remembered for some reason a story she'd once read in a magazine. It seems a U.S. Cavalry horse patrol once came upon a Spanish galleon sitting high and dry out in the middle of the Mojave Desert. The only way they could explain its presence there was on the theory that the seventeenth-century vessel had run aground after sailing up the Colorado River on an exploring mission from the Sea of Cortez. Then, over the years, the river changed course once, twice, several times, and finally went around the other side of a range of hills. And there you had it! An ancient galleon, perfectly preserved in the dry desert air, sitting alone through the centuries, a world away from its Mediterranean home, a hundred miles from water. . . .

Outside Palm Springs, California, with the snows of Mount San Jacinto high above them, flashing up the freeway for L.A., Moke decided she'd make it up with Arv by telling him the story. . . .

Part IV

Part IV

Forty-One

Little Arv, at the end of all endurance, sciatica acting up, radiating down his right leg and back round into his prostate, drove home from Elaine's place and took a good long shit while he read the *New Sonora Times* from cover to cover.

"RACE WAR" IN STATE PRISON
BLACK FENCE BLAMED IN SLAYING
OF WARDEN'S SON

He knew this'd be the only time he'd be able to relax all day long. Did it purely as a measure of self-defense. There would be no other moment of rest. Every other minute of his day had already been booked, overbooked: all night on the road from Mexico, kept awake only with the aid of Moke's powerful meth pills and frequent stops for black scalding coffee, and the popular song of the hour that played every ten minutes from Arizona to New Sonora: Taj Mahal sang it, he sang:

> Six days upon the road and
> I got to see my baby tonight . . .

At Livermore, in California, Moke broke out her hidden stash of brown Culiacán boy and started snorting: SNORT! SNORT! snorting her derision at Arv's stuffy disapproval, snorting SNORT! at her own previous resolution to kick her nasty habit, snorting herself into nodding oblivion, while Taj kept wailing on the radio and the Merc kept wailing too, up through California to New Sonora.

"Why'd you bring that shit across the border?" he asked her. "Lucky we had that New Sonora State Peace Officers' Association sticker or we could've got twenty years!"

Moke merely laughed. "Shit!" she scoffed, "that sticker doesn't mean anything! He knew what we had. He knows me. He's bought. Half the Border Patrol is working for us. And the U.S. Customs Bureau! Christ, we got an easy man at every Mexican crossing!"

And Arv, in the hours later, the hours alone, while she went on her junkie nod, and later, when dawn came riding out of the eastern Sierras, Arv rolled around in his buzzing nervous head the notion that she'd been right in Mexico. They should've split south, and to hell with the consequences. But still, he just couldn't stop that Merc. Couldn't get the bastard turned around. It seemed like it just wanted to keep going toward home.

Now, on Orchard Street in the city, plopping his still-black and solid beany Mexican turds into the pube-scattered porcelain of his unwashed toilet bowl, Arv contemplated his heavily overbooked day, a day already so top-heavy it threatened at only 11:37 A.M. to break down, keel over, die in his head. . . .

At eight o'clock that morning he had driven the zonked and raving Moke to her Molina Valley mansion, carried her up to her apartment and left her passed out on the low Japanese-style bed while the black mynah shouted his outrage in the background: "Black powa, muthafucka, black powa!"

Got back out to the car just as the City of Molina Valley's ancient caretaker rode by in his pickup truck loaded down with garden implements and a miniature snow plow. Managed an almost convincing smile, breath blowing steamy in the frost-tipped air.

Carried Moke's five keys of brown smack up and dumped it behind her potted fern.

Got back in the car, cranked him over, old Merc, the valiant one, the only one who would last, beloved trusty Merc, his 375 horsepower steed, who would see Little Arv through all his trials and tribulations and emerge undaunted with him on the other side . . . Arv hoped.

Switched on the radio, heard the News, same News they'd been hearing all the way from Baja. News, that's all. Just News that Arv listened to on the radio. The same old News: in Vietnam B-52's were going down in flames. Hospitals were burning in Hanoi. In New Sonora, U.S.A., a prison guard had been killed. His name was

Frank R. Miniver, the son of the warden, survived by a wife and four children, beep beep beep. You couldn't take it seriously when you heard it like that. Driving up through California Moke and Arv had heard the News of Fast-Walking's mortal discharge upon the clean-mopped floor of the East Block, but they hadn't taken it all seriously; perhaps they hadn't even heard it. How could they hear it? How could they accept it? The rock station disc jockey just read off the headlines real fast and then beep beep beep a phony short-wave beep signal sounded self-importantly in the background and then the disc jockey went on to the next brief item of his News report: "Three B-52's down over North Vietnam" beep beep beep "Hanoi hospital reported destroyed" beep beep beep "New Sonora prison guard killed" beep beep beep "Waterside 'race war' seen" beep beep beep.

Though he'd cried before, on the way north, cried for the death of his old buddy, Arv hadn't really let it all soak in, hadn't let it really rattle around in his brain, hadn't quite realized that old loose-limbed, easy-riding Fast-Walking wouldn't be around anymore, wouldn't be back again, never. Arv just hadn't let that sift. Not till now . . . Fast-Walking!

Wham! he slammed the door and ran back up the stairs to Moke's place, leaving the Merc idling unhappily on the frost-bit lawn. "Wake up! Wake up, you bitch!"

"Huh? Huh?"

"Wake up, goddamnit! Fast-Walking's on ice!"

"Huh?"

"Wake up!" he shouted, screaming with hatred and rage, "who are you, anyway, you fucking bitch!"

"Huh? Huh?" she said, that's all she could say. Her eyes opened a hair, wavered, and then her heavy black lids dropped audibly down "tock" to close her orbs to the ugly world outside. Zonked, zilched, zapped, lost to the land of humankind, Moke was not the one to answer Arv's pathetic questions.

"Black powa, mothafucka, black powa!" went the wretched mynah bird, locked in his ornate cage.

"Shut up, you black bastard!" Arv hollered . . . "Moke. please tell me," he said. "tell me the truth. I'll forgive you. We'll work it out together, whatever. Moke!"

"Huh? Huh?"

"Black powa, mothafucka, black powa!"

"Shut up!" Arv shrieked, knocking the cage over. The cage went down and struck Moke's glass table, cracked it ZANG! and rolled to the floor.

"Aaaaaaaaaaawk!" croaked the mynah.

"Shut up, goddamnit!" Arv yelled, kicking at the cage. Kicking, kicking. The cage burst open. The bird flew at him, its wings flapping madly, its strong yellow beak snapping. "Aaaaaaaaawk! Aaaaaaaaawk!" Arv swatted at him. Feathers flew around the low-ceilinged tapa and straw room. Arv ran to the window and threw it open. Freezing air blew in. The mynah was right behind him. Whoooooosh! he shot past Arv and out into the icy yard and disappeared over the dense roof of the tangled trees. Wham! Arv slammed the window shut. Warm weather bird, tropical beastie, jungle-born, the mynah would fly on and on, trying to fly out of that midwinter air.

"You take your chances out there, then. You sonofabitch. See how you like it! . . . Moke!" he said, turning to her again. "Moke!"

"Huh? Huh?" she said. And that's all he could get out of her.

Went to her phone and called Control at the Joint.

"Hank?"

"Yeah."

"This is Little Arv."

"Where the fuck you been, man?"

"Took a trip down south and had some car trouble."

"The Warden's after your ass. You be in this afternoon?"

"Sure."

"Okay. I'll mark you down on the roster. You hear about Fast-Walking? Too bad, huh?"

"I can't believe it."

"They're having his funeral today at the employees' chapel."

"Oh yeah?"

"Yeah. At three o'clock. The whole swing shift's gonna be there, in uniform. Gonna show them niggers where we're at."

"The Black Fence really do it?"

"Who the fuck else?"

"Can't convict anyone just through the process of elimination."

"No? Maybe not," Hank growled into the phone, "but I'll tell you what. You can eliminate somebody without any process at all . . . har har har!"

Arv hung up on him, covered Moke with a pile of blankets *you're right we should've split, baby, we should've split* . . . and raced for Elaine's place in the city.

Out over the Alvarez Straits Toll Bridge the wind blew cold and fierce straight down from Alaska, right through the big hole it had battered in the high pressure front in the Aleutian Islands. COLD WAVE! BEEP BEEP BEEP.

Icicles hung fron the huge suspension cables at center span. On the black rocks below, the sea kicked up foam, foam the most extraordinary color Arv had ever seen. What color was it? Extraordinary! The color of bug blood? The color of octopus ink? Dinosaur piss?

Elaine lived on 18th Avenue, near City College, in one of the double-decker white and pink stucco houses overlooking the stormy Pacific. A neat small palm tree suffered silently in her tiny grass front yard. The cold and wind had stripped the poor thing to nudity. It was depressing. All the other little single palms in all the other small yards all the way down 18th Avenue to Fitzhugh Grove were naked too, their branches scattered over the frozen lawns.

Arv rang Elaine's bell, pulling his collar up around his ears. Brrrrrr!

"God, where've you been? I've been looking for you everywhere!" she exclaimed as soon as she opened the front door. "Come in, come in! I can't tell you how worried I've been!"

"Look," he said, seating himself on a yellow Macy's sofa, a sofa that, like the house itself, was probably a remnant of her former marriage to an unhappy army dentist, a relic of her safe middle-class past of over ten years ago that still, somehow, fit. In the classroom Elaine was queen. And yet here she didn't look out of place either, in these decidedly unqueenly digs, in her worn housecoat and curlers and fuzzy pink slippers and her frowsy hair . . . and he wondered for an instant if Galliot's breakup with her had really been for ideological reasons. . . .

"Look," Arv repeated, "there isn't much time. I'm here to do anything you want!"

"Wonderful!" she said, bouncing excitedly on her gray wall-to-wall carpet.

"They're trying to pin those killings in the Joint on the Black Fence. I happen to know three of the people killed. They're absolutely unconnected with politics or racial conflict of any kind. I mean, Christ! The two old black men used to cut my hair and shine my shoes! They're just old . . ." he said, and realized that he'd said the wrong thing. But she hadn't seemed to notice, so he continued, "They haven't been murdered in any 'race war'! They've been killed probably just to stir up racial hatred in the Joint, or maybe to cover up an attempt on Galliot's life. Anyway, that's how I figure it . . ."

"Okay," she said, very serious now, "look, we were able to get an oral message in to him through a guy who was going in from the county jail. But in case he was unable to get to Galliot, let's make double sure. Okay?" she said, hurriedly scribbling a letter on her dining room table, sealing it, handing it to Arv.

"Sure," Arv said.

"Okay. Now listen, Galliot knows they're after him. Needless to say he's doing everything he can to avoid getting killed. I can't tell you any more than that, for the moment. But soon you'll understand."

"Alright," Arv said, "I'll see you tomorrow."

"That may not be necessary," she said. "I'll give you a call."

"Tomorrow's Christmas," Arv said, starting to leave, "would you believe it?"

"Hardly," she said, motioning to the *New Sonora Times* extra edition lying on the sofa, and the headlines:

B-52'S STAGE 5TH DAY OF RAIDS;
U.S. PUTS PLANE LOSSES AT 12

NIXON 'DETERMINED' TO KEEP UP
BOMBING TILL PEACE IS REACHED

WATERGATE BUGGING SCANDAL WIDENS

"Well," said Arv. "Merry Christmas anyway."

"Yeah, Merry Christmas, dear," she said, ". . . and . . . thank you, so much."

"No problem," he said, "it's the least I can do. . . . Say, have you read your paper yet? Do you mind if I borrow it?"

"Not at all," she said. "And . . . oh! I almost forgot. How's Moke?"

"Oh, she's fine. We just got back from a trip down to Mexico. Had a little trouble getting back."

Arv grabbed the paper and went out the door and drove home where he sat reading it now, reading those very headlines over again, sitting on the cold toilet on Orchard Street. Plop!

. . . As soon as Arv had got home he'd gone to Fast-Walking's room, the living room, and gathered up his things to deliver to Marie-Claude at the Joint. Fast-Walking didn't own much. Arv, to dispel his nameless terror, listed the items in his head:

1. 2 pairs slacks
2. 3 shirts
3. 1 pullover sweater
4. 1 extra uniform
5. 1 pair shoes
6. 6 pairs socks
7. 6 pairs shorts
8. 6 T-shirts

Going through Fast-Walking's pitiful belongings made his fingers feel clammy, just like a shakedown at the Joint. He hated going through other people's things, touching their sweaty dirty clothes, he hated it. It occurred to him that Fast-Walking, for some reason, had not been back to Orchard Street since he'd been there himself. Everything was just the same in the living room as when they'd left it, on that sunny winter afternoon how long ago? Fast-Walking's stash of grass hadn't even been touched. Arv went into the kitchen. His same coffee cup he'd left five days ago lay moldering in the sink. Nope. Fast-Walking never came back. What happened? He probably lost the key. Arv tried to imagine Fast-Walking that night, standing out in the middle of Slate Avenue in Mexican Town, all alone in the yellow city fog, no place to go, abandoned by his only friend. Arv felt really horrible for a minute, putting himself in Fast-Walking's lonely unloved shoes. *But we was only kidding, man! And you didn't want to come to Mexico anyway. You wanted to go over and see Marie-Claude, you said, didn't you?* Sure! That's where he went.

Couldn't get in here so he went home. Finally made it back into his happy home, I'll bet . . . before he died. . . .

Squatting on the toilet, pretending to read the newspaper, Arv thought about that now. "I'm sure glad he got to see his wife and kids, at least once or twice . . . I sure am glad!" he said out loud. Thinking: *Fast-Walking, you old sonofabitch, I never knew you.* . . . Thinking of the $587 in cash he'd just found stuffed into Fast-Walking's old uniform jacket . . . *Fast-Walking I never knew you.* . . .

One o'clock. Arv popped another methadrine from Fast-Walking's stash and lay back on his war surplus army blanket looking up at the wishful *Vol d'Oiseau* street map of Paris on his wall, *maybe we'll go to France, get place in Montparnasse. Let's see. Where would we live? How about Boulevard Saint Jacques. That would be nice. Right . . . there!* he thought, and then pulled his hand away from the map in horror . . . and then glee . . . when he found that the place he was pointing to was located just across the street from the notorious La Santé prison.

Arv lay there on his bed for an hour, letting the meth work at him, grind his jaw, blink his eyes, set his heart to racing madly, sorting things out, *what are you gonna do?* sorting out reality from mere appearance, making lists in his head:

1. Moke

. . . I seen her once before, long ago, riding . . . riding . . . on the back of a motorcycle, a great big Harley . . . who's that person she was with?

2. Wasco

Then he got up quickly and began preparing for work. While he shaved he kept looking out at the Alatri Art School across the street, as was his habit. Like he and Fast-Walking used to do it, looking out at those beautiful black and white birds arriving for an afternoon Christmas party. They were all dressed in costume: motley, queens and knaves, cops and robbers, penguins and pelicans.

They looked so gay and young! Old man Alatri welcomed them at the door with a lecherous grin.

"Buon giorno, signorine, buon natale, buon natale!" he effused, leering at them through his salacious black moustache, looking up at Arv with what must have been something very like a . . . wink . . . *probably wonders what happened to old Fast-Walking.*

Arv, in the mirror, regarded his own moustache. It wasn't bad either. He'd let it creep down the corners of his mouth recently. It suited him. Made him look more sinister. . . .

Little Arv got into his uniform. He took his time. Stepped into his forest green U.S. Army pants with the brass clasp belt, into the black government-issue oxfords, pulled on his tan poplin army shirt, his black military tie, thinking about what a clever thing it was that he'd never wasted his money buying an official C of C unee-form, thinking: *I swear that whatever happens I'll never wear a fucking uniform again as long as I live!*

Strangely elated, his heart firing off like an automatic rifle, Arv put on his C of C cop-style billed cap and went down the hall to Fast-Walking's ex-room, Arv's reclaimed living room. The floor and the tattered green and red davenport were still scattered with the already stale newspaper articles Fast-Walking had cut out on that bright winter afternoon long ago, just before he slid up, wobbly, steady, steadily unsteady to his full stable unstable six feet two inches of height and glided tottering and smooth ahead of Arv like the ghost of a giraffe out to the waiting Merc.

"Hey Sylvester!" Arv said out loud, like Fast-Walking used to say it, "should we do it?" and answered himself, "Sho nuff, Jim, let's do it, let's swoop!" trying to get it right, and not quite succeeding, and keeping it just a tiny bit ironic so he wouldn't feel himself ridiculous in the empty apartment. Going for it, going for soul, like old Fast-Walking used to do. And Arv didn't make it, but comforted himself with the assurance that Fast-Walking hadn't made it either.

So Arv went out onto Orchard Street into the freezing winter day. Nobody appeared on the street. Even the pretty art students in their gay party dresses had disappeared into the bowels of the Alatri Art School. The cars

illegally parked up on the curb appeared frozen there under the withering Alaskan wind, their windows frosted
over. Even the normal sounds of Orchard Street and Bird
Park seemed suspended in the extreme cold. New Sonora,
gripped in the jaws of the cold wave, held its breath. The
only thing to be heard was the traffic down on Chase
Boulevard, and a faint drift of Christmas caroling from
within the wood frame Victorian art school building. The
barely heard carols, remembrance of horrid Xmas Eves
spent in the employees' chapel at the Joint, merely increased little Arv's presentiment of approaching danger,
disaster . . . and his bitter resolve and . . . his deep sense
of . . . almost . . . exaltation . . . to be heading off now
to face it.

He got into the old Merc. It cranked over without a
hitch. The Merc was the only thing that never let him
down. He drove out Bird Road past the frostbound park
to 18th Avenue again, and over the white hills and
through the icy silent cypress trees of Fort Riley and over
the Alvarez Straits Toll Bridge again, leaving the frigid
city far behind.

And all the time it was Fast-Walking beside him on the
plastic front seat, rapping his slow-fast rap, his voice
rolling on and on like smooth rolling waves of butter,
reasonable sounding, irrational, beautiful, dangerous. And
he rapped it for Little Arv one last time, old Fast-
Walking did, rapped the last unattainable dream, the one
about the arid south-eastern corner of Oregon, where
the Indians were once so poor that buffalos ate *them,*
the Oregon of a child, the Oregon of wonder, the Oregon
of dreams. . . .

Forty-Two

When Arv finally disappeared from the apartment his anger and excitement stayed behind him, hung in the air like the smoke of battle. Moke had to wait long minutes before his vibrations, taut, fearful, violent, had dissipated. Then she rose cross-legged from her bed and, wearing only yesterday's panties, quickly set about cleaning up Arv's brutal mess. The place was quite warm enough to go about like that. She always left the thermostat at seventy-eight degrees, even when she was gone, so her tropical plants wouldn't die. She bustled about, watering her shrubs and trees, straightening things, dusting, sweeping, vacuuming, putting stuff away, putting the brown smack away that she found where Arv had plopped it behind her potted fern.

Moke's breasts were small and high and firm. She was happy they were like that; when she was working they never got in her way.

In the kitchen she boiled up some morning rice, listening to the nine o'clock newscast on the radio: "Fuel shortage in New Sonora. Consumers warned to conserve gas during cold snap." That's all she had for breakfast, just rice and some chocolate sauce on top, since there was nothing else in the house . . . and she had a craving for sweets.

She sat down on her tatami floor, with her bare legs crossed under the cable spool table, and absentmindedly shoveled the rice into her mouth with her chopsticks, all the time looking around her room where she did all her eating and dreaming, where she'd been happy, alone, many times, indulging all her harmless fancies. *How stupid to fall for the first one who fucks you right.*

Moke would not see her place soon again. That was sure. *Not in this lifetime.* She intuited that quite clearly.

And her intuition had never been wrong yet. Never? No, never. Even with him . . . she'd seen it all coming. Even before Wasco sent her after him. And she'd done nothing to curtail its sure growth within her. It was all written down somewhere anyway, in advance, Moke the fatalist thought, so what the hell! *Yeah, but what if I'm not ready for it?* But she'd made her choice *what choice?* And now she had to accept the consequences *what consequences?* Very grave ones.

After breakfast Moke fixed in the bathroom, skin-popping, jerking it off, letting the blood back up till it filled the dropper, waited for the rush, good rush, then cleaned her fit, boiled her point and cooker, put away her stash, washed the dishes and put them away, and went back out to her now-tidy bedroom.

Stepped out of her nasty Mexican road panties, found a pair of clean sniffworthy today's: SNIFF SNIFF. *How lovely,* she thought, *how simple and nice and lovely to have spotless stainless soap-smelling panties to put on whenever you want.* She scratched her crotch happily, a habit with her when she was alone and wanted to comfort herself.

And sniffing, SNIFF SNIFF SNIFF, Moke thought of her baby, her rectal child, Flo, conceived by anal fluke, residing now far across the sea with Tutu, her Great Aunti Cereza, in the warm wet Manoa Valley, neither of them ever to be seen again . . . unless . . . ?

She went then naked into her bathroom, paused before her full-length mirror, regarding her perfect brown body, little body, but long legged, perfect flat tummy, perfect round little hips, small well-formed titties, perfectly shaped legs, feet, hands, shoulders *how beautiful I am! For what?* Had a nice long shower. Washed her hair twice, rinsed it twice. Sat under her hair dryer on the toilet for ten minutes, combed her black shiny hair out straight in front of the mirror. How it shone! It hung down to her asshole in back. It was gorgeous hair. *For what?*

When she'd finished her toilet Moke just dawdled for a while, puttering about her bedroom, straightening things around again, dusting, wiping her now-cracked cutter's table with a moist rag. Then she got out the five keys of brown Culiacán Boy and, fastening her gauze cutter's mask around her face, wearing only the mask and her panties to cover her nakedness, went to work sifting and mixing and cutting and razor-blading her smack, working slow, working in the mannita and quinine, cutting it at five/one because it was such inferior shit. After that she worked for a long time bagging the cut smack into Sheik rubbers for the Joint trade, doing it very neat, careful, pro, popping the rubbers open with a deft little flip of her wrist FLOMP! then putting it up to her mouth and blowing out the kinks WHOOF! and packing it with fresh-cut junk. She did it good. She took pride in a job well done. She liked to be working, concentrating on the job at hand, behind her black-out windows. Already forgetting her first-time happiness in the sun, her pleasure in bright-lit day with Arv down in Baja, she thought: *more than anything I hate leaving darkness for daylight.* The thought of going out into even this cold gray dismal day was most disquieting to Moke. She would have preferred staying right where she was, alone, working her shit, bagging it, stacking the rubbers in neat piles, snapping them together SNAP! four at a time into neat bundles with rubber bands SNAP! a neat little sound, not seeing anyone, bothered by no importunate young men with messy notions of love and entrapment, notions of owning her, keeping her, taking her possessions, her greatest possession . . . *did he actually suppose I'd strap a rucksack on my back and hitch-hike about the world with him, sleeping in city parks and begging for greasy food? Dumb Haole!* . . . notions that were, in spite of herself, extremely powerful, and drew her, drew her toward him with an almost irresistible force, drew her, therefore, toward destruction . . . *oh love Haole love what you do to me?*

When Moke had cut and bagged two bundles of rubbers she quit. Went over and did her eyes up with black mascara, while she deeply perused the Germanic fjord-gray of old Hiram Todd's hereditary eyes. Got into a pair of heavy winter pantyhose and a black leather jump suit and put a short-waisted fur coat over it. Got into her motorcycle boots. Put on her crash helmet. Stuck the heroin in a large paper bag. Locked her apartment. Went out to the garage, clomping across the brittle cold lawn like a spaceman on a moonwalk. Put the smack in a secret compartment in the Honda's gas tank (a compartment that took up so much room she could only go fifty miles on a full tank of gas), cranked the bike over, let it warm up a long time, and rode it slowly down the winding winterscape drive to Molina Valley Road and the freeway entrance.

Out on the big ten-lane superhighway she goosed it a bit, headed out past her favorite poplar grove, poplars today clean and cold and chaste as Girl, Miss Cocaine, and the same color: white. Past the ugly dick of the Joint, yellow and gray, stuck out in the shitty Sound. Over the humpback West Hazelton Bridge with the Exxon tankers tied up underneath. Along the brown muddy East Sound past the racetrack to the Nueva Ronda Exit, and over the low range of brown barren hills to Evie's low-rent neighborhood in Spic Town. She pulled up under the date palm tree, next to Big Arv's banged-up Chevy Impala, and went without knocking through the front screen porch and into the living room, giggling to herself at the grotesque exchange to which she was unintentionally privy: Evie to Big Arv in the piss-yellow kitchen: "No no, not now you naughty boy! Can't you even wait?"

"At least tell me then, please, tell me again!"

"Alright, you big baby . . . you're gonna get . . . everything, everything you always wanted from Evie and never got . . ."

"When?"

"Today, silly! You've done your part of the bargain."

"Everything? No lie?"

"Everything you can handle . . ." she said, diphthonging the first syllable archly, like maybe she'd heard Alexis Smith do in the movies years ago, "everything you can possibly HANdle," she repeated, and then shut up when Moke appeared at the kitchen door.

"Hey, Big Arv," she said, clomping across the asphalt tile in her muddy motorcycle boots, "can you open up the garage?"

"Sure, honey!" he said, "anything for my gal! Where you been?"

"Getting some more stuff for your Thermos," she said, as he went out the garage door.

Moke went back out and rode the bike into the garage. Big Arv shut the heavy garage door behind her. She opened the secret gas tank compartment and removed the smack. Big Arv carried it into the house through the inside garage door. All but two of the rubbers he took out to Evie's room where she deposited them in a hidden safe. He returned and put the remaining rubbers into two Thermos bottles which he then filled with coffee and capped.

Sanger showed up out front HONK HONK with a vanload of wetbacks eager to buy trinkets. Big Arv put the Thermos bottles into two lunch pails, stored them temporarily in the dish cabinet, and went over to open the Montoya Market for business.

Moke decided to split. She went back out to the garage, pushed the big door open, and cranked over the bike. Big Evie came waddling fast out from her room and caught up with her just as she snapped her visor down. ROOOM ROOOM ROOOM went her little bike as she revved it.

"Everything okay?" asked Wasco's mom, overcoming her distaste for this little "island nigger" only through a visible effort, only for the sake of business.

Moke pretended like she couldn't hear. ROOOM ROOOM Actually she couldn't hear. But she could read her fishy lips.

"Everything okay for today?"

Moke made her yell it again, louder, made her yell it so loud that her kewpie doll's pink face went all red with the effort. And her voice, that high little girl's voice, Wasco's voice, that seemed like it came from a long distance even when there wasn't any noise to contend with, her horrid voice, the voice of vice, finally penetrated the thick plastic of the helmet. It was extraordinary, Moke thought, that Evie's voice, once she got it through all that noise, through the walls of her helmet, sounded just like normal, sounded like it always did: like it was coming from a long long way off. . . . "EVERYTHING OKAY FOR TODAY?"

Moke grinned at her tartly, kind of sharky, as if to say, "I ain't afraid of you, honey," and nodded her head affirmative.

Evie lit up. "Wonderful!" she hollered after Moke as she accelerated down the driveway to the road *fuck you bitch!*

Raced out to the freeway and back over the humpback bridge to the Joint. All the flags were at half-mast. The American flag, and the New Sonora State flag too, all of them at half-mast on poles in front of the Joint, at all the

gates that Moke passed through, and in the garden of the
Ad Building.

The fat butchy Visitor's Matron gave Moke a card with
a number. "Any gifts this time, honey?"

"I rather think not, this time," Moke said in her phony
English accent, as she handed over her purse.

In the Waiting Room all the Spics and Boos and Okies
stared at her black leather getup. The place smelled the
same as last time. It smelled to Moke like bean farts and
chitterling breath and chawing tobacco. It was stuffy and
loud in there, filled with smoke, packed with low-rent visitors on account of Christmas Eve and all. None of them,
however, were bearing gifts. That was against state policy.

"Number forty-seven . . . Weed!" said the loudspeaker.

She followed a tiny wispy young officer out to the
Third Fence Gate where the same old crusty mean gate
sergeant pulled them up. His vicious Doberman Pinscher
strained at its leash.

"Inmate?"

"Weed."

"Relation?"

"Who?"

"What?"

"Who?" she repeated.

"Who what?" he demanded, exasperated.

"What?" she asked again, as his scowl got meaner and
meaner, and the Doberman started to growl and pull at
his leash.

"What's your relation?" the old fart finally said.

"To whom?"

"The inmate!"

"What inmate?"

"The one you're visiting, goddamnit!"

"Oh . . . wife!" she said, and he let her in, threatening
her with the evil dog. But little Moke kept her head,
showed the beast she wasn't scared, and headed across the
lawn directly into the teeth of an Arctic blast off the
nearby Sound.

In the Visiting Room an officer directed her to a chair
in the rear. Wasco hadn't arrived yet. She sat at the end
of a long line of visitors and convicts and twiddled her
thumbs till he came in, not thinking of anything, pur-
posely not, not even listening to the drone of the other
conversations in the room.

Wasco flashed out of the steel door, a flash of red: his hair was already growing out. It was sparse hair, but it grew like hell. He sat down and took the phone off the hook, as she did, and they peered at each other through the reinforced glass window. Moke was afraid it was going to be difficult from now on. And she was hoping she wouldn't show it.

"Hey, baby, what's the haps?" he said into the phone. It was remarkable how much he sounded like Evie. He sounded like he was all the way over in China, rather than right there before her.

"Eh! I do everyteeng you say!" she said, and realized that it would be very difficult not to show it. She always called him *Haole*, before. And now she didn't think she could do it anymore. She hoped he wouldn't notice.

"Everything?"

"Sure!" she said, speaking now in plain American to avoid the necessity of calling him *Haole*. And then she also realized that she had forgotten to take off her panties in preparation for her normal "flashing." And hoped to Jesus that he wouldn't ask her. He didn't. He didn't even mention it . . . *and that's the least I could've done for him . . . Maybe he's really in love like Arv says, with that pretty-ass fag in the Joint* she thought, and then rapidly dispelled it from her mind as a temptation to another disloyalty. . . .

Moke was having problems. She had major problems to contend with while Wasco talked in code to her, in their personal code that they'd developed together over the years outside the law. Wasco told her in code just what he was going to do, how he was going to do it, what he'd do for them all, all his family, Little Arv included, what each of their responsibilities would be, what Little Arv must do . . . Moke's problem was keeping in mind her firm and everlasting commitment to Wasco *all I know is I never met the black guy he doesn't exist* . . . Wasco, this red-headed, bristle-headed convict talking to her now *He's stuck by me. I've stuck by him. That means something.* Reaffirming it in her head. Rerunning all their adventures together. All their separate temptations to break the faith . . . and not one betrayal. Not one? No, not one single betrayal in all their five years together. Except maybe in the beginning. But that didn't count. They'd still been feeling each other out at that time.

Moke, knowing that a second's hesitation on her part, a moment's doubt revealed, a remote suspicion of betrayal in Wasco's mind would mean instantaneous death for Arv, tried hard to establish her old rapport with Wasco through eye contact. So far everything seemed okay. He didn't appear to have detected anything. Wasco would kill her too, if he suspected.

When Wasco finished running down the operation for her, he switched back out of code talk and said, "Well now, baby, so what's happening? How's Flo? You heard anything?"

"Sure, honey, she's okay. Got rid of her cold. Just got a letter from Tutu. Says the weather's beautiful over there. Nothing like here, huh?"

"Hell no! Man, this cold is horrible, ain't it, sugar?"

"Oh yeah, it's murder," she said, going along with the small talk. Wasco always liked to indulge in the little game of small talk at the end of their conversations. The truth of the matter was that he really liked this kind of talk, just a touch of it, not too much. But he liked it.

"Yeah, well, it's sure been real nice, baby."

"Sure," she said, preparing to go.

"Oh hey!" he said suddenly, "by the way, how's old Alii, huh?"

Moke was struck dumb. Wasco never mentioned that bird. Did he know something? But how could he? Flustered, she retreated to pidgin . . .

"Da mynah? Eh! He only a mynah mattah!"

"Har har har, that's real funny," Wasco said, laughing insincerely, "I bet you can't guess what I'm gonna ask you to do with him . . ."

"Geev it to da dumb beast!" she said, attempting a joke.

"Right!" he said, frightening her with his vehemence. "I want you to get rid of that damn bird, honey. It's always stinking up the house. I been thinking about it. I'd hate to have it around when I get out of the Joint. So I want you to put it away, dig?"

"You're kidding."

"No," he said, real cold, "I ain't kidding at all. Drown it. That's how you put a bird away. Now! The minute you get home. Dig?"

"Well . . ."

"Dig?" he asked, and his question left no room for discussion. "If you can't do it yourself then get a vet and tell him to gas it."

"If you say so," she said.

"I do," he said.

"Okay," she said, and thought *where in the fuck am I gonna find that damn bird?*

"Aw, come on, honey," he said, with a phony smile on his fat red face, "it's nothing to sulk about."

"Alright," she said, making an attempt at achieving the appearance of her old placidity . . . *who's got something to hide after all? Who's going to double-cross who?*

"Good. I got to go now," he said, "say it for me, will you? Like old times?"

"What's that?"

"You know."

"No, I don't. What're you talking about?" she said, playing along with the old game. But her heart wasn't in it.

"Say it!"

"Oh, alright, *Aloha,* you sonofabitch!" she said, laughing, but her laughter rang false, almost stifled her in the close air of the prison Visiting Room. And as he left the building she wondered if Wasco couldn't tell. . . .

Forty-Three

Moke wasn't home when Arv got back. He knocked for five minutes and no one answered. He went out to the garage. Her bike was gone. He sat out in the Merc and waited, not even switching on the radio for comfort. After ten minutes he had to turn the engine on so he could get the heater going. It was cold as a tomb within the Merc. Arv's breath fogged all the windows. Another ten minutes and he heard the Honda winding out, coming up the road through the overgrown park.

Moke skidded up alongside the Merc. ROOOM ROOOM ROOOM! went her hot little engine as she revved it. She had her black leather jump suit on, and her white helmet with the red lightning flash. She raised her visor and looked at him. He could barely see her through the fogged window. He rolled it down, took his cop hat off and leaned out . . .

"Eh, *Haole!*" she yelled. "Wa' you do wi' da bird?" Her breath rose white in the icy air.

"Moke," he said, ignoring her question, and yet not ungently, "you're Wasco's old lady, ain't you?" And, considering the fact that he'd seen Moke with Wasco before, and the fact that he'd heard Yuba only five days ago in the barber shop describing Wasco's "foxy" dark-skinned girl friend, and that it was Moke who suggested that Arv carry letters between Elaine and Galliot in the first place, and considering that Moke had not only dropped hints in Mexico but had as much as *told* Arv who her lover was and what her role was in his life, and that Moke had on many occasions revealed by her erratic and irrational behavior not only her feelings of extreme guilt toward Arv, but her dependence on that lethal drug so closely associated with Wasco's name and reputation, considering all this Arv found it damn remarkable now that he hadn't

long ago asked Moke this highly pertinent question, which
he posed again for her:

"You're Wasco's old lady, ain't you?"

"Who tol' you dat, *Haole*, eh?"

So remarkable, so utterly dumbfounding did Arv find
his own inexplicable delay in asking this supremely vital
question that he could not evade the inescapable conclusion that he had been her willing conspirator . . . in hiding the truth.

"Maybe I always knew it," Arv told her, quite honestly.

"Oh yeah? Eh! Why you no say someteeng, eh?"

"I dunno," he said, and he didn't. Was it because he
didn't care to know? He wondered. Was it because he
wanted to grab hold of a slice of life first, grab hold of
Moke, regardless of the consequences? Or was it because,
consciously or subconsciously, he wanted to make good
his old challenge to Wasco, to throw his hat into the ring
at long last? He didn't know.

"To prove you not scared, or someteeng, eh?" Moke di-
vined, rather accurately, smiling a little all the time, like
maybe she was relieved that now it was all coming out in
the open.

"Maybe," Arv said.

"So? Now wa' you do?"

"I'm gonna win you still."

"No, you not."

"Yes, I am!"

"You not!"

"I am!" Arv repeated, trying to overwhelm her with
that frail possibility, loudly uttered, not sure if it was true,
not even sure of his motives in telling her. *Is it to win
her love? Or to win her trust so she'll 'fess up?*

"Eh! Maybeso you do," Moke said, "but you be sorry
eef."

"How come Wasco wanted me to bring letters into the
Joint?" he asked her point-blank. "He's no friend of Galliot's! How come?" he urged. "Blackmail? Was that it?"

"Don' know what you talk about."

"You know, alright. How come he wanted to blackmail
me? What could he possibly get out of me? I haven't got
anything."

"You got talent," she said, and reached out her hand
to touch his on the icy window ledge of the Merc.

"Talent? Shit! I ain't got no talent he could use!"

"Oh yes you have!" she insisted, still holding on to him, her dark slim hand covering his white one on the cold metal. And Arv, thinking of his one talent that Wasco might be able to use . . . the deadly one . . . asked her suddenly, "Does Wasco have the contract to kill Galliot?"

"Don't know," she said, removing her hand from his, shrugging her shoulders stubbornly.

"Was he going to blackmail me into . . ."

"Don't know."

"So, *I* was the hit man!" he said, almost jokingly, as if it were the wildest and most remote possibility. And Moke's response thrilled him, and chilled him, to his very deepest marrow.

"I say you got talent," she said.

Then, caught up in a giddy swirl of impossible revelations, he asked, following a wild hunch, "Who killed Fast-Walking?" and, watching her wince when he said it, added, "Did Wasco?"

"Wa' make you teenk dat, eh?" she parried, still employing her atavistic pidgin English, her Island talk, her old wily defense against the white man and his ways *Orientally obscure this way so she'll be able to tell herself someday that she didn't reveal anything, that I figured it out all by myself.* . . .

"Tell me one thing," he said.

"Eh?"

"Did you know he would . . . before?"

"Know wa', eh? I know noteeng!" she said, shaking her helmeted head and, in this instance, he chose to believe her. Contemplating that image which had now become imprinted, heated up and stamped, branded into his weary brain, that image of poor old daddy-long-legs, wobbly Fast-Walking, standing alone in the fog, in the middle of Slate Avenue in the city, in the middle of the night, thinking of that, and the look Arv saw on Fast-Walking's face in the rear view mirror as he got smaller and smaller, contemplating all of that, and considering too Moke's and Fast-Walking's magical rapport that night, and her surprising interest in and liking for old Fast-Walking, and her cheerful indulgence of his boring rap, and thinking of all the possible ramifications of meaning in Moke's possible duplicity on that joyful foggy night in the city, among New York poets and dewy Chinese bells lost in railroad yards, and at the Mexican restaurant in Spic

Town and *ai Chihuahua!* and all that, and even Arv's old
grandpa Alfonso Encina leading them on, away from poor
Fast-Walking . . . in view of all this Little Arv could permit himself no other choice in the matter. . . .

"I believe you," he said, with passionate conviction.

"Why?" she demanded, genuinely astonished, incredulous enough to drop the pidgin talk, as if she wouldn't
have believed such a far-fetched denial herself.

"Because," Arv said, very carefully, "if I didn't, I
couldn't love you. And I love you."

She started crying in her helmet. Her dark slanted eyes
clouded over and fogged the visor like the windows of the
Merc, and tears then appeared and tracked black mascara
down her cold brown cheeks.

"Baby, baby," he murmured, seeking her hand again,
on the handle-bar of her bike. The sight of her real or unreal tears brought tears to Arv's lighter whiter eyes too,
tears of sympathy for her plight. *It ain't a nice place to
be, between him and me, mortal enemies like this . . .*
"Baby," he said, "I know. He probably just told you to
get me out of the way for a couple of days. You didn't
know why. Or what he'd do. It wasn't your fault."

"No?" she asked.

"Shit no! Listen, here's what we're gonna do. We're
splitting!"

"Oh yeah?"

"That's right. Tomorrow. I'm gonna pull this one last
shift and hand in my resignation and draw my pay and
see my kid one last time and then tomorrow afternoon
we'll get everything together and just split for good. And,
say! Don't worry about anything happening to me in the
Joint today. They won't be able to call me a traitor or
blackmail me into doing anything I don't want to, or pull
any hanky-panky on me at all . . . Look!" he said, and
pulled out Elaine's letter to Galliot and tore it up before
Moke's eyes, "they won't have anything to hold against
me now, no evidence!"

"You sure about that?" she wanted to know, and something in her tone reminded him of another letter, a letter
to Elaine on the night they left for Baja, a letter she tried
her damndest to peek at, get away from him . . . but that
was long ago . . . all of that was behind them now. . . .

"Sure I'm sure," Arv said, "and then we'll be on our
way!"

"Where for?" she asked, with just the slightest trace of irony.

"Where for?" he echoed, and the strangeness of her turn of phrase hung there in the frigid air between them for a moment, like another question, and then . . .

"Anywhere!" Arv said, with real vehemence. "Who cares where? Any fucking place! Wherever you like. Mexico again, Hawaii, Europe, Asia. For as long as the money lasts. Then we'll just let the future take care of itself."

"I got a kid in Hawaii."

"Alright. You want to go there?"

"The kid is related to you."

"I don't care."

"Naw, I don't wanna go there, I don't think. But maybe . . ."

"Good! We'll go somewhere else. Okay?"

"I think I wanna go to Hawaii."

"Whatever you say, alright?"

"If you say so . . ."

"I say so! I'll meet you here after work. We'll celebrate, okay?"

"Whatever you like . . ."

"Right! Then *mañana* we'll be on our way."

"You think so?"

"I know so!"

"Alright," she said, smiling, her white sharp little teeth reflecting in the upturned plastic visor. "But let's go right now. Right this minute! Let's go!"

"Ah," he said, and saw her face fall at his hesitation, and almost decided to go with her, with no further ado, right then and there, "ah . . ." he said again, and thought of Wasco and Galliot in the Joint, and said, "ah, baby! I wish I could! But you know me. Can't leave any strings undone. We'll go tomorrow, okay?"

"Sure, maybe you're right," she said, kind of wistfully. And then, "Eh, *Haole!*" she yelled after him, as he rolled backwards across the frosty lawn, "you ever figure out what those Mexicans were celebrating down there on the twentieth of December?"

"No!" he shouted, snorting with laughter, "I never remembered to ask again!" and he waved to her breezily and whipped the Merc down the curving driveway through the gloomy park to the Molina Valley Road, thinking: *Yep! She was right. We should've just stayed right in Mexico. Definitely never should've come back. . . .*

Over at Bert's Beanery Arv had to wipe the nervous smile off his face, considering the solemnity of the occasion.

"Say Mom, I just thought you might need a ride to the funeral," he said, very respectful of the dead . . . as if Fast-Walking would've given a good goddamn.

There wasn't a customer in the place. On this chill winter's day. Outside, in back, across the sun terrace, the tall redwood trees above the hippy cabins, festooned with silver icicles, framed in the rear bay window, looked as good as a Hallmark Xmas card.

Bert and May, who'd been getting chummier and chummier of late, drinking mates, had been sipping away head to head at their boilermakers at the rustic knotty pine bar when Arv slipped in and surprised them. They'd jumped at seeing him, and Arv thought: *one time Dad came in and caught them kissing, tore the place up, told Bert's ex-wife, dragged Mom home and beat her up, called her a fucking whore, had a minor heart seizure. Next morning they'd made up again. We heard their mattress squeaking all night . . . in spite of Dad's coronary ailment . . . hard to keep a Weed down, ain't it?*

"Oh, thank you, honey," May said, "I would like a ride. Ain't it a shame. And a young wife like that. So pretty. Left with all them kids. Had a little insurance though, I hear . . ."

"Yeah. It's a dirty shame," Bert said, answering for Arv in his haste to be friendly, "but a little insurance sure comes in handy!"

"Well Bert," May said, "if you don't mind . . ."

"Oh no, May! Not at all," he said, too loud, "in this weather even Christmas Eve can't get 'em out!"

"Well, you know, our Christmas Eves here are always kind of slow, Bert," May said, bagging a six-pack of beer, "folks around here spend it mostly with their families."

Arv found their rather sheepish small talk utterly unconvincing.

"Say," Bert said, as they were going out the door, "you ain't seen Moke around anywheres, have you? She ain't showed up for work in days! Had to hire another girl."

"Nope," said Arv, "haven't run into her. . . ."

"Okay, well, anyway, a Merry Christmas to you all!"

"Yeah, Bert," May said. "A Merry Christmas to you too . . . see you Tuesday!"

Arv didn't say anything.

Driving down the slick freeway toward the Joint, May made only one concession to the solemnity that Arv had been striving for, on this bleak funereal day. She didn't just pull out her six-pack of twelve-ounce cans of New Sonora Lager and start guzzling, as usual. This time she asked *permission!* Arv laughed, tight-lipped, in "honor" of the deceased, and said, "Go ahead, Mom, it'll probably help. And old Fast-Walking, he sure as hell would've approved!"

"You think so, Arv?" she said, and then old Mom, May, Lula May Mayhew, May Maiden, sitting there on the front seat with Arv in her white pressed uniform and her wedgie shoes and her hair net, chewing her spearmint gum, May she just laughed and said, "Say, Arv, you're prob'ly right there!" and popped one, two, three, four twelve-ounce cans and chug-a-lugged them down and threw them out on the cold blacktop roadway, never letting her Adam's apple stop rolling and rumbling, never giving her belly even a chance to stop its belching, its resounding liquid echo, never stopping for a breath, or to watch the aluminum beer cans bouncing on the asphalt, banging into the chain-link freeway fences, landing in the clean cement gutters. All the way home . . . riding down the C of C off-ramp, going down along Paradise Cove, past the firing range, through the back gate, and up to Prison Residence #64, May maintained to perfection her normal clucking motherly monologue . . .

"Well, honey. Where you been, anyway? It sure is a terrible thing. So young, and all. They say Warden's all broke up. Like I say. Them Colored. You taking care of yourself over there in the city? Oh this here weather! Ever seen anything like it? You know what, honey? I been thinking. You oughta go back with Deanna. The nicest girl. That Moke! Now, you watch out inside them walls. Them agitators. I pray for you every night, dear . . ."

By the time they reached home it was apparent that Mrs. Weed, May, May's Major Maiden, that sweet woman, that good little lady with the heart of gold, whom Arv loved with all his feeble Weed heart and yet had resolved to never see again, that fine woman, May, May's

Most, was no longer in any shape to attend a funeral.

He'd planned it that way *what the fuck good are funerals when you're dead?*

Inside Arv's childhood house, Prison Residence #64, no one was home. He put May to bed in his parents' room and went out through the living room past the ten-year-old fireproof silver Xmas tree and into the kitchen. Libby's homework, even on this day of feast, was lying all over the table:

1. Tense and Mood=T
2. Faulty Reference=REF
3. Incomplete Comparisons=COMP
4. Paragraph Coherence=PAR COH

Poor Libby. She'll try and she'll try. But she'll never make it into college.

Aw, come on! Won't she ever make it?

Nope she'll never make it.

Arv, whose mouth had become as dry as the desert of Baja, drew a long draught of ice water from the tap, glancing out past Big Arv's giant hanging chile bean pot through the back screen porch at the empty rabbit hutches and empty chicken coops and the empty donkey pen in the back yard, and the wintry hills beyond, glanced too around the eggshell-painted kitchen, the kitchen he'd grown up in, eaten peanut butter and jelly and white bread in . . . looked too at the refrigerator door with the invisible sign on it, and the picture of that eighteen-year-old laughing May Maiden who mocked him now, mocked the sodden beer-drunk lady breathing now heavily in her bedroom dreaming perhaps of a young run across a muddy field toward a loaded troop train . . . mocked them all with those eternally ineradicable words:

DON'T TOUCH KIDS
AND YOU TOO DADDY
LESS MOM SAYS OK

Arv went back through the small tattered living room past the TV set and down the hall to his old room. Nothing of his own was left. All his stuff was in the city. But his smell remained. The smell of his surreptitious teenage come, perhaps, the smell of his piss when he pissed the bed as a baby. That's all. Except the item he pulled off the pegs on the wall now: the shiny well-kept M-16 Assault Rifle he'd stolen from Air Cav Headquarters Supply in Vietnam, expertly disassembled, cached in his overseas bag, and flown with across the Pacific Ocean to the U.S.A. It was the sole item of his belongings that he kept here at home, near the Joint's firing range, where he practiced with it sometimes on days off.

When Arv went back outside an inmate, the Wop gardener who mowed and trimmed their lawn in summer, raked leaves in fall, and unplugged drains and swept the road in winter, was loitering near the Merc, looking in through the rear window. As soon as he saw Arv come out with the big-ass M-16 cradled in his arms he skeedaddled fast *what the hell's he up to?* The Wop hadn't taken anything, though. Arv checked. The only thing he'd left in the unlocked car was his war surplus overcoat and a suitcase full of Fast-Walking's clothes. And that was still lying on the back seat.

On the way down to the Warden's Mansion Arv left Fast-Walking's things off at Marie-Claude's place with a note:

> Frank left these at my place.
> I thought you might want them.
> Also some money I'll leave off
> after work. Chin up, Marie-Claude!
> *Arv Weed*

No one was home, of course, they'd all be down at the chapel on the Sound by now. Arv had no intention of going to that funeral. No matter what anyone said. Fast-Walking would've been the first to understand. He didn't go in for that shit either. Just like he always said, stupidly profound, profoundly stupid:

"When you're dead, you're dead."

Nope! Instead of going to that ridiculous and irrelevant funeral, Arv turned in at the Warden's Mansion driveway.

Ignazio came to the door. "Yes?"

"I'd like to see Wendy, if she's here."

"Aren't you going . . . ?"

"No, I'm not," Arv said, pushing past him into the Mansion.

"I see. Come in," the Filipino said, faced with a *fait accompli,* and led the way across the king-size living room toward the basement. Arv remembered that basement well. . . .

Arv and Deanna, as children, as teenagers, used to wrestle down in that pink-painted basement rumpus room, in the fogs of July and August, the rains of December, vacation times, this time of the year. . . . They used to rub groins for hours, as kids of fifteen and sixteen, seventeen and eighteen, while Wasco her ex-old man was locked up in Prill Reformatory. Every few minutes they'd get up off the couch to do a few quick bars on the piano to keep her mama happy, make her think they were working on their singing technique . . . *"Wonderful, wonderful Copenhagen, salty old dog of the sea . . ."* they would sing, the only number she knew, while she beat out the melody fast and awkward on the baby grand, but with *brio,* while he stroked her pillowed butts, mons veneris, pink-tipped chubs, pearly nubs. And then they'd beat it quick back to the pink modern sofa to diddle some more. Once her big brother Fast-Walking came around to the low-lying basement window, bent the shrubs aside, peeked down. . . . They were playing "Foots," a private game, as it happened. He raced around the yard and up the stairs and told Patsy, Deanna's mom. He was a grown man by then, married, working in the Joint. Arv never could quite forgive the skinny lout for that tattle-telling. Even though, later, Fast-Walking made a big joke out of it. Claimed it was all in fun. Still, Arv figured, what would he want to do that kind of thing for? But now, going down the stairs with Ignazio, the Flip houseboy who'd been around so long he might well have been an unseen witness to those events, Arv forgave his old friend, ironically, as a king forgives a long-ago enemy freshly dead in battle against another king far away. . . .

Ignazio showed Arv into the familiar basement room, turned up the lights, and silently and discreetly exited up the stairs. Arv's three-year-old daughter Wendy lay sleeping entwined in her baby blanket on the pink sofa where he and her mommy, as kids, used to play. Wendy was beautiful. She looked nothing like Arv, nothing like any Weed at all. She was pure prison aristocrat, pure Miniver. And for that, and her slim long limbs, Arv thanked his sweet BeJesus! The only thing he regretted was that she wouldn't be a dancer. The Minivers just didn't have that in them. But, what the hell! She was gorgeous. A princess, a real princess of the Slam, a rose among the stinkweed.

After a few minutes of admiring his lovely little blond daughter's fine hair, her red little pouty lips, her sweet pink cheeks, her long heavy brown lashes, the indescribably soft trailing edges of her earlobes (a special delight of his), her tiny feet and toes sticking out of her baby blanket, her little crinkled-up sucking thumb lying near her mouth . . . and smelling the fragrance of her sleeping baby breath, Arv's mind began to wander. He felt he had to stay there till she awakened. This would be the last time in how long? that he would see her . . . but he just couldn't keep interested in her reclining body all that time. The truth is that Arv didn't relate to kids all that well, and was happy usually to be away from them. It was the same, regretfully, with his own daughter. He rarely came to see her. He was firmly committed to leaving her and her mother forever, without saying good-bye, stealing off in the night never to return, never to be heard of again in these parts, except through word of mouth, perhaps, or through fame . . . worldwide fame. . . . He would steal off, Arv would, and not because he didn't love them, under it all, but because they could get by without him. And he couldn't get by *with* them. It was that simple. For him, staying on at the Joint was death, pure and simple. For them, they'd get by, they'd live. The Warden would see to their financial needs. And Deanna could take care of herself, and the kid. Anyway, Arv was splitting, wailing, swooping out. That was all there was to it.

Arv sat down on the other end of the long pink sofa. Wendy stirred in her sleep, crossing and recrossing her little dimpled knees, and then drifted off again. Arv was left again with some time to collect his thoughts. He figured he needed it. He thought now of the incriminating letter he'd torn up in front of Moke. He'd taken the precaution of opening and memorizing it before he left the apartment. Now, if he got a chance, he could deliver it verbatim to the blackman Galliot in the Joint, a blackman whom Arv felt more and more sympathy with each minute. The more alienated he felt from his own people, the closer he identified with the rebel. The more clearly the lines of battle were drawn up between him and his old-

est enemy Wasco, the more close he felt to the army of
the opposition:

24 Dec. 1972

Dear William:
Your message of 20 December has been received and
understood and your instructions will be carried out
exactly as directed. Count on us! This is a duplicate
message to the one you hopefully received on 23 December. If you didn't, then we're lucky to have taken
this double precaution. I count on seeing you soon,
and remain,

Yours in Revolution,
E.

Going over that message now in his mind he wondered
whether Moke, concerned about his safety, would have reminded him to tear it up, that dangerous letter, if he
hadn't remembered to do it himself. . . . It would have
been damning evidence! With five years in the Joint hanging over Arv's head, Wasco probably could have black-
mailed him into doing anything he wanted! Would Moke
have reminded Arv? He wasn't sure. She hadn't been very
cooperative when he interrogated her on the lawn of her
old house. But, seemingly without meaning to, maintaining to perfection her Asian inscrutability, she'd revealed
nevertheless all the information that Arv needed to fit the
pieces, or enough of the pieces, of Wasco's scheme together. Arv sensed she was still holding a great deal back,
though. Why could that be? Did she see herself as being
in the middle somewhere? The she-wolf sitting back on
the grass, neutral, awaiting the outcome of the battle for
her favors? Or did she see herself as some kind of referee,
in this fierce game between Arv and Wasco? Was she
trying to keep it fair and even between them, and then see
who won? Arv thought that a very real possibility. But it
didn't bother him. Not at all. He'd firmly decided to commit himself to a fight with his cousin. It seemed to him
now that he wouldn't be able to get away, to go on, grow,
without some kind of facing up, some kind of resolution
. . . to . . . what? . . . to Wasco and him . . . to everything, his past . . . the Joint . . . and all that. . . . That's
why the ambiguity, the supposed "neutrality" of Moke's

position didn't worry Arv: he figured he wouldn't have it any other way than even-steven with old Wasco. . . .

Well, anyway, enough of that for now, Arv thought, and turned his attention on the past. To him and Deanna. He figured he might as well finish that off too, since he was "resolving" things today, his last day at the Joint. He regarded the sofa he sat on now while Wendy slept beside him. Old Deanna and him had sure made hay on this pink sofa, this ugly stuffed modern monster. She never would let him go all the way though. Not for the longest time. He tried for all his high school years, working at her for hours, with endless patience, on this monster, with the nervous patience that only horny adolescents can summon, reserves of pimply oily-skinned stamina. He sweated streams and rivulets on her pretty white blouses, summer frocks, dirtying them with the grime of his unclean teenage pores, his filthy Levis, sopping sweatshirts.

The fact is he hated her. He'd always hated her. And she disgusted him. Once he'd dropped his rocks, dry-fucked his load off into his sweaty dribbly boxer shorts, once the gnawing pressure'd been released, he'd leap out of her embrace and make excuses, saying, "Gee, I just remembered, I got to run." And she'd always say, "Oh, you only come over and see me for one *thing!*"

It eventually happened, what Arv'd been seeking. But it happened suddenly and without warning, frightening them both. Arv had come home on his first leave from the army. Sitting in the Miniver living room at the Joint, watching color TV with her family after Thanksgiving dinner, 1968, with Lobo and Patsy and Deanna and Marie-Claude and her kids (Fast-Walking was out rambling, as usual). Arv sat in the semidark playing with Deanna's shapely muscled legs, tickling her, making her laugh, and raised a big hard-on for her. It was at least as much a result of his three-month enforced celibacy at Ford Ord as of Deanna's indisputable and bountiful physical charms.

"Hey Deanna! How's about zipping down to Corky's Drive-in for a Coke?" he had asked far too loudly, unconvincingly, turning everyone's head around just at the moment Marshall Dillon bit through the ropes of his Indian bonds. Everyone in front of the TV (led by Patsy's crazy lewd example) had laughed like hell.

Arv drove her straight up to that same old deserted log-ging road, the one where he'd worked as a kid on the For-estry project, the one he'd sprung suddenly on tens of girls all through his high school career, the one, the very same one where years later he would seal his des-tiny in the arms of mellow slopehead Moke. He parked under the same redwood tree, in the mud and sawdust, under the same late year rain, heavy drops of it dripping off the branches and banging on the roof of that other earlier Merc like ax blows.

"Well," he said, nervous now, with this large scrump-tious creature, the real natural sexual woman sitting next to him, a woman he'd always known, and never known, and him fresh from three months of zero sex, three months of furtive piddly-ass pud-pounding in secret cor-ners of the platoon latrine. And now not knowing whether she would, or wouldn't, or couldn't because of the "curse," and if she could and would, how long would it take, and exactly what would it take, in the way of words or special play in undiscovered erogenous zones?

"Well," she echoed, and laughed, scooting over to his side of the car like a good patriotic American girl, making it easier for him, poor slob, poor GI, bound for the land of Vietnam. . . .

He kissed her thin hard lips, touched her fine blond hair, her noble Miniver eyelids and nose and sprang an-other erection. He touched her tits and she didn't stop him. He stuck his hand inside her blouse and cupped them, her large hard melons, and she didn't stop him. He unbuttoned and removed her blouse and she didn't stop him, nor even slow him down, as he might have even wished. *Where am I going so fast?* he had thought, and *Do I really want to go so fast?* He took her bra off and sucked them, nibbled, love nips, Hard Shell, breast plated, sweet, with a slightly bitter aftertaste: the taste of war. And she didn't stop him. Only giggled and said, "Stop slurping so loud, making those sounds like a baby suck-ing; it turns me off!"

Arv resolved then and there that he would never flag or falter, unless she made him. At least part of him wanted her to make him.

A mere sixty seconds had elapsed since the motor died. Panic-stricken, kissing and sucking her tits very carefully not like a "baby," touching off fearful chemical effects, listening to their results in the pattering rising desire of her young heart, kissing her eyes and hair and ears, Arv pursued his deadly and unwanted little game, impelled by a hundred generations of mindless instinct-ridden Weeds behind him: he ran his hand up her thigh. She didn't stop him.

Didn't she stop him? Didn't she even try?

No, she didn't stop him.

Arv got his trembling hands and fingers inside her pantyhose. He was clumsy and brutal, a rapacious soldier. He touched excited excretions through nylon, sprouting his most powerful erection since the obsessions of earliest puberty. And her smell now struck him a blow hard on the nostrils, a scent he'd never forget, that drove him into madness, folly, to wolfpack dreams of hometown car-park violence and murderous destruction: she fought him. *Why didn't she stop me?* He ripped her hose, her panties. She bit three buttons off his poplin army shirt. *When in doubt* they say *whip it out* whipped it out (all the time with eyes closed, both of them, kissing rapturously as if nothing else were going on), pushed her down on the seat, head banging on the steering wheel, skirt hiked up over her boyish hips *like Okie chicks on the levee.*

"Stop it Arv! Please stop it!" she cried, breaking from his embrace.

But Private Weed, brokenhearted, exhilarated, persisted still, because he had to, though he didn't know why he had to. Even though he should have gotten out his Sheik rubber, and the Nupercainal ointment he always spread on the red head of his duddle so he'd last longer, considering his youthful tendency to ejaculate prematurely . . .

"Stop! Oh stop! Stop!"

And then the hated words, the death wish, the mother love, mamalove, mamaluke, motherfuck, and the desire of murdering flesh, the daddyof all spermatozoa . . .

"But take care, please Arv! . . . you understand? You pull it out before . . . before . . . promise?"

"Yes, yes, yes, I promise, yes!"

But Little Arv had already spoken. Already barked and howled and yodeled and honked, already pissed and shit and puked and cried . . . Arv had already spit into her earthy furrow, like a sowing farmhand with a dry phlegmy throat . . . Wendy!

His cookies popped, Arv went on, snuffed, dissimulating, but persistent till he went limp and flappy. . . .

Then, still dissimulating, as Deanna herself was probably doing, feigning the last crazy edge of sexual frenzy, Arv whipped his joint out of her cunt and with bated and guilty breath beat it against her matted pubic hair, undulated on her sweating mound, outside her still probably barely aroused hole, far above her probably untouched clitoris, imitating the convulsions and cries of spermatic release . . .

"Oh! Oh! Oh!"

With which she gamely chimed in:

"Oh yes! Yes! Oooooh yes!"

And all the way back down along the Coast Highway to Ford Ord that night, with only the placid Pacific Ocean as witness, snoring its naïve moonsleep, the sleep of the merciless and the cold, and the new moon coming in low across the water like a torpedo, a submarine conning tower, cutting the silver waves, Arv exulted over his battle won. Abolishing his fear, his mortal trepidation, he reran his grand coup, his felling of the giant, the Amazonian, conquering the unconquerable: Eagle-Woman, Swift-Foot, Moon-Maid, Valkyrie, Invert, knocked over and brought to bed by the hand of the mighty psycho-midget, the poison Weed, the sting of the flea, the nip of the shrimp, the body louse, little old Private Little Arvin Weed, Air Cav, gung-ho, and bound for the land of Vieeetnaaaaaaaaaam, goddamn!

Down there in the basement, in the rumpus room now of the Warden's spacious Mansion, Little Arv wiped the tears from his narrow Indian-Weed eyes, tears of frank self-indulgence . . . *poor Deanna,* he thought, *poor Libby and me, poor Marie-Claude and kids, poor little Wendy and her poor poor dead old Uncle Fast-Walking Miniver* . . . Arv wiped his doleful eyes and looked over at his sleeping little daughter again . . . in all her innocence . . . *she too is a child of the Joint, conceived under the signs of Merc and Moon, the most starcrossed combination of all* . . . and then dismissed the whole idea as the sheerest and most self-pitying sentimentality.

She was watching him the whole time, Wendy was, wide-eyed, unmoving, her baby's mouth hanging open in wonderment, almost as if she could read his mind.

"How're you, Missy?"

Nothing.

"You ain't talking to Daddy today?"

Nothing.

"Daddy's come all the way over here to say hello and you ain't talking, huh?"

Still nothing.

"Well, look, I tell you what, I got to go over to Nueva Ronda now, and then I got to go to work in the Joint, so if you won't talk to Daddy he's just gonna have to leave you all by your little self."

Nothing. Just those wide rapidly blinking Miniver-blue eyes looking at him. Eyes that were not at all like those mirrored in hers. Eyes like her old dead Uncle Fast-Walking's eyes, which would go with him into the cold ground, on this cold day, never to be resurrected.

Arv crawled over toward her like a little kid himself, crawling half on and half off the pink sofa. Wendy did not make room for him. He lay down beside her anyhow, with his chest under her baby blanket and his heavy short legs pulled up so his knees almost touched his chin. She smelled delicious, little Wendy did. Delicious too the smell of baby girl on and under the pink flannel baby blanket.

But she wouldn't talk.

Arv lay there for quite a while, crying, while his daughter stared at his teary excesses in open-mouthed disbelief. He kissed her on her dry white little forehead just before he left. But still she made no response.

"You know, don't you?" he asked finally, abandoning the baby talk entirely, talking to her exactly as if she were an intelligent fully matured girl, talking to her like Moke sometimes did to him when she switched from pidgin to English . . .

"Well, I wish you'd tell *me!*" he said, and then got up to go.

"I don't *like* you!" she cried, as he went up the stairs, "I don't *like* you!"

Forty-Four

Dear Harriet:

If I see you this afternoon as planned this message will be irrelevant. But if, as I now suspect, the plans did not reach you, then I suppose this letter will have to serve as a kind of final soliloquy, a comment on my own tragic fate.

One of the brothers is being released on parole tomorrow and, since my destiny will have been permanently decided by tomorrow, one way or the other, I can afford the risk of conveying to you these words . . . that is, if our courier's bowels cooperate and he's successful in excreting out the swallowed plastic capsule which will be, not inappropriately somehow, my last testament.

It is the gray stormy morning of Christmas Eve, the ice-cold morning of the day of my greatest trial, my greatest and, quite likely, last adventure. Now, on the very brink of destruction, I feel my lifeblood coursing through my veins like never before. Adrenalin pumps through my system, readying my mind and muscles and nerves for the coming "impossible" struggle with the Pig, the force of evil, and his howling squealing minions. I feel total, complete man, every part of this human machine is perfectly tuned, perfectly tested and oiled and ready for this fateful encounter with the Porker, the wild boar, this last and fatal ride upon the hog's back, the tusker, thrusting at his neck and eyes, thrusting and thrusting, attempting to destroy him before he gets me, and all my black kind. Never have I felt more truly alive and willing.

The setting here in the East Block at the moment is not exactly of the proper tragic solemnity, however. Instead of the gloomy beat of the tambour, the keening sound of the fife, my ears are offended by the rattle of tin cups and spoons, the eating utensils convicts tie to their belts and take to the chow hall. In place of the tragic chorus, I hear the rude calls of a prison braggart:

"So, pink toes, she colly the jive, dig it? She suck Soul fo' once, gatemouth it! Oohie!"

"Go 'head, Brother, go 'head wit' yo bad self!"

. . . and the sound of a hundred other unpleasant noises: radios blaring, Mexican music, Soul music, Country and Western music, the sound of electric shavers, steel cell doors slamming, the sound of lewd singing, farts and belches, the clink of feet on the metal walkway, the "pling" of a guard's metal tester as he walks down the tier checking metal cell bars, the sound of the Chicano dude two tiers down who brushes his thick wiry moustache with a toothbrush, the sound of loud speculation concerning my highly uncertain fate:

"Galliot into that shit, ain't he?"

"He do an escape number I'm gon' fall out. I gon' be right behine that motherfucker."

Lies, lies, lies, the Joint stinks of self-deception. With me probably the worst of the bunch. Maybe, after all, it's necessary in order to survive. I sit here trying to convince myself that I've got a good chance of making it today. . . . Though I haven't even got a fighting chance.

My man, my courier, the Honkey in whom I foolishly placed all my trust, has not appeared in the Joint in four days. When last I saw him I gave him a letter of the most vital importance to the success of my self-liberation. I assume it never reached its destination, and never reached you. I deduce, moreover, that he turned it over to the authorities who have now the perfectly legal excuse to lie in wait for me and murder me as I walk out of the Joint.

Nevertheless, I have made my peace with myself. I even let go the broken-winged sparrow I'd kept in my cell. It flew up and out of the cell, beautifully! Its wing had mended perfectly. All the brothers cheered as it made one final full circle of the block, found an open window, and fled into the cold daylight, daring its fate, daring its freedom. I must confess to you I envied that little bird, and sought to anthropomorphize its experience, to see something portentous for myself in its flight from prison. But I didn't succeed. Not at first, at least. In the last few moments, however—since I began writing you this letter, in fact—my spirits have soared like a bird. How could I ever explain it to you? Suffice it to say that, even at the risk of death, the notion of a run for the walls, the notion of sweet escape, even temporary, leaves the prisoner breathless with excitement, and hope.

Regardless of the almost nil chances of my successful self-liberation, I've decided to attempt it. I won't have another chance. By the time I got together another plan they'd have murdered me. I can be offed at any moment. Even now. I could be offed right here in my cell, like Roundo and Yuba, two old black queens a couple of tiers down . . . with gasoline and a match, or a zip gun, a thrown knife, anything!

Certainly, if I remain here in the Joint, I will be iced within the next two or three days. The Pig didn't start this phony "race war" for nothing. It is an attempt to create the proper conditions for my efficient removal from the land of the living. I even know who the murderer is. But he is nothing more than a pawn in the State authorities' game, whatever he may think of himself. If he were lost or removed or got offed himself, they'd simply find another one.

Therefore, my decision is not at all difficult: escape or be killed. You'd be surprised how fast you can become totally committed to an action if your life is at stake. . . . What is difficult for me now is facing the almost total certitude of death . . . death not at some vague and unspecified time in the remote future when I'm old and tired and gray, but death now! This very afternoon!

The strange fact is that I can't! As I write these words to you I realize that I simply cannot accept the notion of death this afternoon. I can't believe I'm going to die any more than these convicts can believe they'll spend the rest of their lives behind bars. I won't believe in my death! I'm going to make it, I tell myself fiercely, in spite of their certain ambush. This nigger's gonna beat the Pig, even if it requires levitating over his bloody walls!

And if I do make it . . . am I joking? I don't know. If I do make it . . . it will only be justice, won't it? Surely that's so. If there is any such thing as cosmic justice operating in the universe then I *will* make it. After all, what was my crime? My crime was nothing more than that of Tantalus who, "having been privileged to eat Ambrosia with the Olympians, later invited the commoners to try it."

I ate of the Pig's goodies. Then when I proffered those precious goodies to my black brothers, what happened? The Pig slapped me down, condemned me to a lifetime in Hades.

Perhaps that is the reason I feel so exhilarated now about my desperate adventure this afternoon: I have the wonderful feeling that right is on my side! At the risk of tremendous oversimplification, in this complex world of human affairs, human destiny, I dare shout out, "I am good! They are bad!" I see it as a conflict between good and evil. The Pig is the handman of Evil. I represent goodness. When I think of it this way, that I've got all the weight of good behind me, then I'm overwhelmed with a desire to get on with the job, to join in mortal combat with the snorting squealing dangerous Pig, like an old-time preacher wrestling with the Devil.

A big-city newspaper columnist once called me "anti-white, anti-motherhood, anti-capitalism, anti-Vietnam War, anti-private property, anti-every-thing!" But he was wrong. You see, it's him and all the other piglets like him who are "anti." They are the ones who are negative, anti-life. They are the killers of black men in the ghettos of America and yellow men in the rice paddies of Asia. They are the "anti's." I feel myself to be, in my very deepest consciousness, profoundly positive about the human race, and its future on this planet, and beyond. I believe that right will prevail. That power will re-turn to the People. I believe it. I'm the one who's pro-man. Profoundly so. And that's what's going to make my sacrifice or success, or whatever, this afternoon, mean something. If I get iced, my death will mean something. It's that simple. Why try to fancy it up with big words? To have lived forty-three good and bad years, to have learned a few things, to have loved, to have learned to love your own despised race, to have learned thereby to love yourself, and then your black woman, and then to have your death mean something, what more can a man ask of life? Few are offered more in this existence. Certainly I ask for no more.

Good-bye, dearest Harriet, my only love. And if I should die, give yourself to another black man soon, love him in my place, have black babies, children that will one day ride like dark sailors to the stars, conquer the universe, discover the black and beautiful God that has lived within us all the time, unrecognized.

ALL POWER TO THE PEOPLE!
William Galliot, Revolutionary

Forty-Five

Deanna rode toward the chapel on her father's arm. The Warden, apparently disconsolate at the loss of his beloved and only begotten son, had in his adversity become like a cruel and willful boy, like the Old Testament's random boy, Yahweh, smiting out at anything near. Deanna leaned on his arm almost as if she were thus preventing him from smiting her.

In her gray woolen dress and her belted black flannel trench coat and her high-heeled black boots, Deanna marched ceremoniously with her handsome grieving father across the chill slippery lawn, watching the yellow-gray snow clouds move slowly in through the Alvarez Straits, across the Sound, over the Santa Caterina Peninsula past Holly Island and Paradise Cove to the prison chapel, where they appeared to hover menacingly just over the steeple, threatening to drop a whole ice-locked Alaska upon the already boreal Jam.

Tramp tramp tramp Deanna marched along with her dad, Daddy, whom she did not know. Knew even less than her toothpick brother, who was now no more, whom she never knew either, whom the Warden himself had never known, though he now pretended he had, and appeared to be enjoying immensely his own orgy of lawful grief. . . .

An organ played in the chapel. She did not know the homely old song. Something horrid and funereal, she thought. Above the wooden chapel gleamed the glassed-in steeple like a lighthouse in the storm. "The Lighthouse of God," a neat little sign on the lawn proclaimed it. And indeed the steeple had actually once been a lighthouse, and capped perfectly this nautical little chapel with its circular porthole-like windows that overlooked the rough Sound. The chapel proper had been constructed from the wood of the broken-up nineteenth-century prison ship that had formerly been the Joint. The steeple had originally been a government lighthouse warning off ships from the rocks at Paradise Point. Now, in the twentieth century, the two were joined together in holy matrimony, and dwelt here on this frozen promontory above the water while wind-driven waves worked away on the cliff below, undermining it all . . . Deanna laughed bitterly to herself at the little alliterative allegory she had devised, the meaning of which she hadn't the slightest notion. . . .

Everybody was inside the prison ship, the chapel, waiting for them now. Waiting for their solemn entry, solemn soulful tread down the bare concrete floor like a bride and father, or groom, down the aisle to the altar . . .

Deanna and the Warden entered, arm and arm, everyone stood and watched them, respectul of their natural grief, while they marched slow-step down to the front pew. There they all were: the angry nigger-hating swing shift and graveyard shift officers in full uniforms, hats off . . . Sanger and Betty, Arv's punchy uncle and fat aunt . . . Lieutenant Marty Boudin, red-faced and gouty . . . Associate Wardens Acuff and Rademaker in black overcoats and black ties . . . Tessy, Alexandra and Meg, three ancient cronies, prison guards' widows who wouldn't die, obscene, mean-mouthed old things who were lone and scurrilous backyard gossip mongers even when Deanna and Wasco and Arv and Fast-Walking had been tiny kids and used to call them the "Sweetheart Sisters." They stood now in their center pew, happily dressed in black, their favorite color. Big Arv, Fast-Walking's enemy in death as in life, was conspicuously absent from the assemblage of the swing shift. There were murmurs among the guards that "Now this here is goin' a little too far, don't ya think?" Little Arv, Deanna saw, the dirty little coward, he was absent too, at this funeral of his only real friend. Too scared to look him in the face and say good-bye. *The dead don't bite, you little twirp!* . . . May was not present either. Everyone knew where she would be: beer-drunk, liquid mourning, distraught over the untimely death of her boy's only friend. . . . And Patsy too, she was absent too, generously left in the dark about her son's tragic murder, and would now be glued to the afternoon TV in her room, catered to by gin-bearing Ignazio laughing like a child when Bert Parks, or his successor, cracked a particularly risqué joke for the ladies in his studio and listening audiences.

Deanna and the Warden sat down in the front pew next to the red-eyed, guilt-ridden foreign woman who had been Fast-Walking's wife. Marie-Claude's two puzzled little kids sat there fidgeting and wondering where their beloved young Daddy'd gone *surely that thing up in the box, that can't be Daddy!*

The chapel organist, a black prisoner who'd played here at services for the past six years, handled the Hammond very well, but he played a little too upbeat for these sober-jawed, proudly dull, middle-American WASPS and their sympathizers gathered here today. Something about his playing was too vital, too lively and good, smacked of a New Orleans street marching funeral. Fortunately there was only the faintest hint of this in his playing. And the huge storm waves crashing against the piled rocks below the cliff drowned out most of the music anyway.

The chapel was decorated with sprigs of pine and mistletoe, green and red wreaths of holly and a Christmas tree. Only the streamers and colored lights remained unstrung and unhung for tonight's annual Christmas Party for the employees' kids—those yearly Xmas events that Deanna remembered so well: the inmate-made white cake that tasted of sweat and spit. The human finger they found in it one year, chopped off by one of the antique kitchen machines and left there on purpose as a protest of prison conditions. The fat jolly old convict Santa Claus. The gifts made in the Joint machine shop and upholstering factory and print shop and jute mill. The blood-red Hawaiian Punch that someone spiked with LSD one year. The children's choir that she and Arv and Fast-Walking used to sing in, singing Christmas carols to the assembled trusties and guards and families. The song that rebel Wasco sang one incredible year, wonderful hateful Wasco who had more gusto and life and spirit and rebellion in him than all the other prison-bred prison-bound kids put together . . . "Can I sing a song about the Virgin and Child, Warden?"

And Daddy, very surprised, said, "Sure Wasco! What an honor!" And then he sang it. Did he really sing it? In front of all those people? And only eleven years old? Yep, by God, old Wasco, he certainly did sing it! In limerick he sang:

There once was an angel "Canary"
Who fucked sucked and stroked Virgin Mary
And Christ was so bored
At seeing Mom whored
That he set himself up as a fairy . . .

Forty-Six

Lobo sat between his daughter and daughter-in-law before the chaplain, who was now wringing his pink hands in his unctuous clerical manner, salivating in anticipation of the coming event. Lobo had always found him odious, this small fastidious Southern Baptist with his blue bald pate. And yet Lobo was not habitually a man of strong or extreme likes and dislikes. He could think of only one other person in the Joint community, as a matter of fact, for whom he'd felt this gut-level antipathy: Wasco Weed . . . especially when he'd been just a kid, hanging around the housing area . . . and then the time he ran off with Deanna . . . and sullied her for good. But that was long ago. And Lobo'd mellowed since then. And anyway, he'd never been the kind of man to hold a grudge. It didn't do you any good. And one didn't survive the ups and downs of life, the political and ideological and military and financial upheavals that Lobo'd gone through, by nursing grudges or strong emotions of any kind, or by resisting the powers that be.

Lobo therefore prepared himself to enjoy the coming sermon, which would be, he was sure, the very finest in Chaplain Edwards' long career in state service, a ringing panegyric to the Warden's only begotten son, dead on the field of battle, "foully slain" by certain vague and undefined "forces of darkness" which Lobo and everyone else in church would hear as just plain "niggers." And that would be quite alright, Lobo thought now, in his secret heart, and even embellished it in his own mind, enjoying the new role he'd worked out for himself . . . *my son, killed at the behest of a nigger radical. . . .*

Then Chaplain Edwards began it, his greatest hour, intoning it, his voice rising to a mummer's incandescent wail: "Ummmmmmm, ummmmmmmm, ummmmmmmm . . . Officer Frank Miniver, fondly known far and wide as

'Fast-Walking,' beloved son of . . ."

Son of whom? Lobo wondered, now that his boy was gone. *And what does that mean, that word "son"? It doesn't mean anything. We are all just people here, who are alive. And life goes on. And that's all.*

As Chaplain Edwards went on, raising his voice higher and higher above the guards and their families gathered together in "The Lighthouse of God," Lobo allowed himself a second or two of self-pity. He figured he had it coming to him: *My God,* he thought, *what have I done to deserve this dog's life? My wife an endless trial, my son now dead. . . .* But he knew in his heart it was merely sham, mummery too, just like the Chaplain's. Like most people with his particular survival instincts, Lobo was really a cynic at bottom. He preferred to call it "being philosophical about life," but it all came to the same thing. Even Fast-Walking's death he had taken philosophically. It was sad, untimely, unfortunate, but Lobo was far from disconsolate about it, at least on a personal level. The grief that he displayed now was like the mourning he wore, a show for the world. The world assumed he'd be grief-stricken today, so Lobo gave them what they seemed to want. Privately he accepted his son's death in the same way he'd accepted the new state government's harsh new penal directives: with complete equanimity. Both were, as far as Lobo was concerned, simple acts of fate. His survival training had taught him one thing: 'Don't fight it, roll with the punches." Not that he didn't think he'd had more than his share of hard knocks. *Lord knows I've suffered plenty,* he thought, allowing himself just one more little necessary injection of self-pity. *Yes, I've had to suffer for it, but I've lasted, goddamnit, and that's something!* he thought. And he had no intention of quitting now. The harder life pushed, the more accommodating Lobo would become. The important thing was to let the stream of life carry you with it. If you fought the current, Lobo figured, you'd soon tire and drown.

Yes, they all thought Lobo was dying of grief for his boy. Well, damnit, he'd give them what they wanted! And tears miraculously appeared at the corners of his cold blue eyes. And everybody at the Joint thought he would come around now, leave off his wishy-washy reformer's ways, come down hard on the black militants, just like the governor'd been pushing for all along. Everybody expected him to seek rapid vengeance for the slaying of his beloved boy. Well, damn them, he would not disappoint them! Not on any counts. Let everyone believe he was vengeance-bound, tough as nails, after a while he'd even believe it himself . . . this was the way Lobo succeeded at life. He admitted it to himself frankly. *Bury the dead,* he thought, *the living have to go on.* He had a family to support, two families now! What would his defeat serve? What would another failed washed-up liberal do to change the world? *What purpose resistance?* he thought, and got angrier and angrier and angrier about the murder of his young son, at the hands of . . . of ungrateful Blacks . . . godless Reds. . . .

Off across the cold church Lobo looked to where under his huge white Easter lilies as big as trumpet horns the corpse in person lay, him, Lobo's only begotten son . . . the subject of all of Chaplain Edwards' fustian twaddle. Under a wreath he lay too, a wreath of white and red carnations in the shape of a heart, with cheap gold lettering on a ribbon across the middle. . . .TO FRANK MINIVER, FROM HIS LOVING FRIENDS, THE WEED FAMILY, "MAY HE REST IN PEACE." Lobo was convinced that May had bought that wreath. Somehow its grossness was more fitting, more honest than his own flown-in lilies. *There's something genuine about May,* Lobo thought, *something that all the rest of us missed.* What was that? And then he thought of her possibly traitorous son, her son who might now be the only one who could and would expunge his guilt, or possible guilt, all of their guilt, the only one who would do it . . . and only one way . . . in blood . . . blood for blood . . . and thought: *guilty or not, he will be the one because guilt is irrelevant when the dice are rolling. . . .*

That morning, when Lobo'd first become privy to that tenuous *and now redundant* possibility, the possibility of Little Arv's blood guilt, delivered to him in person by Little Arv's own cousin, Lobo had been extremely doubtful, and he still was. He'd never trusted Wasco. Never liked him. And Little Arv was a boy he'd doted on, someone he'd helped along in life in any number of different ways. . . .

"Warden," Wasco said, "I got some real sad news to

lay on you, sir. Far be it from me to have to snitch on my own flesh and blood . . ."

"Come on, Wasco," Lobo said, pretending to be angry, "what is it? Get to the point!"

"Sir, pardon my French, but I got some info that that little fucker's working in secret for Galliot and the Black Fence."

"What are you talking about? I don't follow you, Wasco. You'll have to speak more plainly."

"Little Arv, sir," Wasco said, leaning over the Warden's desk, *breathing* on him. "I can prove he's in that whole nigger conspiracy . . . and that . . . I hate to say it, but he's . . . he's . . . involved some way, sir, in the murder of your son."

"Now wait a minute!" Lobo protested. "I can't believe that, Wasco! Little Arv? Why, I . . ."

"I said I could prove it, sir."

"How?"

"First off, don't you think it's a little weird that he just happened to mysteriously miss work for three days while Fast-Walking was getting killed? Now, think a minute, Warden, sir. If Arv had a been at work that night, like he was supposed to, he'd a been with Fast-Walking up on the tiers. They always worked as partners. Fast-Walking woulda had someone to cover his rear, see? Why, hell! Fast-Walking woulda been alive today if Arv had a been there!"

"Surely Wasco, you're not intimating . . . ?"

"And that ain't all, sir!" Wasco interjected again, "not by a long shot!" Lobo allowed him to interject it. "I can prove," Wasco continued, "that Arv's involved in a scheme to spring Galliot and get him on a plane for Cuba! I can prove that he's also a courier, a 'mule' between Galliot and his girl friend on the outside!"

"These are very serious allegations, Wasco . . ." Lobo said, voicing the trite phrase intentionally, knowing he could keep neutral that way, for a while.

"Sir," Wasco said, very confident, "if you'll just pick up that there phone and call the County D.A.'s office and speak to Mr. Crow in person, I think you'll be satisfied. . . ."

Lobo was momentarily nonplussed by Wasco's mention of the D.A. Old Jack Crow had been his bitter political foe for years, and Crow had been itching to get him, tor-

pedo him some way, ever since he'd become Warden back
in the rosy days of the Kennedy era. Lobo finally managed a smile and said, "Let's try to keep the D.A. out of
this if we can, Wasco. Can't you furnish any proof right
here and now?"

"Yes sir, sure I can!" Wasco said. "I got lots of proof,
Warden. I got . . . let's see . . . well, for example . . . I
got information that Arv's gonna be carrying a letter to
Galliot when he comes on duty today!"

"Really? Alright then, we'll arrange to have him
searched."

"Yeah? Then what're you gonna do with him, sir?"

"Well, if we find any incriminating evidence on him,
we'll hand him over to the proper authorities for arrest,
indictment, trial and conviction, if he's proven guilty."

"Sir," Wasco said, and his voice had that wheedling inmate con-man tone to it that Lobo detested, "wouldn't
you hate to see someone so close to us, and our . . . *rep-
utations* . . . get into this kind of a jam . . . ?"

"What are you getting at, Wasco?"

"Warden, I'm gonna be frank with you, sir. Like I told
you before, I been sent here to perform a real sensitive
mission in the Joint . . . to make sure this here state is se-
cured and content in racial quiet and prosperity . . . to
bring this nation of ours back to where it once . . ."

"Alright, alright! I see what you're driving at!" Lobo
said, sickened by Wasco's unbelievable corn, but anxiously
avoiding an argument. He had checked out Wasco's
claims—discreetly to be sure—after their first meeting,
and the response he'd gotten from C of C headquarters
and the governor's office had been sufficiently vague and
noncommittal to convince him of their absolute validity.
"But, I tell you, this is very very hard to believe . . .
about Little Arvin. . . ." Lobo concluded, wondering if
all this could be true about Arv, and rejecting out of hand
his implication in the murder of Fast-Walking, and accepting the possibility that he had perhaps got mixed up
somehow with the niggers, seduced into helping them
somehow *that would be more in character*. But what Lobo
was most concerned about now was not so much the truth
or falsity of the allegations. What he wondered about
now, and puzzled over, was the exact reason for their existence, their *purpose*.

"There's only one way to prove I'm telling the truth,

Blow" rubberband fly-killer that Lobo remembered him making as just a little boy of ten.

Sure, Lobo's kid was dead . . . and, yes, the possibility that he'd been offed by other than black hands, other than Arv's hands, had presented itself to Lobo's unwilling consciousness . . . even that perhaps the overanxious Wasco might have had some little thing to do with it. . . . But life must go on! Lobo's boy was dead and gone and nothing would bring him back. Lobo was still alive and kicking, vibrant with health, for his age! And he had a load of responsibility besides, a damn sight heavier responsibility than Fast-Walking'd ever dreamed of!

In his mind the Warden suddenly changed the subject . . . *There's no man,* he thought, *no man in the entire C of C who's done more over the years for the Negro prisoner in this state . . . but this time, with the killing of my own son . . . they've gone too far, too damn far, and there's gonna be the devil to pay for it!*

And only when Lobo had confirmed himself in this belief, and resolved firmly in his mind to do everything in his power to carry out its resolution, was he able to start listening to Chaplain Edwards' excellent sermon in earnest, and listen to the organ, and offer up to Fast-Walking's extra-long coffin tears of his natural fatherly condolence and affection. . . .

Later, waiting in line to view Fast-Walking's elegant wax face, Lobo surprised himself with his own morbid curiosity; he knew the Brian Brothers, as had Fast-Walking: incestuous homosexual twins who ran the local mortuary. Lobo wondered: *did they shave my son? What did it sound like when they ran the razor over his face?*

Lobo had run his hand over Fast-Walking's rough stubbly face while he lay . . . lay splattered on the concrete floor of the East Block . . . ah! But it seemed such a long time ago now. . . . Now it was time to go.

Now it was time to go. The music stopped, as did Chaplain Edwards' sanctimonious voice. Through the high portholes of the chapel Lobo could see his towers . . . towers #1 and #2 . . . and the gunmen leaning over the railing, smoking cigarettes, their rifles pointed into the invisible Big Yard across the wall.

Outside it was snowing. The uniformed pallbearers marched in cadence behind Lobo, Deanna and behind the red-faced Marie-Claude.

Tramp tramp tramp tramp they all marched into the swirling unfamiliar Alaskan snow *in this temperate land* while inside the chapel behind them the black organist played his funeral march, a touch of boogie to it, just a smidgen, but enough to give Lobo, the terrible Warden, Bigman of the Joint the excuse he'd been waiting for . . . enough to make him frown, frown deep, a widow-making maledictory frown that boded no good toward that black man, nor his unfortunate black African Negroid nigger race. For there was brand new vengeance in Lobo's frown, vengeance in his very mouth and head and neck, vengeance in his nose and in his hard-set jaw and his eagle eyes, vengeance in his bones, vengeance that was its own *raison d'être*. Look out niggers here come de Man!

And he almost pitied them now, Dem, the Joint's "groovy ones," but knew there was nothing he could do for them anymore, and that's all there was to it. . . .

No man in this state has done more for the Negro prisoner than . . . he began, and was honestly pained by what he felt to be their callous betrayal of an old friend. . . .

On across the snowy lawn, slipping and sliding, came the funeral procession, headed for the little "historic" Joint cemetery on a bleak heathery headland above the Sound, above the humpback bridge to West Hazelton and the Standard Oil refinery, headed for that cold and lonely place where ex-Sergeant Fast-Walking Miniver, penal minion, aristo of the Joint, child of prison, would be set into the chill slushy hillside and covered over with the black mud of the Mud-Hen Indians and laid to permanent rest alongside prison guards and wardens killed through the Will of God and inmate insurrection, through riot and heart attack, heat stroke and knife stroke, old age and too much gun-tower solitude, laid to final endless sleep in the State Employees' section of the segregated graveyard, right across the picket fence from nineteenth-century oyster pirates and Mexican bandidos and hanged rustlers and horse thieves and Gold Rush highwaymen and the large subsegregated plot where lay the gassed and hanged and electrocuted lower-class and black convicts publicly executed by writ of law in this the twentieth century after Our Lord's execution upon Calvary alongside two other mean-ass cons. . . .

Forty-Seven

"Take it easy, honey, don't work so hard!" Evie said, as Big Arv frantically chopped peppers for his chile beans.

He'd been working fast and smooth all morning and afternoon with a singing skipping heart, confident that at the end of the workday he'd be granted the favor he'd been wanting and needing all his life, the favor he'd been waiting for since that fateful morning in the chicken house when he was just a little boy, the favor he'd earned with great labor and great risk, the favor of his beloved's indescribably delicious charms, promised as a reward for his services above and beyond the call of duty to the State and the Free Enterprise system it stood for.

Evie, bundled up in her new Alaskan sable coat, with only her stained pink dressing gown underneath, had fondly followed him around all day long, watching him fulfill his various duties. She even got into the VW van with him and Sanger when they went out to round up the wetbacks at the labor camps, laughing when Sanger sang out *"Vamos a la tienda!"* in his croaking broken-windpipe fighter's voice. The van filled up with cheery coldfoot Spics. Business was good that day 'cause they couldn't work the celery in the cold. She watched with approval as Big Arv and Sanger drove them to Montoya's Market, opened up, vending trinkets for Christmas presents and candy for *piñatas* and dry goods, liquor, and the usual vast quantities of hot sauce. She watched later while Big Arv fed and watered the goats, the donkey, the chickens, rabbits, and the gangly bawling white-face calf. Watched him install electric heaters in the chicken houses for her, both the chicken house of the chickens and the chicken houses of the whores. Watched him supervise the freezing lineup of Mexicans waiting for a quick fuck. Watched him accept and ring up each man's ten bucks as he stepped into the coop. Watched him oversee Lola's and Honey's assembly-line tricks. Made sure that they were warmly wrapped up in the big old war surplus army overcoats she'd recently provided for them, made sure they didn't catch their death of cold. She cursed the weather the whole time: "Damn, you know, Big Arv, this Black Home cold is enough to change your life style out here on the Coast!" Evie stood by also later out in the garage while Big Arv performed his daily ritual bath and sprayed Lola and Honey down good with hot water. Watched him send Sanger out to drive the greasers back to camp.

Big Arv liked it so much, her hanging around him, watching him like that, that his old ticker started acting up, started that one potater, two potater, palp pitater palping again, that ran in the family.

Evie watched him with such adoring eyes.

"Why you following me around so close today, darlin'?"

"Shucks, Big Arv, you know, you finally come to be a man. I just can't leave off looking at you, now that you come to be the man I always wanted."

At the end of the workday, with Sanger gone off early to Fast-Walking's sad and unfortunate funeral, and all the work done, and still two hours to go before the swing shift at the Joint, Evie said, "Now, come on into the kitchen, dear, and make me up a nice batch of chile beans while I brew us a hot cup of coffee!"

Big Arv trembled as he chopped tomatoes, cut garlic for his beans. "Now damn it, I said take it easy!" Evie warned again. "Don't get yourself all worked up over nothing! Am I that exciting? An old bag like me!"

He cut his hand with the paring knife. "Stop it!" she said, "that's enough of that! You're acting up like a little kid, honey. Like some little feller that ain't had no poon-tang before. Now, I'm gonna get mad if you don't quit it. Remember, you're my love, my love, my one and only heart . . . I been waiting all my life for you, for you to grow into the man I knew you was . . . remember that about your old Evie. No need to get all shook up. Hell, I'm yours, honey! Or . . . Listen! Is it me or that damn nigger-loving Commie kid of yours that you're acting up about?"

"Now Evie . . ." Big Arv protested, but his heart wasn't in it. What she said was true! And the persistent nagging idea that he was gonna have to get rough with his own son today in the Joint, that him and Lobo and Sanger and Wasco were gonna have to confront that guilty god-damn kid with unassailable evidence of his complicity in a Black Fence plot to riot, murder, destroy state property and aid in the escape of a dangerous nigger militant . . . kept preying at his mind, to say the least! *If it ain't one damn thing it's another!* he thought, and cursed his peren-nial bad luck. Fuck! The notion that his own son, Little Arv, his own kid was a proven traitor to Big Arv's be-loved America . . . as Wasco and the squeeze had re-vealed to him in the East Block the day before yesterday, when Little Arv was unexplainably absent from work on the very day of Fast-Walking's death . . . as Evie had strongly confirmed only yesterday . . . the notion that Little Arv had suddenly become the *enemy* spoiled even Big Arv's anticipation of his coming "reward."

"Well," said Evie, "hell, Arv! You're always apologiz-ing for that kid!"

"No I ain't!" Big Arv whined. "But shit! The way I figure, I still got hope for the boy, Evie. You know he ain't all bad. He just fell in with an evil crowd over there at that damn City College. You know what Gov-ernor Riley said about that place on TV the other day . . ."

"Sure I do," Evie said, "he called it 'a haven for every half-baked hippy and hirsute hermaphrodite, every car-rion-bird, Com-Symp and queen in the State of New Son-ora!' That's what he said!"

"That's right!" Big Arv agreed. "That's what I mean! So, the way I see it, we're gonna knock some sense into that boy yet . . . if we can get him out of their clutches over there . . ."

"I tell you, Big Arv," Evie said doubtfully, "I don't know. But one thing! I feel the kid is lucky, in a way. He's gonna be offered a golden opportunity today . . . to pay for his sin against Jesus and everything we hold dear . . . an opportunity to achieve forgiveness from his family, be redeemed by the State, and receive the absolu-tion of Our Lord and Savior Jesus Christ all in one lump . . . by performing a patriotic service for America . . .

That's his one and only opportunity, Big Arv. And if he flubs this one . . ."

"He ain't gonna flub nothing!" Big Arv insisted. "I'll see to that!"

"I hope so, Big Arv, cause, as far as any more . . . lovin' . . . I mean . . . after your reward today . . . a man has to prove himself for Evie, you know . . . over and over . . ."

"Don't worry, honey! Your Bibi, he's gonna deliver! Don't you worry your pretty head about that! See, Evie, I got faith. Now, Little Arv, he's been acting up. And there just ain't no two ways about it. And he's guilty, I know, just like you all proved to me. But he'll come out alright in the end. You'll see. I got faith in the young people of this country. Now, just like Little Arv, they been acting up lately, all through the sixties, like we seen on TV every night. But they'll settle down yet, you mark my words!"

"Okay, okay," Evie said, reaching out to stroke the back of his reddish neck, "if you say so, sweetie. But just cool down a bit, huh? You're gettin' all worked up, honey, ain't you?"

But Big Arv just couldn't calm down. His face got redder and redder. He chopped those peppers faster and faster. The green just flew. His heart just a-beating away in the center of his chest like a jackhammer.

"Here, damn it! Have some coffee," she said, when he put the beans on to boil, "sit down and relax a minute . . ."

BOOM! a loud report like a rifle shot rang out, echoing off Evie's cinderblock wall.

"What's going on out there?"

"Aw, shit, calm down!" Evie said, "it's just them greaser kids next door, honey, with that goddamn hot rod chili wagon of theirs. It's always acting up like that, back-firin' all up and down the street . . . I declare, sweetheart, I just don't know what I'm gonna do with you today . . . I tell you, if you're done with them beans, I guess I'm gonna have to take you on out now and give you your damn old reward. Otherwise, you're just gonna keep acting up like an old hound dog that wants his bone. Come on!" she said, untying the apron around Big Arv's large waist, "come on, big boy, let's see what you can do . . ."

Evie led him out across the cemented inyard and
through her pedestals and statues and her grassy outyard
to the first chicken house. Big Arv, now that his moment
was here, felt almost reluctant, in a way, almost held back
. . . a little. But Evie tugged at him stoutly. And there
was no going back.

Beyond them, out toward the back fence, Big Arv could
hear his animals. The rabbits scratching in their clean
hutches, the goat snuffing in the dirt, the calf chomping
hay in the rick, the chickens clucking. The donkey was
quiet as usual, a good sign. Only his hee-haw meant trouble. Everything was just right in the yard, just the way Big
Arv liked it . . . and, yet, still his fucking old heart ran
on, beating madly in his chest . . .

"Come on in, now, you silly fellah, come on!" Evie
urged, tugging at his sleeve. "I'm gonna give you your
surprise now, darlin' Arvie! Your reward! Right out here
in Lola's chicken house. Har har! Cause I don't want
you dirtyin' up my clean white bed sheets with them big
old dirty feet of yours! Come on, honey! This is gonna
make you feel a lot better. Come on! You'll see!"

Big Arv was weak, staggering, near collapse. WHAM
WHAM WHAM WHAM! His heart just wouldn't hold him up
no more. Evie helped him inside, laid him on Lola's
come-stained sleeping bag, turned on the new electric
heater, switched on the radio to hide their anticipated
cries of love, removed her sable coat, and her stained pink
dressing gown. Slid it over her red head. Ran a wire
hanger through each item of clothing and hung it neatly
up on the wall.

And then there she was, standing before him, a monument in skin, a fleshy monument to Big Arv's lifetime of
carnal devotion. There she was in the flesh, in all her
glory, from her strawberry blond Shirley Temple curls to
her tiny squinting Indian eyes to her rosy healthy cheeks
to her flat Weed nose with its flaring nostrils to her peach
fuzzy moustache to her cupid's-bow mouth to her five
chins and six necks to her wondrous breasts, those tits like
Hindenburgs, like great punctured zeppelins, those teats
you could shelter between. And, as she fell to her dimpled
knees above him, they swung over him, those heavenly
hanging udders of hers, pink-tipped, freckled . . .

And his heart then went out of control, crash-dove,

went down in flames. She bent over him. Let them drag in his face. He licked at the pimpled nips each time they swayed by his nose. She opened his fly . . .

Brought him out into gray day . . .

Heart going faster . . . faster . . . spinning toward earth . . .

And she, his love he'd been pursuing with constancy for nearly forty years, since deepest Depression days, since he was nine and she was thirteen, out in the chicken house behind her daddy's place, under the pepper tree the smell of which he still remembered now . . . She, his love, went down upon him now, sucked him with her little girl's mouth, little girl's lips, fell upon his overalls with her massive marvelous body, rolled him over, *roll me over, roll me over, roll me over in the clover and do it again*, rolled over and under, with him now by magic firmly mounted . . . Opened her powerful thick All-American girly legs, wiggled her fatty high-protein American ass, and presented him her secret, her secret he had not seen or smelled these forty years, her gray fishface he still remembered with bliss, her open mouth like the mouth of a beached yet still breathing flounder, with dry scaly skin and a proud dull dribbling mouth. . . .

And her voice, beloved voice, coming from a long long distance away, far away across her mammoth belly and pendulous breasts, across her necks and chins . . . far away he could hear her tiny quavering baby girl's voice speak up encouragingly:

"Touch me . . ." she said, sighing like a virgin.

And he did. Did he really? Sure he did! He touched it and it felt just like it used to. It felt like melted margarine in a hairy dish . . .

"Now, sniff it!" she commanded, exactly as she had done when they were children. And Big Arv could no more have disobeyed that command than he could have resisted the command of Duty, Race, State, Country or Commander-in-Chief, no more than he could have hushed his speeding palpitating ticker . . .

"Ugh!"

"Sniff it!" she repeated, urgently, breathing hard, like a bitchdog in heat. So Big Arv, always the gallant, brought his thick rough finger up to his fat nose and sniffed. SNIFF! SNIFF! It smelled what it looked like: trout.

"Now you're my man!" she screamed, while the *ranchero* music played airs from their South Texas borderland youth in the background, sparing the neighbors Evie's mad cries of love.

And Big Arv's heart broke the sound barrier then, strove for the speed of light. He could no longer hear her, but he could still read her scaly lips:

"Fuck me, big boy, fuck me good!" Evie shrieked, wide-legged, and Big Arv drove his powerful challenger into her heaving snorting fish.

He was blind now, having gone far beyond the speed of mere light, couldn't see a thing . . . at 186,000 miles per second. But he could still feel. He could sure as hell still feel, goddamnit, and thrust at her faster and faster . . . till finally he could go no faster, no further . . . and broke his poor heart strings. TWANG! He heard them go just like the strings on an old banjo.

The last thing he'd heard was Evie talking. It seemed like her voice was coming from a long way off. It seemed just like normal to Big Arv at the time:

"Shitfire!" she said, "you lead a damn mule to water and he drinks himself to death!"

Yet, Big Arv died a happy man in spite of it all. Sure, he cursed his fate, his early meaningless death, his eventless years in the Joint, his drunken wife and traitorous son. But, the way Big Arv figured it, he'd achieved the greatest desire of his life, and that was a damn sight more than most dudes had done.

As his blood ran cold and stopped flowing within him, Big Arv had approximately twenty seconds before his brain shut down for lack of nourishment. During those long seconds that lasted for the rest of infinity, he abolished all his worries, all his trials and tribulations . . . the Joint, his wife, his son, to concentrate on Evie . . . and died right then and there, Big Arv did, of fatty degeneration of the heart, arteriosclerosis, "the American Disease," mounted upon the bucking fucking bod of his one and only love, in the chicken house of his desire. . . .

Forty-Eight

"Tweet, tweet, tweet, tweet!" Wasco, lying up in the Chief Tier Tender's day bed, was practicing his bird calls and listening to the radio: "After killing spree IRA provisionals announce three-day Christmas truce." He was getting pretty good now. Sounded just like an East Block sparrow. "Tweet, tweet!" Pretty soon he'd have 'em eating out of his hand. The squeeze and the old Portagee day sergeant, Boa, were snoring away in the guard shanty with Wasco, all of them wrapped up in heavy state-issue blankets.

Beyond the shanty the block was cold and still as the grave. Only the sick-call people remained, zonked in their cells on legal doctor-dealt downers to keep 'em quiet and happy. *That is one area of diversification we got to look into: organize the Joint docs. Why not? If I don't, somebody else will. If somebody else don't, they will themselves, if they ain't already.*

Wasco playfully reached up and stuck his hand in the squeeze's pant cuff to see if he was still carrying around them dirty fingernails. Nope! The fastidi-ass little punk had cleaned 'em all out. Wasco laughed to himself, raised his big feet off the electric heater, took off his right shoe and sock, clipped his toenails quickly with the shanty's scissors PROPERTY STATE OF N.S. and stuck them in the squeeze's cuff. See how long he carries 'em around this time! Har har har!

"Tweet, tweet, tweet!" went Wasco, imitating almost perfectly the tweet of the sparrows, snow birds now, almost, in this cold, snow birds that fluttered and flirted in the rafters and the barred windows.

Wasco was thinking. He had plenty of time to think. He liked that. Nobody would be in the block for another three and a half hours, not until the prechow First Count.

And by then everything'll be settled. Wasco was a happily contented man, almost. Everything seemed to be just turning up roses. He was so happy with things that he kept dropping off to sleep. The trouble was, every time sleep came over him, his bliss disappeared. And he was susceptible to bad dreams, daydreams, "napmares," as he called them.

A few minutes before, he'd dropped off and dreamed he was lost in the maze of a nighttime West Coast trailer-court, tripping over the kitchen garden pea strings of the retired elderly residents, a white searchlight from a police prowl car in his face, blinding him . . . And before that he'd dreamed of being woke up again by his dead-drunk dad in the middle of the teenage night and hit around the eyes again with that double-tongued prison guard belt. Half-awake, he reached for his knife, Boy Scout knife, hunting knife, again, beside his bed. But it wasn't there! This time it wasn't there, Wasco realized in a terrible panic. His old man just kept beating him till he was nearly dead, till everything went green like spearmint gum, all sticky, gluing his lids down. Then he screamed and woke up. And dreamed again. Dreamed of riding Canary when he was a kid. Riding him backwards looking at the ass of the ass, getting a big fat hard-on and only eleven years old. Riding up into the Soundside Hills, up to the secret fort where him and Arv used to hang out, going up there to diddle, feeling that special sexy way, going up to diddle, diddle Arv or diddle the burro, didn't matter much which. But this one time, he got up there alone and what was hanging around grazing in the pasture but Deanna's little trim virgin white filly, white mare to be. Wasco rode the donkey fast across the yellow grass and the donkey bucked up on his short goaty hind legs and mounted her. It was like Wasco himself was mounting her. "Oomph oomph oomph!" went the donkey. "Oomph oomph!" went Wasco. Tupping at that white mare. Then Wasco woke up suddenly, startled, frightened terribly, for some reason, and he didn't know why. Cause it seemed like to him a real pleasant little dream. The drippy wet in his jockey shorts told him that. Just couldn't figure it out. Fell asleep again, nodding, screamed out, "Aaaaah!" Woke the squeezy.

"Wha'? What is it?"

"Nothin! Go back to sleep."

The old Portagee just kept snoring.

Fell asleep. More bad dreams. Woke up again with a start. The squeeze was awake too by then. Watched him jump.

"What'sa matter, honey?"

"Bad dream."

"I don't like that."

"How come? Got nothin' to do with you."

"Bad luck."

"Shit!"

"No jive. Listen, I don't like the look, the feel of things. How come we don't just zap him ourselves? I don't like getting tied up with a bunch of amateurs."

"Oh no? Well, you might like it a little more if you figured like I do."

"How's that?"

"I figure they'd love to pin it on us, them Front Street dudes, if they had the chance. The whole fucking beef. Take it from me. We don't want to get tied up in no killing if we can help it. Don't worry though, I got it all worked out."

"Well, like I say. I figure it's an error in tactics. And how you know that cuz of yours is gonna come through? And listen, how you know he won't blow you off instead of the spade?"

"My own cousin? My own flesh and blood is gonna blow me off? Come on, man. Old Marvie-Arvie, he'll come through alright."

"But how you gonna make him?"

"Me and the Warden," Wasco said, leaning toward the squeeze, "we had us a little talk this morning . . . dig it! We're gonna make Little Arv such an attractive proposal he ain't gonna be able to say no. Especially when he fully appreciates the possible penalties for a negative attitude. Like I always say, the way you got to do it, Squeezy, is to just accentuate that old positive. Otherwise you ain't gonna get anywhere in life. Right?"

"Yeah," the squeeze said doubtfully, "but what about the . . . ?"

"Now damnit Squeezy," Wasco said, pointing over at the radio which was blaring out the latest news on the Watergate scandal, "I don't want you to be asking too many questions. Take a tip from that there Watergate thing. What you hear on the radio, man, that's only the tip of the iceberg, the tail of the dragon, the rattle of the snake. Them boys, they didn't want to know too much. That way they wouldn't have much to tell. Dig?"

"Okay," the squeeze agreed finally, "but will you just listen to one piece of advice from your baby?"

"Sure, honeybuns, what is it?"

"You got to plant another letter on him. What if she gives him an oral message? Then how you gonna blackmail him into doing it?"

"Don't worry. Just the accusation'll be enough. When he finds out his own dad, and his uncle, his cousin, the woman he loves, and the Warden, and everybody's coming down on him all at once, accusing him of being a traitor, a Commie, an agitator who wants to bring down the American Way of Life, a criminal who's consorting with and aiding a dangerous nigger, he'll come through alright. We'll demoralize him into it. I know him. Once he knows for sure that Moke's lied to him and played him dirty and set him up and ratted on him and used him and betrayed him and never even liked his cock, dig, he'll fucking fold like a marshmallow, cave in like rotten fruit, dissolve like cut Boy. I know that cat. Once we got him down, real down, he ain't gonna sacrifice his life for no joe-college nigger. No way!"

"Maybe," said the squeeze doubtfully, "but I'd be happy just the same if you'd do that for me. Will you? We could get the Wop to do it. He owes you a lot. Just to make it fail-safe."

"Whatever you say, tickle-tongue. But, I'll tell you. I I'm gonna do a favor for you, you're gonna have to do one for me."

"What's that?"

"I want you to run up and unlock Galliot's cell with your tier key while *he's*" (Wasco gestured toward the sleeping Portagee) "asleep. Go in and get that cage he keeps in there and bring it to me with the bird in it."

"What bird?"

"That broken-wing sparrow he keeps in there."

"Oh, that one! He let that go yesterday. Said its wing was all well. The whole nigger tier sent up a cheer when it flew out of the cell. Then it went one time around the block, like a matador when he's made a good kill, found the window, and flew out over the wall. The niggers went crazy."

"You're shucking!"

"No, I ain't."

"Come on!" Wasco growled, dragging the squeeze roughly out of the shanty. They ran up the spiral metal staircase to the fifth tier. Wasco pulled the lock pin. Wham! It flew open. Then him and the squeeze went down to Galliot's cell and opened it up with the big brass key. The cage was in there alright. But no bird.

"Goddamn!"

"What you so pissed off at?"

"It's the principle of it."

"What principle?"

"The nigger outfoxed me."

"Shit, it was only a little bird."

"It's a bad omen."

"What omen?"

"Shut up!" Wasco yelled, cuffing him across the face SLAP SLAP! "Take that fucking cage and throw it over the tier!"

"What?"

"You heard me."

"But he'll know who did it."

"He ain't gonna know nothing after today."

"Now you're talking!" the squeezy shouted brutally, flinging the colorless, intricately carved plastic cage over the side. It spun round and round as it fell, and then shattered with a loud PLAK! on the concrete floor of the block.

"Hey! What's that? What's that?" the Portagee yelled up from the guard's shanty.

"Tell him we're destroying contraband we found on the tier," Wasco commanded.

The squeeze hollered out, "Contraband, Sarge!"

"Oh! Okay!" the Portagee said, and went back to his nap.

"Now, look at that," Wasco said, real mean, gesturing to the inscription on the wall of Galliot's cell, an inscription written very carefully with black charcoal:

> RHYTHM: THE PULSE OF SOUL
> SOUL: THE PULSE OF LIFE

LIFE: THE PULSE OF ETERNITY

"Squeezy, I want you to go down and get some paint in the shanty. Tell the Sarge what you're doing. Come back here and paint that out. Out! Oh-you-tee, out! It's strictly against the rules."

"Sure, but why bother? If he ain't gonna be around . . ."

"Do it!"

And the squeeze did it. He did it just like Wasco said. While Wasco went down and brewed up another cup of Nescafé. sssssssss, the electrified water sizzled and jerked in the Mason jar.

After he was done the squeeze locked the fifth tier, let the bar go ZING! back into place, and hauled ass down the spiral metal staircase CLANG CLANG CLANG. Wasco heard him coming all the way down and knew by his step that he was gonna be asking another favor. You could always tell like that with the squeezy. Just like a woman.

"Let me come with you over to the Sign-in Room this afternoon!" he said, as soon as he came into the shanty. He was breathing hard, all out of air. Wasco was bent over the stinger jar. He looked up and didn't say anything, just looked at him, made him repeat it . . .

"Won't you?"

"No, goddamnit! N-oh spells no!" said Wasco, who didn't like the omens, for the moment. At least he didn't like this last bird omen up in Galliot's cell, and figured him for more powerful medicine than he'd discerned before. Nope. The squeezy definitely couldn't come. Wasco didn't want anyone underfoot.

A few minutes later the squeeze dropped off again, pouting like a chick. Wasco watched him with love, true love, love in his eyes for his honey, his nightfuck, darkdick, buttbitch, watched him, his little poopoo-prick, lost in the luxuria of infatuation . . . and the Portagee snoring away . . . Wasco watched his love for the longest time and then he dropped off again himself, though he resisted it mightily . . . for damn good reason. . . .

Now in his dream, napmare, he dreamed the worst one, bad omen, the one he didn't want. Little Arv blew him off, hit him in the belly by mistake . . . or was it on purpose? Got *him* instead of the proper nigger. Bowels dumped out into the Yard. But still alive and kicking.

Kicking at the ground. Like a chicken on the asphalt of the Yard. Kicking his heels into the blacktop. Digging a hole with his metal boot heel CLINK CLINK. Little Arv shot and shot, making his body quiver and dance on the ground with every hit, making it move, summoning it back POW POW POW almost, to another kind of life, making it live again with every round. Wasco heard him screaming up in the tower while he danced. Arv screamed out, "Let me go! Let me go! Let me go!" as if it was him getting shot, him dying an ignoble death in the dirty Yard. Soon the ambulance came. Took him out past his old house in the housing area, past the ball diamond and the football field where they all used to play, past the abandoned World War II airfield, through the back gate to Mission Santa Bonita and New Sonora County Hospital. Lying in the back of the ambulance, pale as a lover, Wasco dreamed within his dream. Dreamed of rolling out the back of the Caddie ambulance, Jimmy Dean rollout, running across the weeded-over airstrip to the rusting old C-46. Bullets pattering all around. PING PING! Cranking the old baby over. Taking off. Circling over Paradise Cove at two thousand feet. Circling the Joint, firing a gatling gun into the yard, watching the spurts kick up black on the macadam, white in the Sound, yellow and gray in the walls. Firing and firing, hitting cops and cons, Spics and whites and niggers and Flips, hitting them all indiscriminately, till he got hit himself, engines flaming, and crashed his fucking bomber into the East Block with a mighty roar. Stepped out into the burning East Block unscathed by his uncontrolled plummet. Surrounded suddenly by laughing convicts, scoffing at him, pointing, "What to hell's the matter with you, Wasco? You just gone and jumped from the fucking frying pan into the fire!"

"Shit man," Wasco said, "the Joint is my home!"

That was what he dreamed, as he dreamed, riding in the Caddie past the firing range where him and Arv used to practice with their .22's, the cove where they went crabbing, over the low range of snowy hills where they used to ride their donkey on yellow summer days. They rolled him inside the County Hospital and down a long egg-shell and institution-green corridor. He smelled that good smell again, that hot sweet bittersweet institutional smell he loved. They put him in a long roomful of old crazy dying men. They put him next to his grandpa Alfonso the Spic and they died together soaked in their own piss, happy as little larks in their blue and white striped PJ's, county issue, and their first white sheets, starched and clean and gleaming, dreaming within dreaming within dreaming of the future and the past, the present total and under complete control. . . .

Then he woke with a start. For a moment he didn't know where from.

"Squeezy?"

"Yeah?"

"Run up to the fifth tier and yell to the Wop in the Yard. Tell him to go ahead and make the plant. No use taking chances, you're right."

"You bet!" smiled the squeeze, and went like a whirlwind up the spiral stairs not like Fast-Walking used to do it, smooth and easy, going fast. No, the squeeze went like a little steam switch engine in the rain, breathing fire and smoke, making a lot of noise, but never seeming to get anywhere.

Later on, 3:30 on the shanty's clock, the phone rang, waking them all from the deepest slumber RIIIIING! waking Wasco in fact from the deepest sleep of his life, bringing him back, as it were, from the very gates of perdition . . . "Whew!"

"East Block!" said the squeezy, picking up the old-fashioned wall phone receiver. "Who? Oh, of course, Warden. Just a moment, sir! . . . Wasco? . . . The Warden!"

"Hello . . . Warden Miniver? Yes sir. Yes sir. Yes sir. By all means, sir! I'll be right over. Good-bye."

"Let me go with you!" the squeeze begged.

"Now, honey, I said you couldn't. And that's that," Wasco said. And then, just to embarrass the wide-eyed Portagee, just to shake him up, Wasco said, "Come here now fuckypie, and give your Ma a little kiss-poo goo'bye. Yeah! That's what she likes!" The squeeze and him sucked spit for a while, and rubbed joints, grabbed ass, copped a little dryfuck, and all the time Wasco was watching old Boa. He just wasn't a very contemporary cat, that old Portagee, and couldn't relate to their good lovin'. It scared him half to death to hear them heavy male beards scratching against each other in true and hungry passion. Scared him shitless. His blue Portagee lips started quivering, spittle started dribbling at the corner of his ugly satchel. his eyes went like sapphires in righteous fear of the princess, Ma Weed, the Queen of the Joint, King Dog, Hitler's Little Helper, the Devil's Disciple, Hell's Angel, Anti-Christ, Scourge of BeJesus, Doom of God! Yeah!

When Wasco wanted to go, when he'd kissed his caca-cock bye-bye and wanted to split, he didn't even have to say nothing. That terrified little Portagee ran out ahead of him to the steel gate like a footman of the Queen, opened it, swung it wide, bowing and scraping, and showed Big Ma Weed out into the Main Yard. . . .

Wasco went across the Yard and through the Isolation Yard Gate thinking . . . *never are you more alive than when you're working a dangerous scam.* . . .

Over in the Sign-in Room Wasco encountered Warden Miniver and Uncle Sanger. They were standing around amongst the piles of mothballed inmate denims, sober-faced, the Warden in a black suit and black tie and Sanger in his uniform. Wasco had to wipe the happy grin off his satchel. He'd forgotten. They'd just come from the funeral of the Warden's only begotten son.

"Warden, Uncle Sanger, I hope the services were worthy of the man . . ."

"Yeah," the Warden said impatiently, "but frankly, Wasco, that's all past now. We've buried the dead and must concern outselves with the living. Now is the time for sweet revenge . . ."

"At our convenience too, sir," Wasco said, concealing his rapture not too well.

"Revenge!" the Warden repeated.

"Right, sir!" the ever-loyal Sanger shouted, coming to attention in front of the high-piled stack of numbered blue shirts, clicking his buffed black jodhpurs.

"We're with you, sir!" Wasco said, enjoying the fake stentorian tones, the phony authoritarian bombast that Lobo figured would win stupid impressionable old Sanger to their cause.

"I don't know," the Warden said, looking a bit preoccu-pied, "but I don't like it one bit. He didn't even attend the funeral. I was aware of their mutal antipathy. But I had no idea he'd carry it this far."

"He"ll show up, sir." Sanger assured the Warden. "Evie wanted him to cook up some chile beans for her, and . . ."

Wasco and the Warden permitted themselves a brief smile, Wasco discreetly following the Warden's lead, in response to Sanger's almost comic naïveté. . . .

They spoke together in low voices for a few minutes, pacing up and down the stuffy room smelling of mothballs and stored clothes, looking at their watches all the time. The Warden got more and more nervous. The more nervous he got, the more Wasco liked it.

Finally the Warden said, "Sanger, call Evie's place and find out if he's left yet."

Sanger dialed the number and got no answer.

"What the hell's going on here?" the Warden wanted to know, and picked up the phone to dial the barber shop, the Staff Dining Room, and the Briefing Room to see if Big Arv'd showed up yet. No luck. He phoned Big Arv's private home and no one answered there either. "This is absurd," the Warden fussed, "he's getting as bad as his damn kid!"

"Warden, sir," Wasco said, "I suggest we forget him for the moment and consider how we'll operate without his fatherly influence on the boy."

"I suppose you're right, Wasco. Let's see . . ."

"I further suggest, sir, that we . . ."

RUUUUNG! The phone sounded very dead in the close quarters of the room. It was a very loud but very dull sound, a sound that flattened itself out real disquieting in the piles of wool and cotton clothing. The Warden answered.

"Hello. Yes. Yes. Yes. I see. Most regrettable. I see. Unfortunate as that may be, we shall have to carry on as usual. Please have Sergeant Morgan take his place in the East Block tonight. Move Blair to the swing shift sergeant's position, and inform me of any new developments. Stress to Sergeant Blair, if you will, our very considered opinion that the possibility of a riot situation is very great this evening, especially just before the First Count. I want each and every gunman standing alertly outside his wall post shanty, rifle loaded, in hand, and safety off. Is that clear? Good. And . . . oh! Will you please send Officer Arvin Weed, Jr., to me at once? We shall not want to be disturbed. Understood? Very good, Hutchins. And keep me posted, okay?"

The Warden then turned to Sanger, sober and serious, and said, "I'm very sorry to have to tell you, Sanger, that your brother Arvin has died of a coronary at his part-time job. They tried everything, even an open-heart injection of adrenalin, but nothing worked."

Sanger dissolved into a veritable flood of boozy tears. "What's a coronary?" he asked, plaintively, raising his eyes up to the Warden like a hound that wanted to be punished.

"A heart attack."

"Heart attack? Big Arv? No! No!" Sanger cried, the tears flowing in unclean streams down his dented fighter's cheeks.

"Yes, I'm afraid so," the Warden said, and then he turned to Wasco, "they say he died cursing his son. Blamed him for his death. Accused him of being a coward, and a traitor to his family, his race, and his country. . . ."

"Wha'zat?" Sanger angrily demanded, wiping his wet face with a dirty blue work handkerchief.

"Now, you know, Sanger," Lobo said, with a great show of deliberation. "I explained it to you once. And Big Arv told you too, I believe . . . we have information which leads us to believe that your nephew Arv may have become a courier for the Black Fence, that he's entered into a conspiracy to help Galliot escape from this institution so he can continue his subversive work of overthrowing the lawful government of his state and this nation. You are aware of that, are you not? Stand up straight! Pull yourself together, man! You're a prison corrections officer, not a woman! Now, answer my question, Sanger. Are you aware of what I've been saying?"

"Well, uh, sir, Big Arv told me today that Little Arv's mulebacking. But I figured we'd just kind of shake him up a little and find out how far he was mixed up . . . I mean, I never did get along with the kid too good. He was always kind of a weirdo, if you know what I mean. Not like the other kids. But I figured, since he was one time your own son-in-law, sir, we'd give him a chance to explain hisself a little and . . ."

"Explain shit!" Wasco said, wiping a tear from his eye too. "He's responsible for the death of my uncle, his own father! And worse than that, he's a traitor! You know what that means, Uncle Sanger? A fucking traitor! If you'll excuse the expression, Warden . . ."

"A traitor," Sanger repeated, letting it soak through his cauliflowered ears and right into his ring-battered brain, ". . . a traitor, a traitor, a traitor . . ."

"That's right, you damn tootin'! You heard the Warden. A traitor. Cursed by his own daddy on his death bed!"

"A traitor," Sanger repeated in tones of wonder. "A traitor, a traitor, a traitor, a traitor . . ."

And then Wasco figured that maybe they should have shut the punchy motherfucker up cause he got to be a broken record . . . "a traitor, a traitor, a traitor, a traitor . . ." getting louder and louder, pounding his huge scarred mitt on the table. But Wasco and the Warden didn't say a thing. Considering the circumstances, they had to take the risk that he'd beat the aim out of Arv, break his trigger finger, or get his twenty/twenty sharp-shooter vision. They had to take that chance, hoping they could stop the old ex-pug in time to save their plans. And, after all, it turned out to be well worth it. The Warden succeeded in getting the authority-loving old boxer calmed down just before Little Arv came in the door . . . "Listen, listen," the Warden coaxed, "Sanger, let's do this fair and square. Like we always do. Let's give him a fair trial. Let's allow the man to defend himself. If he proves to be guilty, then we'll have to punish him. Right here and now. No telling what may happen in a court of law. He'll get himself one of those long-haired lawyers and some bleedy-heart judge and get off scot-free, for all we know, right?"

"Uh . . . yeah! Right, Warden, you never know. Never know," Sanger said, trying to get his color to come down from the ruddy height his blood-pressure had taken it to. . . . "Right, Warden, whatever you say, sir . . ."

"Yes, we'll have to punish him. Punish him. Crime must be punished. The criminal is to be penalized, punished, not coddled!" the Warden said, "but not too hard, Sanger. You understand?"

"Uh . . . I think so . . ."

"Take it easy on him. Don't hurt his eyes. Don't hurt his trigger finger especially. I've got something real special for him. You'll see. I've got something in mind for him, something to make him pay back, poetic justice. . . . He's going to be . . ." the Warden said, poking Sanger hard in

the ribs with his elbow, laughing suggestively, "he's going
to be the one who gets the man behind all this. . . ."

"Who'zat? Who'zat?" Sanger asked, barking it eager,
like a dog straining at his leash.

"Galliot!" said the Warden. "We have information
which leads us to believe that he and his group are agi-
tating a racial riot for today, on the scale of Africa, just
before the First Count whistle . . ."

"Galliot! Galliot, huh? Galliot!" Sanger said, sniffing
loudly, dancing on the balls of his feet, ready for action.
The Warden had handled him like a master con. . . .

It was Little Arv's great misfortune to bang on the door
just at that moment.

"You wanted to see me, Warden?" he asked, as soon as
Wasco let him in, and Wasco felt almost kind of sorry for
him.

"Lock the door behind you!" the Warden ordered. The
Warden was holding Sanger back from the attack by the
scruff of his neck . . . "Traitor, traitor, traitor . . ."

"Shake him down, Wasco!" the Warden yelled, when
Arv had closed the door behind him.

Wasco jumped. He ran at his littler cuz and hit him
with his heavy shoudler right in the solar plexus, bowling
him over into the door. WHAM!

Little Arv got up right away, still dazed. "What's going
on? What's going on?" he asked, kind of plaintive. Wasco
felt almost bad about it. But you could tell by the shifty
look in his little Weed eyes that he knew damn well what
it was all about . . . and was racking his brain to find a
safe way out of it.

"Never mind!" the Warden said. "Search him, Wasco!"

"Sir," Arv said, "I must remind you that it's against
regulations for an inmate to even touch an officer."

"Alright! Alright! Wasco, come here!" the Warden
shouted.

Wasco did as he was told.

"Now," the Warden yelled, releasing his hold on Sanger's straining neck, "go shake him down, Sanger!"

Sanger streaked across the room like a pointer after
quail, like a bull after tail. Little Arv dropped neat to all
fours at the last minute. Sanger tripped over him. He did
a full flip and smashed into the door upside down. His
lower back hit the doorknob with a CRACK that made you

wince, cracking his genetically inferior and feeble Weed sacroiliac. He fell down at the base of the door all in a useless pile of arms and legs. Unable to get up or even ease his position, with his head bent under his huge chest, and his heavy legs wrapped around his neck, Sanger just lay there moaning in agony . . . "Oh my back . . . my back!"

Arv got up fast, but not fast enough to avoid a rapidly aimed dropkick from Wasco that sent him flying on top of Sanger. SNAP! went Sanger's neck. And nobody heard a peep out of the old Golden Gloves champ for the rest of the struggle. Wasco ignored Sanger, grabbed Arv by the hair, bent his head back, bent his left arm around behind him in a hammerlock till it too was about to snap, planted his big knee in the center of his back, and held him down while the Warden hastily phoned for reinforcements, *selected* reinforcements, since he didn't want the whole Joint in on the caper.

"Hutchins? Send me Sergeant Monte, and Lieutenant Marty Boudin immediately!"

When Boudin and Monte showed up, two beefy veterans with always-angry eyes, the Warden let them in, pushing Sanger's limp body out of the way, and said, "We're having a little trouble here, men. Take over from the inmate, will you? I want you to search this man. I have reason to believe he may be carrying contraband."

Marty took Wasco's place holding Arv down while Boudin went through his clothes like a pro, calling off the items as he found them:

1. one wallet
2. one handkerchief
3. one letter
4. spare change
5. one pocket knife
6. one set of keys
7. one roll of cash

Wasco handed each item to the Warden, who called out loud what he found inside:

1. $587 in cash
2. an unaddressed letter to inmate William Galliot

        a. subject:
            1. advocates insurrection
            2. advocates escape
            3. offers help
        b. Signed: Arvin Weed, Jr.
    3. one snapshot
        a. subject:
            1. an Oriental girl

"Okay," the Warden said, "that's enough incriminating evidence right there. Let him up! Wasco, call the infirmary. Get a stretcher over here for Sanger."

Wasco made the call.

The two big burly guards let Arv up and stood one on each side while the Warden interrogated him.

"Where'd you get the $587 in cash?"

"It belonged to your son, sir. I was bringing it to his wife," he said, scared looking, breathing hard, scared peeless, but facing up to the Warden a lot taller than Wasco'd expected . . . and old Uncle Sanger lying over there, not breathing too hard.

"I'm Frank's father. And I can tell you he's never had $587 in cash in his entire life."

Boudin and Monte chuckled, remembering old Fast-Walking.

"Begging your pardon, sir, he got the money in a dope deal with Wasco."

"What did you say? Are you accusing my son, not an hour in the grave, of complicity in a criminal action?"

"Yes, sir," Arv said staunchly. Old Wasco, he had to give the kid credit. . . .

"Well," the Warden said, "I've heard the limit . . ." and the way he said it left it in the air that it'd be okay to poke him or hit him a little to bring him around to a more credible statement. Monte poked him . . . hard.

"Oomph!"

"Alright. What about this letter?"

"It was planted on me . . . oomph!"

"You've got a ready answer for everything, haven't you?"

"No sir, I'm only telling the tru . . . oomph!"

"Do you deny you've entered into a criminal conspiracy with inmate Galliot to bring letters in and out of this institution?"

"Yes sir, I . . . oomph!"

Someone knocked at the outside door. Wasco let the stretcher-bearers in. They gathered up the remains of Sanger and carried him off to the infirmary, shaking their heads.

Arv made no attempt to turn around and watch.

"You've got all the answers, huh?" the Warden said, as if that in itself was an accusation. Which it was. The way Wasco figured, anybody who thought he was smart-ass, who thought he knew all the answers, he was damn suspicious, probably subersive.

"No sir," Arv persisted, real sincere-sounding, "I don't believe I do. I'm only trying to . . . oomph . . . tell the . . . oomph . . . truth . . . oomph!"

"We'll see about that," the Warden said threateningly. "Marty! Leave the prisoner in Sergeant Monte's custody. Go over to the Visiting Room. There you'll find a young woman. Bring her here immediately."

"Wait a minute! Who's that?" Arv asked suddenly, and Wasco knew they had him. They had the little sonofabitch running now, nearly broken. He was sweating like a pig. His eyes were pinned with fear.

"Who's whom?" the Warden asked, raising an eyebrow.

"Who's the girl?"

"Oh, her? She's just a little Hawaiian girl who's agreed to testify against you if she's guaranteed immunity from prosecution . . ."

"Okay. You got me," Arv said, sighing like his heart was broken . . . poor kid! "I guess I'm your hit man, right?" he said, and Wasco pitied him with his whole soul.

"Hit man?" the Warden asked, incredulous, turning his palms up. "No C of C employee ever has been nor ever will be a . . . 'hit man,' as you so quaintly phrase it, so long as I'm Warden of this correctional facility. Our offer is merely this: since we're in a rather tight spot just now, with explosive tension building in the Big Yard, and a major black riot obviously brewing for this afternoon, we need your expert help as a rifleman on the Yard gunwalk. You are a very lucky young man. We're prepared to forget your serious crimes if you'll offer us your aid in quelling any racial disturbance that may take place."

"You win," Arv said, kind of draggedy-ass. And again, shit! Old Wasco, he felt kind of sorry for the kid. But he figured it was for his own good.

Forty-Nine

Officer Little Arvin Weed, no longer Junior, stood up on the gunwalk of Wall Post #8 smoking a Kent and scanning the Big Yard. Pigeons, sparrows, and sea gulls whirled over the heads of the frozen-ass convicts and then landed skidding on the icy mud puddles, flapping their wings comically to avoid falling on their tail feathers. The Yard was teaming with cellbound cons in denim blue trying to keep warm in their thin jackets, waiting for the First Count whistle, waiting to be shook down, locked up, counted, and let out again for chow. Their heavy respiration, the white vapor of four thousand hard-breathing, hard-timing cons, rose up as high as the walls in some parts of the wintry Yard, obscuring it in man-made mist. The snow flurries of earlier afternoon had ceased. The little snow that had drifted up against the walls had melted away. Still, in this usually temperate Pacific land, this usually more comfortable prison yard, the prisoners shivered and danced and blew on their cold red hands, unprepared for this sudden onslaught of Alaskan fury.

In spite of what the Warden had said just a few minutes before, there seemed to be little evidence of that potential "racial violence" of which he'd so strongly warned. Tension? Yes. But murder? Certainly not. Not at least from the black quarter of the Yard. Those warm-weather Afros, they seemed too busy just keeping their blood going. There would be no riot today, not from the black man. Arv confirmed that observation with a lifetime's experience of the Joint's sudden and violent moods. Scanning over across the entire range of the Yard and its encompassing high stone walls, looking on the gunwalks, in the wall posts, gun towers, looking under the big tin-roofed rain shed, looking around at the Dining Hall Rotunda, the South Block, the Honor Block, it seemed to

Arv that the only really nervous and distracted people in the Joint were the officers themselves, especially the gunmen, who paced up and down the railing, chain smoking, throwing the butts over the side onto the asphalt, constantly checking and rechecking their equipment, their ammunition, their weapons, flares, smoke bombs, tear gas projectiles.

But, of course, Arv had known that all along. The only riot that would occur in the Joint today would be the long-planned riot of Sate authority, oink-war, pork-fight, hack-battle, with Little Arv, Arvin Weed Sr. now, as hitman-in-chief. Irony of ironies . . . he who would raise himself above the pig-stench through an act of conscience, an act of great moral determination to resist the Pig, and all he stood for, would fall deeper into the stench precisely because of that determination.

Or would he? Smoking his weed, leaning over the iron railing above the Yard's ugly black macadam, watching inmate movement, watching Galliot, the leader of his people, the last militant, over near the Honor Block, Arv thought, *I've got to think! Haven't had time to think!* But it was so hard to think. His belly ached terribly where Wasco'd hit him. His lower back hurt bad too, where he'd fallen into Sanger. The pain radiated down his right thigh in the familiar sciatic pattern, reaching round his thigh, going up along his ass, into his asshole, all the way to his prostate gland, which pained him greatly too. He'd gone to the Joint doc over it once, Doc Wakefield, when he was still with Deanna. "Nonsense!" he'd said, "it's all in your head!" Head or no head, it hurt now, hurt like hell, and his slippery slipping lower vertebral disc too, and his head, his neck, his knees, the glands under his arms and on his neck, his ears, where he experienced sharp shooting pains, spots before his eyes, shaky legs, and his heart, his poor weak Weed heart . . . palpitating, palpitating, palping harder and harder and harder till he was afraid he'd lose his breath, till it made him see the future, made him see his own future. . . . He too would die young, would die as rumor already had it his dad had died: die of that high-protein, fat-infected, quintessentially American disease, Weed disease, sickweed, mounted on a woman not his wife, riding her, ridden himself, guilt-ridden . . . ridden dead of Protestant guilt and fatty American degeneration of the muscle that is the heart, fat heart, fat head,

fat floated brain . . . that's how he would die . . . Arv
felt almost as if he were dying now. The Yard reeled
beneath him. The sky spun. Round and round it went. The
Alvarez Straits rode around to Funland Amusement Park
in the city, the city went around to Holly Island, Holly Island raced toward the Pony Island Naval Base, the humpback bridge to West Hazelton spanned the Joint, and Arv
was flung momentarily at the stars as the Joint catapulted
to the New Sonora Alps on the horizon. Then the horizon,
after passing the Pacific Ocean, crossing Quintana Sound,
flew home to normal, and Arv knew he was safe. Meanwhile, however, his entire life had fled before his eyes, like
a drowned man going down, and then he started working
on the future near and far. . . . And that's what got him
calmed back down to a more reasonable panic. He saw
his death now a long way off. He would die like the Merc
had finally died on the bridge coming back from Evie's
place not an hour ago. He would run fast till he finally
sputtered and just pooped out. He still had a long way to
go. The Merc died on the wayback from murder. Died on
the swayback bridge on the wayback from swayback don-
key-dusting, assicide, burrocide . . . Merc conking out
like the old man's heart must have conked . . . sput, sput,
sput, . . poop . . . dribble . . . sput . . . dead! Valiant
Merc! Brave steed, having carried his little master far and
wide, over hill and dale, mountain and river, forest and
desert and great plateaus and plains . . . having nearly
done it for him, having nearly saved his pathetic existence, having tried, in its very death, to save Arv's life
. . . gallant Mercury!

When the Merc finally went dead on the freeway, Arv
coasted the old beauty down the first hump to the swayback middle of the bridge, and tried to make the second
hump too. But the Merc, privy to info of which Arv was
unaware, refused. Pooped to a stop halfway up the hump.
While Arv, uninformed of the Merc's last great self-sacri-
fice, cussed it brutally . . . you motherfucking cocksucking chickenshit . . . pulled the emergency brake, cussing
to beat hell. Then, when he'd calmed down, and begged
forgiveness, he felt kind of bad. Still didn't know why the
Merc had decided to give up, but felt kind of sad and
grateful for all the Merc had done for him anyway. If it
had been possible he would have picked the Merc up and
given it honorable burial at sea. If he'd been muscleman

Wasco he would have done it. Or if the Merc had been a Fiat. He could imagine it tumbling over and over and over to the shitwater Sound to a final resting place in the sumpy waters by the Exxon tankers. Arv, valiant captain, might have even ridden it down to the sea like a ship. Might have even gone down to it like Captain Courageous.

But nope! Like a prudent captain, a modern captain, Arv had abandoned ship, stuck his thumb out, abandoning hope, and hitchhiked in his C of C uniform over the hump to the gates of the Joint, where fate intercepted him just outside the Xmas-decorated little chapel where the last rites of his old friend Fast-Walking had so lately been administered. Fate intercepted him in the guise of old Widow Tessy who had informed him that his daddy was dead on the field of honor, in the chicken house of his desire. Or maybe the chicken house came later, and only through uncorroborated rumor. Maybe he'd heard it referred to approvingly in the barber shop, strangely empty and echoing barber shop, with no Roundo and no Yuba in there. Or perhaps it had been in the Staff Dining Room, or the Briefing Room before the swing shift began. But it didn't matter. Because Arv had read it all in the eyes of the donkey, the canary yellow eyes of the burro, Wasco's stolen ass, the ass of the ass, had read the entire life and history of the Weedy race in its pissy eyes, before it turned into a huge white stallion and rose up on its hind legs in a desperate and nearly successful attempt to off the offer, ice the ice man, hit the hit man, zap the zapper. But, in the nick of time, Arv, brave Arv, had evaded the sharp thrusting dangerous hoofs, and BOOM! let go a quick round of powerful NATO-approved international M-16 high-velocity peril, and felled the little yellow bastard forthwith, right there in Evie's far back yard, with no regrets . . . *and he lay there stiff as a board, upside withers, legs pointing straight up at Jesus . . . looked like he was just standing calmly up on the sky. . . .*

And were there really no regrets at the callous death of his childhood pet?

Nope, there were no regrets.

And now Galliot too, whom Arv watched at this very moment maybe only a couple of hundred feet away, one hundred NATO meters away across the yard, Galliot too, like the Merc, like a noble vessel that was going down, bottom bound, a doomed liner, would have to be abandoned. Arv had admired Galliot with his whole soul. And his great struggle for his people. Those same black people Arv could see now running around down in the Yard, shucking and jiving and sparring and singing Temptation numbers in trios. And practicing dance steps with transistor radios to their ears. Snapping their black fingers. Clapping their pink palms to keep their minds off the Man. Them black motherfuckers out there now. . . . Arv had read the future in Galliot's black face. Would have sailed with him into the sunset—albeit for selfish reasons, ambiguous reasons, even to himself—nevertheless, he would have done it! He really would have if . . . if . . . *Anyway, even when done for selfish motives, good is good, ain't it?* Arv would have sailed with this black man, this black ship, slave ship, doom ship, to the end of time. Really! He would have! But, pure and simple, Galliot's boat got hit, torpedoed, was shipping water fast, about to sink. And there was no way to save her. And Arv, like the prudent captain he was, like the ship's rats, couldn't see riding it down to the murky bottom for the mere sake of outdated form. . . .

Abandon ship, motherfucker! Every man for himself when the water comes down!

Abandoned Galliot's doomed cruiser as Arv himself had been callowly abandoned high and dry by his soul's companion, his heart's navigator, beloved Polynesian, intrepid island-hopping sailor in whom all his stars had been spotted. *Why didn't we just keep going south in Mexico? Everything would've been so different . . .* or would it?

"Dirty fucking bitch! Black bitch!

Did I dream her? Was she ever fucking real? Did I love her? Do I love her now? How much? Enough? Enough to kill?

What did Arv feel? He didn't feel anything yet. He didn't know yet, up there on that metal gunwalk above the wheeling convicts in the freezing cold, with his war surplus army overcoat *the overcoat the Wop planted with the phony letter while he was fucking around out at my car* the collar pulled up over his numb ears, and his ciggie hanging out of his mouth, and his hat pulled down Pig-style to keep his scalp from freezing. . . . There was no time to think. No time at all. This much was clear: his dad, Big Arv, Daddy, the old man, he was snuffed. So was punch-drunk Sanger. Fast-Walking was already interred under six feet of Indian shit and mud-hen clams and peaty earth. Galliot would soon be blown away too. And what did Arv think? What did he think? He didn't know what to think. He felt empty. The only thing he could think was that personally he still wanted to go on existing till his inevitable forty-eight-year-old All-American fatty heartbreak. He knew in his genes he would die young. He wanted to live at all costs. Yet he felt absolutely vacuous.

Could he do it? *All the time I was on his side he was whining and carping that hacks were all stupid sadists, even me, Pigs. I knew better. I pitied him with my whole soul.* What? Could Arv pull the trigger? *His was a niggardly generalization, the evil of a prejudiced mind that condemns an entire segment of the white race to the level of the animal, the brute, the evil that calls the pot black,* Arv thought, and then dismissed the thought as a cowardly rationalization. Though he believed it, at least partially. But . . . again . . . could he pull that hair trigger on the M-16? Just like he'd done on the ass. Could he do it? Sure he could do it. He was empty. Anyway, he never knew Galliot. Who was Galliot, anyway? Just some spade cat he'd had one all-too-brief shower-time conversation with up on the tiers. Aside from that one face-to-face exchange Arv only knew him through his letters. . . . What can you know of a man through his letters? Letters make everything prettier. Arv had known Galliot not at all. He had known him in the only way white men ever know black men in America. He had perceived him only in sketch, shadow, print, one or two dimensional, bas-relief, viewed through "colored" glasses. Arv didn't know him, couldn't ever know him, and that's all there was to it! What, for example, made Galliot give up everything for his people? Arv didn't know, hadn't a fucking clue! He didn't know him. Galliot was simply an abstraction to Arv, the color black. Therefore he could and would pull that hair trigger if it meant his life against Galliot's. He could do it. Was that sure? Sure. Galliot was merely a shadow to Arv, a black shadow. Wasn't he? Wasn't he?

Arv was empty still. And it went beyond death, or murder. He would have been empty anyway. He was empty because he'd lost. He had dared, and he'd lost. Fully

aware of what he was doing, and the possible consequences of his actions, Arv had accepted the challenge,
thrown his hat into the ring as soon as he recognized
Moke for who she was and what she represented, had
joined in mortal combat long ago, with his hereditary enemy, part of himself: Wasco, his cousin, his brother, his
hated and loved bugger brother, brother of . . . *Did he
like it? Sure, he liked it alright.* . . .

And lost . . .

Arv had loved and lost. But who was it he was loving?
Arv had fought his enemy. But who was his enemy? What
was lost? Who won?

Wasco won. Wasco'd done it again, goddamnit. De-
feated them all. Every fucking one of them. Wasco it was
who'd won the deadly game, just like when they were kids
on the ball diamond.

Was it?

After the Warden had split, leaving them in private for
a few minutes, in the Sign-in Room, Wasco said, "Hey
man, I know about your scene with Moke. How was that
shit? Getting into my old lady's panties like that . . . you
oughta be ashamed of yourself! But it's wild stuff, ain't it?
Listen, baby, no hard feelings. Really! And look, all this,
it looks kind of bad now. But I done it for your own
good. You ain't gonna work for nothing, man. I got a dynamite proposition here for you! I'm always looking out
for your best interests, kid, you know that! Now, the
Warden, you dig, he don't want to be involved in this part
of the operation. But, let me tell you, here's what the
State of New Sonora is prepared to offer you, backed up
by me, the County D.A. and, I hear tell . . . old Uncle
Sam hisself!

1. fifteen thousand dollars in cash
2. two one-way tickets anywhere
3. guaranteed executive clemency in case of
   (unlikely) prosecution
4. honorable retirement from State service at full
   pay for 'severe mental strain incurred in the line
   of duty'
5. Moke"

Moke?" Arv wondered.

"Well," Wasco said, "that's not the State's. That's mine.

Like I told you, kid. I want whatever's right for you. And she digs you too. I can tell. And I oughta know, right? No hard feelings. She's all yours, baby, and my blessings . . . if you just pull this very important caper for your race, your State and your Country!"

And Arv said, "Uh . . . okay, whatever you say, Wasco."

Did he really say that? Sure, what else could he do? They had him trapped. There was no choice in the matter. And anyway, he offered up his assent to their plans as merely a coverup, a play for time. He needed time to think, to find out whether there was an alternative, whether there was a way out.

But now he had his time, of course, up on the wall. And he couldn't think. *Don't you know what you're gonna do? Nope. I really don't. I don't know what I'm gonna do!*

They strapped him into his ammunition belt, and his rifle safety harness, handed him his Winchester, gave him the .38 Police Special . . .

"No!" he yelled, "gimme the M-16."

Wasco was pleasantly surprised. The M-16 was automatic, and very dangerous, not generally employed for yard work.

The Warden, who'd just come back in after their private conversation, said, stroking his handsome jaw, "It has a tendency to jam, I believe."

"Not for me!" Arv bragged, playing his new role, playing for time, "I know these weapons!"

They clapped him on the back, shoved him out on the gunwalk gate, and locked it behind him. Even if he'd had a change of heart, he had no choice but to continue along the gunwalk to Wall Post #8, relieve the day shift man, and assume his duties. They'd never have let him out, no matter how hard he pounded on the steel door. He was locked into the Joint, locked into its system, both real and moral, just as surely as any convict, more surely, as a matter of fact, than inmate Wasco Weed.

"We're putting you at Wall Post #8, 'cause that covers the Honor Block corner of the Yard, where Galliot's been hanging out lately," Wasco had said, when the Warden had given them their time alone. "We'll take him as soon as the First Count whistle goes off. I'll be out there with my boys. I'll stroll over and hit on one of his bodyguards.

He's been sticking to the new rules so he'll only have two men around him. That'll leave you a pretty clear shot. If you hit the other nigger it don't matter. We can just say you was breaking up a fight, right? It's been done before in this same Yard, right? But I don't think you'll hit the other one. I seen you plug a garbage dump sea gull in flight at a hundred and fifty yards, so I know you're gonna squeeze off a minimum of shots and nail him good. But keep firing till you're sure you blown him off. Anyway, hitting Galliot, that ain't gonna be the major problem. The trouble's gonna come afterwards, I figure, when them niggers find out their massa's been snuffed. They're like honeybees, niggers, once they get stirred up, it takes a whole shitload of firepower to calm 'em down. But, like honeybees, or Indians, once you got their queen the motherfuckers just run around in circles. Dig it? Anyways, me and my boys will retire to the other side of the Yard. The niggers are gonna be isolated then. And the Warden's got enough cross fire coming at 'em from up there on that gunwalk today to either shut 'em up or snuff 'em out. That's up to them, as far as I'm concerned. I been hired to do a job, the way I figure it, and once I done it, then it's the Warden's baby, see? The main thing is, though, like the Warden says, kid, try to avoid anything that looks too much like an Attica-style massacre. That might stir up negative public opinion, dig? Try to make it a good clean kill."

Arv stood up on that gunwalk now, chain-smoking, surveying the Yard, trying to think . . .

Oops! He'd forgotten to flick his safety to ON. He did it now. Checked the .38 too. Six bullets. Twirled it. It wouldn't fail or misfire or jam either. That Arv was certain of.

Trying to think . . . what the fuck was there to think about?

Did he want Wasco's gift, for instance, his Christmas gift? Did he want Moke? Now that she'd callously betrayed him? Assuming that Wasco wasn't lying about his intentions. Did he want her? Did he?

When he thought of her, when he thought of Moke, and her heady brown essence, he felt a great feeling of warmth creep all over him, all up and down his body.

Even her betrayal made him feel warm in his loins. Because he knew it hadn't been easy for her. And he, accurately, he thought, perceived that the betrayal itself had been a kind of perverse act of love . . . for she knew he'd had to take up that old challenge. Knew he'd thrown his hat into the ring. . . . And he'd read the true distress in her eyes, when last he saw her on the frozen lawn of her place in Molina Valley. *I know she loves me, I know!* And the thought that she loved him, the utter certitude of that love, which overwhelmed him now in warm shivering waves on the gunwalk, made Arv feel certain he could even kill for her, if he had to.

Yet, he still didn't know. Not for sure. Not yet. He couldn't think straight. There was no time. He glanced at his watch. Fifteen minutes till the First Count whistle.

Would he be able to pull the trigger then?

He couldn't think.

Did he really want to kill a man to save himself from prison? To possibly win a possible mate?

He couldn't think.

Alright, wait a minute! Are there any alternatives? Escape! Grab the wall post rope and run for the outside wall. Tie it to the railing, go down hand over hand to the dairy yard. Run across the cow pasture to the jute mill, through the metal shop and out onto the airstrip. Get in the C-46. Fire the engines, after all these years, push the throttle forward, take off, fly away, away, away . . . bullshit!

Suicide! Turn the M-16 around, take off your shoe, and pull the trigger like Ernest Hemingway did, with your big toe. Shit!

What have I done to deserve this? Kill or be killed. Dog eat dog. Is this really all there is? Is this where the world is really at? And . . . why me? Why me? Why me?

Arv's back was killing him. His eyes, ears, legs, lungs, glands, prostate, and his heart hurt too. He hurt all over. And he just couldn't think straight. So he did nothing. In fact, after a few more minutes, he thought nothing at all. What was there to think about? He just stood up there on the cold metal walkway, wrapped up tight in his overcoat, watching the yard carefully, just like the other ten gunmen on the other gunwalks surrounding the packed yardful of cons.

RIIIIIING! The phone went off in the wall post, making Arv jump. He hustled along the slippery walk and picked it up.

"Officer Jackson'll be coming out of the Honor Block in a few minutes. He's being relieved by the reserve man, Billings."

"Ain't that kinda dangerous right now?"

"Emergency. Besides, between you and me, because of the riot situation and all, the Warden's trying to ease the colored officers out of the tender areas . . . you never can tell."

"Yeah, always best to be safe," Arv said. As soon as he hung up he could hear the Control man ringing up everyone else on the gunwalks, warning them about movement in the Yard.

Five minutes later Billings, a slope-shouldered, four-eyed officer, appeared below Wall Post #8. Arv let him into the Big Yard with the bucket key, and wound it back into the wall post. Billings went across the yard and banged at the Honor Block door. It was a big heavy steel door, and began to open very slowly.

Suddenly, out of nowhere it seemed, a restless crowd of black men materialized, surrounding Billings!

Billings panicked, banged on the metal door.

"Let me in! Let me in!" he screamed, convinced he was done for.

Finally Jackson opened the Honor Block door wide enough for him to squeeze in, closed it behind him and locked it. But the crowd of black men stayed put in front of the block.

"Break it up! Break it up!" Arv hollered, as duty required.

Jones, on the gunwalk under the rain shed, yelled too, "Break it up! Only three men in a group!"

"Yeah! Break it up, damn it!" someone yelled from within the closely packed crowd of blacks, "this is an emergency! Lemme through here! Break it up! Break it up!"

Suddenly they broke up, just as the voice demanded. And out stepped Officer Jackson, lunch pail in hand, heading for the gate under Arv's wall post. It was Jackson alright. A small mild-mannered brownish black officer, he'd been one of the first two Negroes hired at the Joint, back in the early sixties, and had worked in the Honor Block ever since. The captain kept him there because the convicts liked him, even the white ones, and he ran a "smooth clean show."

"Break it up, goddamnit! I'm in hurry!" Jackson hollered again, motioning to the remaining small groups of black men in his way. "Break it up!" he shouted. And they did. They broke right up into groups of permitted threes and dispersed across the Yard. The tension in the Yard died down. Jones under the rain shed, and Bailey across the Yard, and the other wall post gunmen calmed down, lit up cigarettes, and leaned on the railings, blowing smoke out over the icy metal barrels of their Winchesters.

Arv's problem was this: he'd seen no one come out of the Honor Block. He'd seen Officer Jackson welcome the reserve man, shut the door, and go with him back inside the block. Officer Jackson was inside the Honor Block now. This small brown black man proceeding briskly across the slippery frozen yard toward Arv now was, therefore, not who he appeared to be at all! He was, obviously, an inmate attempting a surprisingly ingenious, daring, and well-timed escape, an escape that might well succeed, since none of the other guards had yet detected it.

Who was that inmate? It could be no other than Mr. William Galliot himself, dressed up in prison guard's gear, heading toward Little Arv to solve all his problems. . . .

Galliot hurried along, waving at Jones under the rain shed. Jones cupped his hands and shouted down, "Sorry to hear the bad news, man!" Galliot merely nodded his head sadly in reply.

Here he came now, old Galliot! Striding rapidly on his way out of the Joint. PLONK, PLONK, PLONK across the cold stone Yard. There was a queer silence in the black section of the Yard, as if seventeen hundred niggers had suspended breathing till he reached the gate. You could almost hear them tighten ass—SLOMP! Just like Arv.

"Come on, baby!" he breathed, and his breath carried it swirling upward toward the icy sky above the gunwalk like a prayer, like a prayer to his God, the Southern Baptist God of his childhood, his dirt-eating Okie Jehovah whose doubtful existence he'd ignored completely since the last tight spot he was in: 1968, the Tet offensive in Vietnam.

Here came old Galliot! Seventy-five feet away. He looked up at Arv, recognized him, smiled. Arv hesitated, afraid Wasco or one of his boys would notice. Finally he smiled down at him very, very slightly, and nodded his head just a tiny bit. Galliot understood that his danger was not over yet, and nodded too, very slightly, thanking him . . .

Fifty feet.

Galliot was coming. Nobody recognized him. If none of the other guards recognized him, then, who could blame Arv? He was no more responsible for the escape than they were . . .

Arv went over to the wall post, put the gate key in the bucket, and lowered it down along the high stone wall. Galliot came for it. *Never have I been so alive,* Arv thought, silent, holding his breath, suspending the beat of his heart, like the black men in the Yard.

Never had he been so alive as precisely then, never had Arv felt more intensely his own essence and identity. And his thoughts turned for a last time toward Moke . . . and the warmth of love for his beautiful Island Moke he could not contain, it ran through him undiminished, undaunted, all-forgiving, and he could do nothing to stop it, nothing . . .

Galliot came closer.

Twenty-five feet.

His hand was already outstretched for the hanging key when a streak of blue and red appeared out of nowhere *Life just won't give you any easy outs, will it?*

Wasco! He came thundering across the Yard like white lightning with a red prime, like a wild bull of the Joint, like a fiery two-legged chopper 74, CLOMP CLOMP CLOMP CLOMP he came in his heavy high-style stomper Motopsycho boots, headed for Galliot with murder in his crimson orbs. Wasco didn't yell. He didn't say a word. Little Arv watched him real close, and he didn't say nothing.

Didn't he say anything at all?

"Nope, he didn't say a thing.

All he had to do was yell "Galliot!" and Arv's decision would be made for him. He'd have no alibi, and would be obliged to shoot and not miss. But Wasco kept his own counsel, and his mouth shut. And ran for that black man hard, eyes fixed firmly upon his objective a short distance across the yard.

Galliot turned around. Saw his assailant. He was so close to freedom! Not fifteen feet away! He paused, did a little nervous shuffle, nervous but graceful little shit-pants soft-shoe blackman's dance, doing the Desperation Boogie. Arv could see the expression on his face very clearly when he realized that Wasco would catch him. Arv watched him read with terror what was in Wasco's bloody eyes: fulfillment of the prophecy he'd heard the minute he walked in the Joint with his black brothers, the apocalyptic augury laid upon him by the premonitory Vine, the infallible oracle of the Slam:

THE HIT MAN COMETH

"Aw, fuck!" Galliot said, out loud, faced with destruction just at the moment he was reaching for liberty. "Aw, fuck!" he said again, turning to meet his killer, as a driver on the freeway says it when faced with his own death barreling down upon him in the person of a big red semi-trailer truck . . .

A shot rang out. The blacktop behind Wasco kicked up. Wasco hesitated in midstride, looking puzzled, and then started up again. Arv could see Jones out on the gunwalk under the rain shed. Jones was shooting at Wasco! *Fire when inmate attacks or menaces officer in performance of duties. . . .*

PING! Another clink of asphalt jumped, this time to Wasco's right. Wasco stopped for a second, looked around wild-eyed, and started up again.

Yet still, even now, Wasco did not speak. Nothing would deflect him from his bloody purpose.

Galliot, encouraged by Jones's shots, turned and ran for the gate again, for the key that dangled tantalizingly in the bucket at the end of the rope.

Now he had the key! He put it in the lock, turned it.

PING! Another bullet ricocheted off the wall. Wasco stumbled. Was he hit?

Galliot swung the steel gate open.

Wasco got up and ran at him. Finally Wasco spoke . . .

"Shoot him!" he screamed, and someone shot. Right between Wasco's ruddy eyes.

"Who shot him?" Arv yelled.

Galliot, calm and sure, closed and locked the gate behind him.

"You did," he said.

Moke lay up in her apartment plucking pubes out of her perfect triangular black muff and piling them on a neat small stack on the tatami mat beside her low Jap-style bed, waiting for another omen. The black bird's cage was still empty. No mynah, no matter how minor, sang beside her.

She'd been lying there ever since she'd come home from the Joint, and her unnecessary appointment with *cause I no can choose da one kine Haole over da other I got to geev eet to da both* the Warden, appointment with *though it's not my fault I am faulted, fated* destiny. She did not turn the radio on. The report that would soon come over the air waves had nothing to do with her now, no matter what the results. Her fate was wrapped up already, like dope, cut and packed and folded like a dynamite half-load of smack, like the beautiful shit she'd just gotten off with in the bathroom. Mainlining it for the first time in her life, Moke's fate was already junk, already heavy into shit. All she was waiting for now, listening to the Christmas season traffic pick up on the freeway above the rickety mansion, was a final omen.

She'd already thrown the *I Ching*. When it came up pointing to a death in the family she'd pretended to be delighted. Yet still she dawdled, lying on her low bed, plucking her pretty pubes from her naked Hawaiian box, stacking them in a neat pile like so much loose thatch. She was almost bald now. . . .

The freeway noise got louder and louder as December's early nighttime fell. Giant petroleum tankers rumbled right over her head, shaking the foundations of the City of Molina Valley's ancient nineteenth-century manor house. High school kids in stroked Xmas gift Camaros rapped their pipes out, showing off in the passing lane,

rattling her windows. Fords and Chevys and big Buicks, all
headed for Christmas Eve parties and celebrations at
Grandma's, or Cousin Jim's, or Aunt Penny's, heading
out, all of them, to the festivities, while poor Moke lay
there in all her brutal baldness now, awaiting *her* Xmas
gift! Her omen. "Oh man!"

The traffic noise got worse and worse. Giant semitrailer
trucks sounded their air horns. Car horns honked. Brakes
screeched. Police sirens wailed. Right over poor Moke's
head. While she waited, baldly, waiting now, waiting for
her . . . oh man!

More and more sirens wailed in the distance. More
than was normal even at this accident-prone season of the
closing year. Something was up. AAAAAAAAAAAW went the
sirens. AAAAAAAAAAAAW! Tens of them, dozens. All seemingly converging here at the Molina Valley Interchange.
Lights, red and blue, flashing. *Is that all there is to it? Is
that it? Oh, man! What a half-assed ordinary little omen!*

Moke rose now in one easy cross-legged motion from
her hard bed. She felt . . . "Oh man!" It was coming.
"Oh man!" The sirens grew louder and louder and louder.
With purposeful quick strides she went to her closet, got
out her black rubber dry-suit, her rubber hood and pro-
tective face mask and her long-distance swimming fins.
She put on the dry-suit, listening to the sound of the
sirens pick up. Put on her waterproof hood and mask.
Threw the fins over her shoulder and headed for the door,
never to return. She paused for a moment in her "living,"
appreciated for one last time her handiwork on the tapa
walls, her drawing, her story, her heraldry, her myth,
went to the kitchen, got some lighter fluid, threw it on the
straw floor of the living, dropped a match on it, and split.
AAAAAAAAAW went the sirens on the freeway, getting real
close now, as she clomped across the frozen lawn to her
bike, cranked it over, let it warm up, adjusting her face
mask. Before she closed it she sniffed the cold winter air.
It smelled good to her. It smelled like New Sonora. It
smelled of redwood trees and wet closed-cone pine trees
and damp wax-myrtle and glasswort and greasewood and
silver Spanish thistle and salt and sea and fog . . . and
gas and oil and burning plastic and hot rubber and heavy
exhaust fumes. *Oh Haole Love, what you do to me?* she
sighed. What had mattered more than anything was trust,

trust and money. When *Haole* Love, that absurd notion, began to matter more, she had to flee. *When what really mattered no longer mattered, then I no longer mattered either.*

Then she closed herself off entirely from the freezing air, switched her headlight on, whipped the Honda around, stem-turning expertly on the icy grass, and wailed under the freeway bridge and over the misty coastal mountains to Pacific Beach, where nude hippies played in summer, and picklewood, salt grass, sea blite and dogtail grew untrammeled in wintertime, close in to Point Asunción, westmost salient of the entire New Sonora coast. Turned off the blacktop road and bumped over a dirt road, slipping on frozen mud puddles, and roared out onto the hard blackmud beach. ROOOM ROOOM ROOOM! went the Honda as she wound it out.

She took two high-speed spins to the end of the dark beach and back, her headlight reaching far out into the ocean on each turn. And then, just like in her dream of Balticoast, presentient dream, the dream she'd last told her last lost *Haole* lover, her only love, the prison hack, Officer Little Arvin Fucking Weed, just like in that long-ago dream she recounted to her love on a brief southern journey, just like she loved him, just like that, like the one and only red and yellow striped chickenshit fastest human unicycle alive, just like that, Moke gunned that hot little Nip bike and, her back tire spinning mud clods high up into the air behind her, she accelerated down the long black beach, leaning farther and farther forward as her speed increased till it seemed her nose would skim the fast-passing mud below her. Moke streaked at seventy miles an hour like a rocket-propelled unicycle for the hill, the bluff above the cold and most unpacific ocean. Soared out over the cliff and felt the norther wind upon her face, saw black waves far below. The earth fell away. Airborne, she climbed the cold western sky, up, up, up . . . Wisely separated herself from the shuddering machine when it finally stalled at the top of its glide and went into its last and fatal dive. Pushed off. Watched it tumble faster and faster and fall into the heaving sea with a cold empty heart *it was not my life but my goods that I had valued. I watched that pretty little red Honda tumble into the water, however, this time, with disillusionment of a kind . . . perhaps, but no sadness. . . .*

None at all?

No, none at all. No grief for a cold and dead machine.

Then Moke herself hit the water, black nightwater, boots first. SPLASH! Went down, down, down into her home, resisting the strong impulse to relax, to just keep falling and falling to sleep with her brothers, the shark and the whale and the mahi mahi, lying close to the bottom, waiting. She resisted this impulse. After all, she was no cowardly *Haole* suicide! She removed her untied boots, let them drop away, swam for air. Broke the surface. Gulped oxygen . . . HAAH HAAH HAAH! It tasted good, so good. Checked herself carefully for injuries, sprained bones, torn ligaments . . . "All systems Go!" . . . and struck out south and west for her native place, home of her ancestors, fiftieth state of the American union. A bold and hardy navigator, like the stout Polynesian sailors before her, she set out bravely into the icy tempest. Swimming strongly, buoyed up and kept warm by her rubber dry-suit, Moke swam away from New Sonora, swam hard for warm water, three thousand miles away. . . .